G. BAILEY & REGAN ROSEWOOD

SECRET WOLVES

G. BAILEY & REGAN ROSEWOOD

SECRET WOLVES

SECRET WOLVES

SUPERNATURAL SHIFTER ACADEMY SERIES

G. BAILEY

REGAN ROSEWOOD

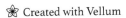 Created with Vellum

DESCRIPTION

Secret societies. Magical boarding schools. Supernatural beings...
What could go wrong?

I'm Millie Brix and apparently, I'm a supernatural shifter. Funny
eighteenth birthday present, right?

Chosen for Supernatural Shifter Academy, I have to learn which
Shifter Clan I belong to and how to use my powers that are slowly
growing out of control.
Supernatural Shifter Academy only has five hundred places, and if
I'm not strong enough to survive, I won't get to walk away.
The Sirens lure you in, the Wolves bite first and ask questions later,
the Dragons only care for themselves, the Vampires plan to own the
world and the Witches will do *whatever* it takes to win.
I'm not going to let the academy beat me, that's for sure.

With a Prince of the Vampires seducing me, a secretive Siren dead set
on making me his, a gorgeous wolf shifter who wants to claim my

heart, and an alpha dragon who sees me as a prize he wants to keep... the academy is far more dangerous than it looks.

In this academy, secrets are the only thing you can trade with and I'm right in the middle of the biggest secret the academy has.

And when the truth comes out...the academy will fall.

17+
This Collection includes:
Crescent Wolves
Azure dragons
Demonic Vampires
Unpredictable Sirens
Regent Witches
Plus exclusive bonus scenes.

CHAPTER 1

S ometimes when I look into the light of the sun, I can only see the shadows around the edges, waiting for their chance to smother what brightness is holding them back.

But looking up at the sky, as I make my way down the sloping drive, I can only see big black thunderstorms forming on the horizon. I'm only just past the top of the hill on Bowery Street, and considering how quickly the weather is going sour, the odds of getting home before it starts to rain are slim to none.

"Damn," I mutter, pulling my backpack up higher on my shoulders and shaking my head. It's times like these when I really wish Central High's bus route included my neighborhood. Well, *our* neighborhood. *Their* neighborhood. Whoever's neighborhood it is, it's too far outside the city center for the school bus to reach, and since I don't have a car, I'm what some might call shit out of luck. Normally I don't mind the long walk home—in fact, I usually enjoy it. It's a chance to listen to some music, stretch my legs after eight hours of sitting at a desk, and, most importantly, it means less time spent around Mark. When the weather's bad, though...

Kicking myself for not thinking to bring an umbrella, I continue down the road, hoping I'll get lucky and not end up soaked by the time I reach the house. Doubtful. All I can reasonably do at this point is try not to get water all over the front entryway and pray that Mark won't be in one of his moods when I get in. I can practically hear him snapping at me already, slurring his words as he gestures at me with an empty beer bottle: *Damn it, Millie! You couldn't even dry off before getting mud all over the front porch? What's wrong with you, huh?*

I shake my head, feeling the first raindrop plop down on my shoulder like a warning. *Yeah, I know,* I think. *It feels like I'm on my way to the gallows.*

Okay, maybe that's a little overdramatic. But not by much. I've been living with my most recent foster parents, Mark and Tonya Stone, for going on a year now, and things haven't been peachy. It's not like I'm not used to bad foster family situations--in fact, that's basically all I've ever known, with a few exceptions. It's like the start of every fantasy story I've ever read: a baby girl, abandoned at the hospital when she was born by parents she never knew, drifting from one abominable living situation to another and wondering why she was put on this planet. Except if this was really a fantasy story, a fairy godmother would have appeared at my bedroom window a long time ago to whisk me away on some whimsical adventure.

Instead, the only things that have ever appeared at my bedroom window are the eggs thrown by neighborhood pranksters and the occasional crow.

It hasn't been all bad, though; I think as the ground levels out beneath my feet. The raindrops are coming more frequently now, and I see the horizon light up briefly with the flash of lightning. Mollie, the foster mother I lived with from when I was nine to when I was eleven, was easily my favorite of the bunch. *Mollie,* I remember her saying when she first introduced herself. *It's only one letter away from your name, Millie. It's like it was meant to be.*

And for a while, I almost believed it. With Mollie, I actually felt like I had a home, not just a place to stay. She showed me how to cook, let me watch her TV programs with her, and actually seemed interested in me as a person, not just a source of government-provided income. She even gave me a necklace—a little sterling silver pendant in the shape of a crescent moon—that I had worn until the clasp broke. Now I keep it tucked into the worn combat boots that I wear every day, no matter the weather. If I can't wear it, then at least I can keep it—like a good luck charm, or something.

But, as I've been forced to learn again and again as I'm passed from one set of strangers to another, nothing good is meant to last. The economy took a hit, Mollie had to close down her bakery, and it was determined that she was no longer fit to support me. So off I was packed, to a new family, a new set of introductions, and a new set of disappointments. Rinse and repeat.

With every good thing in my life, shadows seep into the edges and make it impossible to stay good for long.

As I turn off the main road and into Mark and Tonya's neighborhood, I remind myself to stop ruminating. What has that ever gotten me, other than resentment? Feeling the reassuring pressure of Mollie's necklace against my ankle, I speed up a little, motivated to at least minimize my time outside in the rapidly increasing downpour. Once I get home, I'll have to finish my trigonometry homework, as well as work on the English paper that's due this coming Monday.

It's as I'm contemplating my schoolwork that I'm hit with an increasingly familiar new wave of anxiety. I turned eighteen last month, which means that not only am I in my last year of high school, but my days in the foster care system are numbered. One would think I would be happy to be finishing the endless cycle of lousy living situations, and I am, but I'm not blind to what this next transition will mean: I'll be on my own, for better or worse. And given my luck so far, my money's on worse. I'm going to have to decide what to do about university, about getting a job, finding a place to live... the training wheels are coming off, and I'm in no way prepared for it.

I guess that's something every foster kid has to face, I reason, feeling the raindrops now pelting down on me. I lift my backpack and hold it above my head like a shield, aware that my papers are going to get wet but hardly caring at this point. *But not every foster kid has had as hard of a go of it as I have.* I know I'm just feeling sorry for myself, but it's almost impossible not to.

The truth is that I've never really felt at home anywhere, with the exception of those two wonderful years with Mollie. No matter where I go or who I live with, I've never really felt a sense of belonging. I've made friends here and there, but by the time I'm ever really starting to find a niche in one place, it's time to pick up and move somewhere else. It's like my life has never really begun, leaving me with a lingering sense of emptiness and dissatisfaction everywhere I go.

By now, my blonde hair is beginning to dampen, and I pick up my pace, practically jogging now in a desperate attempt to stay dry. *That's enough chewing the cud*, I tell myself. *Just take things one day at a time. That's all you can manage.* By the time I reach Mark and Tonya's old, single-story house, I'm thoroughly soaked and shivering. Like a lost kitten... or something. It takes me a minute to fumble my house key out of my dripping backpack, but eventually I get the front door open, pausing on the threshold like one wrong move will set off an explosion.

And for all I know, it will.

"Tonya, honey, is that you?" I can hear Mark's voice coming from the kitchen. Good. If I'm lucky, I can get down to my basement room and change my clothes before he's any the wiser.

"It's me, Mark," I call back, hoping my tone comes across as jovial and unbothered.

"Hmph," he says, and then goes quiet. Judging from the sound of his voice, he's been hitting the bottle for at least an hour already. Ever since losing his job at the factory on the other side of town, he's been taking full advantage of the unemployment checks and letting Tonya put food on the table by herself.

Tonya, a mousy woman who probably won't ever have the gumption to divorce her deadbeat husband, pulls odd hours at the diner down the street to support his drinking habit. Funny how they should take me away from someone like Mollie and then stay silent when I end up in a legitimately dysfunctional living situation. But what do I know, right?

I manage to slip out of the entryway and down the basement stairs, doing my best not to drip water on the grimy linoleum floor. The basement is half-finished, with a pull-out couch serving as a bed and my meager possessions all crammed into the closet by the back wall. It's more or less a glorified storage area, but at least nobody comes down here to bother me. Down here, I can re-read my worn copies of *Narnia,* the *Harry Potter* series, and yes, even *Twilight,* in peace, daydreaming about being swept away into a life full of purpose and magic, where tragedy and boredom were always just the precursors to a grand new adventure.

The grimy mirror on the back of the door makes me pause, looking at my blonde wet hair falling around my shoulders, dripping rainwater onto my drenched clothes. My very dark blue eyes stare back at me, daunting me with how much they look like the very water that smothers my clothes. Not for the first time, I wonder what my parents looked like. Do I look like my mother or father? Or neither of them.

But the mirror doesn't have answers for me. Of course it doesn't. No one does.

I'm just pulling on a dry sweater when Mark's gravelly voice shatters the silence into a million pieces. "Millie, what the hell?!"

My eyes go wide. "Yeah, Mark? What's wrong?"

"Get up here," he yells, and even from down here I can hear the alcohol in his voice. Swallowing hard and bracing myself for the worst, I pad back up the basement stairs to find Mark standing in the entryway. His hulking figure makes me feel even smaller than I normally do, and with his shoulders hunched, his beer gut sagging over the top of his trousers, he looks more like a troll than ever before. "What the fuck is this?" he demands, pointing down at the floor by the welcome mat.

"What...?" I begin, taking a step closer, and then I see it. A set of streaky, damp boot prints leading to the basement door. Shit. Why the hell didn't I take my shoes off?! "Oh," I say, blanching as I turn to look at him again. "I, uh... I'm sorry. It's pouring outside."

"Yeah?" Mark rounds on me, his bloodshot eyes flashing. "Is that right? And why the hell didn't you think about that before you went and got mud all over the floor?"

"I'm sorry," I repeat, inching back as he takes a step toward me.

"I'll clean it up. I didn't even think about it—"

"Of course you didn't, because you don't think, *period,*" Mark says, swaying slightly on his feet, and I can smell the stench of booze coming off him. Not beer this time, either. Something heavier. Whiskey, maybe. And there's something in his voice that floods me with unease. Have I ever seen him this drunk before? "Sometimes I wonder why the hell we're even keeping you," Mark continues, running a hand through his thinning hair. "I mean, you're useless, do you know that? We spend all this time and money providing for you, and what do we get?" He advances on me, making my heart jump to my ears. The unease is turning into full-blown fear. "Nothing," he finishes. "That's what."

"Mark," I say, my voice coming out embarrassingly small, "please... I'm sorry. Really. I'll—"

"Did I say you could talk?" he roars, and then he does something I've never seen him do before, no matter how drunk he's been. He takes a swing at me. It's sloppy and uncoordinated, and I'm able to duck out of the way. His fist connects with the wall, and he roars in pain. "You little..." he begins, winding up to throw another punch.

Where's Tonya? She won't be back until dinner time, at the earliest. It occurs to me that he could do whatever he wanted to me right now, and no one would be the wiser.

He's going to hurt me, I think, heart thundering as I continue to back up. *He's actually going to hurt me.*

In that instant, with that realization, I feel something strange welling up in the pit of my stomach, something cool and insistent—a feeling I've never experienced before. For a moment it's enough to draw my attention away from Mark, away from school, away from everything. The *novelty* of it makes me wonder if this is how newborn babies feel.

I can feel something in me waking up, something I couldn't put my finger on even if I tried. And one thing becomes clear to me, a truth I think I've known for a long time but was unable—or unwilling—to face until now.

I need to get out of here.

CHAPTER 2

I don't have time to think before Mark is winding up to hit me again; I turn on my heel and make a break for the basement door like my life depends on it. I almost slip on the rainwater staining the floor, and I feel the air behind me move as another one of my foster father's uncoordinated swings narrowly misses me. My heartbeat is so loud it's all I can think of, all I can worry about. Scrambling to keep my balance, I throw the door open and bolt through, barely remembering to lock it behind me before Mark arrives, his slurred yelling muffled as he pounds on the door.

Racing down the stairs, I begin to frantically gather up my things. There isn't much to collect—a half a dozen articles of clothing, a couple of books, my cell phone—and before I know what I'm doing, I'm dumping out the contents of my school backpack, papers and pencils showering onto the carpet. I cram the backpack full of my stuff and look around. My mind is already made up; I'm not staying here a minute longer. It doesn't matter where I go, as long as it's away from here. Because if Mark can cross that line once, then he sure as hell can do it again, and I might not be so quick next time.

Being hurt at this place isn't worth the roof over my head.

Shouldering my backpack, I turn to the other set of stairs, the ones leading out to the garage, and head for the door. I feel a pang of regret that I won't get to say goodbye to Tonya--she was always nice to me—but there's no looking back now. After taking one last look around the basement to make sure I'm not forgetting anything, I shove the door open and leave the house through the garage. I am half-expecting Mark to be waiting for me, but he seems to have given up and stumbled back to his booze. *Thank god for small favors,* I think.

It's not until I'm outside again that I realize it's still pouring. At least I didn't forget my umbrella this time; the last thing I need right now is all of my clothes getting soaked from the rain. Not sure where I'm heading, I pick a direction and make my way down the street, feeling cold again as the downpour continues.

I start to calm down as I walk, my heart rate slowly returning to normal, and it occurs to me that I don't have a plan, or anywhere to go. The child services offices won't be open until tomorrow morning, and they might not even care that I ran away. I'm eighteen now; it's not like I'm their responsibility anymore. I take stock of my few school friends, who are really more like acquaintances, and it's immediately clear that my options are limited as far as places to stay.

At the very least, you can find somewhere to wait until this storm passes, I tell myself, and keep moving. The clouds still seem thick overhead, and that doesn't seem like it's going to be anytime soon. Still, all I need right now is a place to rest and figure out what to do next.

As I walk, I think back to that feeling I had when Mark took a swing at me. There was the fear, yes, and the realization that I needed to leave, but there was also something else--something I couldn't put my finger on. Have I ever felt something like that before? It was almost like there was something inside me, trying to get out. *Maybe it was just the adrenaline,* I reason. But I've felt adrenaline before, and this wasn't it. I can't fight the feeling that it has something to do with the growing sense of unease and foreignness I've been feeling increasingly lately. It hasn't just been the new foster family, or the fact that I'm an adult now. There's something more to it, but I can't figure out what.

I lose myself in thought for a while, the events of the past hour

8

feeling more and more absurd as I walk. The rain continues, and before I know it, I've left Mark and Tonya's neighborhood and am entering an industrial area of the city. It only takes one look around to tell me this isn't the place for a girl, especially a girl alone. I can feel the passerby giving me strange looks as I continue down the street, wondering all the while if I should turn around.

Yeah, I ask myself bitterly, *and go where?* It's not like I can return to the house, and at this point I have no idea where I am. I could end up wandering in circles for the rest of the night. I can see that the sun is dipping low on the horizon. Soon it will be nighttime, and the last thing I want to be doing when the sun sets is walking around this part of the city. Eyeing the buildings as I go, feeling increasingly self-conscious under the scrutiny of the strangers around me. Eventually a dilapidated warehouse around the corner from a run-down apartment complex catches my eye. On the door is a sign reading, "CAUTION - CONDEMNED", but the padlock keeping it shut has been broken. I'm probably not the first squatter to turn up here. All I can do is hope it's empty as I try the door. It groans open stiffly and a flurry of rust flakes showers down on me.

It seems like some kind of abandoned storage facility, with debris and evidence of more vagabonds scattered around the floor. There's no electricity, so I use my phone flashlight to look around as I make my way to the back corner. It occurs to me that if the place is condemned, the roof might fall on me at any minute... but I'm past thinking about that now. *Hell, maybe that would even be a blessing,* I think dryly. When I reach the corner, I catch a glimpse of my reflection in the dirty, boarded-up window on the far wall. Blonde hair--wet, dirty, and tangled. Dark eyes--so dark they could almost be black. I look like I've aged ten years in the past few hours. If this is what one evening on the streets does to me, how am I supposed to survive after tonight?

Whatever, I tell myself. *We'll worry about that later. For now, just try to get some sleep.*

There's a flat piece of cardboard on the floor in the back of the room, and I decide it will do as a makeshift bed. Using my backpack as a pillow, I curl up on the hard concrete and listen to the rain fall outside. As I do, I find myself thinking about my parents once again, but I'm not sure why they keep coming to my mind tonight. Why did they leave me in the hospital all those years ago? What made them leave me to a life of bouncing from foster home to foster home, listening to drunk old men yell and having to run away to get away from it all? And what's going to happen to me now?

At some point the sound of the rain lulls me into an uneasy sleep, and for a few blissful hours, I forget all about where I am or how I got here. Eventually, though, the sound of voices breaks the fitful sleep, and I begin to drift awake. For a moment I'm disoriented, missing the pullout couch, but then everything comes flooding back to me and I jerk awake.

There are two men standing over me.

Scrambling to get back into a sitting position, I stare up at them in shock. They're dressed in baggy clothes, their shoes ragged, and in a heartbeat I realize why this place was empty.

"What do we have here?" the first one asks, staring down at me with bloodshot eyes.

My mind is racing—I should have locked the door, or barred it, or... something. Shit. Another mistake in a long string of mistakes. "I-I'm sorry," I stammer, still trying to get a handle on the situation. "I didn't realize this place was occupied."

"Damn right, it's occupied," replies the second man, peering down at me. "What the hell is a little girl like you doing here?"

"I..." I fumble for a response. "I just needed somewhere to get out of the rain." Still disoriented and foggy from sleep, I sit up straighter. "I'm sorry. I'll get out of your hair." I get to my feet, backpack clutched to my chest, and begin to retreat.

"What have you got there, huh?" asks the second man, his interest piqued now that he's seen my backpack. "Did you bring us a present?"

"Huh?" I ask, shaking a little.

The first man points to my backpack. "Think of it as an apology gift. For wasting our time."

"I..." I glance down at the backpack, containing my only possessions, and shake my head. "I'm sorry. This is all I have. If I could just go, I would..."

"Fine," the second man says. "Just your wallet, then."

I take another step back, my heart beginning to beat more quickly. The door is on the other side of the room. Do I make a break for it?

The first man must have seen me steal a glance at the door, since his eyes narrow and he advances on me another step. "Thinking of running, little girl?" he asks. "Don't bother. You're outnumbered." He licks his lips, his eyes sweeping me, and I can see the wheels in his head turning. Whatever he's thinking, it's not good--of that I can be sure. The second man is taking another step forward when the first man stops him with a hand on his arm and says, "You know what? Wait a minute. Maybe we can figure something out."

I can feel my stomach drop at his words. "I... I'm sorry?"

"Pretty thing like you..." the first man says, his voice trailing off as he appraises me with his eyes.

Now the second man is catching on, a knowing smirk creeping onto his face. "I like the way you think," he comments to his friend, before turning back to me and saying, "Maybe we could trade. We let you keep your stuff, and in exchange, you—"

The fear is too much at this point, and the scream is leaving my mouth before I can stop myself. "Help!" I yell, but not a moment later I realize how pointless it is. We're inside, and even if we weren't, the sounds of the storm are still raging outside.

The second man seems to be thinking the same thing, darting forward and seizing me by the arm. "Not happening," he hisses, and I can smell the stench of his breath. "No one can hear you."

Out of the corner of my eye, I can see the other guy approaching, and for the second time today I realize I only have seconds to react. I have my backpack in a death grip, and something tells me that even if I handed it over, that wouldn't stop them. Not now that the idea's in their head.

It's as the panic is surging through me that a familiar feeling—

that same feeling that began to well up when I realized Mark wanted to hurt me—begins to surge through me again. Like a rush of strange, cool energy that is also nice to feel takes control of me. The fear bleeds away, like a wave in an ocean brushing everything in its path to the side.

And that's when I begin to transform.

CHAPTER 3

The closest thing I can compare it to is being plunged into a pool of cold water. The cool feeling that welled up inside me expands suddenly, faster than I can keep up, shooting out from the pit of my stomach and into my arms, legs, and head. It's overwhelming in its intensity, as if every nerve in my body is suddenly bursting with energy, the cells struggling to contain it. I feel like there's an electric current coursing through me, uncontainable and unrelenting as it pulses from my core out to my fingers. For a moment, I wonder if I'm dying. Is this what a heart attack feels like?

My body seizes up all at once, my back going rigid at the new sensation, and I see the two men look at each other--first in confusion, and then in fear. I don't understand why they look so panicked until my eyes travel down my own body and see my skin beginning to... change color? Yes, it's definitely taking on a reddish tint. Is this some sort of physical reaction to the adrenaline? A panic attack? It's like nothing I've ever felt, but I'm willing to chalk it up to some kind of medical problem. That is until I see little concentric arches rippling up my hands, first becoming hard and then flaking off my skin, like scales. They're a shimmering metallic green, almost iridescent in the dim light streaming in from outside, and it's at that moment that I realize this isn't something medical--at least, nothing medical that I've ever heard of.

"What the fuck...?" asks the first man, taking a step away from me and grabbing his friend's arm. "What is she...?" The second man just shakes his head in disbelief, looking at me like I'm a cornered animal that might attack at any minute.

The changes don't stop there. I let out a surprised cry as I feel something happening to my teeth; first they feel like they're falling out, but then I realize that's not what is happening. They're *growing*, getting longer and pointer at the same time, digging uncomfortably into my lower lip.

This has to be a nightmare, I think, plunging my hands into hair that no longer feels quite right, it's softer and longer. *I'm asleep back on the pull-out couch in Mark and Tonya's basement. I fell asleep in front of the TV or something, and this is what I'm dreaming about. Right? Right?!* But it sure as hell doesn't feel like a dream. The sensations are all too real, too logical, and that unfamiliar feeling in my torso is stronger than ever.

"What the fuck are you doing, kid?" demands the first man, digging in his pocket and pulling out a switchblade. "This isn't funny!"

He's scared, I realize with a start. *They both are. I don't blame them. I'm scared, too.*

"Get... away... from me..." I say, groaning with the discomfort that has now swallowed me completely. These men, and the possibility of them hurting me, is suddenly the furthest thing from my mind. I'm entirely focused on what's happening to me--what's *wrong* with me--and trying to contain the explosive, frigid energy that feels like it's threatening to burst out through every pore and cell. The men stare at me, looking uncertain. "Please," I tell them again, my voice rising. "I don't know what's happening!"

"Look," the second man says in a low tone to his companion, "she's not going anywhere. Let's just take the backpack and go."

The first man gives him a doubtful look, but nods after a moment, and the two of them begin to move back towards me. "No!" I yell, unable to think of anything else to say; my mind feels like it's falling apart almost as quickly as my body. My nails, which I normally keep short and neat, are getting longer at this point, too, extending past the ends of my fingers and turning hard, durable, and pointy. Like claws.

It's all I can do to move backwards as the two men approach, some part of me wondering if I can somehow escape out the window, and another part telling me that's impossible. Soon they have me backed up against the wall, the rigid concrete hitting my back as I look around frantically. I'm desperate for something to do, something to use... anything so that I can get these guys away from me and focus on more important things. Like the fact that something very wrong is happening to my body, and I have no idea how to stop it.

They're almost on top of me now, the first man reaching his arms out as he rushes forward, grabbing for my backpack. If I lose it, I'm screwed. Desperate, fear taking hold of me completely, I let out an incoherent scream, louder than I think I ever have.

And that's when a jet of fire bursts from my mouth, reaching as far as one of those makeshift flamethrowers you make with a lighter and a can of hairspray. The guys stop, the fear back on their faces. I'm left to just stare as the fire burns out, dissolving into a waft of smoke, wondering how the hell it was possible. How the hell any of this was possible. The fact that my mouth feels fine when it should be scorched, burned beyond recognition, occurs to me moments later For a split second I wonder if it's not a dream at all, but a hallucination. That would explain why it didn't hurt me, but it wouldn't explain why the men are staring at me like... well, like I just breathed fire.

"I don't like this," says the first man, eyeing me warily. "Whatever this is, I don't like it. We should just go. We can bring the others back and deal with her then."

"No," snaps the second man. "Nobody muscles in on our territory, especially a little girl. Grab her, keep her from doing that again. I'll get the bag--"

But at the sound of their words I'm doing the only thing I can think of: screaming again, as loud as I can, praying more fire will come out of me and not caring about how that is physically impossible. And it does. Another blast of flame shoots out of my mouth, coming dangerously close to reaching the two men.

"Fuck this," the first man says, shaking his head. "You're on your own." And then he's turning around and sprinting for the door, not looking back even as his companion yells threats and obscenities.

The second man stares me down for another moment, calculating his odds against someone who's mutated into some kind of fire-breathing freak, and eventually drops his shoulders, taking a step back. He opens his mouth like he's going to say something else to me, but then closes it. He backs up a few paces before turning and bolting the same way the other guy went.

I'm left standing there, shaking and staring down at myself. Do I dare?

Before I have time to think about it, I'm turning around to face the window, looking at my reflection once again in the grimy reflection. I'm nearly unrecognizable. I look like a monster. My arms and legs are covered in scales, my hair has turned almost white and coarse, my skin still has that red tinge to it. There are claws on my fingers and fangs protruding from my mouth. It's not something I think I could describe to anyone, and even as the sheer impossibility of everything that just happened continues to flood my mind, the aftershocks are taking over, and I realize I'm shaking.

Breathing hard, trying not to hyperventilate and pass out, I drop back down to the floor, trembling with chills and cold sweat. Two near-misses in one day, and I'm not out of the woods yet. What do I do now? Go to the hospital? Will they even be able to help me?

Of course they will, the rational part of me desperately pipes up. *It's obviously some kind of medical condition. There's no other explanation.*

Okay, sure. I could buy that for the scales, nails, and red skin, but what about the fire? When in history has a person breathed fire outside of the circus? And how am I supposed to explain that to any doctor who comes to examine me? I can already see the headlines, the documentaries, the men in black from the government and the scientists taking me away to some lab or quarantine somewhere, doing tests until the end of time and never letting me see the light of day again. What else would they do? No way. I'm on my own.

I realize I'm crying from a combination of exhaustion, the trauma of the attack, and my fear about my physical condition. Taking a shaky breath, I close my eyes, putting my head on my knees and praying this is all some sick joke. The hidden cameras will be revealed any minute now, and I'll go back home to apologize to Mark, whether he deserves it or not. That has to be better than this nightmare I've ended up in.

It's not until my panicked tears are drying that I notice something. The icy cold feeling from before, that freezing energy that overtook my body when I changed, is starting to subside. My hands are starting to feel normal again, and when I look down, I'm shocked to see that my nails are retracting back into my fingers, my skin beginning to go back to its normal color. And there's more; the scaly patches crawling up my arms are disappearing back into my skin, absorbed under the surface. I touch my canines, which are already returning to the length they were before. I run a hand through my hair and pull a strand into the light, seeing my blonde locks back. Glancing behind me at the dirty window one more time, I see that, as far as appearances, I'm back to normal again.

Okay. So it wasn't permanent... whatever it was. That doesn't make me feel a whole lot better, though; I felt the same thing back at the house, after Mark tried to hit me. It didn't escalate this far that time, but it's proof enough for my scared, sleep-deprived mind that if something else happens to trigger it, it will happen again. And I don't know how to prevent it.

I'm just beginning to rifle around in my backpack for my cell phone, wondering if there's anyone I can turn to for advice, when there's a loud booming noise on the other side of the warehouse. It sounds a bit like a firecracker going off--a short, loud *crack* that pierces the air and nearly makes me jump out of my skin. This is followed by the sound of footsteps scuffing on the concrete, and I can make out two figures in the shadows. For a moment I panic again, thinking that it must be the two men. *They came back,* I think, eyes widening. *They came back; they brought their friends, and I'm back to normal. I'm dead.*

But then the footsteps approach and I'm able to make out two figures, svelte and feminine. Women. Did the others send them?

"Hello?" I call, my voice unsteady. "Who's there?"

Eventually the moonlight illuminates them more easily, and I see immediately that they don't look normal, the same way I didn't look normal a few minutes ago. Their skin is a deep ruby red, similar to the way mine was, and their eyes and hair are pitch black.

I gasp, scrambling back, and the women look at each other for a moment. Then they're changing, too, as easily as taking off an article of clothing, their skin going pale and their skin and eyes going back to looking normal. They look human now...not whatever they actually are.

"Sorry to have frightened you," the first one says, continuing to move forward until she's standing in front of me. The other one hangs back, crossing her arms over her chest.

"What..." I'm at a loss for words for a moment, and then the questions start to tumble out all at once. "What is this? How did you do that? Who are you?"

"Millie Brix," the first woman says, "we've been looking for you."

CHAPTER 4

I stare at her in shock, the fact that I just watched her body transform the same way mine did is temporarily forgotten. "I... How do you know my name?" I ask.

"We've been keeping an eye on you for a while," the woman responds, extending a hand to me. "My name is Samantha Gold-stein." Tentatively, I reach out and shake her hand, feeling numb. Samantha gestures to the other woman, who still hasn't said anything. "This is my colleague, Josie Everhart."

The other woman gives me a thin smile. "Pleasure to meet you, Ms. Brix," she says quietly.

"You too," I say, fully aware of how absurd this situation is. I'm standing in an abandoned warehouse, having just turned into some kind of fire-breathing monster, and now I'm greeting two other mutant women like it's the most normal thing in the world. I turn back to Samantha. "What do you mean, you've been keeping an eye on me? Are you from the foster agency? Is this about what happened with Mark?"

Samantha beckons to Josie, who wordlessly walks over to join us. "Why don't we sit down for a while? We have quite a bit to go over with you and believe me when I say I think you're going to want to be sitting down when we tell you this."

"Are you serious?" I ask. "You just show up and... and transform like that, and now you want to sit down with me and chat? What's going on? What do you want with me?"

"Ms. Brix," says Josie, gesturing at the now-forgotten cardboard sheet on the floor, "please."

I look from one woman to the other, eyeing them suspiciously. Samantha is a statuesque blonde, while Josie has dark skin and the face of a supermodel. I don't see malice in their eyes, even though I have no idea who they are or where they came from. For a moment I hesitate, debating making a break for it, but I push the idea away. I still have no idea where I'll go, and something tells me that these women might be my only hope for figuring out what's wrong with me.

Slowly, I sit back down, still clutching my backpack to my chest like it's a lifeline. The other women follow suit, taking a seat on the cardboard and crossing their legs. For a minute I have the absurd feeling that I'm back in kindergarten again, sitting in a circle with the teachers as I wait for them to start the day's story.

Samantha eyes me for a moment before starting to speak, looking like she's choosing her words carefully. "Something happened to you just now, didn't it?" she asks. "Something you can't explain."

"I..." I clear my throat, the idea of not telling her what happened flashing briefly through my mind, but I dismiss it. "Yes," I say, my voice barely above a whisper. "Something happened to my body. I can't even describe it. It was like..."

"Like you were transforming?" asks Josie gently.

I nod. "These two guys came in here while I was sleeping. They were trying to steal from me, or... or worse." I shake my head. "I was scared. They came towards me, and then it was like I started changing. My skin turned red. It looked sort of like yours was when you first showed up. There were these scaly things popping up on my arms, my teeth turned into fangs, my hair got thicker... and then I breathed fire." I take a shaky breath, hardly believing the words even as they come out of my mouth. "I guess I scared them away, because they ran. I don't know if they're coming back. That's when you guys arrived."

Josie's eyebrows raise slightly, but Samantha just nods slowly, knowingly, like she's seen this all happen a dozen times before. "For what it's worth, Millie--can I call you that, by the way?" I hesitate for a moment and then nod. Samantha continues, "For what it's worth, Millie, you're not alone in this. I've seen more people your age in this exact situation than you can count." She takes a breath, as if steeling herself before making a big announcement, and then says, "The truth is, you're a shifter."

I stare at her blankly. "Huh?"

"We use the word shifter as a shorthand for 'shapeshifter'," Josie adds.

My expression must be giving away how confused I am, because Samantha says, "I get that this must be coming as a surprise to you. Up until tonight, you probably thought shapeshifters only existed in stories, right?"

"Yeah," I say dryly. "That's because they *do* only exist in stories."

"Do they, though?" Samantha asks, holding her hand up in the beam of moonlight that's coming in through the window. As if on cue, her skin begins to turn red again, the color deepening until her whole hand is the same shade of bright scarlet. She snaps her fingers, and suddenly her hand starts to glow, radiating white light as if it were a luminescent bulb. "Can you really say that this is anything other than magic?" she asks me, meeting my eyes with her own.

I scoot back, my head spinning with fear and confusion. "How are you doing that?"

"Josie and I are witch shifters," Samantha says. "Yes, you heard that right--witches. We have the ability to turn into another form. The red skin, the black eyes, the magic... that's all witch stuff, and we access it by... well, by shapeshifting."

"So you're saying I'm a witch?" I ask, shaking my head in disbelief. "Like Harry Potter?"

Josie chuckles. "Hardly." Samantha shoots her a warning look, and she quiets, returning her dark eyes to me.

"It's more complicated than that," Samantha says, closing her hand as it returns to normal. "There are more types of shifters than just witches. Dragons, vampires, wolves, sirens..."

"And up until now, you probably didn't know any of those things even existed," adds Josie, tucking her legs under her. "You're probably thinking we're crazy, right?"

I let out a long breath, biting my lip for a moment. "I don't even know what to think anymore."

"Well, that's progress," Samantha says. "Confusion is normal at this point. The truth is, you shapeshifted back there when those guys attacked you. The fear response is what activated your powers. That happens a lot when shifters come into their own--usually right around your age. As witches, we have charms in place to locate and track the source of any new shifter magic--in this case, you."

I run a hand through my hair, feeling more tired than ever. "This is crazy. I don't... I mean, *what*? You guys show up here out of nowhere and tell me I have magic powers, and you're acting like this is all normal."

"That's because it *is* normal," says Josie. "For us, at least."

I stare at them, looking from one to the other. Their expressions are frustratingly calm and casual. I feel like my life has been turned completely upside-down, like I can't get a grip on anything that's happening to me anymore. The rational part of my brain is fighting against all this, telling me they must be lying, this must be a joke, magic isn't real, humans can't transform... But the other part, the part that knows deep down that this isn't a dream, is whispering that I might as well listen to them, that this is as good of an explanation as any for what happened to me earlier. *You were wondering why you breathed fire,* that part of me murmurs. *You know it's physically impossible, but it happened anyway. Who says this isn't the reason?*

I find myself thinking back to that growing feeling of being out of place, that sense of non-belonging that I've felt growing inside me all my life, that cool, foreign energy that I felt coursing through my body. It's all too much, and I just want to go to sleep for about a year. But that's not happening, and I know it. "Let's say I believe you," I say slowly, pursing my lips. "Let's say I believe that shapeshifters *are* real, that I'm one of them. Why did you come find me? What do you want with me?"

"That's the big question," Samantha says, nodding approvingly. "If you thought this was like Harry Potter before, Millie, you have no idea what is coming."

I raise my eyebrows. "What do you mean?"

"There's a reason most humans don't know that shifters exist," she replies deliberately. "You can probably imagine what would happen if all of society knew about magic and magical beings. Scientists would never leave us alone. There could be fighting, discrimination, full-on wars, for all we know. That's why we let them believe we're just the stuff of fairy tales. But there are a few humans who know about us. Heads of government, trusted members of our society. People we can be fairly sure will have the best interests of shifters in mind."

"Okay," I say slowly. "I guess I'm with you."

"Good," says Samantha. "Things between humans and shifters haven't always been peaceful, though. There was a period of time when even the humans who knew about us seemed ready to take action against us."

"Why?" I ask, finding myself intrigued even though what they're telling me is absurd.

"They were afraid, I think," Samantha answered. "When we started becoming more common, it shook up relations between shifters and humans. Many of us didn't even know we were shifters, and our abilities were unstable and unpredictable. It looked like things were going to get ugly, especially with the possibility of shifters forming an army and making a move against them. But it wasn't like they could get rid of us, so eventually, our two societies came to an agreement."

Josie met my eyes. "The humans founded a series of schools on every major continent, academies where newly-discovered shifters can learn to use their powers under supervision. There, they are taught how to coexist with humans, how to keep their powers under control, and how to keep the secrets of our society safe. Samantha and I are representatives of the English-speaking branch of Shifter Academy."

"So let me get this straight," I say, my sarcasm just barely masking my confusion. "You guys are... what, recruiters? And somehow your witchy powers told you that I had transformed, so you came here to pick me up and bring me to this Shifter Academy. Do I have this right?"

"That's the long and short of it, yes," says Samantha.

"Shit," I mutter, staring down at the floor. "You guys realize how insane this sounds, right? I mean, it does. It sounds insane."

"I know," Samantha says, and I can see sympathy in her expression. "We realize this is a lot to put on you. The truth is. A lot of shifters are like you: orphans or transients, who either didn't know their parents or were abandoned by them after they found out what they were. Not everyone can handle the truth of what we are."

My eyes widen. "Are you saying that's why my parents left me in the hospital when I was a baby? Did they know what I was?"

Josie and Samantha exchange a look, and something that I can't identify crosses their faces. "That's not clear to us," Samantha says, not looking at me.

"But how did you know my name, then?" I ask. "You must have more information about me."

"We only know your name because we sensed it," Josie replies. "We're highly trained in the use of our witch powers. They allow us to get bits of information about the source of an unexpected burst of magical energy. We've been following you ever since you left your house. That was when your shifting magic first appeared on our radar."

I think back to the incident with Mark, nodding. I had to admit it made sense. There's a long moment of silence as I struggle to process everything they've just told me, but soon it becomes clear that it's going to take longer than a few minutes to come to grips with it. "So what now?" I ask at last, looking back up at the two women.

"Now," Samantha says, "you're going to come with us. The Academy is waiting for you."

CHAPTER 5

I wish I could properly put into words the combination of thoughts and emotions that are swirling around in my head when Samantha tells me this. The look on her face is irritatingly calm, like she's a parent patiently waiting for her kid to grasp a simple math concept. But my mind is a mess. I find myself thinking back to the fact that yesterday morning I was waking up at home in bed, the only worries on my mind was the fact that I had an upcoming history exam and that we were out of instant coffee. Now here I am, sitting across from two strange women with magic powers who are telling me that I, too, have magic powers.

Secret societies. Magical boarding schools. Supernatural beings. And I still haven't even fully processed the fact that I breathed fire a few minutes ago. It's all too much. I drop my head and cover my face with my hand, my shoulders slumping. I don't think I've ever felt so tired. "You have to be kidding," I mumble into my hands, not looking at Samantha or Josie. Suddenly the idea of meeting their eyes is too much for me.

"We're not," Samantha says, "but I can see that you're feeling a little overwhelmed."

"A little overwhelmed?" I ask, lifting my head. "A *little* overwhelmed? You're telling me that you're going to whisk me away to

G. BAILEY & REGAN ROSEWOOD

some kind of boarding school for shapeshifters, and you think I'm just a *little* overwhelmed?"

"Okay," Samantha concedes, "fine. Very overwhelmed. But trust me when I say that with time, this will all stop being so scary. Once you're at Shifter Academy, things will start to feel more normal. I promise."

"You're assuming I'm even going to go with you," I say slowly, my eyes narrowing. "I never agreed to this."

Josie raises her eyebrows. "Are you saying you're not going to come with us?"

I shrug my shoulders, even though I can already feel myself making up my mind. My world has been turned upside-down already. I'm not about to shake it up any more. "Are you going to force me?"

The woman exchanged another one of those cryptic looks, and it's enough to make me want to scream. It feels like this is all a joke, and I'm the punchline. "If you're asking whether we'll take you there against your will," Samantha replies slowly, "the answer is no. We're not authorized to do that. Even if we were, we wouldn't be able to teach someone who's hellbent on not participating."

"Good," I say, a little smugly, finally feeling like I'm getting a scrap of power back. I get to my feet, dusting the dirt and grime off my hands. God, I need a shower. "Then I guess we don't have anything else to talk about."

"Just a minute, Millie," Samantha says. The women both stand up, their expressions unreadable. "I would advise you to think long and hard about this," Samantha continues, staring at me with her big blue eyes. "It's true that we can't force you to come with us. But that doesn't mean your life can just go back to normal now."

My eyes narrow. "What do you mean?"

"For starters," Josie chimes in, "your powers have been activated now. There's no undoing that once it happens. Sooner or later, you'll end up with your back against the wall again - and I'm guessing sooner, considering you seem to be living on the streets - and you'll shift again. It's a dangerous ability, and if you don't learn

26

how to control it, then you may end up hurting someone. Or yourself."

"I'll take my chances," I snap, not liking the condescension in her tone.

"Second of all," Samantha adds, crossing her arms over her chest, "you're on the grid now, Millie, whether you like it or not. We detected your identity and your magic, and if we could do it, then others will be able to as well. Other shifters, for example, and eventually, humans, too. If our liaisons with the human community find out that there's a rogue shifter out in the world, they'll watch you. And if - *when* - your powers start to cause problems, because you've never been trained in using them, they will come after you."

I swallow, feeling my confidence falter a little. "And then?" I ask, not sure if I really want to know the answer.

"And then they'll deal with you as they see fit," Josie finishes. "Humans may be our allies, but make no mistake: they're not our friends. This school is a way of protecting you from their perception that shifters are a danger to the world. If you don't accept our help, you're taking on the risk of living your life as a rogue shifter. And trust me when I say that rogue shifters don't last long."

I shake my head in disbelief. "But that's not fair," I protest. "I didn't ask for any of this! Now you're saying that if I don't give up everything I have here, they'll never leave me alone?"

"No," agrees Samantha. "It's not fair. But it's the reality of the world we live in."

"Besides," Josie says, her tone gentle but firm, "what's left for you here, anyway?" I feel like her eyes are boring a hole into me, seeing more about my life than she has any right to know.

And why shouldn't she? some part of me asks. *Look at you. You're dirty, you're alone, you're lost, and you have nowhere to go. It doesn't take a genius to see that.*

True enough. But I'm not about to give up my freedom so easily. I've spent my life being passed from one person to another, never getting a say in it and never being in charge of my own fate. I'd rather be alone than be a prisoner. "I don't have much," I agree, "but I'm not giving up any more of what I have to make other people happy." I square my shoulders, looking from one woman to the other. "Thank you for the offer," I say, "but I'll take my chances."

Josie bows her head, and Samantha gives me a curt nod. "Okay," she says at last. "If that's what you want. You're making a mistake, though, and I think you know that." I open my mouth to argue, but she holds up a hand. "Relax," she says. "It's all right. I'll tell you what, though..." She turns to look at Josie, who nods, seemingly already knowing what she's going to say. "We aren't leaving the city until the morning," Samantha tells me. "It's a little past midnight now. We're going to depart from the docks on the south side of the city--the pier down by the old marina. If you change your mind--and I strongly suggest you do--come meet us there at nine AM. We'll be going whether you show up or not. Think hard about this, Millie."

"Okay," I say, nodding. "But I'm not going to change my mind."

"If you say so," Samantha says. "In that case, we'll say goodbye now." She motions to Josie, who nods to me before turning and heading in the direction of the door. "Be seeing you," Samantha says, and follows her.

I'm left to watch them go, feeling more alone than I ever have before.

IT TAKES me a long time to go back to sleep. After setting an alarm on my phone, and noticing that the battery is getting low--I'll have to find a place to charge it before too long, I spend a long time back on the sheet of cardboard, staring at the ceiling. For a while I'm afraid to go to sleep, wondering if the thugs from earlier are going to return--this time with friends--but after more than an hour I let myself relax a little. If they were really going to come back, they probably would have done so already. Most likely they don't want to take the risk, and I don't blame them. I'm not under any illusions that these powers--whatever they are--aren't dangerous.

The longer I lie there, trying to find sleep, the more I start to have second thoughts. Was I too hasty to send the women away? It was obvious they wanted to help me, and as shocking as this all is, wouldn't it be better to have someone in my corner, someone who understands what's happening to me? What if I transform again and hurt myself... or someone else? Then there's what they said about humans coming after me if that happens. With no family to speak of, it would be easy enough for them to make me disappear, to whisk me off to some black site where I'll never be heard from again, all in the name of keeping the human world safe from shifters.

I can feel a fresh wave of anxiety bubbling up inside me, and if it weren't for the fact that I'm physically exhausted, I probably wouldn't be able to fall asleep. Eventually, though, I drift off, uncomfortable as I am on the hard concrete floor, and when I do, I dream.

I'm in a police interrogation room. The detective has his hands on the desk, his eyes furious as he stares down at me. I don't feel quite right, and there's a creeping, haunting sensation that I've done something terrible. "Why did you do it?" he asks me, slamming his hand down on the desk. "Why? People are dead because of you, Millie. Innocent people. All because you were too selfish to think of anyone but yourself."

"I'm sorry," I begin, desperate to explain myself, even though I don't even know what I did to end up here. "I didn't mean to. You have to believe me."

"Oh, I know you didn't mean to," the detective says, "but that doesn't change the fact that you did it. You thought you could mess around with things you can't control and look at what's happened. You're a murderer."

"A murderer?" My eyes widen. "No, that's not true. There has to be some mistake." I lift my hand to try to placate him, and that's when I notice two things.

The first is that my hand doesn't look human. It's red and scaly, with razor sharp claws where the nails should be.

The second is that it's covered in blood.

I sit bolt upright on the cardboard, gasping for breath. There's sweat staining my clothes, and my heart is pounding out of my chest. I look around as I try to collect myself after the nightmare and notice that light is streaming in through the window. I'm still in the warehouse, it's morning, and the storm from last night finally seems to have let up.

There's a lump in my throat, and I'm filled with the sense of guilt, terror, and unease that always comes after a bad dream like that. *Relax,* I tell myself. *It was just a dream, probably because you were still thinking about all this shifter stuff. You're fine. You didn't hurt anybody.*

No, the other part of my mind argues, *but you could. You know that, don't you?*

"Damn it," I mutter, raking a hand through my dirty hair. I can already feel the stubborn resistance I had to the women from the academy melting away, the dream having planted a paralyzing seed of fear and anxiety in my chest. Who am I kidding, anyway? It's not like I have any other options. Even if the dream doesn't end up coming true, even if these abilities don't cause a disaster, I'm still alone, jobless, and friendless. How long will I last on the streets, anyway? Maybe before I turned into some kind of supernatural being, I could have made it work. It would have been hard, sure, and I might not have been cut out for it, but I could have at least given it a shot. But things are different now, and there's no denying that. The scope of my world has been changed, whether I like it or not.

I let out a long sigh, feeling the resignation wash over me.

I don't have a choice--I never had a choice.

Stretching, I grab my phone to check the time, and my eyes widen. It's a quarter to nine. If I'm not at the dock in fifteen minutes, Samantha and Josie will be gone forever.

CHAPTER 6

The fact that I'm not at all familiar with this part of town isn't doing me favors, and by the time I've scrambled to my feet, gathered up my stuff, and bolted out of the warehouse and back into the bright sunshine, I'm almost positive I'm not going to make it. Frantic, I pull out my phone, feeling half-insane as I bring up the maps app. If I miss this chance, I'm screwed, and it's rapidly going up on nine.

Yeah, I think dryly, *and whose fault is that, exactly?* Okay, fine. Mine. Point taken. But can you blame me?

I'm in luck; the marina Samantha mentioned is close--less than ten minutes away, if I run. Not wasting another minute, I jog down the street. The passersby are still giving me dirty looks, but for some reason--whether it's the fact that I'm in such a hurry or the fact that I now know I have the ability to breathe fire--they don't scare me as much as they did last night. All I care about at this point is heading those two witches off before they take away my only chance to make sense of this new situation.

Rounding onto a busier street, I pick up my pace, nearly crashing into a couple that's walking in my direction. I call an apology over my shoulder as I go, feeling the necklace that Mollie gave me digging into my heel against the sole of my boot. There's no time to adjust it; I bolt forward, passing confused-looking pedestrians as I make a beeline for the docks. Soon I can see the outline of the pier in the distance, dark against the sun that's glistening off the water. And there... yes, I can see them. Two, by now familiar, female figures. It's a minute to nine; all I can do is pray that they'll see me coming and wait.

I sprint the rest of the way to the pier, kicking myself all the while for telling them to go away. As I get closer, I see that their backs are to me, and they're facing out towards the waves, shielding their eyes from the glaring sun with their hands. "Hey!" I yell as soon as I'm in shouting distance. They don't seem to hear me, and I can see Samantha extending her hands, as if she were praying... or casting a spell. Her skin has gone red again. "Hey!" I shout again, tearing across the wooden planks as I reach the end of the dock.

Finally, I seem to have gotten their attention. Josie is the first one to turn to look at me, raising her eyebrows slightly when she sees me jogging towards her. She nudges Samantha on the arm who then lowers her hands and turns in my direction. I think I see the hint of a half-smile on her face when she realizes I've changed my mind, and I'm willing to let her have the satisfaction, considering how narrowly I almost missed them. "I'm sorry," I say, breathless as I slow to a walk and close the distance between us. "I'm sorry. I almost didn't make it."

Samantha quirks an eyebrow at me. "Are you saying what I think you're saying?"

"If you think I'm saying I've had a change of heart and want to come with you after all, then yes," I reply without missing a beat. My face feels a little flushed, both from the exercise and from the embarrassment.

Samantha's smile grows. "I'm glad to hear it. I had a feeling you might end up coming here after all." She holds her hand out to me, and I can see the honesty in her eyes. Not hesitating this time, I reach out and take it, giving it a short, firm shake. "You made the right choice, Millie. Seriously."

I nod, still breathing hard, and the sense of relief that washes over me is enough to make me agree with her. "Well," I say, trailing behind them as they return to the end of the pier, "what happens now? Horse-drawn carriage? Flying carpet?"

Josie chuckles. "Don't you think that would be a little cliche?" She turns to Samantha, who nods and extends her arms again. I watch as her skin turns red, the color rippling up her arms to her elbows, her palms beginning to glow with an eerie light in a matching shade of crimson. I glance behind us. If someone happened to pass by, they would be in for one hell of a sight. But there's nothing to worry about; the marina is deserted, and even on the farther docks there's hardly a soul to be seen.

Overhead, a seagull shrieks down at us. For a moment, there's just the silence of the pier, the lapping of the waves, and my own heart beating in my ears. Then I notice a tingling sensation in my body. It starts in my fingers and then begins to vibrate upwards, growing stronger each time. Seconds later, my eyes widen as I stare down at my body. If I hadn't seen everything I've seen in the past day, I would think I was hallucinating. I can see through my legs. Underneath my feet, which have gone translucent, I can make out the shape of the boards we're standing on.

I snap my head back up, panicking a little, and grab Josie by the arm. "It's okay," she says, nodding down at her own legs. They're turning see-through as well, as are Samantha's. "Just relax. It will be over in a minute."

Fighting my instinctive reaction to freak out, knowing already that at this point I'm better off just sitting back and enjoying the ride, I drop my shoulders and let the sensation wash over me. Soon, the planks under my feet are changing color, going from brown to vibrant green, and I can see the shapes of grass blades becoming clear. It's like a Polaroid photograph that's slowly developing in front of my eyes, except instead of the changes happening on a piece of celluloid, they're happening to the ground beneath me. The next thing I know, the cool breeze off the ocean is dying down, the sky turning overcast, the sounds of the waves fading into the background.

I look around again, and my breath catches in my throat.

We're no longer at the Marina. In fact, it's becoming increasingly clear to me that we're no longer in the city, period. We now stand on top of a sloping hill, with green fields stretching out as far as the eye can see. In the distance is a forest, following more rolling hills onto the horizon. It's nowhere I can recognize, and for all I know, we could be miles away from where we just were. In fact...

"Where are we?" I ask, my voice barely above a whisper.

"A few minutes off campus," Josie replies. She points behind me, and I follow her motion, eyebrows raising as I take in what's on my other side. The hill continues downward, lush green grass carpeting the ground, and at the bottom is an enormous, old building. It reminds me a little of an old-fashioned boarding school, like something out of a movie, supported by tall marble pillars, with balconies on every story and ivy creeping up the outer wall. In front of it is a paved road that wraps around in a loop before snaking away towards the forest in the background.

"Is that...?" I ask, not able to pull my gaze away. Samantha nods.

It's unlike anything I've ever seen, and I can't help but suck in a breath. This can't be real, can it? None of this is possible. Again I wonder if I'm dreaming, and again I have to remind myself that I'm not. "Where are we?" I ask, my voice sounding soft and far away. "How did we get here?"

"A teleportation spell," Samantha replies. "It's a taxing form of magic, especially when we're going this far, but it's more efficient than other human forms of transportation. Sometimes I forget what it's like to experience it for the first time." She puts her hands on her hips, and I can now see that she looks a little drained. "We're on an island," she continues. "Not far from Scotland, actually. It's not huge, but it's all property of the academy."

"Now you see why coming with us was so important," Josie adds. "This is a place away from prying eyes, where you can train in peace and safety." She turns to Samantha, raising an eyebrow. "Although I don't see why you couldn't have just brought us to the front door, while you were at it."

Samantha shoots her a look. "You try jumping three people this far. I'm beat. Besides..." She nods to me, smirking a little. "I always like to see the looks on their faces when they see it from up here."

I clear my throat, unable to disagree with her. I feel like I've stepped out of the real world and into the pages of one of my fantasy books. "So what now?" I ask. "Do I have to sign up for classes? Where am I going to live?"

"All in due time," Samantha says, holding up a hand. "We'll start by taking you to the registrar's office, and from there we can figure out what classes you'll need to take first."

"Speaking of which," I say, "that reminds me. You said that there are - what, five different types of shifters?" Josie nods, and I continue. "But you never told me which kind I am." I see something cross her face, but it's gone too quickly for me to identify it. Now that the danger is over for the time being, I can't help but feel a little curious which type of shifter I am. *That's a weird thing to think about,* I think.

"I mean," I continue, "I turned red like you guys, but I also had claws, and fur, and scales, and fangs..." I shake my head, thinking back to my monstrous appearance when I looked at my reflection earlier. "So what am I?"

Josie clears her throat. "Why don't we start walking, and we'll tell you what we know on the way? Would that be all right?"

I nod, and the three of us begin to make our way down the slope and towards the front of the building.

"The truth is," she says, not looking at me as we pick our way over the grassy ground, "we're not sure what kind of shifter you are."

My brow furrows. "What do you mean?"

"Your magic signature was unlike anything we've ever seen before," Samantha chimes in. "At first, we weren't even sure if we had detected a shifter. I was wondering if my charm was faulty and needed to be replaced." She turns to look at me. "So far, you've described characteristics of several types of shifters. The fur is typical of wolf shifters, but the claws and scales sound like a siren--or maybe a dragon."

"I did breathe fire earlier," I admit. "When those guys attacked me." Samantha raises her eyebrows but doesn't reply, looking thoughtful.

"And then there are the fangs, which makes me think vampire," Josie says, "but you said your skin turned red, like ours."

"So you're saying I'm... what, just a mish-mash of all these different kinds?" I ask. "How is that even possible?"

"It's not," replies Samantha. "At least, not as far as I'm aware. That's why we need to talk to somebody else and get more information. Someone who knows more about these things might be able to get to the bottom of it."

"I guess I have two reasons to thank you guys for bringing me here, then," I say quietly. "I'm sorry I was so rude to you earlier. I was just scared, I think."

"That's normal," Josie replies. "What matters is that you're here now, and you're safe. Now your training can start." We stop where the circular drive passes in front of the building. The giant front doors stare me down, and I'm struck by the sense that after I walk through them, my life as I knew it, as much of a life as I had, anyway, will be over. Josie smiles at me as if she can read my thoughts - and for all I know, she can.

"Millie Brix," says Samantha, starting toward the doors, "welcome to Shifter Academy."

CHAPTER 7

The women push the doors open and we find ourselves in a large entrance hall. The ceiling seems almost impossibly high, with marble floors underfoot and an enormous staircase in the back leading to the upper levels. Hallways and classrooms stretch in every direction, and as tranquil as it looked from the outside, inside, the school is bustling with life. Students and teachers mill about, some looking like they're on their way to classes and some looking like they've just gotten finished. They jostle each other as they move through the entrance hall, passing papers back and forth and moving in gossiping clumps.

The students all wear pristine white uniforms--skirts or leggings for the girls and slacks for the guys. I suppose if this *is* some kind of ancient magical school; it makes sense that there's a dress code. The thing that startles me, though, is how *normal* they all seem: no claws or fangs to speak of, just a plethora of normal skin tones, with no scales, fur, or magical powers to be seen. If I didn't know better, I might mistake this for just another European boarding school.

"Cat got your tongue, Millie?" Josie asks, a gleam in her eye as they lead me across the foyer. We turn a corner into a hallway full of old-fashioned classrooms and offices, the kind you would find in a

1900s boarding school. Part of me wonders how the hell I'll ever find my way around this place.

"The students," I reply quietly. "They all seem so..."

"Human?" offers Samantha. "Don't be fooled. They're all shifters, like you."

"Like me?" I ask.

"I see where you're going with this," Samantha replies. "The answer is no; none of them have shown characteristics of more than one clan... until now."

"I see," I say, heart sinking a little. "But why haven't any of them... you know, transformed?"

"Excellent question," replies Samantha. "Transforming is strictly forbidden outside of class, at least until you've shown to be competent at controlling your powers. Of course, many students break the rules and do it anyway, but if you want to stay on the good side of the faculty here, you won't test your luck."

"Got it," I say, nodding. "No unsupervised transformation." Again I'm struck by the absurdity of this whole situation, but at this point I'm too far in to start questioning my sanity again. At least if this is just some crazy hallucination, so far, it's not a bad one.

I gape at my surroundings as we go, lagging behind the other women as I try to take in the strange new world around me. Even without levitating bookcases and magic wands, it's unlike anything I've ever seen. After eighteen years of bouncing from one public school to the next, passed from one disinterested foster family to another, I'm overwhelmed by the newness of it all. Briefly, and not for the first time, I wonder about Mollie--what ever happened to her? Is she safe? Will she ever find out what became of me?

I'm jostled away from this train of thought when the witches come to an abrupt stop in front of an office door marked "Registrar". Not bothering to knock, Samantha pulls it open and waves us through to an enormous wooden desk. Behind it is an ancient woman with a pair of enormous glasses balanced on the end of her nose.

She looks up when we enter. "Ms. Goldstein, Ms. Everhart," she says, pushing aside the stack of files in front of her. "To what do I owe this pleasure?" Her eyes settle on me. "A new student?"

"Yes, Mrs. Fairbanks," Josie says, taking a seat on the other side of the desk. I follow suit, finding myself between the two witches. "We were alerted to her early last night, and we tracked her down in an abandoned warehouse."

"I see," says Mrs. Fairbanks, scrutinizing me. "A runaway?" I stare at her, feeling like she's looking right through me. "It's all right, my dear," she adds. "You're not the first. Do you have a family that needs to be notified?"

"I..." I begin, and the truth of my situation falls on me again. "No. No family. My foster dad was trying to hurt me, so I... I ran away from home. That's when they found me." I don't know what's compelling me to tell her all this, but I can't help it. It's like she's opening me up just by looking at me.

"Ah," Mrs. Fairbanks says, nodding. "Well, it's a good thing we found you, then. Now, tell me, Miss..."

"Brix," I reply. "Millie Brix."

"Ms. Brix," she continues, "what kind of shifter are you, exactly?"

I stare at her, wondering what on earth I'm supposed to say. A hybrid? Some kind of freakish combination? Again, my mind flashes back to the hideous monster I saw in the reflection of the warehouse window, and I suddenly feel like I want to cry. I can feel that old, familiar worry welling up inside me as I look at this kindly woman with her wrinkled face, that fear that I'll never properly belong anywhere. It looks a little different now, but at the end of the day, it's the same old anxiety.

"I don't know," I breathe. "What's wrong with me?" I'm not sure who the question is directed toward, but it's out before I can stop it.

Mrs. Fairbanks' brow furrows, and the others exchange a look.

I turn to Samantha. "You said you couldn't figure out what kind of shifter I am. Does that mean there's some kind of problem?" A horrible possibility comes to me then, and I touch her arm. "Can you even teach me here?"

Josie puts a gentle hand on my shoulder. "It's all right, Millie. It's all right." She looks up to address Mrs. Fairbanks. "Her shifter signature was all over the place, and her aura back at the warehouse was... Well, like a rainbow. She showed signs of all five clans."

"Really?" Mrs. Fairbanks' brow furrows, and she leans forward, examining me with her large, inquisitive eyes. "That's unusual." She reaches out for me and then hesitates. "May I?" Hesitatingly, I nod, and her eyes suddenly go black, the same way the other witches' did back at the warehouse.

I guess we know what kind of shifter she is, I think dryly.

Taking my chin in her hand, the old woman stares at me, turning my face this way and that. "Mm," she says, nodding. "Mm-hmm. Very unusual." She lets me go, and her eyes go back to the watery blue that they were moments before. "You're certainly right, Ms. Everhart. I have to admit, I've never seen anything like this before, and I've been working at the Academy for fifty years." Seeing the dismayed look on my face, she rushes to add, "But that's no reason to worry! We'll find a place for you here, Ms. Brix." She turns to the others. "I think it might be a good idea to bring President Hawthorne here and get his opinion."

Samantha nods. "I think you're right."

"Who's President Hawthorne?" I ask, feeling stupid.

"He's the headmaster of this Shifter Academy," Samantha replies. "Since you've shown signs of multiple shifting abilities, he'll be the best one to decide how to design your schedule."

"And I don't have to wait for the next term to start?"

Samantha shakes her head. "Most of our new students are like you. Their powers manifest at random times after they turn eighteen, and they master them at different rates. We've made it easy to integrate new students into our program by dividing classes up based on skill level. You won't have to worry about getting lost--all of your classmates will be relatively new shifters, like yourself."

"I'll put a call in to President Hawthorne," Mrs. Fairbanks volunteers, already reaching for the old-fashioned rotary telephone on the desk. Before I can say anything else, she's dialing a number and speaking rapidly into the phone, talking for less than a minute before hanging up. "He'll be down shortly," she informs us. "Feel free to wait here."

I stare down at my lap as we wait, unsure what to do or say. At least it sounds like they're not going to turn me away for being a freak, but that doesn't do much to put my mind at ease. All I can do now is wait... and hope this President Hawthorne feels the same way as the others.

A few minutes later, the door to the office opens, and I look up. A guy who looks to be around my age pokes his head into the room. "Mrs. Fairbanks?" he says. His voice is melodic, with a slight Cheshire lilt in the accent. His hair is an ashy shade of blonde, his eyes a bright gray. "Professor Abernathy sent me to ask you about wolfsbane. Tomorrow's a full moon."

A full moon? I think. *Does this mean he's a wolf shifter?*

I'm once again a little surprised by how nonchalant the students here are about their abilities--will I ever get to that point? *Not if you only ever turn into an abomination like you did earlier,* sneers a cynical part of me, but I do my best to ignore it.

"Ah, Mr. Ivis," says Mrs. Fairbanks. "We received a new shipment this morning. Would you be a dear and make sure it got to the nurse's office?"

"Of course," the guy says, giving her a nod. He glances at Samantha and Josie before his eyes come to rest on me, giving me a curious once-over. I'm not sure whether it's the fact that he's obviously handsome or the fact that I must look a mess, but I duck my head a little. His eyes linger on me for a moment longer before he clears his throat and leaves the office.

"Good kid," remarks Josie. "That was Shade Ivis, Millie. He's a wolf shifter. Before long you'll learn the names of most of the students here."

I open my mouth to respond, but then the door opens again, and a tall man enters the office. He's stately, handsome, and well-groomed, with salt-and-pepper hair and a trim goatee. His dark suit is a stark contrast to the white school uniforms. "Good morning, ladies," he says, approaching Mrs. Fairbanks' side of the desk. "May I?" he asks, indicating a free chair. Mrs. Fairbanks nods, and he sits down, leaning back and folding his hands. "I was told we have a bit of an unusual case here," he says, his dark eyes settling on me.

I listen as Josie and Samantha reiterate the story, from their charm alerting them to a new shifter to bringing me back here. Mrs. Fairbanks chimes in to confirm what they saw in my aura. For a long while after, nobody speaks, and I feel incredibly small under the headmaster's unreadable gaze.

Finally he speaks up. "Well, you're right that this is an unusual case," he says. "In fact, I've only heard of something like this happening once before. It was centuries ago, when a group of rogue witches tried to create a hybrid shifter using the abilities of the other clans. It was deemed an abomination and destroyed." My heart sinks.

Samantha's brow furrows. "You're not actually thinking about--"

"Of course not," Hawthorne replies. "That was a long time ago. We're more civilized now, more evolved. Obviously, we'll want to see how your abilities manifest, Millie, and some research will need to be done into your background and parentage, but you're entitled to an education here, the same as everyone else." He smiles at me.

Did they ever tell him my name? I wonder. They must have, right? I honestly can't remember. Before I can consider this further, he's standing up, straightening his suit. "You said she showed signatures of all five clans. We'll have to start her in introductory courses for each of them. As for her last period..." He considers for a moment. "Coexisting with Humankind. That will give you plenty to do this semester, I think." Once again, he gives me that toothy grin. "It's a pleasure to have you here, Ms. Brix. I'm sure we'll be seeing more of each other."

With that, President Hawthorne excuses himself.

"See?" says Mrs. Fairbanks, turning back to me. "Nothing to worry about. Our headmaster is very progressive."

"I can see that," I say, nodding. "What kind of shifter is he, anyway?"

Mrs. Fairbanks blinks. "Why, he's not a shifter at all, Millie. President Hawthorne is a human."

CHAPTER 8

The dormitory was an equally ornate building on the other side of the drive from the academy itself. "You'll be on the fifth floor," Josie says as she leads me down the cobblestone path. Samantha stayed with Mrs. Fairbanks to do my intake paperwork, and with President Hawthorne having gone back to his offices, that only left bringing my stuff to my new living quarters, which I can only hope won't be too difficult to find. "Everyone has a single room, so privacy won't be an issue. Lights out is at ten PM, after the last bell rings." She glances at me, frowning. "Are you okay? You look... I don't know, worried."

"I'm sorry," I say, shaking myself. "I'm still just trying to process everything. Yesterday I was going to regular high school and walking home in the rain, and now... It's just all so surreal." A beat passes, and I add sheepishly, "Come to think of it, I'm also pretty tired."

Josie laughs. "You've had a long twenty-four hours. Well, don't worry--you won't be expected in classes tomorrow, so you can spend the rest of the day decompressing."

"Maybe this is a stupid question," I say as the road levels out beneath our feet, "but do I need to bring anything tomorrow?"

"There should be notebooks and pencils in your dorm room,"

Josie replies, "but other than that... Oh, wait! That reminds me: what's your clothing size?"

I purse my lips. "Medium, I suppose."

She nods. "Okay. I'll run down to the laundry and have them drop you off a uniform later today. Do you prefer skirts or pants?"

Glancing down at my dirty, torn jeans, I can't help but chuckle. "Pants. Definitely pants."

By now we've reached the front of the dormitory. The circular drive is lined with trees and hedges, reminding me of some kind of Victorian manor, and all around me are students going to and from classes. Josie turns to me and fumbles in her pocket before pulling out an old-fashioned skeleton key. "Here's your room key. Quaint, I know. Yours is number 12-B. Fifth floor, remember."

"You're not coming with me?"

She shakes her head. "I have to get back to my office and check my charms. There may be others like you out there who need to be picked up. But the dormitory is pretty straightforward--you won't have any trouble. Here's a copy of your schedule, as well," she adds, producing a printed sheet of paper. "The breakfast bell rings at seven every morning. If you're worried that won't wake you up, set an alarm on your phone. Just follow the other students to the dining hall, and if you get lost, you can ask the faculty for help getting to your classes."

"Got it," I say, nodding. "Thank you, Josie."

"You're welcome, Millie," she replies, giving me a long look. "And listen," she adds, "if you ever need anything, or even if you just want to talk, my door is always open. I know how it feels to be new to all this--I was in your shoes too, once."

I can't help but wonder if she knows anything about being in my shoes, considering what the headmaster said. An abomination, he had called it. If he's to be believed, then I'm only the second shifter like me in history. Still, I appreciate her kindness, and when she extends her hand, I shake it. "I'll take you up on that, I'm sure," I tell her, smiling. She takes a step away, giving me a professional nod, and then begins to make her way back towards the academy building.

On my own now, I turn and walk the rest of the way down the

drive until I find myself facing the dormitory doors. I probably look pathetic, standing there in dirty clothes, all my possessions on my back, clutching my schedule like a lost puppy. The fact that I don't have a uniform yet only makes me feel like more of an outsider as I glance over my shoulder at the campus around me.

As if to confirm my fears, the sound of a female voice over my shoulder makes me turn back around. "You don't look like you've been here more than five minutes." I look to see a svelte girl with freckles and a mess of blonde curls that bounce around her face when she moves. She has her book bag over her shoulder and her arms are full of school supplies, having just emerged out of the building through the double doors. Her expression is curious but not unkind. "Yikes," she says, in an accent that might be American, or maybe Canadian, stopping beside me and giving me a once-over with her jade green eyes. "You've certainly had a bit of a rough go of it, haven't you?"

Shrinking a little under her gaze, I reply, "You could say that."

"So what was it?" she asks, either oblivious to my embarrassment or too brazen to care. "Did you set your house on fire? Attack one of your classmates? One of the girls on my floor nearly drained her sister dry when she first shifted. You know--vampire." She makes a face and shakes her head. "I'm more into chocolate than blood, personally, but to each their own, I guess."

"Uh..." I begin, caught off-guard by her willingness to talk to me.

The blonde girl laughs, a tinkling, girlish sound that probably makes every guy she meets fall head over heels for her. "Sorry, sorry," she says, shaking her head. "This is probably all pretty new to you, right? Let me guess: you didn't even know shifters existed until, like... now."

She's really on my wavelength, I think, and reply, "Damn. You're reading me like a book."

The girl waves a dismissive hand at me. "Hardly. I've just been there before, that's all. Just two months ago, actually. When the recruiters tracked me down, I thought I'd completely lost my mind. Thought it was all bullshit."

"Really?" I raise my eyebrows. "Are you... I mean, do you have parents?" It comes out sounding more insensitive than I intended, and I wince, but she doesn't seem to notice.

"Oh, I have parents," the girl replies, "but they're human, both of them."

My curiosity is getting the better of me, and I ask, "How is that possible?"

She shrugs. "I think being a shifter is more like a genetic mutation than something hereditary. That's what they say, anyway... whoever "they" are. It sounds like they still don't know what causes some people to be born with shifter magic. But I guess that's why we're here, right? Sorry," she adds, going a little red, "I'm rambling. My name's Hazel, by the way."

She sticks out her hand, and I shake it. "Millie," I reply. "It's nice to meet you."

"Nice to meet you, too, Millie. Listen, I've got to get to class--I'm already on thin ice with Professor Freemantle. But I'll catch you later, yeah? Got dinner plans? Of course you don't. We can eat together, if you want."

"Okay," I say, my smile growing. I'm already starting to like this girl. "Sounds good. I'll see you later." She nods, grinning, and starts away. "Good luck with that professor," I call after her, and she raises a hand in acknowledgement.

Feeling a little better after my interaction with this bubbly class-mate, I push open the heavy wooden door to the dormitory. I find myself in what looks like a parlor, with couches and ottomans all around. On the opposite side is a fireplace, but given the weather, there's no fire burning in the hearth. To the left and right are two narrow spiral staircases, disappearing into the upper levels. Aside from hallways leading to washrooms and what looks like a study area in the distance, there's nowhere else to go. There are a few students around, and some of them shoot me curious glances from their seats around the common area.

There's a sinking feeling in my stomach when I look around and realize that I don't know where I'm supposed to go from here. Why the hell didn't I ask Hazel for directions? The others in the room don't seem nearly as friendly at first glance, and by now Josie is long gone. Sighing, I take a few steps forward, realizing that there's nothing for it but to try. The left and right wings of the dormitory aren't marked, so I pick the left one at random and head for the stairs, not wanting to waste any more time. I need a shower and a nap.

If I was expecting the stairs to move or somehow teleport me to the fifth floor, I was sorely mistaken. By the time I'm two flights up, I'm already breathing hard, and I'm just glad nobody is around to see me struggling. Have I always been this out of shape? Gritting my teeth, I power up a few more levels, finally arriving at the fifth floor landing and turning into a long hallway. Nondescript wooden doors line either side, along with windows that let in a great deal of the daytime light. I start to hurry down the hallway, keeping my eyes peeled for my room, and I'm so distracted that I don't see the guy heading my way until it's too late.

I collide with him, coming to a sudden stop in the middle of the hallway and staring up at the newcomer with wide eyes. He's tall and sturdily built, and bumping into him seems to have done more damage to me than to him. His eyes are a golden brown, standing in sharp contrast to his jet-black hair. His features are rugged, and I notice a scar running from his upper lip to just above his chin on the left side. Embarrassed, and a little intimidated, I take a couple steps back. "I'm so sorry," I say, holding my hands up. "I was completely distracted. I didn't even see you."

"Don't worry about it," the guy says, giving me a half-smile. "I'm pretty hard to knock down."

I chuckle, rubbing the back of my neck. "I can see that, yeah."

He takes in my clothes and says, "You're new here, aren't you?"

Sighing, I reply, "I guess it's pretty obvious, right? You're the second person in, like, five minutes who's asked me that."

"Well," he says, his smile growing a little, "considering the rest of us have to dress like we're in some kind of new-age cult, it's pretty easy to tell." He gestures down at his pristine white uniform, and I snort. "Anyway," he says, "I'm guessing you're looking for your dorm

47

room, right?" I nod, and he replies, "That's what I thought. Some bad news for you, though: this is the boys' wing."

Groaning, I run a hand through my hair. "That means I'm going to have to walk up all those stairs again, doesn't it?"

The guy laughs at that. "You'll get used to it. Anyway, though, it's nice to see a new face around here. I'll see you around."

He turns to leave, looking surprisingly happier than he did when I first ran into him. He's almost out of sight before I think to call after him. "Hey! What's your name?"

The guy turns back around, an amused but thoughtful look on his face. "Silas," he calls back. "Silas Aconite." And before I have the chance to say anything else, he's turning the corner and disappearing out of view.

I'm left to go back down the stairs and slog up to the girls' wing, where I easily find room 12-B and unlock the door with the skeleton key. It's not elaborately furnished--no more than a double bed, desk, and dresser--but the window is big, with a view of the sunny campus and the rolling hills and forests stretching into the distance beyond. I pause for a minute to take it in, still unable to quite believe I'm here, but too caught up in it at this point to do anything but marvel.

Soon, though, I'm hit with another wave of exhaustion, and it's all I can do to strip off my threadbare jumper and collapse into bed, the weight of everything that's happened falling on me all at once. Before I even get around to pulling the covers over myself, I'm already asleep.

CHAPTER 9

I've never been a heavy sleeper in my life, so I'm astonished when I start awake, roused by what sounds like the chiming of an old church bell. It's loud--loud enough to carry into the dormitory, even though it's clearly coming from outside. Frowning, I clamber out of bed, peering out the window and trying to find the source of the noise. Sure enough, around my corner of the building, practically out of sight in the courtyard between the dormitory and the main academic facility, is an enormous brick clock tower, the bell ringing rhythmically. Part of me wonders if its volume is due more to the acoustics of the dorm or the fact that this is a school run by magical beings. Maybe both. Either way, the sun is low in the sky on the horizon, and one glance at my phone tells me it's seven PM. I slept for eight hours, something almost unheard of for me under normal circumstances. Then again, these aren't normal circum-stances.

Someone has laid a fresh set of clothes outside my door, several clean sets of white leggings and white shirts. Realizing I won't be able to track down the washroom and take a shower in time for dinner, I change into these, fighting to get my hair in some kind of order before leaving my room and following the crowd of other girls down the hallway and to the lower level. A few of them cast me sideways glances as we make our way across the quad, but being in new clothes puts me at ease a little, and I find myself examining the others, wondering what kinds of shifters they are. The truth is, I have no idea how to identify them when they're in human form, if there even is a way, and my knowledge of supernatural lore is limited at best.

I'm eyeing a group of older-looking students as we file into the main building when I hear a familiar voice behind me. "Staring's not polite, you know." Turning around, I see Hazel sidling up to me, smiling. "Fancy running into you here. Millie, right?"

I nod.

"I was looking for you back there," she continues. "Didn't think you'd have changed already. It's damned difficult to recognize people in these uniforms." She shakes her head. "Anyway, how are you liking it so far? Are people being nice to you?"

"So far, yeah," I reply, thinking of Silas. A cluster of students moves to the opposite side of the front room, where a couple of paned glass doors lead into the dining hall. I don't think I've ever seen so much food before. At a buffet table on the far wall are heaps of meat, tossed salad, grains, and gravy. Tall bottles full of soda and water stand at one end, with stacks of plates and utensils on the other. I follow Hazel's lead to the line, almost paralyzed with indecision. Eventually I pile things onto a plate, wondering when I last had a meal that wasn't microwaved. *Keep going at this rate, and you won't be able to fit into this uniform,* I think dryly.

Hazel leads me to one of the long, bench-style dining tables, where a mix of boys and girls are seated. We take a seat side-by-side, and I'm glad to know someone here as I look from one unfamiliar face to the next. "Can I ask you something?" I say, turning to Hazel.

"Sure," she replies. "Go ahead."

"What kind of shifter are you?" It's a question that dawned on me after she left me earlier. "If that's not, like, a breach of etiquette, or something."

She laughs her tinkling laugh again. "Hardly. I'm a siren."

"Like the sirens from Greek mythology?" I ask, raising my eyebrows.

"A little," she replies, "although maybe not like you're picturing. Here," she adds, leaning in close to me, and I see the tips of her curly hair go briefly from blonde to sea green. "We have scales, too," Hazel continues, lifting her hand to show me an array of shimmery green scales, much like the ones I saw growing from my own skin back at the warehouse. Quickly she returned to normal, stealing a glance around to make sure no one had caught her shapeshifting, and then turned back to me. "The fun part is the singing, though," she said in a conspiratorial voice.

"Do sirens really sing?" I ask, my curiosity getting the better of me.

"Sure we do," she replies. "Although don't be expecting Adele or anything. It's more like screeching, really, but it does wonders for getting people to leave us alone. Men, especially. Advanced sirens can lure people to them and seduce them with song. Even to the point of mind control but it takes years of practice, apparently."

I nod, pursing my lips as I begin to dig into my food. "Speaking of which," I say, "are all sirens female?"

"*That's* where the myth gets it wrong," Hazel replies, taking a bite out of a heel of bread. "There are plenty of male sirens. Like Landon, here, for instance." She nods to a boy sitting across the table from us. "He's a siren. In my class, actually. Landon, this is Millie. She's new."

The boy looks up from his food. He's quite possibly the prettiest guy I've ever seen, with softer features and skin of a dark caramel brown. There's a dusting of freckles across his nose, and his hair is dark, curly, and unkempt. He smiles broadly at me when I meet his black eyes. "Pleasure," he says, reaching across the table.

I shake his hand, a little amused at the gesture but appreciating the friendliness in his expression. "Landon Thyme. It's always nice to see a new face around here, especially one as lovely as yours."

I feel a blush creeping into my cheeks, and Hazel kicks at him under the table. "Come on, Landon."

"What?" he asks innocently, grinning at her.

"She's been here for all of a day and you're already hitting on her!" Hazel retorts, but her tone is light-hearted.

"I was stating a fact," Landon shoots back, his eyes meeting mine for a moment. "That's different than hitting on someone."

Hazel rolls her eyes, turning to me. "Don't listen to him. He's full of shit."

I chuckle. "He seems okay to me,"

"Checkmate, Hazel," Landon says, laughing. "Everyone knows I'm the best thing to ever have happened to this school."

"You know, just because you're a siren, you don't have to be so predictable," Hazel retorts. "Landon's the biggest player in the school," she tells me. "Or at least, he seems to think so."

"I *know* so," Landon replies. "But for your sake, Millie," he adds, making a put-upon face, "I'll tone it down a little. Don't want to spook you or anything."

I shook my head, grinning. *I like this guy.* "Hazel was just telling me a little about sirens," I tell Landon. "I'm not really familiar... I mean, like she said, it's my first day."

"No classes yet, then?" Landon asks.

"Not yet," I answer. "I start tomorrow."

"Nice," he observes, nodding.

"So what classes do you have on your schedule?" asks Hazel, leaning an elbow on the table. I can feel a surge of nervousness at the question. I guess I should have known it would come sooner or later, but I was still futilely hoping that I would be able to fly under the radar for a little longer before explaining my situation. I lick my lips, my shoulders slumping. "Was that the wrong question to ask?" Hazel says. "Do you have Professor McDonald for History of Shifting or something?"

I shake my head. "I'm actually not taking that class. That's the thing." I take a breath, feeling self-conscious. Will these tentative new acquaintances think I'm some sort of unnatural adnomination? But by now they're both staring at me pointedly, and I can sense the curious gazes of some of the others at the table who have been listening in. "They don't know what kind of shifter I am," I reply, chewing my lip as I look from Hazel to Landon.

Hazel frowns. "What do you mean, they don't know? Usually that's the first thing the recruiters tell you when they track you down."

"I know," I say with a sigh. "This is the part where you guys will think I'm a freak and you'll never want to talk to me again." My tone is joking, but there's real worry beneath it.

"Listen, Millie," Landon says, "we're all freaks. That's kind of why we're here. I don't think anything you could tell us would surprise us at this point."

Hazel nods, eyes wide, and I can tell they mean it. Steeling myself, I reply, "The thing is, back when I first transformed, I sort of... shifted into all five clans at once." Seeing the others' confusion, I elaborate. "I mean, I had fur and claws, right? But also fangs, and red skin, scales like yours... and I breathed fire."

I'm half-expecting them to move away, or burst out laughing. A lifetime of difficulty making friends has me prepared for the worst, so I'm surprised when Hazel just purses her lips. "Interesting," she says. "The fur and claws would mean wolf shifter--werewolf, to the uninitiated." She gives me a conspiratorial grin. "The red skin means witch, obviously, and the fangs..."

"Vampire," Landon adds, nodding. I pull a face, and he laughs, adding, "Don't worry. They only need to drink blood when they're in vampire form."

"Thank god for small favors, I guess," I mutter, and he snorts.

"The scales are a siren thing," Hazel continues, glancing at Landon, "so welcome to the club. And as for the fire breathing... Well, I'm sure you can figure that out."

"That's wild," Landon remarked. "I can't imagine having to learn to control any more powers than I already have."

"But it's cool, too," Hazel rushes to add. "It means you'll have access to every shifter form. That's, like, unheard of. What were your parents? Were they humans or shifters?"

I shake my head. "I have no idea, actually. They left me at the hospital when I was a baby and never came back. They ended up placing me in the foster system, and that's where I've been... until now. My whole life I've just been going from home to home. I've never really settled down." Almost instinctively, I reach down and finger the necklace Mollie gave me, which is still tucked into my boot.

London seems to have perked up when I said that. "I'll be damned," he mutters, his food completely forgotten.

"Why do you say that?" I ask.

"Because the same thing happened to me," Landon replies, and I see that his amused expression has dissolved.

My jaw might as well have hit the floor. "Are you serious?" This is the first time I've ever met another orphan. I never shared my foster homes with other kids, and in retrospect, I'm sure that contributed to my sense of isolation along the way. The idea of someone else having gone through the same thing--especially another shifter--is almost too impossible to believe. For the first time since arriving here--the first time since before that, actually--I'm starting to feel at ease with the people around me.

Landon nods. "Dead serious. Same story, down to the foster families. An anonymous kid in a hospital in Glasgow. The only difference is that I can't shapeshift into anything other than a siren."

"Wow," I say in disbelief. "You know, you're the first person I've ever met who's been in the same situation."

"Likewise," Landon says, smiling a little, and our eyes meet for a moment. He clears his throat and leans back in his seat. "So does that mean you'll be in every shifting class?"

I nod. "Every shifting class, as well as one about mingling with humans... or something."

"Well, one thing's for sure," Hazel says, draining her glass of soda and pushing her plate away.

"What's that?" I ask.

Hazel turns to me. "You're in for a busy day tomorrow."

CHAPTER 10

"I'm going back to my room. I'm super tired," Millie says, brushing a strand of her light blonde hair over her shoulder as she softly smiles at me. Her dark blue eyes remind me of an ocean when a storm is above it. Dangerous. Seductive and so damn beautiful. But I know better than to stare for too long...or at least part of my mind tells me to look away. I could stare at this girl forever and never stop finding beautiful things about her. I struggle to take my eyes off her as she stands up and walks off, her tight pants showcasing the amazing ass she has. Sure, I've seen lots of stunning girls but there is something different about Millie Brix.

Something that I'm certain I'm going to get addicted too and not care one bit.

"Nope. Don't even think about going there," Hazel interrupts my gaze and I turn back to her. I like Hazel in a weird sister kinda way. I saved her ass from drowning in Siren Studies a month ago and since then she has my back and I have hers. In fact, she is the only girl my age I don't get sexy vibes from at all. Not that she isn't pretty.

"I have no idea what you are talking about," I say, raising an eyebrow.

She snorts. "You've slept with every girl in our siren class and I want Millie not to hate me for being your friend. So nope. Millie is off-limits. I need a girl to talk to."

"I can't make any promises," I say, crossing my arms. "I like her."

Hazel rolls her eyes. "You like anyone with a pulse."

"What about you? You never date anyone and being a siren, that's strange," I point out and her cheeks suddenly burn red. "Shit, I was just deflecting. I didn't mean to upset you."

"No, it's okay," she answers. "I do like someone, but I'm certain they don't know I exist."

"Who?" I ask. "I could introduce you to pretty much anyone."

"No, this one you couldn't," she answers, picking up her bag and standing up. "Thanks though. See you around, Land."

"See ya," I say, wondering who exactly it is she likes. It has to be someone in our siren clan at the academy, but I don't know who. There are one hundred-odd sirens in the academy, far less than the other shifters who dominate the academy spaces.

Gathering my stuff, I walk out of the dining room and nearly crash into Mr Hawkthorne in the middle of the corridor.

"Landon, just who I was looking for," he says as I step back. "Walk with me." Knowing I don't have a choice, I fall into step with him and he is silent until we get outside and there is no one around.

"Many of the siren leaders are stepping down and they have asked me to look into the students at the academy for recommendations," he remarks, holding his hand behind his back. "All of your teachers say you are extremely talented and they all think you would make a good leader."

"Thank you," I reply, but the truth of it is, I don't want to be a leader of a world I know little to nothing about.

"Have you met the new student? Miss Brix?" he asks me, eventually.

"Yes," I answer.

He hums, nodding his head once. "Many are interested in her powers, much like I am. Would it be too much to ask you to stay close to her? To pull out her siren shifter powers?"

A sinking feeling drops into my gut. He wants me close to Millie for whatever reasons he has, but he is also trying to bribe me with being a leader of the sirens, a big step up from whatever I will leave the academy to do.

I don't have any family, unlike every siren at this academy, and I don't have a clan home to actually leave for.

Which makes me the most disposable siren at this place.

"I don't have to remind you that our places at the academy are extremely limited...do I?" he threatens with a smile.

"Of course not," I tightly answer.

"Now, just for safety, I need you to swear on this stone never to speak of our conversation," he picks out a witch stone from his pocket. Witch stones are a foolproof way of making sure someone keeps their promise. If you try to break the promise, the Witch Stone will take your life. I grit my teeth and take the stone into my hand.

"I promise never to speak of this conversation," I say, feeling the stone warm in my hand.

"Perfect," he grins, taking the stone from me and putting it in his pocket. "I do hate gossip. Secrets have a way of becoming messed up truths if they are spoken too much."

"And how many secrets do you have, Mr Hawkthorne?" I ask and he simply smiles.

"Too many," he answers and turns around, walking in the other direction. I watch him walk away, the magic in the air thicker than the salt in the sea air I loved when I was a kid.

I might be a siren, but I just got lured into a trap and I have a sinking feeling Millie will pay the price.

CHAPTER 11

Even though I slept like a zombie most of the day, I'm still tired when I get back to my room after dinner. I have enough energy to drag myself to the washroom--there's one in the girls' wing and one in the boys' wing, with multiple showers and stalls--and take a much needed shower before returning to my room and crawling into bed. I feel a little more at ease after dinner--a *lot* more, actually. The idea of actually having acquaintances here, let alone friends, wasn't something I was expecting, and the dinner conversation with Hazel and Landon was a pleasant surprise. All I can do now is hope that the rest of my classmates will be equally accommodating.

The breakfast bell rings at seven on the dot the next morning, and for the first time in my life I actually feel a surge of excitement about going to class. I shake my head as I climb out of bed and pull on my crisp new uniform. *Who would've thought?*

The rest of the dormitory migrates back to the dining hall, where a full English breakfast spread is laid out, and it takes me a while to locate Hazel in the throng of people. I make a mental note to ask her which room she's in--maybe next time I can meet her beforehand. *We could make a routine out of it,* I think, with a sense of almost absurd glee.

Eventually I find her, and the two of us chat about things that seem frighteningly banal compared to the world we've found ourselves plunged into. She seems more interested in which upper-classman pissed off which professor than the fact that we're about to go to a shapeshifting class, at a secret boarding school on a private island. *It's not going to seem this strange forever,* I remind myself as we bring our dishes to the bus tubs. *You feel this way every time you change schools.*

Sure, but most schools aren't full of dragons and werewolves.

"So what do you have first?" Hazel asks as we step out into the entrance hall. The sunshine of the quad is streaming in through the windows, nearly blinding in its intensity.

I rummage in my bag and withdraw my schedule. "Looks like... 'Introduction to Vampire Shifting'," I read.

"Nice," Hazel says, nodding approvingly. "Between you and me, the vampires are the most annoying guys at this school."

I raise my eyebrows. "What makes you say that?"

She rolls her eyes. "They all have the dark, brooding thing going on. The girls always go for that in the movies, but in real life it's a hell of a lot more bothersome. You wouldn't believe what it does to your social life to never smile. Usually by the time they graduate, they'll have figured out that being a dick isn't a good way to make friends."

I chuckle. "I guess I'll have to try to avoid falling into the stereotype."

"Please do," Hazel agrees, laughing. "Although between you and me, there's no harm in eating the eye candy."

"Eye candy?"

She tips me a wink. "Wait and see."

I'm almost more nervous about finding the classroom than about going to the class itself... almost. Thankfully, I spot Samantha hanging around in the back, monitoring the outgoing students, and approach her with the kind of frantic desperation that's only found in a kid on her first day of school. She laughs when she sees me. "Let me guess," she says, "you're not sure where the classroom is."

I nod. "How old is this building, anyway? It's so complicated."

"It dates back to the 1500s, believe it or not," she replies. "It was originally used by a coterie of witches living in the Scottish Isles. Which classroom are you looking for?"

"1301," I reply. "Huxley's the professor."

Samantha nods, although she briefly pulls a face that could be a wince. "I see." My stomach drops. Coming from a faculty member, that's not a great sign. "It will be on the ground floor," she says, pointing in the direction I came from. "Down the hall--the odd numbers are on the left."

"Thank you," I say, and scurry off. I nearly have to go all the way to the end of the hall before I find the classroom, but I manage. Barely. The classroom is well lit, with a tantalizing view of the campus outside. Old wooden desks sit in neat rows, with a teacher's podium at the front of the classroom. Behind it stands a stern-faced older gentleman dressed in the dark faculty uniform. His hair is white and a little messy, and even from a distance I can see that his face is lined with wrinkles. *Weird,* I think. *I thought vampires were supposed to be immortal.*

Most of the other students have already settled in by the time I arrive, and they look up with vague interest when the door opens. Professor Huxley glances over at me, his eyes narrowing for a moment before going wide with recognition. "Ah, Ms. Ash! It's nice of you to join us!" He bustles up to me, not giving me a chance to get a word in edgewise. "The registrar had told me we had a new face in our class, but I must have forgotten. Too many things to think about at once!" Putting an arm around my shoulders, he turned to face the assembled students, who had all gone quiet. "Everybody, this is Amelia Ash. I'm told she's an exceptional student, so follow her example."

I clear my throat, already turning red. "I'm sorry," I say, turning to the professor, "I think you have me confused with someone else."

Professor Huxley frowns, his big, watery eyes looking both curious and half-mad. "Don't be ridiculous. I was told we would have an Amelia Ash in this class, so if that's not you, then who *are* you?"

I can feel the eyes of my classmates on me, and whatever excitement I was feeling before evaporates under their gaze. "My name is Millie Brix," I reply, handing him my schedule. "I'm in your class this period."

He sniffs, holding the paper at a distance and squinting at it. "Well, I'll be," he says, shaking his head. "My apologies, Ms. Brix. It's so dreadfully difficult to keep all the new faces around here straight. Well, go ahead and take a seat. There's an open desk in the back, next to Hunter." He points toward the back of the classroom, at an empty desk in the corner.

Good, I think. *At least I'll be in the back.* I hurry toward it, eager to have the others stop staring at me, and find myself sitting down next to a silent boy who's hunched over the desk closest to the window. His hair is a shock of bronze red, the color of a new penny, and his eyes are bluer than I would have thought humanly--or inhumanly--possible. His attractiveness is more alien than some of the other guys I've seen around the academy, a more clear reminder that he's not a human... and as I glance around the room, I see that the others have a similar otherworldly beauty. Now I understand what Hazel was saying about eye candy. Hunter's features are sharp and chiseled, and his skin is so pale that he might be mistaken for a corpse. Go figure, right?

As if sensing my eyes on him, he hunches lower over his desk, his eyes sliding over to look at me. Raising my eyebrows, I look away, remembering what Hazel said about new vampires' attitudes and doubting that I'll be cozying up to anyone in this class anytime soon.

Professor Huxley has returned to the podium, rustling a stack of papers, he's clearly scatterbrained, but so far he seems more or less harmless. I'll take it, even if it means being mistaken for someone else. Hell, maybe that would even be a blessing. "Now," he says, "while we're waiting for Amelia, let's start the lesson off with a simple exercise. Today we'll be discussing blood drinking, but no vampire worth his salt drinks blood without first knowing how to use his fangs." He spreads his arms out, a gleeful look on his face. "With that in mind, I'd like you all to partner with the person closest to you and take turns manifesting your fangs. *Just* your fangs, mind you--you're all beginners, and I don't want anyone else sent to the nurse this week. I'll be making rounds to monitor your progress. Don't worry, Millie," he adds, looking at me, "if you're stuck, just follow along and you'll get the hang of it. Practice is the best way to learn!"

He makes a shooing motion with his hands, signal enough to get started. Immediately, the classroom erupts with activity as the students turn to their partners and begin the exercise. I find myself looking to my right to see if my other neighbor seems friendlier than this Hunter guy. No such luck; she's already partnered up with someone else, barely sparing me a second glance.

Shoulders slumping, I turn back around to Hunter, who still looks like someone just told him his mother died. "Hi," I say tentatively. "I'm Millie. Should we...?"

Hunter takes a long breath before turning to me. "Yeah," he says. "Sure. Fine. You first."

"I, uh..." I clear my throat. "I'm totally new to this. I mean, I... I don't know how to..."

"Fine," says Hunter, crossing his arms, his expression still stoic. "I'll keep my expectations low."

I can feel the blush returning to my cheeks as I glance around at the other students. Some of them are already baring their fangs, while others seem to have gotten too gung ho and are struggling to transform the right parts of their bodies. I know this is supposed to be a beginners' class, but I don't even know where to begin. The only time I've transformed, I had adrenaline on my side, and I hadn't been thinking about it. I don't know if I could transform now if my life depended on it. "That's the thing," I say, biting my lip. "I've never done this before."

Hunter snorts. "You had to have. You're here, aren't you?"

Now I can feel myself getting frustrated. "Come on," I say, "the professor said you'd be able to help me. Don't tell me you knew how to transform after a single time!"

"No," he replies. "And I still don't, so I'm about as useful as you are right now."

I blink. That wasn't what I had been expecting. "You can't make fangs?"

"Or anything," Hunter answers dryly. "Hence, I suppose, why I'm in the back of the classroom."

"Oh." I frown. "How long have you been here? At Shifter Academy, I mean."

"Going on a month now," Hunter replies, his expression still stony. "And from the looks of it, I'll probably be stuck here in this intro class for the rest of my life."

"Well, I guess that makes two of us," I remark, and there's a flicker of something that might be a smile on his face, but it's gone before I can identify it. "I guess I'll ask the professor," I say, and raise my hand, but the professor is busy giving pointers to a pair of students in the front who are having the same problem.

"...You have to feel the magic inside you first," he's saying. "It's a little different for everyone, but it's always a sort of energy in the pit of your stomach. Once you feel it, you have to visualize the transformation you want to make."

Squaring my shoulders, Hunter forgotten for the moment, I close my eyes and fish for that cool pool of unfamiliar energy I felt on the day I first transformed. But it's nowhere to be found, and even as I set my jaw and furrow my brow, I can't for the life of me make myself feel it. It's hard to even remember what "it" felt like.

I'm just starting to grow frustrated when the classroom door opens. I open my eyes and look up, Hunter following my gaze, to see a hauntingly beautiful red-haired girl standing in the doorway. Her eyes are the same ocean-blue color as Hunter's, and she has the curves of a classic pin-up girl, the kind of body that probably earns her stares everywhere she goes. Her eyes settle first on me, and then on Hunter next to me, and her face immediately twists into a look of disdain. "So," she says, crossing her arms, "the freak is in our class."

CHAPTER 12

I have to give her credit for her audacity, even if I'm shrinking in my chair, staring across the room at the newcomer like she might attack me or something. Professor Huxley looked up from the pair of students he was helping and gave a sniff. "Amelia Ash, I presume?"

The girl gives Professor Huxley an appraising look, one eyebrow raised. "That's right," she replies, her Irish lilt unmistakable. "Sorry I'm late."

The professor eyes her for a moment before replying slowly, "All right, then. I suppose you can just take a seat where you like. We're doing a basic shifting exercise--fangs only. I assume you know how to--"

Amelia shoots him a look of barely disguised condescension. "I think I can handle it, yes." With that, she strides across the room to where Hunter and I are seated. By now, most of the other students have returned to their activities, unbothered by the new student or simply past caring.

Professor Huxley returns to desperately trying to coax his charges back into human form, and aside from an occasional sideways glance from the others, we're left alone. Amelia stops in front of my desk, looking down at me. She's tall--tall enough to cast a shadow over me-

-and she looks at me like I'm something unpleasant she's just found on the sidewalk. "You're in my seat," she tells me, crossing her arms.

Huh? I shift uncomfortably. "I didn't realize we had assigned seats. The professor just told me--"

"I'm going to be honest with you," she says, "I don't really care what the professor told you."

Shit, I think, a sinking feeling in my stomach, *she's going there.* It should probably be obvious by now that I don't handle confrontations too well, and this was no different--I found myself slowly sinking in my chair, as if by hiding I could somehow avoid a conversation that has already become uncomfortable. "I... I'm sorry," I stammer, looking around the room. It looks like there's one other open desk on the other side of the classroom, which I point to. The truth is, the idea of drawing any more attention to myself right now is enough to make me want to cry. "I think that one's free."

Amelia doesn't even glance that way, instead turning to Hunter, who's been watching the exchange with a look of vague discomfort on his face. "Hunter," she says, "tell her to move."

Hunter turns to me, an apologetic look flashing across his face, and opens his mouth to speak, but I beat him to it. "It's okay, it's fine," I rush to say, already struggling to gather up my stuff, which has somehow spread out. "I'll... uh... leave you alone, I guess." I turn to Hunter. "It was nice to meet you," I say hurriedly, and turn to go.

Amelia's voice stops me in my tracks. "Are you really doing this in front of me?" I turn back to her, and her mouth twists like she's just tasted something sour. She shakes her head, laughing a little. "You know, I'm not sure if you're incredibly brave or incredibly stupid," she tells me, eyes narrowing.

"I..." I look to Hunter as I stand up, hoping he'll step in and intervene, but he's just watching the exchange, his brow furrowed. So much for that. "I'm sorry," I begin, wanting to be anywhere else in the world right now. "I didn't realize--I, I mean, I didn't mean to offend you or something--"

"Offend me?" She snorts. "How adorably naive. I'm not worried about you offending me, *Millie Brix,*" she says, leaning forward and punctuating the last two words for emphasis. How does she know my name? Come to think of it, why did she call me a freak when she saw me.

Come on, I think to myself. *The cat's out of the bag, that's how.* Briefly, I wonder if Hazel or Landon might have let something slip, but I push the idea away. They wouldn't have.

"My brother, though," Amelia says, nodding at Hunter, "that's a different story. I would recommend not dragging him any further into your shit." I open my mouth to reply, but she doesn't stop. "I heard about you," she says, eyes flashing. "You're the hybrid everyone's been talking about. They're being generous, I think. 'Mistake' might be more appropriate. Stay away from my brother if you know what's good for you." That's all she has to say. The conversation apparently over, Amelia turns, tossing her scarlet hair over one shoulder and dropping into my desk, crossing her legs like it's the most normal thing in the world.

"Still no progress, huh?" I overhear her asking Hunter, but I don't wait to listen to his response. I'm already shuffling over to the free desk on the other side of the room. A few other students are staring at me, having watched the exchange, but Professor Huxley is still blissfully distracted, now at the podium desperately trying to sort out a pile of documents. Maybe it's for the best that he didn't witness that. The last thing I need is a teacher rescuing me from bullying on my first day here. That's a guaranteed way to ruin one's reputation at a new school, if experience has taught me anything.

So much for making new friends, I think, awkwardly inviting myself into another group and returning to my efforts to make my fangs appear.

No such luck on that front, either.

The rest of my vampire shifting class goes by in a blur, but at least there are no further incidents after the Amelia Ash debacle. Occasionally I look over at her and Hunter, seeing her making animated gestures in her attempts to show him how to make his fangs appear, something she seems to be able to do effortlessly. Eventually we stop the practical drill and do a guided meditation, something I never would have imagined them teaching in school, before a brief overview of the way shifting magic moves through the body. The information is interesting, but I'm too rattled from the confrontation to do much more than take notes and bite my nails.

After that is siren shifting, and I'm blessed to have Hazel and Landon in my class. Once again, I don't manage to change during any of the transformations, but at least I don't get chewed out by a stranger this time, so I suppose I'll take it. At the end of the class, the lunch bell rings and the academy students disperse, heading for the quad or the cafeteria. The others invite me to eat outside with them, and I eagerly accept, grabbing some food from the dining hall before following the two sirens out onto the grass. Around us, students sit in groups, talking and eating, and Landon leads us to the shade of an enormous oak tree, its branches casting a shadow almost all the way to the road.

There's a guy already sitting under the tree, sprawled out with an open book in his lap, and Landon waves to him as we approach. "Hey, Silas!" he calls.

The boy looks up, and I realize with a start that he's the same tall guy I met yesterday, when I ended up in the boys' wing of the dormitory. *Small world,* I think, unable to keep the smile off my face. "Hey, Landon," Silas says, closing his book and sitting up. "I figured I might see you out here today."

"You know me," Landon replies. "I'm a sucker for nice weather. Anyway," he says, stretching a little, "I heard something about a pop quiz in Morris' class today."

"Damn, really?" Silas wrinkles his nose. "Well, I guess I know what I'm doing for the rest of the period." His eyes turn to me, and he gives me a crooked smile. "You look strangely familiar," he says, pulling a face and stroking his chin. "But I can't put my finger on it."

"I'm the girl you saved from untold amounts of embarrassment yesterday," I remind him, laughing.

Hazel raises her eyebrows, looking between the two of us. "Oh? This I have to hear."

Silas scoots back to make room for us, and we sit down in a loose circle. "It's not that dramatic," he explains.

"Oh, no, it really is," I say, letting my eyes go wide with mock-seriousness. "I was trying to find my room yesterday and I ended up on the boys' side of the dorm."

Landon laughs. "Classic. Happened to me on my first day, too."

"Well," Silas says, his amber eyes settling on me, that knowing half-smile still on his face. "I'm glad you found your room. Eventually, anyway."

Hazel sighs contentedly. "See? This is what I like: when the introductions have already been made."

"Actually," Silas replies, his eyes still on me, "I don't think I ever got your name." His tone is calm, not revealing much, and I wonder if anyone's ever been able to avoid answering a question from him. The combination of curiosity and faint amusement in his voice is enough to make me want to start talking and never stop.

I feel a faint burst of color come to my cheeks under his thoughtful gaze, and I bite my lip. "Millie," I reply. "Millie Brix."

What looks like a faint flicker of recognition passes over Silas' face, and I see his eyes narrow for a moment, but his expression remains pleasant. "It's good to meet you properly, Millie Brix," Silas says, holding a hand out to me, and I take it and give it a gentle shake. For a moment, our eyes meet, and there's something in his expression that I can't identify. A brief surge of electricity runs up my arm, but the contact is broken before it can distract me too much. "I have to admit, though," he continues, "your reputation kind of precedes you."

My eyes widen. "Really?"

Silas laughs. "Don't look so freaked out. I just mean I heard there was a hybrid starting here. I just didn't realize we'd met already."

Hybrid. There's that word again. I guess it's as good a term as any for what I am, and he isn't using it with the same disdain that Amelia did, so I nod, replying, "Not everyone here seems okay with that. The hybrid thing, I mean."

"I don't think anyone here actually thought hybrids were real," muses Hazel. "You're rare, Millie. Like a unicorn." Her eyes go wide, and I have to chuckle at the seriousness of her expression.

"I mean, we've all heard the stories," elaborates Silas, "but I don't think anyone thought they were true, you know?"

"I would be curious to know how it happened," Hazel remarks, looking at me. "Was it a ritual or something, like back in the olden days? Or did you just hit the gene jackpot?"

"I'd be curious, too," says Landon, but Silas remains silent, not meeting my eyes. Once again, that unreadable look passes over his face.

For a moment, no one speaks, all of us just looking at one another. I clear my throat. "Well, you guys have certainly been a lot more... accommodating than some of the other people I've met so far."

Hazel's eyes go wide. "What do you mean?"

I sigh, tugging a piece of grass out of the ground. "There was this girl in my vampire shifting class," I reply. "She seemed to have a problem with me. She showed up late and she just... started going after me."

"Well, who was she?" asks Landon. "Although now that I think about it, that's about par for the course for vampires."

"I think her name was Amelia," I reply, frowning. "Amelia Ash."

"Amelia Ash?" Hazel asks with clear suspicion in her eyes. "But she's an upperclassman--one of the best shifters in the school, from what I've heard. What would she be doing in an introductory class?"

I shrug. "I don't know. They said she transferred. I think maybe she wanted to be in the same class as her brother."

"They usually don't let anyone change classes," remarks Silas.

Hazel gives him a look. "Come on. This is Amelia Ash we're talking about."

"What do you mean?" I ask. "Who is she?"

Hazel turns to me. "Her father is one of the board members. Human, but powerful. If anyone could get their schedule changed like that, it's her. Still, I don't know why she would..."

Landon cuts her off, his expression going sour as he sits up and looks over my shoulder. "Well," he says, "speak of the devil."

CHAPTER 13

I turn around, fully expecting to see Amelia coming after me and wondering once again what I've done to piss her off so much. Instead, I'm mildly surprised not to see her, but her brother, Hunter, making his way toward us across the quad. "Yikes," mutters Hazel, fidgeting slightly. "I wonder what he wants."

There's only one way to find out, and I try my best to look non threatening as Hunter approaches us. He has an awkward, uncomfortable expression on his face, and he looks even paler in the sunlight than he did back in the classroom. Almost sickly. "Hey," he says, coming to a stop in front of us and looking down at me. "Can I talk to you for a second?"

"Uh..." I glance behind me at the others, who sit there, looking bewildered. "Sure," I say, shifting to make room in the circle. "Do you want to sit down?"

He shakes his head, swallows, and chews his lip for a moment before saying, "Listen--about earlier, in Huxley's class..."

I raise my eyebrows, wondering where this is going.

"I just wanted to apologize," he says. "My sister, she's..." He rubs the back of his neck like he's looking for the right word. He sounds almost... sheepish. Embarrassed. A far cry from the dark, stoic guy I sat next to just this morning.

"A handful?" I supply, feeling a strange sort of sympathy for him, but I can't put my finger on why. Maybe it's because he, like me, can't seem to get the hang of shapeshifting.

Hunter chuckles without much humor. "You could say that, yeah," he replies.

"Why is she in your class?" Silas asks, shifting a little in the grass. "She's supposed to be past the beginner level."

"It's a long story," Hunter replies. "I don't really want to get into it right now. I just wanted to tell you I'm sorry for her," he continues, looking back at me. "You didn't deserve to get called out like that in front of everyone. You didn't do anything."

I blink, feeling myself relax just a little. "It's okay," I reply, giving him a small smile. "Thank you. I appreciate it." Glancing over at the others, who seem as bewildered as I am, I ask, "Do you want to come sit with us?"

"I..." Hunter takes a nervous glance over his shoulder. "Okay, sure. For a little while, anyway. Is there room in the shade?"

"For you, vampire boy, always," Landon replies, scooting over.

Hunter is just making a move to sit down when a yell pierces the tranquility of the quad. "Hunter, what the fuck are you doing?!"

We all look up to see Amelia making a beeline towards us, seemingly out of nowhere. How did she even know we were here? "This ought to be good," Landon mutters, getting up. The rest of us follow suit, and I dust the grass off my behind just as Amelia approaches, looking fit to be tied.

"Amelia," Hunter begins, "I just came over here to--"

"I can't believe you," she says, her eyes flashing. "I literally just had this conversation with you. What did I say about hanging around the hybrid?"

Her pseudo-maternal tone seems to light a fire in him, since Hunter crosses his arms, his expression going cold again. "Amelia, I'm nineteen years old," he snaps. "And the last time I checked, you were my sister, not my mom."

Amelia isn't fazed. "And the last time *I* checked," she shoots back,

"Dad told me to look after you, and that means keeping you away from *her*." She nods in my direction.

"Listen," I plead, not wanting this to escalate, "I don't know what I did to you, but I'm sorry. I really don't want you to think that I'm--"

"Was I talking to you, hybrid?" she demands, rounding on me. I feel my heartbeat pick up a little. "My brother has been here for six months, and he can't even transform yet. What he needs is support, not some freak who will put him in danger."

I bristle at the word freak. "That's not fair," I reply. "I didn't ask for any of this!"

"But you got it," Amelia fires back. "You're an abomination, and you're a danger to everyone here."

Silas takes a step forward. "What the hell is your problem?" he demands. He dwarfs Amelia at his full height. "Do you just get off on being a bitch to the new girl? Is that it?"

Out of the corner of my eye, I can see Hunter putting his head in his hands. To my left, Hazel is watching the exchange with wide eyes. Landon, meanwhile, looks like he's debating whether to get involved. "What's it to you, dragon?" Amelia asks Silas. "She your girlfriend? The latest and greatest?"

Silas bristles. "No," he replies, "but I guess common decency is a foreign concept to you."

Amelia quivers for a moment and then turns back to me. "Stay away from my brother, hybrid. If I need to have him taken out of that class, I will."

"Oh, sure," says Landon, rolling his eyes. "Get Daddy to fight your battles for you, right? Is that what the problem is--you've finally found something his money can't buy, princess?"

"Who the hell are *you*?" Amelia demands, shooting him an incredulous look. Not waiting for a reply, she shakes her head, looking from each one of us to the next angrily. "You know what? This doesn't concern any of you guys."

"I think it does," Silas says, and just having his presence next to me is enough to make me feel more safe. "You don't get to just chew out the new girl because you're afraid of her powers." Amelia goes rigid, staring at him, and Silas continues. "That's what this is about, right? You're afraid of her." He glances over at me.

"Guys," pleads Hazel, "let's not go there."

"Too late for that, Hazel," snaps Amelia, and she takes a step closer to me.

"Come on, Amelia," Hunter pleads, but she doesn't listen, already glaring down at me, the sun gleaming on her impeccable auburn waves.

By now, my heart is racing, and my stomach feels ice cold. This isn't how I was hoping my first day would go. "Okay, okay," I say, holding my hands up. "If it's this much of a problem for you, then I'll--"

"It's not my problem!" Amelia yells. "*You're* the problem, freak!"

There's that word again. I can feel myself getting frustrated--angry, even--in spite of my intimidation. "Stop calling me that," I tell her.

"Why?" Amelia demands. "It's what you are."

"Do you think I want any of this?" I demand, my voice rising. The fear is giving way to rage. Everything was finally starting to feel like it was going right last night. And now, on my first day, this girl won't leave me alone. Is this what I'm going to have to deal with for the rest of my time here? How many more Amelias am I going to encounter? *This was exactly what I was afraid of*, I think, stiffening. "My parents abandoned me," I say. "I don't even know where I came from, or how I got this way! I just want to learn how to control this thing, not start shit with people!"

Amelia shakes her head. "You'd better get used to *that*," she says, "because that's all you're going to find at this school. Did they tell you that if you can't learn to control your powers, they will kill you? You don't walk away from the academy, little girl. Foster kids like you are freaks, and in my opinion, should just be killed."

"Guys..." Hazel says again. She looks totally panicked now. We're far enough away from the main square that none of the others seem to realize what's going on.

It's as I'm staring defiantly up at Amelia that I feel a familiar feeling rising in the pit of my stomach. I had almost forgotten what it felt like, but my heart almost stops when that cool sensation floods my body once more. Shit. No, no, no. Not now. I take a step back from Amelia. "Listen," I say, "can you please just--"

"I don't take orders from *freaks*," Amelia sneers, and the poison in her voice is enough to do the trick. Before I'm even consciously aware of it, I can feel the transformation starting again, and in spite of my efforts to control it, it hits me like a freight train. Fur begins to sprout on my arms, my nails turning to claws and my teeth turning to fangs. I'm losing control of myself, only vaguely aware of the others staring at me as I shift. Amelia's eyes go wide, but she stands her ground. "Damn," she mutters. "You're even uglier than I was expecting."

"Stop it!" I yell, and a burst of fire explodes from my mouth, the same way it did back at the warehouse.

Amelia darts back, looking startled, and before I can even react, she's changing too. Her eyes go red, her hair turning the color of blood as fangs sprout from her mouth. "You *bitch!*" she yells, and then she lunges for me. She's startlingly fast, like a bolt of lightning. Is this a vampire ability?

I don't have time to wonder, since she's already knocked me to the ground. Everything feels like it's happening in slow motion. I catch a glimpse of Hazel taking off towards the campus, while Landon and Silas exchange a look before beginning to transform, as well. Their clothes shift into their skin, Landon going sea green and scaly, his hair turning the color of aquamarine. Silas, meanwhile, seems to be doubling--no, tripling--in size, blue-gray scales rippling up his body as a pair of batlike wings sprout from his back. For a moment I'm stunned by the fact that I'm looking at a dragon, but then Amelia slams my shoulders into the ground again, her red eyes raging.

I try to shove her off me, but it's no use; she seems to have the strength of ten people in this form. I'm half-wondering if she's going to kill me, but then Silas in dragon form slams into her from the side, knocking her off me like a bowling ball. Amelia gets up quick and runs at me but Hunter stops her, trying to pull his sister away, yelling at her to stop, but she's past listening to him. I look up to see Landon joining the fray, stopping her from getting close, only for Hunter to curse and push him away from his sister. I catch a glimpse of Amelia hitting Silas hard enough to make him take off, flapping his wings to get out of range. How strong *is* this girl, if she's able to fight off a dragon that's four times her size?

In fact, I notice with a sinking feeling that she seems to be getting the upper hand, throwing Landon off of herself like he's nothing and taking a flying leap towards Silas, teeth bared. I become aware of shouts in the distance, and all I can hope now is that this won't get any uglier...

Except it does. Because of *course* it does. I don't know if it's the adrenaline or the concern for the guys' wellbeing, but I feel something else well up inside me, some new aspect of this magic that bursts out through my fingertips. A shockwave manifests in the air, sending Amelia flying out of the air, mid-jump. It's enough to knock her to the ground.

For a moment I stare down at my hands, wondering how the hell I did that, but then the sound of a woman shouting draws my attention away. "What on earth is going on here?!" It's a male faculty member who I don't know, following behind a frantic-looking Hazel. "What is the meaning of this?" he demands, stopping at the base of the tree.

Silas shifts back into human form and opens his mouth to reply, but Amelia beats him to it. "She attacked me!" she cries, pointing at me. "She shifted into... into... *that.*"

I look down at myself and realize belatedly that I still look like someone put a bunch of fairytalecreatures in a blender. "I'm sorry," I begin, eyes wide as I look at the professor. "I don't know what... I didn't mean to."

Landon shifts back, making it look easy, and takes a step towards the newcomer. "Professor Drysdale," he begins, "listen, she's new. And Amelia was--"

"I don't care what Amelia was doing, Mr. Thyme," replies the professor. "Shifting outside of class is strictly forbidden. And make no mistake, I saw you two doing it, too," he adds, looking from

Landon to Silas. "I would expect better of you--all of you." He glances at me, his expression softening, but only a little. "Picking fights with other students isn't a great way to start your first term," he tells me.

"Wait a minute," Silas says, "Amelia transformed, too."

Professor Drysdale glances at her briefly. By now, she's turned back into a human, her red hair mussed and her uniform covered in dirt. "Self-defense is another matter," the professor says. "She can't be blamed for protecting herself."

Landon snorts. "Sure you'd say that if her dad wasn't a leader? If she wasn't a princess of the shifter world?"

"Watch your attitude, Mr. Thyme," snaps Professor Drysdale. "And as a matter of fact, this has nothing to do with nepotism." He glances at Hunter. "You were involved, too, Mr. Ash."

Hunter's eyes go wide. "Wait a minute, I didn't even--"

"Brawling," replies the professor. "Prince or not, we do not accept this behavior at the academy."

"That's not fair," Amelia says, getting to her feet. "My brother was trying to protect me from these guys! He shouldn't be punished for..."

Professor Drysdale shoots her a withering look--enough to, miraculously, make her shut up. He crosses his arms, looking between me, Landon, Hunter, and Silas. I have no idea what's coming, but I can already tell it won't be good. "For brawling on campus and unsupervised transformation," he says, "I want to see all four of you after class tonight. In detention."

CHAPTER 14

Detention.

Unbelievable.

Just for the record, I've never been sent to detention in my life. In spite of the fact that my social life has been nearly nonexistent at every school I've attended, and the fact that I'm lousy at almost every subject, the one thing I've always had going for me is a spotless record. Until now, I guess.

The rest of the day feels like it slogs on ad infinitum. I do my best to pay attention during my next batch of classes, but between what happened during lunch hour and my inability to transform for the teachers' exercises, none of them goes decidedly well. To make things worse, I feel like the other students are looking at me more, leaning in to make whispered comments to one another and staring at me with cautious expressions. I can't tell if it's because they heard about the fight, or because by now they probably all know just how strange I look when I transform, but I know I'm not just being paranoid. First, I had to watch Amelia strut away without getting punished, and now it seems like the student body has been turned against me.

I don't know anybody in my witch shifting class, although I do learn that the shockwave I unleashed during lunch break is a witch power, a spell that can only be cast in full or partial witch form. I guess that's progress... if only I could actually make it happen consciously. After that is my dragon class, with Silas on the other side of the room, although aside from a shared glance when we arrive, we don't interact. Nobody in my wolf shifting class looks familiar either, and by the time the last period arrives, all I really want to do is go back to my room and sleep the day away.

Unfortunately, that's not meant to be. As I drag myself out of the lecture hall where I've spent the past hour listening to an old woman explain shifter etiquette to a group of bored-looking students, I can see the others heading out for free time. Dinner isn't for another three hours, all of which I'll be spending in the detention hall.

At least the others will be there, too, I think as I make my way to the ground floor and down a winding hallway that leads to the older offices. The detention hall is a stuffy room that doesn't get the same light as the other classrooms, a faculty member slouches at a desk in the front, dozing. Silas has taken a desk near the window, while Landon sits near the front, making a paper airplane. Hunter has, as per usual, claimed the desk in the far corner of the room, and next to him sits a blond guy who looks oddly familiar.

We seem to be the only five people here. I give a resigned sigh and move to one of the desks in the middle of the room, prepared to ride out my punishment in silence. That's when a voice from behind me pipes up, "You're Millie Brix, aren't you?"

I turn around to see the familiar-looking guy staring at me, a grin on his face. His voice is what makes it finally click. "Yeah," I reply. "You're the guy who came to Mrs. Fairbanks' office yesterday, aren't you?"

"One and the same," the guy replies, putting his feet up on the desk.

"What are you doing in detention?" I ask.

"Sitting," he replies. "Talking. Thinking."

"We just had to get stuck in here with you, didn't we, Shade?" mutters Silas, shooting the guy a look.

"I don't know what you mean," the new guy, Shade, retorts. "I thought *I* was stuck in here with *you*. What'd you do this time? Beat up an old lady? Set fire to the boys' bathroom?"

Landon rolls his eyes. "Guys, come on. Can't we just go back to sulking in silence?"

"No way," Shade replies, leaning forward in his desk. "Silas and I are just joshing each other, aren't we, Silas?"

Silas rolls his eyes.

"Besides," Shade continues, "I want to hear more about the new girl." He grins at me, his gray eyes sparkling. "I heard you kicked Amelia Ash's ass at lunch today."

"Hey," snaps Hunter. It's the first thing he's said since I got here. "That's my sister you're talking about."

"Yeah," Shade says, "and you still ended up in here, didn't you?" Hunter doesn't reply, hunkering lower in his chair, and Shade turns back to me. "So is it true? Can you really shift into multiple forms?"

"That's what they tell me," I reply, "but right now I can't even do that right. Whenever I do shift, I just end up looking like some... hideous blob of body parts."

"Ha! Nice!"

I can't help but chuckle. "Easy for you to say. You're a... what are you again?"

"Wolf shifter," Shade replies proudly. "Listen," he continues, a thoughtful expression appearing on his face, "if you need help learning how to shift, maybe I can help you."

I raise my eyebrows. "Yeah?"

He shrugs. "Sure. It's always come pretty naturally to me."

Hunter makes a scoffing noise but doesn't say anything.

"Well, I..." I blink. I hadn't considered the possibility of someone tutoring me before. Considering how well my classes have gone so far... "Yeah," I say, smiling a little. "That sounds good."

Shade smiles, his silver eyes meeting mine for a split second. My heart flutters a little in my chest. "How's tomorrow morning before breakfast?"

I purse my lips. "Aren't we, like, not allowed out before breakfast?"

Shade shrugs. "What's the worst that they're gonna do to you if they catch you? Send you back here?"

"You have a point," I reply.

"Then it's settled," Shade says, sitting back in his chair. "Tomorrow morning at six, on the quad. I'll show you a thing or two about turning into a wolf."

"Come on," Hunter says finally. "Can you not ask the new girl out right in front of me?"

Before I have time to process the implications of his anger, Shade is already replying gamely. "Hey, I never said it was a date. You can come too, if you want. I've heard you're not doing so well, yourself."

Hunter snorts. "Not happening."

"You don't know what you're missing," Shade tells him. "So, Millie," he says, "how did you end up winning the shifter lottery, anyway?"

"No idea," I reply. "I never knew my parents."

"Damn, really? Join the club."

My eyes widen at the same time as Landon's. "Seriously?"

"Yeah," Shade replies. "I was adopted."

"Holy shit," mutters Landon. "I spend my whole life angsting about my past and then I meet two others like me in less than a day? It's a small world, I guess."

Silas, who's been silent for some time now, speaks up. "It's even smaller than that," he says slowly, turning around in his chair to look at the rest of us. "I'm an orphan, too." There's a pause, and he adds, "That sounds pretty pathetic when I say it out loud."

"I'll be damned," says Landon, looking between the three of us with newfound respect.

"Well, looks like we're a regular Breakfast Club in here, aren't we?" says Shade. "Next thing you know we'll be dancing on the desks and confessing our darkest secrets to each other."

Silas snorts, but there's humor behind it. "I wouldn't count on it."

"To be honest," Landon says, "until I met you, Millie, I thought hybrids didn't exist."

"Oh, they existed, all right," replies Shade. "They say they were experiments done by witches, but then the humans took them out."

Silas clears his throat but says nothing.

I open my mouth for a moment and then close it, debating, before asking, "So what happened, Silas? To your parents, I mean." There's a pause, and I realize how insensitive the question must have sounded. "You don't have to talk about it if you don't want to," I add hastily, already feeling my cheeks going red. What the hell came over me?

"It's all right," Silas replies. He takes a breath, meeting my eyes, and replies, "They were killed."

The room goes completely silent, except for the snores coming from the teacher's desk. The others are staring at Silas, eyes wide. Even Hunter seems to be both intrigued and scared.

"How?" Shade asks, the only one bold enough to break the silence. "I mean, who by?"

"Jeez, Shade," snaps Landon.

Shade puts his hands up. "Sorry, sorry."

Silas shifts in his seat, not seeming particularly bothered. "Humans," he replies, swallowing before he continues. I'm surprised at how composed he is, considering what he's discussing, but maybe that's just how it is when enough time has passed after a tragedy. "My mom and dad were both pretty pro-shifter," Silas says. "They were always suspicious of them--raised me in a shifter-only community, away from civilization. They were always telling me not to trust them, calling them violent and xenophobic. I kind of brushed it off. I mean, I was a kid back then, and I didn't even know if I was going to end up with shifter powers, you know?"

The others nod.

"Anyway," Silas continues, "my parents paranoia eventually started to get the better of them, I think. They started coming up with all these crazy conspiracy theories about how the humans who know about shifters don't actually want to coexist with us. The humans apparently wanted to enslave us, or use us, experiment on us... It was a different story every day. It got to the point where they tried to stop interacting with humans at all. It went about as well as you'd expect."

He takes a breath, fidgeting. "At one point, I remember coming home every day to see a new group of shifters in our living room, discussing conspiracy theories and talking about how they were going to 'escape enslavement', or something like that." He shakes his head.

"I can't imagine that ended well," says Landon.

"No," Silas replies. "It didn't. By the time I was ten, they had basically turned our lives upside-down. Then, one day, they pulled me out of school, packed up our stuff, and got in the car. They wouldn't tell me why, or where we were going. It didn't matter anyway--we hadn't made it that far when we were stopped by a couple of humans. Apparently, the word had gotten out that my folks had been stirring the pot, and the governments needed to do damage control. So they took me out of the car, hauled my parents away, and that was the last time I ever saw them."

There's a long moment of silence as we process all this. Finally Landon turns to look at him. "You okay, Silas?"

He nods. "Yeah, I'm fine. It was a long time ago, and my parents were... unwell. That much was obvious." He shakes himself, sitting up in his chair. "But enough about that. Let's talk about something more fun, yeah?"

"Well," Shade remarks, "I don't think any of us are going to top that."

Silas snorts and the others laugh, the tension in the room breaking up. I stay quiet, Silas' story still bouncing around in my head like a pinball. The idea of having parents and then losing them... I didn't think anything could be worse than not knowing one's parents at all, but I'm realizing now that I'm wrong. Absently, I reach down into my boot, touching the necklace given to me by the only real family I've ever had. *I do know what that's like*, I think, the memories of Mollie flooding back to me. *I wouldn't wish it on anyone.*

"What are you doing, Millie?" asks Shade.

The others turn to look at me with my hand in my boot, making me blush a little. "Sorry," I respond. "I just..." I never talk about Mollie with anyone. She's always been sort of an unspoken guardian angel, one I look to with a kind of superstition, as if one wrong step will corrupt her memory, too, leaving me alone for real. But now I find myself relaxing as I speak, the words coming out as easily as if I've known these guys my whole life. "That story of yours got me thinking, Silas," I reply. "I never knew my parents, but one of my foster mothers gave me a necklace. I keep it in my shoe, since the clasp is broken." There's so much I want to say, want to explain, but somehow, none of it seems right--or necessary. "I was just thinking about family," I say simply, shrugging.

I have no idea what's compelling me to open up like this in front of a bunch of people I've known for less than a day, but I'm past questioning it at this point. My first day at Shifter Academy has been a shit show; maybe a little solidarity is exactly what the doctor ordered.

"You're a funny girl, Boots," remarks Landon, and I blink at him. He looks around at the others for support. "Come on, Boots? Because she keeps it in her boots? Guys?"

The others laugh. "I can get on board with that," says Silas.

"It's got a nice ring to it," remarks Shade. "Boots Brix. Hunter, thoughts?"

"Whatever," Hunter murmurs, but there's a ghost of a grin on his face.

"Boots," I say, testing out the nickname. For the first time since lunch, I find myself smiling. "I like the sound of that."

CHAPTER 15

Hunter

"Dad is going to be so mad," Amelia all but huffs as I walk into my room and come to a halt. *How the fuck did she get in my room?*

"And for the second time today, you are not my mother therefore you can't tell me what to do. What the hell are you doing in my room?" I demand, dropping my bag onto the floor and kicking off my shoes. Amelia sits on my chair in front of the window. This room is pretty big and I even have a kitchen area. Nothing but the best for a Prince of the Vampires.

Except I don't want it. I don't want anything that comes from my father or that I didn't earn on my own.

And no one in my family seems to understand that. To them, blood and what family you are from is all that matters.

Hard work is for the poor, as my father likes to remind me.

"You need to stay away from the hybrid," she tells me, and I ignore her like I always have since we were kids. Amelia was always the bossy one, the sister who thought she needed to look after me just because my powers don't work. I appreciate that she cares, but sometimes it feels like she wants to control me rather than try to understand me. Amelia catches my arm as I walk past, making me stop. I effortlessly pull my arm from hers and she raises an eyebrow. "You little liar, your powers work fine enough when you need them."

"Strength is one thing. Everything else just feels blocked," I all but growl at her. "Now get out. I'm tired."

"Dad called me today--,"

"Good to know he calls one of his children. How is mum?" I question and she narrows her eyes, a touchy subject for us both. Dad is domineering and always in control...and mum is shy and weak. She is the complete opposite to him, and he controls her every waking move. If he could control her dreams, he would.

"Don't be like that. Dad loves you," she says, lying so effortlessly and avoiding the subject of mum all together. Typical Amelia. And Dad wonders why his kids are cold and emotionless assholes. "Anyway, he said the hybrid is dangerous to the whole shifter world and the shifters of every clan are watching her. You can't be noticed at her side, so drop the tramp and find someone else to bang. She isn't even that pretty!"

I lean against the wall, crossing my arms as I swallow the anger that bubbles in my throat. I'm usually the master at controlling my emotions, but something about Amelia calling Millie a tramp has me wanting to scream at her. And about her not being pretty? Amelia must be fucking blind. Any shifter in this academy can see that Millie Brix is fucking gorgeous. She could bring any man to his knees. Me included.

I can see why Boots would be a big interest to the shifter community if I really think about it and why my sister would want me far away from her. They really don't have anyone like her, and she is clearly linked to every clan. Effectively she could lead all of us when she is older and if she is as powerful as I suspect she actually is.

Either way, I have no intention of staying away from her. I feel something, some kind of connection to her that I don't know how to explain exactly. Either way, I want to find out more about her life, and whether she feels anything for me.

I don't give a shit if my controlling sister and father want me away from her.

"I'm going to say this once. I love you, Amelia. You're my sister and I care about your opinion usually, but not this time. I'm friends with Millie and you need to get over it," I tell her. The moment the words leave my mouth she growls, and stands up from the chair. If looks could kill, I'd be a dead vampire right about now.

"Hunter!" she screeches.

Sighing, I walk to the door and hold it open. She stares at me like she has never seen her brother before. I smile as she stomps to the door, coming to a halt right in front of me. "If you won't save yourself, then I will have to."

I grab her arm before she can escape. "Hurt Millie and we will have a problem."

She smiles sweetly as I let her go and she leaves my room. As I shut the door, I rest my head against the cold wood and pray to the shifter goddess that Amelia lets this go.

I will protect Millie, even against my sister.

CHAPTER 16

Maybe it was the story that changed the dynamic between the five of us, or maybe it was just the fact that we were all stuck in detention together. Whatever the reasoning, by the time the dinner bell rang and we were allowed to leave, I felt a strange sense of camaraderie with the other guys. It wasn't like we suddenly became friends or something, but even after the professor who was still half-asleep at his desk, waved us out the door and we went our separate ways, I found myself hoping I would see them all again. Even Hunter, as quiet and broody as he is.

I ate dinner with Hazel, and she spent the whole time asking me questions about detention, about the brawl, and about the others. I didn't mention anyone's past, as it didn't seem like my story to tell, but that didn't stop her from being intrigued, her eyes wide as she gave me the update on what I missed on campus. Having someone to socialize with continued to improve my mood, and by the time I went up to my room to turn in for the night, I was feeling almost as good as I had been before the whole Amelia business went down. I spend the night sleeping like a baby, exhausted from the first day and ready to put the unpleasantness behind me. I'm so comfortable in bed that when the first light of the morning makes me stir, I almost nestle back into my covers. Then my eyes fly open and I sit up in bed. I said I would meet Shade today before class.

By the looks of it, we're well before the breakfast bell, but I can't tell by how much, so I scramble out of bed and get dressed rather than waste any more time. I feel a surge of nervousness as soon as I poke my head out of the door; the dormitory is quiet, with only the occasional scuffling of feet on the floorboards to break the silence. There's no rule against getting up before the bell, as far as I'm aware, but I can't help but feel like a delinquent as I pad down the hallway, off to more illicit shapeshifting under the tutelage of the wolf shifter I met yesterday. At one point, I nearly jump out of my skin when I pass one of the housekeepers, who is in the middle of distributing fresh uniforms to each of the dorm rooms. But she barely spares me a second glance, and I tell myself to calm down. Nobody seems to care what I'm up to, and besides, Shade seemed pretty well-acquainted with rule breaking yesterday. In all likelihood, he has unsupervised shifting down to a science.

Shade is waiting for me in the quad, shielding his eyes from the rising sun as I make my way across the lawn to him. "I almost thought you weren't going to show," he says when I approach.

"Sorry," I reply, feeling sheepish. "I almost overslept. Almost."

"Well, you're here now," he says, grinning, and I find myself admiring his gray eyes once again. Boys have never really been a big part of my life--always moving from place to place makes it hard to date, let alone form a relationship with someone. But I can still appreciate his sharp features, and the effortlessness with which he carries himself.

A blush begins to creep into my cheeks and I say, "Well, shall we?"

"Here?" Shade snorts. "No way. We're out in the open. Here, follow me. Once we're under the trees, no one will be able to spot us." Without another word, he turns and begins to walk out of the quad, heading in the direction of the trees in the distance. I have to hurry to catch up to him, and he doesn't bother to check to make sure I'm still with him; we continue in silence until we arrive at the edge of the forest. The trees tower over me, making me feel even smaller, and the dense foliage makes it difficult to see very far in. That doesn't deter Shade, however, and he strides in between the trees, hands stuffed in his pockets, with me following uneasily behind him.

"Is it... safe in here?" I ask, my voice low.

Shade laughs. "As safe as any forest can be, I guess. If you're asking whether there are monsters living here or something..." He shakes his head, turning to me. "Not likely. Although the faculty will probably tell you differently--it's an easy way to make sure everyone stays within the bounds of the campus."

"I see," I say, looking around. I can hear the sound of a wood-pecker tapping away at a tree in the distance, and all around us, birds shout and crickets chirp. It's quiet, almost tranquil, and I allow myself to relax a little as I turn to Shade, spreading out my arms. "All right," I say. "Here we are. Do your worst."

There's a gleam in Shade's eye as he replies, "I like your style, Boots. All right." He takes a step back, giving me an appraising look before continuing. "So tell me a little about what your magic feels like."

"I..." I think back to that feeling in my stomach, those cool fingers branching out and radiating through my body. "I guess you could say it feels cold," I reply. "A bit like that feeling you get after drinking ice water--that sort of coolness in the pit of your stomach." I shake my head, realizing how ridiculous that must sound. "God, I sound like a lunatic."

"Not at all," Shade replies without a hint of sarcasm in his voice. "Everyone's magic feels different. Mine feels a bit prickly--like, itchy, you know? Sometimes it can be hard to pinpoint it at first."

"I'll say," I mutter.

"But you're already a step ahead of the game if you can recognize it," Shade continues. "It took me nearly a month just to get that part down."

"Really?" I raise my eyebrows. "You seem so confident."

"Damn right, I'm confident," Shade replies. "But I was a late bloomer. Anyway, I want you to close your eyes."

"But I already did that," I protest. "In every class I've had, they say that's the first--"

Shade holds up a hand. "Who's the one doing the teaching, here?"

I give an exasperated sigh. "Okay, fine." My eyes drift closed. "Now what? They kept talking about trying to concentrate so I can find my magic, but I have no idea how."

Shade snorts. "And that there is why the teachers at this school are idiots. It's not about concentrating, Boots--it's the opposite. It's about letting go."

"Letting go?"

"Yeah. Hippies might call it meditation, but I like to think of it more as letting your senses experience the world around you. In my experience, the key isn't to focus on the magic itself--that's like trying to hold on to water. You can't force these things."

"So then how am I supposed to control it?" I ask.

"You have to let it come to you," replies Shade. "And the best way to do that, at least at the start, is to stop trying so hard." There's the sound of crunching leaves, and I open my eyes to see that Shade has moved closer to me, standing to my right. There's silence between us, but I'm intensely aware of his proximity to me. If he moves any closer, his chest would be brushing my shoulder. "Here," he says, putting his hands on my shoulders. "Don't be so tense. Let your body relax. And keep your eyes closed, damn it."

"Okay, okay." I do as I'm told, and I feel his hands gently smooth my shoulders down. I didn't even realize how much tension I was carrying until just now.

Slowly, Shade moves one hand to my lower back. "That's it," he says. "Now take a deep breath. Forget about the magic, forget about where we are, forget about everything. Just listen to the forest and let the world around you come in." He goes quiet again, and I take a slow breath in, trying to force myself not to think about the magic itself.

Instead, I focus on the sounds of the woods around me: the rustling of animals in the high tree branches, the gentle whisper of wind, the distant chirping of birds. I can still feel Shade's hand on my spine, and its presence is both comforting and thrilling.

"There you go," Shade murmurs, his voice close to my ear. It sends a shiver up my back. "Now, when you're ready, start feeling for the magic. Don't try to grab onto it. Just become aware of it." His other hand moves to my stomach. "Look for it here," he says quietly.

I don't know if I've ever been so flustered in all my life, but even still, as I continue to breathe, absorbing the feeling of Shade's hands and the sounds of the forest, I gradually become aware of something below his hand, in my abdomen. It's that familiar, cold feeling, like a pool in the pit of my stomach. For a moment I feel a surge of triumph. It's working! I force myself not to pounce on it, instead just continuing to feel it. It's almost comforting, like meeting an old friend who you haven't seen for a long time. "Do you feel it?" Shade asks quietly.

"Yes," I breathe, my voice barely above a whisper.

He hums in approval. "The key is to not jump on it. Just let it do its thing, okay? When you're ready, visualize your form. Think of every detail."

"Okay," I reply, taking another deep breath as I let an image come to mind. A wolf: not a werewolf, but a timber wolf, with gray-brown fur and bright, watchful eyes. I remember what I can about the partial transformation I managed earlier--the texture of the fur, the way the muscles felt, and throw myself into perfecting the image, all the while aware of the cold sensation of my magic running through me. And just like that, I can feel the energy start to branch out, flooding through my body like a cooling wave.

The hairs on my arms stand on end, bristling into fur, and my muscles lengthen. Then I'm leaning forward, dropping onto all fours as my senses grow even more powerful. I can feel my teeth changing, the shape of my skull shifting under my skin into something canine and primal. And then I'm on the forest floor, feeling like both a human and an animal, the current of shapeshifting magic buzzing through my body.

"Yes!" cries Shade. "You did it, Boots!"

For a moment I'm afraid to open my eyes, afraid I'll lose this progress, but I slowly allow them to come open, looking down to see that my body is no longer human. It's lupine, and enormous--larger than a wolf has any right to be. The smells of the woods are enhanced, and my vision feels more acute. I feel strong... powerful. And I'm all wolf, no other clan features to be found. I turn back to Shade, watching as he grins electrifyingly at me...

And then the breakfast bell rings, its loud chime echoing all the way across the campus to where we are. It startles me, and in a split second I lose the thread, bursting back into my human form in an instant. Now I'm just a girl again, on all fours on the ground. For a moment I stare at Shade, wide-eyed, and then he starts to laugh. "Not bad for a first-timer, Boots." I can't help but laugh, too; I probably look ridiculous.

Getting to my feet, I brush the leaves off my pants and follow him triumphantly back to the quad. "Thank you, Shade," I say when we arrive on the main path. "I mean it. I was starting to think I would never..." I shake my head.

"My pleasure," Shade replies, giving an exaggerated bow. "I'll be here all day."

I meet his gray eyes with my own, and I swear something passes between us. I'm on the verge of asking him what made him offer to help me in the first place when the sound of a familiar voice draws our attention away. It's Hazel, jogging down the road towards the two of us and looking distraught. "Millie!" she exclaims when she approaches us. "There you are. I've been looking everywhere for you." Her eyes narrow a little when she sees Shade. "He's not bothering you, is he?"

"No," I assure her. "The opposite. He was helping me."

"Huh." She raises her eyebrows, looking skeptical, but then shrugs and turns to me. "Listen, we all need to get back to the academic building. Right now."

I frown. "Didn't the breakfast bell just ring?"

Hazel shakes her head, eyes wide. "The president called an emergency assembly. One of the Academy students has gone missing."

CHAPTER 17

S hade and I stare at each other. "Missing?" I ask, turning to Hazel. "Who?"

"One of the upperclassmen," she replies, beckoning to the two of us. We follow her in stunned silence, walking fast. "A guy named Brody Patton. At least, that's what people are saying."

"How do they know he's missing?" asks Shade, falling into step next to me.

Hazel looks at him. "I'm sorry, who are you, again?"

"Shade Ivis," he replies.

Her expression darkens. "Right. Shade. I've heard about you." She looks like she's going to make another comment, but then she shakes her head. "Apparently he wasn't at dinner last night. Everyone thought he was sick. But then he wasn't in bed this morning, either. Apparently they searched the dorms and the academic building. But there's been no sign of him."

"Could he have just wandered off?" I ask, thinking back to my training session with Shade. Considering how big the forest is...

"I don't know," Hazel replies. "All I know is that they can't find him anywhere. Hawthorne wants everyone to meet him in the East Lecture Hall. It's the only space big enough for the whole school."

I nod, mind reeling, but don't say anything else. By the time we get back inside the main building, it's immediately clear that something isn't right. Students hurry through the foyer in clusters, murmuring urgently to one another, and faculty members weave through the crowd, doing headcounts while shooting each other concerned looks. We follow the crowd down the east hallway, and I spot Josie herding confused-looking students in the right direction. "Save me a seat," I tell Hazel, before jogging over to her. "Josie," I say, "what's going on? I heard someone's gone missing."

"Hi, Millie," she replies, looking distracted. "Listen, I'm not allowed to say much right now. The president will explain everything at the assembly. Where were you, by the way? I didn't see you in the dorm, so I thought maybe..." Her voice trails off.

"I, uh... I took a walk," I reply. "I just needed some air."

"I'm glad you're alright," she says. "But you need to stay inside until the president gives us more information. It's possible this will turn into a..." She stops herself.

"A what?" I ask.

"Nothing," Josie replies. "Go find a seat. I'll see you after the meeting."

Unable to get anything more out of her, I weave through the crowd in search of Hazel. She's already seated in the auditorium by the time I arrive, looking uncomfortable next to Shade. To his left are Landon, Silas, and Hunter, all looking equally concerned. I squeeze in alongside them, thankful that they're all here. It's strange how... *necessary* they feel all of a sudden, even though I've only known them for a short time.

"Boots," Silas says. "There you are. I was getting worried."

"I *told* you she was fine," Landon says. "She was training with Shade, remember?"

Silas blinks. "Oh. Uh, right." He clears his throat, a tinge of color entering his face. There's also a hint of something else as he glances at Shade. Jealousy? No. I push the idea away. That's ridiculous.

"Do any of you know what's going on?" I ask the others.

"No more than you do," Landon replies.

"What about this Brody guy?" Hazel asks. "Do any of you know him?"

The guys shake their heads. "I think he's a friend of my sister's," says Hunter.

Landon snorts. "Charming."

Hunter shoots him a look. "He's a siren, Landon. Like you. Be careful, or you might be next."

Landon raises his eyebrows. "Was that a snarky comeback, Hunter?" He laughs. "Maybe there's hope for you after all."

Hunter glowers but says nothing more. Moments later, I see President Hawthorne walk onto the lecture hall stage, flanked by a few people who I can only assume are either faculty or board members. I can make out Mrs. Fairbanks and her enormous spectacles, as well as Samantha, who is standing off to the side, arms crossed. One of the board members has Hunter's fiery red locks--no doubt his and Amelia's father.

Hawthorne approaches the podium, tapping the microphone a couple times and clearing his throat. It takes a moment for the assembled students to quiet down, but soon a hush falls over the auditorium. "Good morning, everyone," President Hawthorne says. "Firstly, I wanted to thank you all for coming here, and apologize for the interruption to your morning routine." He clears his throat. "No doubt you're wondering why I've brought you all here today. By now, some of you may have heard rumors of an... incident that has taken place on campus. I wanted to address those rumors now, to prevent the spread of misinformation.

"Last night," Hawthorne continues, "a student by the name of Brody Patton did not come to dinner. The faculty was informed by some of the other students on his floor that he wasn't feeling well. This morning, however, he was gone from his room before the first bell rang. We've had staff searching both the academic facilities and the student housing areas top to bottom to find him, and we will continue to do so, but so far, there has been no sign of him."

A panicked murmur rises up from the assembled students. I stare at the others. Landon's lips are pressed into a thin line, while Hazel is nervously whispering to the girl on her other side. Hunter's expression has gone from broody to concerned, while Shade just stares down at the president, his eyebrow raised. Silas' face is stony, his eyes practically burning a hole in the floor. His shoulders are hunched a little, and he looks ready to get out of his seat at any minute.

"Given the circumstances of Mr. Patton's disappearance," Hawthorne continues, "it's possible that he is no longer on campus. As most of you are aware, this island encompasses thousands of acres of undeveloped land, most of which is forest, with the exception of the faculty housing. With that in mind, it may take quite some time to locate Mr. Patton if the search extends past Academy boundaries. But I want everyone here to rest assured that we are doing all we can to find him, and we will continue our search until we learn his whereabouts. This kind of incident has never happened here before. We take situations like this very seriously here at Shifter Academy, and I want to take this opportunity to remind you that our students' safety is our number one priority."

Hawthorne clears his throat, and for a moment the auditorium is silent save for the shifting of students in their seats. The president's eyes sweep the room for a moment, as if gauging the reactions of all the students present. For a moment I could swear that his gaze settles on me, but as soon as I narrow my eyes, he's moved on.

"Now," he says, "I know that this is probably very confusing, and perhaps a bit frightening to all of you. I want you to know that you will be informed of any relevant new developments as they come up. That said, this is an unusual situation, and it's not clear yet whether Mr. Patton is simply lost, or met with foul play."

My heart drops at the idea. Shade said that the woods were safe, but what if he was wrong? What would he know about it, really? Hawthorne himself just said that the island is thousands of acres. What if there's something in the forest? Or some*one*? My mind is already swimming with possibilities, the paranoia that only comes from a lack of information already sinking its claws into me. I tell myself to calm down, glancing at the others for reassurance, but none of them seem particularly calm, either.

"I have spoken with the rest of the school board," President Hawthorne says. "We have determined that, until we know what became of Mr. Patton, we are going to make a few temporary adjustments to the rules at the Academy. This is first and foremost for the safety of the students here, so that we can err on the side of caution and prevent something else like this from happening. Therefore, effective immediately, we will be instating a mandatory curfew of nine PM. Additionally, no students are to be allowed off campus for any reason without express permission and a faculty escort. This means that you will be required to stay within the Academy buildings and on the lawn. The forest is off-limits until we have more information.

Additionally, no students are to leave the dormitory before the breakfast bell sounds. We will have faculty members patrolling the grounds to enforce these new policies and help maintain security while we search for Mr. Patton. We are taking this situation very seriously, and we expect you all to do the same. Now," he says, putting his hands behind his back, "I'm going to give the mic over to our head of security and co-chair of the board, Ms. Evelyn Rose. She will answer any questions you may have, and then you all will be able to resume your day. Thank you for your time and attention. Ms. Rose…"

He steps away from the microphone to allow a gorgeous, dark-haired woman to take his place. "Hello, everyone," she says. "Some of you may know me. My name is Evelyn Rose, and I'm in charge of campus security here at Shifter Academy. I wanted to take this time to address any concerns you might have before we continue…"

What feels like every student in the lecture hall raises their hand at once, but I'm already tuning the discussion out, my gaze instead lingering on Hawthorne. He has moved off to the side again, but his eyes are sweeping the room once more, and I can't shake the sneaking feeling that he's looking at me.

"Well," says Landon as we slowly file out of the auditorium ten minutes later, "that was… a lot."

The hallway is choked with students, all looking bewildered as they make their way back in the direction of the cafeteria. All in all, the meeting took about half an hour which at least gives us enough time to get some food before we head off to class, but I can't fight the growing sense of unease that I'm feeling in the aftermath of Hawthorne's announcements.

"That's putting it mildly," Shade mutters. "It's always overkill with them, isn't it?"

"What do you mean?" Hunter asks.

"Calm down, daddy's boy," Shade says. "I'm talking about the school in general. This is total overkill, and I'm willing to bet most of the other people here agree with me."

"You think this is overkill?" Hunter asks. "Someone's gone missing!"

"Yeah, and he'll probably be back by the end of the day," Shade replies dismissively. "If you ask me, the guy just got lost. They'll find him cowering under a tree somewhere, and then we'll all be wondering why the hell any of this was necessary."

"You're not at all worried something might have happened to him?" Hazel asks incredulously.

"No," Shade replies. "Like what? Eaten by a monster? There's no one on this island except for the people at this academy."

"Exactly," Hazel points out. "That's what makes me nervous. If it was foul play, how do we know someone at the school wasn't responsible?"

"Great," says Landon. "Now I can add 'trapped on campus with a serial killer' to my growing list of phobias."

"You really think a student would have done something to that guy?" I ask, frowning.

"Maybe not a student," Landon replies. "Maybe a faculty member."

I shiver, muttering, "Glad I asked."

Landon laughs, slinging an arm around my shoulders. His body feels warm and sturdy against mine. "Don't worry, Boots. I'll protect you."

Hunter snorts and rolls his eyes, while Shade raises an eyebrow.

We come to a stop outside the cafeteria, each of us still processing everything that was said.

"Silas?" I say, turning to the dragon shifter. He's been strangely quiet this whole time, his head low and his shoulders hunched. "Are you okay?"

"Yeah, I'm fine," Silas replies. "It's just... something the president said is bothering me a little, that's all."

"Which part?" I ask.

He looks up at me with thinly veiled worry, and something in his expression makes a fresh surge of fear rush through me. "The part about nothing like this ever happening here before," he replies in a low voice. "That was a lie."

CHAPTER 18

"Hey, bestie. I love your hair today," Hazel comments, sitting next to me in the cafeteria and flipping my braid on my shoulder. The sun is just coming up outside, marking a new day. "Can you show me how to do that kind of braid."

"It's called a waterfall braid and sure," I reply. "Did you get the message that we have siren studies all day for a special class?"

"Yup," she replies, before taking a bite of her toast. "That's why I'm here early. I wonder what it's about."

"Same," I say, just as Silas and Landon sit down opposite us.

"Morning, Boots. Hazel," Silas grumbles, never the morning person until he has had a few cups of coffee.

Landon grins and winks at me as Silas drinks his first cup of coffee and then picks up his second. "You look lovely today girls."

Hazel just rolls her eyes as I focus on Silas. "How come you are up early? I know why we three are."

"Early morning flight training," he tells me. His third cup of coffee is empty now and normal Silas is here. "It's an advanced year class, but the professor wants me to learn with the higher-ups."

"Congrats man," Landon pats his shoulder. "So, girls, we should get a move on. We have ten minutes to get to class."

We all gather up our things and get a move on to the classroom because none of us wants to be late to Mrs Leggers class. I'm intrigued by what goes on in the siren class other than reading books, which is all we have done in the lessons up to this point. I know pretty much all the history of the Siren's now. How they were created by turning seals into humans, but the magic got stuck in their souls and bred a whole new race. Sirens are faster than any creature in the water, and they can breathe underwater.

And sing. Their songs are meant to be the most enchanting sound in the entire world if they use their magic in their songs.

Landon chats to Hazel about some party coming up, but I pretty much tune them out as I try not to be nervous about whatever today holds. As much as I want to learn what clan I really belong to, at the moment it feels like I am just hovering between all the clans and never really finding a home.

At some point, we get to the classroom and I walk in first to see the room is full of students on the one side. This room is newer than most of the academy and almost shaped like a giant dome. The one side has pure glass walls, with views over the fields and trees in the distance. Right in front of the glass is Mrs Leggers and Mr Hawthorne, both of them talking quietly and not looking away from each other. Hushed whispers fill my ears as I find three empty seats and Hazel and Landon sit to either side of me.

Landon's knee presses against mine and I turn to him."You okay?" he quietly asks. "You look lost."

"Out of place, I guess," I softly admit.

He takes my hand, surprising me a little. "We all feel that way in our little group, but you aren't out of place with me. Not one little bit."

I link my fingers with his as the room quiets down, and Mr Hawthorne claps a few times.

"Welcome young members of the Siren Clan. We are delighted you could join us here for the day," he starts off. "We have a very special visitor here today who will spend the day teaching you many new things about the world of Sirens."

Mr Hawkthorne claps his hands, and so do all the students as a red-haired woman walks to his side. Her long red hair falls in waves down her back, like a river of red curls, and she wears a skintight costume of some sort. It's thin, almost leather-like in texture and covers her from her neck downwards, showing off way too much.

"Hello everyone. My name is Crystal, and I am a leader of the sirens in the Great Council. I am proud to be here today to show you what you can become if you truly try," she tells us, and I look to Landon. His jaw ticks and his hand tightens on mine. "Have any of you heard a siren's song?"

Resounding no's come from the crowd, and Landon finally looks down at me.

"She is testing you. There is no way this is random," he tells me. "You need to pass whatever test they are going to do."

"How?" I whisper back, but Landon doesn't seem to have an answer.

"This isn't good," Hazel tells me, looking worried. "You're not all siren. The siren's song hurts other races, it can even kill them."

Figures.

I go to stand up, but Landon pulls me down, holding me to his side. "I got you."

Before I have a chance to ask what he means, Crystal lets out a tune like nothing I have ever heard. I turn to her as her skin changes from normal to beautiful blue scales and her red hair changes to pure silver. Every word that leaves her mouth is seductive until suddenly it isn't anymore.

My mouth opens in a silent scream as every part of my body feels like it's being stabbed. Suddenly Landon cups my face and brings my lips to his. The kiss is soothing, washing away the sound of Crystal's voice, and slowly I realize Landon is humming his own song against my lips. His siren song.

And it doesn't hurt me.

If anything, it pulls me to him like a gentle wave brushing against my skin. I sink my hands into his hair, forgetting the world except for Landon's kiss.

I forget everything except for how perfect Landon feels.

"Guys, stop!" Hazel whispers, grabbing my arm and shaking me a little.

Landon breaks away from me, but I'm still in a haze as I stare at him.

He looks in exactly the same haze as me, like both of us just realized something big. And we kind of did. I don't see how we can be just friends after this.

"I hope you all enjoyed my song. For the rest of the day, you may ask me any questions you like," Crystal says, and I turn to see Mr Hawthorne's eyes on me, a frown etched onto his face. He shakes his head and walks out as Crystal starts answering the many questions thrown at her.

Landon was right, that was a test.

And I clearly just failed.

CHAPTER 19

"How was dragon shifter class?" Shade asks as I leave the table and he walks with me to our joint wolf shifter class in the forest. Out of all the classes, wolf shifter class is where I feel a little bit at home. We spend most of the classes in the forest, searching for our connection to nature and everything around us.

"I could hold my fire breathing for a minute. I see it as process. The teacher does not," I answer as we head outside and across the green to the meeting point.

Shade hums. "Even though you are connected to all the clans, I sense your wolf more than others. Maybe that is just simply because of my wolf."

"Will you shift for me today?" I ask as we head into the trees.

Shade smiles down at me and shakes his head. "I'm not allowed to shift around others," he tells me, running his hand through his hair. "My wolf...has issues with dominance."

"Explain that one to me," I ask, feeling a little confused.

He sighs, looking around like something will save him from telling me this. "My wolf is an alpha, and he expects everyone to bow to him. Until we leave the academy, we can't make a pack and while I'm here, I'm protected from the alpha leaders challenging me."

"Would they challenge you?" I ask.

He nods, meeting my eyes. "My wolf would not rest until he is in charge and their wolf would not like having a threat out in the world. It would be a deathmatch with one alpha winning in the end."

Something in my chest hurts at the idea of Shade fighting anyone to the death for alpha rights. I don't get to reply as we come into the clearing with ten other wolf shifters waiting around Mr Hexin, the temporary wolf shifter teacher we have. Apparently there is a permanent teacher, but she is on maternity leave for the year.

I like Mr Hexin anyway, he has a warm feeling about him and he bothers to learn all his students' names.

"Today we do not have much time in the forest. A storm is coming in and we all need to be inside. So off we go, find your place in the forest!" he shouts to us all. A student I don't know, a guy with brownish hair and blue eyes smiles at me as he passes us.

Shade places his hand on the middle of my back, leading me in the opposite direction of the guy, and I look up to see his usual playful smile gone, and instead he looks rather serious.

"Everything alright?" I ask Shade as we get deeper in the forest and Shade doesn't stop, his large footsteps eating up the ground. He comes to a halt and quicker than I can think, he pushes me behind his back.

"It's rude to follow someone in the woods, Tedore," Shade dryly comments. I peek around his shoulder to see the brown-haired guy from earlier and he isn't alone. At his side are three other guys, and I don't recognise them from our class. "And with three higher years to protect you? Are you afraid to challenge me alone?"

"Shade, get out of the way. It's the hybrid we want," Tedore admits, and my hands shake as fear takes over. "Our families want the hybrid gone."

Shade laughs and looks over his shoulder at me as he says one sentence that all but melts my heart. "Boots is mine."

The word mine is growled out, and he shifts almost effortlessly into a giant black wolf. The wolf is huge, stretching above my head, and I try not to be scared of him as I stumble out of the way. Shade's wolf growls low and hard, and lightning snakes across the sky, like the weather is backing up his protective call.

Tedore shifts into a much smaller brown wolf and the three guys behind him shift too, but Shade is already running at them. They clash in the middle of the forest, clawing and ripping at each other as they smack into trees, breaking them.

I jump out of the way of a fallen tree as Shade battles all four of the shifters on his own. One of them, who I'm pretty sure is Tedore, breaks away from the battle and stalks towards me. Blood drips from his mouth onto the fallen leaves and branches between us.

A cold feeling drifts over me and instead of fighting it, I let my wolf take over and shift me almost effortlessly into my wolf, landing on my four paws. Taking Shade's idea, I charge at the wolf and aim for his throat. He catches me with his mouth and throws me across the woods. I slam into a tree, shifting back without meaning to and freezing as the wolf slowly walks towards me. I can't see anything but the blood in his mouth, feel the pain in my shoulder from his bite as he opens his large mouth full of sharp teeth.

Suddenly Tedore's wolf is thrown away from me and Shade's wolf holds him down on the ground, his mouth around his neck. A scary growl comes from Shade's wolf and Tedore goes still under him.

I think he is submitting.

After a long pause, Shade's wolf lets him go, and he runs into the forest and out of sight. Shade shifts back and rushes to me, kneeling in front of me. He cups my cheek and lowers his hand to my shoulder.

"Close your eyes, boots," he softly suggests.

I nod and close my eyes, trusting him completely. He is my alpha wolf and I think he will always save me. A warm feeling fills my shoulder for a moment, and then it's gone. I open my eyes and look down at my shoulder. My shirt is torn and soaked with blood, but the bite mark is gone.

"How did you do that?" I ask Shade as he helps me stand. Shade might have blood on his clothes and a few bruises, but he doesn't look as hurt as he should be after fighting off four wolves. "In fact, how are you okay?"

"Alpha wolves can heal their pack. My wolf and I see you as ours," he softly tells me. "And my wolf will bow to no one. Especially not another wolf."

We smile at each other just as the skies open and heavy rainfalls down on us. I laugh, grabbing Shade's hand and we run through the forest towards the academy.

My alpha wolf saved me, and one day, I'm going to save him from the biggest danger I can see: Himself.

CHAPTER 20

"It's weird to be in nice, normal clothes," I admit to Hazel, who moves to stand at my side in front of the big mirror. I'm wearing high-waisted dark denim skinny jeans and a shimmery silver top tucked into them, a gift from Hazel. She said she bought them and they didn't fit her right and thought they would look amazing on me. I think she bought them for me, judging by the tags I found on them, but I don't want to point that out. I know she's being a good friend and knows I don't have any nice clothes with me. "You look amazing, Hazel."

And she really does. Dressed in a tight red dress, her blonde curls pulled back into a braid I did for her, and silver high heels, she is stunning.

"I hope he likes it," she admits.

"Who?" I question and she shrugs, avoiding my eyes.

"No one you'd know," she tells me. "It's complicated."

"I get complicated," I reply, thinking of all the guys. I'd be lying if I said I didn't feel something for each one of them. Shade is protective, Silas is secretive but makes me laugh, Hunter is mysterious but always there for me and Landon feels like he effortlessly takes my heart without trying too much.

The door is knocked twice, snapping me out of my thoughts. I rush to the door, pulling it open, and Hunter walks in first, followed by Shade. They both look strange to me in normal clothes, but oh so sexy. Hunter looks almost not real like I'm staring at a man in a magazine with deep red hair and pale skin. His flawless looks are only made stronger by his casual grey t-shirt and jeans. Shade has a leather jacket on over a black t-shirt and it is tucked into dark trousers. He looks like a bad boy dream and I have to clear my throat as I look away. Silas is at late training tonight but he plans to get to the party later and Landon can't come because he has detention for not attending class earlier this week as he didn't feel like going.

"Do you have the powder?" Hazel asks Shade. He nods, pulling out four tiny bags of yellow powder.

"What is that stuff?" I ask them, stepping closer.

"Travel powder made by witches and sirens. You pour it into a bottle of water and drink a tiny bit, thinking about where you want to go. It's nice and easy," Hazel explains to me.

"But I don't know where we are going," I point out.

"I will travel with her," Shade announces and Hazel rolls her eyes.

"No fucking way," Hunter grumbles.

"Why?" I ask, confused.

"Traveling together means you need to kiss after drinking the water. I'm all for it," Shade suggests with a cheeky grin. Hunter glares at him, and he turns to glare right back. If we aren't careful, this is going to turn into a fight in no time.

"Wanna do something about it, vampire prince?" Shade taunts.

"Oh for heaven's sake!" Hazel grumbles. I turn to her as she drinks glowing white water from a bottle and drops it on the floor. She walks to me and pulls me to her, kissing me once. The world spins and I gasp as I fall on my ass onto grass, staring at the garden we are in. Behind me is a giant pool full of teenagers and dozens of seats.

"You kissed me," I point out as Hazel pulls me to my feet.

"Shut them up, didn't it?" she shrugs. "Stops them from fighting in my room. It didn't mean anything."

"Okay," I say just as Shade appears, followed by Hunter. Both of them glare at Hazel like the enemy, and I chuckle as I walk around them. The party is being held in an abandoned house and I can't stop staring in awe at the building. It's falling apart, sure, but some kind of magic is holding parts of the roof and walls together, making see through rooms almost.

"Oh, no, you aren't welcome here," Amelia states, stopping right in front of me. Dressed in a near to nothing black dress, she looks amazing but I'm not going to tell her that. She crosses her arms, a sneer on her lips. "Leave."

"Honestly? Make me," I suggest, standing up to her.

"Woah," Hazel mutters and the guys all but laugh even as Hunter moves to my side.

Amelia's eyes widen as Hunter wraps his arm around my shoulders.

"Better yet, make me leave, sis," Hunter suggests. "I've warned you once when it comes to Millie. Don't make me say it twice."

"Why her?" Amelia all but shouts. "She is a hybrid and this will get you in trouble with dad."

"Really that has nothing to do with you," I say. "Hunter can choose his own friends."

"Yeah, you seem to like to collect friends you kiss, huh, Boots?" Amelia sneers and my cheeks redden. "No wonder all the guys like you. You seem easy if the rumours are true."

"That's it," Hunter growls and grabs his sister's arm with impressive strength. We all watch as he drags her away and they both argue the entire time.

"I've never seen Hunter stand up to anyone," Shade comments, crossing his thick arms. "And what Amelia said is bullshit. She is just jealous."

"Totally," Hazel agrees. "Now let's go and dance, drink and be normal-ish teenagers for the night."

"Good plan," Shade agrees, taking my hand and making me walk fast with him into the house. The inside is crazy, all multiple levels of magic floors and a floating dance floor in the middle of the room. Heavy music makes it impossible to hear anything Shade says, but I get the gist when we get to the edge of the floating floor. He jumps on and pulls me up with him before wrapping his arms around me. We dance for ages, to many different songs, and soon the start of the night is completely forgotten as I enjoy this time with Shade. Eventually, we climb off the dance floor and make our way to a room at the back. Shade stops me in front of the door and points at the bar.

"I'm gonna get us a drink. Stay here," he all but shouts and I nod once. The crowd soon eats him up and I lose track of Shade at the bar. Turning around, I open the door behind me and step into a quieter room. There isn't much in here, Just a few sofas positioned around the space. I nearly jump when I see Hunter sitting on one. He is drinking something red and thick from a tumbler and I know exactly what that is.

"Hey," I whisper, and he looks over at me, lowering his glass. Hunter runs his tongue over his lip and smiles.

"Hey," he replies. I walk over and sit next to him, slipping off my shoes and curling my legs underneath me. "Are you thirsty? I don't even know if you drink blood yet."

"Yet or ever," I remind him. "Vampire clan classes don't go well for me."

"Me neither," he shrugs. "Something is holding me back, but recently it comes out. Only when I'm protecting you though."

My heart beats hard in my chest. "Thank you for sticking up for me against your sister."

He meets my eyes. "If you haven't realized it by now, I'm fighting for your heart, Boots. I know I have competition and I've never been a fighter, but hell, I am going to be one now."

"Hunter," I whisper and he reaches up, tucking a little strand of my blonde hair behind my ear.

"Don't give me an answer, I'm not expecting one. I just want you to know," he explains to me. "I'm not here for friendship and I don't care who you kiss. I want us to be Endgame."

"Like the movie?" I ask and he laughs.

"You like those kinds of movies?" he asks, and I nod.

"Guardians of the Galaxy is my favourite Marvel movie," I admit. "What's yours?"

"Hmm, that's a hard decision, but I always loved Spiderman," he tells me. "Now what's your favourite food?"

"Peanut butter cups," I say, remembering how nice they were. "One of my foster parents, the only one I liked, Mollie, made me a peanut butter cupcake once for one of my birthdays. We didn't have much money, but it didn't matter to me. That was the best present."

"Noted for your next birthday," he replies with a grin.

"What's yours?"

"Pizza with lots of different meats," he answers.

"I still can't get over how vampires can eat food and the movies lied to us," I sigh, making him laugh.

"We also don't shine," he tells me, but I figured that detail out.

Shade comes tumbling into the room, a few drinks in his hands and followed by Silas. They both camp out on the sofa. Even though Landon isn't here, this is the perfect way to party.

CHAPTER 21

The days turn into weeks, and gradually I begin to settle into a routine. Get up with the breakfast bell, have breakfast with Hazel and the guys, go to class, eat lunch on the quad, go back to class, dinner, free time, bed.

There's no news of Brody Patton; on the contrary, the staff seems reluctant to talk about him, as if saying his name will jinx it somehow. I can't say I blame them--in spite of Shade's reassurances, it makes me nervous to think about what might have happened to him. Even if he *didn't* meet with foul play, the idea of wandering off somewhere and falling off a cliff--or into a ravine, or getting attacked by a bear--doesn't sound much better. An air of unease seems to have settled over the school. The new restrictions placed by the board just serve as a reminder that something isn't right, and I'm surprised by how stir-crazy I feel being restricted to the immediate school grounds. I catch myself stealing nervous glances out the window toward the stretching expanse of the forest, wondering what's out there, and I'm not the only one--the other students seem equally nervous.

Silas, in particular, seems more bothered by all this than the others. I think I understand why, too. Even if the disappearance was an accident, his parents instilled a fear of humans into him from a young age, and being trapped on an island run by them probably isn't doing much to assuage his fears. But I also have to remind myself that their paranoia was what got them killed, not some conspiracy by the humans themselves, and besides, even if the Academy board is run by humans, the school is staffed by shifters. They wouldn't let anything happen to us if they could prevent it, I'm certain of that much.

The only thing that still bothers me is his comment about Hawthorne having lied about a lack of prior disappearances. Silas seems reluctant to elaborate, and when I ask Hazel, who seems to be in the know about everything important at the school, she has no idea. All I can do now is tell myself that's just him being overly worried and throw myself into my classes.

I think Shade's lesson was a bit of a game-changer for me as far as shifting. Not being able to access my reserves of power was what was holding me back, and now that I've learned to tap into them, the transformations are coming much more easily. I'm no longer just shifting when I'm scared, and when I *do* shift, it's not into a hodge-podge of magical creatures anymore... unless that's what I want.

Granted, I'm still nowhere near mastering it yet: even when I do manage to successfully get into a new form, the smallest distraction is enough to make me change back, and the specific abilities of each being are as elusive to me as ever. The witch spells are especially difficult, especially since I can only manage to change for a few minutes at a time, at most. That's hardly enough time to learn how to cast spells, and I'm having similar difficulties with using the siren abilities. The one form that I still can't get, no matter how hard I try, is the dragon. The best I'm ever able to do is breathe fire, which almost caused an accident during one of my classes. The form itself still escapes me, but I try to tell myself to be patient, that it will come to me eventually.

Having the others around has been a big help, too, and not just because they can give me pointers on shifting correctly; I feel a sense of camaraderie with these guys, and I think they probably feel the same. We're a group that never would have existed if we hadn't been in detention together, and for that I'm grateful, especially since Hazel's social life doesn't revolve around me, and there are times when she's too busy to hang out. The guys, though... They always seem to be there. I've never had a group of friends like this before, and I find myself basking in it. *This* is what it's like to be a normal student.

I'm just getting out of my last class before lunch, ready to stuff my face in the cafeteria, when I almost bump right into Silas. He's standing outside my classroom door, worry etched onto his face, his hands in his pockets and his shoulders hunched. "Hey," he says as soon as he sees me.

"Hey, Silas," I say, grinning. "Did you get out early or something?"

He shakes his head. "I was actually..." He glances at the floor, fidgeting for a moment, before saying, "I was actually wondering if I could talk to you. Alone."

I blink. "Okay," I say, chuckling at the mysteriousness of it all. "All right. Where?"

"There's a corridor in the West Wing," he replies. "No one ever goes there. Follow me--this won't take long, I promise."

Curious, I allow him to lead me down the hall and away from the other students, who all seem too distracted by the idea of lunch to care what we're up to. I can't help but admire him as we walk. His grizzled, masculine features, his perpetually tousled hair, the way he carries himself... but then I catch myself, start to blush, and tell myself to snap out of it. Eventually we come to a stop in an empty hallway. There's a couple darkened faculty offices at the far end, but otherwise, it might as well be abandoned. I turn to Silas. "So what's up?"

"I've been thinking," he replies. "About... Well, everything. The lockdown, most of all. Remember how I said Hawthorne was lying when he said no one had disappeared from the Academy before?"

"Yeah," I reply. "You didn't seem too keen on talking about it then, though."

He nods. "That's because I..." Suddenly he looks hesitant. "Listen, Boots... I don't want you to think I'm crazy or something, okay? I know after I told you that stuff about my parents, you probably think--"

"Hey," I say, looking earnestly up into his dark eyes. "It's okay. I would never think that, Silas. You must know that by now."

Silas swallows, the hint of a smile appearing on his face. "Thanks, Boots. I mean it. You're..." For a moment I wonder what he's about to say, but then he finishes with, "a good friend. Anyway," he continues, lowering his voice and leaning closer to me, "I did some digging into the Academy's history. This was back before I met you. It wasn't because I was really that interested in it--it was for a project for Human Shifter Relations. You're not in that one, are you?" I shake my head, and he continues. "Apparently, around twenty years ago, there were five students who went missing, all around the same period of time."

"Really?" I frown. "Well, that's..." What do I want to say? Absurd? Conspiratorial? But something in the dragon shifter's eyes gives me pause, enough to make me instead ask, "Why hasn't anyone talked about it, then? Do more people know about this?"

"Why do you think?" he asks. "Because they don't want anyone knowing about it. Hell, *I* didn't even know about it until I went to the library that weekend. I had to parse through about three books on the school's history before I dug it up. Just a footnote in the section about the dangers of keeping this many shifters all in one place."

"So what happened to them--the students who disappeared?" I ask. "Did they say?"

Silas shakes his head. "No. It wasn't even written whether they *found* them or not."

I swallow, afraid to ask the question even as I can feel it coming up. "So why are you telling me this, Silas?"

"Call me a lunatic," Silas replies slowly, "but I'm wondering if maybe those disappearances are somehow... I don't know, connected to the disappearance of this Brody guy."

I blink, staring up at him. "You really think so? Couldn't it just be a coincidence?"

"Sure, I guess so," Silas replies, "but I don't know, Boots. I just have a weird feeling. About this whole thing. I mean, why the curfew? Why all these new rules? Have you seen the way the teachers are looking at us lately? It's like they're watching us."

"Silas," I begin, "I'm sure they're just trying to keep an eye on us--"

"Maybe," he says, "or maybe they're not as clueless about what happened to Brody as they claim to be. Think about it, Boots--if he really just wandered off and got lost, why all these new security measures? There's something they're not telling us, I can feel it."

My mind is in pieces. Part of me wants to tell him to relax, that they're protecting us, but another can't help but wonder why the school would have kept quiet about earlier disappearances like this. If anything, one would think they would *want* to bring something like that up, if only just to reassure the students that this isn't nearly that severe. Briefly I think back to Silas' story, his claims that his parents were growing suspicious of the humans. Is it possible that they weren't just paranoid rabble-rousers? "So what are you thinking?" I ask.

Silas glances over his shoulder for a moment, lowering his voice. "I want more information," he replies. "This thing has me too wound up to focus on anything else. My grades have dropped, I'm having trouble sleeping... I can't stop wondering about my parents, about what it was they claimed to be protecting me from. And maybe it *is* nothing. But if it is, then I want to at least be able to put my mind at ease."

"Okay," I say, nodding. "What are you going to do?"

"I'm going to sneak into the registrar's office," Silas replies. "That's where they keep the files on all the students who have been students here, as well as all of their confidential information."

My eyes widen. "Silas, are you serious? What if you get caught?"

"I won't," Silas replies. "At least, I don't think so. I volunteered to help Mrs. Fairbanks out after class tonight. If I get the opportunity to get a look at the student records, I'm going to take it."

I swallow hard, staring at him. "Okay," I breathe finally. "But be careful, okay?"

"I will," Silas replies. "And Boots..." His voice trails off, and my heart flutters in my chest as I become aware of how close he is to me. His shining eyes meet mine, and he takes a step closer, the distance between us narrowing...

Until we're interrupted by a familiar voice. "What do we have here?"

I whirl around, heart hammering, to see President Hawthorne standing at the end of the hall. How long has he been there? Has he heard us talking?

He smiles, striding down the hall to where we are. "Ms. Brix," he says, nodding to me before turning to Silas. "Mr. Aconite. What are you two doing in the West Wing? Shouldn't you be at lunch with the others?"

Silas and I stare at each other for a minute, and then I blurt out the only thing I can think of: "I'm sorry, President Hawthorne. I, ah... I asked Silas to give me a few pointers on dragon shifting. It's the form I've been having the most trouble with." For an extra pinch of sympathy, I add, "It's embarrassing seeing all the other kids able to do it when all I can do is breathe fire."

"I see," says Hawthorne, crossing his arms. "You do realize that unsupervised shifting is against the rules?"

"Yes," Silas says, stepping forward. For a moment, his eyes flash as he stares at Hawthorne. "We weren't actually shifting, though. I just wanted to give her some theoretical tips, you know?"

I nod eagerly, realizing how hollow the excuse sounds but unable to think of anything else that will get us out of this jam. God only knows what the Academy staff would do if they overheard a student conspiring to break into the registrar's office...

Mr. Hawthorne looks between the two of us for a moment, his eyes eventually settling on me. "Ms. Brix," he says slowly, "I'd like to have a word with you in my office."

"But--"

"Now, if you please." Hawthorne glances at Silas for another moment, expression darkening, but all he says is, "Mr. Aconite, I suggest you go to the cafeteria. Lunch will be over soon and we can't have anyone going hungry." He beckons to me and I reluctantly begin to follow.

Over my shoulder, I catch a glimpse of Silas staring after us. Our eyes meet for a moment before he turns and retreats away down the hall.

CHAPTER 22

The sound of our footsteps echoing down the hall is deafening. I cast a nervous glance toward Hawthorne, whose expression is stoic. He doesn't say anything as he leads me back towards the main faculty wing, where a large wooden door with frosted glass paneling leads into an enormous office. If he was going for intimidation when he decorated the place, he succeeded. Against the far wall is a tall oak desk that could easily be a hundred years old. The window shows a view of the area beyond the immediate campus where the dark, quiet forest lurks on the horizon.

"Please have a seat," Hawthorne says, indicating the chair facing the desk. He takes a seat on the other side and folds his hands on the table, a placid smile on his face.

Slowly I do as I'm told, my heart in my throat and my body suddenly feeling stiff. How much did he hear of my conversation with Silas? I've already had detention once, and I haven't even been here a full term; could this kind of thing be grounds for expulsion? *Then* what will I do?

As a whirlwind of dreadful possibilities swirls through my mind, I manage to clear my throat and ask in a small voice, "So, what did you want to talk to me about, President Hawthorne?"

He laughs. "Relax. You look like you're going to faint. You're not in trouble." I feel the knot in my stomach relax, if only a little. "To be honest, Millie--can I call you that?" Swallowing, I nod, and he continues. "To be honest, Millie, I've wanted to sit down with you for a while, just to get a sense of how you're settling in."

"Oh." I blink, the tension leaving my shoulders. He really didn't overhear us... did he? I want to believe he didn't, but there's a gleam in his eyes that gives me pause.

"Yes," Hawthorne says. "I think it's fair to say that you're a special case, wouldn't you?"

Clearing my throat again, I nod. "I guess so, yeah."

"I mentioned when we first met that hybrid shifters are exceedingly rare--so much so that nowadays, people tend to believe they don't exist... or fear them." His dark eyes meet mine, and I shrink under his gaze. "I heard about the fight you had with Ms. Ash."

Damn. Busted. Shifting a little in my seat, I reply, "I, ah... I'm really sorry about that, President Hawthorne. I hadn't figured out how to control my powers yet. I still don't--not really. I didn't want to hurt her, I just... I panicked, and..." I'm babbling, feeling more on edge by the second in spite of Hawthorne's reassurances. "I'm sorry," I say again.

"It's all right, Millie," Hawthorne says gently. "You're not the first shifter who's lost control of their powers. That's why this school exists, isn't it?"

Is it? "I guess so."

"So how are you doing, really?" he asks, leaning forward and giving me a scrutinizing stare. I feel like his eyes are going to bore a hole in my head. "I mean truly--how are you liking it here? Do your classes feel like they're going well? Has the transition become easier?"

"Yes," I reply. "I mean, I still wouldn't say it's *easy,* but... I do feel comfortable here. More comfortable than I've felt at other schools, actually."

Hawthorne nods approvingly. "Glad to hear it." He leans back and crosses his arms. "And you're making friends?"

I nod. "A few, actually. They've... they've made it easier. I mean, they've helped me learn to transform, they've stood up for me..."

They make me feel less alone, I want to say, but I don't think Hawthorne would understand. "They're a good group," I finish instead.

"And Mr. Aconite?" Hawthorne asks, his eyes narrowing slightly, almost imperceptibly. "He seems to have taken quite a liking to you."

My eyes widen, and I feel a blush creeping into my cheeks. "Really?"

Hawthorne chuckles. "Come on, Millie. I was your age once, too. A long time ago. I've spent enough time around boys to know how they think. I actually wanted to talk to you about that," he adds, his expression going stony again.

"What do you mean?"

"Mr. Aconite is..." He steeples his fingers, pursing his lips. "You could say that Mr. Aconite is... troubled. I'm not sure how much he told you about his childhood, but--"

"A bit," I reply. "He said his parents were paranoid. About humans, I mean."

"Paranoid is putting it lightly," Hawthorne replies. "They were conspiracy theorists who thought humans were out to... I don't know, enslave shifters, or something. Hogwash, obviously." He gestures around the room, grinning. "I mean, does this look like enslavement to you?"

I give an uneasy laugh. "No, I guess not." For the first time in a while, I'm reminded of the fact that President Hawthorne is, in fact, human.

"Shifters and the humans who know about their existence have cooperated for hundreds of years," Hawthorne continues. "We support each other, coexisting as we help strengthen each other. *Learn* from each other. Is that enslavement?" He shakes his head, looking thoughtful. "Shifters are more powerful than humans can ever hope to be," he muses. "It's an honor to be able to help your kind assimilate, to study your abilities in a mutually beneficial relationship. Don't you agree?"

"Yeah, sure," I reply.

"It's views like the ones Mr. Aconite's parents held that jeopardize the relationship humans and shifters have cultivated for so long," says President Hawthorne. "Paranoia breeds irrationality, which breeds violence. Mr. Aconite's parents were violent."

My eyes widen. "Really? He didn't mention..."

"No, I doubt he did," says Hawthorne. "He probably isn't even aware. His parents were revolutionaries, radicals who wanted to overturn the system, at the expense of both humans and shifters. They and their co-conspirators were in the midst of planning an attack when we managed to intercept them."

I swallow, unable to respond.

"You see why that kind of ideology is dangerous," Hawthorne continues. "And I fear that..." His eyes flicker away from me.

"What is it?" I ask, leaning forward.

"I fear that Mr. Aconite's parents may have poisoned him with their beliefs," Hawthorne says, sounding almost reluctant to tell me, like it pains him to deliver the message. "He was, thankfully, taken out of that situation as a child, but he spent a great deal of his life learning to be suspicious of humans and our motives."

"Are you saying Silas is going to turn out like his parents?"

Hawthorne shrugs. "It's impossible to predict what will happen to the boy. But I want to warn you now, Millie: spending time with shifters like him is a dangerous game. He could be indoctrinating you, and you wouldn't even know it. I want you to be careful."

I take a breath to steady myself. "Is that why you called me in here?" I asked quietly. "To warn me about Silas?"

Slowly, Hawthorne nods, that thoughtful look still on his face. "I would hate to see you get caught up in whatever delusions his parents might have instilled in him. It wouldn't end well. And you... well, you're special." He shrugs. "Those are just my two cents, of course. You're free to do what you want, but I would warn you to think carefully about who you associate with around here. Do you understand?"

I nod, my heart hammering in my chest. "I think so."

"Good," Hawthorne says, and nods towards the exit. "Then you're free to go."

It's after curfew, and the students are all in bed. There are a few lights on in the individual dorm rooms, but the hallways are empty and dark. I lie on top of my sheets, staring at the ceiling.

Did Hawthorne threaten me today?

That's debatable, I suppose, but the message behind his words was crystal clear: stay away from Silas. But why? He's just another student at the Academy, right?

That business about his parents planning a coup bothers me, though. If Silas' parents were dangerous, Hawthorne would know, right? Unless he was lying. There are too many questions, and my nervousness about the disappearance isn't helping matters. I'm too new to this world, I think, and I don't have enough information to think about any of this objectively. I haven't heard from Silas since our last conversation, and that makes me nervous, too; did he break into the registrar's office? What did he find? Was he discovered?

Maybe he is just paranoid, I think. *Maybe Hawthorne was right, and Brody going missing is just the excuse he needed to lash out against the Academy.*

As if on cue, there's an insistent rapping at the door, enough to make me jump. The knocking pauses for a moment and then resumes with renewed urgency. Sitting bolt upright in bed, I go to the door and hiss, "Who is it?"

"It's me," Silas' voice comes from the other side, making my heart beat a little faster. "Boots, I need to talk to you right now."

I pull open the door, once again surprised by how much he towers over me. He nearly has to duck to enter the room, and I can tell just from his posture that he's on edge--frightened, even. But Hawthorne's warning is still fresh in my mind, and I cross my arms warily. "What's this about?" I ask.

"I did it," he replies, his tone intense. "Mrs. Fairbanks had to step out. I don't know where she went, but it doesn't matter. I got a look at the student files."

My eyes widen. "And? What did you find?"

"Millie, it's..." He shakes his head, looking like he doesn't know how to proceed. "It's bad," he says after a moment.

I clear my throat. "Silas, look," I begin, "I know you wanted to find out the truth, but are you sure this is--"

"It involves you."

My mouth drops open. Those three little words hang heavy in the air, and for a moment I don't know what to do with the information. Me? What the hell does Brody's disappearance have to do with me? "What are you talking about?"

Silas opens his mouth to reply and then closes it again, tunneling a hand through his hair.

"I... Boots, there's no easy way to say this," he says, slowly taking a seat on my bed.

I sit down next to him, eyes wide.

"They had a lot of documents back there," Silas says, turning to me. "And there was a whole file on you."

"A whole..." I shake my head. "But everyone has a file, don't they?"

"Sure," Silas replies, "but yours was enormous. I'm talking hundreds of pages."

"But why?" I ask. "Why would they have that much information on me? I just got here!"

Silas takes a long breath. "Because they made you," he replies. I stare at him, not understanding. "I don't mean the Academy itself made you," he continues, "but the humans. The ones who founded the Academy."

"What do you mean, they *made* me?" I ask. "How do you know? What did my file say?" The questions are coming almost faster than I can keep up with them, but the need for the truth has overtaken any caution Hawthorne might have put in me today.

Silas swallows. "Nineteen years ago, the group in charge of policing human-shifter interactions began a project."

"What kind of project?" I ask, my voice shaking.

"They were trying to create a hybrid shifter," Silas replies. "It had been done before, a few times, but it had always been magic-based, and the lore was lost. It had always been frowned upon, seen as unnatural, but that..." He shakes his head. "That didn't stop them. They spent years trying to recreate the ritual using modern science, taking newborn shifters and experimenting on them, trying to combine their abilities."

"But why?" I ask. "Why would they want to do that?"

Silas shrugs. "I don't know. Power? Control? It could be anything. But what I do know is this," he continues, putting his hands on my shoulders, "They finally succeeded. Eighteen years ago, with four shifters, one from each clan, and a human child. That child's name was--"

"Millie Brix," I breathe.

He nods. "You were their first success," he says. "The only one who didn't die from the experiments."

"What about the others?" I ask. "The shifters from the other clans--what happened to them?"

A grim smile appears on Silas' face. "I'll give you a hint: you were in detention with all four of them."

The news is enough to rock me to the core. How was it possible? It's almost too perfect, the kind of thing that happens in movies. Then again, when I think about my connection to these guys--how sudden and seemingly out of nowhere it felt wonderful and strange and almost *predetermined.* I feel a chill go through me. "Are you saying...?"

"Yes. Me, Landon, Hunter, and Shade. We were all taken from our homes, used to give you your powers, and then..." He shakes his head. "I think my parents knew," he says, more to himself than to me. "I think they figured out what the humans had used me for, and they wanted to take me away. That's why..." His voice breaks. "That's why they tried to run away with me."

"Silas," I say quietly, looking into his eyes, "are you sure?"

He nods. "It was all there, in your file. Paperwork, notes, lab tests, medical records... Millie, they did this to you, to us. The Academy."

"I..." I feel like I'm at a loss for words, both numb and overcome with emotion at the same time. All my life I've wondered about my past, all my time at the Academy I've wondered about my powers, and now... It feels like my world--whatever tenuous version of it I've created for myself since arriving at the Academy--has been turned upside-down. They used the guys to create a hybrid shifter. Me. I'm the result of experiments performed by humans. Is that why Hawthorne said I was special? And what about my parents? Did they give me up willingly? Did they know what was going to happen to me? Or what if...

A horrible idea occurs to me. What if my parents, like Silas', found out about what the humans were doing, and were snuffed out? Could that be what happened to them? And what about the others'? It's all too much, and I suddenly feel like I want to cry. "I don't know what to say."

"Me neither," Silas says quietly, looking away from me. "And the worst part is--" But he stops himself, and I see a hint of color in his cheeks.

"What is it?" I ask.

"If this was all planned," he says, voice barely above a whisper, "then how do I know any of it is real?"

"What do you mean?" I find myself reaching out to touch his arm, and a spark passes between us. Silas meets my gaze, his eyes smoldering, and I'm very conscious of how close we are on the bed.

"You," Silas replies. "Us. Any of this. What if it was all just a plan? Is it all just a game to them? What if the Academy wanted us to meet, to become friends? Did they want me to have feelings for you, too?" There's a long pause as the meaning of his words hits me. I think back to what Hawthorne said, my heart fluttering in my chest. Silas' eyes go wide as he realizes what he just said. "I'm sorry," he says. "That was... forget I... I didn't mean to--"

"Do you have feelings for me, Silas?" I ask quietly, my hand still resting on his arm. The thought of breaking the contact seems impossible.

The silence in the room grows almost unbearable, and I'm unable to tear my gaze away from Silas'. A truth I've been dancing around for a while--possibly since the beginning--is looming over me, and I feel like I'm on the brink of something.

"Yes," Silas replies, his voice heady. "Ever since that first day in the dorms. But I couldn't--I mean, I didn't want to... presume. Or ruin what we had. I just feel like you're mine and I would do anything,

anything to keep your heart." Tentatively, almost shyly, he reaches out to touch my face. His hand is warm and steady, and I find myself leaning into his touch. It feels like there's a fire burning in my stomach as I look up at him, this dark, thoughtful dragon shifter who risked everything to find out the truth about my past.

"Silas," I say quietly.

His lip twitches in a small smile, and then he kisses me. My head feels like it's going to explode, his soft lips gentle against mine, the fire in my stomach now a raging inferno. In what little kissing experience I've had, I've never experienced anything like the passion I'm feeling right now, as his other arm wraps around me, pulling my body close to his.

Finally he pulls away, his eyes searching mine. "Boots?" he murmurs.

"Don't stop," I reply, and within moments my lips are on his again.

CHAPTER 23

I wouldn't have thought I would end up sleeping well , but for the first time since the assembly, I find myself sleeping soundly. Having Silas next to me is comforting, and even though we're cramped in the little dorm room bed, the feeling of his arms around me is enough to make it all worth it. We stopped kissing sometime later in the night and fell asleep, which I'm glad of. There's no use denying now that I *do* feel something for Silas, and the more I think about it, the more I realize that it's a connection that's lasted ever since I first met him. What this means for the future, I can't say, but I feel safe in his arms. My mind is still in pieces over what he told me, but in the shelter of my dorm room, I'm able to put thoughts of experiments and conspiracies out of my mind.

The first thing I become aware of when I awake the following morning is the fact that Silas is no longer in bed with me. Groggy, I sit up in bed and see that light is streaming in through the window, and the sun is already high in the sky; it's a Saturday, which means no classes, although activities have been fairly limited ever since the new security measures went into effect. Brow furrowing, I peer out the window to the clock--it's almost eleven AM.

Slowly I get out of bed and get dressed out of my pajamas, wondering if maybe Silas has already woken up and gone to the bathroom. I take my time dressing, then return to sit on my bed for another few minutes while I wait for him to come back. It's quiet in the dormitory, and I can hear the sounds of the other students beginning to move about. Still, nobody comes to my room, and after another spell of waiting, I pull out my phone and send Silas a quick text: *Hey, where'd you go?*

The message arrives but remains unread. Maybe he left his phone in my room...? But upon checking, I see that none of his stuff is here; he must have dressed and left. Sighing, I leave the room, glancing around at the other girls in the hallway as I make my way down to the common area. He might have gone down there to meet me, although why he wouldn't wait for me, I have no idea. Maybe guys are just strange about these things.

The common room is bustling, but there's no sign of the tall dragon shifter anywhere, and I begin to feel the first stirrings of unease. Silas still hasn't opened my message. Not wanting to wait any longer, I approach the first boy who comes down from the dorms and ask, "Excuse me--did you happen to see Silas Aconite up there?"

"Silas?" The boy frowns. "Now that you mention it, no. He didn't come to bed last night. Hey," he adds jokingly, "maybe whatever got that Brody kid got him, too."

I give him a thin smile but don't laugh. *Stop it,* I tell myself. *You're just being paranoid.*

Am I, though?

My worry only grows as I leave the dormitory building and begin to wander around the campus, asking the people I pass if they've seen Silas. Those who even know who he is tell me that they haven't seen him since last night, and his dorm room is shut and locked. I make a sweep of the campus, eventually ending up in the academic building, and begin to prowl the halls, uneasy as I look for Silas. I send him a couple more texts as I go, both of which go unread. The academic building might as well be deserted on a day like this, and it soon becomes clear that I'm not going to find him here.

Feeling a lump forming in my throat, I wander back outside, scanning the quad once more for any sign of Silas. There's none to be found. Horrible scenarios are already drifting through my mind, and all of them revolve around what he told me last night. Is it paranoid to wonder if someone saw him in Mrs. Fairbanks' office? And what about his speculation that his parents were killed because of their suspicions? The campus suddenly doesn't feel as safe as it once did, the tall doors and yawning corridors seeming to glare down at me everywhere I turn.

My feet are taking me in the direction of the faculty offices before I'm really even aware of it. I'm gripping my phone until my knuckles turn white, my eyes flitting in every direction as I go. I want--no, need- -to talk to someone. It's as I'm passing the registrar's office that I notice Mrs. Fairbanks isn't at her desk. Could she have stepped out for something? I pause at the door, peering in, my eyes drawn toward the large file cabinet in the back of the room. Could there be more information there that Silas didn't see? Would it be worth looking to see if there's something on my parents?

But a familiar voice snaps me out of it. "Millie? What are you doing in here?"

I turn around to see Samantha watching me from just outside the door. How long has she been there? "I, ah..." I swallow. "Listen, Samantha, I--" I lean in closer to her, and my eyes must betray my panic, since she looks a little taken aback at my expression. "I think Silas Aconite might be missing," I tell her, the words sounding ridiculous even as I say them.

She frowns. "Why would you think that?"

"He wasn't in the dorms today," I say, talking quickly. "I've already looked everywhere on campus for him, and there's been no sign of him anywhere. Everyone's saying he didn't come to bed last night."

Samantha's eyes dart up and to the left for just a moment before her expression softens and she chuckles. "It's all right, Millie. Silas is fine."

"Really?" I stare at her. "Where is he?"

"He was admitted to the infirmary earlier this morning," Samantha replies. "Stomach problems, I think."

I blink. Part of me wants to believe her, but the other part is hung up on her brief hesitation before she answered me. "Is he okay?"

"Yes, he'll be fine," Samantha says, giving me a thin smile. She doesn't say anything else.

"Can I see him?"

"No," she says, a little harshly. "Sorry, Millie," she adds. "It's against school rules."

"Since when? I thought students were allowed to visit the infirmary."

"They are, most of the time," she replies. "But it's our policy to keep students with unknown conditions isolated from the rest of the school. I'm sure you can understand, given how... on edge everyone has been, lately."

"Unknown condition?" My eyes narrow. "I thought you said he was having stomach problems."

"I... yes," she says. "Yes, stomach problems. But we don't know what caused them,"

There's a pause.

"I want to speak to President Hawthorne."

"I'm afraid that's not possible," says Samantha.

"Why not?" I demand, face flushing. "Is he suddenly not taking visitors?"

"There's no need to get angry," Samantha says, her patience unnerving. "President Hawthorne is a very busy man, and this isn't a matter of concern to him."

"What do you mean, it's not a matter of concern?" I ask desperately. "What aren't you telling me? Where's Silas?" I can feel my heart hammering in my chest as we size each other up for a moment. Part of me wants to push further, but another part already knows it would be a waste of time. *She knows something,* I think. *There's something she's not telling me.* Samantha just keeps watching me with that unnerving look on her face, to the point where my shoulders slump and I let out a defeated sigh. "I guess I'll just wait for him to get better, then."

"You should do that," says Samantha, still with that wan smile on her face. "And Millie," she adds as I turn to go, "you should really relax. It looks like the stress is starting to get to you."

"WHAT DO YOU MEAN, he's missing?" asks Hunter, his arms still crossed in front of his chest. The four of us are standing in the shade of the dormitory building, a ways away from the other students.

"*That's* what you're worried about?" counters Landon. "Not the part where we were all experimented on as kids?"

"Come on," says Shade. "Silas has always been paranoid. It runs in the family. Millie, I'm sure whatever he found wasn't--"

"No, listen to me," I protest. "He said he found proof--documents. Records. And now he's vanished off the face of the earth, and the faculty won't help me. Doesn't that strike you as a little suspicious?"

"Maybe a little," Shade admits.

"Are seriously none of you worried about the fact that, if he wasn't lying, this means the five of us were part of some kind of... conspiracy?" Landon asks, sweeping his arms out. "Does that not bother any of you?"

"Obviously, it does," snaps Hunter. "But if Silas is missing, then we have more urgent things to deal with."

Landon blinks. "Damn. I think that's more words than you've ever said, Hunter."

"Not now, Landon," I say. "Guys, come on. We need to focus here. Samantha was lying to me about where he was. Why the hell would they stop letting students into the infirmary all of a sudden?"

Shade purses his lips. "I guess you have a point."

"Look," I say, my tone pleading now, "I know none of us have known each other for very long. But if what Silas was telling me is true, then think about what it means for the rest of us. If we were all used by the humans when we were babies, and now we're all here at the Academy, what does that mean for us? What if these disappearances have something to do with it?" I cross my arms. "And even if they don't, that doesn't change the fact that, as of this morning, another student is missing. One of us could be next. I don't know about you guys, but I want answers. Answers that the school isn't giving me."

Landon sighs, scuffing his foot against the ground. "So what are we supposed to do, then? Form an angry mob and storm Hawthorne's office?"

"Like that would help," mutters Shade.

"Okay, thanks. Got any ideas of your own?" Landon fires back.

"I might have one," Hunter pipes up, and the rest of us turn to look at him. He sighs, raking a hand through his red hair, and then says, "I can't believe I'm actually saying this, but... I might be able to get us into the faculty offices tonight, if you guys really want to dig deeper into this."

"How?" Shade asks incredulously.

"My dad's a board member," Hunter reminds him, and thanks to a few lessons, I know board members are the leaders of our community and come from old families in the shifter world. Mostly people refer to them as royalty, as they might as well be. That's why people call Amelia the prince and princess of the academy. "I might be able to get a hold of his keys. *Might*." He shakes his head and sighs. "Amelia will kill me if she finds out."

"Better her than the school," I point out. "This is the kind of secret that could make the academy fall."

Hunter just stares at me. "You don't know Amelia."

"So are we really doing this, then?" asks Landon. "Are we going to look for information in the offices?"

"It's our only option right now," I reply, turning to look at each of them in turn. "Listen, you guys... I know this is crazy. And I know it's probably not what you want to be doing right now. But Silas needs help--I can feel it. And there's something the Academy isn't telling us. That said, though..." I swallow. "If this isn't a risk you want to take, then I'll understand."

There's a long pause, and none of them speak. Then, finally, Shade meets my eyes, the ghost of a smirk appearing on his face. "I don't know about the rest of you," he says slowly, "but I like risks." He turns to me, straightening up and crossing his arms. "So when do we go?"

CHAPTER 24

Waiting for the day to end is one of the hardest things I've ever done. Even though I'm with the others for most of the afternoon, I find myself constantly looking around, seeing an enemy in every staff member I see, wondering who the next kid will be to inexplicably vanish. Most of all, though, I'm worried about Silas, and about what breaking into the faculty offices will mean. I don't want to endanger any of these guys, or get them in trouble... whatever that would entail. I'm not sure I want to think about it.

At one point, Hazel comes to join us, but I resist the urge to tell her what's going on. I think she picks up on the fact that something is strange, because she keeps glancing at me with a worried look in her eyes. Still, the last thing I want is anyone else getting involved in this. And besides, Hazel wasn't named in the documents that Silas found. This doesn't affect her, at least not yet, and she shouldn't have to be dragged into it just because she was kind to me on my first day at the Academy.

By the time dinner rolls around and it gets dark outside, I feel like I'm about to go crazy with anticipation. I'm aware that what we're planning could land us all in deep shit, and as much as I don't want to risk my place in this newfound home, I want answers more. And besides... what if this isn't as much of a home as I once thought it was?

We decide to wait until it's dark out, when most of the faculty has already gone to bed. In spite of my concern that there would be monitors in the dormitory, it's empty when I finally creep out of my room and into the hallway, doing my best not to make the old floorboards creak as I move. At one point I hear footsteps on the stairs, and I find myself paralyzed with fear until a bleary-eyed, confused-looking student passes me. My nerves are all frayed, and by the time I make it down to the common area and out to the front, the smallest sound is enough to make me jump.

The others are waiting for me when I step outside. They all look uncomfortable and vaguely nervous, but looking into their eyes shows me nothing but grim determination.

"I still can't believe we're doing this," Hunter mutters as we begin to make our way across the quad to the academic building. "If my dad finds out-"

"He won't," Shade says, waving him off.

"How do you know?" Hunter hisses. "What if someone walks in on us?"

"Then just tell them you wanted a secret place to make out with Boots," Shade says teasingly.

It's hard to tell in the dark, but I could swear I see Hunter go a bit red at the thought. "Whatever."

"Guys, can we focus, please?" asks Landon as we come to a stop outside the administration side of the building. "We're not--"

Shade claps a hand over his mouth.

Landon struggles for a moment before he notices what has the wolf shifter's attention: a light has come on in one of the upper rooms. "Shit," I hiss, and the four of us press ourselves up against the side of the building. We're in the shadows, but the light shines like a beacon in the darkness, and it's all I can do not to panic and make a break for it. My mind is racing: what if they see us? Shade's jokes aside, how on earth are we supposed to explain this away? What will they do to us?

Relax, I tell myself, closing my eyes. *You knew there was a risk when you decided to do this.*

Unthinking, I find myself reaching out and grabbing Landon's hand as we wait in tense silence in the shade of the building. He looks surprised, his eyes meeting mine for a moment, and then he grins, giving my hand a squeeze. His touch is both comforting and electrifying, and for the next several seconds I just try to focus on the feeling of his hand in mine.

What feels like an eternity later, the light upstairs finally goes off, and I let my breath out in a whoosh.

"We have to be careful," whispers Hunter. "I think they heard us."

"Go slow," I whisper back, nodding at the door. "You have the key, right?"

"Of course," Hunter replies, and fumbles in his pocket for a moment before extracting a skeleton key like the ones that unlock the dorm rooms. He stares at it for a few seconds, biting his lip, and then shakes his head, sighing. "Here goes," he says, and slides it into the lock. There's a click, and I watch as the vampire pushes open the heavy wooden door. He does it slowly, deliberately, to avoid squeaking, and I hardly dare to breathe as I creep through, the others following behind me.

As soon as the door shuts behind us, we're in complete darkness. "Does anyone have a--" I begin, but Shade beats me to it, turning on his phone and using the light to illuminate the hallway. It's strange seeing this place in the dark; it feels eerie somehow, not homey the way it did when I first arrived at the school. Things were simpler then, I realize: no conspiracies, no vanishings, no worrying myself sick over the fate of someone I cared about...

But, I realize as I glance behind me at the others, that was because back then, I didn't have anyone I cared about. I had never been this close to anyone before, and I never in a million years would have expected to bond this profoundly, this *naturally,* with a group of people the way I have with my friends at the Academy. Maybe it really is predestination or something. Could we have always been meant to cross paths again?

We follow the hallway to the registrar's office, which is locked up tight. Hunter pulls out another key and lets us in, looking nearly crippled with fear. I can't blame him.

"So what are we looking for?" Shade asks, pushing the door closed behind us.

"My file," I reply. "Yours, too. All of ours. Is it alphabetized?"

"Looks like it," Landon says, squinting at the filing cabinets in the darkness.

Shade seems to be having no trouble reading the labels. "Do you have super vision or something?" I ask incredulously.

"No," he says, turning to me, and I start when I see that his eyes have gone a bright amber color. "Wolf vision."

"Lucky," mutters Landon, craning his neck as he continues to search.

"You should give it a try, Millie," Shade says. "Maybe you could--"

But at that moment the light comes on in the room, nearly blinding me for a second. "What on earth are you kids doing in here?" asks Mrs. Fairbanks, who is standing in the doorway in a nightshirt.

"Fuck," moans Hunter, putting his head in his hand.

"I-" I begin.

"Are you looking through the student files?" Mrs. Fairbanks takes a few steps closer to us, and I notice that her eyes have gone the telltale black of a witch. While once that was comforting, however, now it's terrifying. "What are you doing outside at this hour? Breaking into the registrar's office, and... Hunter Ash, is that you?" She rounds on Hunter, who is shrinking in the corner of the room.

"Mrs. Fairbanks, please--" begins Hunter.

"Break in!" she yells, at a surprisingly high volume considering her diminutive size. "Break in in the registrar's office! I need security, now-"

But before I can react, I see a flash of sea green out of the corner of my eye. Landon has transformed into a Siren, his lean muscles on full display as he shimmers with iridescent scales. He opens his mouth, but instead of a reply, what comes out is a shrill, high-pitched tone that's enough to make me clap my hands over my ears.

"Landon, what the hell--" I begin, but then my eyes go wide as I see that Mrs. Fairbanks' posture has changed. Her shoulders slump, her eyes return to their normal color, and the twisted expression of upset confusion on her face smooths out. Within seconds, she's quieted, and she stares at Landon with a docile look as the frequency dies down to a low thrum. "Leave," Landon tells her, his voice like silk in his siren form. "Go back to bed."

Mrs. Fairbanks blinks. It looks like part of her is trying to fight it, but back in human form, there's nothing she can do. "I... yes," she says quietly. "Yes, bed would be a good idea. Excuse me." And with that, she turns around and waddles out of the registrar's office, switching the light off as she goes.

Landon is already shifting back by the time I turn around. The others are staring at him, stunned.

"What was that?" I ask, eyes wide.

"Siren song," Landon replies. "She's female, and she wasn't prepared, but that's the only reason it worked. I'm not powerful enough to make it last, either. Between that and her yelling, I don't think we'll have long here, guys."

"Then we'd better hurry," says Shade, turning back to the filing cabinets. The rest of us don't need telling twice, and I hurry to resume my search, still reeling from Landon's magic. I guess it's a good thing it wasn't directed at me.

The seconds tick by, the only sound is our frantic scrabbling as we look for our files. As hurriedly as we're searching, it's damned near impossible to find what we need; it seems like the student records are dated all the way back to the mid-twentieth century, at the latest. I can practically hear Mrs. Fairbanks coming back, this time with help, and adrenaline rushes through me as I desperately sort through folder after folder. I'm on the verge of yelling in frustration when Hunter's voice draws our attention. "Guys, look at this." We cross the room to where he is, and I'm surprised to see that he's not looking at the files themselves, but rather the cabinet. He points to it, running a hand through his hair. "Do you see that?"

"As much as I'd love to sit here and admire the furniture with you, Hunter," Landon says, "we've got more important things to--"

"No," insists Hunter, his voice sharp. *"Look."*

I have to squint in the darkness, but a second later I see what he's pointing at: in the place where the cabinet meets the wall, there's what looks like a seam of hinges. The kind that would be put in if there were a...

"A door?" asks Shade, frowning.

"I don't know," Hunter replies. "That's what it looks like though, right?"

We stare at it for a moment longer, and Shade runs his fingers along the seam. "I'll be damned," he murmurs, and then nods to Hunter. "Here, help me. Let's try to open it."

"Guys," I begin, "what if it's not--"

But they aren't listening to me, already putting their weight onto the filing cabinet, Hunter pulling and Shade pushing. For a second nothing happens, but then there's a low groaning noise as the filing cabinet swings outward on its hinges, revealing a gaping doorway. It's impossible to make out where it leads; all that's visible from here is a long, steep set of stairs descending into the floor. "A secret passage," mutters Landon. "We really are in a movie, aren't we?"

The sound of muffled voices and echoing footsteps makes us all jump, and a light comes on in the entryway. "What do you mean, they were in the office?" comes a male voice.

"They were rooting through the filing cabinets, Sir," I hear Mrs. Fairbanks saying, the sound of her voice growing closer by the second.

There's the sound of the office doorknob jiggling, and the male voice asks, "Isn't the office usually locked?"

"Usually," replies Mrs. Fairbanks.

"All right, let me take a look."

None of us say anything, instead making panicked eye contact before our gazes settle on the passageway. We're all thinking the same thing, and the four of us bolt through the doorway and onto the stairs.

Shade remains for a moment longer to pull the door shut moments before the newcomers enter the room. We're left in darkness, breathing hard as we listen to the staff members moving through the office.

"I'm telling you, they were in here," Mrs. Fairbanks says.

"I believe you, I believe you," the man insists. "They can't have gotten too far. Go get the other on call security guard. I'm going to keep looking."

There's the sound of retreating footsteps, and we're left in silence, with only a sliver of light from below the door to illuminate the stairs. "What do we do now?" Hunter asks, sounding vaguely sick.

"There's only one thing we *can* do," Shade replies, turning to glance down the steep flight of stairs leading into the bowels of the building.

He doesn't have to finish the sentence; we all know what he's thinking.

CHAPTER 25

With the limited light from the office, it's nearly impossible to see in the stairwell, and even when Shade turns his phone flashlight on, I have to grip the railing just so I don't slip and fall. The stairs are steep and narrow, descending farther underground than I would have thought possible. Faintly, we can hear the sounds of people moving around in the building above us; it looks like we got down here just in time. "You know what's weird?" murmurs Landon in the echoing silence of the stairwell.

"What?" I ask.

"It sounded like Mrs. Fairbanks didn't know about this passageway," he replies.

"Neither did the other guy, by the sounds of it," adds Shade.

"This place looks ancient," Hunter remarks, craning his head to get a look at the dimly lit concrete that surrounds us on all sides. "Do you think many people know about it?"

"I don't know," I reply. "For all we know, this could be a dead end."

"I'd rather find out while we're here," Landon remarks. "The fact that this was in the registrar's office makes it seem important."

"I guess there's only one way to find out," I say as I continue to lead the group down the stairs. It feels like the walls are pressing in on us on all sides, and the air is stagnant, like no one's been down here in a very long time. A horrible image of the tunnel collapsing on us comes to mind, and I have to grit my teeth against the urge to freak out; that won't do us any good. We've already been found out by the faculty; we have nothing to lose now and everything to gain. Maybe this leads to some sort of top-secret information storage facility, or an Illuminati bunker, or something? Whatever it is, the Academy clearly has dirty laundry that they don't want the students accessing, and if there were ever a place to put it, it would be in a secret hideout under the building, I reason.

After what feels like ages of carefully climbing downward, I notice that it seems to be gradually getting lighter in the passageway. As if reading my mind, Hunter says, "I can see a bit better now."

"Same here," says Shade. "We must be getting towards..."

But he trails off as I come to a sudden stop at the bottom of the stairs. The passageway has flattened out, and we're now facing a large steel door. There's light filtering through underneath it, and an experimental push causes it to glide open, not making the slightest sound as it does. Fluorescent light nearly blinds us, and we make our way into an industrial looking hallway. The floor and walls are concrete and sterile, and as we walk down the hall, I can see doors leading to banks of computer monitors and laboratory equipment. It's a far cry from the old-fashioned decor of the rest of the Academy, and the others gape as we peer around. The sound of clanking machinery echoes down the hall, and I find myself shivering in the cold air. "What is this place?" wonders Hunter.

"You don't know?" asks Shade.

The vampire shifter shakes his head. "My dad never mentioned anything like this. Is it for storage, maybe?"

We all jump at the sound of a yell. It's a male voice, cracking with pain, and it's nearly deafening in the confined space. "What was that?" asks Landon.

"Silas," I breathe, and begin to run in the direction of a lone doorway at the end of the hall. I can't say what drives me in that direction, but my feet carry me, anyway; it's just a sense that I have, impossible to ignore.

"Boots, wait!" yells Landon, but I don't listen to him. I would know that voice anywhere, and the agony in it is enough to send chills down my spine. The others catch up to me just as I'm pulling the door open, and we all stop dead in our tracks as soon as we see what's going on in the room.

It's a large space that reminds me a little of a doctor's examination room, except instead of the usual jars full of cotton swabs and tongue depressors, the counter is covered in medical equipment that I don't recognize. A bank of beeping computer monitors stands against the opposite wall alongside a sinister-looking device that could have come straight out of a science fiction film. In the middle of the room are two examination tables. Strapped into one is a blond boy I don't recognize, although I would wager a guess that this is Brody Patton. His eyes are wide and staring, his face frozen in terror, and one glance is enough to tell me that he's dead.

On the other exam table is Silas. He's writhing in pain, desperately trying to free himself from his restraints. Needles attached to the unknown medical device protrude from his arms, and he looks worn and battered, as if the energy has almost gone out of him completely.

Examining the readouts on the machine is Samantha Goldstein, and she turns around, her eyes flashing black as soon as she sees us. "What the fuck are you doing down here?" she demands.

"What are you doing to Silas?" I ask in response. I'm trembling with fear and adrenaline, my eyes wide as I stare at her.

She ignores the question, taking a step forward and making us balk. "Didn't Hawthorne tell you to stay away from Mr. Aconite?" she asks, her voice low and menacing.

"You've been keeping him prisoner down here!" exclaims Landon. "Why?"

Samantha glances back at Silas, who has gone still, his eyes clamped shut. "He poked his nose where it didn't belong," she replies. "We've needed a shifter for some time now. Especially now that *this one* is no longer with us." She nods coldly at Brody's body. "A shame, too," she mutters. "He was strong. I thought he would last longer than he did."

"What are you doing to them, you insane bitch?" Shade demands, lunging forward, but I grab hold of his wrist.

"That's none of your concern," Samantha replies. "Now, if you would be so kind as to stand where I can see you all, I would appreciate it. This doesn't need to get uglier than it already is."

"Like hell," I snap.

"I'm telling my dad about this," Hunter says, his eyes wide. "Whatever this is, it can't have been sanctioned by the board."

"How terribly naive of you to think so," Samantha says, her black eyes turning on Hunter. "It's unfortunate that you'll have to die, too, Mr. Ash. But your father will understand."

"What are you saying?" asks Hunter, his eyes going wide. "Does my father--"

"Don't listen to her," snaps Shade. "She's trying to manipulate you."

"Manipulate?" asks Samantha. "No. I don't need to *manipulate* you. You're nothing but a bunch of first-year students who can barely transform. And you, Ms. Brix," she adds, turning her dark gaze on me, "I expected better from you. Really, I did. It's a shame that you had to keep pulling on this thread. But," she says, her tone businesslike, "that's the reality of the situation. Close the door behind you, Mr. Ash. You aren't going anywhere."

Hunter turns to the door, but hesitates, and once again I find my body acting before my mind has a chance to catch up. The cool presence of my magic is rearing up inside me, and I barely have time to visualize my wolf form before I'm transforming, lunging at Samantha from across the room. But even as I land where she was just standing, she's disappeared, manifesting on the other side of the room. "Come on, Ms. Brix, you know I can teleport," she says. "Now let's put the toys away. There's no need for this to get violent."

"Too late for that," says Landon as he shifts into his siren form.

Shade follows suit, letting out a snarl as the three of us surround Samantha.

Hunter stays back, his eyes closed in concentration, his hands clenched into fists.

"Really?" Samantha says, laughing. "I've been at this school for twenty years, guys. But," she continues, letting out a disappointed sigh as her skin begins to turn red, "if you really want to get nasty, then so be it." And with that, she lets out a burst of energy that's enough to send me sailing off my feet. I strike the back wall with a groan, pain shooting through my body.

"Millie!" yells Landon, and moves towards me, but then he's being lifted up in the air by some sort of telekinetic spell and launched across the room in the other direction.

Shade, still in his wolf form, charges for Samantha, and actually manages to get close enough to her to swipe at her with his claws, but once again, she blinks out of existence and reappears right next to me, staring down at me with her bright eyes. Her hands begin to glow with energy, and I clamp my eyes shut, bracing myself, but that's when Landon lets out another siren song, the shrill frequency enough to drag her attention away for a split second. She sets her jaw, looking like she's struggling against the siren magic, and begins to advance on him, momentarily distracted.

Not wanting to waste the opportunity, I visualize my vampire form and feel the fangs burst out of my mouth, my stature going humanoid again and my strength and agility shooting up. I dart across the room, slamming into her from behind and knocking her off her feet.

"How's that for nasty?" I yell, shoving her shoulders onto the ground the same way Amelia did to me all those weeks ago.

A pulse of energy explodes out of Samantha's body, and it scorches me enough to make me yell in pain. It's searing hot, like being set on fire, and it's all I can do to stay standing as the pain courses through my body.

Landon yells again, at a louder volume this time, and I can see that he's putting everything he has into the song.

Samantha growls in frustration and turns back to him, but not before Shade charges across the room and clamps his strong wolf jaws onto her arm, tearing clothes and flesh into ribbons with an aggression I've never seen in anyone before.

I glance over my shoulder at Hunter, who is still cowering in the corner, trying desperately to transform but still having no luck.

Samantha begins to chant under her breath, her black eyes starting to glow with magical energy, and Landon's eyes go wide for a split second before his scream is suddenly silenced, as if his voice has been plucked from his body. He puts his hands to his throat, eyes wide, and my heart sinks when I realize she must have hexed him somehow.

"Shit," mutters Shade.

Without the distraction of Landon's powers, Samantha is free to send a bolt of energy flying into Shade, who yells in pain and collapses on the floor, struggling to get back to his feet even as the magic sinks into him. He's losing concentration, and a moment later, he's shifting unwillingly back into human form, gritting his teeth in a desperate attempt to stay a wolf. But it's no use. Within moments he's a guy again, pinned to the ground by magic.

Landon is still struggling to get his voice back, his hands clawing at his throat as he is silenced by an invisible magic, and Hunter remains behind me, as feeble as ever.

Fuck, I think. *It's just the two of us, now.*

As if reading my mind, Samantha sneers, "So much for your little harem, Brix." Then she's teleporting across the room to me, lifting me into the air with her telekinesis. I feel the magical force squeezing around my throat, cutting off my air supply and making me see stars. Within seconds, I'll be unconscious or dead, and with the others incapacitated, it will be easy for her to finish us off... Or worse, subject us to the same treatment that she's using on Silas and Brody.

Darkness threatens to close in on my vision as I gasp for breath, twisting around in midair as my body goes from vampire to human again. *I'm going to die,* I realize with a start. *She's going to kill me. Just like Mark was going to kill me, just like those guys at the warehouse were going to kill me.*

That revelation seems to wake something up in me, even as the last of my consciousness begins to ebb away, my muscles going weak from the lack of oxygen. With one final burst of desperation, I visualize a dragon: all powerful muscles and hard scales, enormous in its size and power. I think back to the times I breathed fire, to the lesson Shade gave me on transforming, and throw myself into the image. *Come on,* I pray as my vision goes dark. *Come on, come on, come on...*

And then, like magic, the hold on my throat is loosening, the invisible hand opening ever so slightly, and I draw in a shaking breath.

My eyes open again and I look down in astonishment to see that I am no longer a human, but a dragon, my golden scales iridescent in the fluorescent lights of the laboratory. Magic is no longer what's holding me in the air; rather, it's my wings, flapping with enough power to create gusts of wind.

Samantha looks taken aback as she stares up at me, moving backwards a step, hesitating a little...

But that second of hesitation is all I need. Embracing the second wind, I fill my lungs with air and scream out, a jet of fire lighting up the room and hitting Samantha squarely in the chest. She shrieks as the flames engulf her, frantically swatting at her clothes as she tries to put the fire out. The distraction is enough to make her form waver, and in the instant she becomes human again, Landon finds his voice once more. "Get down!" he yells at her, his voice tinged with the siren frequency. "Surrender!" There's a moment of futile resistance, but then Samantha is dropping to the ground, her clothes and hair still on fire as she is forced to obey Landon's command.

I flap my wings again, sending another gust of air at her, and it's enough to extinguish the flames, leaving Samantha a trembling, scorched wreck on the floor.

I drop back to the ground, shifting back into human form, too focused on taking stock of the others to process the fact that I finally managed to transform into a dragon. Shade is groaning as he picks himself up off the ground, while Landon is advancing on Samantha, his song down to a low thrumming as he works to sustain the command. Hunter, who has been watching the fight with wide eyes, shuffles slowly forward. "Is it over?" he asks, but I don't respond. I'm bolting across the room to the table where Silas is tied down. The dragon shifter's eyes are closed, and although he's breathing, he doesn't seem to be conscious.

"Silas!" I yell, touching his face. "Wake up!" He doesn't even stir, his complexion still ashy and sickly. Quickly I feel for a pulse; it's there, but faint, like his heart is struggling just to keep beating. "Come on," I say, shaking his shoulders. "Come on, wake up. I'm here--we're here. Silas, please!"

Still nothing. I turn back to the others. Shade's eyes are wide as he approaches. "What's wrong with him?" he asks.

"I don't know," I reply, and I realize that my eyes are brimming with tears. "What do we do?!"

"What are they injecting him with?" Shade asks, pointing to the needles in his arms. I follow his line of sight to the IV tubes, which are hooked up to the monitoring device; not daring to think about it any further, I reach down and yank the needles from Silas' arms one at a time. A little blood trickles out of the puncture wounds, but otherwise, there's no response.

A minute passes, and then two, as we all stare at the dragon shifter with bated breath.

At first I can't tell if I'm imagining it, but it almost looks like his breaths are coming more easily now, and when I put my fingers to his neck once more, I feel his heart beating with a little more strength. Moments later, I feel a warm hand cover mine, and I look up to see Silas's dark eyes opening. He groans, shifting a little as he stares up at me. "Silas," I breathe, leaning in closer to him.

He gives me that tentative, crooked smile, the same one he gave me the other night, and says two words: "Hey, Boots."

CHAPTER 26

"Would you stop leaning on me?" Landon says, sounding exasperated. "God, Shade. I know I'm attractive, but I have a personal bubble."

"Don't stress yourself," Shade fires back, shifting away. "You're not my type, anyway, Thyme."

"Guys, come on," Silas pleads. "You're gonna crush me."

We're in the infirmary, all gathered around Silas' bed. He's being given fluids and anti-inflammatories, and his cot clearly isn't meant for the number of people it's currently supporting. Shade and Landon are sitting on either side, their bickering reaching nearly comical levels, while Hunter lingers next to the bedside table with Hazel by his side. I'm at the head of the bed, arms crossed over my chest as I watch the others' antics, occasionally sharing an incredulous glance with Hazel.

It's been a day and a half since we broke into the faculty building, and I still feel a little bit surreal about the whole thing. As soon as we stumbled out of the basement, supporting a weak Silas as we went, we found ourselves surrounded by faculty and security. Judging by their horrified reactions, most of them had been unaware of what was going on in the basement--or at the very least, were good at pretending so. The questions are enough to make me paranoid when I think about it too hard.

"I'm glad to see you're all right," Hazel said, patting Silas's shoulder for a moment before taking a step away from the bed. "When are they letting you come back to class?"

"They're saying they just want to make sure I'm stable, and that I should be clear to go by the end of the week," Silas replies.

"You're not worried they're going to try to kidnap you again?" Hazel's tone is joking, but there's genuine worry in her eyes.

"Hawthorne's claiming it was an isolated incident," replies Landon, rolling his eyes. "Guess he's got a handy scapegoat in Ms. Goldstein."

"Yeah, what's happening to her?" asks Hazel.

"I don't know," I reply. "I saw them hauling her away after our meeting with Hawthorne. She's being put on administrative leave until the board decides what to do with her."

"Forgive me if I don't find that very reassuring," mutters Shade.

"Yeah," I agree, turning to him.

"But it seems like the danger is over, for now at least," Hunter says. "Although whether more students are going to go missing..."

"I don't know," Landon says, shaking his head. "Something tells me this is far from over."

"It *is* far from over," replies Silas. "Whatever they were doing to me and Brody, Samantha mentioned that more people were in on it."

"Poor Brody," murmured Hazel, shaking her head. "I'm glad they got there when they did, Silas."

"Believe me," Silas replies, glancing at me, "so am I."

"I don't trust Hawthorne," I say. I haven't forgotten the conversation we had in his office, when he warned me to stay away from Silas. It's easy enough for him to feign concern for us, I think, while behind the scenes he's working with whoever gave the order to kidnap the students in the first place. It's not clear to me whether he's behind it, but one thing is for sure: anyone who believes Samantha was acting alone is naive.

"Me neither," Hazel says, biting her lip. "But I guess there's not much we can do, is there? Aside from staying vigilant, I mean."

"And looking out for each other," I agree, nodding.

There's a moment of silence as we look around at each other, me and all these friends I've made since arriving at Shifter Academy. Finally, Hazel straightens and says, "Well, I guess I'd better get back to class. I've got Houston next period."

"Damn," Landon says, laughing. "Good luck."

"Thanks," says Hazel, grinning. "I'll see you guys later." And with that, she turns and walks out of the infirmary.

The five of us are left looking at each other. "You're right about looking out for each other," mutters Shade. I glance at him, surprised. "We owe each other that much," he says. "And I agree--whatever this is, it's far from over."

"And there's still this whole issue of our past," Landon points out. "I don't know about the rest of you, but I want answers. About all of it."

"Then let's find them," Silas says, and we all turn to look at him. He shifts a little in his bed, sitting up with a grunt. "Together, I mean. Look, I..." He clears his throat. "I know we haven't always gotten along perfectly, but at the end of the day, this affects all of us. I want to make sure we're all on the same page, here."

"You're right." Before I really even know what I'm doing, I'm reaching out and grabbing first Silas's hand, and then Landon's. They look at me, confused, but it's almost as if something passes between us then.

Wordlessly, Landon takes Hunter's hand, Hunter takes Shade's, and Shade takes Silas's. We're left standing there in a circle, looking from one to the next as the invisible bond we share--whether it's predestined or not--weighs us down. I've grown close to these people, and I find myself vowing that I'm not going to let anything happen to them. Whatever it takes. The room seems to crackle with energy, and I meet each of the guys' eyes in turn, nodding. "We're in this together."

"So what now?" Hunter asks quietly.

"We survive," I reply. "As far as what comes after..." I take a long breath and square my shoulders. "We have work to do."

CONTINUING READING MILLIE'S STORY IN AZURE DRAGONS BY CLICKING HERE.

DESCRIPTION

Wolf, Siren, Dragon, Witch and Vampire shifters in one academy? Make that two academies and then there is a big problem.

Our magical boarding school is in danger and its students are being hunted. With the humans blaming the supernaturals and the supernaturals blaming the humans, no one knows who is doing this. But everyone knows they are no longer safe.

With a trip to Boston suddenly coming up, my five "friends" becoming more than I ever imagined they would be to me. Supernatural Shifter Academy is no longer a safe place.

For my heart...and my life.

Someone wants us dead and the secrets we have found out buried with us.

But I won't let that happen.

18+ Reverse Harem Romance which means the main character will have more than one love interest. This is book two of a five-book series and will be rapidly released.

CHAPTER 27

My life is insane. In a good way.

A little less than a year ago, my school guidance counselor sat me down for one of our requisite meetings. I think it was meant to help get us thinking about life after graduation and figure out a game plan for our future—one of those misguided things that the administration thinks is more helpful than it really is. I remember her asking me where I saw myself after finishing school, no doubt fishing for some answer about university, picking a career, and soldiering out into everyday society without a care in the world. In the end I made up something about "seeing where things went", because the answer *I'm probably going to end up burning out in a dead-end job, since I have no friends, no family, and no connections"* somehow didn't seem like it was going to placate her.

How could I have known that by this time the following year, I would be standing in the middle of a forest with a shapeshifter, desperately trying to master the art of transforming into a wolf in time for next week's practical?

It's funny how these things work out.

"Boots. Earth to Boots." A familiar voice breaks through the reverie, and I shake myself as I cast the memories aside. Shade Ivis, the handsome, lanky, ash-blond wolf shapeshifter and U.K. Shifter

Academy's resident criminal is standing a few feet away from me, his hands cupped around his mouth in an exaggerated gesture. "Are you still with me?"

"Sorry, sorry." I clear my throat. "I just zoned out for a second, there."

"Really?" he teases. "I never would have guessed." Taking a step forward, he crosses his arms over his chest. "You're not going to impress anyone by zoning out, though, Boots."

Boots. Even though it's only been a few months, the name already has a homey ring to it, like an old coat or a used car. It *suits* me, but more than that, it makes me feel like I'm a part of a bigger group, which isn't something I would have ever expected. I think maybe that's what's struck me the most about all this, in the end: the ease with which I've connected with the people here, in the aftermath of a lifetime on my own.

They say people change after leaving school, but usually they don't mean it *literally*. In my case, though, instead of a new set of goals or a new lease on life, a few months ago I found myself with a new body—five new bodies, to be exact. What started out as a day on the run, a desperate attempt to get away from my alcoholic foster father and his escalating temper, ended in a night of being attacked by squatters in a building I had thought was abandoned. That was when everything had, as the saying goes, gone pear-shaped. Looking back on it now, I can still hardly believe it—it was the kind of thing I thought only happened in stories: the cornered orphan discovers that she has magical powers and uses them to save the day before being whisked off to a new home and new life. On the surface, it was almost too perfect.

They say that shifter magic usually first presents itself during young adulthood. The jury's still out on where the magic comes from, exactly, with theories ranging from a genetic mutation to occult meddling hundreds of years ago. Either way, what do you get when you cross a runaway foster kid with unknown superpowers?

Me, of course. The only difference being that instead of having access to just one shifter form, like pretty much every other shifter in the world, I have access to all five: witch, dragon, wolf, siren, and vampire. It's like something out of a comic book, except usually comic book characters don't have as much trouble using their powers as I do. I've made a decent amount of progress since first coming to the Academy, but I've got a long way to go before I'm on par with the upperclassmen—and even longer before I'm capable of handling myself in a world that I now know is nowhere near as straightforward as I once thought it was.

"You're not giving up, are you?" Shade asks, smirking. "And here I was thinking you *never* gave up, Boots."

"You're damn right, I never give up," I fire back, rolling my shoulders and widening my stance. Closing my eyes, I follow the advice he gave me all those months ago and casting away the outside world. It's not an easy thing to do, especially for someone like me, who would rather overthink everything than let instincts do what they're supposed to. Everyone says that's the key to mastering your shifter form: to learn to *let go*. The only problem is that it's easier said than done, and I've only really ever gotten the hang of it in life or death situations. But that's a story for another time, I think.

I suck in a long breath, focusing on the feeling of the cool autumn air on my skin and the sounds of the leaves rustling in the trees overhead. It's a Sunday, and there are no classes today, which means the students of the Academy have free reign to roam about the campus, study, and practice their forms. It's a simple life, but I'm not complaining, especially now that I've seen what it's like to have the Academy on lockdown. It's been a bit more than a month since that student, Brody Patton, disappeared, and the faculty has only just eased up on the curfews and restrictions. How many of them know the *real* reason behind Brody's disappearance, I can't say.

I feel my breathing start to slow down, that cool, familiar feeling that I've come to know as my magic making itself known in the pit of my stomach. I resist the urge to reach for it, to try to grab onto it; Shade was the one who told me how counterproductive that is. The key is to let go and let it come to you. So I do... or at least, I try to.

The truth is that I'm finding it incredibly hard to focus with

Shade in such close proximity to me. He's close enough that I can feel his breath stirring the chestnut flyaways on my forehead, and can *smell* him—earthy and musky, with a layer of danger that sets my heart pounding whenever I catch it. Not for the first time, I catch myself wondering if he's picked up on my feelings yet. What do I even call it, anyway? A crush? A friendship? An attachment? Somehow, none of those feel quite right, and that's the problem.

That's the problem with *all* the guys.

"Take your time, take your time," Shade says dryly. "It's not like it's almost dinnertime or something."

I open my eyes and give him a playful shove, sending him stumbling back. "You're making it hard to concentrate."

Shade gives me a devilish grin that sends a swarm of butterflies moving through my stomach. "That's the point."

My eyes go wide, and I open my mouth to ask what he means by that, but think better of it at the last second. That's opening a door I'm not sure I want to open.

Aside from Hazel, the siren shifter who I met on my first day at the Academy, most of my friends here have been guys. It's not like that's a problem, or anything—I don't discriminate—but when I arrived here, I wasn't used to being close to people. After a life of bouncing from place to place, never able to settle down and form real connections, I had almost forgotten what it was like to care about someone—let alone multiple someones. The fact that each of the guys is compassionate, handsome, and intelligent? *That's* the issue, and it's complicated even further by the fact that they, in a sense, made me.

I straighten up and redouble my efforts, forcing all thoughts of the guys, my past, and the Academy from my mind as I bring the image of a timber wolf to mind. Focusing on every detail, I back away from the pool of magic, allowing it to branch out and envelop my body. Within moments, I can feel the telltale prickling of fur emerging from my skin, my posture changing and my muscles shifting. It's a bit like meditating, in a sense; the second you think about it too much, you lose the thread, and then you're a human again. So instead I open my eyes as I become a wolf, focusing on something else instead—namely, the tall student who stands watching me with a crooked smile. Not for the first time, I find myself lost in his gray eyes, my wolf's vision allowing me to see flecks of color and tiny details that I can't as a human.

He's so handsome, I think, and nearly kick myself. But I can't help it, especially now; I can feel the heat rolling off him in waves, sending fresh shivers up my spine as we stare each other down like predator and prey... except which one of us is the predator, and which one of us is the prey?

The tension mounts until Shade finally speaks up, that cocky grin still on his face. "Take a picture, Boots," he tells me. "It'll last longer."

"Ass," I mutter, still struggling to form the words around my wolf's snout and thankful he can't see my embarrassment at being called out like that. And then, without thinking about it, I lunge for him, sending him tumbling to the ground as I pounce on him playfully. The forest floor is carpeted with leaves and fallen pine needles, cushioning the fall, and Shade lets out a laugh as I land on top of him, my weight pressing him against the ground.

Weird, I think. *Usually I can't hold the form this long.*

And that does it. In an instant, the control slips away from me, and I pop back into my human form in a split second—which, as you might imagine, leaves us in a rather compromising position. For a moment we just lie there, staring at one another with me on top of him in a tangle of limbs. The seconds tick by, seeming to stretch on into infinity, and it dawns on me how close I am to him; my face is inches above his, close enough to make out the scar on his temple and the blasé look in his eyes. "You don't look so bad from this angle, Boots," he remarks, and I groan, rolling my eyes.

The moment broken, a familiar nervousness seizes me, and I scramble off him, dusting leaves and dirt off my pants as I hold out a hand to help him up. He takes it and gets to his feet, his skin cool against mine, and I realise my heart is pounding wildly. In spite of his arrogance, I think Shade realises it too; he tips me a wink before turning around. Through the trees, we can make out the shape of the

Academy in the distance, a campus of stalwart brick buildings that have been on this remote Scottish island for years.

Even now, though, I can't help but wonder—is it a refuge, or a prison?

The sound of the clock tower bell ringing shakes us out of our thoughts. "Come on," I say, nodding in the direction of the quad. "You said you didn't want to miss dinner."

Shade smirks. "There are more important things than dinner," he observes. "I could maybe be talked out of it, if it means spending more time rolling around on the ground with you."

I raise my eyebrows. "Oh? Is that why you offered to help me get ready, then?"

"I'll leave that for you to figure out, Boots."

Shaking my head in a combination of exasperation and self-consciousness, watching as the wolf shifter turns on his heel and heads off in the direction of the campus without so much as a glance back over his shoulder.

A moment later, I straighten up, square my shoulders, and follow him.

CHAPTER 28

Even though I'm finally starting to learn my way around the main academic building, I find myself occasionally getting confused by the winding halls and endless doorways. The only way I'm normally able to navigate the place is by following the crowd and hoping it leads me where I need to go... unless, of course, we're talking about the dining hall. When food is concerned, I have a sixth sense—although the fact that everyone else is heading in the same direction doesn't hurt either. It's a sea of starched uniforms and buzzing weekend energy, and all the students seem supercharged with the respite of a day off. I fall into step beside Shade as we allow the crowd to sweep us away and catch myself eyeing him out of the corner of my eye as we navigate the hallway that branches off the foyer. His hair is getting long, and a lock of it falls into his eyes as we walk; I'm struck with the urge to reach out and brush it out of his face, but manage to stop myself—that's not a road I'm ready to go down right now. Or ever. Still, I can appreciate him from a distance, even if he *does* need a haircut.

I'm pulled out of my thoughts by a familiar lilt off to my left: "There you two are."

I turn around to see Hazel muscling through the crowd to sidle up next to the two of us, smiling broadly when she sees us. "What are you up to?"

"Just trying to help Boots here practice her wolf form a little more," Shade replies, elbowing me playfully. "She has a practical this week, and believe me, she's *screwed.*"

"*She* is right *here,* you know," I retort, pushing between the two of them and linking my arm through Hazel's. "And *she* is going to ace that damned test if it kills her."

"Well, I guess positive thinking is the first step," Hazel says, smoothing things over as she shoots Shade a look over my shoulder. The two of them haven't exactly gotten on swimmingly in the weeks that I've known them, and I suppose I can understand why: Shade's personality is a bit abrasive—certainly more so than our other companions—and his reputation around the Academy precedes him. It sounds like he's a bit of a problem child, which makes some sense —all of us are castaways, in some way or another, either separated from our families, with no families to speak of, or with families we don't get along with. We needed each other, I think—more than any of us ever really expected to. That said, I don't know much about Shade's story other than the fact that he was adopted. From the sounds of it, he didn't exactly get on swimmingly with his new family, either. He doesn't seem too keen to talk about it, so I don't push the issue.

The three of us make our way into the large dining hall, where the students are fanning out to find seats at the long tables and pounce on the buffet which is stocked with an assortment of delicious foods. I pause in the doorway, looking around until I catch a glimpse of a familiar face near the back of the room: Landon Thyme, the siren shifter, is sitting at one of the far tables, and he seems to have cleared a space for us. Next to him sits Hunter Ash, the surly vampire shifter who might as well be a self-parody, if it weren't for the difficulty he also has changing into his form. We're two of a kind in that sense, which is for the best, considering that we couldn't be farther apart in every other way. His father is one of the Academy board members, and it's obvious from square one that it's a family of stuffy, uptight over-achievers and high expectations.

None of this is helped by the fact that his sister, Amelia, is an overly protective upperclassman hellbent on getting her little brother's shapeshifting abilities up to the same level as her own. She also seems to take issue with me on the grounds that I'm a hybrid, although part of me can't help but wonder if her reasons go deeper than that. My origins, while clearer to me now, are still shrouded in mystery, but Hunter's family has connections with the Academy and, most likely, to the experiment that brought me here in the first place. It was a bastardization, if the most vocal opponents are to be believed, a repetition of the kind of horrific rituals used by witches hundreds of years ago in order to combine shifter powers. A child, taken from the hospital as a baby, was used as a test subject, a blank slate for men in white coats to give her the powers of one of each of the other shifter species. I'll give you one guess as to who that child was.

The twist, of course, was that the other children used to grant me my abilities turned out to be the same guys in my friend group now. The fact that we all ended up in detention together only lends credence to the idea that we're all in this together, pawns in some game that we don't understand just yet. All we know is that all subsequent attempts to recreate that experiment failed, but that hasn't stopped the powers that be—the alliance in charge of making sure humans and shifters could coexist, without ever revealing our existence to the world—from continuing their attempts. It all came to a head soon after I arrived at the Academy, with Brody's disappearance; one of the two recruiters who brought me to the Academy in the first place was overseeing the experiment that killed the poor guy, and if we hadn't stumbled on the plot, others would no doubt have followed suit. She was hauled off by the bureaucrats and never seen again. But I don't believe the conspiracy ends there.

Not for a second.

We make our way across the dining hall and to the table Landon's saved for us; I slide into the spot next to him while Shade and Hazel take seats on opposite sides of the table. "I heard the two of you were getting up to some 'extracurriculars' out in the woods earlier," Landon remarks, his eyes gleaming.

I groan, rolling my eyes. "It was nothing like that." Shade catches my eye then, smirking, and something passes between us, but I push it away. "I've got an exam this week. Aaronson wants to see how long I can hold my wolf form."

"That shouldn't be too hard, should it?" Landon replies. "You held it for a while when we fought Samantha."

"Yeah," I reply, "but that was an emergency situation. I don't know if I can replicate it. I certainly haven't been able to with my other forms."

Hunter frowns. "At least you *can* shift," he remarks. "I'm stuck listening to Amelia give me shit every other day."

"Why the hell do you put up with that, anyway?" Shade asks, turning to the vampire shifter. "You're a big boy—can't you just tell her to lay off."

"Charming," mutters Hunter, before sighing and running a hand through his red hair. "If your dad was on the school board, you'd be talking differently, Ivis."

"If *my* dad was on the school board, maybe I'd have an easier time passing my Integration class," Shade fires back. "I swear, now they're just holding me back for the hell of it."

"I seriously doubt that," comes a familiar voice, and I turn around in my seat to see Silas Aconite, the tall dragon shifter, making his way over to us with a tray of food in his hands. He sits down next to me and leans forward, glancing at the others. "What did I miss?"

"Just Hunter bitching about his sister," Shade replies. "You know —the usual."

"You're in top form today, you know that?" Hunter fires back at him. "You're just *trying* to piss me off, aren't you?"

"It took you long enough to catch on." Shade turns to Silas, raising an eyebrow. "You look like you've been run over by a train."

"Gee, thanks," Silas replies, rolling his eyes. "Rehab hasn't exactly been easy, for your information."

Shade clears his throat, looking down at the table. "Right," he mutters. "Ah, sorry. Forgot." It's the first time I've ever heard the wolf shifter apologise, but we're all treading a little lightly around Silas in the aftermath of our showdown with Samantha.

The tension propelling the current state of affairs hits closest to home for Silas. His parents seemed to be on the verge of acting against the humans overseeing the shifter community when they were taken away from him, never to be seen again. It's possible they knew something about the experiment, and were on the verge of saying too much, but it's never been clear. Silas was the one who discovered the truth about my origins, and my ties to the other guys, and that revelation nearly got him killed. If we hadn't come to rescue him from an underground testing facility beneath the registrar's office, he *would* have been, and that thought is enough to make my blood run cold.

I'm not sure if I can even put my finger on the nature of our relationship, exactly. It's certainly not platonic, but even after kissing each other, we've been dancing around labels as if trying to define it will jinx it somehow. Maybe he's picked up on my attraction towards the others, or maybe he's shying away from anything that might put us in danger the way that his discovery of the truth did. Either way, my heart skips a beat when he settles into the seat next to me, and his presence is enough to make me flush a little. "Boots," he says, nodding to me, "are you okay?"

"Yeah," I reply, a little too quickly. "Just wondering how you were holding up."

"Could be worse," he says, shrugging his broad shoulders. "At least my powers seem to be more or less back to normal. Using them still takes it out of me, but they *are* coming back."

I clear my throat, feeling a little awkward under the scrutiny of the others. "I'm... glad to hear it."

He gives me his signature crooked smile, the one that always sends me reeling, and the feeling of his leg brushing up against mine is nearly enough to make my head spin. I was never a very romantic person before coming to the Academy—chalk it up to years of moving from place to place; I guess—but the kiss I shared with Silas seems to have awoken something in me, something as alluring as it is dangerous.

Fuck. Who would have thought university would end up being this complicated?

"Look," says Landon, nodding, and the rest of us follow his gaze to the raised platform at the front of the room. The setting sun casts a bright glare through the side facing windows, illuminating the poised figure of President Hawthorne as he makes his way onto the platform and clears his throat. Something about his presence is always enough to instill a sense of awe and dread, in spite of the fact that he's only human, and today is no different: a hush falls over the assembled students as they realise he's waiting for them to quiet down.

"Great," mutters Shade, "this ought to be good."

"It's good to see so many smiling faces here tonight," Hawthorne says, clapping his hands together with a smile that doesn't quite reach his eyes. "Before you get started on your meal, I wanted to address something with you while I have you all here today. This will save you from having to go to an assembly before class tomorrow morning, so bear with me."

I exchange a look with Silas, who seems just as concerned as I am. The last time Hawthorne made an announcement to the school like this, it was to tell us that we were going on lockdown until further notice. There's nothing quite so ominous as watching the guy speak, and a chill runs up my spine as his gaze sweeps the dining hall. "I'll keep this as brief as I can," he continues, putting his hands behind his back. "We are witnessing something of great concern for both the student body and the shapeshifting community as a whole, something I fear could have dire consequences for everyone at this school - faculty and students alike."

My heart sinks, my stomach drops, and my mouth goes dry, but not because of the words he's saying.

It's because, in that moment, Hawthorne's eyes have settled directly on me. And no matter what I do, I can't seem to pull my gaze away.

CHAPTER 29

I nearly jump at the feeling of a hand on mine, and my eyes are wide when I look to see Silas watching me with a concerned expression. "Boots," he whispers, "are you okay?"

Wordlessly, I nod, swallowing hard as I return my gaze to Hawthorne. Whatever ominous spell he had me under seems to have broken, but the silence in the room is nearly oppressive, and an uneasy murmuring passes through the crowd of assembled students.

Hawthorne shakes himself and clears his throat. "We take great care to not cause unnecessary panic when a situation like this arises," he continues, "but it's also important to acknowledge the gravity of what is happening outside this island." He takes a breath, moving back a step. "Some of you may have heard of a certain level of... unrest between the shifters of the world and the humans who know about their existence. Obviously, the human-shifter coalition exists in order to help keep this a secret from the general population, but there are subsets of humanity who know the truth about shifters." There's something I don't like under his words, and it feels as though they carry a double meaning.

"These groups have been causing a bit of a stir amongst shifter communities around the world of late," Hawthorne continues. "I can't speak to any talk of a so-called 'uprising', other than to assure everyone here that they have nothing to be afraid of. That said, though..." He straightens his dark jacket. "This isn't something to be taken lightly. Skirmishes in shifter communities are increasing, and more and more humans are beginning to buy into conspiracy theories about the existence of magical beings. We've seen it here, too, at this very school - the incident involving a missing student and one of our faculty members has been treated with the utmost severity."

I catch a glimpse of Shade rolling his eyes, and Hunter elbows him. I can't blame him - if the Academy administration thinks for one minute that I'll buy this being an isolated incident, they're sorely mistaken. They had a whole underground testing facility, one that seemed incredibly active and state-of-the art, in spite of Hawthorne's claims that it was long defunct before Samantha began to use it for her own purposes.

Hazel shoots the two shifters both a withering look, and they return their attention to the President, who continues his speech. "For this reason, the human-shifter coalition has organised a conference to address this shifting dynamic, the precautions our communities must take, and steps that will ensure the continued coexistence of our species. Ambassadors from both groups will be there, as well as the presidents of all the world's Shifter Academy branches. As for what this has to do with *you* all," he goes on, "the conference is scheduled to be held next week, in the city of Boston in the United States— the location of the North American Shifter Academy. I have consulted with the board members, and we have decided that this is an excellent opportunity to introduce the student community to the inter-species politics that are a reality for shifters living in the modern world. For this reason, we've decided to bring the students at the academy to Boston to witness this historic event and continue their studies in an urban setting."

It's like a jolt of electricity bursts through the crowd. Everyone starts talking at once, their eyes lit up and their voices excited as the news of the field trip sinks in. I turn to look at the others; Landon has a broad grin on his face, and Hazel looks like she's ready to burst with excitement. "Class trip," says Hunter, giving a slow nod of approval.

"Did you know about this?" Landon asks him.

The vampire shifter shakes his head. "Why would I? My dad never tells me anything."

Hawthorne holds up a hand to quiet the group, although a few snippets of conversation carry on. "We have already arranged travel to Boston this Wednesday," he says when he has the room's attention once more. "This will allow you a week of seeing the conference first-hand, as well as a weekend of supervised excursions in the city. That said, you will be expected to continue with your studies, which is why we have arranged boarding for you all at the American Shifter Academy."

There's another burst of activity from the group at the prospect of an exchange program with the American school. I've never been outside the U.K. before, and in spite of my unease around Hawthorne, even I'm delighted by the idea. It's times like this that I'm reminded that, in spite of the experiments and decades-old conspiracies, this is still a school setting, and an opportunity to have experiences I never would have gotten otherwise. The others seem to feel the same way; even Shade, who never seems impressed by anything, has a fresh gleam in his eyes.

"You will be provided with more information over the coming days," Hawthorne finishes, "but I would advise you to begin preparations for the journey. If you have outstanding assignments or anything to clear with your professors, make sure you finish them before we go, as you will be studying under the American instructors while you're in Boston. Now..." He glances over his shoulder at the line of other faculty fellows, who nod their approval. "I believe I've covered everything. Without further ado, I'll let you all have your meal now. Enjoy your evening, ladies and gentlemen." He gives a slight bow before retreating to the admin table, where the other instructors and board members are starting in on their food.

"This is so exciting," Hazel exclaims as we tuck in ourselves. "Vacation! I mean, I'm from California, so it's maybe bigger for you guys, but still... I've never been to Boston."

"Do they do this often?" I ask, looking around at the others. "Field trips, I mean."

"No," Landon replies, shaking his head. "I mean, last year they brought us to London to see one of the oldest siren communities, but that was just for a day trip. Nothing this big."

"I'll be curious what the American students are like," Hunter admits, picking at his food thoughtfully.

"If they're anything like you and your sister, I'm guessing uptight, boring, and bummed out," Shade tells him. Hunter kicks him under the table.

"Boys, boys!" I say, laughing. "Am I going to have to separate you two?"

"Not a terrible idea," Hunter mutters. "Absence *does* make the heart grow fonder."

"Damn, your sarcasm is improving, Ash," Landon observes. "Looks like we're rubbing off on you."

The vampire shifter gives a dry laugh. "Yeah. Maybe. Don't tell Amelia."

Silas has remained quiet, and I turn to him. "You okay?"

He nods. "Just thinking."

"'Just thinking,' eh?" teases Landon, although his tone is good-natured. "What else is new?"

There's a long pause, and the big dragon shifter sighs. "Actually, I, ah... I think I might head up to bed, you guys. It's been a long day."

"Already?" asks Hazel. "You've hardly eaten anything."

Silas glances down at his plate. "I'm not really hungry anymore. This whole trip thing is putting me off a little." Getting to his feet, he nods at the rest of us. "Might as well get a head start on packing though, yeah? I'll see you guys tomorrow."

"Later," Shade replies, and we watch him disappear into the crowd.

"Wonder what's gotten into him," Landon says, frowning.

"Hawthorne," I reply, leaning an elbow on the table. "And I don't blame him."

Hunter's brow furrows. "What do you mean?"

"I mean..." I shrug. "Don't you think it's a little odd that they'd decide to bring us all out to America so soon after what happened with Samantha?"

"I don't see how that tracks," Hazel replies.

"I'm not sure I do, either," I admit, looking down at my hands. "It's just a little weird, that's all. It feels like all this stuff with humans and shifters has started happening all at once, you know? I mean, had *you* guys heard about any of what Hawthorne was talking about back there - riots, skirmishes, conspiracy theorists?"

"My dad's mentioned it a few times," Hunter admits. "We were talking to him last weekend, actually. He said one of the shifter settlements in Russia was attacked by a pro-human fringe group. It sounds like the government is doing an okay job of keeping a lid on the rumours, but..."

"It can't be an easy job," Hazel remarks. "Think about it - you're basically having to keep the existence of a whole species a secret from the general population. And with the internet and everything..." She shrugs. "I'm honestly just surprised this hasn't happened earlier."

"It's a strange time to be a shifter," Shade comments.

"Yeah," Landon agrees. "Damn right, it is."

THE EXCITEMENT DOESN'T SEEM to die down, even after dinner concludes and the students start making their way up to their rooms. I say goodnight to the others, and I'm on my way to the girls' wing of the dormitory when I catch sight of Silas in the downstairs common area. He's looking out one of the broad bay windows, his arms crossed as he sits slumped in one of the armchairs. "Hey," I say, coming to stand next to him.

He seems a little surprised to see me. "Hey, yourself," he says. "You guys finish dinner already?"

I nod. "The others are headed to bed. I was thinking of going too, but..." I chew the inside of my lip. "I wanted to make sure you were okay."

"I appreciate it." He stands up, and I'm stunned again by just how much he towers over me. "I think this trip thing just caught me off-guard, that's all."

"Yeah," I say, rubbing the back of my neck. "You and me both."

"Do you feel a little like..." He purses his lips. "Like this is a bit sudden?"

"Yes," I exclaim, relieved that someone else had the same reaction. "Yes, I was just saying that to the others!"

He nods in the direction of the stairs leading up to the boys' dorm, and I follow him to the door. There aren't many students left in the common area, but Silas keeps his voice low when he turns to me and says, "I'm worried, Boots. What if this is just some kind of ploy to get us away from the Academy? What if..." He trails off, but I see where the question is going.

"You're worried they're going to use this as a way to continue the experiments."

Silas nods. "Maybe that's just my paranoia talking. I don't know. But if it's not..." He looks down at his hands, which are still shaking a little - the tremors have gotten a lot better since we first broke him out, but he's still not back to a hundred percent.

Instinctively, I reach out and take his big hands in my own, looking up into his dark eyes. "We're not going to let them," I tell him, even though I know there's no way I can really promise something like that. "They're not going to pull that shit again, Silas. I swear. I'm in your corner on this - we all are."

"That makes me feel better than you would believe," he tells me, a small smile creeping onto his face.

"That's what I'm here for," I joke, my voice chipper. "Now if I could just find the bright side to this wolf shifting exam..."

Silas laughs. "You'll do fine, Boots."

"I'm glad at least *one* person thinks so," I say.

He takes a step closer to me, his eyes meeting mine, and my stomach floods with warmth. "That's what I'm here for," he says quietly, echoing my earlier words, and then he leans forward and kisses me. It's gentle and brief, but sweet enough to leave me swaying on my feet when he pulls away and flashes me his crooked grin. "Goodnight, Boots," he says, before turning and heading up the stairs towards the boys' dorms.

I'm left to watch him, my insides like jelly. But a small part of me feels conflicted. *How can a kiss feel guilty and perfect at the same time?* A scoffing sound is the only thing that's able to pull my attention away, and I turn to see Amelia Ash watching me from the opposite corner of the room, her arms crossed over her chest and an unimpressed look on her face. Our eyes meet for a moment and she raises an eyebrow, but before I can say anything, she's turning on her heel and disappearing into the downstairs bathroom.

I sigh—she's got eyes like a hawk, and I'll no doubt have to deal with more of her snark sooner or later. There's no winning, it seems. Running a hand through my hair, I make my way in the direction of the girls' rooms. It's getting late, and by the sounds of it, we have a big week ahead of us.

A very big week.

CHAPTER 30

"What's the weather like in Boston, anyway?" asks Landon, scratching his arm as he looks around my room from his seat on my bed. He's kicking his feet, leaning back as he watches me pack; my meagre possessions are all strewn about, littering the floor around my still-empty duffel bag. Who would have thought packing would be this difficult when we wear uniforms, for god's sake? But I'm having trouble figuring out what's important. I left home in such a hurry last time that I wasn't really even thinking about what I brought, but this is a different situation. We're talking about an international conference here, and I've never felt so woefully unprepared.

It's been a couple days since Hawthorne's announcement, and the student body has been abuzz with excitement about the trip. Even the professors seem to be in a better mood than usual, and if I didn't know any better, I'd say they've started to ease up on the workload just a little. My wolf shifting practical was yesterday—it went okay, but the knowledge of the upcoming conference has been looming in the back of my mind, bringing with it equal parts excitement and nervousness. In spite of my reassurances, I haven't been able to shake the feeling that Silas was right—that this all feels a little too sudden, in the aftermath of the disappearances. I guess time will tell if I end up having to repeat the class or not. Shade's not going to let me hear the end of it, either way.

"I've heard it's nice this time of year," I reply, although what they mean when they say "nice," I have no idea. "I just don't know if I should even bother with normal clothes. We're still going to be wearing our uniforms, right?"

Landon shrugs. "I don't know. Maybe they'll give us new ones." He grins, lifting his head and meeting my eyes. "That's why I came in here to watch you. I figure I'll just copy whatever you pack."

"Gee, thanks," I say, giving him an exaggerated eye roll. "I'll make sure to stick with the girliest stuff I can find, then."

"Hey, who says I can't pull off girly?" Landon retorts. "I bet I could rock one of those skirts."

"It's an interesting image, that's for sure." I sigh, shaking my head, and then throw my hands up. "You know what? Screw it. I'm just going to pack one of everything and hope for the best."

Landon laughs. "You're starting to sound like me."

"Thanks for the company," I tell him as I begin to fold my clothes and stuff them into my bag. "It's kind of a weird time right now."

"My pleasure," Landon replies, giving me a mock bow. "It wouldn't be right to leave the lovely Millie Brix to do the packing all on her own."

I raise an eyebrow. "'Lovely,' is it?"

"Sure," he responds gamely, without missing a beat. "Lovely, ravishing, gorgeous, noble... Give me a thesaurus, and I can come up with even more."

I snort. "I can guarantee that's not necessary."

"Maybe," Landon replies thoughtfully. "But you can humour me, can't you?"

I meet his eyes again from where I'm kneeling on the floor, and my heart skips a beat. I'm struck with the same pang of guilt and confusion that I felt in the forest with Hunter the other day. An image of Silas pops into my mind, but Landon's presence in this moment is damn near overwhelming, and I find my reply sticking in my throat. As if reading my mind, Landon clears his throat and begins to examine his fingernails, saying, "I don't want to step on any toes, though. You and Silas seem... close. If I'm making you uncomfortable, just tell me."

"You're not," I assure him, getting to my feet and rubbing the back of my neck. The scattered clothes suddenly don't seem as important as they did a few minutes ago. I feel the words threatening to spill out even before I can stop them. "I mean... close? Yeah, I'd say we are. But I don't know *how*, exactly, you know?" I frown. "He hides it well, but I think he's still struggling to get over what happened with Samantha."

"Yeah." Landon sighs. "I can't even imagine what that must have been like. He's strong to even have survived as long as he did. I'm glad you've been there for him."

I blink, surprised. "Really?"

"Well... yeah." He shrugs. "Is there some reason I shouldn't be?"

I bite my lip. "I don't know. I guess I just thought..." Shit. My words are getting away from me. I didn't think we would end up here. "You were saying all that stuff just now... I kind of figured you were..."

Landon raises his eyebrows. "Jealous?" A grin spreads across his face, and he hops down from my bed. "Come on, Boots. Give me *some* credit. I'm pretty good at picking up on these things. I'm a siren, you know? We have a nose for romance."

"I..." I clear my throat. "I guess that's true." Meeting his eyes, I bite my lip. "So that doesn't bother you, then? Me and Silas?"

He shrugs. "Should it? I mean, it would be a little weird if you guys *weren't* close, considering everything that's happened. And as for the flirting..." The corner of his mouth twitches, setting off another rush of adrenaline in the pit of my stomach. "Like I said, I don't want to make things weird for you. If it bothers you, tell me."

"It doesn't," I reply honestly. "I... like it."

"Good," he says, taking a step closer to me, and the tension mounts even further. It dawns on me that we're alone together in my room, with nothing to stop *something* from happening, if we wanted it to... But that familiar confusion is threatening to rear its ugly head. God, why is it so hard for me to talk about my feelings all of a sudden? "You know, I meant what I said," he adds in a husky voice, reaching out and brushing a strand of hair out of my face. "None of those adjectives really does you justice."

"Sweet talker," I say, unable to pull my gaze away from his eyes, like chips of onyx gleaming against his dark skin.

He leans forward, and my heart threatens to beat out of my chest. Thoughts of Silas seem to flit away in the face of this gorgeous siren, and it's all I can do not to *swoon* at the waves of sensuality that I feel coming off of Landon. He moves closer still, his hand lingering on my cheek, and I feel my eyelids flutter - this feels so dangerous, so complicated... Am I really about to go there with another one of my friends? His face is inches from mine, and I can make out the dusting of freckles on his nose. Landon pulls me close, closer still...

And then he flicks my nose. "Gotcha."

I shove him playfully. "God, you're starting to sound just like Shade."

"Hey, hey, easy," he laughs, rubbing his chest. "I can't help it that I'm sexy. I'm a siren."

I groan. "You use that line much, Landon?"

"All the time." He grins. "Is it working?"

"You know," I tell him, crossing my arms, "I think it just might be."

Damn. I'm in so much trouble.

LUNCH BREAK IS OVER, and Landon and I have gone our separate ways for the next classes of the day. I'm still reeling from what happened—what *almost* happened—but I can't help but chuckle when I think about it; this is what I like about these guys. Even in the most awkward of situations, they're able to make me feel comfortable, and that's a feeling that's more foreign to me than I can describe.

I guess now's not the time to try to sort out my feelings for them all, anyway. We've got bigger things to worry about, and from the sounds of it, this conference isn't going to be the kind of thing I can just push to the background, anyway. Better to keep my eyes peeled for more shenanigans from the school administration—not that I'm sure I'll even be able to do anything to stop them if they pull something, but that's beside the point.

I'm so lost in my own thoughts that I don't even realise Amelia Ash is waiting for me at the end of the hall until I bump into her, taking a few stumbling steps back as I'm brought reeling back to the present. My heart sinks as soon as I see her; I've done a decent job of avoiding her ever since Silas' kidnapping, but I should have figured I would run into her sooner or later. I suppose I at least owe her for indirectly leading me to the group of guys; if we hadn't gotten into a fight with her in the schoolyard that day a couple months ago, we wouldn't have bonded during our time in detention. But that's all beside the point, and it doesn't make my current situation any less uncomfortable.

Running into her is like running into a brick wall, and she doesn't seem fazed in the least by the collision, standing with her arms crossed over her chest and a put off expression on her face. "Where are you headed now, hybrid?" she asks. Her voice is cool and steady, but there's a note of barely disguised contempt in it that sets my teeth on edge.

"Class," I reply, struggling to keep my unease from creeping through in my tone. "Last I checked, I don't have an off period right now."

"Sure, sure," she says. "What form is it this time? Actually, never mind - I just remembered I don't care."

"Great," I mutter, moving to the left in an attempt to sidestep her. "In that case, I think I'm going to go. Excuse me."

She moves along with me, blocking my path, her blue eyes flashing. "We need to talk, Brix."

I sigh. "I'm kind of busy, Amelia. I need to get to class."

"Class can wait." She stares me down, her pale skin lending her an inhuman quality in the low afternoon light that streams in through the hallway windows.

Clenching my hands into fists at my sides, I say, "Fine. What is it?"

"You've been avoiding me," she says, "and with the field trip coming up, it's high time we talked about my brother." Ah. Of course.

What else would it freaking be? It wasn't enough for her to retake the elementary vampire shifting class with Hunter and I; now she needs to harass me in the hallways. "You've been spending an awful lot of time with him lately," she observes, putting a hand on her waist and tilting her head to one side.

"I guess that's true," I admit. "Hunter's a big boy, Amelia. If he wants to hang out with me, that's his call."

She sniffs. "Maybe. But what's *not* his call is getting dragged into conflicts with the school faculty."

My stomach drops. I guess I should have figured she would hear about what happened sooner or later. I have been banking on later, though. I clear my throat. "I needed his help," I tell her. "There were students going missing. He was the only one who could get us into the-"

"By breaking and entering," she snaps. "Do you have any idea what could have happened to him? Did you even *care*?"

"Look," I say, putting my hands up, "I didn't want to put him in danger. And I don't plan on doing it again."

"You'd better not," Amelia warns me, her voice taking on a new edge. "Especially now that we're all going to Boston. You heard Hawthorne—things are dangerous out there right now. I don't want my brother getting caught up in any more of your bullshit."

"Language, Ms. Ash," comes a new voice from behind us, sending a fresh pang of dread through my chest. I turn around to see Hawthorne approaching us from the other end of the hallway, his footsteps eerily quiet. "I heard my name mentioned," he adds, coming to a stop next to us and crossing his arms. "Is everything all right?"

Amelia clears her throat and looks away, while I remain frozen to the spot.

Out of the frying pan and into the fire.

CHAPTER 31

S omething about President Hawthorne has put me off since long before he started making veiled threats and sweeping the faculty's experiments under the rug. It has nothing to do with the fact that he's human, and everything to do with the fact that there's nothing behind his eyes. His face is like a mask of kind expressions and soothing words, but his character doesn't match up. Mollie, the one foster mom I actually loved, always told me that you shouldn't look at a person's mouth when they speak if you want to know what they're really thinking- you should look at their eyes. And Hawthorne's eyes display nothing but cold calculation and secret plans. Whether he's picked up on my suspicions is another story, though.

"Shouldn't you ladies be in class right now?" he asks pleasantly. "Just because we're having a school trip doesn't mean you can stop taking your lessons seriously."

"Er, yes," I reply, standing stiffly. "We were just-"

"I was just explaining to Millie here that she can't go stirring up trouble when we're in Boston," Amelia cuts in. "Especially when my brother is involved. You know Hunter has been having some trouble mastering his form—he's not cut out for rule breaking and wild conspiracy theories." Her face has taken on an angelic cast, and I have to admire her ability to change tones on a dime, even if she is a manipulative snake.

"Well, I'd say you're quite right, Ms. Ash," Hawthorne agrees, nodding. "In times like these, we need to focus on supporting each other in our studies, not in stirring up trouble. Wouldn't you agree, Ms. Brix?"

I look down at my shoes. "I guess."

"Good," he says, clapping his hands together. "I'm glad we're all on the same page. Now, Ms. Ash, feel free to head to class. Ms. Brix - a word, if you don't mind."

My stomach drops as I watch Amelia saunter away, looking like the cat that ate the canary. And here I was thinking that school bullies didn't exist in university. Slowly I turn my gaze back to Hawthorne, pasting an accommodating smile on my face. "Yes, President?"

He puts his hands behind his back, looking thoughtfully out the window. "Ms. Ash is a good student," he says. "A little preoccupied, maybe, but bright. Her head is in the right place. I think you could learn a thing or two from her."

"I..." I clear my throat. "I'm not sure I follow, Sir."

"I realise you haven't had the easiest go of it in the months you've been here," Hawthorne replies. "Part of that's on me, I think—it's always difficult to integrate students whose parents weren't shifters, and I understand that it's difficult to find a community here—especially when, like Hunter, you've been having such a hard time mastering your abilities." I grit my teeth at the subtle dig, keeping my expression neutral. "I can understand wanting to know more about your past," he continues, still not meeting my eyes. "It makes sense that you would fall in with someone as paranoid as Mr. Aconite."

"Paranoid?" I shake my head. "I'm sorry, Sir, but I don't think Silas is paranoid. He..." I catch myself, stopping abruptly mid-sentence.

"Yes?" Hawthorne raises an eyebrow. "You can speak freely, Ms. Brix."

There's a long pause. "I know he shouldn't have broken into the registrar's office," I reply, my voice barely above a whisper. "But imprisoning him and torturing him?" I shake my head. "It's not right."

"As we've discussed, what happened with Ms. Goldstein was an isolated incident," Hawthorne replies coolly. "You know she is—was —a witch shifter. They have a history of meddling in magical genetics —they were, after all, the ones to pioneer hybrids. I have no doubt that her intentions were good, and that she wanted to make sure Mr. Aconite was punished for what he did, but she was misguided. These kinds of experiments are forbidden, and there was no excuse for performing them on one of our own students. That's why we've... dealt with Ms. Goldstein."

So that's the story he's sticking with. Part of me does want to believe him, to let him lead me to think this really was just a faculty member gone rogue, but another, saner part is railing against it. Samantha was a patsy, and now that the rest of the students know what happened, she makes a convenient scapegoat. It blew up in their faces, and now they're doing damage control.

It really is the same no matter where you go.

"And Silas?" I ask, afraid to know the answer. "What happens to him?"

"I think Mr. Aconite has learned his lesson about prying into school records - don't you?" Hawthorne gives me a thin smile. "To be perfectly honest, it's you who I'm most concerned about. Don't let what happened with Ms. Goldstein fill your head with strange ideas."

"You don't have to worry about me, Sir." I meet his gaze, staring up at him as defiantly as I dare. "I'm going to be fine - on this trip, and afterward."

"I hope so," says Hawthorne, nodding slowly. "Because getting in over your head with these kinds of things never ends well, and this academy has a limited amount of places. And none for students who cause trouble. Have a good rest of your day, Ms. Brix." And with that, he turns on his heel and disappears down the hallway.

I watch him go and realise after a moment that my hands are balled into fists at my sides.

I may not be a very good shapeshifter, but I recognize a threat when I hear one.

"You don't look so good, Millie," Hazel informs me, swatting at a fly that seems very interested in her blonde curls. "A little queasy, actually."

"It's the travel," I lie, not making eye contact. "I've only teleported the one time—when Samantha and Josie first brought me here."

"For whatever it's worth, it gets easier every time," she says. "I almost puked the first time."

"Call me crazy, but I don't think reminding her of that is going to make it any better," mutters Hunter from where he's standing off to the left.

"I'm just trying to help," retorts Hazel.

"It's fine," I tell them. "I'm fine." Teleportation has never been an issue for me—at least, it *wasn't*, the only time I've ever experienced it. The truth is that I'm still uneasy after my run-in with Hawthorne. It didn't help that he made me late for my next class, either, but that's beside the point; I don't like the idea of his eyes on me, or any of my friends. And something tells me that we've only just hit the tip of the iceberg when it comes to what the administration will do to keep things under wraps. But I'm not about to dump that all on my friends right now - especially when they all seem thrilled to be leaving for Boston.

The students are all assembled in the quad, a thick throng of people all jostling each other and talking in excited voices. The rest of the week seemed to crawl by at a snail's pace, to the point where I was almost going stir-crazy. After finalizing the logistics and finishing our packing, the day has finally arrived, and in spite of my nerves, I couldn't be happier to be getting a change of scenery.

I was actually wondering how we were going to travel to America; there are hundreds of students at the Academy, and it seemed like a tall order to transport us all, but the faculty seems to have it all figured out. I suppose this beats an eight-hour flight followed by another hour going through customs, at any rate. I've heard they're pretty uptight about that sort of thing.

Either way, here we all are: huddled in a cluster around one of the low stone benches in the courtyard while we wait for things to get underway. Faculty fellows are milling about, doing head counts, while the professors and President stand off to the side, talking in low voices as they watch the proceedings.

"I'd rather we do it the old-fashioned way," Shade remarks from where he's sprawled out on the bench.

Silas turns to him, looking surprised. "Seriously?"

The wolf-shifter nods. "Don't tell me you don't miss plane travel. Tiny drinks, standing in line for hours, getting felt up by security agents..."

"I can't tell if you're being serious or not," Landon says.

Shade just grins at him.

I turn to Hunter, who's standing a little ways away from the rest of us. He's the quietest of the group, with a glumness about him that seems almost cliche, considering he's a vampire shifter. He's always struck me as a bit fastidious and neurotic, but then again, if I had Amelia as a sister, I would probably be, too. At the end of the day, he's a good guy, and he came through for us when it mattered. That matters more to me than how talkative he is. "I kind of figured you would be traveling with the rest of the Board members," I say, putting my hands in my pockets as I peer at him. "I saw Amelia over there with your dad."

"Right." He sighs, glancing in their direction; the fiery redheads of his family are engaged in some sort of deep conversation, although I could swear I see Amelia shoot us a contemptuous look. "Believe me, they wanted me to."

I raise my eyebrows. "You said no?" He nods. "Why, though?" I ask. "It would probably be easier for you all. First class treatment, and all that."

Hunter looks at me, and something flickers across his face. "I..." He sighs, rubbing his arm. "Maybe I'd rather travel with you," he says finally, looking like he's struggling to stay composed. Seeming to realise his mistake, his eyes go wide, and he struggles to course-correct. "I mean, you *guys*," he adds hastily. "All of you. You know."

I come close to asking what he means, but the poor guy already looks painfully flustered, so I let it go. "Well, we're glad to have you along," I tell him, clapping him jovially on the shoulder. He stiffens at my touch, like an electric shock has just gone through him, but says nothing else.

At that moment, Josie, one of the faculty fellows, approaches us, rubbing her hands together. Josie was one of the two recruiters who found me after my powers first manifested, along with Samantha. Both witch-shifters, they were the ones who brought me to the Academy in the first place. She's gorgeous, with dark skin, a cascade of glossy curls, and a kind smile, but I feel myself bristle as she approaches, even still. After Samantha showed her true colours, I'm not about to let my guard down again. As far as I'm concerned, everyone working for the Academy is suspect.

"All right, guys," she says in a commanding voice, loudly enough that the talking dies down. "We're going to be transporting you in groups of around ten. The faculty and administrators will be going separately as soon as we get there, you are all to wait on the school grounds until everyone has arrived." She nods to a couple of other women dressed in faculty uniforms, and they begin to shapeshift in unison, their skin going red and their eyes turning black. This makes sense, as powers can only be used in full or partial shifter form.

Josie steps forward, beckoning to us and a cluster of other students. "You all will be with me," she says, extending a hand to me and smiling. "Good to see you again, Millie."

"Likewise," I reply, returning her smile as I take her hand. Hunter comes to stand on my other side, joining his hand with mine, and the six of us form a chain along with the others in the group.

"Well," Josie says, checking one last time to make sure we're all accounted for, "enough of these formalities. Let's get this show on the road, shall we?"

CHAPTER 32

The sensation is familiar, and I'm reminded of the time not so long ago when I was first introduced to teleportation magic. That day on the docks feels like a lifetime ago, and in a sense, it was, but I don't miss the panic I felt when the witches' magic began to work on me. This time it's less frightening, although I chalk that up partly to the fact that Landon's warm hand is in mine, steadying me on my feet as pulses of tingling energy begin to course through my body. It's still a little off-putting to open my eyes and see that my limbs are starting to turn translucent, as if in a slow dissolve in a movie. The energy continues to grow in intensity, and I remind myself to relax so that Josie's job can be made easier. I can't help but steal a glance at the ground beneath my feet to see the grass of the courtyard begin to waver and shift before my eyes. It slowly fades, going from a verdant green to a shade of dull grey as the magic continues to course through me. One look at the others tells me that they're in the same boat, their bodies taking on that same noncorporeal look as we hurtle through time and space, jumping across the planet in a matter of seconds. It's truly astounding.

Suddenly, almost as soon as it begins, the sensation subsides, and a warm breeze whips my hair as I look around. The Academy lawn is a world away; gone are the stone benches and old-fashioned buildings of the boarding school, replaced by one of the most modern campuses I've ever seen in my life. We're standing on the curb at the bottom of a gently sloping hill that leads up to a sleek, squat building. Paneled glass windows stretch practically from floor to ceiling, and thin yellow columns support an asymmetrical geometric roof that tilts upward at an angle. Trees line the sidewalk, and as I look around, I see that this isn't some isolated island like the one where our school is located; in the distance, buildings break up the horizon on all sides. This area seems vaguely suburban, but farther out, I can make out the shapes of skyscrapers, clock towers, and colonial-style municipal buildings. I can only assume that's downtown Boston, and we're somewhere on the outskirts. It's astonishing to me that they would put a shapeshifting academy right in the middle of human society like this, and I wonder if the unrest Hawthorne mentioned has affected the students here in any way.

Josie lets go of my hand and rubs her palm down her face. She looks tired from the exertion, but she handled the teleportation spectacularly, all the same. Her body is still red and glowing with her magic, and she turns around after composing herself for a moment to make sure everyone is here. All around us, I can see other groups beginning to manifest, the witches keeping a careful eye on their charges as more and more students appear in the lot. "I'm heading back for another round," Josie tells me. "Stay put here until we've brought everyone over."

I nod, and watch as she vanishes in an instant. Off to go collect more students. It's only then that I realise I'm still holding Landon's hand, and I our eyes meet briefly; he grins, giving my hand a squeeze before letting go, and I cross my arms as I turn to face the rest of my group. "This is amazing," Hazel says, her eyes wide as she stares around at the campus. "I wasn't expecting something so modern. I mean, don't get me wrong, our Academy is nice and all, but..."

"Don't kid yourself," Shade tells her. "It's stuffy as hell. This is much more my speed."

"Would you mind at least waiting until we've settled in before you start setting things on fire, or whatever it is you do?" Silas asks, rubbing his forehead.

Shade shoots him a look. "No promises, big boy."

My attention has already returned to the buildings in the distance. "It's awfully bold of them to put it right in the middle of a city," I remark. "Aren't they worried humans will stumble across it or something?"

"Why would they be?" Hunter asks, turning to me. "This is a shifter suburb. It's obvious—everywhere around here. I'm guessing it's a gated neighbourhood, too."

"How on earth do you know that?" Landon asks him.

Hunter just shrugs. "Spend enough time with the mucky mucks of the shifter community and you start to get a nose for these things." There's a brief pause, and then he adds, a little gruffly, "Now if I could just get a nose for actual *shapeshifting*, I'll be golden."

At that moment, the group of board members and professors appears on the grass of the hillside, with Hawthorne at the front. He says something to one of the others, and they turn around to assess the assembled students. More and more are manifesting every minute, and before long what seems like the entire student body is crowded on the sidewalk, talking excitedly and waiting for instructions.

"Hawthorne," comes a new voice from the top of the hill. It's honey-sweet and crystal-clear, belonging to an attractive, dark-haired woman dressed in a blue uniform, not unlike our own, that matches her ocean-blue eyes. "I'm glad to see you all made it here okay." Her accent is distinctly American, with an unmistakable East Coast twang. She sweeps us with her gaze, clasping her hands in front of her. "I knew there would be a lot of you, but I wasn't expecting quite *this* many."

"We've brought along all our students," Hawthorne replies. "If that's going to be a problem, though..."

"No, not at all," she replies, shaking her head. "We actually just remodeled, and we've got plenty of open dorms. The students have been buzzing for days about getting to meet some of their counterparts from across the pond."

"As have we," Hawthorne agrees, before turning to the assembled students. "Ladies and gentlemen," he says, "I would like to introduce you all to Rosemary Russo. She's the President of the American branch of the Shifter Academy. I expect you all to treat her with the same respect you would show to me, or any of my colleagues. Is that clear?"

There's a murmur of assent from the crowd of students, but Russo waves him off. "Don't get too hung up on formalities," she tells him. "This is a once-in-a-lifetime opportunity. I'm sure we're all itching to see where this little conference of ours takes us."

"On that, we can agree," Hawthorne says.

"Well," continues Russo, "I don't want to keep anyone waiting. If your students are all here, then we can give them a quick tour of the campus and let them get set up in their rooms. No sense in sticking around in the parking lot, yeah?"

Hawthorne gives her a brisk nod.

"You heard the lady," Josie says, ushering us up the path onto the hill. "Let's go see what this place has to offer."

We head up the slope and into the front lot, looking like a herd of white-clad horses on the fresh green grass. Hawthorne and Russo are at the front of the group, and the rest of us follow them like ducklings, making our way into the front entrance hall. A long, windowed hallway extends in the back, leading to a set of twin staircases. There's a reception desk, along with a bunch of smaller, branching hallways lined with classrooms on either side. The ceilings are high, letting in an absurd amount of light. A few students dressed in gold uniforms are milling about the room, and they look at us like we're a new, exotic species of animal as we flood the entrance hall. A couple of them jostle each other and point, while a few more murmur excitedly to one another.

"This is the main hall," announces Russo, making a sweeping gesture with her arm. We have the reception desk here, and off to the left is the registrar's office. Those stairs in the back lead to the upper floors - there are three, altogether, divided into wings based on shifter form. On the east side is our auditorium, as well as a couple lecture halls for the theory classes, and the nurse's office can be found that way." She points over her shoulder towards the far corner of the room.

We come to a stop in front of the reception desk, where a tall, handsome older guy dressed in the gold student uniform is looking at something over the receptionist's shoulder. His hair is dark brown and on the long side, and he has the inhumanly pale complexion that I've come to see as characteristic of vampire shifters. He straightens up when Russo approaches, giving her a brisk nod. "President Russo," he says, turning his gaze to the rest of us. "I assume these are the U.K. students?"

"That's right, Mr. Morgan," Russo says. "I'm wondering if you wouldn't mind showing them to the dorms? If everything is taken care of, that is..."

"Of course," he replies. "I was just going over the living arrangements with Mrs. Palmer, here."

"Excellent." The President turns back to us, rubbing her hands together. "All right, everyone," she says, "I'll have the faculty accompany me to the guest house where they'll be staying. As for the rest of you..." She puts a hand on the tall guy's shoulder. "This is Lyle Morgan. He's in his third year here, a vampire shifter, and one of our Resident Assistants. He'll be explaining your housing assignments for the time that you're here. If you have any questions about where to find things on campus, he's who you should turn to. But I'll let him handle that, himself."

"Gladly, President," the guy, Lyle, replies, his eyes sweeping over the crowd. For a moment, they settle on me, and the corner of his mouth quirks up, but I don't have time to think about it; the look is gone in an instant as he clears his throat and beckons to the assembled students. "All right," he says, accepting a paper from the receptionist before taking a step backward to look at us. "The dorm building is just on the other side," he says. "If you'll follow me this way..." He leads the throng of students down the main hall and out a separate door on the other side, where a lawn full of modern sculptures and flowering plants gives way to a set of equally gorgeous buildings.

"This is nice," Silas observes, falling into step alongside me.

"Damn right," agrees Landon. "I think I could get used to this."

"Don't get too comfortable," I warn them, laughing a little. "We're not here for long."

"Exactly," Landon replies. "Which is why I plan to make the most of it." He winks at me, and I stifle an eye roll, even though I can feel my heart do a little flip-flop.

The dorm building reminds me a lot of the one back at our campus, except with modern architecture and furniture that reminds me a little bit of a hotel lobby. The biggest difference is that the rooms start on the ground floor and there doesn't seem to be a division between male and female dorms. Lyle turns to us, examining the piece of paper. "Well, let's not drag this out," he says. "This is a new building, and there are only a handful of American students currently rooming here. We have suite-style dorms here, which means a shared common area with four connecting rooms each. We were originally planning to give assignments ourselves, but this was a bit of a rush job. So..." He shrugs his shoulders. "They've decided to leave it up to you guys to pick your rooms. Any issues you have, I would be happy to assist. So... I guess that's all she wrote. Go crazy, or whatever."

He puts his hands behind his back, and the rest of us look around in confusion, waiting for some kind of further instructions. When none come, and it becomes clear that we really are being left to our own devices, the students begin to disperse in a practical frenzy. I glance back at the others with a questioning look on my face. "Well, you heard the man," Shade says, crossing his arms and smirking. "Let's figure out where we're gonna be shacking up for this little adventure."

CHAPTER 33

I can't help but feel a rush of excitement as I follow Hazel and the guys out of the common area and up to the dorm level. While the dorms back home have a bit of an austere feel to them, like a convent or a monastery, the upper floor here looks practically like a hotel room, with modern glass fixtures and numbered doors stretching along either wall. On the front of each suite door is a white board marked with the names of the residents inside, although as Lyle said, it seems like this building is mostly empty. Other students are already peering into rooms with an almost childlike glee, and I can't blame them—we've more or less been given free reign here, and Landon was right: we ought to make the most of it.

"What about this one?" asks Silas, pausing in front of one of the doors on the right.

"Sorry, taken!" comes a voice from inside, followed by a chorus of muffled agreements.

"This is why you've got to be on the ball, Aconite," Shade tells him, continuing down the hall. "First come, first serve."

"All right, all right," Silas says, rolling his eyes. We share a brief look, and I quirk an eyebrow at him, making the big dragon shifter break out in a grin.

"You know, I wasn't expecting them to have coed suites," Hazel remarks thoughtfully, crossing her arms as I push open another door and peer cautiously inside. "These Americans are... progressive."

"What do you mean by that?" I ask, glancing over my shoulder.

She winks at me. "I think you know what I mean, Brix."

"Ladies, ladies," Landon says, pushing between us, "there's no need for such risque talk. You're looking at a group of bona fide gentlemen. Isn't that right, Hunter?"

The vampire shifter rolls his eyes. "Try telling that to Shade."

Shade just grins at the rest of us as he comes to stand beside me in the common area. It's surprisingly roomy, with floor to ceiling windows on one side, along with a balcony that overlooks the vast lawn, with a view of downtown in the distance. There's a small kitchenette, along with a table and chairs and a sofa. "Is this what the high life feels like?" he asks with a mocking wonder in his voice, his gray eyes wide.

"I have to admit, it's impressive," observes Silas, hugging his elbows as he stops on my other side. "Why can't we have rooms like this back home?"

"That would go against their whole vibe," Landon responds. "Self-flagellation is kind of their thing." Landon replies.

"Easy there," Shade warns him. "Keep up that flagellation talk and things might just get interesting."

Landon stares at him for a moment and then bursts out laughing, clapping him on the shoulder. The ease with which we've all learned to banter with one another is astounding, especially considering the tension between us when we first got to know one another. But these guys and I are tethered to one another through more than just a shared detention, and that fact has never been lost on any of them. For all our distances, we share a common thread, one that's stronger than anyone - the Academy included - gives us credit for.

"Well," I say, putting my hands on my hips, "I guess we'd better claim this place before someone else does."

Hazel hangs back by the door. "Looks like you guys have found your place, then."

I turn back to my friend and immediately feel a pang of guilt at having forgotten about her. Guiltily, I look around the room. There are only five bedrooms connecting to the suite. "Listen," I say, clearing my throat, "maybe it would be better if we leave the guys in here. You and I can find another suite with a couple of free rooms." Glancing back over my shoulder, I add dryly, "Maybe it's for the best we let the boys here have some space."

Hazel laughs good-naturedly, holding up a hand. "Oh, please, Millie. Who am I to step on any toes?"

I give her a questioning look, crossing my arms. "You guys should be able to stick together," she elaborates. I open my mouth to protest, but she shakes her head. "It's not just because the chemistry between you guys is off the charts," she says, grinning, "although it *is*."

I duck my head, my face flushing bright red, and steal a glance back at the guys. Silas' expression is unreadable, while Landon and Shade exchange a look. Hunter just stares at the floor, although if I didn't know better, I would think the slightest smidge of a blush is lighting up his deathly pallor. Hazel continues, her expression turning serious again. "Look, there are other things to consider, too. The Academy fucked with all of you guys when you were babies - those are the facts. And if—*if*—something happens while we're all here for this conference..." She shakes her head. "I'm just saying, they've tried to pull this shit once already, with the kidnappings and experiments." Her eyes move to Silas, who shuffles his feet. "You guys need to be able to protect each other, especially in a new place like this. It makes sense."

"Are you sure, Hazel?" I ask, even though what she's saying makes sense. If Silas is right, and Hawthorne has something up his sleeve for this trip... then she's right. We need to be in each other's corners. I made a promise to survive this while protecting the people I care about, and the best way to do that right now is to keep my friends close. As for Hazel... "This goes for you, too," I tell her. "They know you're our friend, too, Hazel. I don't want you getting dragged into this, either."

"I'll be fine," she begins. "I-"

The sound of a clearing throat draws all of our attention back to the door. Standing in the doorway are two of the American students. They're both slim, with black hair and dark eyes, and it's obvious that they're brother and sister—maybe even twins. "I hope we aren't interrupting something," says the guy.

I shake my head quickly. "No, nothing. We were just trying to figure out this room situation." Eyes widening, I hasten to add, "If you guys were already in this room, we can leave, though!"

"No, no, it's not that," the girl assures us, holding up a hand. "We just couldn't help but overhear. This is the problem with the suites here—five rooms is such an odd number." Putting a hand to her chest, she says, "My name is Ruby Murakami. This is my brother, Xander."

"Nice to meet you," the guy, Xander, says. "We're in the suite across the hall. It's just the two of us there right now, so if you want, you can come room with us." He gives Hazel a winning smile that lights up his face. "I know it's not right next door or anything, but if you guys all want to be close..."

In spite of the obvious problem that they must have overheard us swapping conspiracy theories about the Academy, I feel a wave of relief as I turn to Hazel. "I... Wow," she says, blinking, a small smile of her own echoing Xander's. "That would be fantastic, thank you."

"You're welcome," Ruby replies. "We'd be lying if we said we weren't excited about having U.K. students here. You guys will be the first international shifters we've ever met."

"Likewise, actually," says Silas, and he begins to nod to each of us. "My name's Silas Aconite. This here is Hunter Ash—his parents are on the Academy board. Then we have Shade Ivis, Landon Thyme..." His eyes come to rest on me. "And this is Millie Brix."

"And my name is Hazel," Hazel finishes. "Hazel Harris. AKA the person who owes you guys both a big favour."

"Oh, please," Ruby laughs, flapping a hand at her. "It's our pleasure. Although..." She and her brother exchange a look, although the look in their eyes is one of good humour. "What's all this about kidnappings and experiments?"

IF YOU ASKED me a while ago how I would feel about the prospect of sharing a suite with four other, incredibly attractive guys—who also happen to be both my classmates and the source of my powers - I would have balked. Surprisingly, though, our first night in the dorms wasn't nearly as awkward as I was expecting it to be. I think it helps that even though our rooms are connected, there's still a level of privacy in each having our own bedroom. Even more surprisingly, instead of nerves or jitters at being within feet of these guys—all of whom have me feeling more confused than I've ever been in my life —there's something *comforting* about it, a sense of oneness that I can't put my finger on. As cliche as it sounds, being in the same living quarters as the guys feels right, somehow, like it's meant to be, and when I'm not struggling to put labels on my feelings for each of them, I find myself put at ease by their presence. The last time—the *only* time—I've been in such close proximity to a guy was the night that I spent with Silas, which I haven't forgotten... but having them all near is a nice feeling, at the end of the day.

Unlike at our campus, the dining hall at the American Academy is a separate building from the academic one. Although the breakfast spread this morning was no less impressive, although a touch more heavy. The only downside to this all is the fact that the very next day, our classes have already started back up, and that means we'll have to wait until the first day of the conference to really experience the city. Still, you can't win them all, I guess, and it's still an adventure. Funny that I should be so used to the Academy already that just a change of scenery qualifies as an adventure.

Hazel and I have already parted ways with the other guys now that breakfast is over, and we're standing in one of the upstairs hallways now, trying to make sense of a campus map that was provided to us at dinner last night. "God, this place is confusing," she mutters.

"I think you're holding it the wrong way," I tell her, pointing. "*That's* the Siren wing, right? So you should go up a level."

"Really?" She frowns. "I thought that was down a level."

"Is it...?" I furrow my brow. "Shit, I think you're right. So then where the hell do I go? I have vampire shifting next!" I rake a hand through my hair. "I should've stuck with Hunter."

"Come on, you know his sister's going to make life difficult for you," Hazel tells me. "Better to just give her a wide berth, I think."

I sigh. "Maybe you're right. So how are the Murakami twins?"

"Fantastic," she tells me, her eyes bright. "Seriously. It's nice to know I'm close to the rest of you guys, and as for them..." A sly grin appears on her face. "That Xander isn't too hard on the eyes, is he?"

I raise an eyebrow. "I guess not. Are you interested?"

She just winks at me. "That would be giving it away," she teases, and then nudges me playfully. "Well, I guess I'd better go upstairs, then. Don't want to be late to my first class here. Do you think you can make it to yours okay?"

I shrug dismissively. "I'll figure it out."

"Godspeed," she replies, giving me a mock salute before tipping me a wave and disappearing down the hall.

I'm left to try to make sense of the map on my own, and I end up surprising even myself by making it to vampire shifting class a minute before the bell rings. It's a sea of white and golden uniforms, and I can see Amelia and Hunter on the far left side of the classroom, talking in low voices. In the back corner, I see Lyle, whose eyes drift unnervingly over to me as I enter the room. The teacher, an older woman with graying hair, holds out a hand to me as I come to a stop. "Nice to meet you," she says. "I'm Professor Cochran. It's free seating here, so feel free to take any of the open desks, Ms..."

"Brix," I reply, shaking her hand. "Millie Brix."

She raises her eyebrows. "Wow," she says. "I think we lucked out today, everyone."

I balk when the other students' attention settles on me, feeling put on the spot. "Sorry," I say, brow furrowing. "'Lucked out'?"

Professor Cochran nods eagerly. "I've been teaching here for nearly forty years, and I've never once had the privilege of having a hybrid as a student!"

Just like that, all the air seems to go out of the room. There's an awkward rustling amongst the other students, followed by hushed whispers as their eyes practically burn a hole in my forehead.

I grimace.

So much for flying under the radar.

CHAPTER 34

I clear my throat, continuing to balk under the gazes of seemingly everyone in the classroom—specifically Lyle, who is giving me a look I can't put my finger on. "Well," Professor Cochran says, when the silence finally becomes unbearable, "I think this is a bit new for everyone here. Hybrids are exceedingly rare, so I think we should all take this as an opportunity to expand our knowledge. Sorry to put you on the spot like that," she adds, leaning in closer to me.

"Don't worry about it," I tell her, relaxing a little. "I guess I'll go find a seat, then."

She nods. "We'll get started in another couple minutes."

Clutching my bookbag to my chest, I work my way to the back of the room and dropping into a desk. Hunter glances at me over his shoulder, and our eyes meet for a moment; he gives me a questioning look, and I shrug my shoulders. Could be better, could be worse. At least no one is giving me shit for my origins, the way Amelia does—although I don't miss the stink eye she shoots me when Hunter finally turns his attention away.

I'm only just starting to get situated when Lyle comes over, taking a seat in the desk right next to me. He continues to give me that penetrating stare, made all the more unnerving by his corpse-like appearance. Finally, I can't stand it anymore, and I turn to look at him. "Sorry, was I in your seat?" It's a stupid question, but anything to get him to stop giving me that look.

He gives me a thin smile. "So *you're* the hybrid," he says, and my shoulders slump. If this is any indication, the rest of my time here is going to be equally coloured by my unique abilities. I can only hope it's in a positive way, although I know better than to get too optimistic. I return his smile, nodding. "You were in my tour group yesterday," he observes, leaning back in his chair. "I remember you. There was something about you, although I couldn't figure out what... I sort of just had it chalked up to you being - well, gorgeous."

I blink, startled. This just took an interesting turn. "I... thank you," I say, feeling my face heat up a little. "I appreciate it."

"No need to thank me," he says. "It's true. I mean, I have to admit, the whole hybrid thing's a bit odd, but not a deal breaker. Call it a case study in interspecies interaction, right?" His smile turns a bit predatory, and I stiffen in my seat. I don't like the way he's looking at me, like I'm some kind of novelty - a snack he's eagerly getting ready to devour.

"Well," I reply, a little dryly, "I'm so glad I have your approval."

"Hey, hey, I mean no disrespect," he protests, putting his hands up. "I'm just curious, is all. I've heard rumours about hybrids, but I never thought I'd actually meet one."

I open my mouth to ask what sort of rumours he's referring to, but think better of it at the last minute. I'm already on edge from my introduction to the class, and I don't like where this conversation is going. There's something off-putting about this guy, and I feel exposed under his gaze. I clear my throat and return my gaze to the front of the room without responding.

"Silent treatment, eh?" Lyle sighs, shaking his head. "You girls are all the same. Offended by a bit of friendly conversation. You'd think shifters would be better at it than humans, but I guess you'd be wrong." I set my jaw, not responding. I can't tell if he's intentionally trying to provoke me or just being an ass, but I can feel myself getting agitated, the magic in my stomach waking up even as I try to keep a level head. Lyle doesn't seem to take the hint. "What, you're just going to ignore me? Not very nice, considering I'm your RA."

Hunter turns back around in his seat, his blue eyes darting from me to Lyle as the older student speaks. He's gripping the back of his chair so hard that his knuckles are turning white, an uncharacteristically fierce look appearing on his face. He looks like he's about to speak up when Professor Cochran begins to talk, silencing the class and bringing our attention back to the front of the room. Saved by the bell, so to speak.

As per usual, the class consists of theory and practice, similar to how the lessons are structured back at the home campus. Cochran takes her time lecturing us about a couple of significant events in the history of vampire shifters, and then we break into groups to practice shifting. I end up with a couple of other girls who seem to be having an easier time with it than I am, although my struggles are as much due to anxiety as to problems concentrating; I can feel Lyle's eyes on me throughout the class, even though he's on the other side of the room, and every time I look up he just gives me that wolfish, unsettling smile, like he's reveling in my discomfort. It's only by watching Hunter that I'm able to calm myself down, although he seems as distracted by Lyle's words as I am. He's partnered with his sister, whose demeanor softens around him as she patiently tries to coax any sort of transformation out of him, but no dice. In spite of his best efforts, he remains thoroughly human, if pale, and the frustration on his face is evident by the time the exercise ends.

Vampire form is one of the easier ones for me - that and siren seem to have come to me most easily since I started at the Academy. Granted, I've managed to get into all of my forms at least once, although some of them are more a struggle than others - dragon, especially, which I haven't been able to replicate since the one time I transformed while fighting Samantha. It doesn't help that Lyle has me shaken up for the remainder of the class, and it's almost a relief when the bell finally rings and we begin to file out. I hang back until most of the students have dispersed, and then make my way outside and onto the quad, hoping to get some fresh air. Not the best start here, all things considered, but at least there was no overt crisis - even if Lyle is shaping up to be a thorn in my side.

Famous last words.

Almost immediately after I step onto the grassy lawn, I find myself face-to-face with the older shifter once again. He's leaning against one of the statues, his arms crossed over his chest, seemingly waiting for another chance to talk to me. "So, I was thinking," he says, coming to stand in front of me, "maybe you and I should have a drink together. I know *you're* not technically old enough here, but I am, so..." He shrugs, smirking. "It might loosen you up a little bit."

I glare at him. "And why do you think I need to loosen up?"

"You just seem so tense," Lyle replies coolly, raising an eyebrow. "I mean, listen, Millie, now's your chance to open up a bit. You're here, you're unsupervised... and you've got an upperclassman who's *very* interested in getting to know you." That predatory grin appears on his face again. "Trust me when I say that doesn't happen very often."

"Lucky me," I mutter, looking up at him defiantly. The height difference is staggering, and I can't help but feel a little intimidated. "Thanks, Lyle, but I'll pass."

"That's a shame," Lyle says, taking hold of my upper arm, "because people don't usually say no to me."

"I just did," I snap, trying to wrench free. "You'll have to forgive me for not wanting to be a project for someone with a hybrid fetish."

That seems to set him off, and his eyes flash as his grip tightens. "What the hell did you just say to me?" he demands, and a wave of panic shoots through me. We're far enough away from the main building that I doubt there's any faculty around, and it's not lunch yet, so the courtyard is more or less deserted. Fuck. This isn't where I wanted this to go.

Entitled asshole, I think, still struggling against his hand, which is like a vice around my arm. I can feel my shifter magic starting to flare up again, and I struggle to stay calm in the face of what might happen; I've gotten into one brawl already since starting my training. I'm not looking to get into another, so instead I just say, "You heard me."

"You're new around here, so I'll let you off easy," Lyle says, his voice dangerously low, "but you're going to learn very quickly that you don't just get to insult me to my face."

"Let me go." I take a step back, but he moves with me, and my heart rate speeds up.

"You first years are all the same," he sneers. "Someone ought to teach you some respect."

"Get the fuck off her." We both whip our heads around to see Hunter stalking up to us, his hair like fire in the midmorning sun.

Lyle raises his eyebrows. "I remember you. You're that kid who can't even grow fangs yet. Are you sure you want to get involved in this?"

"That's funny, coming from an RA in the beginners' class," Hunter fires back. "They must've held you back longer than *me*."

The anger in Lyle's eyes is sudden and intense, and within moments he's transforming, his vampiric strength increasing his hold on my arm as his eyes turn red and his fangs extend from his mouth. "You tell me," he says, rounding on Hunter. "On second thought, maybe you ought to stick around, too," he adds after a moment. "It sounds like you and your girlfriend could *both* use a lesson on the way things work at *our* school."

He wrenches me toward him painfully, and I cry out. Hunter's eyes flash, and he lunges for the older guy, slamming into him at full force. I've never seen him get this aggressive before, and it stuns me more than the pain in my arm, but Lyle just lets out a barking laugh and shoves him away. His vampire strength is enough to send Hunter flying, landing in a heap a few feet away.

"Hunter!" I yell, my eyes wide with panic. The redhead struggles to sit up, blood on his face, and a rush of anger and fear take me over. The world narrows around me, I feel my magic surge, and I summon the first form that comes to mind: in an instant, green scales are rippling up my arms, my physique becoming svelte and reptilian as I transform into a siren. That seems to throw Lyle for a loop, and his grip loosens for a brief moment, long enough for me to shove him away.

204

I've never done it before, but I've seen Landon and Hazel do it enough times to give it the old college try, as they say, letting out a loud, shrill shriek that's enough to make Hunter clap his hands over his ears. Almost as soon as he hears it, Lyle's demeanor changes, his eyes going wide and fixing on me at the first sound of my siren song.

Damn, I think, with a touch of surprise, *that was cool.* Then I turn back to the older student, my eyes flashing with anger. "Get out of here," I tell him, "and leave us the hell alone."

I'm not under any illusions that my abilities are on par with Landon's and Hazel's, but the scream I managed seems to be enough to get him to follow the basic command, and wordlessly, the vampire shifter turns on his heel, brushing past me and moving with unnatural, lurching steps back towards the main building. I watch him long enough to make sure he goes inside before shifting back to human and hurrying to where Hunter is.

"Are you okay?" I ask him, holding out a hand and helping him to his feet.

He wipes the blood off his upper lip, looking away. "What do you think?" he asks.

"I'm sorry he hurt you," I say, touching his shoulder. "If you need the nurse, we can-"

"What? No." He shakes his head. "I mean, that's not the problem." He turns in the direction Lyle went. "I can't believe he talked to you that way," he says, his voice shaking a little, and I'm taken aback. I don't think I've seen him quite like this before. He looks angry, frustrated, confused... but most of all, embarrassed.

"Thank you for intervening," I tell him. "I don't know what would've happened if you hadn't shown up."

Hunter just snorts, shaking his head. "Right. Intervening. For all the good *that* did." He kicks a loose stone, sending it rolling away in the grass, not meeting my eyes as he jams his hands in his pockets. "I'm useless. I can't transform, not even to help the girl I-" But then he stops short, his mouth closing so hard I can hear his teeth click. Ducking his head, he takes a step away from me. "Fucking *great.*"

I feel a burst of colour in my cheeks, and think back to our conversation before we left for Boston as I watch this brooding, self-loathing vampire-shifter, this guy who's spent his life in his sister's shadow. I've spent so long thinking about my own difficulties that I've practically forgotten I'm not the only one who's struggling. And *my* dad isn't on the school board. A wave of emotion hits me then, and before I can stop them, the words come tumbling out. "Maybe I can teach you. How to transform, I mean."

Hunter meets my eyes then, a glimmer of hope on his face, along with a healthy dose of skepticism. "You... want to teach me?"

I shrug. "I mean, no promises, but... Shade really helped me figure out what was holding me back before. I'm not a master, by any means, but maybe you just need the right perspective, you know? Someone who's not a teacher or your sister."

He looks at me for a long time, seemingly torn. Several emotions flit over his face, and I can see the conflict in his eyes - as well as a hint of what might even be desire. Then he finally clears his throat. "I mean... I can't say I'm expecting much, but... I wouldn't mind." He gives me a rare smile. "What do I have to lose at this point?"

I grin back at him, nudging him playfully with my elbow, and a familiar spark passes between us. "That's more like it," I say. "How's eight tonight, then? Professor Brix, Vampire Shifting 101. Don't be late."

CHAPTER 35

The American campus isn't nearly as big or spread out as ours, which doesn't exactly make it ideal for practicing magic, but I've always been told to make do with what I have, and tonight is no exception. I'm not about to let something as simple as not having enough space prevent me from helping Hunter, if I can.

The rest of the day's classes were quiet and uneventful compared to what happened with Lyle, which is saying something, considering we're at a new school on the other side of the world. The American teachers have a different sensibility about them than ours, along with a tendency to be less formal, but there's no mistaking the power each of them holds. Silas mentioned to me that the East Coast has a higher density of shifters than other areas of the country, which explains why there are so many students here - and why the conference would be called in a place like Boston, right under the noses of hundreds of thousands of people. I guess that's what they mean when they talk about hiding in plain sight.

The curfew isn't until around nine-thirty or ten, which gives us plenty of time to wander - or, in my case, try to coach Hunter into his form. I can't say I have high hopes, which is as much a reflection on my self-confidence as it is on his abilities; I'm not exactly the prime example of a capable shifter, but if there's anything I can do to make it easier for him, then I'm willing to give it a shot. Especially after watching him put himself at risk for me like he did earlier.

I dig in my pocket for my cell phone as I make my way down the sidewalk and up onto the grassy hill that borders on the parking lot. I end up coming to a halt right where we stopped after transporting yesterday, squinting against the darkness to see if Hunter's here yet. I'm halfway to sending him a text when there's the crunching of grass behind me, and I turn around to see the ginger vampire shifter climbing the hill, his hands in his pockets. He's wearing his classic look of slightly on-edge concern, and it's endearing; this is clearly a guy who isn't used to breaking the rules, and he seems as unsure of himself as I am of myself. "Hey," he says, hunching his lanky shoulders and looking around.

"Hey," I say, scratching the back of my neck as an awkward silence mounts. Okay, so maybe I didn't exactly think this all the way through.

"Well," he says at last, "I'm here, professor." He spreads out his arms. "Work your magic."

"Okay, let's not get too ahead of ourselves," I reply with a nervous laugh. "Let's face it - I'm not the best shifter in the school."

He returns my chuckle with a dry one of his own. "I didn't want to say anything, but..."

"But we're going to give this a try," I finish for him, putting my hands determinedly on my waist.

"I swear, Boots, if this works, I'll be shocked."

"I know, I know." I bite the inside of my lip, debating as to how we should proceed. The first time we worked together, Shade had me start by relaxing and getting in tune with my breath. "Okay, so... close your eyes."

Hunter raises an incredulous eyebrow. "Seriously?"

"Seriously."

"No offense, Boots, but I'm not totally sure how I'm supposed to get in fights if I have to close my eyes every time I transform."

"Not *every* time," I protest, crossing my arms. "Just at first! You need to focus on tuning the world out before you transform."

He snorts. "Right. Like *that's* going to happen."

"Okay, enough with the surly broodiness," I tell him, moving to stand in front of him. "Just trust me on this, okay? Close. Your. Eyes."

Hunter sighs, rolling his eyes, and I raise a hand to his face to smooth his eyelids shut, leaving it there for a moment while I wait for his fidgeting to stop. He reminds me a little of myself, the first time I tried learning how to transform, and I'm struck by an odd feeling. It hasn't even been that long since my powers first manifested, and now here I am, trying to pass what little I know on to someone else. Talk about the blind leading the blind... literally. But I push the self-doubt away and drop my hand. Hunter's eyes are closed but still fluttering with anticipation and thought. "Boots-" he begins.

"Not a word," I tell him, rubbing my chin as I think back to that first training lesson with Shade. "Okay, so..." I purse my lips. "Tell me about your magic. What does it feel like?"

Hunter frowns. "I don't know."

"What do you mean, you don't know?"

The vampire shifter shrugs. "I mean... It doesn't really feel like anything. What's it *supposed* to feel like?"

I run a hand through my hair. "Shade told me it's different for everyone. But you know it's your magic because you feel it right in the pit of your stomach, just below your tummy button."

Hunter scoffs. "That's ridiculous."

"It's not ridiculous, it's true!"

He groans. "Okay, okay, let me think for a minute." His brow furrows and his hand drifts to his stomach, almost unthinkingly, and there's a long pause as he struggles to articulate what he's feeling. "It's a bit uncomfortable," he says at last, "like there's something in there that's trying to get out. My sister always told me it was probably a stress thing, like an ulcer."

I stifle a laugh and reply, "Well, maybe that's your problem. You've spent all this time thinking your magic is a *medical* condition."

"If *your* sister was like *my* sister, Brix, you would understand."

"Ha. Fair point. Okay..." I take a hesitant step toward him, and then another. Hunter has always been the most aloof and standoffish guy in our group, and as I watch him, I think I'm starting to figure out why: the feelings of inadequacy that he must feel, seeing the rest of us shapeshift with relative ease while he can't even master the most basic of transformations, can't be easy. Add to that his overbearing family and the fact that everyone in the school knows who he is, and you've got yourself one unhealthy combination. I'm almost hesitant to touch him, as if he's some cornered, frightened animal, and I'm the person who's trying to gain his trust.

Tentatively, I reach out, the distance between us feeling miles long, and let my hands settle on Hunter's shoulders. He straightens up, stiffening almost immediately at the feeling, as if my touch has sent a bolt of lightning through his body. "Easy," I murmur. "Drop your shoulders. Let go of the tension you're holding."

"How am I supposed to do that?" he asks. "How am I supposed to concentrate at *all,* come to think of it? Amelia always says you should-"

"Amelia's not here right now," I tell him in an overly haughty tone of voice. "Now for the next..." I glance at my phone clock. "Hour, I want you to forget everything Amelia's ever told you about shapeshifting."

"I don't think that's-"

"Hunter. I'm the one in charge, here."

"Great. Now she's gotten power-hungry." He throws his hands up in defeat, making me laugh.

"Focus," I tell him, still with my hands on his shoulders. "I'm not moving until I feel you relax."

Slowly, he lets out a long breath through his mouth, softening his posture and straightening his neck. I feel his shoulders drop ever so slightly, although there's still a tension in his stance, and I can't help but wonder whether it has more to do with the stress of the lesson... or our close proximity. "That's it," I say, letting go of him and taking a step back. "Now, I want you to just let your mind relax," I tell him.

"Stop paying attention to your powers for a while. Stop *thinking* altogether, if you can. Let your mind wander."

"Boots," Hunter protests, "this makes no sense."

"I know it sounds counterintuitive," I tell him, "but you have to trust me. This is what really opened the door for me with Shade. Your powers will sneak up on you when you're ready, but first, you have to let them in."

"I... okay," Hunter says at last. "I *do* trust you, Millie."

"Good," I reply lightly, "because I trust you, too. Now listen to Professor Brix."

Hunter chuckles. "All right, all right."

I leave him to focus in silence, and the sounds of the night fill my ears. It's cooler after the sun goes down, and a crisp breeze gusts over us as we stand here on the hill. We're the only students out here, and in the distance, I can see the lights of the academic building slowly going out, one by one. Farther out than that, the Boston skyline twinkles against the dark sky, and it strikes me that shifters are arriving from all over the world right now, all in search of a solution that will keep both us and humans happy. It's a tall order, not least of all because our existence is a secret, and I can't help but wonder if this conference will bring any real solutions... or leave us even worse off than we were before.

But now's not the time to focus on that. Hunter needs my help, and he's been standing there quietly this whole time. I shake myself and turn back to him. "How do you feel?"

There's a long pause. "Relaxed," he replies finally.

I nod. "Good. Now, what I want you to do is visualize your form. Picture everything about it that you can—think of Amelia when she's transformed. Focus on all the details and try not to leave anything out. The rest will come naturally." I *hope.*

Hunter continues to breathe deeply, his eyes closed and his red hair ruffled by the wind. I can't help but appreciate his beauty while we're out here like this; under the moonlight, he looks more like a vampire than he ever has, his skin pearlescent and pale, his body radiating power...

Wait.

My eyes widen as I see it: fangs, razor sharp and deadly, emerging from under his upper lip. I have to clamp my hands over my mouth to keep from exclaiming with delight, and when Hunter opens his eyes, I see that they've gone blood red. "Is this...?" he begins.

I nod. "Don't look now, Hunter, but I think you might have just passed my class."

"Holy shit," he murmurs, staring down wonderingly at his hands before looking back up at me. I've never seen him so excited before; his face is lit up like a kid's on Christmas. "Holy *shit!* Boots, it worked!" And just like that, he pops back to normal, his fangs receding and his eyes going back to blue in an instant. "Damn," he says, and I can't help but laugh.

"You did it," I tell him.

He's practically glowing with pride, his eyes wide with excitement and an exuberance I've never seen on him before. "I thought I was a lost cause," he says quietly, staring at me.

"Nobody's a lost cause," I reply, and before I even realise what's happening, he's leaning forward, taking me by the back of the neck and pressing a quick kiss to my lips. Heat builds up in my body, a blush rising rapidly in my cheeks, and when he pulls away, he leaves me swaying on my feet.

"I... Sorry," he mutters, looking at the ground. "Impulse."

"Turnabout's fair play," I tell him, and kiss him back. This time it's longer, less cautious, and I can't help but let my arms creep around him as the vampire shifter pulls me close, his lips exploring mine with both sweetness and trepidation. It feels strange, but in a good way... It feels right.

Finally, we pull away from each other, each looking sheepish, and I clear my throat. "Well, I think that's probably good for one night, wouldn't you say?"

"That's more progress than I've made since I started school," Hunter says earnestly, and grins at me. It lights up his face, and I'm struck by just how rare and beautiful it is when he smiles. My heart beats faster, and for a moment I forget how to use my legs.

It's not until he begins to head back towards the school that I'm able to pull myself from my trance, feeling both exhilarated and hopelessly confused.

CHAPTER 36

The fact that we only had three days of classes at the American campus before our first weekend in Boston is both a blessing and a curse. It's a blessing because, let's face it, I'm not someone who's used to plunging into anything headfirst. Ironic, I know, considering that I spent most of my life moving from new school to new school, but there it is. It's a curse because that means we won't get any downtime during our first weekend here— something I could desperately use right now. It's not even a question of being rundown from the travel, which I am, but a question of where my head is at; in the aftermath of what's happened with me, Lyle, and the rest of the guys, I could use some time to parse through everything before being plunged headfirst into the shifter-human conference. But that's not going to happen, apparently, and on Saturday morning I find myself being roused bright and early by the bell, an automated sound that stands in sharp contrast to the chiming of the clock tower back home.

Groaning, I fling the sheets off myself and sit up in bed. My room is on the left-hand side of the suite next to Silas' and Shade's, with Landon and Hunter taking the others. As I poke my head out my door, my hair slightly mussed from sleep, I see that Shade and Landon are already dressed and seated at the kitchen table. "She rises," Landon exclaims, grinning when he sees me. "We were wondering if you'd died in your sleep."

"I might as well have," I protest, running a hand through my tangled locks and stretching my arms up over my head. "What time is it? Seven?"

"Seven-thirty," Landon replies. "We're supposed to head straight out to the quad as soon as we're dressed."

"What, no breakfast?" Shade asks, crossing his arms. "This is just getting into torture territory, if you ask me."

"Thankfully, no one *did* ask you, Ivis," comes Silas' voice from over my shoulder. I turn to see him emerging from his room, eyes still clouded with sleep. There's good humour in his tone, though, and he gives me a very subtle wink as he heads into the kitchen alcove. "God, I need some tea."

"You're out of luck," Landon tells him. "We're in the *States*, remember? They don't *believe* in tea."

Silas groans, rubbing his hands over his face. "Seriously? Coffee makes me sick to my stomach."

"Aren't you precious," Shade mutters dryly, leaning back in his chair. Silas just shoots him a dirty look over his shoulder as he fumbles with the coffee machine, leaving me to retreat back into my room and get dressed. The sound of the guys' bickering continues on the other side of the door until it's joined by additional voices that I recognize as belonging to Hazel and the Murakami twins. By the time I emerge, it's damn close to a party in the common area, with the others all hovering around the table.

"I hope you don't mind if we tag along with you," Hazel says when I enter the room. "It's going to be crowded today, and if they let us roam around, we might lose track of one another." She's sitting between the twins, who are in the middle of an animated conversation with Landon. The others quiet at her question, all turning their gazes on me at once as if waiting for me to give my permission.

I blink, realising in an instant that they've come to see me as some sort of *de facto* leader—or at the very least, someone they can trust to make decisions. I'm not sure I like that, not least of all because that implies that this is an us versus them situation, but I guess I can't blame them. For better or worse, I'm in the middle of all of this, and the sooner I can accept that fact, the better.

Clearing my throat, I reply, "Of course. The more the merrier." I turn to the Japanese-American siblings. "You guys are... Ruby, right?" I ask. "And Xander?"

"In the flesh," Xander replies, grinning. "And you're the hybrid."

I rub the back of my neck. "I guess Hazel must have filled you in."

"I'm sorry," Hazel says, holding up her hands, "I didn't mean to-"

"No, no, it's all right," I assure her quickly. "Any friends of yours are friends of mine."

"And *we're* no friends of the Academy administration," Ruby adds, meeting my eyes with her own. "We won't go around blabbing about your history. At least... *I* won't. I can't speak for my brother, but-"

Xander elbows her. "Ruby!"

They both start to laugh, and the rest of us join in after a moment's pause. It's nice to know that all the U.S. students aren't as mean-spirited as Lyle. Maybe things will turn around, yet.

"So what are we waiting for, then?" Hazel asks, getting to her feet. "We've got a peace talk to attend - don't want them leaving without us."

"REMIND me again why we're using human transportation," Landon says, taking hold of one of the railings in the Blue Line train car, a wave of white and gold clad students that couldn't stick out from the Saturday-morning traffic more if we tried. It's impressive to me that we were even all able to get underground and into the metro station without incident, although with a dozen magically equipped faculty fellows herding us around like sheep, maybe I shouldn't be so surprised. We didn't get nearly as many weird looks from the humans as I was expecting us to; considering the campus' proximity to the city, they're probably used to seeing Academy students out and about. If only any of them knew what we *really* were.

"If you were a witch, would you want to bother tapping out your powers just to jump us from the suburbs to downtown?" Hazel asks him. "It's exhausting."

Landon sighs. "Fair point. It's just weird, is all. I'm not used to public transport."

"None of us are," Hunter replies from his seat.

"Think of it as a learning experience," I say. "That's what this is all about, right? Learning to coexist with humans?"

"Fair point." Although he looks visibly uncomfortable amongst the crowd, the vampire-shifter's blue eyes meet mine for an instant, and something approaching a smile appears on his face. We haven't really talked since last night, and the kiss we shared; I don't think either of us is really sure what to say. It's not that I'm worried about him blabbing about it—Hunter's always been reserved, bordering on shy, and I doubt he'll bring it up unless I do. The problem is how he fits into everything else, and what a certain dragon shifter might say if he found out that we kissed. I realise I'm making a lot of assumptions about Silas here, but I've never been in a situation like this before, and overthinking things is sort of my specialty.

Deciding it would be better to focus on something else, I let my eyes drift to Hazel, who's standing next to the twins. Her eyes slide over to Xander for a moment before meeting mine, and she winks at me before sticking out her tongue. I can help but laugh, disguising it as a cough at the last second.

"This is how we usually get downtown," Ruby explains. "If we were witches, I suppose we could transport, but there's always risk to that, you know? The campus is isolated enough, but it's pretty much open season once you get into the city proper.

"Come to think of it," I say, turning to her, "what kind of shifters *are* you guys? I just realised I have no idea."

"I'm a wolf shifter," Xander replies. "Ruby here's a dragon."

"Seriously?" Shade raises his eyebrows. "I didn't know siblings could be different kinds."

"It's rare, but it does happen," Ruby replies. "We used to get a lot of shit for it when we were younger - even our parents took a while to warm up to it. It's a little taboo in the shifter community - sort of like hybridism. We're in the same boat, Millie."

"Boots," I say, feeling a sudden sense of camaraderie with the siblings. "Call me Boots."

Xander's brow furrows. "Boots?"

I nod, instinctively reaching for my foot and fingering the broken pendant I keep in my worn shoe. It was a gift from Mollie, something of a good luck charm. Although I feel a twinge of sadness whenever I think about her—whatever happened to her, anyway?

"All right," he says, laughing. "Boots it is, then."

IT TAKES us less than half an hour to reach our stop, emerging from the metro station in a wave of excited chatter. I do my best to stick close to the others as we walk, but it's difficult when there's so much to take in, and I find myself pausing at practically every street corner to gawk at something or another. The streets are tight and winding, lined with buildings dating back hundreds of years. We pass parks, clock towers, fountains, and flowerbeds, all crammed in next to hole-in-the-wall Italian restaurants and Colonial museums.

I'm so caught up in the sightseeing that I don't even notice Amelia flanking me until we come to a stop at an intersection and she sidles up next to me. "Brix."

I glance at her before looking frantically for the others; they've already crossed the street, and the light has gone red, leaving the rest of us behind. Not looking forward to whatever it is she wants to discuss, I slowly turn to her. "Was there something you wanted to talk about, Amelia?"

"I... Yes." Her voice is uncharacteristically soft, and she crosses her arms over her chest, looking at the ground. "Look," she says, finally making eye contact, "this isn't easy for me to say, so I'm only going to say it once. I wanted to thank you."

I blink. "Thank... me?"

Amelia nods. "Hunter transformed for me out on the quad this morning. He wasn't able to hold it for more than a few seconds, but it's more than he's ever done before." She clears her throat. "He said you were the one who showed him how to do it."

"Er... right." I rub the back of my neck sheepishly. "I just felt like maybe he needed a different approach. I gave him a few pointers last night, and he trusts me, which I think helped." Rushing on, I add, "It wasn't anything dangerous, though. He seemed pretty down about it, so I thought, if I could help..."

"I know." There's a look on her face that it takes me a moment to identify, before suddenly it hits me—gratitude. And a hint of remorse. She shuffles her feet. "You know, I've been trying to show him how to shapeshift ever since we were kids. He could never get it right. I was always the quick learner, and I think maybe some part of him resented me for it... I don't know." She shrugs. "I was starting to wonder if he'd ever get there."

"Maybe you just needed to have a little more faith in him," I suggest gently.

"Maybe." She looks at me thoughtfully. "And maybe he's not the only one." Biting her lip, Amelia looks as if she wants to say something else, but then the light turns green, and we begin to cross the street. "I'll see you around, Millie," she says at last, before moving away and disappearing into the crowd.

"What was that about?" Landon asks as I rejoin the group. "Amelia giving you more problems?"

"Actually... no," I reply. "I think maybe she was trying to apologise. In her own way."

"Well, I'll be damned," Landon says, shaking his head. "An apology from Amelia Fucking Ash. What else does this trip have in store?"

"I don't know for sure," I say, nodding towards the end of the street where the Boston Convention and Exhibit Center towers in front of us, "but I think we're about to find out."

CHAPTER 37

I don't think I've ever seen anything quite like it, not even the time Mollie took me to a concert in London for my thirteenth birthday. It seems like practically the whole city of Boston is crammed into this one multi-block area, and what's even more spectacular is the fact that, if the administration is to be believed, everyone here is connected somehow to the shifter community.

The Boston Convention and Exhibit Center is a modern building a lot like the Academy, with a massive overhanging roof supported by hundreds of crisscrossing beams. All around us, people are moving about, jostling and murmuring to one another while they press forward in a rush to get into the building. You'd think it was Comic Con and not an international peace conference, but then again, I would be lying if I said it wasn't exciting to be here. It's astonishing to me that they've managed to put this all together in such a short amount of time - the only explanation is that the diplomats in charge of the conference have ties to some very important people, and why wouldn't they? They would have to, in order to keep an entire species' existence under wraps for this many centuries.

I can make out the figure of Josie at the front of the group, but once the rest of the students are all assembled, she quickly moves aside to make room for Russo and Hawthorne, the latter of whom straightens up and projects his voice so that everyone can hear him when he speaks. "The official talks will be happening on an ongoing basis, every day until the end of the convention. I would like to remind you all to be on your best behaviour - you're not only here as representatives of the Academy, but as representatives of the shifter community as a whole. This could very well end up being a critical moment in the history of shifter-human relations, and I would strongly encourage you all to remember that."

He takes a step back to allow Russo to move forward and speak, her hands behind her back as she clears her throat. "In addition to the main diplomatic talks, there will also be several other sessions led by important figures in both our communities, all with the goal of strategizing and encouraging integration. I would also personally recommend listening to some of the lectures on keeping a low profile while living in densely populated human communities, such as Boston. Again, though, it will be up to you all how you decide to spend your day. The Academy faculty fellows will be around the convention center until the day is over, and you will be free to spend your time here as you see fit. Remember, though," she adds, a knowing gleam in her eye, "this is an *academic* trip. Don't take this as permission to run wild around the city. Our resident witches will be keeping an eye out for your magical signatures, so it's in your best interest not to stray too far from the convention center. Other than that, though..." She spreads her arms out. "Enjoy yourselves, and I hope this experience is an educational one for all of you."

Silas and I exchange a look. He shrugs his broad shoulders, and I nod. Seemingly finished with their speeches, the two school presidents turn around and retreat into the building, leaving the rest of us to trickle in on our own. The guys and I linger behind for a moment, waiting for the crowd to clear up, and Landon turns to us as the students disperse. "So," he asks, "where to first?"

"Anywhere that's *not* here," Shade replies haughtily. "As if listening to a bunch of brown-nosing politicians is *anyone's* idea of a good time."

"You heard Russo," Hazel shoots back at him. "They're going to be tracking us. We have to at least put in *some* effort."

"Just think of it this way," I say, "it's better than class, right?"

"It would be," Shade agrees, "if it weren't a Saturday."

I purse my lips. "Good point."

"Well, I don't know about the rest of you," Silas says, "but I actually want to see these so-called peace talks. This affects all of us, whether we like it or not, and if a bunch of bureaucrats are going to be deciding our futures, I'd like to hear what they have to say."

"Same here," Hunter puts in. "Most of the board members are going to be there, and I ought to go there to support my dad - at least, for a little while."

"Screw that," Landon replies. "I want to learn about blending into human society."

"I wouldn't mind just poking around for a bit," Hazel adds. "You know, to see what looks interesting."

"Maybe we should split up, then," I suggest. "We can all meet up around lunchtime and go get something to eat together. Until then, we can go do our own thing."

"That works for me," Shade replies. The others murmur their agreement.

"I guess we'll see you guys later, then?" asks Xander, turning to us.

"Sounds like a plan," I reply.

The group disperses into the building, Hazel, Xander, and Ruby heading in one direction and Landon and Shade heading in another. I'm left standing between Hunter and Silas. "Well," the dragon shifter says, turning to me, "do you want to come with us, Boots?"

"Yes," I reply. It's not even a question; Silas is right. This could end up being a landmark event, and like it or not, we're smack in the middle of it. This could also be a chance to learn more about the experiments the humans conducted on us, and one look at Silas tells me he's thinking the same thing. Now is the time to be strategic, especially if it means getting some insight into the humans' plans for us.

Wordlessly, the three of us file into the building, taking in the soaring ceiling and massive banks of glass windows on all sides.

Everywhere I look, I see booths with conflicting messages and themes - some are clearly geared towards shifters, while some seem to be more human-focused. Opportunists using this as a chance to sell their services to the magical community have staked out at a lot of the tables, and the walls are littered with signs declaring messages of coexistence and unity. It all feels a bit disingenuous.

I follow the two guys down the length of the hall, weaving my way between other attendees as I do my best to keep up with them. At one point, I almost run smack into a security guard who's no doubt here to make sure unsuspecting humans don't wander in, thinking it's some kind of public access event. I'm struck by the fact that there's no easy way to tell which of the attendees are humans and which are shifters; if you didn't know any better, you'd think there was no way to distinguish them at all. I spent most of my life thinking that, and yet here I am. Talk about getting thrown into the deep end.

There are signs directing us up a steep set of stairs and towards the main auditorium where the peace talks are being held. There's already a crowd forming outside, although the number of students waiting to get in is surprisingly small; the others are likely more interested in the glamorous aspects of the conference than the messy political stuff, which only makes me feel even more out of place. Silas comes to a halt on one side of me, with Hunter on the other, and as we stand there, pressed body to body while we wait to be let inside, I feel more aware of their presences than ever before. On one side, Silas: big, thoughtful, and determined to find out the truth, even if it means walking into danger himself. On the other, Hunter: lanky and brooding, with an inferiority complex that he's been nursing all his life that belies a more fun-loving side underneath. Both incredibly handsome, both so different... and yet both more similar than one would realise. And I'm what links them together, in more ways than one. It's... a heavy notion, and it makes me feel something I can't quite put my finger on. Once again, my mind drifts back to the kiss I shared with Hunter, only for me to be struck with overwhelming guilt at having done it behind Silas' back; part of me wants to blurt it out right then and there, just to be rid of the tension, but I'm paralysed with indecision.

Finally, they let us inside the auditorium where a banner reading, "Human-Shifter Peace Summit" hangs over the stage. A roundtable sits in the middle, with well-dressed men and women on all sides, and I can see the Academy executives already sitting in prime spots in the front few rows. It's silent inside, and the talk seems to have already started; a moderator is in the midst of asking whether the shifters' policy of secrecy is sustainable in today's culture.

The three of us are relegated to one of the back rows, and I slide in between Hunter and Silas, my eyes wide as I watch the politicians below us. "That's hardly the point, and you know it," says one of the speakers, a dark-skinned woman in an impeccably tailored suit. "The discussion isn't about secrecy—it never was—and I think questions about shifter culture is a diversion from the real issue, here."

"With all due respect, Ma'am," replies one of the older men flanking her, "the issues are linked. We have to face the fact that keeping the existence of shifters a secret from humans is becoming less realistic by the day. It's only giving these fringe groups more ammunition against us."

"And why should that be *our* responsibility?" pipes up another speaker. "We should be addressing how this information keeps getting out, instead of throwing the baby out with the bathwater."

I lean in to Hunter as the moderator struggles to keep a hold on the increasingly tense debate. "Do you know who any of these people are?" I whisper.

Hunter's brow furrows. "I recognise a few of them from my father's meetings. The ones on the left look like some of the shifter representatives. I'm guessing the others are the human ambassadors."

"They're the ones with the leverage here," Silas states flatly. It's not a question. I can see his hands gripping his armrests tightly, and part of me wants to reach out and smooth the tension out of them, but I can't bring myself to, not with Hunter on my other side.

"You're arguing in favour of secrecy," the moderator says to the first woman. "Do you have any thoughts on protected communities, then?"

"If by 'protected', you mean 'segregated,' then yes, I have quite a few," the woman replies shortly. "This isn't an either-or situation. Humans and shifters have lived together for hundreds of years - there's no reason to change that. It would just be caving to the humans who want us out of the way."

"Who said anything about us wanting shifters out of the way?" replies a man on the other side of the table. "Everyone has to realise that we're talking about a small fraction of humans who know about shifters, and an even smaller fraction of those who want to subjugate them."

The debate rages on, replies firing back and forth so quickly that I can hardly keep up. Hunter watches them intently, leaning forward in his seat, his eyes occasionally moving down to where his father is, while Silas frowns, lost in thought as he listens. I'm left wondering how on earth anything is going to be resolved in the short time that this conference is set to go on... until my cell phone vibrates in my pocket.

Frowning, I dig it out and glance at the screen. It's a text message from an unknown number.

Watch your back. It isn't safe for you here.

CHAPTER 38

My body is tense as we emerge from the assembly room an hour later, my shoulders hunched and my fingers nervously carding through my hair as I stare down at my phone. I know I should have been paying more attention during the peace talks, but as soon as I got that text, it was more or less over for my focus. Could it have been a wrong number? Sure, but I doubt it; even after replying with multiple messages asking who the sender was, I received no response, and my mind has been a mess trying to figure out who it might be. It sure as hell doesn't *feel* like a coincidence, especially now that the whole Academy has up and left the island to surround ourselves with humans for the next week in an unfamiliar city. The idea that the warning might actually be a threat has crossed my mind, although from whom? Hawthorne? That would be bold, even from him, especially considering that the number could be traced, in theory. Another student? That hardly seems more likely; if it were someone I knew, why wouldn't they tell me to my face? I'm left spinning out with more questions than answers, and I think Silas and Hunter can tell that something is wrong. They keep shooting me glances out of the corners of their eyes as we head back down the stairs and make our way towards the entrance.

"Are you all right?" Silas asks, putting a hand on my shoulder as soon as we get outside and into the blessed fresh air. "You look a little shaken up."

"It's just... everything they were talking about," I reply, lying through my teeth. "It's unnerving, listening to them discussing our futures like we're just pawns in some game."

"Is that not what we are to them?" The dragon shifter asks, crossing his arms. "To the humans, at least?"

"Maybe you should have more faith in them," Hunter speaks up, putting his hands in his pockets. "It's only the first day of the conference. They've got more time to figure out a solution."

"For all the good that will do," Silas says, shaking his head. "I'll be curious just how much of a say they give the shifters, at the end of the day."

"What do you mean?" I ask him, brow furrowing.

"Do you really think the humans care about resolving this peacefully?" he asks. "I've seen how they operate. They made my parents disappear because they were talking about changing the status quo. I don't expect this to be any different—the only question is how many people they'll end up throwing under the bus just to make this all go away."

Hunter looks like he's about to reply, but we're interrupted by the sounds of familiar voices approaching us from the left. I look up to see Hazel and the twins walking over to us. She's laughing at something Xander said, and judging by the way they're looking at one another, I'd say that their first foray into exploring the conference was a success - more of a success than mine, at any rate.

"Hey," Ruby says as they come to a stop next to us.

"Hey," I echo. "Where did you guys end up going?"

"This breakout session about integrating with human society," Xander replies, "although it was all bullshit. Just a bunch of pro-human propaganda."

Silas shakes his head. "I'm not surprised."

"How are the talks going?" Ruby asks.

"About as well as you'd expect," Hunter admits. "They're deadlocked. Nobody can agree on anything."

"Figures," Hazel says, frowning. "I'm just surprised they've even been able to keep a lid on things as long as they have. I'm starting to see now why there's so much tension between the two groups."

"Which is exactly why this whole thing is pointless," comes a new voice, and I turn around to see Shade coming to a stop on our other side, Landon following him. "I'm telling you, we'd be better off just fucking around for the next few days."

"Easy for you to say," Hunter mutters, looking at the ground.

For his part, Landon just turns to the blond boy. "What did you have in mind, Shade? I've already had about enough of this place."

A sly smile appears on the wolf shifter's face, and he leans back with mock thoughtfulness. "The seaport is just over there," he says, nodding over his shoulder in the direction of the highway. "I say we go make some memories of this trip that *don't* involve listening to politicians drone on."

"But the witches-" begins Hazel.

Shade waves her off. "It's less than half a mile from here. It's practically in the backyard of the convention center. You think they're going to notice us if we're that close?"

I purse my lips. "You may have a point, there."

"I knew there was a reason I liked you, Boots," Shade says, giving me a grin that can only be described as... well, wolfish. I feel my ears heat up a little.

Silas clears his throat. "I could stand some time away from the politics, myself."

"So it's settled, then," Shade says, crossing his arms and looking from each of us to the next. "We're gonna go have some real fun. What about you two?" he adds, turning to the Murakami siblings. "You in?"

Ruby and Xander exchange a look. "I could be convinced," he says, winking at Hazel, who bursts out laughing.

"Better than waiting for someone else to tell us how kowtowing to the humans is our only hope of surviving," Ruby adds.

"Right on." Shade nods. "So what are we waiting for?"

SHADE IS RIGHT; the seaport is within walking distance, just on the other side of an underpass flanking the convention center. We probably look weird: a group of young adults in brightly coloured uniforms, a tour group that got separated from their bus, maybe. But it doesn't matter; Shade's instincts were right on the money. Being outside in the sun is what I needed right now, not being trapped at the conference ruminating over the text I received. A fresh breeze buffets us from over the ocean, bringing with it the smell of sea salt and old wood and putting a fresh spring in my step. It's less than ten minutes before we arrive at the port, and although it's not exactly picturesque, with a concrete walkway instead of a boardwalk, it's a pleasant enough change of scenery. Behind us is a stretch of storefronts and well-tended greenery, and we find ourselves leaning against a rusted railing, staring out across the ocean toward the eastern part of the city on the other side of the channel.

We slowly branch away from one another, unbothered by the distance and each lost in his or her own thoughts. I remain where I am; the wind tossing my hair around as my eyes drift closed, slowly relaxing for the first time since the peace talk.

Landon's voice breaks me out of my trance. "Looks like those two are getting on like a house on fire." He nods in the direction of Xander and Hazel, who are standing in the shade of a nearby building; she's jostling him playfully with one shoulder while he feigns outrage.

"I'm happy for her," I reply. "Xander seems like a good guy."

"He does," Landon agrees, "although with only a week here, I wonder how attached she can afford to get."

"Well," I say, turning around and leaning back against the railing, "that's what phones are for."

Landon laughs. "Touche, Boots." There's a pause, and then he grins at me and asks, "So, do you think that would work on you?"

"What?"

He sidles up next to me, his arm brushing mine. "Oh, you know, gentle touches, long, meaningful looks, telling bad jokes and then pretending they're the funniest thing in the world... It's sort of flirting 101."

"Well, unfortunately I'm not familiar," I reply, meeting his dark eyes. "But I've never thought flirting should be reduced to just those things, either."

"Thank god for that," Landon replies, the corner of his mouth turning upward as his eyes sear into mine.

I'm on the verge of asking him what he means when a new voice pulls my attention away. "Look who it is."

I turn around, and my heart immediately sinks; Lyle is standing behind us, on the other side of a bench. His arms are crossed, and there's a haughty look in his eye that I don't like. "What?" I ask, my tone short.

"Just out for a stroll," he replies, "same as you. Is that not allowed?"

"Depends on your reasons," I shoot back.

"Don't flatter yourself, I wasn't following you," he says, waving a hand dismissively. "I know better than to pick another fight with the infamous *hybrid,* right? Knowing when to fold 'em was always my strong suit."

"Good," I reply curtly. "Then you'll leave me alone."

Landon looks from me to Lyle, raising his eyebrows. "Is there a problem, here?"

"No," I tell him, not breaking eye contact with the older student.

"And who might you be?" Lyle asks, turning his attention to the siren shifter. "Another one of her boyfriends? You know, Millie, if I didn't know better, I'd say you were some kind of slut."

"Seriously?" Landon crosses his arms. "Do people seriously still say things like that?"

"Evidently," I reply flatly, mimicking his posture.

Lyle ignores the dig, taking a few slow steps closer to us. I can feel myself tensing up, but Landon's presence steadies me, and I force myself to calm down; I don't want this turning into another fight. "You know, I've been asking around about you," Lyle says, staring down at me with derision in his eyes. "Call it... professional curiosity. Especially after you sent me packing the way you did after class the other day. They always hype hybrids up, you know? But you're never expecting them to actually be able to do it."

"Well," I reply, "I'm happy to disappoint."

"It wouldn't be the first time," Lyle says, a cruel smile appearing on his face. "I did some digging on you, Brix," he continues. "By the sounds of it, you stirred up all sorts of trouble back at your home school. What was it I heard, again...? Something about top-secret experiments?"

"Not so top-secret now, I guess," Landon remarks dryly.

"How the hell did you find all this out about me, Lyle?" I demand, staring defiantly up at him.

The older boy sniffs. "It's not that hard to find information, if you know where to look. Working for the school administration doesn't hurt, either." He turns back to me. "You know, it's almost enough to make me feel bad for you. Almost. A poor little human girl, abandoned by her parents, left to the whims of a bunch of sadistic human scientists... it almost makes up for the fact that you're just like all the other girls at this school."

My eyes narrow. "Abandoned? What the hell are you talking about?"

"Boots," Landon says, taking hold of my arm and tugging at it gently, "leave it. Just ignore him."

I shake his hand off, taking a step closer to Lyle. "What the fuck are you saying?"

Lyle raises his eyebrows. "You mean... you didn't know? Your boys here didn't tell you? Granted, they were just babies then, too, so I guess they wouldn't know either, but still..."

"Know what?" I can feel my nails digging into my palms, my heart leaping to my throat. I'm taking the bait, and I know it, but I can't help it. There's something in Lyle's eyes that gives me pause - a look that says he knows that he has the upper hand.

"Boots," Landon warns me again, "he's not worth it."

"I think that's for her to decide," Lyle says, not breaking eye contact with me. "What do you think, Brix?"

"What are you talking about?" I ask him. "What did you find out about my parents?"

"If you thought the humans took you away from them, you were wrong," Lyle replies, his tone sharp and cutting. "Your parents were the ones who gave you up. They *abandoned* you."

CHAPTER 39

"You're..." I swallow the lump in my throat, trying desperately to fight off the dreadful sensation I can feel rising in my chest. "You're lying."

"Am I?" Lyle crosses his arms. "I took a little field trip to the registrar's office. I'm an RA, so they won't let me look at *everything,* but... I saw enough." There's a pause, and he furrows his brow thoughtfully. "It's funny, though. The one thing I couldn't find any information on was the witch shifter - you know, the baby. You've got one of every form, so there had to have been one. It would've had to have been a girl, since witches are always girls, but it sounds like she's long gone... Although maybe that suits you just fine, Millie. This way you don't have to share the rest of your little boy toys with anyone else."

"Shut up." My hands are clenched into fists, and I realise that I'm shaking, although not from anger, but from dread. "You don't know anything about me, Lyle."

"Are you sure about that?" he asks, advancing on me. "I know *enough* about you, Millie Brix. Enough to tell you with complete certainty that you never had any chance of having a normal life. I guess that's what happens when your parents don't want you, though, right?" He shakes his head in a mockery of sadness. "Poor, sweet, little

Millie, with no one to love her... except for the people who had their powers *dumped* on you."

"Knock it the fuck off, Lyle," Landon tells him, his voice venomous as he comes to stand by my side. "That's enough." I see his eyes flash green, and I can tell he's on the verge of shifting. One panicked look around us tells me that would be a recipe for disaster; there are humans everywhere, and we're no longer in the safety of the convention center. I grab his hand, giving him a warning squeeze as I shoot my eyes over to his. That seems to calm him a little, his eyes going back to normal, although he still looks like he's ready to kill Lyle with his bare hands.

"Easy there, tiger," Lyle says, holding his hands up and taking a step back. "I've had my fill of siren songs for one lifetime, thank you very much." His eyes dart over to me. "I just figured I'd come share the love. That's what you guys are all about, right? *Sharing the love.*"

"Leave. Us. Alone," I tell him, and although I'm trying for dangerous and intimidating, my voice quivers in spite of myself. It's enough to make me want to cry, and I bite down hard on the inside of my lip.

"I'm going, I'm going." The vampire shifter backs up another few steps and turns to go, but not before giving me a venomous smile over his shoulder. "See you around, Millie. I'll be curious to see what ends up happening to you." And with that, he saunters away, holding up a hand in a jovial wave, as if we were old friends parting ways. The fucking nerve.

Still trembling with anger and fear, I drop my shoulders and fall onto the bench with a hard thud. I can feel Landon's eyes on me as I run my hands through my hair, my face flushed and my heart pounding. I can hardly bring myself to look at him as he comes to sit beside me, putting a gentle hand on my arm. "Boots," he says quietly, "are you okay?"

I take a shaky breath and turn to him, swallowing hard. "No, Landon," I reply flatly. "I don't think I am."

"He went through your *records*?" Hazel's eyes flash as we walk back in the direction of the convention center. "How is that even allowed? He could get expelled for something like that, couldn't he?" An air of tension has fallen over the group in the aftermath of what happened, and I can see the guys looking at each other. The question on all their faces is clear: they're wondering whether saying something will make it better or worse. I don't blame them; hell, *I* don't even know the answer to that question.

Hunter sighs, rubbing the back of his neck. "Privacy rules don't apply to shifters, Hazel. You know that. He works for the school - he can pretty much dig up whatever dirt he wants."

"How is that *fair*?" She shakes her head, her blonde curls bouncing around her face.

"It's not," Ruby replies, and sighs. "Lyle's always been an asshole. One of those guys who's on a major power trip because he's in the Academy's pocket." She blows a stray strand of dark hair out of her face, her expression frigid. "He tried to get me to go out with him my first month here - got all pissy when I told him to fuck off. If Xander weren't here, he probably would've pulled something similar." She turns to me. "I'm sorry you have to deal with this, Millie. You're not seeing the best our school has to offer."

"It's fine." I sigh, rubbing the back of my neck. "I guess I should just ignore it, right? Don't give him the satisfaction."

"You shouldn't have to," Silas puts in. "We came here to see the conference, not listen to a bunch of bullshit about your parents."

"What if it wasn't bullshit?" I ask, turning to him. "He said it himself. He has access to my records."

"Look, Boots..." The dragon shifter runs a hand through his hair, looking like he's struggling to find the right words. "Don't listen to him, okay? I'm sure there was a good reason your parents did it. And if not..."

"If not," Hunter finishes, his eyes meeting mine, "it doesn't matter."

"That's right," Landon agrees. "*We're* your family, Boots. And nothing's going to change that."

I turn to look at them: Landon, his arms crossed, Silas and Hunter, watching me with concern on their faces, Shade, who's been quiet this whole time, and Hazel. The twins are new to our group but slowly creeping into my heart. The family I chose.

"Maybe you're right," I say, smiling a little, but there's still a rotten feeling in the pit of my stomach, and I can't fight the sense that it might be here to stay.

"REMIND me again why we're going up here," I say, breathing hard as I round what feels like the hundredth corner in the narrow stairwell. We might as well have been climbing for hours, given how badly out of shape I feel, and I have to pause and lean forward, putting my hands on my knees.

Shade turns around to look at me, ahead of me on the stairs. It's embarrassing how much easier of a time he's having. "Better view," he replies, not sounding out of breath in the slightest. "Besides, practicing is always more fun when there's the danger of falling to your death, don't you think?" He frowns as I continue to suck in air. "Unless... You're not going to like, pass out or something, are you?"

I wave him off. "No. I mean, probably not."

"Good," he says, "because we're almost there."

I follow him the rest of the way up, and we finally arrive at the top of the stairs, where a metal doorway waits for us. Shade pushes it open unceremoniously and steps out onto the roof, and I follow a moment later, still struggling to catch my breath.

The view from on top of the academic building might as well have taken my breath away all over again, and my exhaustion is momentarily forgotten as I gape at our surroundings, my mouth dropping open. It's well past curfew, and going on the roof is against the rules, but neither of those things has ever stopped Shade in the past, and I'm beginning to see why.

It feels like we can see everything from up here. Below us, the grassy hills and modern buildings of the American campus stretch out like a tiny city. I can see the sculpture garden and the student housing on one end, as well as the lot where our group arrived on the other side. Farther out, the suburban houses of the local shifter community surround the campus, with the outline of downtown Boston visible beyond that. The city is lit up for the night, a sea of twinkling lights and shadowy buildings - inside which, right at this moment, politicians could be deciding the fate of our entire species. The stars are more visible from this far out, and a full moon looms overhead, just above the horizon.

The perfect moon for wolf shifting, I think.

I'm snapped out of my thoughts by the feeling of something crashing into me from behind, barrelling me onto the concrete of the roof and making me let out a little yelp. I struggle to get my feet under me, confused and in a panic, until I turn around and see that it's only Shade, already in the form of a giant timber wolf, his silver eyes now gold and glowing in the dark. "Too slow," he says, and I could swear, even though he's no longer a human, there's still a teasing look on his face.

"What the hell was that for?" I demand, getting to my feet and dusting off my trousers.

"You're going to have to do better than that, Boots," the wolf says. "And here I was thinking you were making progress."

I set my jaw, giving him a determined smile, and close my eyes, reaching for the magic that I'm only just beginning to get a feel for and letting it take hold of me. It takes a moment to get started, but before long I'm shifting into my wolf form, landing on all fours and staring Shade down with my newly acquired night vision. "That's more like it," he remarks, and moves gracefully to the left. Slowly we circle each other, two predators under the moonlight, but there's a playfulness to it that keeps me at ease.

Shade lunges for me, and I narrowly jump out of the way, struggling to balance on my paws. Thinking fast, I feign to the right, sending him pouncing in that direction before springing the other way at the last second, leaping into him and pinning him underneath me. "Not bad," he observes, but in the instant that my guard is down, he gets control and rolls me over so that I'm under him, our snouts so close they could touch. There's something animalistic about it... and alluring.

Overwhelmed by the intensity of it, I find my voice and force some humour. "Okay, okay! Truce!"

"Do you surrender?"

"Okay, let's not go that far."

He laughs and gets off me, shifting back into human form easily. I follow suit, and we're left as people again, sitting side by side on the roof. I turn to look out at the city in the distance, and Shade follows my gaze; for a few moments, neither of us speaks. Finally, I break the silence. "You know, I'm surprised you haven't said anything about what happened today. With Lyle."

Shade frowns. "What's there to say?"

I shrug. "I don't know. Nothing, I guess. It just kind of felt like the others were walking on eggshells with me today, you know?" I turn to look at him. "Is that why you brought me up here? To take my mind off what he said about my parents?"

The wolf shifter clears his throat. "I guess I thought it might cheer you up, yeah."

"Thank you."

His grey eyes meet mine. "Good, old-fashioned violence always makes things better. For me, at least."

I raise an eyebrow at him: the school criminal, ignored by everyone but seeing everything. "Should I be worried?"

He snorts. "Nah. I wouldn't hurt you, Boots."

"Glad to hear it," I reply.

There's another long moment of silence, and as I stare out at the cityscape, I can feel his eyes on me. That same nervous energy fills me up, sparks flitting up through my stomach and my heart beginning to beat faster. I feel like a deer in the headlights, and it feels *good*. A shiver goes up my back, and he seems to notice; there's a subtle shift in his posture, like he's on the verge of moving closer, and I would be lying if I said I didn't want him to.

"You know," Shade says slowly, breaking the silence, "I can think of a couple other ways to make things better." There's a sly half-smile on his face, and it's nearly enough to make me sway.

My better judgement is warning me not to be stupid, not to make this any more complicated, but a baser part of me is winning out as I stare up into the blond boy's face. "Is that so?" I ask, almost not believing the words coming out of my mouth. He nods, and I scoot closer to him, tilting my head to the side. "And what would those be, exactly?"

"I would have to show you," he replies, his smirk growing.

More adrenaline floods through me. The rest of the world is momentarily forgotten. "Then show me," I tell him, my voice barely above a whisper.

Now his smirk has grown into a full-on grin, and when he reaches up to tuck a stray strand of hair behind my ear, his hand feels like it's setting my skin on fire. His lips are like fire, too, and his kiss is as fierce as he is, scorching me in the best way possible as his hand comes up to tangle in my hair and my arms wrap around him.

Keeping me warm in the moonlight.

CHAPTER 40

If we thought we were going to get a breather from the constant politics and rumours today, we were sorely mistaken; Sunday is another day at the convention center, and although I now know what to expect, I'm still dreading it... and not only for the obvious reasons.

The others were all in bed already by the time Shade and I came down from the roof last night, and for that, I'm thankful; the last thing I would have wanted was to have to explain why I was out so long past curfew, or why my clothes and hair were rumpled when I got back. Shade gave me another long kiss before disappearing into his room, leaving me swaying on my feet as I went to bed, still basking in the afterglow of the love we had made. I slept like a baby, a dreamless sleep for which I'm especially grateful for now; now that the adrenaline and endorphins have worn off, I'm left to face the truth of what happened last night, and the overwhelming sense of guilt and confusion that accompanies it.

Once again, I hooked up with one of the guys I met at the Academy. Once again, I was overcome with emotion and desire in the moment, and now I'm having to deal with the aftermath. I was reeling from what Lyle told me about my parents, that much is clear, and the conference has been taking a toll on me, yes. But that's a cheap excuse, and I know it; the conference has been taking a toll on *every-one*, especially in the aftermath of what the school did to Silas. Pretending it was a moment of weakness diminishes what it really was - what *all* these moments between me and the guys have been: some part of both of us, feeding on the thing that connects us, that string of fate that's had us tethered together in some way since we were babies. Would they understand if I told them it all felt almost *preconceived,* like the feelings I'm developing for them are just a natural result of our relationship, the next logical step in a long line of fateful events?

It's all too much, and at the end of the day, none of that even matters; a conversation needs to happen between Silas and me, and I'm not sure if I'm ready for it. I know we've never officially put labels on our relationship, but that doesn't make me any more nervous as we file out to the metro station for another day at the conference; I don't want to jeopardize my relationship with any of these guys, espe-cially not now, and no matter what they all have in common, they're still people with their own emotions... and their own hearts capable of being broken.

I look up from my seat on the train so see Shade sitting across from me; his gray eyes meet mine for a second, and his mouth twitches in a knowing smile. We haven't said much since last night, and I can appreciate that. He's always been a bit of a wild card, and I'm not under any illusions that what happened last night was some kind of a *commitment,* but I would be lying if I said I wasn't glad it happened.

Realising I'm staring at him, I feel myself blush, and the wolf shifter just winks at me as if it's the most normal thing in the world. Charmer.

"You all right, Millie?" Hazel asks from the seat next to me. I watch as her eyes dart from me to Shade, and she raises an eyebrow; I just give my head a nearly imperceptible shake to warn her off.

"Later," I murmur, my voice muffled by the sound of the other students talking. "After we get to our stop."

"Got it," she says, giving me a knowing nod as we lapse back into silence.

"Where the hell is Hunter?" asks Landon, breaking the tension a little as he picks his way up to the front of the car where we're sitting. "I thought we were supposed to stick together, here."

"He said something about his dad," Hazel replies, glancing up at her fellow siren shifter. "It sounds like the school board is having their own meeting today, and he wanted to see if he could get in on it. Not a bad idea, if you ask me."

Landon raises his eyebrows. "You think?"

"I mean, yeah." Hazel crosses her arms. "Don't you? The faculty will probably have a better nose for what's going on here than we do. If they're planning some kind of major policy shift, better to hear it from the horse's mouth. And Hunter is the son of the horse."

Landon laughs. "I never thought about it that way. You know, he's pretty sharp, now that I think about it. If he can learn to take advantage of his dad, that could help all of us."

"Strategising, exactly." She nods. "Don't count the guy out just yet, Landon."

"I never did," Landon replies, before turning back to me. "So has Amelia given you any more trouble, Boots?"

I shake my head. "None, believe it or not. I mean, I haven't talked to her since yesterday, but..." I shrug. "No dirty looks, no snarky comments, nothing. I'm honestly a little surprised."

"We'll see how long *that* lasts," Shade mutters.

"I'll take as long as I can get," I reply, and the wolf shifter grins at me. A shiver runs down my back as I remember the feeling of his hands on my body last night, the intensity with which he kissed me. The spark between us continues to grow until I break it off, turning away and shooting a guilty glance at Silas, who's leaning against a railing by the doors, looking thoughtful. This clearly isn't lost on Hazel, who follows close behind me as we get off the train, falling into step next to me as we climb the stairs and step out into the bright Boston sunshine.

"Okay," she says, putting her hands in her pockets, "spill."

I laugh. "You're making it sound like I killed a man, or something!"

"More like kissed one," Hazel retorts, giving me a sly grin. "Which one was it? Wait, don't tell me - Shade. You guys have been making eyes at each other all morning."

"Jeez, not so loud," I protest, laughing. "The whole school's going to hear us!"

"Oh my god, I was right!" She squeals, clapping her hands. "Millie Brix kissed the school bad boy! So how was he? Tell me everything!"

I feel my cheeks heating up again as we continue to walk. "It was... good," I reply. "Really good, actually."

"Okay," she says, "so then... What's the problem? You're walking around looking like your grandma just died."

I sigh. There's no getting away from it; Hazel is perceptive as hell, and I knew the conversation was going to go this way before I even started it. "It's Silas," I reply reluctantly.

"Ah." The siren shifter nods knowingly. "The classic love triangle."

"It's not a love triangle," I protest. "At least, I don't *think* it is." I let out a frustrated groan. "That's the problem, Hazel. I don't *know* what it is - I don't know what any of it is. I mean, I like these guys, there's no denying that. But as far as how they feel about me, or how they'll feel finding out that I feel that way about them all..." I shake my head, rubbing the back of my neck. "God, I don't think I've ever been this confused in my life."

"See, this is what happens when communication falls apart," she says, frowning. "All these assumptions and no straight facts. I think your problem is that you're expecting this to turn into a full-blown drama, Millie."

"Won't it?" I turn to her as we stop at an intersection, a sea of blue and gold, black and white.

"I don't know," she replies honestly. "You're the one in the middle of it, not me. But if you ask me..." She gives me a gentle nudge with her elbow. "The surest way to find out is to just talk to them."

I sigh. "I was afraid you were going to say that."

G. BAILEY & REGAN ROSEWOOD

"Well, it's true," she protests, throwing up her hands. "You should just tell Silas. Let him decide for himself, and then you won't have to worry anymore."

"Tell me what?"

My heart drops at the sound of an all-too-familiar voice behind me, and I whirl around to see the dragon shifter approaching the two of us, the sun gleaming on his brown hair. "Uh..."

"I think I'll leave you guys to talk about this one," Hazel says, shooting me a glance before falling in with the rest of the group. "I'm going to go find Xander and Ruby—I'll meet you guys at the entrance!"

Traitor. Slowly I turn to Silas, who's watching me with a curious look on his face; I should have known this would happen sooner or later. At the end of the day, Hazel is right: things are getting too complicated for me to keep ignoring them. I need to clear the air once and for all, and the time to do it is now. "I... was hoping I could talk to you," I tell him, walking slowly alongside him as we trail behind the rest of the group.

"Well," he says, holding out his arms, "here I am." He turns to look at me, a concerned expression on his face. "Are you okay, Boots?"

"I'm fine," I hasten to assure him. "It's not *me*, exactly... I mean, it has to do with me, but it's not..." I sigh, pinching the bridge of my nose. Why is this so damn difficult? "The thing is," I say slowly, starting over, "something happened that I think you deserve to know about... but you might not like hearing about it."

Silas gives me a small smile. "Well, how am I supposed to know if you don't tell me?"

"I..." I'm struggling to spit it out, and at the moment I feel like I'd rather be anywhere on earth but here.

"Millie." He stops, turning to face me. "You know you can tell me anything. I thought that was clear."

"But this..." I swallow hard. The trust in his dark eyes is both heartwarming and heartbreaking. Biting the inside of my lip, I look down at the ground, struggling to make my mouth form words. "I kissed Shade," I say, my voice barely above a whisper. "Last night. I...

244

I'm sorry. I wanted to tell you, but I didn't know if... I mean, you and I..."

I'm babbling, and it takes Silas putting a gentle hand on my cheek to make me finally look up at him. "It's okay," he says simply.

I stare at him blankly, almost sure I misheard. "Huh?"

He laughs at the look of sheer confusion on my face. "Millie, come on," he says, his hand moving to my shoulder as he stoops to look me in the eyes. "You think I didn't know that?"

I blink. "I..."

Silas just grins at me, and relief washes over me when I see that it's in good humour. "Come on, this isn't grade school," he says. "We're all adults here. If you want to spend time with the others, you have every right to."

"Oh." My shoulders slump with relief. "I, um... Wow. I wasn't expecting that, Silas."

"I mean, it makes sense." He holds his hand out to me and I take it gratefully as we begin to walk again. "There's something special connecting all of us," he continues. "I mean, we share an origin, for god's sake. And what happened between you and me, well..." He shrugs. "Frankly, I would be a little surprised if it didn't end up happening with them, too."

"That's... very progressive."

Silas bursts out laughing. "Are you surprised?"

"I don't know," I reply, blushing. "I've never been in this situation before."

"Me neither." He glances down at me. "But for whatever it's worth, what matters to me most is that you're happy, Boots. Whether that's with me, with Shade... with any of us. That said, though," he adds, pulling me against him, "I'd be disappointed if I couldn't still do this." And he plants a soft kiss on top of my head.

I laugh, letting him draw me into a full-on embrace. "Thank you, Silas," I murmur into his shoulder. "I mean it."

"So do I," the dragon shifter replies, and I can feel him smiling against my ear. "But we'd better go catch up with the rest of them now. People are starting to give us weird looks."

CHAPTER 41

I don't think I've ever felt relief as palpable as the relief I'm feeling now, with the exception of when we found Silas alive after he'd been taken by the Academy. I feel like there's a renewed spring in my step in the aftermath of our talk, and even though the sun is beating down on us and I can already feel sweat forming under my uniform, I have a feeling things are going to work out. It's amazing what a little romance can do for a person's mental state.

Silas lets go of my hand when we arrive at the convention center, smiling at me as we break off from the main group and head over to the place near the entrance that we've been using as a meeting point. It takes several minutes for the others to arrive, coming in groups of two and three. It's only after everyone is here, talking excitedly and looking around at the guests for the day that I realise Hunter still isn't here, and I immediately feel a pang of worry in my stomach. My mind is already going to worst-case scenarios, visions of the vampire shifter strapped to a table in a laboratory somewhere while the humans suck the life out of him, just like they tried to do to Silas. I'm on the verge of full-on panic when Hunter's familiar voice sounds over my shoulder, and I turn around to see him jogging up to us, a look of concern on his face. "Sorry, sorry," he says, running a hand through his red hair as he comes to a stop between Hazel and Landon.

"Where did you go?" I ask. "We were starting to get worried."

"You should be," Hunter replies grimly. Seeing the looks of confusion on our faces, he sighs. "Look, it's about my dad," he elaborates, crossing his arms. "He told me the school board is having a meeting with a bunch of the other Academy representatives from around the world. I'm usually able to get more out of him on stuff like this, but he wouldn't tell me anything—just that they'll be discussing 'measures' to be taken in the aftermath of the riots."

"'Measures'?" asks Shade. "What kind of 'measures'?"

"Like I said, I don't know," Hunter replies. "I even asked Amelia. She said he wouldn't tell her a word about it, and he tells her *everything*. I..." He swallows. "I have a bad feeling about all this, you guys."

"You're not the only one," Landon adds grimly. "We're talking about Academy-wide decisions, here. The last time they did that, we were on lockdown for weeks."

"And they weren't talking about the future of the whole shifter community back then," Silas adds, crossing his arms. "I don't like the sound of this."

"Do you know where this meeting is being held?" Xander asks.

"It should be in the auditorium," Hunter replies. "This afternoon, if I remember right."

The twins exchange a look, and Ruby's mouth drops open. "You're not seriously thinking...?"

"I seriously am," Xander replies. "If they're making decisions about our future, I want to know what they decide."

"Well, how are we even supposed to get in?" Ruby demands, throwing her arms up. "We're talking about sneaking into a board meeting, here. That's not exactly an easy task."

"Wait, we're talking about sneaking into a board meeting?" asks Landon.

"*He's* the one who's talking about it," Ruby responds, nodding at her brother. "*I* think it's impossible."

"It might not be," Hunter speaks up then, and the rest of us go quiet as we turn to look at him. He sighs, looking suddenly put on the spot. "Look, I can't promise anything," he says, holding up his hands. "Ruby's right; anything administration-related won't be open to the public. They'll probably have bouncers, and a group of students trying to muscle in through the front door will stick out like a sore thumb."

"So then what are you suggesting?" Silas asks.

"*We* won't be able to get in," Hunter replies, looking at him, "but *I* might be able to."

"Because you're the son of a board member?" asks Landon.

Hunter gives him a grim nod. "Again, no promises. They might tell me to fuck off the second they see me. But maybe if I can tell them I'm there for my dad... If I could come up with some kind of excuse..."

"You could at least stay long enough to find out what they're planning," I finish for him.

The vampire shifter nods. "Exactly."

There's a long moment of silence as we consider his offer. "Damn, Ash," Landon says at last, raising an eyebrow at him. "Daddy's little boy is finally starting to grow up."

"Shut up, Landon." Hunter shoots him a glare, but looks like he's struggling not to smile.

"So are we doing this, then?" Hazel asks finally. "Hunter's going to try to listen in?"

"I'm in if Hunter is," I reply, turning back to him. "Are you sure about this?"

"Not at all," Hunter replies, "but if this lets us get a step ahead of the Academy, then I'm willing to give it a shot. It still hurts knowing that my dad might be in on this... but then again, he might not be. How will I ever know if I don't try to find out, though?" The corner of his mouth twitches. "Besides, I shouldn't be thinking too hard about this. I might chicken out."

"This could be our shot at finding out the humans' plans," Silas says thoughtfully, nodding. "I'm for it. We'll need some way of listening in, though." He turns to me. "Boots, do you have some kind of witch spell? Something you could do in-form that would let us hear what they're saying?"

"I can barely even get *into* my witch form, let alone cast complicated spells," I reply. "Besides, they're probably going to have wards up against magic. I have another idea, though - something a bit more... *old-fashioned.*"

"ARE you sure this is going to work?" Silas asks incredulously as we sit together in the shadows. We're back at the seaport, our backs against one of the nearby buildings as we watch the water lap at the docks and the passersby move back and forth near the railing. With any luck, we'll be inconspicuous here - just a handful of convention-goers who wanted to take a break from the endless meetings. My cell phone is in my lap, and my knee is bouncing up and down in anticipation as we wait with bated breath for Hunter's call.

"Have a little faith," Landon says, elbowing him playfully. "Boots has got this."

"I don't doubt it," Silas replies, shooting me a grin. "I'm more worried about Hunter, if I'm being honest. What if they catch him?"

"We'll be on mute," I reply. "He's going to put us on speaker so we can hear what the board is saying. If everything goes the way it's supposed to, they won't be able to hear anything we say."

"Emphasis on everything going the way it's *supposed* to," Shade remarks dryly. "Let's just hope Hunter's dad hasn't already sold him out."

"He wouldn't," I reply, although deep down I'm not so sure. I can't shake the feeling like we're about to find out something that will turn the whole world upside-down, but I'm afraid that saying it will just make it real, so I keep my mouth shut. We're all nervous enough as it is without any more ominous predictions.

As if on cue, my phone begins to vibrate, and I quickly hit the answer button before muting our end. Hunter's voice comes through, speaking in a hushed whisper: "Okay, I'm by the back entrance to the auditorium. There's a bouncer there—I'm going to try to talk to my way in. If something happens to me, then... call the cops, or whatever."

Shade snorts. There's the sound of rustling fabric, and I realise Hunter's put his phone in his pocket. We look at one another as we wait for something to happen, nearly jumping at the sound of a gruff American voice. "I'm sorry, but this meeting isn't open to the public."

"Oh, I know," comes Hunter's reply. "I'm actually the son of one of the board members—David Ash. I brought him something."

There's a sigh. "Look, kid, I don't care if you're the president. I was told not to let anyone in here who's not on the board."

"Do you want to see proof?" There's a rustling sound. "Look, here's my ID. My dad is David Bartholomew Ash, and he's on the school board for the U.K. Academy. I have a blood bag for him."

"A blood bag?"

"Hello - he's a vampire shifter." Hunter's tone is making him sound eerily like his sister. "He needs to feed or he's going to pass out."

"I... didn't know vampire shifters worked that way."

"Well, of course you wouldn't. Where did you get your education? The American Academy?" he snorts. "Honestly, I've heard your school system was bad, but I didn't realise it was that-"

"All right, all right, enough," the bouncer says, sounding exasperated. "You're giving me a migraine. Get your dad his blood, or whatever, and then I want you out of there. Do you understand?"

"Absolutely," Hunter replies, sounding overly chipper. There's the sound of a door opening and closing.

"I'll be damned," Shade says, shaking his head in disbelief. "He actually got through."

"He really ought to pull out that Amelia voice more often," quips Landon. "He could get us whatever he wants."

I hold up my hand to silence them; the sound of more voices is coming through. It's muffled, like they're on the other side of a partition, but if I concentrate, I can just barely make them out. "...I really think we should be focused on the matter at hand, Hawthorne," comes an American voice. Russo's, if I'm correct.

"This *is* the matter at hand," comes another voice, this one I recognise as Hawthorne's. "You've heard how the peace talks are going. The politicians are deadlocked. How many more skirmishes are there going to be before you realise that the humans are outmatched, here?"

"Outmatched?" This one I don't recognise. "You're making this sound like it's a war, Hawthorne."

"It *is* a war," Hawthorne insists. "You all know this; I'm just the one brave enough to say it out loud. We're woefully unequipped to deal with the shifters anymore. Not with them mobilising, threatening to rise up. The dam *is* going to break, ladies and gentlemen; the only question is *when*. The only way we'll have any hope of surviving when it does is by leveling out the playing field."

"You're talking about restarting the hybrid experiments," someone else pipes up. My eyes go wide as I look up at the others; they look as stunned as I feel.

"That's a dangerous proposition, Hawthorne," Russo replies. "The U.K. Academy already tried that; we've seen how it ended."

"There were... outside factors," Hawthorne concedes. "It's unfortunate that we weren't able to continue our research. Don't you people understand? Granting humans shifter abilities will make the whole conflict *irrelevant*. We won't have to worry about regulations and integration if we do this. Hell, we might not even need *Academies* anymore."

"But it's a dangerous procedure," pipes up another board member. "Even if it does work, we're talking about hundreds of shifter lives lost. You can't just replicate magic like that without a sacrifice."

"And what would you rather sacrifice," Hawthorne fires back, "a few thousand shifter lives, or a few million human lives? Because these are the stakes we're talking about, here."

"That's hyperbole!"

"I do think President Hawthorne has a point," Russo says with a sigh. "It's clear that the landscape is changing for us, and this conference isn't getting us anywhere. It might be time to take things into our own hands."

"What you're suggesting is *unethical*," protests another board member.

"Not to mention unsanctioned," adds another.

"Enough," snaps a new voice, this one deep and authoritative. "Hawthorne, you've said your piece. We will... need to think about this, before we take any further action. Maybe it would be best to take a recess for a few days and consider this proposal. We can reconvene and take another vote when we're all fresh."

There's an uneasy murmur from the assembled board members, followed by a rustling sound that signals some of them are getting to their feet. Hunter begins to move away, making it harder to catch what they're saying, but it hardly matters; we've gotten the gist of it.

And the gist is not good.

CHAPTER 42

The next twenty-four hours pass by in a haze. Whatever sense of excitement permeated our group before has vanished entirely in the aftermath of the board members' meeting, replaced by a shroud of unease that has us all on edge. Everything said at the conference suddenly feels like white noise, a bunch of nonsense compared to what we know is happening behind the scenes, and the worst part is that I should have known it would come to this sooner or later. *This* was exactly what Silas was talking about when he mentioned being worried before we even left the U.K.. This is what comes of leaving the fate of an entire population up to a handful of bureaucrats. It doesn't matter that there are shifter representatives involved in this too, because the humans are the ones who run the Academy. It all feels too cunningly perfect, engineered so that no matter what we do, as students, there's no way to fight their decisions. I can't help but wonder how many of the shifter politicians have any real power, and how many of them are just puppets, put in place to keep the shifter community from rebelling. It's a system that's worked fine until now, but for some reason—maybe the modern world, maybe the fact that shifters have finally seen through the bull-shit—it's not working anymore. I should be grateful for that, but I'm not; everything feels like it's about to fall apart again, and we're hopeless to stop it.

I try to tell myself at dinner that night that maybe things won't take a turn the way they did last time. The board didn't seem too keen on Hawthorne's proposal; at least, *most* of them didn't. Maybe he's an outlier, and the humans really *are* just trying to promote peace and coexistence between our species. But maybe not. Is that really a chance we can afford to take, anyway? What happens if they decide Hawthorne is right, that the lives of the many are worth more than the lives of the few? What happens if, with the board backing him, Hawthorne is finally able to come out of the shadows, to restart the experiments with the permission of the entire administration? Images of my friends tortured and drained of their magic flit through my mind, making it hard to choke the food down, and it's all I can do not to fall into a complete panic attack at the prospect of that kind of subjugation.

I'm sitting on my bed in my room that night, staring down at my hands, which are balled into fists in my lap, when I hear a quiet knock at the door. "Come in," I call listlessly. Moments later, the door opens, and I see Landon standing there, looking apprehensive.

"I hope I'm not interrupting you," he says after a long pause.

I shake my head. "No, not at all. I was just... thinking, I guess."

"You and me both." He shuts the door quietly behind him and comes over to me; I pat the spot beside me on the bed and he takes a hesitant seat, folding his hands in his lap. "You know, I *do* really like this set-up," he remarks, looking around the room. "All of us being in the same suite, I mean. It's nice. Forget about all the talk of conspiracies and experiments, and I could get used to this."

"Yeah," I agree, adding dryly, "although it's a little hard to see the bright side when the Academy is talking about turning us into test subjects."

"Well, we've been test subjects once," the siren shifter remarks, "and we survived *that*. I'd say we have a pretty good track record."

"Thank god for that," I agree, turning to him and forcing a smile. "I just hope that's not a theory we have to test out." There's a long moment of silence, both of us struggling to think of something to say. I bite my lip, but the words come tumbling out before I can stop them. "I got a text message," I blurt out. "From an unknown number. It was during the peace talks the other day."

"Really?" Landon frowns. "Can I see it?"

I nod, fishing my phone out of my pocket and handing it to him. His eyes narrow as he reads over the anonymous message, his forehead lined with worry. "What does this mean?" he asks finally.

I shake my head hopelessly. "I don't know. But it feels like a warning. Do you think whoever sent it to me knew Hawthorne was planning on converting the rest of the school board?"

"I mean... maybe." He sighs, handing me my phone back. "Any idea who it was?"

"No," I reply. "None. For a while I thought maybe it was Hawthorne himself, but now I'm not so sure. It could be anyone here. Whoever it is, though, they seem to know something that we don't."

"Let's just hope they're on our side, then," Landon remarks grimly. There's a long pause, and he looks at me, his dark eyes meeting mine. "Listen, Boots," he says, "today was rough. For all of us. I don't want to think about what will happen if the Academy listens to Hawthorne, but I wanted to see how you were doing. I can't even imagine what this must all be like for you."

"Not great, Landon," I reply, a humourless smile appearing on my face. "Not great." I reach out and take hold of his hand, the warmth of his skin filling me with a sense of hope I didn't even know I needed. "Thank you, though," I tell him quietly. "It's nice to know I'm not alone in this."

"You're not alone, Boots," Landon replies, leaning forward to kiss me quickly on the cheek before pulling back. "You never were."

"I'm surprised they're even still doing this whole song and dance," Shade remarks as we come to a stop outside the convention center the next morning. It's a routine that's getting old for all of us now, and I think it's starting to wear on the other students; allegedly, this is the last day we'll be spending at the conference before it's back to classes as usual at the American Academy. I wish I could say that's a relief, but at this point, I'm not sure anything is going to be enough to quell the growing dread I'm feeling.

"What do you mean?" asks Hunter.

The wolf shifter shrugs. "I was half-expecting them to drag us out of our beds kicking and screaming in the middle of the night. They're obviously thinking about it."

"A little optimism would be nice, Ivis," Hazel fires back from where she's walking next to Xander. They've been joined at the hip all morning, and she has a glow about her that suggests something more than just idle chit chat happened in their dorm room last night. I'm happy for her; a little comfort goes a long way in times like these. "They didn't *agree* to anything."

"No, but they sure as hell might," Shade replies, crossing his arms. "And what are we going to do if they do, huh?"

"As much as I hate to admit it, Shade is right," Silas agrees. "We're going to need to think about some kind of exit strategy."

"Exit strategy?" I ask, shaking my head. "What does that mean?"

The dragon shifter turns to me. "Who do you think they're going to start with if they do decide to start this project up again, Boots? The answer is you. You're one of the few successful hybrid experiments, and they're going to want to study you. The rest of us, too, probably. We need to consider the possibility that the Academy might not be safe for us anymore."

"Was it ever?" I ask, feeling hopeless.

None of the others respond, looking away from me, but that's all the answer I need. Silas is right, even if I don't want to admit it; it's not a possibility I want to consider, but this is the reality of the situation. "So what are you saying?" Hunter asks finally, breaking the silence. "Are we going to have to run away or something?"

"I don't know," Silas admits, shrugging his shoulders. "Maybe. All I know is that we're going to want to get ahead of the school board, no matter what the Academy ends up deciding to do. We're going to need a plan if things go south."

"I don't know about the rest of you, but I can just up and leave," Hunter protests. "I have family here."

"You're our family, too, Hunter," I protest. "How do you know your father won't end up siding with Hawthorne?"

"He won't," the vampire shifter snaps. "He... he *can't*. I won't believe that."

"But what if-" begins Hazel.

"What are you all doing standing about?" comes the sound of a new voice, making all of us jump. I turn around to see Josie approaching us, her hands in her pockets and her dark hair pulled up in a ponytail. "Last I checked, the conference was happening *inside.*" In spite of her scolding, there's a twinkle in her eyes, and she grins when she comes to a stop in front of us.

"Sorry," Landon mutters, looking at the ground. "We were just... uh..."

"Trying to figure out where to go next," Ruby hurries to supply. "To be honest, it feels like we've sort of exhausted our options."

"You're telling me," remarks Josie. "Try spending three days going to nothing but faculty meetings. It's enough to drive a person insane."

I exchange a look with Silas before turning back to her. "Josie," I say tentatively, "can you tell us anything about what the faculty thinks? About this whole conference?"

The recruiter gives me a long look. "Are you asking on the record, or off the record?"

"Off," I reply without hesitation. "It seems like not much progress is being made."

"I..." She hesitates, a flicker of doubt passing through her eyes. "To be honest, I really can't say. It sounds like something's been put to the board, but they're deadlocked right now. A lot like the politicians, now that I think about it."

I don't need to ask what it is that's been suggested to the board. "What do you think is going to happen?"

Josie just gives us a sad smile. "That's getting into dangerous territory, Ms. Brix." There's a long pause, and it seems as if she's getting ready to say something else, but then decides against it. "You all had better get inside," she says at last. "They're going to want us to do a headcount before too long."

"Understood," Hunter says, giving her a stiff nod before turning to the rest of us. "Shall we?"

We give him a reluctant nod and begin to follow Josie in through the front doors. She frowns when we reach them, an odd look passing over her face. "That's odd," she remarks, her brow furrowing.

"What is?" I ask, coming to a stop beside her.

"There's usually a security guard right here," Josie replies, peering in through the entrance doors. "And where is everybody? The whole floor looks empty."

I can feel the buzz of adrenaline beginning to pulse through my veins, some primal part of my brain sending up warning signals. Something is wrong; Josie senses it, and so do I. I glance back at the others, who have tensed up, and are watching the building with guarded looks. For a long moment, no one says anything, and I realise how thick the silence is in the entrance hall of the convention center. A second ticks by, and then another, and an instant later, Josie's eyes are going black, her skin turning red as she whirls around on her feet, her expression frantic.

"Josie...?" I prompt, eyes wide.

"Run," she says, and moments later, an explosion rocks the building with a shock wave strong enough to knock us all off our feet as the convention center is consumed by fire.

CHAPTER 43

I t feels like everything is moving in slow motion. I can see the ground racing up to meet me, slamming to the floor hard enough to knock the wind right out of my lungs, leaving me gasping for breath. The air goes out of the building at once with a whooshing sound, a shock wave shattering the glass of the windows and sending sharp fragments flying. I suddenly feel a presence over me, and crane my neck to see Hunter covering me with his body, shielding me from the flying glass. His fangs are out, although whether he's even aware of it, I can't say. He seems to have transformed the rest of the way, too, as the high speed glass shards bounce off of him like he's made of steel. I guess the adrenaline must have let him access his powers, and I can't help but feel a smidge of pride in spite of our situation.

The shock wave dissipates, leaving us in the midst of what might as well be Armageddon: fires lick up and down the walls all around us, and panicked students, teachers, and assembly guests run around like chickens with their heads cut off. Some of them are using their powers, others are cowering in corners, and some are making a break for the exits, pouring out of the conference rooms and auditoriums in a stampede. Hunter gets off me then, and I feel a pang of regret at not having his protective presence guarding me anymore; he seems embarrassed as he gets to his feet. "Er... sorry," he says, holding a hand out to me to help me up.

"You shifted," I tell him, aware that I should have other priorities but unable to keep from pointing it out.

"I did?" His eyes go wide and he stares disbelievingly down at himself. "I'll be damned. I wasn't even thinking about it. I just..." He looks away, sheepish. "I wanted to keep you from getting hit."

"Thank you," I tell him, my hand lingering in his for just a moment before we pull apart, looking around at the others. They're all struggling to get to their feet; Xander is helping Hazel up, a concerned expression on his face, while Ruby has already shifted into her dragon form: a deep scarlet red with vibrant green eyes. Shade and Landon have already gotten up, and are both halfway transformed already, while Silas, in spite of the look of concentration on his face, is still struggling to shift, still not having fully recovered from the Academy's experiments.

"What the fuck is going on?" Shade yells to Josie, who's already moving forward, rushing to herd the panicked students out the door.

"I have no idea," she replies, not looking back. "We-"

But she's cut off by the sound of screams coming from the other end of the hallway. I whip my head around to see what looks like a fight breaking out amidst the fire: students are still desperately trying to escape, but a group of armed humans has emerged from one of the back rooms. They're dressed in combat gear, armed to the teeth, locked in battle with the amateur shifters as magic, fire, and smaller shock waves fly through the air, alongside bullets. I don't recognise any of the humans as either politicians or security guards, and there's something in their eyes that has a cold jolt of fear running through me: hatred. Pure, unadulterated *hatred*. And whoever these people are, they've turned it on us.

"Get out of here!" Josie calls over her shoulder. She's already deep in concentration, her hands up as she pushes a wave of psychic energy forward from her body; it slams into a couple of oncoming attackers, sending them flying back, but that doesn't seem to deter them for long. They scramble to their feet and charge forward again, armed with knives and baseball bats. "Go! Get back to the Academy where it's safe!"

"Like hell!" I yell back, digging for my shifter magic. It's mostly students here, and their skill levels vary, but most of them are like us: amateurs. And these humans know it.

Frantically, I look around. I don't see any other faculty fellows or professors; they must be on the upper floors. Reaching deep, I close my eyes for a moment, summoning the first form that comes to mind: my witch form. My body begins to buzz with magic, my skin taking on a red hue as my powers come to me and I move to stand between Silas and Hazel, who are now in their forms as well. "We need to help her hold them off!" I yell at them.

"You don't need to tell me twice," Silas replies, flapping his reptilian wings and launching off the ground before unleashing a spray of fire down onto a couple of the humans. It seems to deter them for a moment, but I realise with a sinking feeling that the clothes they're wearing seem to be fireproof; in an instant, the flames vanish, leaving them no worse for wear than they were before.

They planned *this,* I think, my eyes going wide.

"Move!" yells Shade, charging at one of the attackers in his wolf form. The man swings his baseball bat, but the wolf shifter knocks it out of the way, pinning him to the ground as he begins to rip at him with his teeth. I see Xander following suit out of the corner of my eye, tackling another human with his fangs bared. Ruby flies over to where Landon is standing, slamming a couple of the attackers with her wings; she must have seen that fire isn't going to work on these guys.

Landon and Hunter rush forward, the siren shifter fixated on a couple of female humans as he lets out his grating scream while Hunter barrels into one of the others, knocking him off his feet. All around us, students and conference attendees are rushing for the doors, creating a bottleneck in their desperation to get away from the chaos.

"You need to go!" Josie screams at us, still weaving spells to hold off the next wave of attackers. I fall in beside her, raising my arms and letting loose a chaotic golden bolt of energy; I haven't really gotten the hang of casting spells in witch form yet, and all I really know how to do is aim wildly and unleash, but whatever I do sends a couple of the humans flying. I grin with triumph only to feel something slam into me from my right, knocking me to the ground and breaking my concentration. Terrified, I snap back into human form as I grapple with a human woman in a kevlar vest. She has a knife and a look of wild agitation on her face; I struggle to keep it from connecting with my throat even as I desperately try to concentrate on returning to one of my shifter forms, but it's impossible to multitask, and she's a lot stronger than I am.

"Millie!" yells Landon, turning to me, but Josie is faster, whirling around and extending a hand. The woman is lifted off of me telekinetically before the witch launches her into the far windows, sending her crashing through the glass. I scramble to my feet, shooting her a grateful look. She turned around to save me, and that was exactly the opening the humans needed.

I watch in horror as one of the attackers pulls the pin out of a grenade and hurls it at the ceiling; as soon as it connects with the tiles, the whole roof gives out, sending chunks of concrete and mortar raining down on us from above. Landon yanks me away at the last second as I stand there gaping, letting out a strangled cry as more guests - along with a giant piece of the ceiling - come crashing down on Josie, burying her in the rubble. "No!" I yell, my eyes wide, and I struggle out of Landon's grip to rush forward, trying to get at the faculty fellow.

"Boots, we have to go!" yells Shade, grabbing me by the wrist. He's back in human form, looking uncharacteristically scared as he pulls me back.

"We can't just leave her!" I yell.

"We have to! This whole place is collapsing!"

Looking up, I see that he's right; the second explosion seems to have destabilised the upper floors, and the building lets out a low groaning noise as the pillars supporting the floor begin to give out. The convention center is falling down on top of us, and if we don't get out, we're going to end up buried. I glance at the others; they're making for the doors, beckoning to me, and with a sinking feeling I realise that it's now or never. I give one last, regretful glance to the pile of rubble where Josie is before following Shade, tears streaming down my face from the smoke and the trauma as we race for the exit. With one last sprint, we force ourselves out the door, running faster than we ever have out into the courtyard and towards the street. All around the convention center, bystanders are staring with their hands to their mouths, and in the distance I can hear police sirens and fire engines.

We've barely even made it to the curb when a great, thundering rumble emits from the building. I turn around just in time to see it give a last shudder before the whole convention center collapses in a heap of rubble. All any of us can do is stare in horror.

I FEEL numb as I sit at the kitchen table back in our suite, my head in my hands. I'm filthy, still in my torn and rumpled uniform. Some of the others have showered and changed, but I can't bring myself to do anything other than stare into the distance, the tears on my face stinging my eyes along with the coating of dirt and grime. Hazel and the twins have gone back to their room to clean up, leaving me and the guys in our suite, trying to process what happened.

None of us says anything; we're all standing around the common area, listening to the broadcast on the TV.

"...Tragedy struck this morning when an occult convention being held in downtown Boston was attacked in what authorities are calling a terrorist bombing. The current death toll is around 79, including several faculty members of a nearby boarding school, as well as six international business-men. The conference, which was advertised as a "by invitation only gathering of supernatural enthusiasts from around the world", was the first of its kind, and has been surrounded in secrecy ever since its announcement. Authorities have not released a motive, and no known group has yet taken responsibility for the attack. The story is unfolding."

Landon shakes his head and mutes the TV. "This is unreal."

None of the others speak immediately, until finally Silas asks, "Does anyone know if Josie made it out?"

Shade snorts dryly. "You think she would've? The whole ceiling came down on her."

"Hey," Hunter snaps, glaring at the wolf shifter, "don't talk like that."

"What? I'm just being realistic!"

"You're not helping."

"Guys, stop," I tell them weakly, lifting my head with great effort. They all turn to look at me, and I can feel fresh tears welling up in my eyes. "She got buried saving me," I murmur, my voice barely above a whisper.

"Boots," Silas says, moving over to me, "that wasn't your fault."

"Oh, it wasn't?" I turn to stare at him incredulously. "I lost my form. If I'd been able to hold it, she'd still be alive right now."

"You don't know that." But there's doubt in his eyes.

I can feel myself getting choked up, and I squeeze my eyes shut, shaking my head. "This feels like a bad dream."

"Well, what the fuck *was* that?" Landon asks. "They were humans, that was for sure. Some kind of extremist group?"

"It has to be," replies Hunter. "This is what we get for publicising the conference. I guess we should have known it was going to happen."

"But why?" I ask, running a hand through my hair. "I mean, I thought the point of all this was to find a peaceful solution."

"I guess the humans didn't get that message," Shade remarks.

We all look up at the sound of a knock on the door, and Silas gets up to answer it. Standing behind it are two men dressed in the uniform of the American Academy; their eyes are dark and their expressions serious. "Is everything all right?" Silas asks.

The two men look at each other. "As a matter of fact, it's not," the first one says, before nodding to the other. "Count them. Make sure they're all here."

"Wait a minute-" begins Landon, but the men are already forcing their way inside, taking note of all of us, watching them incredulously.

The second man nods after a moment. "Yes," he says. "They're all here."

"Excellent," says the first. "We're on first watch."

"What the hell is going on?" Shade demands, crossing his arms. "What are you guys doing in our room?"

The second man turns to him. "The five of you are being restricted to your dorm until further notice. Effective immediately, on orders of President Hawthorne."

CHAPTER 44

For a moment, all any of us can do is stare at them. Shade is the first one to speak up. "What the fuck do you mean, on orders of President Hawthorne?!"

"Yeah," Silas adds, taking a step closer to them, "what the hell is going on? What about the rest of the Academy students? And why does it matter if we're in our rooms or not?"

The two men look at each other, and I can see the wheels turning in their heads; I know that look—it's a look that says they're debating whether to tell us the truth or not. These aren't the decision-makers, they're the cronies, and that doesn't bode well for us. These orders came from the top, and I suspect, if the American Academy is involved, that Hawthorne wasn't the only one giving them out.

The first man sighs, running a hand through his hair. "Listen," he says, "it's really not our place to discuss this."

"Like hell it's not," Landon pipes up. "If we're being put on lock-down again, it had better be for a good reason. Is the school in danger? Is that it? Do they think another attack like the one that happened at the convention center is going to happen here?"

"There... *is* a possibility," admits the second man. "This sort of thing has never happened before, not with so many shifters in one place."

"So it *was* an extremist group, then," Landon confirms, crossing his arms. "That's just great."

The second man nods grimly. "The humans are lashing out. Somebody in the know organized this. We can't say more—we don't really even *know* more, to be honest, other than the fact that-"

But the first man elbows him, shutting him up. "Confidential," he hisses, and Hunter and I look at each other.

"Well, what about the other students here?" I ask, stepping forward. "The kids across the hall - Hazel, Ruby, and Xander. Can we see them? Wouldn't it be enough to just restrict us to the school grounds?"

"That's not possible," the first man replies.

"Why not?"

He heaves a sigh, exchanging another glance with his partner. "There *is* a schoolwide lockdown in place, that's correct," he replies. "The witches already have plans in place to expedite travel back to the U.K. campus. That doesn't apply to you five, however."

I could swear I feel my heart stop in my chest. Now isn't the time for us to be getting "special treatment" from the Academy, especially in the aftermath of what we overheard being discussed by the school board. "Why?" I ask in a weak voice. "Are we in trouble or something?" I'm not even sure why I bother to ask the question; some part of me deep down already knows the answer, and one look at the other guys is enough to tell me they do, too.

"It's not that," the second man, clearly the more sympathetic of the two replies. "You've been... selected. All five of you. In the aftermath of the attack, the school board called an emergency vote—they've decided that drastic measures are necessary in light of what happened at the convention center."

"The experiments," Silas murmurs, his voice barely above a whisper. "They're going to restart the experiments again. That's why you're isolating us. That's why you're sending the others home, but not us. We're not on lockdown - we're *prisoners*." It's not a question, and the looks on the men's faces are enough to confirm as much.

"I'm sorry," says the second man. "Really. We don't like doing this, but the decision has already been made. The five of you are to remain here until arrangements can be made to take you to a special testing facility."

"What? No!" Hunter cried, pushing forward. "This isn't legal! My dad is a board member. If he knew about this, he wouldn't-"

"I'm afraid your father was out-voted," replies the first man coolly. "This is an urgent situation, and it sure as hell isn't normal. We're under orders to make sure the five of you are transported securely without causing a disturbance to the rest of the students. We're going to be stationed outside your room, and we would strongly advise you not to make a scene. This will be much easier for all of us if we can-"

"Bullshit," exclaims Shade. "You can't just trap us here! We'll fight our way out if we have to. There's no way in hell I'm going to let you use us as guinea pigs."

The first man gives a heavy sigh, as if he was expecting this, and moments later, he's pulling something out of his pocket—it looks like a normal stone from a distance, but when he places it on the floor, it begins to glow, a rune-like shape carved into its surface lighting it up with a red glow. "I'm really sorry that we have to do this," he says, "but believe me, this is for your own good - and the good of the shifter community."

"What the hell is that?" I demand, pointing at the stone on the floor.

Hunter groans. "I've seen one of these before. It's a charm - probably enchanted by a witch, if I had to guess."

"You would be correct," says the first man. "It's a ward, and it's been charmed to keep the five of you from accessing your shifter abilities."

"Are you serious?!" Landon demands. "This is insanity!"

"A violent reaction isn't something the Academy wants to risk," the second man explains. "We're sorry, but this is the only way to keep the situation from getting out of hand. Please don't touch the rune; it will only hurt you if you try to destroy it. As soon as you've all been safely brought to the testing facility, we'll have it deactivated by one of the resident witches."

"Fuck you!" yells Shade, lunging forward, and I can see he's trying to access his form, but it's no use; the stone gives out a pulse of red light, and in spite of his best efforts, nothing happens. The wolf shifter stares down at his hands in disbelief, his grey eyes wide, before leveling an angry, betrayed gaze at the newcomers.

"Someone will be by shortly to bring you your dinner," the first man says, his tone businesslike and his expression verging on smug. "I would advise you all to save your energy; you'll probably need it for what's coming." He nods at the second man, who shoots us a regretful look over his shoulder, and then the two men make their way down the hall and to the door. I hear the sound of it opening and closing, followed by the muffled noise of their conversation resuming once they're outside. They're settling down in the hallway, guards for a dorm room that has now become a jail cell.

"This is fucked up," Landon mutters, kicking a chair and rubbing a hand across his forehead. "This is *so* fucked up."

"You're telling me," Silas replies dryly. "I'm only just now getting my dragon form back, and they're about to ship us off to have our powers drained. Again."

"They're sure as hell *not*," snaps Shade. "I'm getting out of here. I'm not about to let them turn me into a test subject."

"Good luck with that," Hunter replies, snorting. "How are you going to leave, exactly? We've got to be more than fifty feet up. You couldn't make that drop if you tried."

"It has to be better than getting tortured to death in a lab some-where," the wolf shifter fires back.

I slump into a chair, feeling like the world is collapsing around me. Is this how it's going to end, with us waiting to get carted away to some underground bunker, never to see the light of day again? The thought of it is enough to bring tears to my eyes, and I wipe them feverishly with my sleeve, ashamed of myself. It's all too much, and some half-mad part of me wonders if maybe Shade has a point, if I shouldn't just throw myself off the balcony and hope for the best? At least then Hawthorne wouldn't have the satisfaction of knowing he got the best of me, got the best of *us*. At least then they wouldn't be able to use me to hurt anymore shifters. But even as I think about it, I know I can't do it; I don't have it in me, and in spite of his bravado, I'm pretty sure Shade doesn't have it in him, either.

"I can't believe the board voted in favour of this," Hunter mutters, running a hand through his hair. "Why the hell would they do that? I know the politicians are human, but the school board is mostly shifters. Why would they just sign away our rights like that?"

"They probably felt like they didn't have a choice," Silas replies, sighing. "If humans were willing to destroy a convention center full of innocent people, then they sure as hell won't have any qualms with coming after the Academy, if it comes to that. They probably figure this is the only compromise that won't lead to even more death."

"That's such bullshit," Shade mutters. He has his arms crossed over his chest and is pacing back and forth by the windows. "The whole point of this damn conference in the first place was figuring out a way to put a stop to this *without* more people getting hurt."

"Yeah," Landon agrees, "but that was before a bunch of military types attacked us point-blank. They're scared—we *all* are."

"So what now, then?" Hunter asks, sitting back in his chair. "We can't just wait for them to come take us, can we?"

"What choice do we have?" Landon demands. I watch as he rolls his shoulders, closes his eyes, and tries desperately to get into his siren form, but nothing happens, even as he strains. The stone on the floor flares a bright red, and when Silas moves to pick it up, he lunges away from it, cradling his hand and letting out a hiss.

"Are you okay?" I ask, eyes wide.

"It *burns*," he replies, examining his hand. "It's like it knows who we are."

"Damn it," I mutter, putting my head in my hands. I can feel the tears coming, and I'm hopeless to stop them. As much as I don't want to look weak in front of the others, I can't help it. Here I was, finally having found a place—a *family*—and now the same people who made me what I am are trying to take it all away from me. Slowly, I raise my head and look around at the faces assembled in the dorm room: Silas, Landon, Shade, and Hunter, these guys I've come to know so quickly, so *honestly,* in spite of everything that makes us different. We're the same, in the end, we're on the same side, and I...

I love them; I realise with a start. The revelation is so sudden and so strong that it's nearly enough to knock me out of my seat, my eyes going wide and a warmth flooding my chest. *Holy shit, I actually* love *them. Not like, but* love.

It feels so simple, and yet so powerful. Maybe it's a truth I've known for a long time, but been afraid to admit to myself. But now, in the face of torture and death, in the face of losing these guys to Hawthorne's treachery, it's become as unavoidable as it is magnificent. It doesn't matter that I feel this way about all of them. It doesn't matter that our connection comes from an unethical experiment. It doesn't matter what the future holds.

I love them, and no matter what Hawthorne might have to say about it, no matter what ugly ways he has of trying to bend us to his will, I'm not going to lose them. Not now.

CHAPTER 45

I sit in silence, the wheels in my head turning, as the others continue to debate our current situation. I feel strangely calm all of a sudden, like the newfound revelation has brought with it a sense of security I didn't even know I was missing until just now. I have to remind myself that we're not out of the woods yet; nothing has *actually* changed and now isn't the time to get complacent. It's one thing to promise yourself you're going to do something, and it's another entirely to actually do it.

"So what do we do, then?" Hunter asks, crossing his arms. "I'm not about to just sit here and wait for them to come take me away." None of the guys seem to have noticed my sudden change in demeanor, which is fine by me; there will be time to talk about our relationship - to talk about everything - but that time isn't now.

"All right," Silas says, running a hand through his brown hair, "we need to think. We can't use our powers to get out, so what *can* we do?"

"Maybe we should just bite the bullet," Shade suggests. "We can just pick the damn thing out and chuck it out the window. Hope for the best."

"Forgive me for not wanting to touch that thing," Landon replies. "For all we know, holding onto it for that long will kill us."

"Okay, fine," Shade says. "Let's go out on the balcony and pretend we're going to jump. I say, they want to run tests on us, we might as well make them work for it."

"And what the hell is that going to accomplish?" Hunter asked, exasperated. "Other than making them *more* pissed off at us."

"Listen, I'm open to suggestions here," Shade snapped. "I don't hear *you guys* getting any bright ideas."

"What about Hazel and the twins?" I ask, lifting my head. The others turn to look at me as if they've forgotten that I'm here. "I mean, they're in the next room over. Maybe they can get us out of here."

"I don't like their odds, even if it would be three against one," Silas admits. "I don't like *any* of our odds against those guards, actually. We're students, and they're not. They have the upper hand. Besides, for all we know, the Academy has already moved them out. They're trying to isolate us, and so far, it's working."

"All right," I say, sighing and putting a hand up. "You have a point. We can't depend on them breaking us out, so we're going to have to break ourselves out." I purse my lips, brow furrowing as I look around the room. There has to be a way out of this, there *has* to be... And then, in an instant, an idea comes to me. "Wait," I exclaim, standing up. "We don't *have* to use our powers!"

"What are you talking about?" Hunter asks incredulously. "How are we supposed to beat them if we can't shapeshift?"

"We do it the old-fashioned way," I reply, giving him a crooked smile. "We fake an emergency, get them to come in here, and then we jump them. If we can hit them with something, knock them out..."

"That's... not a bad idea, actually," Landon admits, crossing his arms. "We just need long enough to get out of range of that charm. Then we can find Hazel and the others and high-tail it the hell out of here."

"Exactly," I agree, nodding. "It's not the best plan, but we can't afford to be picky right now."

"All right, then," Silas says, beginning to pace. "Landon and I can wait on either side of the door. Boots, if you can come up with a way to lure them in here..."

"Are you sure Millie should do that?" Hunter asks, glancing at me. "I mean, we can't afford to let you get hurt."

"It's fine," I tell him, squaring my shoulders. "I'm willing to bet they're under orders not to let any of us get hurt. They can't have their prized lab rats getting damaged. So are we doing this, then?" I ask, getting to my feet and putting my hands on my waist.

"It's not like we have much of a choice," Shade replies.

The others murmur their agreement, and moments later, the guys are assembled on either side of the door. They've grabbed what makeshift weapons they can find - Silas is holding a chair while Shade and Landon have kitchen knives, and Hunter has armed himself with the coffee pot - and are watching me tensely as I steel myself. I give the others one last glance as I move to stand in the front hallway; they nod to me, signaling that they're ready.

Time to put those improv skills to use, I think dryly, before I let out what I hope is a convincing moan of pain. There's a long silence, and nothing from the other side of the door, so I do it again, louder this time, stumbling to the ground for added effect. "Hey..." I call weakly. "I don't feel so good!" Low voices can be heard outside, but I can't make out what they're saying. "There's something wrong with me," I insist, practically yelling now. "It's this fucking charm you guys put on the floor! I'm not even touching it!"

There's another pause as we wait with bated breaths for them to respond. "What the fuck is she talking about?" one of the guards mutters to the other.

"I have no idea," comes the reply. "She's probably faking it."

"I'm serious!" I protest, letting out a choked groan. There's no such thing as melodrama in a situation like this. "What the hell are you doing to me?! Did Hawthorne put you up to this - torture the hybrid to make sure I'm weak? Is that it?"

"Listen, kid," begins the first guard, "I don't know what you're going on about, but-"

"For fuck's sake!" Shade yells, sounding surprisingly genuine. "She's dying in here! Do you really want your prized pet showing up at the lab coughing up blood?"

"Blood?" The second guard sounds concerned. "You never said there would be-"

"There shouldn't be," the first guard snaps. "Probably something wrong with her powers. Fucking hybrids, I swear. They never tell me anything around here..."

There's the sound of movement and then fumbling with the door-knob. I can see the others tensing up, and a bead of sweat runs down the back of my neck. We'll only get one chance at this. One wrong move and it will all be over. I can hear the lock being undone, can see the knob twisting - we're seconds away now, split seconds...

But before the door can even open, the sound of a blast echoes down the hallway, sending my heart rate flying. I scramble to my feet, glancing at the others, who haven't even moved yet. My first reaction is panic—are the humans attacking again? Have they really gotten that bold as to try something at one of the Shifter Academies? How are we supposed to fight them with no powers? I open my mouth to cry out as the sound of grunts and scuffling can be heard from the other side of the door, followed by another blasting sound and a yell of pain. Fuck. We're in trouble now. I'm on the verge of telling the others to run for it and hope for the best, but then every-thing goes quiet out in the hallway. It was like an earthquake—intense and loud, but over in seconds. I'm left to exchange a confused glance with Silas, who can only shrug his shoulders in wonderment. Slowly, I straighten up and creep down the hallway, coming to a stop by the door. I can hear heavy breathing, and there's a shadow under the door; someone is out there. The only question is, who?

A tense moment follows, and then another, the sound of my heartbeat loud to my own ears. And then, as if in a dream, a familiar voice comes from the other side, a voice I was already convinced I wasn't going to hear again. "Hello? Millie? It's me, Josie!"

"Josie?" I hiss, hardly daring to believe it. "What the hell? What are you doing here?"

"I came to get you out of here," she replies, her voice barely above a whisper. "Can I come in?"

"Uh..." I glance over my shoulder at the guys, who are watching me with shocked expressions on their faces.

"Be careful," Landon warns. "It could be a trap."

"I say let her in," Shade counters. "If she tries anything, we'll kick her ass."

"I can assure you, that won't be necessary," Josie responds. "I'm here to help you. All of you."

"I... Okay," I reply at last. "Give me a second. I'm going to open the door." Moving slowly, as if one wrong move will set off another explosion, I take a step back and pull the door open, bracing myself for some kind of trick - a hostage situation, maybe, or an imposter posing as the deceased school recruiter. It's more astonishing than I can express when I find myself standing face-to-face with Josie herself. She's looking decidedly worse for wear; there's a nasty gash on the side of her face, and she's battered and bruised, a far cry from the elegant woman who first found me in that abandoned warehouse. But she's *here,* and very much alive; before I even realise what I'm doing, I'm rushing forward and flinging my arms around her, pulling her close. "You're okay!" I cry.

"I am," she says, grunting a little. "Although I broke a couple ribs back there, so..."

"Oh. Right. Sorry." I let her go. "It's just... you're a sight for sore eyes. That's all."

"Well, don't speak too soon," she replies as I close the door and she makes her way into the common area. "Gentlemen," she says, nodding to the assembled guys, who look like they've seen a ghost. "It's good to see you all in one piece."

"We should be saying that to you," Silas replies. "We saw you get buried back at the convention center! How the hell did you make it out of that?"

"You of all people should know how sturdy these shifter forms can be, Mr. Aconite," Josie responds. "You've survived a lot worse than a bit of falling rubble. If you must know, though, protection spells are sort of a specialty of mine. More so than teleportation, even."

"What are you doing here?" Shade asks, crossing his arms, ever suspicious. "It seems awfully convenient that you just happen to show up and take out those guards right when we're trying to get out of here."

"I understand your concerns," Josie replies, "but for what it's worth. It wasn't a coincidence. I spent the last half hour waiting for those guys to get up and leave. You gave me the perfect opening."

"Why, though?" Landon asks. "I mean, I'm not complaining, but still... I thought the Academy was on orders to resume the experiments."

"That's exactly the problem," Jodie responds. "I'm afraid that the school board has lost control of themselves. Things are going downhill, fast." Her expression hardens, and she turns to face the rest of us. "I'm not Samantha," she says, sounding like she's trying to convince herself as much as the rest of us. "I don't care what Hawthorne says— I'm not about to just stand by and let him take advantage of the students here. If that means risking the wrath of the board, then so be it. But we can discuss all that later," she adds, putting her hands on her hips and focusing on me. "We have more important things to worry about right now. Ms. Brix, how would you like to find your friends and leave this place?"

"That would be really nice, Josie," I tell her, relief washing over me.

"Good," she says, turning to the charm that still sits on the dorm room floor. "Let's start with this, then. I've always hated these things."

CHAPTER 46

It's eerily quiet in the hallway when we finally creep out of the dorm, one by one, on edge with wide eyes. The first thing I notice is the two guards, seated on either side of the door, and when I see that their eyes are open and staring, I jump. "It's okay," Josie murmurs, putting a hand on my shoulder. "I paralysed them. It should wear off in an hour or so, which is plenty of time for us to high-tail it out of here."

"When can I learn to do that?" I ask dryly, stepping around the two men with the others following closely behind. I come to a stop outside the opposite door, which is closed and locked, turning back to the others. "Hazel and the twins are in here," I say. "We just need to figure out a way to get their attention, and then-"

But Josie is already shaking her head. "Don't bother. They've already been taken downstairs. Hawthorne wants your friends and acquaintances out of here first - we're going to need to go intercept them before they can teleport back to the island."

"Why is he doing this?" Hunter asks as we make our way down the hall. "It all feels so... so..."

"Calculated?" Josie supplies, her expression grim. "That's what I thought, too. I don't want to jump to conclusions, but I'm afraid that maybe Hawthorne..." She bites her lip and trails off. "Never mind."

"What?" asks Silas as we reach the top of the stairs. No one is out and about, which is just as well; a ragtag group of shifters led by a battered-looking witch would attract attention that we can't afford right now. "What do you think Hawthorne is doing?"

Josie sighs, turning to look at him, and for the first time I notice how much of a toll the last day has taken on her - she looks utterly exhausted, and this is far from being over. "I think Hawthorne may have orchestrated the attack on the convention center," she says at last.

My hand flies to my mouth, and the others come to a sudden stop. "You... You think he would go that far?" I ask, not wanting to hear the answer, even though deep down I know it already.

"Again, I have no proof," Josie tells us. "I can only go on what was being said in the board meeting. The others weren't amenable enough to get him what he wanted. So..." She shrugs her shoulders. "Was it just a coincidence? Maybe. But I'll tell you one thing: that attack was planned and organized. This wasn't just some random pro-human riot. They would have needed inside information, equipment... And this was exactly the push the board needed to resume the experiments. They're backed into a corner, and they're panicking."

"I can't believe this," Hunter mutters, running a hand through his hair.

"*I* can," Shade shoots back. "It was only a matter of time before he went completely insane."

"Come on," Josie says, turning back around as we begin to descend the stairs. "We don't have much time."

I take the opportunity to reconnect with my shifter magic, which was almost unbearably dampened by the charm. In hindsight, it was almost too lucky that Josie was the one to come get us; because it had been enchanted by witch magic, only a witch could have undone the spell, and I'm sure as hell not a good enough shifter to even begin to reverse that kind of magic. I'm only just now beginning to come to terms with the fact that if we leave, it could be the end of my time spent studying—possibly for good.

Am I capable of mastering my forms without the help of my teachers?

I'm going to have to be, I tell myself grimly as we reach the downstairs landing. *There's no other option.*

The common area is blessedly empty, although perhaps that's not a good thing; the dormitory seems eerily devoid of students in spite of the relatively early hour. The faculty is most likely already trying to move the U.K. students back to the island where they will be inaccessible to the rest of us. They're not in for a fun time, either, and I feel a sinking sensation in the pit of my stomach when I realise that they're being pulled into this too, whether they like it or not. If we make it out of here, the Academy will start testing on the general student population again, like they did with Silas and that kid Brody. If we leave, we're signing them up to be next in line, but what choice do we have? Letting them take us will just expedite the process, and no matter what Hawthorne claims, giving a bunch of trigger-happy humans shifter abilities will make things worse, not better. There has to be a way out of this that doesn't involve upsetting the balance of the whole world... doesn't there?

We've just made it out to the sculpture garden when Josie stops dead in her tracks; looking up, I can feel my heart pounding in my chest when I see Lyle standing a short distance away, his arms crossed over his chest. "What do we have here?" he asks, taking a few steps forward. "I thought students were restricted to their dorms."

"I could say the same to you," I fire back. "What are you doing out here?"

"If you have to know," Lyle replies, "I'm under orders to make sure nobody wanders outside without express permission from President Russo."

"I guess we're in luck then," Josie says, "because I'm one of the faculty fellows for the U.K. Academy. I'm bringing these five to the -"

"You really expect me to buy that?" Lyle demands, scoffing. "I was warned about you. The board sent me here to make sure you didn't try anything while they're taking care of your friends."

Hunter's eyes widen. "You mean Hazel? Are they taking her away right now?"

Josie moves forward, glaring down at Lyle. "Listen, kid," she says, "I don't know what kind of instructions you've been given, but *I'm* under strict orders to get these students out to the main building in time for the first group to be transported, and you're in my way."

"Bullshit," Lyle replies without missing a beat. "Russo would've let me know. You know what I think?" he continues, giving Josie a menacing look. "I think you're having a crisis of conscience, and you're trying to fuck with the board's plans. I've got news for you: it's not going to happen."

Landon snorts, shaking his head. "You really are a piece of work, Lyle. Do you know that?"

Lyle just smirks. "So I've been told. You're not going anywhere."

"He's stalling us," Silas says, sounding panicked. "They're probably taking Hazel and the twins away right now!"

"How observant," Lyle mutters.

"I say we just go through him," Shade snaps. "We don't have time for this shit."

"You can certainly try," Lyle replied, and in an instant, he's shifted into his vampire form, his eyes glowing red, his face twisted with hate. "And don't bother trying your little lullaby again, Brix," he adds, turning his glare on me. "You're not going to get the jump on me this time."

"That's it," Shade mutters, rushing forward and transforming. He springs towards Lyle, but the vampire is stronger, and he knocks the wolf out of the air like he's nothing.

"Shade!" I yell, running to his side.

"I'm fine," he growls. "Worry about Lyle!"

I look up to see Josie already transformed, her brow furrowed in concentration as she works a spell, but she's flagging, and we can all see it; between her injuries and the magic she used to break us out, she's running on empty. Silas is standing beside her, struggling to get into his dragon form, but he's not back to a hundred percent either, and it's just the opening that Lyle needs. Striding forward, he picks

Josie up by the neck and lifts her into the air, squeezing hard enough to make her gasp and sputter. Her focus broken, she snaps back into human form, clawing desperately at his hands.

I close my eyes and summon my magic, struggling to concentrate, but before I'm even able to transform, there's a sudden movement to my left, as quick as a gust of wind. Opening my eyes, I see Hunter charging forward, transformed into his vampire form, his eyes blazing and his fangs bared. It's something to behold, especially considering how much trouble he had before, and Lyle seems taken aback. A split second later, he's dropping Josie to the ground as Hunter knocks him down, the two vampires clashing in a battle of supernatural strength and speed.

Landon helps Josie to her feet as I help Shade, who lunges forward again, ready to continue the fight, but Hunter yells out to stop him. "Go!" he cries. "We don't have time!"

"What about you?" I ask, frozen with fear.

Hunter glances over his shoulder, and for a brief moment, his eyes, now red, meet mine. "I've got this, Boots," he says, and something in his tone makes me believe him. "Go rescue Hazel!"

The rest of us don't need telling twice. "Come on," Josie says, gritting her teeth and beginning to run. The rest of us follow suit, although I can't help but pause to take one last look at Hunter, who is grappling with Lyle as if his life depends on it. Sending up a silent prayer that he'll be okay, I follow the others out of the sculpture garden, skirting around the side of the administrative building. "They're doing the transports from the parking lot," Josie says, peering around the corner.

I follow her gaze and see that she's right; already, a cluster of about half a dozen students have assembled on the hill, alongside a couple of faculty members, who are busy doing headcounts and preparing their spells. Hazel is among them, along with Ruby and Xander, which surprises me; as American students, they shouldn't be sent back to the island, should they?

Of course they shouldn't, some cynical part of me thinks. *Hawthorne knows we're friends. It was never about the education - they want us separated, and that means getting the people we love as far away from us as possible. For all we know, they'll bring them back to the island, lock them up, and throw away the key until it's time to strap them to a lab table.*

"Do you recognise any of those faculty members?" Silas asks, coming to a stop alongside us.

"One of them is American," Josie replies. "The other is Myrtle Thorne; I've done a few jobs with her in the past. A fight will just draw attention, so we're going to have to talk our way out of this. Follow my lead, okay?"

We nod in agreement and trail behind her as she straightens up and heads down the path towards where the others are assembled. As we get closer, Hazel notices us and her eyes go wide; I give my head the slightest shake, and she seems to understand, not saying anything. "There you are," Josie says, really playing it up as the other faculty members turn to her. "I was worried we wouldn't get here in time."

"Josie?" The blonde woman on the left looks surprised. "What are you doing here? I thought you were-"

"Dead?" Josie shakes her head, giving a dry chuckle. "You're not the first one." Turning back to us, she continues, "There's been a change of plans. Hawthorne wants these students transported to a different facility, ASAP."

"Really?" The second woman frowns. "We haven't heard anything about a transfer."

"It's last minute," Josie replies. "Something about substandard testing equipment - the facilities at the Academy haven't been used in years."

The two women look at each other. "That's... odd," the blonde woman says.

"Of course it is," comes a new voice. I whirl around to see the man himself, President Hawthorne, coming over the rise of the hill, his hands in his pockets and a dangerous gleam in his eyes. He's flanked by two other faculty members I don't recognise, but they look ready for a fight. "That's because it's not true." He raises his eyebrows at

Josie. "Long time no see, Ms. Everhart. You're looking a little worse for wear."

"Hawthorne," Josie says, her eyes widening. "What are you doing out here?"

"I came to make sure the transport of these fine students goes smoothly, of course," Hawthorne replies, "and by the looks of it, it's not." He nods to the men flanking him. "If you would be so kind as to restrain Ms. Everhart, here, it would be greatly appreciated. It looks like the students aren't the only problem that needs to be addressed, here."

The men move forward; I tense up, and all of a sudden there's a great gust of wind; Silas has transformed, shooting up into the sky like a firecracker before letting loose a jet of fire that lights up the night air.

That one burst of magic is like a starter's pistol at a race, and in an instant, we've descended into chaos.

CHAPTER 47

Hawthorne's men are on us before I can even react, charging forward and changing in one swift movement. Suddenly they're both in dragon form, too, their great wings generating a large enough gust of wind to send us all stumbling back. Hawthorne hangs back, letting his henchmen do the dirty work, and I realise with horror that the two faculty fellows are shifting too, and they're not on our side: the blonde one shifts into a witch, while the other shifts into a wolf, and now all four of them are charging us. Silas lets out another burst of flame, which buys us a little more time as it forces the others back, and I see Landon and Shade shifting out of the corner of my eye. I summon my own power, calling to mind my witch form, and in a few seconds my skin is turning red as my body pulses with magical energy.

If only I knew more spells, I think, raising my hands, *but now isn't the time to be picky.* Trying to emulate the ease with which Josie uses her powers, I unleash a burst of telekinetic energy at the wolf shifter, who is already nearly on top of me. Shade takes advantage of the opening and jumps into action, tackling the other wolf as they tumble away in a blur of claws and fur. Landon, meanwhile, his scales shimmering in the moonlight, lets out a siren scream so powerful that it sends a shock wave up into the air, which collides with the dragons' most recent gust of wind, preventing it from knocking us over. I watch as Silas shoots across the sky, locking in close combat with one of the two dragons while I launch another blast of magic at the other. His scales are too hard for it to do much, but it *does* get his attention, which is more than enough for me. *Maybe if I could lead him away from the others...*

Quickly I begin to back up, nodding to Josie, who's doing her best to summon what remains of her magic. The dragon is hot on my tail, and I see that all around me, the other students are transforming, realising that these people aren't on our side, and they're out for blood. Hawthorne is watching gleefully from a distance, as if we're nothing more than a bunch of prized fighting dogs. The air crackles with heat as fire builds up in the mouth of the dragon pursuing me, and I get my hands up just in time to deflect it with a minor force field, nearly getting my hair singed in the process.

"Millie!" yells Hazel, who has already transformed and is standing shoulder to shoulder with Xander. "Get him to come this way!"

I don't bother to ask her why, and do as I'm told, sprinting over to them as fast as my legs will carry me. The dragon follows us, but realises what's happening an instant too late, as Hazel echoes Landon's siren song, this time in the form of a command: "Get Hawthorne!"

The dragon resists for a moment, thrashing in midair as it struggles against her magic, but Hazel is a powerful siren, and her brow is furrowed in concentration; a moment later, the dragon is changing course, turning around and making a beeline for the president. Hawthorne sees what's happening and dives out of the way just as the dragon sprays at him with fire, setting the grass ablaze under his feet. The other witch notices and summons a force field around him, shielding him just in time from another burst of fire. I curse under my breath, but I guess it was never going to be that easy.

It's pandemonium on the grounds, fire lighting up the night sky, as students and faculty clash in an impromptu battle. It's clear who the experienced ones are here, though, and in spite of our superior numbers, the adults have the upper hand when it comes to their power levels, and they're gaining on us. Hazel's command has already worn off, and the dragons are now flying in formation as they swoop down to claw at us with their sharp talons. Ruby collides with one of them in midair, knocking him off course, while Silas grapples with the other, more fire flying every which way as they let out grating screeches and roars.

Realising my witch form is too vulnerable, I scramble to shift into my vampire form, the sturdiest of the five shifter species, and feel a surge of renewed strength as I lunge for the witch shifter protecting Hawthorne. She fends me off with a pulse of magic of her own, but I manage to hold my ground, my heels digging in as I throw my new strength into my effort.

"Need a hand with that?" comes a familiar voice, and I turn to see Hunter moving to stand beside me. He's still in vampire form, and although I can see him fighting to keep his concentration, he seems to be holding steady so far.

"What about Lyle?" I ask as he leans in against the magical barrier with me.

"He started wearing me down," Hunter admits, his face set with determination. "I threw him off and made a break for it. He'll be here soon, though, and he'll have reinforcements."

"Then we need to get out of here," Shade growls from a few feet away. "They've got us on the ropes already."

"Go," Josie yells, her voice barely audible above the noise of the battle. "Get out of here before more show up!"

"What about you?" Silas demands, still suspended in the air.

"A couple more shifters won't stop me," she growls, sounding determined. "Besides," she adds with a grim smile, "I've had worse."

"Are you sure?" I ask, eyes wide. "What will they do to you?"

"Don't worry about me!" Josie unleashes another burst of magic, which forces the attacking wolf shifter to retreat a few steps. "Get as far away from here as possible. Tell the shifter leaders what's happening here. Make them put a stop to it." She grunts with the effort as one of the dragons descends on her again, narrowly dodging its fire breath. "Go!" she yells. "Now!"

We don't need telling twice. Shifting back into our human forms, Hunter and I make a beeline away from the battle, Hazel and Landon hot on our heels. Silas swoops down and picks up Shade with one claw and Hazel with the other, while Ruby grabs Xander and Landon. A blast of magic soars over my head, narrowly missing me, although it's not clear whether it came from someone on our side or theirs. It doesn't matter, though. Josie was right - the Academy has been compromised, and there's no going back now.

My heart races in my chest, my breathing coming in short gasps, as our ragtag group makes a mad dash away from the fight. In the distance, I can see lights in the school buildings coming on, and a group of more Academy faculty is charging out of the administration building, clearly having been tipped off by Lyle. I feel bad leaving the other students behind, but I have to believe that Josie will protect them, and we're no use to any of them dead. Everything is falling apart around us, and if Hawthorne has his way, none of us will make it out in time to spread the truth about the Academy. I'm not under any illusions that he's going to leave us alone after this; people will be after us—*powerful* people—and the time for talk is over. The time for action is now.

The sounds of fighting still in our ears, the eight of us make our escape, cresting the hill and disappearing into the night.

EPILOGUE

The underground is surprisingly crowded, even late at night, although maybe that's a good thing; at least this gives us a way of blending in, even if we *are* still dressed in our Academy uniforms. Quite a few people shoot us weird glances as we pile onto the train, and I can understand why - we look a mess, all covered in blood, dirt, and sweat... but we're alive. And we're still together.

It's not until I've taken a seat, Hunter on one side of me and Shade on the other, that I feel my phone vibrating in my pocket. My arm feels heavy and lethargic as I pull it out, almost afraid to see who's contacted me this time.

On the screen is a single text message from an unknown sender.

Come to London if you want to survive this, or he will make you watch them all die.

Continuing reading Millie's story in Demonic Vampires by clicking here.

DESCRIPTION

The Academy is chasing us and if we are found, none of us will get out of this alive.

After escaping the academy and the secrets they found out, Millie and her guys find themselves needing to make new alliances to survive in the human world. But trusting strangers has never been easy for Millie or her guys.

With a face from Millie's past coming back, tension building between Millie and the guys, everything just became a little more complicated. How can Millie protect herself when her heart is torn between more than one of her closest friends?

18+ REVERSE HAREM ROMANCE WHICH MEANS THE MAIN CHARACTER WILL HAVE MORE THAN ONE LOVE INTEREST. THIS IS BOOK THREE OF A FIVE-BOOK SERIES AND WILL BE RAPIDLY RELEASED.

CHAPTER 48

I've spent my life on the run.

It hasn't always been a conscious decision; in fact, a lot of the time, it's been a decision made for me by others. The result of outside circumstances falling on me and moving me around like a pawn in the giant chess game that is life. Hell, it's been happening since before I was even *aware* of it. First, my parents, running away from their responsibilities, running away from a future with their child. Handing me over to the people who would end up shaping my life in indescribable ways. Then there was me, moving from living situation to the next with no end in sight, no goal other than surviving another year on a path with no conceivable future. And once that situation became intolerable, I ran from the system itself, stumbling blindly into my fate like a kid running through a dark forest, and I'll be damned if I wasn't starting to get used to *not* running.

It was just starting to feel like a climax, like all the constant fleeing was finally coming to an end. Yes, I went from being an orphaned human to being a hybrid shifter, part of a secret supernatural community running parallel to the normal world. Yes, the life I knew was turned upside-down, replaced by one of magic, mayhem, and politics far above my ability to understand. And yes, there was a new danger in that, there were new unknowns... but I had a place. The Shifter Academy had felt like the last stop on a long and meandering journey with no destination. I was starting to build something for myself, a community - hell, more than a community, a *family*.

I guess that's the thing about life, though, isn't it? Every time you start to get used to one thing, something else turns up that throws it all out of whack again. There's no such thing as certainty, and I was a fool if I thought that a boarding school for shapeshifters would turn out to be anything but *uncertain*. So I guess I'm the fool in the end, right?

At least, that's what I tell myself when I come to an abrupt stop at the end of a dark alleyway somewhere in downtown Boston, in the United States, my clothes filthy and my eyes bloodshot. Blaming it on having too high expectations is a hell of a lot easier than confronting the fact that it feels like the whole world has turned on me and my friends, seemingly overnight. One such friend comes to a halt beside me, his brows furrowing over his black eyes as he glances around the alleyway, lips pursed. "What's wrong, Boots?" he asks, his eyes darting to me. His arms are full of a grocery bag - not much in the way of provisions, but considering we're both broke college students *and* fugitives, we're going to have to make do.

"Does this alleyway look familiar to you?" I ask with an uncertain look at my surroundings.

The dark-skinned siren shifter frowns. "Shit," he mutters. "Now that you mention it..."

I let out a frustrated groan. "We've been going in circles! Why does this city have to be so damn confusing?"

"For whatever it's worth," Landon replies, "these streets all look the same at night."

"That's exactly the problem," I protest, raking a hand through my chestnut hair as I put the other one on my waist. "How the hell are we supposed to get back to the bridge if we're lost in the middle of the... What the hell is this neighborhood even called?"

"Back Bay?" Landon supplies. "I think. We're by the university.

That's all I know. Remind me again why we're making a supply run at one in the morning?"

"You're asking the wrong person," I reply.

Landon snorts. "I mean, if they're so hellbent on finding us that they're willing to come after us in the middle of the night, then maybe we ought to just let them take us and get it over with."

"You don't mean that," I tell him.

"No," he replies, his shoulders dropping. "It felt good to say it, though. Let's head out to the boulevard," he suggests. "We can make a left this time."

I give him a short nod, and we start towards the other end of the alleyway. It was raining earlier, and the cobblestone streets are still glistening with water. The night is relatively quiet, punctuated by the occasional peal of drunken laughter or burst of music from a car stereo, but I've learned by now that quiet doesn't automatically mean safe.

It's only been two days -- or has it been three? -- since we fought our way out of the Boston Shifter Academy and made a break for it, but it already feels like we've been running for a lifetime. This isn't even *our* city; the U.K. Shifter Academy brought us here for a field trip, an academic experience that couldn't have gone more wrong if it had been planned that way.

Ostensibly, it was a conference to address the escalating tensions between shifters and humans, but if one thing has become clear to me since finding out I was a shifter, it's that nothing between humans and our kind is simple. Now, a terrorist attack, a few lies, and a brief spell under house arrest later, here we are, glancing over our shoulders to make sure Academy representatives aren't hot on our heels whenever we leave the rundown motel where we've been staying for the past two nights, courtesy of our new friends, Ruby and Xander.

Tonight is my and Landon's turn to venture out and get supplies, and as stir-crazy as I've been going cooped up inside with the others, the only thing worse is the uncertainty of venturing outside. As runaway shifters privy to information about the human-run Academy's plans, we have targets on our backs, and we know it well.

I'm so lost in thought that I've let my attention slip away from the present. Only the feeling of Landon's hand darting out and closing around my wrist is enough to make me look at him. His olive skin has taken on an ethereal glow under the moonlight, his eyes glistening. The warmth of his skin on mine isn't lost on me, even as he holds me back to keep me from moving forward. "What's wrong?" I ask him, eyes wide.

"I thought I heard something," Landon replies, glancing over his shoulder.

I pause, concentrating. "I don't hear anything."

He presses his lips together. "Maybe it was just a rat or something." Slowly, we start forward again, Landon's hand not leaving my wrist... and I would be lying if I said I wanted it to. But that's an issue for another time, it seems; moments later, the siren shifter stops dead in his tracks and exclaims, "Nope, not a rat!" I turn to watch as he drops the bag of groceries to the ground, his skin rippling with practiced ease as aqua-green scales begin to cover his body, glimmering with an almost inhuman beauty in the light of the full moon. It all happens so fast that I'm barely even aware of it, the world feeling like it's moving in slow motion as Landon whirls around and yells, "Leave!" His voice has taken on an inhuman, commanding tone, the tone of a siren giving an order, and I follow his gaze to see a figure at the mouth of the alleyway, blocking the exit.

My heart jumps to my throat. "What if it's a-" I begin.

Landon shakes his head. "It's not."

As if on cue, the figure at the end of the alleyway reaches into its coat and withdraws a gun, lining up a shot as casually as if we were on a battlefield and not the middle of a city street. "Boots!" Landon yells, pushing me out of the way seconds before a bullet ricochets off the brick wall behind me. Adrenaline takes hold of me then, and I scramble for that cool blob of energy at the pit of my stomach that I've come to recognise as the source of my shifter magic. In spite of the fact that, as a hybrid, a bastard experiment performed by the humans in an attempt to learn the secrets of shapeshifting, I have access to all five shifter forms -- wolf, witch, siren, vampire, and dragon -- I'm still stumbling to learn to use my powers. This obviously isn't helped by the fact that I'm no longer taking formal lessons, and although I've come a long way since starting at the Academy, it's still a struggle to focus when I'm under stress.

The human -- at least, I *think* it's a human -- at the end of the alleyway begins to advance on us, firing another shot that glances off the tough scales on Landon's shoulder. He lets out a hiss and barks out another command using his siren song. "Get away from us!"

The figure pauses for a moment, bristling, and I can see them struggling not to obey. Landon and my friend Hazel are powerful shifters, and assured in their abilities, but that doesn't make them all-powerful. It doesn't make *any* of us all-powerful.

Moving with difficulty, it continues its forward push, and I see that the figure is a woman. She isn't dressed in Academy colours, nor is she distinguishable from any other human we've seen around the city, but the mere fact that she's not running in fear at the sight of Landon tells me she's one of two things. Either she's a pro-human terrorist or an agent of the Academy who's been sent to retrieve us, and neither option looks great for me and Landon. Gripping the pistol with both hands, she unleashes a flurry of bullets, barely managing to shake off Landon's command. She's had training to combat shifters, that much is clear.

Before I can protest, Landon is moving in front of me, shielding my body with his own, grunting a little at the harmless but still painful impact of the projectiles. "A little help here, Boots?" he asks.

"On it," I say, and summon my siren form. Moments later, my skin is glistening with scales like Landon's, a surge of new power rushing through me as I get access to the form's abilities. "Let's hope she's bi," I mutter, glancing at my fellow shifter. "Count of three. One... two..."

"Leave!" we scream in unison, the combined force of our siren scream enough to send a shockwave rippling down the alleyway. It catches her full-force, and this time, she isn't able to resist for more than a few seconds. The look she gives us is one of pure hatred even as she turns around and walks robotically away from the alleyway,

her movements stiff and controlled as if she were a puppet on invisible strings.

We wait until she's disappeared into the Boston night before either of us dares to breathe again, slipping back into our human forms. There's a long pause and I realise Landon is still shielding me. His body radiating heat that envelops me like an embrace against the cold night air. "Landon..." I say, my heart fluttering in my chest at the sensation of his form against mine.

"Oh. Oh!" He glances down and pulls away from me, getting to his feet. "Sorry about that."

"It's okay." I smile up at him as he extends a hand and helps me to my feet. "I... appreciate it."

"Don't mention it," he tells me, winking, and I reluctantly let go of his hand so he can pick up the dropped grocery bag. "Shit. I think we bruised the apples."

I sigh and stoop down to help him. "They should still be edible ," I say, stealing a glance in the direction the human went. "Do you think she was with the Academy?"

Landon presses his lips together. "I don't know," he admits. "We'd better take side streets back to the motel, though. Just to be safe."

"You don't have to tell me twice," I agree. "The others are going to need to know about this."

The siren shifter gives me a grim nod, and together we make our way back down the alleyway and onto a narrow path that runs parallel to the main road. It's going to take us a while to find our way back, but I feel safer with him by my side than I would on my own, especially if there are more humans on our tail.

Besides, I think grimly, setting my jaw as we round a corner, *running is what I do best.*

CHAPTER 49

Somehow, we manage to find our way out of the tangle of streets, following the winding roads and alleyways nearly all the way to the river which glistens ominously under the moonlight. It's quiet out, and that's almost disconcerting, given how much has happened over the last few days. We were never supposed to get caught up in some sort of war between species. Though you might not be able to tell on the surface, the world feels like it's coming down around us. People -- *innocent people* -- died in the attack on the peace talks, and it feels like we're running headfirst into a conspiracy we can't escape.

Josie, one of the two witch shifters who tracked me down when my abilities first manifested, seems to think President Hawthorne was behind the attack. A way to strong arm the school board into allowing him to continue his experiments. Whether he was behind it or not, though, he got what he wanted out of it. I cringe inwardly as we cut across an abandoned intersection at the thought of what the school must be doing to the other students right this second. *We have to put a stop to this,* I remind myself. *This isn't just about you anymore.*

Eventually, Landon and I arrive outside the rundown motel. We're on a desolate street bordering the river, lined with boarded up buildings and closed down shops. It's not the most savoury area, but it's out of the way, and so far, the Academy hasn't found us. We walk in through the reception area, passing a man dozing at the front desk, and work our way to the back of the building, where we've taken two connecting rooms using what money we had on us. Hazel, Ruby, and Xander are in one, while me and the guys are in the other, the bed stripped of pillows and blankets, which we've scattered around the floor. It looks more like a den than a motel room at this point, but considering we have nowhere to go and next to no resources, our options are pretty limited.

Landon holds the groceries while I fumble the door open, and I'm surprised to see that the light is on. In spite of the early hour, it looks like everyone is up and gathered in the cramped suite, including Hazel and the twins; she's perched on the edge of the kitchenette table, leaning absently against Xander without even looking like she realises what she's doing. The two of them are talking as if they're in their own little world, Ruby watching with an amused look on her face from the corner by the door. It makes me smile a little, in spite of our situation. I'm happy if she's been able to find a connection with someone. And as for me and the guys...

Silas, the tall dragon shifter, is sitting on the edge of the bed, his broad shoulders hunched forward as he watches the near muted TV. On the screen is continuing coverage of the attack at the convention center, as well as several banners speculating the cause of the bombing. *If they only knew.*

His brown eyes catch mine as soon as he hears the door shut behind us, and a look of genuine relief spreads across his face. "You're back," he says, untensing a little. "I was starting to get worried. You guys were gone a long time."

"So was I," Hunter, the vampire shifter, echoes from his seat at the kitchen table. He looks distressed and weary, his fiery hair tousled and his blue eyes bloodshot. He hasn't been sleeping well the past couple nights, that much I know. The truth is I haven't been sleeping well, either. Ever since we arrived at the hotel I've found myself waking up during the night, unspeakable nightmares flying through my head -- *what if something happened to them, to any of them? What if*

Hawthorne realises just how close my relationship with them has actually become? What if...? Each time I lie there in silence, trying to tell myself to breathe. That it was just a dream, as I listen to the comforting sounds of the guys around me.

But Hunter has been restless, too, for reasons I don't know. He's been thrashing in his sleep, murmuring things to himself, getting up to go for long walks outside the motel. I'm aware that he hasn't had the easiest go of it -- not only is his father on the school board, but it took him until just a few days ago to even learn how to shapeshift. I make a mental note to ask him how he's doing as his sapphire eyes meet mine for an instant, something complicated flashing across his face too quickly for me to identify it.

I glance over at the wolf shifter, Shade, who is sitting on the kitchen counter and examining his fingernails. His overgrown blond hair is wild from sleep, and he is more stunning each time I look at him. I feel my stomach turn over when he abruptly looks up, raising an eyebrow at me almost imperceptibly, the corner of his mouth twitching in a knowing smirk. Damn him. In spite of his attitude and constant teasing, he's been here for me more than I could have ever expected over the past few days -- in more ways than one. A chill runs up my spine as I remember the feeling of his skin on mine on that rooftop, the night air whipping at our hair as we pressed desperately against each other, our lips locked. "I wasn't," he quips. "Boots and Thyme can handle themselves."

"'Boots and Thyme'," Landon repeats, grinning. "Sounds like the name of a detective and her sidekick."

"Who said you were the sidekick?" I tease back, giving him a gentle nudge with my elbow. "I'm not nearly competent enough to be the detective."

"Oh?" The siren shifter raises his eyebrows, crossing his arms over his chest. "That's funny, because I could have sworn you were the most competent person I knew. The stunning good looks don't hurt, either." As joking as his tone is, I can't help but flush a little at the praise. A surge of powerful emotion suddenly wells up in me, and for a moment I'm brought back to a few nights ago, when we were trapped in our room at the Boston school. That, I think, was when I realised just how deep my feelings go for all of these guys, and it's a revelation I'm still reeling from days later. Part of me feels like I've forgotten how to conduct myself like a normal person in the aftermath. Do they realise what kind of effect they have on me?

"If you're done flirting with Boots right in front of me," Hunter speaks up, his voice sounding both strained and sharp, "we could stand to figure out our next move."

"Hey, take it easy, Ash," Landon retorts, putting his hands up. "I'm just having a little fun. We could use some levity now, right?"

I watch the vampire shifter press his lips together, his eyes flashing red for a split second -- almost too quickly for me to catch it. Landon's ribbing only serves to make him more tense, and a heavy silence follows that makes my stomach drop. *It's fine,* I tell myself. *It's normal. We've been cooped up here for days -- everyone is stressed.* One look at Hunter's steely expression, though, and I'm not sure I totally believe it.

Ruby clears her throat. "Any trouble on the way to the store?" she asks, moving to help Landon and I unpack the groceries.

I swallow. "We ran into someone on our way back."

"More like, they ran into us," Landon adds.

"Who was it?" Shade asks, a slight crack appearing in his unflappable exterior.

"I don't know," I reply. "She wasn't wearing an Academy uniform. She was human, though, and she knew about shifters."

"Shit," mutters Hazel, running a hand through her honey-coloured hair. "They're getting closer, aren't they?"

"It *could* just be a coincidence," Xander offers, although he seems doubtful. "Maybe just a holdover from the convention?"

"In *this* part of town?" Hazel asks him incredulously. "They must have seen us around, or..." Her eyes go wide. "Unless they have a witch tracking us."

"Do you think they do?" Ruby asks.

"If I find out they planted a tracking charm on us while we were back at the school," Shade begins, shaking his head.

"Look," Silas says, "it doesn't matter. Humans are after us, and they're getting closer. We need to move."

"Move?" asks Shade. "Move *where?* Last time I checked, we don't exactly have infinite resources."

"I don't know," the dragon shifter admits, "but we can't stay here. We need to find somewhere we can lay low until we're ready to take on Hawthorne."

"Take *on?*" asks Hazel. "I don't remember volunteering to take him on!"

I sigh. "We might not have a choice. We can't just hide from the Academy forever."

"Why not?" Shade asks. "That suits me just fine."

"Why am I not surprised?" Hunter mutters dryly.

Shade rounds on him, looking like he's going to say something, but then he shuts his mouth.

"Look, like it or not, this fight has gotten bigger than any of us," I say, feeling I have to motivate them somehow. "And until we can find a way of stopping these experiments, we'll never be able to go back to the Academy." There's a long pause, and I take a shaky breath. "We might *never* be able to go back there."

"Which means we need to find somewhere else," Xander finishes, sighing. "I get it."

"Where, then?" asks Hunter. "I'm open to suggestions."

"Out of Boston," I reply, crossing my arms as the others look at me. "Preferably out of the United States altogether." My cell phone feels suddenly heavy in my pocket, and I bite the inside of my lip to keep from saying something rash. *Too dangerous,* I tell myself. *Too many unknowns.*

"We're not far from the airport," Silas says, glancing at the TV once more. Tomorrow we can walk there, get a flight back to the U.K., and find somewhere to figure out our next move."

The others glance at one another, no one else speaking until Hazel finally gives a firm nod. "That's good enough for me."

That issue seemingly settled, the group disperses, ready to turn in for the night now that everyone is safely back at the motel. I watch as

Hazel, Xander, and Ruby file out of our suite and into their own, leaving me standing there with the guys' eyes on me. I feel unexpectedly put on the spot, and blush a little, ducking my head and turning away from the others. "I, ah... I'm pretty tired," I announce. "I think I'm going to lie down for a bit."

"You're not the only one," Landon agrees, yawning. One by one, the five of us bunker down in our makeshift nests on the motel floor, turning on the lights and curling up in silence. The only sounds are the air conditioning and the guys' breathing. The feeling of their bodies next to mine fills me with more comfort than I can possibly articulate, but even as my eyes drift closed, I can't help but feel like things are only going to get more complicated.

CHAPTER 50

I don't sleep well that night, and not just because I'm sprawled out on the hard motel floor. My dreams are restless and impossible to remember, a nonstop parade of incomprehensible, anxious fragments; I'm reminded of a time back when I was still in human school, the night before one of my most difficult final exams. It was pre-calculus, as I recall, and I've never been what you would call mathematically inclined. That was back when I was living with one of my worst foster parents, a man whose temper and perfectionism extended past his own children and to me as well. Afraid of the outcome, I spent the night thrashing around in bed until my sheets were drenched with sweat, equations, graphs, and numbers floating through my mind one after another. I ended up sleeping so badly that I nearly drifted off during the exam, but I was lucky enough to be moved to a new foster home before having to face the wrath of my then-caregiver.

This time, it's different. Instead of maths running through my mind, it's images of fire, destruction, and death. There's Silas, half-dead and strapped to a laboratory table; the convention centre going up in flames; Hawthorne and his goons closing in on us from all sides...

This last one is what jerks me awake, my breath coming in fitful gasps as I put a hand to my chest, closing my eyes and counting to ten. It's only as I come to that I realise where I am -- or rather, *who* I'm currently curled up next to. Hunter has me safe and secure in his lanky arms, pressed against his lean chest with his body curled protectively around mine.

Slowly, I feel myself start to relax, my heart rate returning to normal as I lean into the warm embrace of the vampire shifter. His breath is slow and quiet, the movement of his chest soothing against my back, and for a moment I wonder if he even intended to hold me like this. Did he sidle up to me before he fell asleep, or is he clinging to me subconsciously, trying to keep me safe even as we all slumber? A bright spot of warmth pools in the pit of my stomach at the notion, and I can feel my skin flushing even in the darkness of the room. Hunter has always been the more reserved type, although what I once mistook for a bad attitude has turned out to be years of insecurity about his own power. I'd like to think I've been able to defrost him a little, and it's true that with my help he's finally, *finally* learning how to harness his abilities, but he has a long way to go before he's fully come into his own.

Part of me feels guilty. Whether I chose to be or not, I was the catalyst for everything that's happened to these guys. Their lives are never going to be the same because of me, because of what they were put through to make me what I am, and now we're on the run together because I can't seem to stop sticking my nose where it doesn't belong. The idea of something happening to Hunter because of me makes my blood run cold, especially when he's the least skilled shifter of all of us, and yet here he is, comforting me in my sleep. It's enough to make my heart melt, and I find myself shifting a little so that I'm facing him, subconsciously tightening my grip on him.

The movement is enough to make him stir, and his bright blue eyes open a moment later. "Sorry," I whisper. "I didn't mean to wake you."

He hums, still half-asleep, and whispers back, "That's okay. I'm a light sleeper." A moment passes, and then, seeming to realise that he's holding me, his eyes go wide, and he lets me go. "I'm sorry," he says hastily. "I didn't mean..."

I raise an eyebrow. Even in the darkness of the room, I could swear it looks like... "Are you... blushing?" I whisper teasingly.

"What? No," he retorts. "Vampires don't blush. Obviously." We lapse back into silence, and I can feel his body tense up next to mine. "You just looked like you were having a bad dream," Hunter explains at last. "I didn't want to make you uncomfortable. I was just trying to get you to calm down, but then you came closer, and I..."

"Hey." I crane my neck to look at him, but he's deliberately not meeting my eyes. Blushing or not, it's clear that he's embarrassed. "It's okay," I whisper. "Thank you."

Hunter hesitates for a moment, and then rests his chin on the top of my head, his hand coming up to brush my arm. "I should be the one thanking you," he tells me. "If it weren't for you, I don't know if I would've been able to hold Lyle off."

Thinking back to the battle at the Boston Academy, when the two vampire shifters went head to head, I'm struck with a fresh surge of affection for him. "It was a team effort," I reply.

Hunter squeezes my arm for a brief second. "The thought of that bastard hurting you, Millie..." His voice trails off, and he pulls back to look at me; my heart is already pounding in my chest, and I'm thinking back to the time he kissed me, the feeling of his lips on my own.

But then one of the others sits up on the other side of the room. "Get a room, you two." I recognise Shade's voice, and bury my face in Hunter's chest to stifle my laughter. I can feel him tense up with embarrassment. Things could be worse, though; considering I kissed the wolf shifter not long ago, he's taking my closeness to the other guys rather well.

As for the others, well...

Now isn't the time to think about that, I tell myself, allowing my eyes to drift closed. Snuggled against Hunter's muscular frame, I let sleep consume me once more, and this time, there are no nightmares.

"ALL RIGHT, LOVEBIRDS, UP, UP, UP." I'm roused by Landon's teasing voice, struggling to separate myself from Hunter as I open my bleary eyes. The siren shifter is standing over us with an amused smirk on his face, his hands on his hips. "Looks like you two were up to more than just sleeping," he teases.

"We weren't," protests Hunter. "I-I mean, it's not like-"

"Relax, I'm just fucking with you." Landon laughs as he steps over us to draw back the curtains, flooding the room with sunlight and making me blink.

Elsewhere, I can hear Shade groan in protest, but as I sit up and look around, I can see that Silas is already in the kitchenette, staring down at his phone. Slowly, the five of us begin to rise, Landon and Shade bickering as they stretch while Hunter pulls me to my feet. I share a small smile with him before turning to my hastily packed bag. We left the American Academy in a hurry, and I left most of my stuff behind, but Hazel and I went on a run earlier to pick up some basic necessities: clothes and toothpaste, mainly.

"Has someone gotten up Hazel and the others?" I ask, pulling out a t-shirt, jeans, and a bra.

"I will," Silas volunteers, straightening up. "We need to get to the airport. The sooner we leave the country, the less heat will be on us." He leaves out the unspoken let's hope, but we all get the message.

I watch as the dragon shifter disappears into the hallway before making my way to the bathroom, nearly bumping into Shade along the way. "Sorry," I say. "Figured I'd go get changed."

"Bold of you to assume you can't change in front of me," the wolf shifter replies with a wicked grin, and I feel a surge of butterflies in my stomach as he leans forward, his lips brushing my ear. "I've been thinking about that night on the rooftop," he murmurs, the feeling of his breath sending a shiver up my spine. "I'm always thinking about it, Boots."

Sure that my blush is giving me away, I give him a playful shove, not wanting him to know how much he's getting to me. Laughing, he reaches out to ruffle my chestnut hair before turning away, stuffing his hands in his pockets. I'm left to watch him go, still trying to get my composure back, before taking shelter in the bathroom. *Take it easy,* I tell myself as I struggle out of my sleep shirt and shorts. *You've got more important things to worry about than romance.*

I finish getting dressed and have my hand on the doorknob when the sound of Shade's jovial voice leaks through. "So what *were* you doing, spooning Boots?"

I hear Hunter let out a muffled growl of frustration. "For fuck's sake, guys, we didn't *do* anything."

"Hey," Shade protests, "more power to you if you did. Is it true that vamps are cold when they're... you know...?" There's a pause, and then the wolf shifter bursts out laughing. "The look on your face!"

"Not funny," Hunter growls.

"All right, guys, take it easy," comes Silas' voice.

There's the sound of the door opening, followed by Hazel: "I picked us up some breakfast. There's a bakery on the corner."

Only the idea of food is enough to get the guys to stop bickering, and they descend upon the breakfast like they're starving. My stomach lets out a rumble, too, and I realise just how hungry I am; shifting is taxing on the body, and my little stint with Landon yesterday must have drained me more than I thought. I push out of the bathroom and walk up to the kitchen counter, where Hazel has laid out an array of pastries. "Damn," I observe, grabbing a croissant. "You really went all-out."

"I sure did," she replies proudly. "If we're going through hell, I'm not about to let us go through it with subpar breakfast foods."

"You *goddess*," Xander says through a mouthful of danish, grinning boyishly at the other siren shifter. Ruby rolls her eyes, but it looks like she's struggling not to smile. The others continue to talk amongst themselves as I wolf down my food, hardly believing how many croissants I'm able to put away; if we weren't on the lam, I would be worrying about my waistline, but I've got bigger problems than putting on a couple of kilograms.

I notice that Silas is back to leaning against the counter, staring down at his phone. I sidle up to him and put my hand on his arm, and he tenses up for a moment before seeming to realise it's me. "Sorry," he says.

"Don't apologise," I tell him, crossing my arms and peering over his shoulder. "What are you looking at?"

"A map of the city," the dragon shifter replies. "We're going to need to find a discreet route to the airport." There's a pause as he shifts from foot to foot, rubbing the back of his neck. "I've also been doing some research," he adds. "About getting my powers back up to par."

"They seemed pretty up to par earlier," I remark.

He shakes his head. "You wouldn't say that if you knew how much of a struggle it was. I'm starting to wonder if I'm ever going to get back to where I was."

"Hey," I say, tugging at his arm to make him look at me. "Don't say that. It just takes time." Spontaneously, I lean forward, touching my forehead to his as I meet his dark eyes. To his credit, he doesn't look away, and the smoldering look he gives me worms its way into my stomach. "We're going to be okay," I murmur.

Silas closes his eyes for a moment, leaning into my touch. "Let's hope you're right, Boots."

CHAPTER 51

I t's becoming clear to me that Boston isn't a city meant for walking. Between the winding cobblestone streets and the oppressive summer heat, I'm sweating by the time we step outside the motel, having packed up, checked out, and paid cash. Silas was right, though; the one saving grace is that we're near the airport which should minimise the amount of time we spend wandering the roads of the city. Still, I'm on edge. Every person we pass is a potential threat, and I find myself holding my breath every time we round a corner, half expecting an Academy representative to spring out at me. The area on the waterfront is sketchy and rundown, not unlike the neighbourhood where I ended up after running away from my last foster home, although at least this time I have more people on my side.

We're clustered together on the narrow sidewalk, Hazel, Ruby, and Xander in the front of the group while the guys and I walk drag. Silas and Shade are talking, their hands in their pockets -- it's nice to see them getting along in spite of their bickering. Hunter trails behind them, looking pensive, while Landon and I bring up the rear, squinting against the bright sunlight. Slowly we make our way west, looking about as conspicuous as can be, considering where we are, but mercifully, we don't run into any Academy agents.

After reaching the wharf, we cross a bridge leading to the downtown area, but my anxiety only increases; we're heading back into the eye of the storm, and if we *do* run into any of Hawthorne's people, it's bound to be around here. Across the water, I can still make out the ruins of the convention centre. The fire has been put out, but search and rescue efforts are ongoing, and there's a crush of people watching the commotion.

"You'd think the interest would have faded by now," Landon remarks, as if reading my mind.

"I don't like how many eyes are on this," I reply in a low voice. "I know most of them are probably just innocent bystanders, but still..."

"There's no real way of knowing," the siren shifter finishes for me. "We just have to keep our heads down until we're out of the country."

"And then what?" I ask, unable to help myself. "We can't just go underground for the rest of our lives."

"No, we can't," Landon agrees as we turn right and head north toward the harbour. "I wish I knew what to do, Boots, but I'm not much of the planning type. You probably ought to talk to Silas about that."

"Talk to me about what?" the dragon shifter asks over his shoulder.

"Damn," Landon remarks. "Your hearing is something else, Aconite."

Silas smiles, but there's not much humour in it. "Got it from my mother, but that's not the point. Since when am I in charge?"

"You just seem to be the most decisive out of all of us," Landon replies. "And you have the most experience with... Well..." He stops mid-sentence, seemingly realising his mistake as Silas' expression hardens.

"I'm not a test case, okay?" the dragon shifter says. His tone is gentle, but there's hurt behind it that makes my heart ache. "I know the Academy thinks so, but I'd appreciate it if you thought of me as more than just a lab rat."

"I'm sorry," Landon says glumly. "I didn't mean for it to come out like that. You just seem to know the most about the unrest, considering your parents." Wisely, he doesn't go into the specifics - namely, the convenient disappearance of Silas' parents before they could take action against the humans. No sense in opening up that wound again.

Silas shakes his head. "I'm good at making decisions, but I'm not a leader." He turns and nods in my direction as we cross the street. "Boots should be the one in charge."

"What?" I exclaim, eyes wide. "Why the hell should *I* be in charge? I can barely get dressed in the morning, let alone keep you g-" I stop, blushing a little, and backtrack. "Let alone keep people from getting hurt."

"Look, we don't want to dump this all on you Millie," Silas replies quietly, "but you're at the heart of this. Hell, you're the only thing connecting the rest of us. If it weren't for you, we never would have even met."

"But that's..." I begin and then trail off. It's the truth, and there's no arguing it.

"Besides," Shade puts in, surprising me with the pensiveness in his voice, "you're the most powerful of all of us, Boots. You're the hybrid."

I snort, shaking my head self-deprecatingly. "Yeah, well, I'll get back to you on that once I'm able to hold a form for more than a minute at a time."

Shade's grey eyes flash up at me, making me feel taken aback. "Don't say that shit, Boots. Seriously. You're worth more than you think."

That stokes a fire in my chest, and I can't help but give him a grateful smile. "Thanks, Shade."

"Don't mention it," he says, adding with a cheeky grin, "Seriously. People will think I'm going soft."

"We don't want that," I reply, chuckling as the wolf shifter bumps me with his shoulder.

We lapse back into silence once more, each of us lost in our own thoughts, and continue to make our way through the Boston morning until we arrive at the harbour. Hazel and Xander run to a nearby ATM to get cash and tickets while the rest of us wait anxiously, looking around for any signs of followers, but there are none. It's all just tourists and businesspeople, and that only puts me more on edge.

"I don't like this," I announce, hugging myself.

"What do you mean?" asks Ruby, coming to stand with the rest of us.

"Where are all the Academy people?" I ask, gesturing around at the plaza. "The convention centre was crawling with them. Hell, the whole *city* was crawling with them. After what happened yesterday, I'd be expecting more. It's almost like..."

"Like it's too peaceful," Hunter says, pressing his lips together. "I know what you mean."

"Do you think they're planning something?" I ask, watching as Hazel and Xander turn around, clutching our ferry tickets.

"Do you really even need to ask that question?" Silas asks glumly. "Let's just hope that whatever it is, we can get the hell out of here before it happens."

"That does raise a good question, actually," Hazel says as she comes to a stop and passes out our tickets. "We need to figure out a plan. A more specific plan, I mean."

We start to make our way over to the docks, and I realise that everyone in the group has their eyes on me, waiting for my call. *Guess this leader thing is happening whether I want it to or not,* I think grimly. "We can't go back to the island, that much is obvious," I say, keeping my voice low as I shuffle up to the attendant and hand him my ticket. "We'll get eaten alive. The trouble is, they're going to have people on us back in the U.K. It would be foolish to think that they won't."

"So what do we do?" asks Shade.

"We'll need to find somewhere to lie low," I reply, running a hand through my hair. "Except I don't know..." I stop then, my eyes going wide as we mount the gangplank and come to sit on one of the benches on the ferry. It's almost the top of the hour, and the dock workers are getting ready to shove off. Good. I've had enough of this city to last a lifetime. I snap my head around to look at Silas, who's taken a seat on my other side. "You said you and your family lived in a shifter community, right?"

"Technically, yeah," the dragon shifter replies. "Although I wouldn't feel safe going back there, considering what the humans did to my parents. I don't even know if anyone is still there."

"But there are others like it, though, right?" I persist. "I mean, that's what they said about the Boston Academy -- there are shifter neighbourhoods all over the place around here. Maybe we can find one back home... the suburbs, maybe? Or somewhere in the countryside?"

"We're more likely to find one in one of the big cities," replies Hunter, crossing his arms. "London, Birmingham, Edinburgh... *Where,* though, I don't know. Maybe if I can talk to my dad..."

"No way," Xander says urgently. "The Academy's going to be monitoring communications, especially with faculty members. They'll be on us in no time."

"You're right," says Hunter, sounding crestfallen. "I just... worry about him. And my sister. That's all."

Instinctively, I reach out and put a hand on his arm; I feel him relax a little under my touch. I don't have to say anything, but he shoots me a grateful look. None of us are having an easy go of it right now.

"Well, it sounds like we have a starting point, then," I say as the ferry begins to move out onto the water. "We'll just have to hope we can afford same-day flights to the other side of the planet."

No one has anything to say about that, and as we bob and lurch over the murky blue water, I'm left to concentrate on not getting seasick. Boats have never sat well with me, and the stress I'm under isn't helping things. My churning stomach has me going pale in the face, clenching my hands in my lap. Silas, seemingly noticing my discomfort, slides an arm around my shoulders, pulling me comfortingly against his side.

Out of the corner of my eye, I don't miss the odd look that crosses Hunter's face, but the vampire shifter doesn't say anything.

Somehow, I make it the rest of the way across the water without losing my breakfast, and hurry down the gangplank on legs that are still unsteady. I'm so preoccupied with getting on solid ground again that I don't even pay attention to the airport ahead of us, and I nearly trip over my own feet when a hand flies out and grabs mine. "What-" I begin, glancing up to see Hazel staring at the terminal with wide eyes.

"Bad," she says in a low, tense voice. "Twelve o'clock, by the entrance."

My brow furrows as I follow her gaze, and for a moment I don't understand what the fuss is about... but then I see it, and my heart sinks. "Shit."

"Yeah," Shade agrees, coming to a stop beside us. "Shit is right."

"Is that...?" asks Landon.

"One of Russo's," Ruby replies, looking around. "Two, actually. No, wait, three. The guy on the left is a dragon shifter. I'm not sure about the others, but I know they aren't human."

"What are they doing here?" Xander asks.

"Three guesses," Shade fires back.

"So *that's* where the Academy people have gone," says Hunter, and as I look around, I can see that he's right: the airport is surrounded by familiar faces, none of them on our side. They might not all be shifters, but they're sure as hell not here to help us, and they seem to be waiting for something.

Us.

"They must have figured we would try to escape," mutters Hazel. "They've got the whole damn place blocked off."

"Well, there goes that plan," gripes Landon. "And here I was thinking we could just catch a ride out of this fucking place."

"Can't we sneak past them?" protests Hunter.

"With this many?" Silas asks incredulously. "Doubtful. And they've probably got humans ID'ing people on the inside. Deep pockets, and all that."

"Fuck," Shade says, throwing his hands up and raking them through his sandy hair. "Now what?"

I can feel the others watching me again, waiting for direction, and the answer comes to me in an instant. I square my shoulders and take out my phone. "I think I have an idea."

CHAPTER 52

My hands are shaking as I bring up the text message that's been burning a hole in my pocket ever since it arrived. *Come to London if you want to survive this or he will make you watch them all die*, it reads, as cryptic and ominous as can be. It came from a private number, and although I've done a little digging to try to locate the source, I'm no closer now than I was before. I hate the fact that I'm even considering this, but we don't have much of a choice. Normally, upon receiving a mysterious and vaguely threatening text message from a stranger, most people would delete it and pretend it never happened.

But I think we've established by now that I'm not most people.

The unknown messenger, whoever they are, first reached out to me during the human-shifter diplomatic conference that brought us to Boston in the first place. The only problem, of course, was that the two communities seem to be past the point of peaceful negotiations. Things are escalating beneath the surface, and the worst part is that most humans, in the dark about supernatural beings, don't even realise how dangerous their world has become. That's not the point, though. The point is that I first received a warning message before Hawthorne even attacked the convention centre, which means whoever is behind the texts has an in with the mucky-mucks. Whether they're on our side, though, is another story.

"Boots?" the sound of Hunter's uncertain voice pulls me back to reality, and I realise with a start that I've been staring down at my cell phone in silence. "We lost you for a second, there."

"Sorry," I say, shaking my head. "I was just thinking. Look, I'm not totally sure on the transportation thing, if I'm being honest, but if the Academy is this gun ho about finding us, then we ought to consider finding outside help."

"I'm all for that," Landon says dryly. "It's not like we're a bunch of half-trained university students or anything."

"Do you have someone in mind, Boots?" Silas asks, brow furrowing.

"Maybe," I reply, biting the inside of my lip. I can feel a blush creeping into my cheeks. "It's... a possibility, anyway."

"You don't sound super convinced," remarks Hazel.

"That's because I'm not," I explain. "The truth is, I got a text from someone during the conference, telling me to watch my back."

"Who was it from?" asks Shade, crossing his arms.

"That's the problem," I say. "I'm not sure."

"You realise it could've been Lyle, right?" asks Ruby. "Or any of the other Academy bastards trying to throw you off."

"I know, and that's what I thought, too," I concede. "At least, at first. But then..." I sigh, looking down. It's embarrassing that I've kept this from the others, but I wasn't expecting to need to resort to this. We're backed into a corner. "After we escaped from the campus, when we were first running back into the city, I got another text," I explain, choosing my words carefully. "Same number, but I have no idea who it belongs to. Hell, I don't even know the area code; it was unlisted. It said that we need to come to London if we want to survive this."

"And that's it?" asks Shade, sounding incredulous.

"I texted them back, asking who they were, but they never responded to me."

"Great," mutters Landon. "That doesn't exactly bode well."

"I know," I admit, "and that's why I didn't say anything earlier. I was hoping we wouldn't have to... But now I'm starting to think we might not have a choice."

"So you think we should do it, then?" asks Xander. He and Ruby exchange a look. "Just like that?"

"I'm not sure it's a good idea," Hunter says, shifting uncomfortably. "We don't even know who they are."

"That's a fair point," Silas agrees. "For all we know, it could be someone from the Academy, trying to lure us back there. What if it's a trap to corner us?"

"To be fair, that wouldn't make a whole lot of sense," Landon points out. "If they wanted us back at the Academy, why wouldn't they just tell us to meet them there?"

"Maybe they're finally realising we're smarter than they gave us credit for," Shade suggests with a smirk.

"I guess that's a possibility," I acknowledge, my face falling. "You know what? Never mind. Forget I said anything. We can figure out another way to-"

"Well, wait a minute," Hazel interrupts, holding up a hand. "I don't think we should just ignore this."

"But we could be walking right into a trap," protests Hunter. "We can't let M-" He stops himself, clears his throat, and says, "We can't let any of us get hurt." His blue eyes flicker to me, and then down to the ground.

"We have to think big picture, though," argues Hazel. "Let's just say this *is* a trap, and someone's trying to capture us. They obviously already know where we are, or they wouldn't have sent that warning during the convention, right? Which means if we don't take them up on their offer, we could just be inviting them to come attack us while we're sitting in Boston with our asses hanging out."

"So we leave Boston," suggests Xander. "We can take a train down the coast, find a way to-"

"Do you really think the humans are going to let us leave the city?" Hazel asks. "They've blocked off the airport. They know they have us trapped here, and they're just going to keep tightening the net. I wouldn't be surprised if the train station already has agents there waiting for us."

I can see the wheels turning in Shade's head, and he nods slowly, looking at Hazel. "You're saying it would be better to have someone spring a trap on us if we're in London."

"Exactly," says the siren shifter. "Boston is crawling with Academy enforcers. Twice as many, with the UK humans still looking for us, and that's not even counting the school board and the ambassadors. For all we know, everyone in the damn city is out to get us. At least if we had to duke it out with your mysterious contact in London, Millie, we wouldn't be running the risk of the entire city coming after us."

"And that's all assuming your contact isn't on their side," Silas points out, sounding thoughtful. "It could be that they *do* want to help us. Remember Josie?"

I hum in agreement, thinking back to the faculty fellow who risked everything to help us escape from lockdown at the Boston campus. God, I hope she's okay.

"Maybe you're right," admits Hunter.

Silas turns to me, putting a hand on my shoulder. "Listen, Boots, we meant what we said. You're running this show, and we'll follow you. To the end of the earth, if we have to." His dark eyes bore into mine, smouldering, and his words fill me with renewed confidence -- as well as renewed longing. "It's your call, at the end of the day. We trust you." He looks up at Xander, Hazel, and Ruby for confirmation, and they nod their agreement.

"Give me a sec," I say, already turning back to my phone and tapping out a message to the unknown number. I'm not expecting a reply, but it's worth getting as much information as I can before I sign the group up for something dangerous.

Where in London? I write before sending the message.

We wait for a few moments; the others looking anxiously around at the Academy agents by the airport, and I'm debating having us return to the hotel when my phone vibrates. Surprised, I pull it back out and glance down at the screen, hardly daring to hope...

But there it is, in plain English. *Hyde Park,* the message reads.

Speakers' Corner. Come while it's light out, and message when you're on route. I will be waiting.

I feel a burst of hope as I relay the message back to my friends. "That's... better than I was expecting," says Silas.

"I'll say," Landon puts in. "I can't think of anywhere more public than Hyde Park. And during the daytime..." He grins. "There will be people everywhere. It would be impossible for them to capture us without a bunch of bystanders seeing."

"Not to mention the space," adds Shade. "I don't mind destroying a few sculptures if it means kicking a few of those bastards' asses."

"The risk *is* lower this way," acknowledges Ruby. "I say we go for it."

"There's still one problem, though," says Hunter, who has been silent the whole time. We turn to look at him questioningly, and he raises his eyebrows, gesturing around. "We still have no way of *getting* there," he says. "Last I checked, we can't just walk across the ocean."

"Maybe *you* can't," teases Landon. "Hazel and I have the swimming thing locked down."

The vampire shifter rolls his eyes. "You know what I mean."

"What about Boots?" asks Shade, nodding in my direction. "You can shift into your witch form. You could teleport us over there."

"That's..." I splutter, feeling put on the spot. "That's not possible. I've never transported anyone before!"

"But you have been taught the spell, haven't you?" asks Silas.

"Technically, yeah," I admit, rubbing the back of my neck. "At least, I think so. If I can remember it. But, guys, come on... the faculty fellows have been doing this for years! You saw how exhausted they got after warping us to Boston. Do you really think I could get us all to London without fucking it up?"

"You're stronger than any of us," Hazel points out.

"What if I send us to the wrong place?" I protest. "Or worse, what if I lose focus and we end up getting dropped into the ocean?"

"Silas and I can help," offers Ruby. "We can carry you guys to dry land, if we have to. I really think this is our best bet, Millie."

I fidget, looking from one hopeful face to the next, not wanting to disappoint them but overwhelmed by my own insecurity. It's true that I learned the theory of teleportation back in one of my witch shifting classes, but theory and practise are two very different things. The idea of any of the guys getting hurt because of me...

So what are you going to do, then? a voice in my head speaks up. *It's not like you have a lot of options, here.*

I can feel myself resigning to it even before I open my mouth. "Okay," I say quietly. "I can try."

"Good," says Silas, looking relieved. "Then we just need to find some place where we won't be seen, and we can-"

"I hate to interrupt," Landon says, his tone worrisome, "but I think it's a little late for that." He nods in the direction of the airport, and when I follow his gaze, my blood runs cold. Two of the Academy representatives by the front entrance are staring straight at us. One of them murmurs something to the other, and then they both begin moving rapidly in our direction.

"*Shit*," says Shade. "We have to get out of here!"

Here goes nothing, I think, and close my eyes.

CHAPTER 53

I n case it wasn't clear already, I don't have a great deal of faith in my own abilities. It's less a matter of self-esteem, although considering the circumstances of my childhood, *that's* not exactly stunning either. The issue is that I've had the equivalent of less than a year's training in something not only incredibly difficult, but incredibly dangerous. It's all made exponentially worse by the fact that I have five forms to keep track of, each with its own devastating supernatural abilities, and the last thing I want is to end up causing more problems than I solve with my own magic.

Even as I clamp my eyes shut, brow furrowing in concentration as I dig for that by-now familiar cool spot in my stomach -- my own personal reserve of magic -- I find myself panicking a little. What if I can't manage it? Or worse, what if I only half manage it, and some of us don't make it all the way? *Oh god,* I think, my heart pounding a little faster, *or what if I end up dismembering us?* I heard stories during my first few witchcraft lessons, cautionary tales about young witch shifters who got a little too enthusiastic with the teleportation and ended up losing limbs and organs because they weren't focused enough to do a fully-fledged job. The idea makes me feel a little queasy, but there's no time to worry about it now; I can hear voices coming from up ahead, and I don't need to open my eyes to know that they're coming from the Academy watchdogs. Those bastards.

"Millie, I don't want to rush you," Hazel says breathlessly, "but you might want to double-time it!"

"I'm trying," I grit out through my teeth, trying to steady my breath long enough to summon enough raw power for the spell. The witch powers haven't exactly come easily to me, and this is something so high-level that I'm not even sure it's in my wheelhouse; that's the problem with being a witch shifter: it's not enough just to get into the form. After that you need to learn how to cast spells, something that doesn't hinder any of the other species. It's like learning an entirely new level of magic. I try to remember my training -- specifically, what Shade taught me about transforming -- and focus on the present moment. Which is not hard to do, considering the people currently coming after us. I bring my powers to the forefront and allow them to seep through my being. A surge of triumph washes over me as I can feel the coolness of my magic permeate my body, a telltale sign that I'm on the verge of transforming, and I open my eyes just in time to see my skin turning ruby red, the magic accessible to this form bursting out of my chest in a tidal wave.

"Atta girl," Landon says, looking at me a little wonderingly as energy begins to radiate from my palms.

"Don't congratulate me yet," I warn him, rubbing my hands together and trying desperately to remember the spell. It sounded easy in theory when it was first explained to me: the key is to focus on your destination while allowing your raw power to engulf you and the people you're transporting. Although now I'm quickly discovering that that's easier said than done. *London,* I think, panic beginning to consume me as the Academy representatives draw ever closer. *Come on. We need to get to London.* Frowning, I try to concentrate on the city, imagining the big landmarks and the skyline over the water, as pretty and picturesque as a postcard. Extending my hands, I allow my powers to flow out...

But nothing happens. I crack open my eye, dismayed to see that we're exactly where we were. Except there's no time to troubleshoot;

within moments the two lackeys are on top of us, and it's clear in an instant that they're no mere humans. The one on the left is already sprouting fur, drawing quite a few stares from the innocent bystanders, although I'm sure the other agents will be around in no time to do damage control. The one on the left exhales a jet of flame so hot that it burns blue in the warm Boston air. My eyes go wide, but Silas pushes me out of the way just in time, taking hold of my hand without even being aware of it.

"We have eyes on the escaped students," the wolf yells, his voice loud and insistent. "We're going to need backup!"

"Like hell," mutters Landon, who is already transforming, and one look around at the group shows me he's not alone; the others are all shapeshifting already, even Hunter, who seems to be having a slower go of it.

Shade is on the other wolf in an instant, the two beasts colliding in a growling mess of fur, claws and teeth. The dragon shifter is sprouting wings before our eyes, swiping out at Hunter with claws as sharp as daggers. The vampire shifter lunges out of the way, his superior speed saving him from being eviscerated, and Hazel opens her mouth to use her siren song, but Xander beats her to it, putting himself in front of her and lunging for the throat of the dragon shifter who has now fully transformed. The skirmish is sudden and intense, and it takes me a moment to remember what I'm supposed to be doing; heart racing, I struggle to picture London again, willing my magic to get us there, but it still isn't working, and I almost cry out in frustration.

It can't have been more than a minute since we were first spotted, but already I can see the other Academy cronies approaching us fast; within seconds, we'll be surrounded. "Boots-" says Shade, struggling to fend off the other wolf.

"I need time!" I protest. "We have to move, *now!*"

To their credit, the others don't need to be told twice, and we pull back from the enemies as quickly as we engaged with them, whirling around and making a beeline in the opposite direction. A blast of fire sails over the top of my head, singing a few of the hairs there and making me wince. Silas, who still hasn't let go of my hand, whirls around and unleashes a fireball of his own, this one considerably smaller than the other dragon shifter's, and I hear him swear under his breath.

More fire rains down on us, and I hardly dare to look to see whether the others are okay. *Just have to find somewhere to work,* I think, *just need to buy a little time --*

But as if on cue, other magic joins with the enemy fire, and I realise with a sinking feeling that they have us outnumbered. "Where do we go?" yells Ruby, ducking to avoid a blast of telekinetic energy from one of the others.

"I don't--" I begin, but then my eyes go wide as I remember that we took the ferry to get here; we're essentially trapped on this side of the city, like sitting ducks. In the distance, I can make out a couple of overpasses leading back in the direction we came from, but they're covered, and clearly not meant for pedestrians; letting out a cry of frustration, I turn around and hurl a bolt of my own witch magic back at the closest pursuer, the wolf. It pushes him backward, and he stumbles, and we don't waste any of the precious few seconds it buys us, tearing up to the edge of the water like our lives depend on it.

"Shit," Hazel exclaims, staring down at the churning waves below us. In the distance, I can see the ferry, but it's stopped on the other side of the water, no doubt waiting to bring another batch of passengers over; no help to be found there. "What do we do?!"

"Jump?" suggests Landon. We all stare at him for a moment and then back down at the murky water. It's not the worst idea and considering our options...

I give him a firm nod, and without hesitation I leap into the water. Hazel yells out at me, but as soon as I hit the water and start paddling like my life depends on it, the others quickly realise I'm not drowning and follow me in. A few more blasts strike the surface of the water, sending up spouts of spray and steam, but our attackers' accuracy is limited from up above, and we swim like we've never swum before, bolting to the left to put some distance between ourselves and the airport. I bob under the water, already digging for my magic, and when I come up I yell for Shade and Hunter to give me their hands. They oblige, linking up with the others so that we form a circle. "Any minute now, Boots!" says Shade.

I'm tempted to snark something back at him, but instead focus on concentrating; we're not out of the woods yet. The water is freezing and filthy around me, getting in my eyes and dragging me down with its weight, but I force myself to think. What am I doing wrong?

It hits me in an instant, and I could almost kick myself for missing something so obvious: I wasn't being detailed enough. It's a bit like shapeshifting -- you need to be specific, or it won't work. Once again I close my eyes and imagine London, but instead of a general view I focus on Speakers' Corner itself: the colour of the leaves on the trees, the feeling of the dirt beneath my feet, the noise of the traffic on the nearby roads. And just like that, we begin to go intangible, the world around us fading to a blur only to be replaced with that same dirt and grass. I struggle to maintain my focus, throwing everything I have behind the spell...

And it works. Wiping the water out of my eyes, I look around to see that we're standing in the late afternoon sun of London, still dripping wet, but exactly where we need to be. "You did it, Boots!" exclaims Landon, and I give him a weak nod before a wave of exhaustion hits me, making me stumble backwards.

Shade catches me, helping me onto a bench. "That was a hell of a workout," he observes. "You all right, Boots?"

"I'll be fine," I pant. "Just need some time to rest."

"I can't believe you managed that," Ruby says wonderingly. "And you took us straight here."

"As long as we're away from those Academy bastards, I'm happy," Silas says dryly, sitting on my other side.

Shade puts an arm around my shaking shoulders, and I lean into the warmth of his body, exhaustion already threatening to overpower me. "Better text your contact now, Boots," he tells me. "No time like the present, and all that."

ALL I GET in response from my mysterious ally is a terse reply of, *Be there in half an hour,* so we're left to sit in the park and wait, hoping that whoever it is will be on our side after all. With the sun streaming down on me, I warm up rather quickly, although I still feel like I've run a marathon, no doubt the result of overexerting myself. I find myself sagging into Shade's embrace, nearly nodding off a couple times as the wolf shifter absently runs his fingers through my hair, working the tangles out.

When I hear a voice calling my name, I'm sure I'm hallucinating. *Not possible,* I think groggily. *I'm cracking up from the heat.* I haven't heard that voice in years. So long, now, in fact, that I had almost forgotten what it sounded like. And yet, my eyes go wide as a figure approaches us from further up the path, a person who might as well have stepped straight out of my past and into this new, crazy world. Disbelief filling me, I struggle to sit up. Peering at her with eyes that don't buy what they're seeing, I manage to utter one wonder struck word, the pendant in my boot rubbing insistently against the sole of my foot like the last piece of a jigsaw puzzle.

"Mollie?"

CHAPTER 54

I feel like I'm in a dream. One would think that by now I would have learned not to make any assumptions about the world around me. Yet I find myself at a loss for words as I watch a phantom from my childhood cross over the swathe of grass to come to a stop right in front of me. She's close enough to touch, and almost everything about her is like I remembered: the crow's feet at the corners of her eyes, which are a bright cornflower blue; her stout stature; the way that she smiles. Her mousy brown hair is shorter than it was when I was living with her, and she's lost some weight, but there's no doubt in my mind that it's her. This is the one woman I could have seen myself living with until adulthood, and yet, like so many other things, she was snatched away from me without any consent on my part.

Beneath the layer of awestruck wonder are so many questions that I barely even know where to begin. Mollie is human -- at least, that's what I *assumed* -- and nothing happened during the time she was fostering me to give me the impression that she knew about shifters. What is she doing in London? How did she get in contact with me in the first place? What is her connection to all this? There are too many loose ends to process, and I find myself standing and staring at her, mouth agape, as I try to make sense of what I'm seeing.

"You probably have questions," she says after what feels like an eternity. Her expression is gentle, understanding, and even as I stand there, I can feel something coming apart inside of me. She shuffles her feet, looking a little uncomfortable, and starts again. "I know this probably wasn't what you were expecting, but-"

I cut her off, shooting to my feet in a heartbeat, my exhaustion from the teleportation spell all but forgotten. I throw my arms around her before I can even think about it, squeezing her as tightly as I dare and burying my face in her shoulder. She chuckles ruefully, a sound I thought I would never hear again, and I realise that I'm crying, staining her jumper.

"I'm sorry," I stammer, pulling back, still at a loss. "Your sweater..."

"Hey, hey," Mollie says, putting an arm on my shoulder as she looks at me. Out of the corner of my eye, I can see the guys watching the display, looking curious and confused all at once. "Don't worry about the sweater, Millie. To *hell* with the sweater."

That gets a watery laugh from me, and I dab at my eyes self-consciously, in spite of the fact that I'm already dripping wet from the harbour. "I don't even know where to start," I say, shaking my head in disbelief. "Why are you here, Mollie? How do you even know about..."

"Shapeshifters? Human splinter groups? The Academy?" At this last word, her expression darkens for a split second. "Would you believe me if I told you I've always known?"

I open and close my mouth a couple times, still scrambling to make sense of the situation. "How...?"

"Why don't we take a walk?" Mollie suggests. "You look like you could stand to dry off a little. You all do, actually," she amends, taking a skeptical look around at my ragtag group.

"Hang on a second," Silas pipes up, taking a wary step forward. "I'm sorry, Boots, but you're going to have to catch me up, here."

"He's not the only one who's confused," gripes Hunter.

"'Boots'?" asks Mollie, laughing. "That's quite the nickname."

"Who is this woman, Millie?" asks Hazel, coming to stand on my other side.

"She's a friend," I explain, putting a hand on Mollie's arm. "She was my foster mother, once upon a time."

"I sure was," Mollie agrees. "I'd *still* be, if I had my way. You were the best kid I ever took in, Millie, and I'm not just saying that because you're a shifter." She frowns. "Too bad we humans can't seem to leave well enough alone."

"Humans?" My brow furrows. "Wait, are you saying you had something to do with the people who run the Academy?"

"Not exactly," Mollie replies, "but that's a long story. How about we get you kids somewhere safe? You look like you could use a change of clothes, too."

"Wait, wait, wait," Shade pipes up. His grey eyes narrow as he sizes up my former caretaker. "Let's not get ahead of ourselves, people. How do we know this lady is who she says she is?"

"I..." My voice trails off as I turn back to Mollie. He has a point.

"I mean, you have to admit, it's awfully convenient that your mysterious contact just happens to be your old foster mum," reasons the wolf shifter. I can feel him shift protectively next to me as he straightens up, his fingers brushing mine.

"I can understand your skepticism," Mollie says, her expression kind. "I wouldn't be so quick to trust me either if I were in your shoes. You folks have been through a lot these past few days, haven't you?"

I swallow, unease settling into my stomach once more. I'm aware that highly trained witches have ways of changing their appearance, creating fetches and illusions of other people, but it's not an easy skill to master. Still, if this was someone sent by the Academy... Squaring my shoulders, I cross my arms. "My... friends are right," I say. "This is a hell of a coincidence, if you're telling the truth." Biting my lip, I think for a moment. What's something only the real Mollie would know? "What made us friends in the first place?" I ask her, raising an eyebrow. "I mean, what *specifically*?"

"Our names," Mollie replies without missing a beat. "One letter difference. I remember when I pointed that out, that was the first time I saw you smile." As if to drive her point home, she nods down at me. "Do you still have that pendant I gave you?"

I can't help but break out in a smile. "Of course," I reply. "The cord broke, but I keep it in my shoe."

"Hence the name," Mollie says, nodding her approval. "It's all starting to make sense." She glances around at the others. "You keep handsome company too, I see." I can feel the colour rising in my cheeks at that, and she laughs. "I'm just teasing you. Come on, we should get out of this park. People are starting to give you weird looks. What the hell *happened* to you guys, anyway?"

"It's a long story," I reply before turning to the others. "Guys, this is one of my foster parents. Mollie."

"Pleasure," she says, extending her hand to each of my friends in turn as they introduce themselves. "Are you all shifters, too?"

"Yes," answers Landon. "We had a bit of a near-miss back in Boston. The Academy has the whole city on watch."

Mollie sighs as she beckons toward the path, and we follow in a cluster, like a group of baby ducklings trailing behind their mother. "I'm not surprised," she admits as we walk, putting her hands in her pockets. "I heard about what happened at the convention centre. Bad business, and it's not going to stop any time soon."

"Speaking of which," I say, "how on earth do you know about... well, any of this?"

"It's a long story," Mollie echoes my earlier words. "The truth is, I've known about shifters since I was a little girl. My parents were on the committee managing human-shifter relations in the U.K. That was before I realised just how corrupt the organisation was."

"So you... what, keep tabs on us?" asks Hunter, sounding incredulous as we come to a stop beside the main road.

Mollie chuckles. "Hardly. Although I've spent enough time sheltering shifters on the run that I have a decent network of contacts."

"Is that why you took me in?" I breathe, staring up at her.

She turns to me, fondness in her eyes. "When I found out they were using innocent children to create hybrids, my heart went out to you. A little girl experimented on as a baby, with no parents to speak

331

of and no understanding of the world she lived in..." She shakes her head sadly. "I thought I could keep you safe. I just wasn't expecting the humans to take you away from me."

"So they reassigned you, is that it?" asks Silas.

"They knew I sympathised with the shifter community, yes," replies Mollie. "When they caught wind of the fact that I was fostering you, Millie, they were fit to be tied. I think they wanted you kept in the dark as long as possible, so that you would be malleable, susceptible to their propaganda."

"Why didn't you tell me any of this when I was living with you?" I ask.

"I wanted to," admits Mollie. "God knows I wanted to. I *planned* on it, too, once your powers started to manifest. Looking back, I could have saved you a lot of grief if I had come clean earlier." She sighs. "At any rate, when I found out they were dragging you kids to the U.S. for some bullshit peace talks, I had a bad feeling. I texted you from a burner phone. I had hoped you would at least be able to keep yourself safe..."

"Well, none of us has died so far," Landon observes dryly.

We continue to weave our way east, towards the centre of the city. The sun is warming me up a little, although my muscles are still fatigued; I end up having to lean on Landon for support as we go, and I'm not oblivious to the curious glance Mollie gives me when she sees the physical affection.

"So, tell me," she says as we turn onto a quiet street, "just how do you kids know each other?"

"We're friends," Xander supplies. "Well, at least Ruby, Hazel, and I are. As for the others..."

"We were the original test subjects," Silas explains quietly. "For the hybrid experiment."

"Then you haven't had an easy go of it," Mollie observes. "For whatever it's worth, you are all welcome to stay at my flat as long as you need to. I can't promise I can keep you safe, but I've done a decent job with the other shifters who have passed through." We arrive outside a pristine-looking apartment, following Mollie inside and up to the second level. She unlocks the front door and we file in one at a time, finding ourselves in a sprawling, well-lit, multi-room flat.

"This place is huge," breathes Hazel.

"The perks of having friends in high places," Mollie says, grinning. "Make yourselves at home. Although, I have to say, this is an interesting situation."

"How so?" asks Shade incredulously.

"All six test subjects under one roof," marvels Mollie, putting her hands on her hips.

"Six?" I ask, my eyes going wide. "You mean, there's another one?" I've always known that there must be, since I have access to the witch form, but so much time has passed that I was starting to think I would never meet her.

"Damn right, there's another one," Mollie says, peering down one of the hallways. "Edith!" she yells. "We have more guests! Come out and say hello!"

"Just a second," comes a muffled female voice.

Moments later, a door opens, and I find myself face to face with the last piece of the puzzle, the last ingredient in my strange past.

CHAPTER 55

To describe her as "pretty" would be an understatement. She was radiant, almost ethereal, like I might picture a fairy, if fairies existed. Her stature is svelte and petite, her skin pale and pearlescent, contrasted by her jet-black pixie cut and vivid green eyes. The girl smiles, and although it only takes a second for her expression to shift from vague distrust to jovial friendliness, a second is all I need to feel a brief pang of unease.

For a moment, neither of us speaks, and I can't shake the feeling that she's sizing me up as much as I'm sizing her up. This is the last test subject, the girl responsible for giving me my witch powers. I'm expecting to feel happy, reassured, even, now that the last question has been answered. By all accounts, it *should* be cathartic, especially considering the danger our little posse is in...

But.

Something about her gives me pause, and the frustrating thing is that I can't even put my finger on it. She's gorgeous, that's obvious, and I can feel the others watching me expectantly, no doubt curious about how I'll react to the new addition, but something still feels *off*.

You're being ridiculous, I tell myself, forcing myself to smile at her. *There's literally no reason to be suspicious. If anything, you should be happy to have finally met her.* So why the hell do I have this strange feeling in the pit of my stomach?

The girl breaks the silence, her voice tinkling with the hint of an Irish lilt. "You must be Millie Brix," she says, extending a delicate hand to me. "My name is Edith Conaway. It's nice to finally meet you."

I blink, my movements stiff and rusty as I accept her proffered hand, half-wondering if I'll break it if I shake it too hard. "You know who I am?" I ask with dull surprise. It's a stupid question, considering who she's been living with, but it takes me aback just the same.

Edith laughs, a bell-like sound that is half-beautiful and half-grating. "Of course," she says. "It would be a bit strange if I didn't at least know your *name*, considering..." She gestures vaguely around. "Well, *everything.*"

"I... guess that's a fair point," I admit.

"Mollie told me about what happened at the peace convention," Edith goes on, sidling up to my former foster mother with a familiarity that makes me bristle in spite of myself. "It must have been dreadful. For the humans to attack like that..." She shakes her head. "Well, you're safe here, at any rate." I glance over at Hazel, who clears her throat. "Oh my god, I feel like a buffoon," exclaims Edith. "Here I am, acting like you're the only one here. Are the rest of you shifters as well?"

"That's right," Silas replies stiffly, indicating the rest of the guys. "Believe it or not, we're the other shifters who the humans experimented on."

"Is that so?" Edith asks, her eyes going wide as she sweeps her gaze from one face to the next. The corner of her mouth twitches, and her eyes linger on each of the guys a little longer than I'm comfortable with .

Landon shifts uncomfortably from foot to foot, coming to stand beside me and slides an arm around my waist. "Boots here is the common denominator," he announces, clearly trying to inject some levity.

"Boots?" asks Edith, tilting her head to one side.

"It's sort of our nickname for Millie," Shade explains, nodding in my direction.

"*Their* nickname, not ours," Hazel adds dryly.

"Well, it's good to meet you all," says Edith, beaming around at the assembled shifters. "It looks like we have more in common than I thought."

"You could say so," Hunter replies, and the witch shifter turns to look at him once more, her expression unreadable.

"Well," says Mollie, clapping her hands together, either unaware of the tension or simply not caring. "There's no need to stand on ceremony, folks. My place is your place. Make yourselves at home." She points first towards the hallway on the left, and then the one on the right. "My bedroom is the last door on the left. There are two other empty rooms, although I've been told the couch is quite comfortable, too. Edith has taken one of the spare rooms, but..."

"I would be happy to share with someone," the witch shifter hastens to assure us, giving me another one of those coy half-smiles. "After all, we might as well be family."

"Ah, right," I say, rubbing the back of my neck before turning to the others. "Guys? Thoughts?"

Landon shrugs his shoulders. "You're the one calling the shots here, Boots."

I snort, rolling my eyes, and make my way to the opposite hallway, pausing to peer into each of the unoccupied bedrooms. In spite of its size, the flat is sparsely furnished, with few accessories and even fewer decorations. As if reading my mind, Mollie says, "I know the trappings aren't much, but I'm afraid we can't get too comfortable here. There's no telling when we might need to leave in a hurry."

"So you've spent all this time sheltering shifters?" Silas asks as he comes to look around with me.

"More or less, yeah," Mollie replies. "Most humans would call it insanity, but I would call it doing the right thing. Anyone who says things between us and the shifters are fine clearly hasn't been paying attention." Turning to address the others, she announces,

"I'm going to go out and get some supplies -- we've got a full house now. You guys make yourselves comfortable, but don't let your guards down. As far as I know, the Academy presence in London is pretty high."

"What about wards?" asks Hunter, looking from Mollie to me. "I don't want to pressure you, Boots, but it might be worth fortifying this place."

"I..." I furrow my brow, biting my lip. The basic protection enchantments I can remember from my time at the Academy might hold against humans, but shifters are another story, and I barely passed that practical. "I mean, I could *try*... I'm still pretty beat from the teleportation, but maybe if I eat something first..."

"No need," Edith announces. "Not to gloat, but I'm pretty skilled at warding."

"Plot twist," jokes Landon, crossing his arms.

"Have at it, Edith," Mollie says, already pulling on her coat. "Don't exhaust yourself. I'll be back in a bit, everyone. Don't get up to too much trouble while I'm gone." She tips me a wink, the friendliness on her face bringing me momentarily back to a simpler time of my life, and I can't help but rush back over to her, embracing her tightly.

"Thank you, Mollie," I tell her, meaning it. "Seriously. We would've been fucked if you hadn't found us."

"Oh, hardly," she laughs, "although I appreciate the compliment." With that, she grabs her handbag and walks out the front door, leaving the rest of us to take in the new dynamic.

"Well," says Ruby, putting her hands on her hips, "I guess we should probably --"

"Wards first," announces Edith, already moving towards the door.

"Wait," I protest. "What about when Mollie gets back?"

"Relax," the witch shifter tells me. "She understands our magic. If it makes you feel better, though, I'll make it semi-permeable."

"I... didn't know you could do that," I mutter, feeling sheepish. Edith doesn't respond. Instead closes her eyes, and when she transforms, it's controlled and precise -- nothing like the struggle I always have when I change forms. Green eyes now onyx black, skin ruby red, she extends her arms, and within seconds the room is pulsing with magical energy.

I exchange a look with Shade, who looks incredulous, and Hunter, who looks dumbfounded, as a bright blue glyph manifests against the door, glowing more and more intensely until its power is nearly blinding. Almost as soon as it appears, it fades away, leaving behind an afterglow that I've come to identify as a sign of enchantment.

"Damn," Hazel says, crossing her arms. "That's impressive. Can you do that, Millie?"

"Not a chance," I admit, swallowing hard. I can't help but feel a twinge of envy at the ease with which she cast the spell -- how long did that take her to learn? I've been practising for almost two semesters and I *still* have trouble just getting into my form. *Sour grapes,* I tell myself. *She's on your side.*

For some reason, that doesn't make me feel much better.

WITH THE FLAT SECURE, the rest of us are left to spread out and explore the place. I'm reminded of our time at the American Academy, but don't find myself missing it all that much; at least there are no asshole RAs getting in our way this time.

"Ruby, Xander and I will take the room next to Edith's, if that's all right," Hazel says, turning to the twins for confirmation.

"Of course," I assure her listlessly. "Go for it."

"I volunteer for the couch," Landon announces, putting a sombre hand to his chest with a tone of mock-seriousness that gets a laugh out of me. "It's a rough job, but someone has to do it."

Shade elbows him. "Good luck getting away with anything squatting in the living room."

"Unlike *you,* Ivis, we're not all delinquents," Landon fires back.

"Okay, okay," I say, laughing. "Shade? Silas? Hunter?"

"The far room is fine with me," Silas says. He turns to the wolf shifter, who shrugs.

"Fine by me," Shade agrees. "Boots? Wanna join?" He raises an inquisitive eyebrow, making my face heat up.

"I mean..." I glance over at Hunter, the odd one out. "Hunter? What do you think?"

"Hunter can stay in my room," Edith offers, coming to stand next to the vampire shifter. "There's plenty of space. We can set up a sleeping bag on the floor, maybe."

Hunter looks torn, glancing with uncertainty from me to Edith. Something passes over his face when he sees me -- a combination of melancholy and frustration -- and then he nods. "Um... yeah, sure," he says, giving the witch shifter a small smile. "That sounds good. Thank you."

"My pleasure," Edith purrs, brushing past him as she saunters back to her living quarters. Hunter shrugs sheepishly before trailing after her.

I'm left to watch him go, brows knitting together. *What was that about?* I wonder. At the risk of sounding vain, I was expecting him to put up more resistance, if not because he got last dibs, then because he'll be rooming with a virtual stranger. I swallow hard, telling myself not to overthink things. I'm tired and I'm not thinking clearly.

The others begin to disperse, Landon flops down on the couch, and it takes me a moment to realise I still don't know where I'll be sleeping. As if on cue, Silas puts a hand on my arm. "Do you want to bunk with me and Shade?" he asks tentatively. "No guarantees he won't set the room on fire, but..."

I turn to him, relieved. "That would be awesome, Silas. Thank you."

The dragon shifter smiles, hesitating for a moment before pressing a brief kiss to my hairline. "I'm going to go change," he announces. "I smell like seawater, and not in a good way."

Shade unceremoniously barges into our room, and I follow him, dragging my bag behind me. "Silas is right," I say, dropping my stuff onto a chair by the window. "We're disgusting. I think I might take a shower."

The wolf shifter smirks at me. "Want company?"

I snort, rolling my eyes. "Nice try, Ivis." Without another word, I grab a towel off one of the hooks on the wall and make my way to the bathroom. Everything will look better tomorrow, and this uneasy feeling will go away with some rest.

I hope.

CHAPTER 56

Silas was right. None of us are exactly camera-ready right now, perhaps me most of all. My hair is hanging in damp strings around my face, and I realise belatedly that I've been tracking ocean water around Mollie's apartment, making me groan. I'm going to have to deal with that, but not now. Right now, what I need is a good cleaning.

The exhaustion starts to creep in again almost as soon as I get to the bathroom. How the hell did Edith cast a high-level spell so easily? *Stop worrying about it,* I remind myself. *You've been doing this for less than a year.* Instead, I focus on disrobing, my muscles feeling weak from our sudden flight. I feel like I've run a marathon, and when I close my eyes to check on my magic, I can barely sense it, like the well of power has been completely tapped out. Shifter magic is like a muscle -- the more you use it, the stronger it gets -- but my *god*, I feel like I've been run over by a truck. Getting my arms up over my head is enough of a challenge to my aching limbs, and I feel glued to my damp clothes, which aren't exactly giving me an easy time. Wincing, I manage to pull my shirt off, and make the mistake of glancing in the mirror.

I look like a train wreck. My eyes are tired and bloodshot -- no doubt courtesy of sleeping on a motel room floor for the past few nights -- and my face looks gaunt and stressed. Worse, however, is the angry red mark that creeps up my left side, from my hip to just under my breasts. I don't even remember getting injured, but the adrenaline of running from the Academy could have easily covered up the pain. In short, I look a mess, and I'm glad no one is here to witness my pathetic struggles. I'm supposed to be in charge here.

The bathroom is big, pristine, and the water runs hot from the shower head almost immediately. I'm grateful for that, and by the time I actually step into the large shower, I feel like I could practically fall asleep standing up. It's only as the water rains down on me, washing away the dirt and muck, that the full extent of my injuries becomes clear: the impact from hitting the surface of the water must have really messed me up. I can only hope that I broke the surface tension in time for the others to avoid the same fate.

Closing my eyes, I let my forehead rest against the wall and breathe deeply for a few minutes, relishing the fact that we've made it this far. Still, I can feel the noose tightening, and no matter what Mollie says, we're not going to be safe forever.

As for Edith... Maybe I just need to get to know her better, I reason. The dynamic has shifted with her around, but for better or worse, she helped make me what I am today, and I owe it to her not to shut her out just because she wasn't at the Academy with the rest of us. It might take some time, but it's not like we have anything better to do while we're hiding out here. Resolving not to let my uncertain intuition muck things up, I'm able to start cleaning myself, luxuriating in the feeling of finally being able to relax.

By the time I step out of the shower, I've managed to steam up the entire bathroom, and end up having to wipe some of the fog away from the mirror so I can rake a comb through my tangled hair. It's only after I do this that I realise with a muttered curse that none of my clothes are clean; they all went in with me, and I have no idea where Mollie keeps her spare stuff. Groaning, I look around, and chance upon a fluffy white bathrobe hanging from a hook on the door. Good enough. I cross the room and bundle myself in it, giving my hair a quick towel dry before I finally feel ready to be seen by other people again. Letting out a long breath, I straighten up and open the door, pausing for a moment to return to the cabinet above the sink and rummage a little. Bandages, ointment, rubbing alcohol... I grab a bottle of ibuprofen and take three tablets, hoping that will take the edge off the pain a little, along with a disposable ice pack, before padding out of the bathroom, my dirty clothes tucked under one arm.

It's cold in the hallway, and I can't help the goosebumps that break out on my arms as I return to the room Silas, Shade, and I are sharing. The bed is enormous, but I'm not under any illusions that the guys will want to sleep together, so we're going to have to dig up some sleeping bags. Shade seems to be elsewhere in the house, and I feel alone enough with the door shut to open my robe and crack the ice pack, relishing in the relief it gives when I press it to the mark on my side. My eyes slide closed, and for a moment I forget where I am...

A moment too long, it seems. An instant later, there's the sound of the bedroom door opening, and a familiar roguish lilt hits my ears. "You know, Boots, you could've..." But his voice trails off when he sees me, half naked and scrambling to cover myself back up.

"Sorry," I murmur, a blush filling my cheeks. "I didn't know where you went."

The wolf shifter stares at me for a moment before slowly crossing the room. I'm surprised to see that his grey eyes aren't locked to my body at all, but rather the welt on my side. And there's something in his expression... *concern*, I realise with a start. The Academy criminal is actually *concerned* about me. "When did that happen?" he asks, tucking his hands into his pockets.

Self consciously, I close the robe more tightly around myself. "Don't worry about it," I tell him. "Happened when I hit the water, I think."

He hisses through his teeth. "They say it can feel like concrete."

Wincing, I give a rueful chuckle. "Wish I'd known that *before* I jumped, but what can you do?"

Shade extends his hand, and it takes a moment for me to realise he's waiting for the ice pack. "May I?"

"Uh... sure," I reply, passing it to him. Unfazed by the cold, he gently applies it to my side over the top of the robe, his movements achingly gentle. He hasn't been this intimately close to me since that night on the rooftop of the Boston Academy, and it's clear that my feelings haven't dulled for him in the slightest since then.

"You're shaking," Shade remarks, giving me a half-smile, but the worry in his eyes is clear as day.

"Just tired," I reply, but I can't bring myself to meet his eyes.

Slowly, the wolf shifter reaches up to place his hand over the skin of my chest not covered by the bathrobe. "And your heart is beating fast," he observes.

I raise my eyes to meet his, and the intensity of his gaze is almost enough to make me forget where I am. "I..." I whisper, my voice breathless, but then the bedroom door opens and Silas enters the room, dressed in a new change of clothes. Shade and I jump apart like we've both received an electric shock, but to my surprise, it's Silas who looks the most taken aback.

"Sorry," the dragon shifter says at once, clearing his throat and taking a step back. "I didn't realise you two were..."

"It's okay," I hasten to tell him. "Silas was just helping me with an injury. Nothing serious," I add when I see the expression of alarm on the dragon shifter's face. "We're not -- I mean, it's not like..." Fuck. Why do I always end up tripping over myself the moment feelings come into the equation? The fact that I'm in love with both of them doesn't ease my discomfort in the slightest.

"Well, gee," Shade jokes dryly, "you could've just told me my kiss was that bad, Boots."

I snap my head up to look at him with an offended expression, giving him a playful shrug. "That's not it!" I insist. "You were fine. No, great. God, I'm terrible at this." My blush intensifies as I glance over at Silas, who is watching the exchange with a mixture of curiosity and amusement on his face. This all suddenly feels too serious, and I feel the need to take the edge off. "Silas, back me up here."

Silas raises his eyebrows, looking from me to Shade. "I wouldn't know-" he begins.

I snort, collapsing onto the bed. "You two are unbelievable," I joke. "You're both *great*, okay? Better than great. Fantastic kissers."

I would've once expected some jibes from the guys, or at the very least a surly look, so I'm surprised when they exchange a look and then burst out laughing. "Relax, Boots," Shade tells me, coming to sit next to me on the bed. "I'm not territorial. Hard to believe, I know."

"And I've told you before, I'm more interested in making sure *you're* happy," Silas adds, sitting down on my other side. "Although," he adds dryly, "I'd be interested in a formal comparison."

"Mm," Shade agrees, and it's only then that I realise just how *close* they both are. "Thoughts, Boots?"

"I..." I feel like I've lost my ability to speak.

"Only one way to find out," murmurs the wolf shifter, nodding once to Silas before nuzzling his mouth into my neck. I let out a gasp as his teeth gently worry the skin there, and out of the corner of my eye I can see the dragon shifter's expression burning with barely disguised lust.

"I-I mean, if that's the *only* way..." I murmur, making the others laugh.

"Come here," says Shade, pulling me to my feet. "Stand up." His hands pause at the hem of my robe, waiting for permission, and I nod to him, allowing him to drop it to the floor.

"Shit, Boots," Shade mutters, running a hand through his hair. "You're unbelievable."

Silas hums in agreement, moving to stand behind me and run his hands over my still-damp shoulders. A shiver goes through me as he buries his face at the base of my neck, one of his hands drifting downward, between my legs, and before I know it he's working a finger gently against my clit, making me tremble and shake with every movement. I shouldn't be in the mood for sex right now, considering my day, but there's no fighting it: I've never thought about a threesome before in my *life*, but I *want* these guys. Both of them, in whatever capacity they'll allow. I let my eyes close, savouring the tenderness of their movements and the affection that seems to pour off them in waves. I know being with them is going to be nothing like

345

my first time with a high school boyfriend that I wish I could forget happened. Not that it lasted long...

By all accounts, it should be awkward. They hated each other when we first met. And yet it feels *right* somehow, like we're three pieces of a jigsaw puzzle all fitting perfectly together, the connection of our childhoods more powerful than any former rivalry.

I gasp when I feel Shade's mouth latch onto my breast, his fingers expertly teasing my other nipple as I quake from their combined touches. Silas peppers kisses over the skin of my neck as his fingers pick up their pace, and it's like he *knows* what I need somehow -- they both do, as if they're reading each other's thoughts. It's impossible, and yet the bliss is all-consuming.

"You're wet, Boots," murmurs the dragon shifter, boldly sliding a finger inside me as his strong arms keep me flush against his chest. Shade, still occupied, hums in agreement, pulling free of my breast to press his lips to mine, his hands tangling in my wet hair as his tongue brushes against my lips. I'm left a shaking mess between the two of them, fully at the mercy of the pleasure they're giving me, and it's like the pain of my injury fades away in an instant under their expert touch. I buck my hips against Silas' hand as I can feel my orgasm building, lost in the feeling of Shade's mouth on mine as he continues to ravish my breasts with attention like his life depends on it.

Working in tandem like this, it's no surprise that I unravel completely, coming with an intensity I didn't know was possible, breathing hard and feeling like jelly under their touch. Shade pulls away, running a thumb affectionately over my cheekbone while Silas holds me tenderly in his embrace, his mouth still on the skin of my neck. "Guys," I breathe, nearly at a loss for words, "that was..." I can't find a good enough adjective, so I resort to throwing my hands up and dropping them, making the other shifters laugh.

"Glad we could be of service," Shade mutters teasingly.

"Well, don't keep us in suspense," jokes Silas. "What's the verdict?"

"What can I say?" I pant. "You're both incredible."

Silas opens his mouth to say something else, but at that moment the door flies open. I whirl around, scrambling to cover myself, and my heart sinks when I meet the eyes of one *very* skeptical-looking Edith.

Fuck.

CHAPTER 57

lmost as soon as her emerald green eyes meet mine, her head snaps away, like she's embarrassed to have been caught watching. I fumble my robe back on, flushing more brightly than I ever have before and thanking all that's holy that at least the guys kept their clothes on.

"I'm sorry, I'm sorry," Edith stammers, putting a hand up and turning away. "I should have knocked. That was my bad." In spite of her sheepish words, she doesn't *look* that put off about it, which somehow only serves to heighten my own embarrassment. "I'll just, ah..." She turns to go.

"It's okay," I hasten to assure her, not wanting to draw any more attention to myself than I already have. "Was there something you needed?"

"I was just..." She takes a hesitant glance back up, her posture relaxing when she sees that I'm decent. "I realised you guys didn't have any clean clothes. I wanted to get yours so I could wash them and maybe see if Mollie has some spares for you until then."

"Oh." Silas blinks. "That's... very thoughtful of you. Thank you."

"I sure as shit could use something else," Shade complains. "I smell like a swamp."

I move to my bag, which is still damp, and pull out a sopping wet bundle of shirts, pants, and underthings. Out of the corner of my eye, I can see the guys going to do the same. Silas looks like he's been caught doing something he isn't supposed to, while Shade doesn't seem put off by the audience in the slightest; I'm starting to think the wolf shifter is just generally unflappable... *Except when it comes to me getting injured,* I realise after a moment, my stomach sending up a rush of warm sparks.

"Here you go," I say, passing my clothes to Edith.

"Are you sure you don't want help?" Silas asks cautiously, giving me an uncertain glance. "First you ward the place and now you're doing our washing for us."

Edith's eyes linger on the dragon shifter for just a *moment* longer than normal, like she's drinking in the sight of him. "I... wouldn't say no," she admits at last.

"I can help," I interject. Edith looks at me with a surprised expression as I add, hoping to lighten the mood, "It's the least I can do, considering you've had to see me naked."

Edith hesitates, looking unsure, but then laughs her tinkling laugh again. "Fair enough, Millie. The laundry room is just on the other side of the foyer. I'll meet you there in five minutes?"

"Sounds good," I say, giving her a curt nod. Seemingly satisfied, the witch shifter backs out of the room, the bundle of clothes tucked under her arm.

Groaning, I run a hand through my hair, turning back to the guys self-consciously. "Sorry about that," I tell them, feeling the need to apologise even though it wasn't my fault. "Does it count as cock-blocking if it happens *after* the fact?"

Shade cackles at that, and even Silas can't hide his snort, although I have to give him credit for trying. "Should've locked the door, I guess," the dragon shifter mutters.

"Why?" Shade protests. "I like having an audience."

"Of *course* you fucking do," Silas retorts, rolling his eyes before turning to me. "Don't apologise, Boots. She didn't knock first."

"Did you see the way she looked at you, though?" Shade asks, raising an eyebrow at Silas. I can feel my hackles go up before I can even stop myself, ashamed at my reaction but unable to stop it. "Probably picturing you without clothes on."

"Give me a break," grumbles Silas, but it's all too good-natured, like neither of them are feeling the same unease that I am, and it's *frustrating* because I know I'm being irrational.

Still, I can't stop myself from asking, "What do you guys think of her?"

"Who, Edith?" asks Shade, raising his eyebrows. "She seems fine to me."

"I don't really know her well enough to say," Silas says. "Why?"

"No reason," I reply, a little too quickly. "She's just... not what I was expecting. That's all."

Damn my lousy poker face. Shade eyes me for a moment before breaking into that shit-eating grin of his. "Wait a minute, Boots. Are you... jealous?"

"What?" I exclaim, shaking my head. "No! Of course not! I just... I mean, it's not like..."

"Holy shit, you *are*," the wolf shifter teases. "As I live and breathe! Millie Brix is getting territorial! What is this world coming to?"

"I am *not*," I protest, my cheeks flaming. "We just don't know her, that's all!"

"Sure, sure," Shade says indulgently, smirking. "Whatever you say."

I stare at him for a moment and then shake my head. "You're being ridiculous. I'm about to go help her with the laundry."

"Uh huh. I'm sure it has nothing to do with the fact that she was just undressing Silas with her eyes."

I give him a playful shove, overhearing Silas' good-natured laughter at my response, and the tension in my stomach eases up a little. "I owe her one," I rationalise. "If it weren't for her, I wouldn't have been able to teleport us out of Boston."

"Fair enough," Silas remarks. "Let us know if you need anything."

"Oh, you've already given me everything I need," I reply coyly, giving the guys an exaggerated wink that has them chuckling again.

"Now if you'll excuse me, I'm going to go be a good houseguest even with slightly wobbly legs."

The guys exchange a triumphant look as I turn and walk out of the room, keeping my head high in spite of my earlier embarrassment. It's only after the door is closed behind me that I give myself permission to ruminate. What is it about her that's bothering me so much? I try to tell myself that I *do* just feel indebted to her -- she did help make me, after all -- but that's about as hollow of an excuse as they come.

Am I really that insecure, that I don't want Silas helping her with something as mundane as washing clothes? What am I afraid is going to happen, exactly? We're all adults here, and the guys can do what they want. I don't have a claim to them; hell, it's pretty damn hypocritical of me to be getting possessive when I'm more or less juggling four different guys at once. It makes me feel shitty, and the guilt only darkens my mood further.

At least the orgasm has me feeling better, the pain in my side having dulled to a distant ache. The fact that Shade and Silas were willing to have a threesome isn't lost on me, either. Who would have thought the two guys who butted heads the most at the beginning would end up in sync when it comes to my place in the group? It's enough to give me tentative hope about the future of my relationship with the rest of them. Maybe I won't *have* to choose. At this point, I don't know if I even *could. Shit,* I think as I walk across the common area. *I'm in deep.*

Landon is sprawled on the couch, fast asleep and snoring softly, looking as gorgeous as ever in the beam of sunlight shining through the back window. I tiptoe around him, listening to Hazel and Xander's muffled voices coming from the other room, and make my way to the laundry room, where Edith is already sorting our clothes. "Hey," I say, hugging myself self-consciously as I come to stand next to her. "Sorry again about earlier."

"Don't apologise," Edith replies, giving me a smile that doesn't quite reach her eyes. "I should have knocked. Thanks for offering to help." She nods to the pile of clothes on the bench. "I'm doing brights first."

"Got it," I say, gamely beginning to paw through the damp clothes. "I'm a little surprised you're not using magic to clean these," I remark. "You did a bang-up job with the glyphs earlier."

"Oh, please." Edith laughs, flapping a hand. "That was child's play."

"Wouldn't be for me," I murmur glumly.

"Well, it's not like I can turn into a dragon or a wolf," she reasons. "We all have our gifts." Her green eyes flicker up to me, her expression unreadable. "Funny how these things work out."

"Yeah," I echo quietly. "Funny."

For a moment we continue to work in silence. "You and the guys are close," Edith observes finally.

I swallow hard. "I, uh... Yeah. I guess we are."

"Is your... relationship like that with all of them?" she asks, sounding almost deliberately nonchalant. "Like with Silas and Shade, I mean."

I close my eyes for a moment, feeling put on the spot. "I mean... not exactly, no," I admit. "That is, I think they all care about me, if that's what you mean. We've... been through a lot together."

"I have to say, I feel a little left out," the witch shifter says with a half-smile. "You guys have known each other longer than I have. It's going to take me some time to catch up."

I balk at that and then kick myself for the knee-jerk reaction. "Well, we've got nothing but time while we're here," I reply. "I'm sure we'll all be too close for comfort by the time this is all over."

"Guess I'd better get started, then," she says indulgently. "That Landon sure is gorgeous, even if he is a bit of a goofball. *Hunter*, though..." She makes a low, appreciative sound in her throat, her face lighting up. "I love the broody, sullen types. Call me a glutton for punishment. I've got a thing for gingers, too," she adds with a wink. I'm stuck wrestling between panic and anger, so I settle on staying silent. Edith seems to pick up on this, inclining her head slightly. "Unless... That's not a problem for you, is it?"

"Of course not," I reply hastily, not meeting her eyes. "They're their own people."

"Sure, but you seem to be the one calling the shots here."

I just shrug, forcing myself to keep my voice level. "It's really none of my business," I tell her.

So why am I so bothered, then?

CHAPTER 58

Edith doesn't say much more to me, seemingly lost in her own thoughts as she continues doing our chores. Part of me wants to stick around, at least *try* to get to know her better, but the other balks at the thought of hearing her opinions on any more of my companions. Feeling surly and frustrated that I don't know *why*, I excuse myself as she starts the washing machine, wandering into the common area at a loss for what to do with myself.

I'm halfway across the living room when Landon's smoky voice makes my head snap back around: "You know I'm a sucker for wet hair, Boots." I duck my head, swiping a strand of still-damp hair out of my face. I didn't realise he had woken up.

I snicker, rolling my eyes. "You're incorrigible, Landon."

"Hey, don't blame me," he protests, holding up his hands. "It's in my *nature.*"

I stare at him for a moment. "Because you're a... right. Well, I guess I'll just have to remember to never dry my hair, then."

"Oh, perish the thought!" the siren shifter exclaims, his voice taking on that melodramatic tone that always makes my heart flutter even as I roll my eyes. "Your comfort is, and always *has* been, my top priority, Boots. And speaking of which..." He leans forward on the couch, the humour vanishing from his tone. "You seem a little... bothered, if I'm telling the truth. Are you all right?"

"Me? I -- of course," I reply, a little too quickly, avoiding his eyes. "I'm just... It's just the let down, you know? We barely made it out of Boston alive. It's weird being somewhere *safe* again." *If this could really be called* safe, I think grimly.

"You sure that's all it is?" Landon asks, scooting to the side to make room for me on the couch and patting the space beside him.

"I mean, yeah," I reply, not very convincingly, as I move to sit next to the siren shifter.

Landon's black eyes bore into me. "Come on, Boots. We both know you have the world's lousiest poker face."

"That's not..." I protest indignantly. "Hunter has a worse poker face than I do!"

Landon laughs. "This is the part where you make jokes to avoid the subject, right? You've learned well."

"God, you're such a smartass," I complain, elbowing him good-naturedly. To my surprise, Landon catches hold of my elbow and pulls me against his side, slinging an arm around my shoulders as if it's the most natural thing in the world. My breathing hitches for a moment, my train of thought slipping away under the electricity of his touch. *He's so cavalier,* I muse wonderingly. Some wicked part of my mind wonders whether he's this self-assured in other, more *salacious* contexts... only prompting me to blush traitorously.

If Landon notices my nervousness, he doesn't remark on it, making me feel a little better. It's astounding how comfortable I feel around him, like we've known each other for years. "So what is it really, Boots?" the shifter asks me gently, his eyes studiously fixed forward. "You're pretty good at ramping down your feelings for the good of the group, but you have to lighten up on yourself. No one should have to shoulder all these emotions by themselves."

I sigh, and then steal a glance over my shoulder, towards the laundry room. The racket of the washing machine muffles the sound around the flat, and Edith is still in there with the door closed. "I wish

I could explain it," I admit. "That's the worst part. It's totally irrational. There's no rhyme or reason to it. Something feels *wrong."*

"About this place?" asks Landon. "About Mollie?"

I shake my head. "Not about *Mollie,* specifically. I know she is who she says she is, I feel it in my bones. I never, *ever* thought I would see her again." I can feel myself getting emotional all of a sudden, the combination of the relief of escaping the U.S. and my mounting unease making tears spring, unbidden, to my eyes. Out of the corner of my eye, I can see Landon watching me, and his hold on me tightens comfortingly, almost imperceptibly. I take a moment to gather my thoughts before continuing, my voice barely louder than a whisper, "It's her. Edith." I'm not in full control of my emotions. I feel raw, *exposed,* and right now, the Academy is just the tip of the iceberg.

"You're shaking," Landon observes quietly, concern on his face. "That teleportation spell really did a number on you, huh?"

I nod weakly, surprised to see that he's right: I'm trembling. Landon makes a small sound of distress, pulling me gently into his lap before I can protest and folding his lean form around my own. He rests his chin on my head. "What about her?" he murmurs into my hair, and I immediately understand that he brought me so close so he could speak quietly.

"I don't *know,"* I reply quietly. "She's powerful, that much is obvious. More powerful than me."

"You're being too hard on yourself, Boots," Landon tells me. "She's been at this longer than you have."

"*Has* she, though?" I reply. " We don't know anything about her, other than that she's a witch shifter, and she was the one who gave me those powers." I shake my head miserably, hating myself for how insecure I sound. "I don't like the way she looked at me when we first met her," I whisper. "I don't like the way she looked at the others."

Landon takes a long time to respond. "It's awfully convenient," he says at last, his tone measured.

"What do you mean?" I ask.

He shrugs his lithe shoulders. "First Mollie shows up out of the blue and offers to take us in. And she just *happens* to have another shifter here, a shifter who claims to have been part of the experiment with us."

"You think she's lying?" I ask, craning my neck to get a better look at him.

"I don't know," Landon admits. "It just all feels like it's worked out too well. After everything going wrong for so long..." He sighs. "Or maybe I'm just being cynical."

"What do you think of her?" I ask cautiously, not sure if I really want to know the answer. "Edith, I mean."

Landon clears his throat. "She's... friendly," he says, choosing his words carefully. "She was certainly giving Hunter an eyeful earlier."

My heart sinks. "Yeah?"

"That doesn't mean much, though," Landon hastens to add, a half-grin spreading across his face. "She pales in comparison to your magnificence, Boots."

I groan in exasperation, shifting a little in his lap, and a small sound issues from him as he adjusts his grip on me. "That's enough of *that,* you... you wannabe Casanova."

He chuckles, but the noise sounds strained, and it's only then that I realise how closely nestled together we've become, my hips settled neatly against his, the only layers separating us the denim of his jeans and the thin fabric of my bathrobe... My eyes meet Landon's, and behind the teasing humour, I can see something more intense on his face, something primal, almost *possessive...*

But then there's the sound of knocking on the front door, and I scramble to separate myself from Landon and the rather incriminating position in which I've found myself.

"Who...?" Landon begins, but before he can even finish, Edith is breezing out of the laundry room, her skin already halfway between the porcelain of her natural complexion and the ruby red of a witch's. She's fully transformed by the time she reaches the door, just as there's another brisk rapping sound.

"I got it," she announces, pausing to peer through the peephole for a moment before her hands begin to glow with power. There's a low humming sound as the wards she put up dissolve seamlessly on the other side of the door which she then unceremoniously pulls open. "I was starting to wonder if you'd gotten lost," she teases as Mollie shuffles into the flat, her arms weighed down with overflowing grocery bags.

"Yes, yes, yes," my former foster mum says dismissively. "You'll thank me for going to three different shops. It gets boring being trapped in here, let me tell you."

"Do you need help?" I offer, already halfway to my feet.

"Don't bother," Edith assures me, her tone overly saccharine. Shifting back into human form, she takes a couple of bags from Mollie and together they make their way to the kitchen area, leaving me to stand there watching them awkwardly. The way they banter is easy, like mother and daughter, as they toss various groceries to each other and laugh about this or that. A twinge of envy blossoms in my stomach, and I want to kick myself; is this all just me being jealous of the bond they have?

It's only after a few minutes of this that Mollie even seems to realise I'm standing there staring. "Millie," she exclaims. "Good lord, here I am blabbing away while you're standing there in a robe! Did you get that from the bathroom?" I nod. "Well, I'm glad you're making yourself comfortable, at least. There are some extra clothes in my bedroom, in the bottom dresser drawer. Sheltering this many runaway shifters, you start to accumulate a decent number of hand-me-downs. I'm sure there's something in there that will fit you until your clothes are dry. Edith..."

Edith moves to approach me, but I hurriedly reply, "That's all right, I can find them on my own. You stay here and just... you stay." Stiffly, I turn on my heel and bolt for the hallway, only to hear Edith clear her throat behind me. "Other hallway, Millie."

Flushing angrily, I mutter, "Right, sorry," and make a beeline in the opposite direction.

I damn near throw the door closed behind me, pinching the bridge of my nose and letting out a long sigh. Is *this* what fleeing the humans has done to me? Turned me into a suspicious, nervous wreck? And that's not even going into what happened with Landon on the couch just now. Was he... turned on? He was certainly starting to seem affected by me, and the worst is that I wasn't even aware of what I was doing. The feeling of being wrapped up in his embrace, allowing him to murmur against my hair in that gorgeous accent of his...

Clothes, I remind myself. Right. Smoothing my hands over my thighs, I turn to Millie's simple dresser and pull open the bottom drawer. Some of the clothes look older than others, things that would have been in style five or ten years ago, and I find myself struck again by how *involved* Mollie has clearly been in the fight for shifter freedom. A lot of them are too big from me -- my height is decidedly *not* one of my strong suits -- but eventually I settle on denim shorts and an oversized tee, tugging them on and bunching up the bathrobe before meandering back out of the room.

What I see in the kitchen is enough to make my thoughts grind to a halt. Millie's return must have drawn the others back out, as our ragtag group in its entirety is now gathered in the kitchen. That's not the problem.

Silas and Shade are still needling each other from the kitchen table, while Landon seems to be teasing a blushing Hazel about something. Mollie is already laying lunch ingredients out on the counter while Ruby and Xander speak to each other in low voices, in that way only twins can.

Edith is sitting on the kitchen counter, looking like the cat that ate the canary. Hunter is sitting next to her, closer than I would ever expect for people who have known each other all of one afternoon.

That's the problem.

CHAPTER 59

For a long moment I can only stand there, paralyzed, until Mollie's voice pulls me out of my stupor. "Millie? Are you all right?"

"Yes," I reply. "Sorry. I was just thinking." Once again kicking myself. I've stood up against powerful Academy representatives, classroom bullies, and human extremist terrorists. So why the hell does it take a coquettish mind like Edith to get me all turned around like this? *Enough is enough.* I'm not some kind of emotionally unstable little girl. I've dealt with worse than a little jealousy. I'm going to try to be reasonable about this. "What are you making?" I ask, creeping up to the stove to stare into the pot Mollie is stirring.

"Pasta," Mollie replies bluntly, although she frowns. The pot looks more like it's full of a congealed mess of tentacles than spaghetti, and the smell coming from the pan on the other burner doesn't *exactly* seem edible. "I know, I know," she says, seeing my expression. "It's supposed to be puttanesca, although I'm starting to wonder if takeout would have been the better option."

"I see your cooking skills haven't improved since I lived with you," I observe teasingly.

Mollie groans. "That's a low blow, Millie," she says, reaching out a hand to ruffle my hair affectionately. For a moment I'm transported back to my primary school days, all the precious moments like this that made me feel *normal* in the face of overwhelming abnormality, an abnormality that pales in comparison to what I'm experiencing right now.

Discomfort washes over me again when I notice that Edith has turned her gaze away from Hunter to watch me, a thin smile plastered on her face, but her green eyes are glowing with something I don't quite like. "Just like old times?" she asks, and although her tone is nonchalant, I can tell that it's masking discomfort. Maybe I'm not the only one with some insecurity about my relationship with Mollie.

"I sort of lost count of the number of times we had cereal for dinner," I reply, relishing the sound of Shade's surprised laughter.

"Wait, seriously?" he asks. "I was starting to think I was the only one who did that."

"Oh, you absolutely *aren't*," I inform him with mock haughtiness. "Frosted flakes were ninety percent of my diet."

"I like you more and more each day, Boots," the wolf shifter says, grinning and giving me a playful nudge on the shoulder. As if he and Silas weren't just sharing me not long ago.

"As interesting as it is to talk about breakfast foods," says Ruby, moving forward to fill up her water glass at the crowded sink, "we should probably figure out a game plan sooner or later."

"Agreed," says Mollie, "although let's hold off until lunch is ready. I find it's always easier to talk serious business on a full stomach."

"Not to look a gift horse in the mouth or anything," Landon says, turning to glance at Mollie, "but I *think* the pasta sauce might have been on the stove too long."

"Shite," Millie exclaims, rushing back to the saucepan and fanning at the acrid smoke with a dish towel. I take an inquisitive glance back at the pasta, attempting to stir it only to discover that it has completely solidified into a block of noodles.

"I think that settles it," says Edith, jumping down from the counter and taking the saucepan from Mollie. "Who here likes Chinese food?"

· · ·

An hour later, we're all seated around Mollie's admittedly sizable dining room table, jammed in shoulder-to-shoulder as we pour over a veritable feast of fried rice, chow mein, and dumplings. My stomach is making its hunger known loud and clear, and I wince when it lets out a growl loud enough to be heard across the street.

"Now tell us how you *really* feel," Landon jokes from across the table.

I stick my tongue out at him. "I'll be sure to worry about propriety as I'm pigging out, Thyme." Without further ado, I begin shoveling food into my mouth.

"You should really slow down," Edith informs me, her tone sounding almost too polite. "Too much food at a time will slow you down. As a shifter, though, I would think you'd know that already."

I blink, seething a little. "I'll take that into consideration the next time I'm *not* coming off a dangerous chase and international teleportation spell."

"That's what practise is for," argues Edith.

"You know, Millie," says Mollie through a mouthful of food, "maybe Edith could teach you a few things. Help you hone your witch shifter skills. She's incredibly talented -- one of the best I've ever seen."

Edith smirks a little, obviously preening. "I would be happy to," she tells me. "My mother was a witch shifter, too. She taught me everything I know."

"So why didn't you end up at the Academy?" Xander asks inquisitively.

"My parents were... anti-establishment," Edith replies, a little evasively. "My mother had classical training, but she hated every second of it. The humans are pretty much all the same -- subjugate, sow discord, keep us under their thumbs... No offense, either of you," she adds, looking from me to Mollie.

"None taken," Mollie says.

I fidget with my fork for a moment. "I'm not a human," I remind her.

"Right," Edith says. "You're a hybrid." There's an unspoken challenge behind her words -- a superiority complex, maybe?

"Boots didn't choose to be a hybrid any more than you chose to be a shifter," Silas comes to my defense. He's sitting to my right, with Hazel to my left, and I shoot him a grateful look. "Hell, she's been the most taken advantage of out of all of us. All the humans wanted was to make her into a weapon."

"And they still do," I add quietly, turning my eyes down to my food.

"Which is exactly why we need to figure out our next step," says Xander. "We're not exactly sitting ducks here, if this place really is off the humans' radar, but we can't stay here forever either."

"True," admits Hunter. "Sooner or later we're going to have to take the fight to the humans themselves."

"That's very noble of you," Edith purrs, scooting her chair closer to his.

"I owe it to Boots," Hunter tells her. "She was the one who made me confident in my abilities." His blue eyes meet mine for a moment, but then he breaks eye contact, almost like he's afraid of how I'll react to the praise.

"Is that so?" Edith asks, her emerald gaze turning on me. "Now if only you could find that confidence yourself, Millie."

"Working on it," I retort curtly.

"All this talk of going after Hawthorne is great in theory," says Hazel, "but I'm pretty sure it's going to take more than a human and a handful of shifters to take down the establishment."

"Right," I agree. "We'll need allies."

"You're talking about building an army," says Silas. "Only problem is, pretty much all the shifters *I* know are right in the eye of the storm."

"You guys aren't thinking big enough," says Edith. "Why look for allies who haven't even mastered their abilities, yet? We should be looking at Academy graduates. Other outsiders, like me. Fully-fledged shifters who can go head-to-head with the professors at the school."

"I'm open to suggestions," I say. "Silas, you mentioned shifter-only communities, right?"

"Sure," says the dragon shifter, "but there's no guarantee they're even still there. They could've ended up disappearing the same way my..." His voice breaks a little, and I reach to him under the table and intertwine my fingers with his. He gives my hand a grateful squeeze.

"Lucky for you, we won't need to look that hard," Edith replies. "I happen to have half a dozen contacts in this neighbourhood alone, and that's not even talking about the rest of London."

"Really?" Landon raises his eyebrows. "And just how did you happen to make so many magical acquaintances?"

"Easy," Edith answers without missing a beat. "I was born and raised here."

"What happened to your parents?" asks Ruby.

Edith doesn't reply immediately, looking away as an unidentifiable emotion passes over her face. "They're not around anymore," she says. "They left me at a group home when I was fifteen. Said they had taught me everything they could, and couldn't protect me any longer."

"That's brutal," Hunter says softly, and she looks at him with a practised smile.

Mollie clears her throat. "That seems like as good a place to start as we have," she says. "We can start knocking on doors, trying to drum up support. If your contacts have contacts of their own, Edith..."

"Then we can build an army," the witch shifter finishes for her.

I nod, grateful, at least, that she's willing to give us actionable suggestions. "So where do we go first?"

Edith thinks for a moment. "I know of a couple not far from here who might be a good place to start. A siren shifter and a dragon shifter. Both powerful, and respected in the community. I can take us there tomorrow."

"We shouldn't all go," warns Shade. "We've all got targets on our backs."

"Hunter and I will go," Edith announces decisively, paying no mind to Hunter's surprised look.

"Millie should probably go, too," suggests Mollie. "She's sort of in charge of this operation."

The witch shifter blanches a little, but then forces a smile. "Right. Of course. Millie can come too."

Landon raises his eyebrows at me, the look on his face telling me everything I need to know. I can only shrug in reply.

The rest of the day wears away without much fanfare. I can feel my powers regenerating, and with any luck, I should be back up to par by the time we go to visit Edith's friends tomorrow.

The others have already quietly made their way to bed, setting up makeshift cots and blanket piles all throughout the apartment. I'm on my way out of the bathroom when I practically bump full-force into Hunter. "Sorry!" I exclaim, pulling back. "I didn't realise anyone was still out here."

"You know me," he jokes weakly. "I always come last."

The casual way he says it is enough to break my heart. "What do you mean?" I ask him quietly, shrinking in his shadow.

He shrugs. "I'm not exactly on the same level as the rest of you. That's no secret."

"But you're getting better," I protest. "Besides, none of us are master shifters, anyway." *Well, maybe except for Edith,* I think, a little bitterly.

Hunter just shakes his head. "I'm starting to think I..." he says, but then cuts himself off, breaking eye contact.

"You what?" I prompt him gently.

"I'm starting to think I'm not worthy to be fighting alongside you," he replies, his voice soft and husky. "You're all so strong. It's like... here I am, taken care of by the Academy all my life, and I can still barely get into my form. And you're this beautiful, strong, smart..." He shakes his head. "I don't deserve you."

"Hunter," I whisper, my hand coming to rest on his cheek. He flinches at my touch, as if the contact burns him. "Don't say things like that."

He takes my hand and removes it from his cheek. "Why not?" he asks, sounding borderline despairing. "It's true." And without another word, he sidesteps me and disappears into the bathroom, unceremoniously closing the door between us. I'm left to stare after him, dumbstruck.

Listlessly, I make my way back to my room, crawling into bed next to Silas as Shade climbs in on my other side. The dragon shifter is already asleep, so I put an arm around him and press a kiss to his neck. Shade pulls me against his chest, tangling me up in his arms, and although I feel safe between the two shifters, sleep doesn't come.

CHAPTER 60

The next morning dawns bright and brilliant, sunlight streaming through the street facing window, warming my face and pulling me gently out of the grip of sleep. For a moment I bury my face in Shade's chest -- somehow I got turned around in the night and ended up tangled up between the two shifters. Not that I'm complaining, mind you -- but then I remember today's agenda and force myself to sit up with a groan.

Silas slings an arm over his eyes while S hade makes a belligerent sound, his grey eyes cracking open ever so slightly. "Big plans, Boots?" he mumbles at me.

"Just going on a run with Edith and Hunter," I reply, keeping my voice low so as not to disturb the sleeping dragon shifter. "Don't worry about it."

"I don't worry about *anything*," Shade informs me with a coy smile. There's a pause, and then he amends. "Well, *almost* anything." His eyes meet mine, and I can tell he's concerned, although he does a damn good job of hiding it.

"Come on, Shade-" I begin, startled when he pulls me down for a kiss tender enough to make my stomach turn to liquid.

"*Almost* anything," the wolf shifter repeats softly, resting his forehead against mine before letting me go and falling back onto the bed. "God, I feel like I could sleep all day. Make me some tea?"

"Nice try," I tell him teasingly, maneuvering around him and out of the bed.

"Ruthless," the wolf shifter complains, but he doesn't sound all that broken up about it. I chuckle, shaking my head, and begin to dress; someone has laid out our freshly-dried clothes on the shelf in the hallway, a welcome alternative to what I was wearing before. Within minutes, I'm ready to go, my hair swept into a ponytail and my eyes blinking against the bright morning sunlight.

The sound of voices from the kitchen alerts me to the fact that I'm not the first one up. I creep out of my room, pausing at the end of the hallway and peering in at the table where Edith and Hunter are already seated. They're talking in low tones, and once again she's conveniently positioned herself a little too close to him for my comfort.

I bite my lip, almost afraid to make my presence known; that moment with Hunter last night is still fresh in my mind, and I'm worried that the instant he looks at me with those ocean blue eyes, uncomfortable questions will start spilling out of me. Swallowing hard, I try my best to look nonchalant as I mosey into the kitchen, making a beeline for the kettle to pour myself some tea before rummaging briefly in one of the cabinets.

"There you are," says Edith, looking up at me. "We were starting to wonder if we should go wake you up. Although after yesterday..." She stifles a smile, making my ears turn red, and the intense look of discomfort on Hunter's face tells me the cat is out of the bag. She must have told him about what she walked in on after my shower.

"Don't worry about it," I tell her breezily. "We're all family here, right?" I give her a thin smile to match the loaded statement, but she doesn't respond, instead turning back to Hunter.

"Anything else we need before we go?" he asks.

Edith shakes her head. "We're all we need, although I appreciate your conscientiousness." She gets to her feet and holds her hand out to him -- *as if the guy can't stand up on his own,* I think bitterly, slinging a backpack over her shoulder. "Charms," she says by way of explanation. "My own work. You never know when they might come in handy."

"Fair enough," I admit grudgingly as I wolf down a biscuit and chug my tea, wincing at the burn in my throat. "Well, there's no use waiting around any longer. Shall we?"

"Whatever you say, Millie." Again with that disingenuous smile. It makes my skin crawl. Is this *really* the person who made me a witch?

Hunter doesn't say anything, following Edith to the door without so much as a glance at me. My stomach drops -- *is he mad at me?* I wonder with a feeling of sudden dread. It's ridiculous, I know; it's not like we've fought about anything, and just last night he was praising my work teaching him! So what gives?

The tension is palpable as we file out of the apartment, Edith disabling her hexes with an enviable ease before pulling the door open and leading us out and down the hallway. Hunter is making a point to avoid my gaze, his expression serious and almost haunted, and it takes everything I have not to ask him what the hell has gotten into him.

At least the weather is on our side. Aside from a cool breeze, the day is gorgeous, and I feel revitalised as we step out onto the street and begin to make our way down the block. Edith clearly knows where she's going, which is good, because this neighbourhood might as well be a maze to me. I feel exposed, like at any moment now an Academy agent will pop out of an alleyway and drag me into the shadows, but at least we have numbers on our side. For whatever else I may think of her, Edith is a strong witch. If anyone tries anything, at least we'll be able to give them a hell of a fight.

Unable to hold my tongue any longer, I fall into step beside Hunter. "So how's the living situation working out?" I ask.

He shrugs, his eyes fixed on the pavement. "No complaints," he says, his voice flat.

Edith shoots him a coquettish look over her shoulder. "None from me either," she adds with a wink. "Here's to not-so-strange bedfellows, huh?"

"Bedfellows?" I ask, blanching a little.

The witch shifter laughs. "Relax, Millie. It's just an expression."

Is it, though?

I swallow hard but don't reply.

We continue on in silence, eventually leaving the shops behind in favour of a block of flats that looks like it was constructed hundreds of years ago. "Well, here we are," she announces, spreading her arms out. "Stop one, right?"

"Right," I echo curtly.

We make our way around a corner and down a side street before coming to a stop in front of a narrow complex. "Shall I do the honours?" Edith asks, nodding at the doorbell. Before I even have a chance to reply, she's ringing it, squaring her shoulders and smoothing her shirt like she's here for a job interview and not a rebel recruitment. "Jennifer?" she says into the speaker. "It's me, Edith Conaway!"

There's a long pause before the person on the other end wordlessly buzzes us in. Looking rather self-satisfied, Edith pulls open the door and leads us to a glass lift, which slowly rises until it slows to a stop at the top floor. We arrive outside an expensive-looking penthouse apartment; this must have been what she was talking about when she said these guys were influential in the shifter community. We'll just have to hope they'll use that influence to our benefit.

Edith knocks on the door like she's done this a million times before, and I'm a little shocked by her nonchalance -- how many times has she visited these people? But before I can think about it too hard, the door opens to reveal a stunningly beautiful red-haired woman who appears to be in her mid-thirties. The siren shifter, I would assume. Her face lights up when she sees Edith. "There you are," she exclaims, holding her arms out to embrace the witch shifter. "I was half expecting not to see you, Edith! You've been off the grid for some time."

"It comes with the territory," Edith replies with a grin. "Dodging the humans is kind of a full-time job."

"I know it well," the woman, Jennifer, says, nodding. She holds the door open for us and we filter into a spacious apartment. "And just who are your friends?" she asks, glancing from me to Hunter.

"This is Hunter," Edith says, gesturing to the vampire shifter. "He's a shifter. And this," she continues, "is Millie. She's the hybrid I told you about."

Jennifer's eyebrows shoot up. "Certainly not something you see every day. Well, come in. Make yourselves comfortable." She indicates a sofa in the living room, where I stiffly take a seat, with Hunter following close behind. "Caleb?" she calls into one of the other rooms. "We have guests! Edith and her hybrid!" I bristle a little at the way she calls me *Edith's hybrid,* like I'm some kind of prized pig at a county fair, but I stay silent, not wanting to jeopardise a potential partnership.

A big blond man breezes into the room moments later, beaming at the three of us as he extends a hand to shake each of ours. He drops into an easy chair near one of the windows, Jennifer following suit. Their eyes sweep over us, lingering for an uncomfortably long time on me before meeting Edith's green ones. If I didn't know any better, I might wonder if they know more than they're letting on, but considering the idea to contact them didn't come up until yesterday, somehow I doubt it. They're probably just amused by the novelty of having a crossbreed in their midst. "So," asks Caleb, leaning back and crossing his legs, "what brings you here?"

"There's no easy way to say this," I tell them, taking charge. "We're on the run from the U.K. Shifter Academy. We've *been* on the run, ever since Boston."

"Mm." Jennifer nods slowly. "Yes, that was... unfortunate."

"That's a bit of an understatement," remarks Hunter. "Dozens of people died. Students."

"Yes," Jennifer hastens to say. "Of course."

There's an awkward pause as they size us up. I wish I could put my finger on what is making me so uncomfortable. "At any rate," I say, "none of us is going to be safe from the humans until we can take the fight to them. And we're going to need help to do that."

"I see," Caleb says thoughtfully. "And you thought to come ask us to help."

"I mean, yeah," I reply sheepishly. "If that's something you're open to. Edith suggested coming to you first. She... mentioned that you have a lot of influence around here."

"*Did* she, now?" asks Caleb, cocking his head to one side. "Yes, I would expect that from you, Edith. You always were... precocious."

"Look," I say, fidgeting a little, "we don't want to make you do anything you're uncomfortable with. I know this is a lot to ask of complete strangers. But don't you think we'll all be safer without the humans trying to control us?"

"I suppose that's a matter of perspective," Jennifer muses. "The humans have given us stability. We've made sacrifices for that stability, yes, but the alternative is so... ugly. Untrained shifters running about, causing untold chaos... Don't you think it's worth counting our angels and moving on?"

"That's no way to live," I reply firmly.

"To each their own," Caleb says, shrugging. "I'm sorry to disappoint you folks, but we're perfectly content with our lot in life. I would rather see a world that *isn't* overrun by magic users."

"I... see," I say slowly, starting to get to my feet. "Well then, I guess we shouldn't take up any more of your time. Edith, should we...?"

Edith, who has been strangely silent for the whole exchange, follows my lead, but when we make for the door, Jennifer is suddenly out of her seat, extending an arm to bar us from leaving. "What's the rush?" she croons, her eyes locking with mine. "Don't you want to stay a while?"

"Thank you," I say, attempting to sidestep her, "but we really should-"

"I'm sorry," Jennifer laughs, giving me a toothy smile. "You misunderstand me. That wasn't a request."

"What do you..." I begin, but I stop mid-sentence, my eyes going wide as my anxiety turns to full-blown fear.

Something is very wrong here.

That's the only coherent thought I have before the violence starts.

CHAPTER 61

Jennifer lunges for me, her eyes blazing with a fury I've never seen before, and it's all I can do to stumble out of the way just as she swipes at me like a feral animal. "Edith!" I yell, glancing around for the witch shifter. She's standing at the far end of the room, eyes wide and watching, but she's not doing anything.

Why isn't she doing anything?!

"Edith!" I shout her name again just as Jennifer leans back and expels a jet of flames from her mouth. I dart out of the way and gape at her for a moment, completely poleaxed. *So* she's *the dragon,* I think. *But that means...*

Oh. Oh shit.

I whirl around, my hands flying to cover my ears as I search the room frantically for Caleb. The realisation has only just dawned on me, but I'm too late; he opens his mouth and lets out an ungodly screech; the soundwaves sending vibrations through the air that are nearly enough to knock me off my feet. He's transformed already, covered in shimmering green scales. On some level, I'm aware of Jennifer transforming as well, the room palpably heating up from the power of the fire she's unleashing, but it all seems so far away all of a sudden.

Caleb's eyes are locked on me, his mouth twisted in what could maybe be a smirk, and blocking my ears might as well be useless. The sound pierces the space around me, digging into the core of my being and twisting up there like a burr, hopelessly tangled in me. I struggle against it for a moment, but it's no use; he has me wrapped around his finger, and I can feel myself slipping away second by second. The fight drains out of me in an instant, and suddenly I find myself unable to pry my eyes away from him. In that instant, he's the most handsome, alluring, *captivating* man I've ever seen, and although some part of me knows I've just fallen victim to his siren's song, that part is trapped behind an impenetrable magical wall.

"Come here, Millie," he commands. "Drop your arms, please." His voice sounding like honey to my bewitched ears, and I'm helpless to fight it, my hands falling limply to my sides and my legs moving as if of their own accord. I've never been on the receiving end of a siren's magic before; it's brutal, like being trapped in a glass cage even as your body is manipulated by someone else, and I thrash against its confines like my life depends on it.

For all I've learned to harness my siren abilities, I never once thought to practise *resisting* them.

"Boots!" Hunter yells, sounding like he's halfway through his own transformation, but a roar from Jennifer silences him, and there's a thud, followed by the sound of shattering glass. My stomach drops -- did she knock him out the window? -- but then I hear him groan as a melee breaks out between him and the dragon. *He's hurt,* I think in a panic.

My muscles are on fire, my brain on overdrive as I scramble to access my magic, to fire *something* back at him, but it's like a barrier has gone up between myself and that by now familiar pool of power. It's as inaccessible to me as Edith is.

Edith...

It takes everything I have just to drag my eyes away from Caleb for a moment, glancing to the left to see what's become of her. She's still just *standing* there, watching it all unfold with Jennifer's dragon form casting a dark shadow over her. For all her abilities, she's seemingly useless right now, like a deer in the headlights. Could she have fallen victim to Caleb's song, too? But that wouldn't make sense, I realise as my eyes are forcibly brought back to the siren shifter. His commands were directed at *me*. And if he had control of her, why would Jennifer even need to bother with her?

That's as far as my thoughts take me before Caleb is speaking again in that ungodly, inhuman voice. "Millie, I'm waiting."

I shuffle forward, hating how easily he bends me to his will.

"There's a good girl," he croons, the sound making me shudder. "Now, I want you to go to the window."

I do an about-face like a marionette on strings, walking stiffly to the bank of glass windows overlooking the London street; it's far below us, multiple stories down, and I realise with a sinking feeling that my theory about Hunter wasn't so far off. There's no way I'll survive that fall in human form.

"Open it," Caleb commands. I'm trapped in my own body as my trembling arms reach out and pull the window open. "That's right," he says. "Now, I want you to jump."

I feel sick. Every movement feels like climbing a mountain. "Please..." I croak.

"Don't argue with me, Millie," Caleb tells me. "The sooner you do as I say, the sooner this can be over."

I slowly approach the window, a zombie in a girl's body. The street glares up at me from below as I bring first one foot to the edge, and then the other...

And then the front door bursts open, nearly flying off its hinges from the force of the vibrations pulsing through the air. "Boots, don't!" I recognise Landon's voice in an instant, my heart leaping to my chest. He's using his siren's song on me, too, but instead of dread, the sound of his fills me with a rush of warm relief. The command stops me in my tracks.

Edith is still frozen in place, Hunter is fighting Jennifer with everything he has, and it's down to me, Landon, and Caleb. How he got here, I have no idea, but there's no time to wonder about that now.

"Jump, damn it!" commands Caleb, and I can feel the force of his words.

"Don't you *dare*, Boots! Do you hear me?" Landon sounds panicked. Within me, the two opposing commands battle each other, pulling me in different directions. I'm stuck, desperate to go to Landon, but Caleb's song is so strong...

At that moment, a blast of pale blue magic erupts from Edith's fingers and collides with Caleb, hitting him squarely in the chest. She's finally gotten a hold of herself, it seems. That's enough to break Caleb's concentration, and I take a few staggering steps backward, nearly falling into Landon's arms. "Where did you come from?" I ask him wonderingly, staring up into his obsidian eyes.

"Don't worry about that," Landon tells me soothingly, brushing a strand of hair out of my face. The relief in his voice is obvious. "I'll always save you."

I glance up. Edith has shapeshifted and is holding Caleb off with some kind of spell. Hunter, on the other hand...

"Hunter!" I yell, struggling to my feet. He's in his vampire form, which has surely saved his life -- the enhanced durability is the only thing keeping him from being eviscerated as Jennifer shakes him furiously in her massive jaws, like a dog with a toy. Without thinking, I reach for my dragon magic, shifting more easily than I ever have in my life. The room seems to shrink as I grow, power rippling through me as I flap my wings and hurtle across the space toward the other dragon attacking one of the men I love. My body collides with hers full-tilt, and the impact causes her to drop Hunter as I rake at her with my claws. She retaliates with a burst of fire, but I manage to bowl her over, pinning her beneath me as I tear at her neck furiously with my teeth. Jennifer lets out a roar of outrage as we grapple on the floor, all other sounds receding in the wake of my blind fury.

It's only Landon's voice that's able to bring me back to the present. "Boots, come on!" he shouts from the other side of the room. "We have to go!"

I glance up from the other dragon to see Caleb unconscious on the ground. Edith, Landon, and Hunter are already at the door. I give

Jennifer one last swat with my claws for good measure, and then leap off her, transforming back into my human form in the process. Together, we make a break for the exit, afraid to even look back.

"So let me get this straight," Shade says, pacing in front of the sofa. We're back at Mollie's place, a little banged up but no worse for wear. I'm curled up against Landon's side, and his hand is idly running through my hair in a comforting gesture. If he hadn't shown up, I would be a puddle on the pavement right now. "You went to visit these guys, they *attacked* you, and then Landon came in the nick of time?"

"That's right," the siren shifter says lightly.

"What made you even decide to follow us?" I ask him.

Landon shrugs, his hand coming to rest on the small of my back. "I had a bad feeling, I guess you could say. I was supposed to be out grabbing a coffee, but I figured I would at least tag along to make sure things didn't go badly. Looks like I was right."

"You were," I tell him softly. "Thank you."

He gives me a crooked smile that makes my heart skip a beat. "'Course, Boots." His expression hardens as he turns to Edith. "Why weren't you helping?" he asks. "When I came in, you were just... standing there."

The witch shifter grimaces, avoiding our eyes. "I'm sorry," she says quietly. "I was just... stunned, I guess. Jennifer and Caleb were always my friends. They were supposed to be on the *shifters'* side, not the humans." She shakes her head disbelievingly. "The Academy must have gotten to them. It's the only explanation."

Silas scrutinises her from his place by the mantelpiece. "You're saying you had no idea they'd switched sides?" he asks, his eyes narrowing.

"Of course I didn't," Edith snaps. "D o you think I would've brought you guys there otherwise?"

"I don't know," Silas admits, his broad shoulders hunching.

"Something about this doesn't feel right," Shade says, still walking back and forth restlessly. "If the humans got to them, how many more shifters around London have also been converted?"

"We can't think like that," Edith insists, glancing at Mollie for backup. The human woman nods.

"She's right," Hazel agrees. "We can't give up just because of one near-miss."

"Easy for you to say," Hunter mutters. I turn to him. He's studiously avoiding my gaze, the pain sharp in his blue eyes.

"What do you mean?" I ask him gently.

He throws his hands up. "What do you think?" he demands sharply. "Caleb had you on that ledge, Boots. You almost *died,* and I couldn't do a damn thing to stop it."

"Hey," I tell him, "you were busy with Jennifer. No one knew *he* was the siren."

Hunter just shakes his head. "It should've been me."

"Don't say that," I tell him, my voice wavering a little. "Don't you dare say that."

The vampire shifter remains silent for a moment, then gets up and walks out of the room.

"I say we stay the course," says Xander, giving Hazel's hand a squeeze. "Tomorrow we can try another group. With more of us as backup."

"What about the humans?" asks Silas. "We're not exactly inconspicuous."

"What choice do we have?" Ruby counters. "The whole city could be out to get us, for all we know."

The conviction behind her words weighs heavy on me, makes me balk. Part of me wants to scream, and the other part wants to bury my head in my hands, because I know she's right.

We've been backed into a corner without even realising it.

CHAPTER 62

The business with Edith's so-called allies has left all of us on edge; that much is obvious. The others don't even have to say anything -- we can all feel it, that awful certainty that things are coming to a head, and we're helpless to stop it. The question remains unspoken amongst us, but I know without even needing to ask that we're all thinking the same thing.

If we can no longer trust the other shifters in London, who *can* we trust?

I disentangle myself from between Shade and Silas the next morning, responding to the insistent growling of my stomach. Ruby, Xander and Hazel are gone when I enter the kitchen, but I notice a hastily scrawled note from the latter on the counter: *Out to track down some more leads. Should be back later -- if not, send help.* Right. Not exactly easy when I don't know where they've gone, but I'm too mentally drained at this point to let the anxiety take hold of me. I'll just have to hope they're okay.

Mollie isn't around either, but I'm actually less worried about her, in all honesty; she's a tough cookie -- I've known that since the day I first met her -- but more importantly, she's human. As long as she takes care not to draw undue attention, she doesn't have to worry about walking around with a target on her back the way the rest of us do. As much of a gift as our shapeshifting abilities are, they've become just as much a curse.

I pile my hair on top of my head in a messy bun before padding over to the refrigerator and grabbing an apple. I would have preferred junk food, but Mollie, for all her culinary ineptitude, is hell bent on keeping us healthy -- chalk it up to her maternal instincts, or something. Either way, beggars can't be choosers, so I dig in with a vengeance as I drop into a chair beside the kitchen table. I can see Landon over on the couch, his arm draped over his eyes -- he appears to be dozing, but it's hard to tell with the siren shifter. I still feel like I owe him for yesterday; he saved my life, the only person who possibly could have in those circumstances.

The sound of voices catches my attention just as Shade and Silas emerge from my room, looking bleary-eyed and out of sorts. "I'm telling you, you're wrong," the wolf shifter insists. "It's all about avoiding concentrating. That's how you get distracted."

"You *would* say that," Silas fires back. "When was the last time your strategy didn't amount to 'charge in, both guns blazing, and watch what happens'?"

"I resent that," Shade mutters.

Silas gives him a daring grin. "You want to put that theory to the test, Ivis?"

Shade raises his eyes. "Is that a challenge, Silas? You'd better be careful -- I hear you're still not back to a hundred percent."

The dragon shifter's expression hardens. "I'm close enough."

The two guys come to a stop by the kitchen table. "We'll get Boots to judge," Shade says, winking at me.

"Nah, ah, ah, I'm not about to get sucked into another one of your arguments," I laugh. "You guys can duke it out yourselves."

"Fine," says Silas. "We'll take it to the roof, then."

"You know you have the advantage in tall places," Shade protests.

"Is that a problem? You just said I wasn't back to full strength."

The wolf shifter grumbles, but concedes, and the two guys make their way to the door. "We'll be outside, settling this," Silas announces, elbowing Shade. "We'll see which one of us is the better fighter. You sure you don't want to moderate, Boots?" He raises his eyebrows at me.

The idea of two gorgeous guys duking it out for my attention *does* sound appealing, but what happened yesterday has me spooked. I'm not even sure I can bring myself to go out and meet our next prospects, and that's something we *have* to do. I don't relish the idea of being forced out a window again. "You guys go ahead," I tell them weakly. "I'm going to rest up in here. Rough day yesterday, you know." They nod in unison, and Shade pushes the door open. "Be careful," I call to them as they file out of the apartment.

"Always am," Silas calls back, and with that, they're gone. I'm left to sit in silence, damn near twiddling my thumbs as I turn over the events of the past few days in my mind. I've tried to tell myself I'm paranoid to be worried about Edith, but there's no fighting it. After yesterday, I'm on high alert; I remember how she stood there watching while the chaos ensued, and while I'm willing to admit that maybe she froze, something about the whole thing rubs me the wrong way. It's like an itch I can't scratch, and it's driving me crazy.

I'm just beginning to wonder if I shouldn't catch up with Shade and Silas, at least for something to do, when the sound of muffled voices catches my attention. I raise an eyebrow -- here I was thinking Landon and I were the last people left here. The voices are coming from the room Edith has been sharing with Hunter, and I can feel my stomach drop even as I slowly get to my feet.

The vampire shifter hasn't spoken to me at all since yesterday, but every time I've caught his eye, he just looks away with a melancholy expression on his face. He's hurting, and I wish desperately that there was something I could say, but *what?* How can I assuage a guilt that he shouldn't even be feeling in the first place?

Carefully, I shuffle down the hallway, doing my best to stay light on my feet. I know I shouldn't be eavesdropping, but I can't help it -- call it morbid curiosity or something. The door to Edith's room is open, and I can hear her crooning voice wafting out like music on the heavy air. "You know there are other fish in the sea, don't you?"

"Not for me, there aren't." That sounds like Hunter.

"Listen," Edith persists, "I get it, okay? Don't you think I understand where you're coming from? I'm an outsider too, just like you."

"It's different," I hear Hunter protest. "You're good at what you do. Hell, you're *incredible* at it. There's no denying that."

"I'm late to the party, though," she points out. "You think I don't see the way Millie looks at me, like she's suspicious of me? I don't know if it's because she feels threatened, or if it's just because I'm not part of your original group, but..."

I can feel my hackles rising at the implication, and struggle to keep from saying something.

"You're not giving Boots enough credit," Hunter insists, making a warm spot bloom in my chest. "She's been through hell these past few weeks. It's not easy living in this world as a hybrid -- take it from me. My family has ties to the community." There's a pause, and his tone grows fond and soft. "Millie has done more for us than anyone," he says.

"Mille, Millie, Millie..." Edith sighs, sounding like a put-upon parent. "When will you realise that the world doesn't revolve around her?" There's a moment of silence, followed by a shifting sound. "I just want you to remember that you have other options," she says, so quietly that I have to strain to hear her. Her voice is like silk, and the sound makes my blood run cold. "I see you for what you are, Hunter."

"I..." I can hear the confusion in his voice, the hesitation.

Don't do it, I tell myself, clenching my fists so hard that my nails bite into my palms. *Don't do it, don't do it...*

"Come here," Edith purrs to him.

I clear my throat loudly and walk to the doorway, already preparing some excuse about why I'm here. My words catch in my throat when I see what's happening. Edith and Hunter are perched on her bed, and she has her hand on his thigh. Her delicate fingers are running through his scarlet hair, and I arrive just in time to see her lips brush against his. I blanch, speechless.

Hunter is the first to see me, and he quickly springs away from the witch shifter. "Boots!" he exclaims. "How long have you been...?" I can feel tears welling up in my eyes, despite my best efforts. "Long enough," I reply quietly, and turn on my heel to escape before they can see me cry. I should have been expecting this, but it still hits me like a knife in the heart.

I can hear Hunter following me. "Millie, wait! Let me explain-"

But I don't want to hear his explanations. I don't want to listen to any more of Edith's platitudes. My eyes have grown blurry with tears, and it's all I can do to make it to my room and close the door behind me before I'm collapsing on the bed, my hands over my face. I can hear Edith and Hunter continuing to speak, but I can't make out the words, and maybe that's for the best. Their rapport is clear enough for my purposes.

I don't know how long I sit on the bed, but Hunter doesn't come, and I don't know if that makes me feel better or worse. My throat feels thick, and as ridiculous as this all is, I can't help it. It's like the house of cards has finally come falling down.

After what seems like forever, I hear a knock at the door. I'm about to tell whoever it is to go away when Landon's voice comes through gently. "Boots? You in there?"

I sniffle and hurry to wipe away my tears. "Yeah," I call.

Slowly the siren shifter enters the room, closing the door behind him. Wordlessly he takes a seat next to me on the bed, putting a comforting arm around my shoulders. "I take it you weren't asleep for that," I mumble.

"Resting my eyes," he confirms, "but I think I got the gist."

I shake my head, turning to look at him. "Am I crazy?" I ask him quietly. "Is this whole thing... I mean..." I sigh, trying to collect myself. "I thought we had something," I whisper. "Something real."

"You do," Landon tells me quietly. "We do."

"We?" Timidly, I look up at him, feeling my cheeks growing hot. For the first time ever, he seems to be at a loss for words. "I never thanked you properly for saving me yesterday," I whisper.

"You don't have to thank me," Landon says, not meeting my eyes. "I'd follow you to the ends of the earth, Boots. We all would."

I can feel my heart beginning to beat faster. "Do you mean that?"

Landon clears his throat. "I mean... Listen, Boots, I..." Finally, he meets my eyes with his own, and I can see the debate on his face. I only have to wonder for a split second before his mouth comes crashing into mine, and *god,* I don't think I've ever felt this relieved in my life.

I sigh, leaning into the kiss as I allow my arms to snake around the siren shifter's neck. He groans, shifting a little, as his hands move up to let my hair down so that he can run his hands through it. His touch is ginger, delicate, a far cry from what I would have expected from the self-confident playboy. I let my tongue brush his bottom lip, and he gently pushes me back onto the bed, his hands trailing my body with a gentleness that's enough to make me want to start crying again. Like he doesn't want to hurt me.

No, more than that; like he wants to keep me from ever being hurt again.

My hands go to his shirt, but he stops me, pulling away for a moment to look at me. "Are you sure?" he asks quietly. "I don't want to-"

I kiss him again. "Yes," I whisper against his lips. "Landon, *please.*" It's more than a want at this point, it's a need, and not just because of what I witnessed with Hunter. This has been a long time coming.

I can feel him smirk against me. "As you wish."

I snort, laughing even as I help him get his shirt off. He tosses it to the side, allowing me to admire the planes of his body - for a swimmer, I've never seen him shirtless before, and the sight of his golden skin is making me feel weak in the knees. I feel him tug gently at my hair, making me groan, and he grins as he moves his mouth to my neck. "Problem?"

"Hardly," I pant as he continues to go lower, hooking his fingers through my belt loops and tugging my shorts off me. I squirm out of my underwear as he continues to lavish my neck with attention, aware that there will probably be a mark there tomorrow, and nearly cry out in disappointment when he pulls away to trail his tongue gently over my exposed skin. "Landon..." I whisper.

He hums against the skin of my inner thigh, his eyes bright as they watch my reactions to his movements carefully. Slowly he lowers his mouth to my clit, and as he begins to eat me out with a patience that makes my head spin, it's all I can do to bunch my hands in the sheets and breathe through his ministrations. No one's ever done this to me before -- I had no idea what I was missing! I can feel a pressure building between my legs, and I can feel Landon's eyes on me, observing how I react to every little thing he does. When he slips a finger into me, curling it slightly, it's enough to make me come undone completely, and I come with a muffled cry, shuddering in ecstasy.

Landon continues to smooth his tongue over me for another few moments, his hands rubbing ginger circles into my thighs. When he finally looks up and smiles at me as he crawls up my body, lining himself up at my entrance.

"One second," he murmurs, leaning back and reaching into his trouser pockets on the bed, grabbing a condom. Sliding it on, he settles back on top of me and kisses me as he thrusts deep. I arch my back at how good he feels as he groans, a masculine and deep groan against my lips. It doesn't take long before he is thrusting faster and I feel another orgasm building up deep within me. The orgasm crashes through me as Landon takes my lips and kisses me deeply, thrusting into me one more time before he comes.

We breathlessly lie together for a moment.

The pain is still there, but in Landon's arms, it might just be bearable.

CHAPTER 63

At some point during the day, Landon and I move out of the room to give Silas and Shade their space back, but I'm not ready to let him go just yet; I'm clinging to him like a lifeline, and the idea of spending the night alone is inconceivable. We end up sprawling out along the large sofa, me with my head on the siren shifter's chest, a blanket draped over us both. He doesn't say much about what I saw, which I'm grateful for -- for all his jibes, he clearly reads emotions well, and knows that I just need quiet comfort right now. Eventually, Mollie and the others come back, and although we get some curious glances, none of them give us any flak. They must just be used to me moving from guy to guy by now, and for some reason, that's not as embarrassing as I once would have thought.

I make a point of avoiding Hunter for the rest of the day, doing everything in my power to not be in the same room as him at any given time. Edith, too, although that's not much of a change from how things were before. My mind keeps replaying what I saw: her lips on his, that coy smile on her face, her beautiful, tinkling voice... A horrible possibility dawns on me -- did she know I was there? Did she kiss him because she knew it would upset me? Or does she truly have feelings for him?

I can't decide which option is worse.

The tension is palpable when we gather in the common room to debrief. I sit perched on the far end of the couch, Landon's hand in mine, while Hunter just stands on the other side of the room, smouldering. I can feel his eyes on me, burning holes in my head, as if by willpower alone he can make me look at him. At one point, Edith creeps up to stand beside him, but he shrinks away as if she's poisonous. Part of me feels bad, part of me feels guilty, but mostly, I'm just confused.

"The good news is, they didn't attack us," Xander says. He's sitting at the foot of the couch with Hazel's back against his chest. "The bad news is, they want nothing to do with any of this."

"Shit," Silas mutters, sweeping a hand through his hair. "That figures."

Ruby sighs and gets to her feet. Most of us are already changed for another night in, and I can see the exhaustion on my companions' faces. "They're scared," she says flatly. "They don't want the humans bringing heat down on London, and I can't say I blame them."

"We're just going to have to keep trying then, aren't we?" says Shade.

"We'll be *trying* for the rest of our lives, at this rate," Landon grumbles. I give his hand a gentle squeeze and see the faintest flicker of a smile on his face.

"That's another three off the list, anyway," says Hazel, getting to her feet. She lets out a yawn, her short blonde curls bouncing. "I'm going to turn in, I think. All this rejection is bringing my mood down."

"You're not the only one," mutters Shade.

"We should all just rest up," suggests Mollie. "We can come back to it fresh tomorrow."

Xander sighs and follows Hazel's lead. Silas and Shade, looking a little worse for wear after their duel earlier, exchange a look as the dragon shifter heads into the bathroom. Shade's grey eyes flicker from me to Landon, and he winks -- how can something so corny be so sexy? -- before turning into his room, shedding his shirt as he goes.

I can feel Landon's grip on me tighten instinctively as the wolf shifter disappears, and just have time to wonder whether there's some tension there before Mollie bids us goodnight and shuffles away with Edith in tow.

Hunter is the last one left, and for a moment he just stands there with his hands in his pockets, staring at the floor. "Millie..." he says quietly, taking a step toward me. "Can we talk?"

"I..." I can feel the emotions welling up in spite of myself and force my expression to harden. "I don't think there's anything to say."

"Please." His blue eyes are imploring me to give him a chance, but the wound is still fresh in my heart, and part of me wants to hurt him the way he hurt me. I shake my head silently.

Hunter opens his mouth to say something else, but Landon speaks up first. "Leave it alone, Hunter. She doesn't want to talk about it." I see the vampire shifter's jaw clench, but then he gives us a stiff nod and leaves the room. Landon turns to me. "You okay, Boots?"

"As okay as I can be, I guess," I say, forcing a smile. "Come on, let's get ready for bed. You and I are up to bat again tomorrow."

TOMORROW'S PLANS, as it turns out, are not meant to be, and that's putting it lightly.

The first thing I become aware of through the fog of sleep is the sound of a loud banging, like someone on one of the lower floors is moving furniture around. Except it's two in the morning, and the banging is getting louder...

I sit up on the couch, rubbing my eyes, and adrenaline rushes through me as I realise the sound is coming from just outside the flat door which is shaking on its hinges. "Landon!" I shake him awake. "Someone's here!"

"Mm... what?" The siren shifter blinks at me, but I don't have time to respond. Suddenly the door flies clean off, landing on the hallway floor with a deafening crash. Lights begin to turn on all over the apartment, but I'm barely thinking now, operating on instinct alone. I don't see who's at the door, and I don't care, already letting my magic take over. An instant later I'm in my wolf form, pouncing on the first of several shadowy figures with a flying leap.

It feels like the world around me is moving in slow motion as chaos begins to unfold. The others come running out of their rooms just in time for a veritable army of black-clad intruders storming in. How did they get past Edith's wards? How did they know there were wards *there*?

But I don't have time to think as I snarl down at the man below me and sink my teeth into his shoulder. He yells, and I realise a moment too late that he's not a human -- just before he shifts into a vampire and throws me off of him with his supernatural strength. I lose my grip on my form as I go flying into a bookshelf, the force of the impact dazing me for a moment as I look around. "Leave her alone!" Hazel yells in her siren voice, drawing the vampire's attention away. Allowing my hands to turn red with witch magic, I unleash a blast of telekinetic energy just in time to shield Shade from a fireball coming from one of the other attacking shifters. The fire begins to lick at the walls and furniture, and within moments the room is filling up with smoke.

"We need to go!" yells Landon, dodging an incoming swipe from an attacking wolf shifter. Concentrating, I lift him up with the force of my mind, struggling to hold him in the air long enough for Shade to tackle him to the ground. Even through the haze and chaos, I can just make out the insignia on the man's jacket.

The Academy. They found us.

How?

It's not a question for right now. Where is everyone? The fire is making me disoriented, and I have to shout to make myself heard. "It's the Academy!" I yell, stumbling on an overturned chair with my arms out, struggling to see.

A strong arm hooks around my waist and helps me up; for a moment I struggle against it before I hear Silas' calm voice in my ear. "Come on -- this way."

We fight our way through the common area, which has suddenly turned into a war zone, but we've only made it as far as the entryway when a telekinetic blast, much stronger than anything I've done so far, sends all of us -- humans, shifters, and furniture -- flying every which way. I feel a sharp pain in the back of my skull, and when I brush my fingers over my scalp, they come away bloody. My ears are ringing, and the world seems to spin around me. A concussion? I stumble to my feet, fighting against the stinging of the smoke in my eyes and the wound in my head to feel my way to the front door. I fling it open to get some relief from the smoke, realising too late that one of our group is still unaccounted for.

It's only as the smoke begins to clear that I see Mollie lying on the ground. There's a gaping wound in her neck, and I don't need to be a doctor to see how bad it is. "Mollie!" I cry out, rushing towards her, oblivious to the commotion around me. I'm back in human form before I know it, taking her by the shoulders and pulling her into a sitting position. A jet of fire shoots over my head -- Ruby's doing -- just as one of the attackers, this one a witch, begins to launch magic in my direction.

Except it's not one of the attackers. It's Edith, fully shapeshifted, her eyes blazing with a hatred I've never seen before. "What are you doing?!" I yell. "Mollie's hurt! Help us!"

She smiles, actually *smiles*. "Why don't you help yourself, hybrid?" she sneers. "You're the special one here."

Hunter lets out a snarl and lunges for her before I can process what she's saying, blocking her attack from hitting me with his own durability.

I glance down at Mollie, whose eyes are growing glassy. "No, no, no..." I murmur, trying desperately to think of something -- a healing spell, an artifact, *something* -- but nothing is coming to me. "Mollie-"

She grabs onto my arm with surprising strength for someone bleeding out on the floor, pulling me close enough that I can feel her weak breath against my cheek. Her voice is barely above a whisper, but I can still make out the one command that she gives me.

"Run," my former foster mother says just before she dies.

CHAPTER 64

I want to scream. I want to tear my hair out. I want to cry. But instead, I just linger there as if the flat isn't burning and we aren't in the middle of a war zone. It feels like the wind has gone out of me, like I can't catch my breath, and it's not just due to the thick haze of smoke that's filling the apartment. I stare down at Mollie. Her eyes are wide and staring now, and her hand has dropped from my arm, frozen in a clawing gesture that makes me want to explode when I look at it.

The closest thing I ever had to a parent, and she's lying dead on the floor in front of me. Because *we* brought them here.

There's a low moaning sound, and it takes me a moment to realise that I'm the one making it. I slump onto the floor in spite of the voice in my head that's crying out for me to leave, leave now or I'm going to die. The fight has gone out of me. My eyes close for a moment, and when I feel a hand gripping my shoulder, I try desperately to shake it off. "No!" I yell, lashing out with my hands at what I can only assume is another one of the Academy representatives. "Let me go!"

"Millie, Millie, it's me!" I recognise Hunter's voice. Isn't *that* just dandy -- the man who broke my heart is now trying to pry me away from my dead foster mother. "Come on, we have to get out of here!"

"Get off me!" I shout, leaning forward over Mollie's body as if that will somehow change the outcome.

"Millie, *please.*" He's imploring now, that same voice he used when he tried to talk to me last night, and god, it hurts. Everything hurts, from my pounding head to my heart, and I've never been so tempted to just curl up on the floor and let death come to me as I am in that moment. I've not only managed to drag a bunch of innocent people into my mess; I've also gotten one of them killed. "Come on!" He leans into me, using his vampiric strength to haul me to my feet. I struggle futilely against him, but I don't have the energy to fight him off, my eyes still lingering on the corpse on the floor.

"We can't just leave her," I protest, tears streaming down my face and leaving clean trails in the soot on my cheeks. "We can't -- we have to do something, we have to..."

"Boots." Hunter takes me by the shoulders and forces me to look at him. "She's gone." His normally blue eyes have gone red with his transformation, making him look borderline inhuman, and I want to scream at the injustice of it all.

Still, something in the way he's looking at me pierces through the cloud of grief that's surrounded me, and somehow I'm able to make my legs work. Nodding curtly to him and wiping my streaming eyes, I allow him to lead me to the door, guided by his superior vision. One by one, we rush out of the apartment, Hunter and I in the lead, and the guys following behind. Xander and Hazel are already outside, and it's not until I hear an explosive roar from behind me that I realise Ruby has been singlehandedly holding the rest of them off. She unleashes a last burst of flame from her powerful jaws to cover us while we make our exit, but moments later I hear a different roar. They have a dragon of their own.

Ruby goes flying out the front door, thrown like a ragdoll and suddenly back in her human form. "Ruby!" Xander yells, letting Hazel go to run to his sister and help her to her feet.

"Too many of them," she pants. "Where did they come from?"

"It doesn't matter," he replies. "We have to -"

But the sound of a telekinetic burst -- Edith's doing, I'd bet a fiver

-- makes it impossible to hear the rest of what she says. Except instead of sending us flying away, it drags Ruby and Xander back into the apartment. Hazel yells something, but I can't hear it over the commotion, and before I know what's happening, she's shifted back and is charging headlong back into the flat. "No!" Silas protests, lunging for her. "We have to stay together!"

"Go!" Hazel yells over her shoulder, barely audible in the chaos. "I'll cover you!" Silas hesitates, but then she repeats her command, louder, in her siren's voice. "*Go!*"

That gets him moving. The big dragon shifter takes me by the hand and pulls me toward the stairs. I try to argue, but Hazel knew what she was doing -- the other guys are hopeless to ignore her command. We forgo the lift and race down the stairs. By the time we emerge back out onto the street, I'm bracing myself, half-expecting another pack of shifters to be waiting for us in ambush. Instead, all I see is a crowd of humans rubbernecking, trying to get a good look at the disaster happening on the top floor. In the distance, I can hear the sounds of police sirens and fire engines, and lights are coming on all over the neighborhood. Worse yet, the spectators all have their phones out to record the scene which makes using our powers a problem.

"Lie low," Shade suggests, pulling the hood of his sweatshirt up.

"Hey!" shouts one of the people watching, a woman trying to herd two young kids. "What happened up there? Do you guys need help?"

"No," I call back to her breathlessly. "I don't know. Please let us go..." In a single file line, the five of us snake past the rest of the bystanders, doing our best to keep a low profile despite the fact that we're all a mess. I steal one last glance over my shoulder: the top floor of the building has caught fire by now, and there's no sign of the others. It's too late to go back up for them, and all I can hope now is that between the three of them, they'll be able to escape. The odds aren't in their favour.

Silas takes my hand and pulls me gently away. I realise I'm crying again as we round a corner onto a side street, this one less hectic and more out of the way. Before I even notice that I'm shaking, my knees give out on me and I slump to the curb. Putting my head in my hands, I let out a harsh sob.

The guys turn around, exchanging worried glances. "Hey." Hunter tentatively rests a hand on my shoulder. "Hey, it's okay."

"Don't touch me," I snap, but there's no fire in it.

Hunter, to his credit, doesn't let up. Instead, he pulls me into an embrace that feels like it's my last lifeline. One by one, the other guys approach me the same way, putting their arms around me and surrounding me protectively. I let the tears fall freely, clinging to them like a drowning person clings to a life raft. If they weren't here, I would truly have nothing left.

After what feels like an eternity, Landon is the first to pull away. "I hate to do this," he says quietly, "but we'd better get out of this neighbourhood. If there are any more hunters around, they're going to be sweeping this whole area."

"Where do we go?" I protest.

"Anywhere," the siren shifter replies. "Anywhere that's far away from here."

Silas gives a stiff nod. "He's right. Soon this place will be crawling with humans -- bystanders, if not hunters. Better we move now."

I let out a long breath, but I know he's right. Shakily I begin to walk again, the guys forming a protective circle around me the same way they did earlier. Everything has fallen apart in the space of a few minutes. Some part of me wonders if I'm going into shock from it all. My normal life has never felt so far away.

For all our precautions, though, none of us are listening to our surroundings very closely, and by the time I'm aware of footsteps behind us, the paralysis spell has already taken hold. My muscles seize up, spasming uncontrollably, just as the guys are blasted back by a wave of magic. Straining against the magic, I look over my shoulder to see Edith approaching, flanked by two of the Academy hunters. She's looking a little worse for wear, but her green eyes are just as piercing as ever, and they flash with hatred as she stares me down.

"You treacherous *bitch*," gasps Shade. He's had the wind knocked out of him, but just as he starts to get to his feet, Edith flicks her hand and moves him back another few steps. The others are struggling against her magic too, and although I can sense that she's flagging, she's powerful enough to keep us all at bay.

"Why?" I croak out. It's the only word I'm able to say.

"Things must come so *easily* to you, don't they?" Edith hisses, slowly walking towards me. "The school. The shapeshifting. *Them.*" She nods in the direction of the guys, and I suddenly see something on her face, something that's been here this whole time without my noticing it: jealousy. "It must be nice, having a harem of guys following you around, being able to shift into any form, having the whole world watching what you do." Her mouth twists with contempt. "You can't blame me for wanting to shake things up a little."

As she speaks, I close my eyes, drawing on my reserves and reaching for my witch magic. If I can just shift my hands, that will be enough. Slowly, red begins to creep up my arms, and with a hoarse yell, I let out my own bolt of magic. It's not much, but it's enough to temporarily pierce the entrapment spell and get the guys moving again. "Get out of here!" I yell at them.

"Millie -" Shade shouts, but upon seeing the look in my eyes, he trails off.

"Don't let them get away," Edith yells to one of the hunters, who takes off after the guys as they disappear around a corner.

I feel a pang of regret, but I don't want anyone else getting hurt because of me. *Especially* not them. At least this way, they'll have a chance.

That's the last coherent thought I have before the rest of the hunters are on me.

CHAPTER 65

I put up a hell of a fight, if I do say so myself. This is the first time I've transformed different parts of myself into different forms at once, and I'm not sure whether it's due to my rage or my exhaustion. One arm is that of a dragon, the other is that of a witch, while my mouth, now a siren's, lets out a scream loud enough to rival Landon's. It's not enough though, none of it's enough, and the fact that the attackers are all women renders my commands to let go basically useless.

"That's enough out of you," Edith says, waving her hand lazily and inducing paralysis once more. I'm shaken back into human form like someone might shake a bothersome bug off their arm, and I'm helpless to fight it as the other shifters surround me, pinning my arms painfully behind my back. I let out a cry of pain as Edith strides up to me, her emerald eyes flashing. "I'm sorry it had to work out this way, Millie," she says, although I don't hear any real remorse in her voice. "It would have been fun to get to know you, but you know what they say ... nothing personal." She pauses, her brow furrowing, and then adds, "Actually, what am I talking about? Of *course* it's personal."

I glare daggers at her, fighting uselessly against her magic, but she seems to be done taunting me. I guess that's something, at least. She turns her back to us. "Keep her still," she commands. "We have a long way to go to get to the safe house." Raising her hand, she releases a haze of pale magical light, and I immediately begin to feel drowsy. I've seen Josie do this once before, to subdue the guards outside our room when we were trapped at the Academy in Boston, but I've never been unfortunate enough to be on the receiving end.

My eyelids suddenly feel immensely heavy, and despite the voice in my head that's screaming for me to *move, move, fight it, do something*, the clutches of the spell are unshakeable. Little by little, the life goes out of my limbs, made useless by the paralysis, and within moments the world has faded away around me.

I FEEL like I'm in a dream. Colours drift in and out, as well as vague bits and pieces of dialogue: *"Get her set up."*

"She has to wake up first, Sir."

"I don't care! We've wasted enough time already!"

"The procedure won't work unless she's conscious! We found that out the hard way with those other boys..."

"Fine. I want to know as soon as she wakes up. Are we clear?"

One of the voices sounds oddly, ominously familiar, but the fog that I'm in is making it hard to listen, even harder to figure out if any of this is real. More images drift through my mind: Mollie's glazed-over eyes. Edith kissing Hunter. Hazel and the twins, trapped in the burning apartment. Most of all, though, I see visions of the guys running for their lives from the pursuing hunters. My heart aches - I was so cruel to Hunter, and now I may never see him again. What if I never see *any* of them again? The most precious thing in the world to me, they've been torn from my grasp by one treacherous betrayal.

And then I lose consciousness once more.

I'm surprised to find that I'm not dead when I finally stir, my eyelids fluttering against the bright fluorescent lights. The pain in my skull has come back with a vengeance, and for a moment I'm struck by a wave of agony so intense that it makes me want to retch. I double over, clutching my stomach and dry heave . How long has it been since I've eaten something?

My head spins, my ears ringing, and it's all I can do to sit there in a shaking heap as the dizziness starts to clear. Eventually, I'm able to force my eyes open, although the harsh lights make it hurt to do so, and look around.

I'm in a room as nondescript as it can get. The walls and floor are made of concrete, and the lights make me think I'm in some sort of basement or storage facility. What did Edith call it? A safe house?

Seems pretty far from safe to me.

I'm surprised to discover that I'm not restrained. I'm slumped forward in a hard wooden chair. My clothes are the same soot-stained ones I had on when the apartment caught fire, and my hair is hanging around my face in dirty clumps. Slowly, agonizingly, I struggle to my feet, having to pause with my hands on the chair to keep myself from passing out from the pain in my head. Once I'm sure I'm grounded, I straighten up and take a slow, shuffling step towards the door in the back.

Even before I reach it I realise it's a pointless exercise. It's padlocked shut on my side, and I'm willing to bet it's been enchanted. Why else would they leave me in here alone with no restraints?

Still, I can't resist the urge to summon a burst of flame from my dragon form, breathing it directly into the padlock for several moments. The metal doesn't even change colour. Of course. Why would it? It's not like I've ever been able to catch a break before.

I let out a yell of frustration and drop my head against the door, banging it uselessly with my hand as if that will somehow change my situation. The gesture sends a fresh stab of pain through me. God, my head hurts -- I go down hard.

The sound of bolts shifting on the other side makes me jump, and for a single crazed second I wonder if my frustration actually worked. But then there's the sound of shuffling feet and I take a few steps back. I'm still weak from the spell and my injuries, but I'm already preparing to fight, my hands clenching into fists as I back up a few steps.

Then the door swings open and Hawthorne, the man who started all this, strides into the room. The smug bastard is smirking, like this is all some big joke to him. And he doesn't look the least bit intimidated by my posture.

I raise my hand to cast a spell, but he shakes his head. "I wouldn't do that if I were you, Ms. Brix," he says, his tone as self-righteous and condescending as ever. "We're underground right now, miles away from anyone who will be able to help you. And we're not alone."

He steps aside to reveal the hulking form of another man, who immediately shifts into a siren. Before I have time to react, he's already growling, "Don't. Move."

For the second time this week, I'm under the thrall of a siren, and I drop my hands weakly to my sides. Still, I'm able to force myself to speak. "Where are we?"

"Nowhere special," Hawthorne replies. "The important thing is that we're safe from prying eyes. Like your boyfriends, for example. We'll find them, I have no doubt, but it's nice to know that they won't stumble across this facility themselves."

I try to lunge at him, but I'm held in place by the command. "Leave them alone."

"You really are feisty , aren't you?" Hawthorne says. "I guess it would take someone with your personality to do all the damage that you've done. Still, that's all in the past. Chin up, right?" He gives me a toothy smile before nodding to his henchman. "Take her to the testing room."

The man turns to me. "You heard him. Follow us."

My feet begin to move on their own as the two men turn and lead me out into a long hallway, their footsteps echoing ominously against the high walls. I struggle, but it's in vain, and this time, Landon isn't here to override this siren's command. The men unlock a door at the far end, and what I see on the other side makes my heart stop: it's a medical examination room, exactly like the one under the Academy where Silas was being kept. A table stands in the middle, manned by a meek-looking woman in a lab coat. The siren grabs my arm and thrusts me onto it, not bothering to be gentle as he secures me in place.

"Thank you, Hugh," Hawthorne says. "That's all we'll need of you."

The siren leaves, taking his magic with him, but by now I'm stuck in place, and even without his magic, I'm not going anywhere. "What are you going to do to me?" I demand.

"The same thing I've always been trying to do," replies Hawthorne. "Level the playing field."

"You just want to give yourself shifter powers," I spit.

"I want to give *everyone* shifter powers!" Hawthorne snaps. "Don't you understand? I'm working towards egalitarianism, Ms. Brix. A world where everyone has the same abilities. And if sacrifices have to be made for that, then..." He shrugs. "It's a worthy cause."

I open my mouth to protest, but there's a sharp pain in my arm; I look down to see that the assistant has put a needle in my vein. "Sir," he says, "I still have reservations about using a hybrid for -"

"We've been over this," says Hawthorne.

"But-"

"Do. As. I. Say." His dark eyes flash, and I feel a lurch of terror as the machine connected to the IV whirs to life, strange blue liquid shooting through the tube and into my arm. My reaction is as immediate as it is violent; the pain in my head is negligible in comparison to this. It feels like acid is running through my veins, dissolving everything in its path. I barely even feel the assistant putting a separate IV in my other arm, which he connects to another machine, but I *do* see my blood beginning to move sluggishly out of it and into the collection beaker. It looks wrong, though, too thick: like it's corrupted.

Or already dead.

The pain rips through me, blocking out all conscious thought. I thrash against my restraints, crying out against the agony, *feeling* the strength going out of me, but it's futile. Time slows to a crawl, my eyes clench shut. I think of the guys, their grinning faces, their gentle touches, and latch onto the image like it's my last hope. That eases the pain, even as I feel tears streaming down my cheeks. I don't know how much time has passed when I hear the assistant's voice. He sounds far away. "Sir," he says, "look at the blood concentration."

Hawthorne steps closer to examine one of the monitors, and then lets out a roar of frustration. "What the fuck is wrong with her?"

"I told you," the assistant protests. "There's no way of isolating the blood serum. Her DNA is scrambled -- that's the whole reason she's a hybrid in the first place."

"Then take more," Hawthorne commands. "Take as much as you need!"

"It's not the device," the other man says. "We could drain her dry and it will still be useless. We need isolated strains from each species, preferably a lot of them. That's how she was made in the first place."

There's the sound of a crash, and I open my eyes to see that Hawthorne has kicked a table in fury, sending medical supplies flying. "We haven't gotten the okay from the board to start testing on the students yet," he says. "Everyone's on edge after that damned convention centre attack-"

I choke out a strained laugh. "*You* organised that!"

"Shut up." Hawthorne doesn't look at me. "Where are we supposed to get more test subjects? I thought the whole point of the girl was to save ourselves the resources."

"We're just going to have to wait," the assistant replies. "I know that's not what you want to hear, but-"

"We are *running out of time!*" yells Hawthorne. I've never seen him lose his composure like this before. "Shifters everywhere are shaking us off. They're mobilising. We don't have time to wait for the fucking school board."

"Then don't," I say quietly, a last desperate hope coming to me. It's a gamble and I know it, but it's like a light at the end of a tunnel, and I cling to it with everything I have.

Hawthorne turns to me. "Excuse me?"

I give him a humourless smile. "I happen to know four good shifters. And if I'm going to die here -- which considering how I'm feeling right now seems pretty likely -- I'd rather have them by my side."

"You would send your boy toys to us?" Hawthorne laughs. "What makes you think I believe that? What makes you think they'll even come?"

"They *will*," I insist, looking at him long and hard out of the corner of my eye. My body is weak, on the verge of giving out, but the anger I feel in me is enough to make my eyes flash just the same. I could almost swear I see Hawthorne look taken aback for just a second, caught off-guard by my sudden spirit. "They'll come because you have *me*."

CHAPTER 66
SILAS

I was the first of their group to be taken by the Academy to be experimented on, so in some ways it feels almost appropriate that my cell phone is the one that rings. We head southwest, on a mission to get as far away from the city centre as possible. My heart leaps into my throat when I see that it's Millie calling, and for one hopeful moment as I answer the phone, I wonder if she managed to escape after all; if anyone could do it, Millie could. Either way, we are going to find her and get her back. Nothing else is important. I know where she is and once we are out of the city, I'm building the biggest army of supes and raiding the fucking academy.

All hope is dashed when I put the phone to my ear. Gone is the musicality of her voice, gone is the touch of self-deprecating humour that sends my nerves into overdrive even as I laugh. She sounds like a shell of her former self, and it doesn't take a rocket scientist to hear that she's not well. "Hey, Silas."

Just those two words are enough to sow the seeds of panic into my chest. "Boots! Where are you? What happened?"

At the sound of her name, Shade, Landon, and Hunter all stop dead in their tracks, whirling around to stare at me . Landon's eyes flash with questions -- *where is she? Who took her? Is she okay?* -- while

Shade looks like a live wire, dangerous and liable to explode at any moment.

For his part, Hunter is suddenly awash with emotion: regret, disappointment, worry, and fear flash across his features in the space of a few seconds. It's like ripping the scab off a wound that's only just started to heal, only to realise that it's been infected since the beginning. He can't help but blame himself for some of this, at least in part for everything that's gone wrong so far.

I know Hunter wishes he could snatch the phone and tell her he's sorry, tell her he was a fool to think himself worthy of her; he's never been under any illusions of superiority. His abilities are pitiful in comparison with the rest of the group's, and he's unqualified to be receiving affection from someone so steadfast, so determined, so *pure*, in spite of everything the world has thrown at her.

When I put the call on speaker, holding a finger to my lips, her rasping voice comes through, and we all share the same emotion. Anger.

"...doing well," she says. "Hanging in there, but I don't know for how long."

"Where are you?" I demand.

There's a sound, followed by a new voice. "Nice try, Mr. Aconite. You will be brought here when you've met with our arranged contact."

The sound of that bastard's smug voice is enough to make me want to break the phone into pieces. It's all I can do is remain silent, to not call the self-righteous prick every name in the damn book. But the thought of Boots tied up somewhere, half-drained and fighting for her life, keeps me quiet.

I never, *ever* thought I would be in this position, bent out of shape over a girl, but here I am, silently panicking. She's beautiful, yes, and she's spirited, but I have had beautiful girls before. And had damn good sex before. This is something else, something deeper, something no piece of shit delinquent like me should be experiencing.

But...

Love. I'm in love with the damn Brix girl.

．　．　．

I CLOSE my eyes and swallow hard. "I want to talk to Millie."

"Are you really sure you want to-"

"I'm not agreeing to anything until you put her back on."

A pause, and then Millie's voice comes through again. She sounds like all the strength has gone out of her. "Silas, please. I need you guys to come here."

"What if it's a trap?" I ask, knowing they're listening but not caring.

Boots hesitates for just a second, but it's enough to tell me everything I need to know. "*Please*," she says at last, her voice cracking. "You guys are all I have left."

"We need to go get her."

"Like hell," snaps Shade. "That has 'trap' written all over it."

"I know," I say. "We don't have a choice."

"Academy agents are going to be crawling all over us the minute we show up," Landon says.

"I *know*," I repeat. "But Millie's there and I can't leave her a second longer, and I'm going to do whatever it takes to save her." *She did the same thing for me once*, I think. *She barely even knew me, and she put her life on the line to save me. Now it's my turn.* Eyes flashing, I look from Shade to Landon to Hunter. "And if any of you guys feels the same way about her that I do, then you'll do the same."

Hunter looks at his feet while Shade and Landon exchange a glance. None of them need to use the L-word; it's there, practically written on their faces, hanging around them in all its fullness and beauty, and they know it isn't a discussion.

It never was.

CHAPTER 67

Time has lost all meaning for me. Have I spent hours strapped to this table? Days? Someone must be giving me fluids, or I'd be dead by now -- that much I'm sure of. Pain has become the centre point for my entire existence, and although god knows I've had plenty of time to get used to it, it hasn't gotten any easier. It feels like my body is giving out on me, all hope of accessing my powers now long gone; the essence of my magic is now dripping into a beaker on the other side of the room, and I'm helpless to stop it.

The laboratory technician doesn't say much during my ordeal, but Hawthorne paces restlessly at the front of the room, his hands clenching and unclenching as the gears turn in his head. He's wondering if the guys will take the bait. To be honest, so am I. If this were a movie or TV show, I would have found some way of warning them, of encoding my words with a secret message about what waits for the guys here, but I'm barely holding together anymore, and even speaking has become an immense challenge. A horrible possibility keeps dawning on me: what if they didn't realise the danger? What if they show up here, expecting an exchange, only to get blindsided and captured? That would be it for me, I think; there's no way I could live with myself if I led them into danger. All I can do now is wait and hope.

Eventually, though, Hawthorne's voice filters back to my ears. "...at the main entrance."

"Will you go meet them?" asks the assistant.

"No," he replies. "Hugh is on his way, along with a few of my other enforcers. I'm not taking any chances until they're inside and prepped for the procedure."

My heart sinks. They came after all, and by the sounds of it, not with guns blazing. I drop my head back to the exam table and squeeze my eyes shut, already bracing myself for the worst. Who would have thought the greatest torture imaginable wasn't being drained of your life force, but having to watch the men you love walk into a trap?

"Yes, Sir." The technician steps away from me. "Should I go prepare the other rooms?"

Hawthorne nods to him, waiting for him to scurry away before turning back to me. "Looks like the gang's all here, Ms. Brix," he says with a smile. "You got what you wanted. Let's just hope it's worth it to the rest of them."

"We'll see," I spit out through gritted teeth. My voice sounds foreign to my own ears, like the voice of a dead person.

Hawthorne chuckles but says nothing. A few minutes later, the sound of approaching footsteps can be heard outside. Hawthorne perks up and shoots me a look before leaving the room to meet the group. If I weren't so weak, I could try to work on my restraints, but I'm past the point of being able to struggle by now. "Well, boys," I hear him say, sounding like the cat that ate the canary. "It's nice to be seeing you all again. I wish it were under better circumstances."

"Cut the crap." The voice is achingly familiar -- Shade's, if I'm not mistaken. "Where is she?"

"Now, let's just take it easy for a minute," Hawthorne begins placatingly. "I don't want anyone doing anything they'll regret-"

"Let us see Millie, or we're going to make this a lot harder for you." That sounds like Hunter, and his tone is brokering no argument.

"Believe him," Landon mutters. "We will."

"You had to know we would want to make sure she's still alive," reasons Silas.

There's a long pause on the other side of the door. I hold my breath. Finally, the bolts slide away and Hawthorne shoves the door open again. I find myself face to face with a cluster of familiar faces, and my breath hitches in my chest.

I can feel Hunter staring at me from the other side of the room, his expression drawn and menacing. Slowly, he turns back to Hawthorne. I feel like we're on the edge of something, and the window of opportunity is shrinking fast. If something is going to happen, it needs to happen now. Otherwise...

"On second thought," Hunter says, his tone more dangerous than I ever could have imagined coming from him, "maybe we'll make it hard for you, anyway."

CHAPTER 68

I t's astonishing how fast everything goes to hell after that, although maybe that's just my altered perception from whatever energy-draining procedure they've been using on me. Either way, the world seems to move almost in slow-motion for the next few minutes, and I'm helpless to do anything but watch.

Hunter is the first to move, shifting into his vampire form with a speed and precision I've never seen from him before. His rage is written all over his face and if it weren't for one of the henchmen -- an equally fast vampire shifter -- he would be tearing Hawthorne's throat out right now. As it happens, though, he ends up locked in close-quarters combat with the woman behind him, the two vampires grappling each other with a ferocity I've never seen before. She appears to be a bit stronger, and I watch in horror as she pushes him into the wall, wrestling to maintain her grip on his arms as Hunter leans back into her with all the strength available to him.

"Get off!" That's Landon, already using his siren's voice , and the command is enough to give the woman pause. She looks like she's resisting it on her end, but the momentary diversion is enough for Hunter to regain the upper hand, whirling around and slamming her face into the wall with an animalistic growl.

Looking now, I can see that there are a handful of other

henchmen escorting my would-be rescuers. Almost as soon as the fighting is going down among the others, everyone seems to be shifting at once.

Silas, whose powers have been giving him trouble ever since he was in my position, seems to shake off his difficulties with no trouble now. I wonder if it could really be because he sees that I'm in danger. Shifting and giving a flap of his enormous wings, he unleashes a massive gust of wind in the enclosed space. The vampire shifters are able to maintain their footing, but Hawthorne, the only human in the room, is blown back by the force of it; he stumbles into the far wall, nearly tripping over his own feet.

"What are you *doing?*" he yells, all of his composure out the window at this point. "*Stop them!*"

One of the other guards looks like a wolf shifter, and he's halfway into his form when Landon charges him, body checking him from the side and breaking his concentration. I've never seen the siren shifter go so readily into the melee before, but a flash of his now-green eyes tells me he's beyond caring about his own safety at this point. The thought brings tears to my eyes, the reality of it sinking in: *they came for me. They actually came for me.*

Shade tag-teams with Landon, lunging for the struggling wolf shifter and completing his transformation before he even hits the ground. He pins the man to the floor, sinking his powerful jaws into his shoulder and eliciting a cry of pain from the trapped guard. It's only as my attention turns to Silas in the doorway that I realise the worst has yet to come.

They have a dragon shifter of their own. Of *course* they do . The giant reptilian beast, his scales a shimmering green colour, is doing his level best to force his way into the room. Silas is keeping him at bay, his wings spread defensively as the two of them exchange blows with their mighty claws. Because dragons are immune to the effects of dragon fire and highly resistant to other kinds, Silas seems to be using his own body as a shield to deflect the majority of his opponent's flames. My heart leaps into my throat when I see that he's flagging a little. The second that dragon shifter makes it into this enclosed space, he's going to light us all up, Hawthorne included.

Hawthorne...

Wait a minute. Slowly I force myself to turn my neck, every single muscle in my body protesting the movement, which feels as difficult as running a marathon. My former school president is nowhere to be seen, but there's an emergency exit door now standing open in the back of the room. The coward can't even be bothered to stand and fight his own battles! Well, no matter, I guess. We've got our hands full enough as it is. If he comes back with reinforcements, though...

I begin to thrash weakly against the straps holding me to the table, for all the good it does. We might be evenly matched right now, but there's no telling how many other Academy loyalists he has working in this facility.

The enemy vampire shifter sees my renewed efforts to free myself and immediately ignores Hunter in favour of lunging at me. Adrenaline rushes through me, and I close my eyes, bracing for the death blow, but a snarl from Silas makes me glance up. He's craned his neck around and unleashed a targeted fireball, not enough to catch me, but enough to hit the vampire squarely between the shoulders.

She gives out an inhuman shriek, self-preservation instincts kicking in as she drops to the ground, giving Shade a perfect opportunity to pounce. This gives the other wolf shifter a window, however, and soon enough there's a second giant wolf charging us. Hunter zooms across the room, picks him up by the neck, and hurls him into the back of the room, where there's the sound of laboratory equipment scattering across the floor.

"Hunter," pants Silas. Hunter and I look up at the same time to see the enemy dragon bearing down on Silas in the doorway; he's the bigger of the two, and it was only a matter of time before he would turn things around.

"Go!" Shade snaps, still in wolf form. "I'll cover you!"

Hunter nods and rushes to help Silas hold off the dragon, and in the meantime Shade, now unoccupied, charges across the room to assist Landon with the remaining guard, another siren. His commands are useless against the guys, and within moments they've overpowered and dispatched him.

With the vampire shifter still fighting the flames and the wolf shifter lying dazed in a heap of medical supplies, all four can now turn their attention to the dragon in the hallway. "Get out of the way," Hunter commands Silas, squaring his shoulders.

"What?" Silas demands. "What are you...?"

The vampire shifter turns his red eyes on the dragon , and I see them burning with a vengeance. "Trust me, Silas."

There's a brief pause, and then Silas releases his grip on the other dragon. They both come tumbling backward into the room, knocked off balance by the sudden shift. Hunter wastes no time seizing his chance. Without a second thought, he leaps onto the dragon's long neck, grabbing it at the base of its head with his powerful arms, and breaks its neck with one swift movement. The dragon shifter crumples to the floor, already changing back into human form as Hunter leaps off. And just like that, it's over. The guys shift back, breathing hard from the exertion. Somewhere in the facility, I can hear an alarm going off.

Hunter is the first to my side, already fumbling with my restraints. "Boots," he says, his voice breaking with worry, "I'm sorry. I'm so sorry."

"Don't..." I rasp. "Don't apologise. Nobody's fault."

"I shouldn't have tried to push you away," he murmurs, pressing his forehead to mine as his voice breaks a little. "I should have listened to you. I should have..."

My left hand, now free, comes to rest on his cheek. "It's okay," I whisper, running my thumb over his soft skin. "I'm here."

"How are you feeling?" demands Shade, now standing at my other side. "Can you stand?"

"I don't... The machine..." I pant.

Landon whirls around to stare at the equipment they have me hooked up to. "Where the hell is the off switch on this thing?"

"There *is* no off switch," Silas tells him flatly, breathing a long jet of fire into the device. There's the smell of burning plastic and noxious steam, and we watch as the machine slowly melts down into a pile of scrap, letting out a few final listless beeps.

Landon gently removes the IV line from one of my arms while Shade works on the other, and within moments the guys are helping me sit up.

"Here, hold on to me," Silas says, putting an arm out. I allow him to support me as I stumble down from the bed, but my legs are too weak to support me, and they crumple out from under me.

Hunter catches me. "Don't try to move. I'll carry you."

"Are you sure?" I ask, eyes wide.

"Of course," he replies. "Vampire, remember?" Without another word, he shifts back into his vampire form and scoops me up into his arms, carrying me bridal-style towards the door.

"We have to leave now," Landon says. "This place is going to be crawling with guards any second."

"Come on," says Shade, taking the lead as we hurry out the exit door. "This looks like a way out."

We find ourselves in another fluorescent-lit hallway, hurtling down with hardly a glance behind us. I can feel the guys stealing concerned looks at me, fear and relief in their eyes. "I can't believe it worked," I rasp, burying my face in Hunter's chest.

"Shh," says Shade, turning to put a hand on my thigh. "Don't try to talk. It's okay. We're here. We're safe."

That's enough for me, and by the time we emerge into the bright sunlight, the pain of the past hours is already beginning to feel like a distant dream. Being surrounded by guys you love will do that to you.

The relief is short- lived, however; the shrill alarm is still blaring out of the facility, and we turn around momentarily to see guards pouring out of the doors and into the remote field where we now find ourselves. "Run," says Landon.

"We can't outrun them," protests Shade.

"Millie," Silas says gently, "can you teleport us? It doesn't need to be far. Anywhere that's not here."

"She's barely hanging on," protests Hunter.

"I can try," I say, struggling to pull myself up in the vampire's arms. It feels like I weigh a thousand tons, but I'm not about to give up now, not when we're all still here and alive. Closing my eyes, I reach for my witch powers. They were elusive before, but I've been able to jump us across the planet once already. If I just dig deep, tap into my energy reserves...

But almost as soon as I begin searching for that cool, familiar magic, my blood runs cold.

I try again, more desperately this time, throwing off all thoughts of Hawthorne and the procedure and concentrating completely on accessing my form. But it's not an issue of concentration, I realise with a surge of dread. It's not a problem with my ability to access my powers, because my powers aren't there. They're gone, as surely as my physical strength is gone, and it doesn't take more than a second for the terrible, terrible truth of my situation to dawn on me.

I can no longer shapeshift.

To be continued in book four of Supernatural Shifter Academy.
Pre-order now.

DESCRIPTION

The academy has taken my powers...and what use is a powerless shifter in a supernatural academy?

The academy hunters chasing us, we have to search for Edith and find out how to get my powers back before it's too late. When I first got my powers, I never thought for a second I'd miss them as much as I do.
Or how weak I actually am without them.
When humans with supernatural powers start appearing and attacking us, finding Edith is going to be harder than it looks.
But I'm not alone.

Falling in love, fighting evil and hiding from the academy was a lot easier with powers.

18+ Reverse Harem Romance which means the main character will have more than one love interest.

CHAPTER 69

The worst part of having something taken away from you is the fact that now you know what you're missing. It's one thing to say you've never experienced something, because at least you haven't known the joys of having it in your life. It's another to be given something, something life-changing, and have it snatched away from you. It's like having a piece of yourself gouged out with a knife, and nothing will ever fill the void that's left behind.

Does it make me selfish that my first thoughts are of myself, and not of the people who surround me? Maybe. But the pain is as poignant as it is all-encompassing, and there's no avoiding the immediate sense of wrongness that I feel as I desperately grope for my powers, only to come up empty.

"Boots?" Landon's voice sounds like it's coming from far away, although that could be as much due to the fact that I'm barely staying conscious as it is to the fact that my world seems to be crumbling around me. "I don't want to rush you, but..." I follow his gaze back to the Academy facility where, up until a few minutes ago, I was being tortured and drained -- and to the herd of oncoming agents charging toward us from the other side of the field.

I shake my head, my heart hammering in my chest. "Something's wrong. I can't -- my powers, they're not..."

"Shit." That's Shade, and I can see he's already getting into a fighting stance on my other side. "What the fuck did they do to you?"

"I don't know," I wail. I've never felt this helpless in my entire life. "You guys have to go. Get out of here while you still can. I'm just going to slow you down."

"Like hell," Hunter snaps. "We're not letting you out of our sight again, Boots."

"Looks like we're going to have to fight," Silas says, squaring his shoulders. "Millie, get behind me."

I swallow and nod, allowing the guys to form a protective wall in front of me. I'm still digging in vain for the shifter magic that has by now become so familiar, but it's no use. That comforting coolness in the pit of my stomach is nowhere to be found. Not even a whisper remains. It's like it was never there in the first place.

I can feel a lump forming in my throat as I watch the oncoming herd of guards -- some humans, but some no doubt shifters -- continue their relentless approach. Is it possible that Hawthorne managed to completely drain my powers? I don't want to think about the possibility, but...

A gust of wind makes my attention snap back to the present, just in time to see Silas, now in dragon form, flap his mighty wings. A burst of fire escapes his jaws, but he doesn't aim for the oncoming agents, instead lighting up a trail on the ground in front of us. The dry grass immediately goes up in flames, creating a wall of fire that instantly begins to spread into a fully fledged blaze. Just in time, too; the Academy soldiers come skidding to a stop on the other side, watching us with barely masked hatred on their faces.

"Come on!" Hunter shouts, already back in vampire form. "Boots-"

I don't need to be told twice, and I allow him to sweep me back up into his supernaturally strong arms. Carrying me bridal style, he backs up from the onslaught, his fangs bared and his eyes blazing red. Shade and Landon have transformed as well, I see, but hang back on our side of the wildfire for a moment before turning and sprinting away. Silas, Hunter, and I follow suit, my consciousness already beginning to waver in the face of the overwhelming heat from the fire.

I give up on finding my powers and focus on staying awake; the least I can do is not become dead weight. A glance over Hunter's shoulder shows me that several of the agents have stopped, but my heart sinks when I see two of them transforming -- into dragons. Because of fucking *course* they would happen to be fireproof. One yellow and one orange, their scales glistening in the light of the flames, race forward on their massive legs, unaffected as they charge through the fire barrier.

One of them locks its jaws around Silas' mouth, restraining him from breathing fire, while the other shoots across the field towards Hunter, no doubt trying to avoid a repeat of the kill inside the facility. Hunter takes a step back, ready to fight, but a blur of grey fur slams into the dragon from the side. Shade. Although as a wolf he's no match for the dragon's raw power, he has agility on his side, and the giant reptile isn't able to keep up with his unpredictable leaps and lunges.

A *distraction,* I realise, just in time for Silas to break free of the other dragon's grip and pin the second one to the ground. The first dragon makes a move to follow him, but Landon's voice, now tinged with the sound of his siren's song, draws its attention away. "Leave him!" he yells, and although the dragon shifter is a male, he isn't going for mind control. He's going for pure power. The sound is earsplitting, and the sonic waves from the scream are visible in the air as they send a shockwave across the field which connects squarely with the dragon's chest. Caught off guard, he's sent flying backward, tumbling to the ground in his human form. And humans aren't immune to fire. He lets out a yell of pain as the flames threaten to consume him, leaving Shade, Silas, and Landon to focus on the second dragon.

My ears are still ringing, although whether that's from my earlier trauma or the fact that I might have just ruptured an eardrum, I have no idea. What I *do* know, however, is that the rest of the facility guards aren't just standing by, and my eyes go wide when I see them bran-dishing weapons.

"Guys!" I yell, my voice sounding pathetically meek in compar-ison to the others' shouts. "Guys, we have to go! They have guns!"

As if on cue, a spray of gunfire cuts through the wall of flames. Silas, aware of his relative durability, lunges to the left to take the brunt of the attack, but he doesn't move quite quickly enough. I'm aware of screaming as one of the stray bullets connects with Shade's flank, and it takes a moment for me to realise that it's coming from me. To my surprise, the wolf shifter manages to keep a hold on his form, although his eyes have gone wide with shock. He stops dead in his tracks, going down to his front knees as blood begins to pour out of the wound in his side, and adren-aline floods me. He can't die. I can't let him die, not after he saved me.

"Hunter," I yell. "Put me down! Help Shade!"

"Are you sure?" Hunter asks, his eyes wide.

I nod, surprising myself with my own coherence. "I'll be okay. Get him out of the line of fire."

Hunter hesitates for a moment, his gaze stormy, and then sets me gently onto the ground. In a flash, he's sprinting back towards the scrimmage, almost too fast for my eyes to track.

"What the fuck are you doing?" Shade yells, still in his wolf form, as the vampire shifter comes to a stop beside him.

Silas and Landon are still working on driving back the dragon shifter, and although he appears to be flagging, I'm aware of the rain of gunfire spraying across the field.

"Can you stand?" Hunter demands, the authority and self-assuredness in his voice enough to catch me off guard. He's come a long way from the insecure guy I met in shifting class all those months ago.

Shade lets out a growl and forces himself back to his feet before shifting back into human form. There's a gnarly gash on his side, I can see, and my stomach drops when I notice that his clothes are already seeped through with red. "Get in front of me," Hunter commands. Shade glares at him but does as he instructs, allowing the vampire shifter to cover him from behind as they make their slow way back over to me. Bullets glance off Hunter's skin like raindrops as they pull back, coming to a stop beside me.

"We have to go," I pant. There's a queasy feeling blossoming in my stomach, a mixture of fatigue and panic, and I focus all my attention on the guys. *Keep them alive, at all costs.* "There's too many of them. And if they send reinforcements..."

"You're right," says Hunter, sliding a hand around my waist to support me. "Can you both stand? I can't carry you both."

"Didn't think you'd ever be the one saving *me*," Shade pants as he slings an arm around the vampire shifter's shoulders. "I owe you one, Ash."

"Save it," Hunter tells him, and the three of us begin to work our way towards the stand of trees on the other side of the clearing. There will be cover there, which is more than we can say for where we are now. It's slow going, and the pained noises I'm hearing from Shade make my blood run cold, but he's tough, and makes no complaint as we stumble into the shade of the forest. I'm reminded eerily of the forest surrounding the Academy building. If only I had known then that it was designed more as a prison than as a boarding school.

Back in the field, I watch as Landon unleashes another shockwave. It's powerful enough to deflect the most recent barrage of bullets, but I can tell that he's flagging; siren songs are meant for mental manipulation and not physical attacks, and if Hazel is to be believed, that kind of power takes a lot out of a person. Silas seems to realise the tide is turning, and before Landon can even protest, he's shooting up into the air and picking him up with his strong talons. Flapping his wings again, he glides out of the range of the attackers, bypassing the brush fire entirely as he swoops in to land beside the rest of us. In the blink of an eye, he and Landon are shifting back into human form, and then we're picking our way through the densely packed trees, disappearing into the darkness of the woods.

"Where are we going?" I pant.

"Anywhere that's not here," Landon replies, shoving a branch out of the way so I can pass. The sounds of shouting and crackling flames can still be heard behind us. If we're lucky, they'll fall back to regroup. If not, though...

The roar of the remaining dragon jangles my nerves, and I force myself to pick up my pace as we hike deeper into the woods. At least the canopy will make us hard to spot. I'm running on pure adrenaline at this point, all hope of using my magic dashed for the time being, and putting one foot in front of the other feels more and more difficult with every step. I grit my teeth, tightening my grip on Hunter, and the feeling of fingers interlacing with my own makes me look up; Shade meets my eyes, giving my hand a squeeze -- although whether that's for my peace of mind or his own, I don't know. His fingers are dreadfully cold and clammy, and the fact that he's not mouthing off for once doesn't bode well either.

"Shade..." I pant, gripping his wrist, "Are you all right?"

"Bastards got me," the wolf shifter replies. "Don't know how deep. Doesn't matter. We have to keep moving."

"Just focus on walking," Silas reminds us. "We'll find shelter and regroup."

"Right," Shade pants, sweat standing out on his temples.

And then he collapses.

CHAPTER 70

"Shade? Shade!" My voice sounds like it's coming from the far end of a long tunnel. Am I panicking, or just about to pass out? Or maybe both? I feel myself drop to my knees, the world already narrowing to a pinpoint before my eyes. My limited grasp on my own consciousness feels dangerously close to slipping away, and a voice in my mind whispers that I've about maxed myself out, even as I grab the wolf shifter by the shoulders and give him a gentle shake.

"Shade, say something!" I cry, desperation seeping into my voice. My breath is coming hard and fast, the combined trauma of the experiments and seeing one of the men I love injured enough to make stars appear in front of my eyes. The idea of dying in the Academy's clutches before having a chance to say goodbye to them was one thing. The idea of any of them being harmed in the process of saving me is another, and my exhausted mind rebels at the notion. A sudden coldness on my face makes me aware that tears are running down my cheeks, although I'm not even sure when I started crying.

"Boots..." Landon's voice sounds far away. "Millie, wait a second. Hold on to me..." He puts a steadying hand on my shoulder, and I lean into his touch, aware that it might be the only thing keeping me from passing out. My eyes are still locked on Shade's unconscious body, and although his chest is rising and falling, the movements are irregular and rapid. Fumbling forward, I press my fingers to his neck to feel for a pulse, but I'm shaking too badly to get an accurate read.

"Here," Landon gently takes my hand and moves it away before taking over, his frown deepening as he holds his fingers to Shade's throat.

"What's wrong?" I ask, my voice trembling. "Landon, what's wrong with him?"

"His heart rate is off the charts," the siren shifter replies.

"What about the soldiers?" Silas, ever the pragmatic one, asks. The others have all stooped down to cluster around the fallen wolf shifter, but I can see the fear in their eyes behind the rallying. We may be adults, but just barely. And now, more than ever, we're in over our heads.

Hunter furrows his brow and transforms for a moment. We all go silent as he cocks his head to one side, listening for any sign of the pursuing agents. What we all know, but don't dare say aloud, is that Shade, being a wolf shifter, has the best senses of our entire group. Unfortunately, he's out of commission... and I don't want to follow that line of thinking any further. "I can hear them," Hunter says at last, "but barely. It sounds like they're heading east."

"Good," Landon says. "Then we head west."

"No way," I reply, already shaking my head. "Not with Shade like this. We need to help him."

"We can't move him," Hunter says flatly. "He's losing too much blood. If we try to carry him out, we might kill him." I can see the flashing of his red eyes, and I'm reminded of vampires' innate bloodthirst when they've shifted. To his credit, though, Hunter doesn't complain a bit, instead setting his jaw and looking from one of us to the other while we debate our next move.

"I'm not abandoning him," I state, my tone brokering no argument.

"We're not asking you too, Boots," Landon reassures me. "We're in this together."

I shoot him a grateful look, and he gives my hand a squeeze.

"Millie," Silas says hesitantly, and the fact that he's using my real name is enough to tell me it's serious. "Do you think you might be able to...?"

He doesn't need to finish his sentence for my stomach to drop. Slumping forward, I bury my head in my hands. "I can't," I say, my voice barely above a whisper. "They did something to me. Took my powers away. I can't shapeshift for shit." If I still had access to my witch form, I might be able to cast a healing spell. Nothing life-saving -- I'm not powerful enough for that yet -- but it might at least stabilise him. Instead, I'm left to watch as one of the guys I love bleeds out on the forest floor, as useless as any other human, and the thought makes me want to scream. The tears are coming harder now, and it's all I can do to bury my face in my hands and stifle my sobs. The adrenaline is wearing off by now, and the ugly, brutal reality of my situation is at last sinking in.

Out of the frying pan and into the fire.

I jump at the feeling of a hand on my back, and turn to see Silas gazing into my eyes. He reaches up to brush the tears off my cheek with his thumb. "Hey," he murmurs, "this isn't your fault. None of this is your fault. We're going to figure this out." Seeing that I'm in no state to be making decisions, he straightens back up and puts his hands on his hips. "We're going to need to treat him enough to get him to a real medic. Millie, can you put pressure on his side for me?"

I nod and do as I'm told. Shade lets out a low moan as I press the palms of my hands onto the wound, and the sound of it makes my throat tighten. "Do you have an idea?"

Silas purses his lips as we all stare at him and then gives a curt nod. "Maybe," he replies, and then turns to Hunter. "But I'm going to need your help."

"Mine?" Hunter's eyebrows shoot up. "What do you...?"

"Vampire blood has anaesthetic properties, right?" Silas asks, cutting him off.

Hunter stares at him for a moment, and then nods. "Yeah," he replies. "It's a bit like an opioid. It's why the witches nearly hunted us to extinction back in the day. I think it's still sold on the black market in some places."

"You're saying it can't heal Shade? Only numb him?" I ask, my heart already sinking. If their plan is just to make him comfortable while he bleeds out...

"No," Silas replies, shaking his head. "But *I* can heal him."

"I didn't realise you'd had medical training, Aconyte," Landon mutters dryly.

Silas shoots him a look. "Not now, Landon. I'm talking about fire. *Dragon* fire, specifically."

I watch Hunter's eyes widen with comprehension. I'm barely following as it is. "You're going to cauterise it," the vampire shifter states.

Silas nods. "It won't replenish the blood he's lost, but if we can keep him from losing any more, we might be able to save him. What do you think, Boots?" he asks me. I'm reminded once again that I'm still the final word in these matters, and for some reason, that only saddens me more. But there are more important things to worry about right now than my own damaged pride.

"Do it," I reply without hesitation.

Hunter is already shifting back into his vampire form. He's really getting the hang of it. "Does someone have a knife?" he asks, rolling up his sleeve.

I pat my hands down Shade's body before extracting a switch-blade from the inner pocket of his jacket. Once a delinquent, always a delinquent. Wordlessly, I pass the knife to Hunter, and watch as he grits his teeth before slicing a long gash down the length of his arm. Blood begins to ooze out, and I see right away that the consistency is different from other shifters': more sluggish, and darker . Wincing a little at the pain, the vampire shifter presses his arm to Shade's mouth while I gently urge the wolf shifter's head up. Blood begins to trickle into his mouth, and the result is instantaneous: immediately, I see his muscles begin to relax, his breathing slowing to a less concerning speed.

"Just enough to put him under," he murmurs. "Have to be careful. It's potent."

We watch in tense silence as Hunter continues to administer his blood to Shade, until at last the fallen shifter looks more like he's sleeping peacefully than unconscious from blood loss. He pulls back, allowing Silas to take his place, and for a moment our eyes meet. I'm still too distraught to express myself coherently, but he seems to see the gratitude in my expression, and nods, smiling just a little.

Silas pulls Hunter's shirt up, exposing the wound which is even worse than I was expecting. The bullet grazed him, but the gash is deep, and I'm pretty sure I can see his rib bone peeking out of the cut. The sight makes my stomach turn, but I grit my teeth and force myself to watch.

"Stand back," Silas instructs us, and once we're a safe distance away, he exhales a thin jet of fire directly onto the wound. Shade immediately tenses up once more, but doesn't seem to be in agony the way I would have expected. There's the smell of burning flesh, the sound of crackling flames... And then he pulls back, the fire going out all at once. What's left on Shade's side is an ugly scorch mark, just big enough to cover the wound, and precise enough not to have damaged the rest of his skin. He's still pale and sweating, but he's no longer bleeding.

Realising I was holding my breath, I slump backward, but the world starts spinning around me once more. I put my head between my knees, struggling to keep a hold on myself, when I'm interrupted by the feeling of someone brushing my hair out of my face. I turn to see Hunter looking at me, his still-bleeding arm extended in an offering.

"Hunter, please," I pant. "I'm fine..."

"Millie." His expression doesn't falter. "Come on. You need it." And then, in a voice so quiet the others can't hear, he adds, "I owe it to you."

I search his eyes with my own for a long moment, my mind wandering back to the image of him kissing Edith, and then nod, taking his pale arm in my hands and lowering my mouth to the cut. The blood tastes nothing like human blood -- it's almost cloyingly sweet, and stickier than it has any right to be. But the moment it passes my lips I can feel a sense of relaxation flooding through me.

It's like taking the world's strongest Xanax, and before long I'm leaning desperately into him, drinking like my life depends on it. It takes everything I have to pull away , wiping my mouth with the back of my hand and feeling better than I have since being taken by the Academy.

"Thank you," I whisper to Hunter, and press my forehead into his chest for a brief moment.

His hands come up to touch my hair, and I get the sense that he wants to keep the contact going, but instead, he forces himself to pull away. "We should get going," he says.

"Agreed," says Landon, extending a hand and helping me to my feet. Hunter assists Silas in supporting the unconscious Shade, and together we start forward again.

Although my physical symptoms have been aided by Hunter's blood, the cause continues to gnaw at me. "I need to get my powers back," I say after a few minutes of silent walking. "I'm useless to us without them."

"Well," Silas says, eyes fixed forward, "I can think of a good place to start." At that moment, we emerge from the stand of trees and into a clearing. Before us, the ocean stretches out like a field of blue, and for a moment I'm not sure what he's talking about.

But then my eyes adjust to the sunlight, and it all becomes clear. On the horizon, shrouded in mist, is an island . Extending from the top of a hill into the sky is a building that is also ominously familiar, enough that the sight of it alone makes my heart race again.

The Academy.

CHAPTER 71

I'm not sure whether to feel angry or relieved. My feelings for the place itself are as murky as the politics governing it; there's no arguing that the Academy saved me, in more ways than one. It gave me a home when I had none, and if I hadn't been found that day after running away, I would probably be dead in a ditch somewhere right now. Then again, it's also responsible for my current predicament, so I find myself torn in multiple directions as I stare across the water at its ornate brick walls and jutting clock tower. Almost unwittingly, I begin to move forward, taking first one step and then another...

And then Landon's hand lands on my arm. "Whoa, whoa, whoa, wait a minute," he says, looking visibly tense. "Can we just talk about this for a second?"

"There's nothing to talk about," Silas replies, already moving forward. "We need to get help for Shade. I'd say our options are pretty clear."

"You're talking about walking right back into the wasp's nest," the siren shifter protests. "Look, I want to help Shade as much as any of us, but..."

"I think Silas is right," Hunter remarks grimly. "These islands are out in the middle of nowhere -- we knew that from the first day we arrived here. And without Boots' teleportation powers..."

"There's nowhere else to go," Silas finishes for him.

As if on cue, the two of them turn to look at me, eyebrows raised expectantly.

Realising they're waiting for my take, I clear my throat, still struggling to shake some of the fog out of my mind. "Won't they attack us on sight the minute they see us?" I ask, crossing my arms over my chest. The thought of turning away when Shade is in such dire straits makes my heart hurt, but the only thing worse than him being injured would be the others being injured as well.

"There *is* my dad," Hunter says, although his tone is doubtful.

"Your dad usually isn't around the campus," Landon points out.

"Amelia, then?" I ask. "If we could somehow get in touch with her..."

"What will that accomplish?" Silas asks, letting out a frustrated growl that might make my heart flutter if we weren't in a life-or-death situation. "She won't be able to do anything you haven't done already, Hunter. We need the nurse. Either that, or someone with healing magic."

"A witch, then," I say, setting my jaw.

I can tell we're all thinking the same thing. "Josie?" Landon asks quietly.

"If she's even still here," I reply, hating the possibility. "If she hasn't..." I can't even bring myself to finish the sentence. Josie was my first real shifter friend, and one of the few Academy members who I feel like I can actually trust. She's saved us from multiple scrapes, and seems disgusted by what President Hawthorne is doing... but I know that puts a target on her back, the same way it puts one on mine. The last time we saw her, she was tangling with Academy loyalists back at the campus in Boston, and the fact that we haven't heard from her since doesn't bode well.

Landon scuffs his foot against the ground. "I guess it's worth a shot," he says at last. "I don't like the thought of you ending up in danger again, Millie. Especially now that..." But he pales, clears his throat, and trails off.

A fresh wave of embarrassment and disappointment hits me at the implication that I can no longer protect myself, but as much as it sucks, for the moment, at least, it's true. "I'll be careful," I reply diplomatically. "I trust you guys."

"I say we go for the infirmary," Hunter suggests. "We can find supplies there, and if we're lucky, potions. I've heard the witches sometimes keep enchantments in there somewhere. We can look for Josie, too, but we'll have to be careful."

"Was that leadership I heard from you just now, Hunter?" Landon teases, elbowing him. "I never thought I'd see the day."

"Yeah, yeah, yeah." Hunter waves him off. "Don't get used to it." But in spite of everything, there's a touch of self-deprecating humour in his voice that gives me a momentary boost.

"So how do we get over there?" I ask. "I can't port us, and with Shade out of commission, it's not like we can swim."

"*I* can swim," Landon points out, and then glances at Silas. "Do you think you can manage carrying three people?"

Silas runs a hand through his hair. "I think so," he says, after a long pause. "We're going to draw attention, though. I'll have to fly low."

"Fine by me," Hunter says.

I nod my agreement, and we watch as Silas once again shifts into his dragon form. Craning his long neck, he nods in my direction. "Climb on my back, Boots," he says. "It will be safest for you up there."

I don't need to be told twice, moving close and clambering onto Silas' warm haunches. His scales glimmer in the daylight, and I'm struck once more by the strength of his body, especially when he's shifted. As I nestle close to his reptilian neck, he lets out a low intonation, a rumbling of contentment deep in his chest that makes goosebumps appear on my arms. I don't have time to think about it further, however, as he unfurls his wings. He picks Hunter up in one of his talons, Shade's limp body in the other, and soon we're lifting off the ground.

Landon, unfazed, becomes a siren and dives into the water as easily as a dolphin, his scales merging beautifully with the water. I watch as his lean body begins to swim in a butterfly motion, faster than any human could accomplish, and Silas catches a gust of wind to glide along above him.

We make good time, and soon we're approaching the island. The salty sea breeze helps to wake me up further, and as I cling to Silas's strong body, I take a moment to appreciate the beauty of the scenery around us. If only it didn't disguise such an ugly truth. As we close in on the rocky slopes, the mist surrounding the island begins to envelop us, making me hopeful that we won't be spotted from the ground.

And just like that, we're touching down on the shores of the unnamed island that houses the U.K. Academy. I slide off Silas' back so that he can change back just as Landon splashes ashore, droplets glistening against his dark skin which is already human again. Catching me staring, he winks at me. I roll my eyes at him, which only makes him laugh as he pulls me in for a brief kiss. Curious, I watch Hunter out of the corner of my eye as my mouth touches the siren's, but the vampire shifter doesn't even bat an eye at the affection. Some part of me wonders if maybe we've passed a threshold in our relationship, but I don't have time to dwell on it.

Silas clears his throat. "Shall we?"

Together we make our way up the sloping beach and into the woods bordering the Academy building, which feels both foreign and familiar to me now. To think that the last time I was here we were only just getting an idea of the humans' treachery...

My breathing is growing faster as we approach the clearing where the campus is housed, but Silas and Hunter, who are supporting Shade as we move, suddenly come to a stop. "What's wrong?" I ask, already going into panic mode.

"We can't just drag an unconscious shifter into the quad," Landon replies. "Someone's going to have to stay behind and take care of Shade."

"I'll do it," I say without missing a beat. My heart aches for the wolf shifter, and I'll be damned if I'm going to leave him behind.

"Millie..." Silas bites his lip. "I understand you wanting to keep him safe, but you're not a hundred percent. Not by a long shot. One of us should probably be the one to guard him, in case we get caught."

My heart sinks, but even as I open my mouth to protest, I realise he's right. Nobility is all well and good, but it means nothing if it will just end up getting us killed. Swallowing hard, I give him a stiff nod. "Okay. Do you want to do it? You could probably use a rest."

"Yeah, go ahead and sit this one out," Landon suggests. "The three of us can handle this."

Silas gives him a wry smile. "Somehow that, coming from you, Landon, doesn't make me feel super reassured."

Landon gives him a shove, but behind his usual playfulness, I can see that he's nervous. I don't blame him; I am too. The administration knows we've gone on the run, and for all we know, they could have scouts patrolling for any signs of our return. Then again, if they think we're still trapped in Hawthorne's facility...

Hunter places his hand at the small of my back, his fingers pressing in ever so gently, and the sensation is steadying. Wordlessly, we walk into the clearing, leaving Shade and Silas in the shadows of the forest outskirts. It feels more and more surreal the closer we get to the quad: what used to be a home for me, a sign of hope, has now become a lion's den, and the worst part is that we don't even know where the lion is.

"Seems awfully *normal*. You know -- considering all the kidnappings and bioterrorism," Landon remarks sarcastically. And he's right. By all appearances, the campus is running as it always has. Uniformed students rush this way and that on their way to their classes -- it seems we've arrived during a passing period -- and nobody seems bothered in the slightest by the disappearances or the convention centre attack.

"People would always rather pretend everything is fine," Hunter murmurs with a frown. "Easier that way."

"Do you think any of them even suspect...?" I ask. "I mean, surely if they've kept running their tests..."

"One would think," Landon says, his brow furrowing.

Upon reaching the stone walkway leading to the academics building, we come to a stop. "What's the plan?" Hunter asks, turning to me.

I think for a moment. "I say two of us go to check the infirmary, and one goes looking for Josie. Two birds with one stone."

"I like it," Landon says. "The less time we spend in this place, the happier I'll be."

"I'll look for Josie," Hunter volunteers, surprising me once more with how quickly he's come into his own. "You guys take the infirmary. We can meet back here in half an hour."

"Sounds like a plan," I say.

As Hunter turns to go, I grab him by the wrist and give him a little squeeze. "Be careful," I tell him.

The vampire shifter gives me a melancholy smile. "You too, Millie." And then he turns and vanishes into the crowd of students, his hands in his pockets.

"You ready for this?" Landon asks, holding his hand out.

"As ready as I'll ever be," I reply, even though it's a lie. I've never felt more vulnerable in my life.

For all his teasing, Landon is perceptive, and I can tell he can sense my fear. Instead of taking my hand, he puts an arm around my shoulders as we walk, his relaxed posture setting me at ease. "It'll be fine," he murmurs in my ear, and the vibrations of his voice make me shiver.

It turns out he spoke too soon. Just as we're skirting past one of the stone benches and making a beeline for the side entrance, a voice makes us snap to attention. "And just who might you be?"

CHAPTER 72

My breath hitches, and for a brief moment I wonder whether we could get away if we made a break for it right now. But then my mind goes back to Shade, lying unconscious on the forest floor, and all thoughts of fleeing go out the window. Slowly we turn around to find ourselves face to face with not a faculty member, as I was expecting, but a student. He looks to be a few grades ahead of us, and he crosses his arms as he waits for an answer.

Landon stares at him for a second before turning his question back around on him: "I don't know. Just who might *you* be?"

"Isaiah Wilson," the other student replies. "I'm part of Hawthorne's campus security cohort. I don't think I've seen you two around the school before."

I stare at him blankly with no idea what he's talking about. *Fake it till you make it,* I decide, and do my best to give him a winning smile. "Oh, right. The security cohort -- of course. I just wanted to thank you personally for keeping all of us safe. It sounds like these insurgents are becoming a real problem." It's a shot in the dark, and it's all I can do not to cross my fingers.

Isaiah's face softens for a moment. "Not exactly my idea of the perfect work study, but I'm not complaining." His tone then goes serious again. "You two aren't in uniform."

Shit, shit, shit. Landon and I exchange a panicked look; I hadn't even thought about the fact that we're in streetwear. "That's completely my bad," Landon says, covering for me. "I was trying to help Boots with her siren form down by the shore-"

"I never learned to swim," I put in.

"-and I didn't want us to get our uniforms wet. Have you ever tried to get salt water out of that fabric?" He scoffs. "Fucking forget it."

"I... wouldn't know about that -- I'm a wolf shifter," replies Isaiah, sounding doubtful. "You do realise that's a dress code violation, don't you? Nonconformity."

It's a struggle to disguise my disgust. The Academy seems to be getting more authoritarian by the minute -- the subjugation is ironic, considering the humans are doing their damndest to give themselves shifter powers.

But I force myself to rein in my reaction and turn on the charm. "Shit," I say, doing my best impression of vapid obliviousness. My weakened state is making it hard to concentrate, but I'm still riding the high from Hunter's blood, and the words seem to roll effortlessly off my tongue. "I keep forgetting about all these new rules. They're changing things faster than I can keep up, I swear."

I glance at Landon for backup, and he nods and holds up his hands. "Idiot freshmen! But hey, now we know, right?"

Isaiah frowns. "I'm supposed to report you guys for this."

My eyes go wide. The last thing we need is for someone to take our names down -- or worse, send us to the office. "Is that really necessary?" I ask, taking a step towards Isaiah. "If we promise not to do it again?"

"Look, it's not up to me," Isaiah replies.

But there's a hint of doubt in his voice, and I seize on it. An idea comes to me, and I slink closer to Isaiah, sweeping my hair out of my face with one hand while putting on what I hope is a sultry smile. "What Hawthorne doesn't know won't hurt him, will it?" I ask in a husky voice. "Can't you make an exception? We -- *I* -- would be incredibly grateful."

Isaiah's eyes sweep over my figure, and I can see more cracks appearing in his armour. Is the vampire blood enhancing my sex appeal, or am I just better at this than I thought? "I mean, I... I don't know if..."

I put my hand on his arm, looking into his eyes. "I'd owe you a favour," I tell him quietly.

And that finally does it. "All right," Isaiah says with a nod. "Go ahead. Just... make sure you stick to the dress code from now on."

"Absolutely." I turn to Landon, and the two of us hurry on our way.

"Can I get your number or something?" I hear Isaiah call from behind us.

"Don't worry, I'll find you," I call back, and before he can respond, we're disappearing into the crowd.

I can feel Landon eyeing me slyly as we head for the admin building. "What?" I ask, blushing a little.

"Not bad, Boots," Landon remarks. "If I we re the jealous type, I'd be pretty pissed off right now."

"Let's not get ahead of ourselves," I reply, pulling him close so I can kiss him on the cheek. "I know where my priorities are."

Landon only laughs. "Thank god for that."

ALTHOUGH WE AREN'T STOPPED AGAIN on our way into the admin building, I'm now painfully aware of the fact that Landon and I stick out like sore thumbs. We do get our fair share of raised eyebrows as we pick through the crowd in the direction of the infirmary; we probably look either brave or stupid, considering how severely the humans have clamped down on the rules, and I'm actually a little surprised that none of the teachers do more than give us a strange look or two. Then again, they're shifters too, and Josie can't be the only one dissatisfied with the way things are going.

The infirmary is blessedly empty when we creep inside. Not even the school nurse is around, and I wonder if our luck is finally turning. Behind the rows of beds partitioned by curtains is a supply cabinet, which Landon and I make a beeline for. "What do we need?" I ask.

"We need to prepare for the worst," Landon replies. "If we can't find Josie, we'll need an elixir, or a healing potion. Bandages, too, and antibiotics."

"Got it," I say, and tug on the door. It doesn't budge. "Fuck, it's locked. I should've figured it wouldn't be this easy."

I bunch my sleeve around my fist and swing back, ready to break the glass by hand, but Landon reaches out and seizes my wrist. "Hold it," he says. "It might be enchanted."

"What do we do?" I ask.

The siren shifter frowns for a moment. "I might have an idea," he says finally. "If I can just manipulate the tumblers without tripping whatever spell is on here..." I move back to give him room as he lets out a targeted gust of soundwaves. It's a narrow stream, and I can see the vibrations in the air as he directs it towards the keyhole. The concentration is written on his face, and I can tell he's having a diffi-cult time maintaining precision with the makeshift lockpick. Almost instinctively, I find myself getting ready to shift so I can help, only to discover that I'm completely empty of magic. To his credit, if Landon sees my obvious distress, he doesn't make an issue of it.

A few tense moments pass before the lock gives a satisfying click and the door pops open. We open the doors wider and together we stuff our pockets with supplies. Most of them I don't even recognise; enchanted balms and poultices, talismans, boxes of herbs, and even a few human remedies, so I don't discriminate as I cram them all into Landon's backpack.

We're just shutting the cabinet and preparing to make a break for it when the sound of footsteps makes us both jump. I whirl around, expecting to see the school medic ready to sound the alarm, but what I see instead makes me breathe a sigh of relief.

Standing in the doorway is Hunter, and next to him is someone I wasn't sure I would ever see again: Josie, the witch shifter. Before I even realise what I'm doing, I'm running across the room and throwing my arms around her. "You're alive!"

"Easy, easy," she says, wincing, and I pull back to see how gaunt she's become.

"What happened?" I ask. "What did they do to you?"

"Let's just say the administration wasn't too happy that I helped you guys escape in Boston," she replies with a pained smile. "The Board won't approve of disposing me without a full inquest, so Hawthorne settled on confining me to my room. They've been trying to get me to tell them where you guys went, and their methods have gotten... extreme."

"Josie, I'm so sorry," I tell her. "This is my fault."

"Don't worry about it," she replies. "I'm just glad you're safe. Your friend Hunter here pulled rank down in the registrar's office. This is the first time I've been out of my room in two weeks." In spite of her obvious trauma, she still has a determined look on her face. "So," she says as we head out of the infirmary, "what can I do for you guys?"

BACK IN THE woods where we left the others, I watch as Josie works her healing magic on Shade as I explain what Hawthorne's scientist did to me. The fact that we can save the supplies we stole is an added bonus. "He's going to sleep for some time yet," she says, standing up, "but he's stable. Give him some more rest and he'll be okay." Relief washes over me, but it's short-lived. "As far as your powers," she continues, "that's going to be a little more complicated."

"How much more complicated?" Silas asks.

"The good news is that if they had drained you completely, you would be dead," Josie explains. "Remember what happened to that other student, Brody?" I nod, thinking back to the poor boy we found in the basement all those weeks ago. A little later and the same thing would have happened to Silas. "The issue is that, whereas Silas still had some control over his powers after being kidnapped, you can't access them at all," the witch shifter goes on. "That means they got farther in the process with you. The core of your magical energy is still there, but until it's reactivated, you won't be able to transform again."

"Okay," says Hunter, crossing his arms, "so how do we reactivate it?"

I can tell from Jodie's look that the answer isn't going to be simple. "You were created using the blood of five other shifters," she says. "If we can distill the essence of their powers from their blood and transfer it to you, I believe we'll be able to give you your magic back."

"I'm sensing a 'but' coming," Landon remarks.

Josie nods glumly. "Normally this type of rejuvenation would demand the DNA of the shifter's parents, since these abilities are passed on genetically. In your case, Millie, being a hybrid, your parents didn't carry the shifter gene."

"Right," I say. That makes sense. It sucks, but it makes sense. "So this shouldn't be too hard then, right? Between you and the guys, we can perform the procedure now."

"I wish it worked like that," Josie says with a sigh. "You have to think of this process like a transplant, or a blood transfusion. If you're a human, you're a blank slate, so under the right circumstances, you can receive shifter powers. It's rare, but it is possible. That's what Hawthorne is trying to do. The issue is that once you have shifter magic in you, the source of the magic needs to be the same. Otherwise, your body will reject it, and the process could kill you."

"How do you know so much about this, anyway?" asks Silas, sounding curious.

Jodie gives him a dry smile. "Witch, remember? Meddling with shifter genetics is something we've been doing for centuries." Turning back to me, her smile fades. "All this is to say, Millie, that you're going to need the precise donors whose magic you were infused with as a baby. The point is to replicate that original experiment on a smaller scale in order to re-up your powers. Which means…"

The implication finally sinks in, and I can feel concern taking me over. Silas, Shade, Hunter, and Landon are all here with me, and would no doubt willingly assist me. But there's one missing ingredient, one remaining shifter, the ultimate snag.

And her name is Edith Carlyle.

CHAPTER 73

For most people, the idea of dealing with an enemy in order to achieve a greater goal is a worthy sacrifice - hell, maybe even a noble one.

I guess I'm just not that noble.

I can feel the others' eyes on me as I wordlessly walk over to the nearest tree and drop my head against the rough bark of its trunk, my eyes drifting closed as I grapple with the worst case scenario. Edith rubbed me the wrong way from square one, and I'll be the first one to admit my initial misgivings had as much to do with my jealousy as they did with her potential to betray us. Either way, though, I was right about her in the end, even if for the wrong reasons: she single handedly caused the death of my former foster mother, Mollie, and put us back on the Academy's radar after our return to the U.K. I can't confirm it, either, but I suspect she also led us into a trap back when we still considered her an ally, pitting me, Hunter, and Landon against a couple of her human-loyalist friends. She also happens to be an insanely skilled witch shifter, with power levels high enough to rival some of the professors at the Academy.

Oh, and she's where I got my witch form from. I almost forgot.

All this is to say, there couldn't be a worse missing piece of the puzzle, and whether the others express it or not, I know they're thinking the same thing. I become aware of a frustrated groaning noise and realise with a start that the intonation is coming from me as I press my forehead into the tree like somehow I can make it swallow me up. It just couldn't be easy, could it?

"Is she okay?" I hear Hunter murmur to one of the others.

"What do you think?" Silas grumbles back.

"Boots?" Landon asks cautiously, and I feel him rest a hand gingerly on my shoulder. "I know I said I wasn't the jealous type, but you're getting awfully cozy with that spruce."

That surprises a laugh out of me, and I open my eyes and turn back to them. "Sorry," I say, rubbing the back of my neck. "I probably sound whiny as hell."

"Considering what you've been through in the past twenty-four hours," Silas replies, "I think you've earned the right to whine a bit."

"Thanks." I give him a weak smile. "I was just hoping this wouldn't involve tangling with Edith again."

"I take it she's the other witch shifter?" Josie asks.

I nod, sighing. "Smart. Crafty. Hella powerful, too. And gorgeous..."

"She's no you," Hunter blurts. I meet his ocean blue eyes, and a flush creeps across his pale face, but he doesn't look away. "I mean it," he adds quietly. "We all do."

That's enough to make me want to cry. Even as borderline-useless as I am right now, they still care about me. It almost doesn't seem fair. "So what do you propose we do?" I ask Josie once I've gotten my emotions under control.

"Get away from the Academy, for a start," she replies. "I'm weak, but I should be able to jump us to the mainland, at the very least. I have an apartment in the countryside, away from prying eyes. By the time you've collected the DNA, I should be recovered enough to perform the procedure. We can plan on meeting up there."

"What about Edith?" Silas asks, crossing his arms. "She's going to be a problem."

"You're telling me," I mutter. "She's clearly on the wrong side.

There won't be a way of getting her to go willingly, that's for sure. And she'll probably have Academy agents with her."

"There's also the matter of where she is," Hunter points out. "We don't even know where she got off to after she turned you in, Boots."

He has a point, as much as I hate to admit it. Considering how far we've seen the humans' influence extend over the past few weeks, she could very well be on the other side of the world, and we would have no idea. I can already feel despair creeping back in, and it must be written on my face, since the others exchange a look of concern.

"Hey," Silas says, putting a hand on my shoulder, "we're going to fix this, Boots."

"Are we?" I ask quietly. "I mean, *are* we, really?"

"Boots-" Landon begins.

I cut him off. "Look around," I say, making a frustrated gesture at where we are. "We're in the middle of nowhere. We've only got a few allies, and next to no resources. We don't even have a place to stay. And the Academy's only going to get stronger."

"That's exactly why we need you back up to par," Hunter argues. "You're the biggest weapon we have against them, and they know that. Why else do you think they've wanted you out of commission for so long?"

"But what if it's not worth it?" I ask, running a hand through my hair. It hurts to even verbalise the fear. "I mean, we don't even have a guarantee that we'll be able to get my powers back. What if we just end up wasting our time on a wild goose chase when we should be strategising against Hawthorne? What if he actually succeeds in his experiments while we're fucking around with my powers?"

"It's not 'fucking around' if it means solving your problem," says Landon. "If anything, this is a detour we *should* be taking. We can use it to gain allies, maybe even find out where some of our friends are."

I purse my lips. Truth be told, I haven't given much thought to my other friends since being taken by Hawthorne. The last I saw of Hazel, Xander, and Ruby, they were vanishing in a burning apartment building while being dogpiled by Academy loyalists. For all we know, they could be dead by now, or worse...

Hardly daring to ask the question, I turn to Josie. "I know you've been sort of out of commission," I acknowledge, "but have you happened to hear anything about Hazel Van Buren or the Murakami twins? I know they're not technically students here, but..."

Josie sighs and shakes her head. "I wish I could tell you they were safe," she says. "I've been keeping my ear to the ground -- not much else to do when you're trapped in your room 24/7 -- but the only mention I've heard of them is from the higher-ups who've passed by on my floor, and a few of the students who have dared to pass on some information."

"What have they said?" asks Hunter.

"From the sounds of it, they aren't here," Josie replies. "Rumour has it some of the Board members are getting antsy that there are still missing students after the attack in Boston. It's bad publicity for them, and Hawthorne and Russo are getting pissed that there are still loose ends running around."

"That's a good thing, right?" asks Landon. "Means they haven't been recaptured."

"That's a fair point," Silas acknowledges, "but for how long? They're no better off than we are, and they don't have the advantage of running with a hybrid."

"Then you need to find them," Josie says. "The more people you have on your side, the better. It's also possible that they'll have leads to Edith -- or vice versa."

"Sounds like we know what we have to do, then," Silas says matter-of-factly. "We have to go back to London. It's as good a place to start as any, and we know that was where they were last. If they're thinking strategically, they won't have gone somewhere else, especially with all the other shifters in the city."

The sound of distant shouts makes me jump, and when I turn around to glance through the trees, I can see uniformed security officers combing the quad like ants. The other students are nowhere to be seen.

"...to be around here somewhere," I overhear one of the men saying. "She was half-starved. She can't have gotten too far."

"Sounds like they've finally noticed I'm gone," Josie says. "That's our cue to leave. I need everyone to join hands, please."

I chew my lip for a moment, wondering if a transport spell in her current state will even work, or just drop us somewhere over the Irish Sea, but I know better than to bring it up. She healed Shade after all, even in her weakened state. Wordlessly, I move to take her hand, linking my other with Shade's limp fingers. The other guys form a circle, relaxing in preparation for the spell. In the distance, I can hear the sounds of the search party growing closer, and a surge of fear rushes through me. I watch as Josie closes her eyes, her brow furrowing in concentration.

For one terrifying moment, and then another, nothing happens. The witch shifter continues to strain, letting out a grunt as she digs deep; I know the feeling all too well by now, and I wish I could do something to help her. There's the sound of rustling branches, shouting voices, and I can see the others preparing to shift in self-defense. Two security officers appear in the clearing and charge for us, weapons brandished...

And then the ground begins to shift in that telltale sign of teleportation, our bodies becoming translucent. One of the attackers fires his gun, but the bullet passes directly through my torso, which has become intangible. The world around us morphs, and suddenly we find ourselves standing behind an old stone wall in the middle of one of the most picturesque villages I've ever seen. A cathedral juts up in the distance, and a country road winds down between thatched-cottages and pristine green grass, disappearing up a hill and towards the waterfront. A woman pushing a tram along the other side of the street freezes when she sees us appear, her eyes going wide, and then lets out a shriek and rushes to escape with her baby.

"Guess she doesn't know about shifters," Landon remarks.

"Where are we?" Hunter asks. "This doesn't look like London."

"It's not," Josie says, breathing hard and putting her hands on her knees. "We're in Gloucestershire. I was aiming for London, but I'm fatigued, and those agents were closing in on us. This was the best I could do."

"Well, at least it's off the radar," says Silas, shielding his eyes from the sun and peering up the road. "I think there's a train station in the city proper. We can rest here tonight and leave first thing in the morning. No one's going to come looking for us here."

I turn to Josie. "Thank you," I tell her, and mean it. "You're welcome to come with us."

"Thank you," Josie says ruefully, "but if we're going to give you your powers back, I need to start preparing. I think I'll hitch a ride from here. The sooner I can get my strength up, the better."

"Are you sure?" asks Landon.

The witch shifter nods. "You could very well be the key to defeating Hawthorne, Millie," she tells me without a hint of face-tiousness in her voice. "I want to do everything in my power to make that happen. Focus on finding your friends and getting Edith's blood. I'll take care of the rest." She turns to head up the road, but then stops and glances over her shoulder. "And Mille?" she says.

"Yeah?"

"Good luck. And stay alive."

CHAPTER 74

By the time we walk the rest of the way into town, half-supporting and half-carrying Shade as we go, the sun is already low in the sky. We take out rooms for the night in the first inn we come across, courtesy of Hunter and his father's not-inconsiderable means. After a rather awkward conversation with the receptionist, we're at last able to relax. For the time being, anyway.

Once we're settled in -- two to a room, split over three connecting suites -- I allow myself to flop backwards onto the plush bed, my eyes closing as I try to process the events of the last twenty-four hours. It isn't easy, and just when I think I'm all cried out, I feel more tears welling up . Am I being stupid, I wonder, for mourning the loss of my shifting when there are people whose lives are on the line? Hazel and the twins could be dead in a ditch somewhere, but here I am, lying in bed and feeling sorry for myself. It's ridiculous.

I sit up, stretch, and go to the window. Wallowing won't do me any good. Exhaling, I lean against the frame, staring out over the pastoral fields and winding roads and trying to let my mind wander. I'm not sure how long I stand there, but before I know it, the sun has dropped past the horizon and it's getting dark in the room. We'll have to leave early tomorrow if we want to get back to London by the end of the day, and given how exhausted I am, bed sounds like an excellent idea.

I'm just changing into my night clothes when the door opens and Hunter appears. He looks tired, no doubt from his own blood loss, and his red hair is sticking out in all directions. As I turn to him, he runs his hands through it.

"Are you all right?" I ask uncertainly.

Hunter nods, sighing. "Just tired," he replies. "I'm guessing you can relate."

I nod, sitting down on the bed and scooting over to make room for him. He drops down beside me, running a hand down his face. "Look," he says after a long pause, "I wanted to see how you were doing. I understand if you don't want to see me right now, believe me, but..." He meets my eyes with his own. "I care about you, Boots."

"I care about you, too," I tell him.

"So how are you, really?" Hunter asks.

"Alive," I respond, "but that's about all I can say, to be honest. I feel so... useless." My shoulders slump. "It's like they took part of me away."

Hunter puts his hand on my knee. The touch sends sparks of electricity up my leg, but I don't push him away. "We're going to fix this," Hunter says. "We're going to find a solution, Millie."

"What if we can't?" The words come out barely a whisper. "What if I never get my powers back? The things they did to me back there, Hunter... You can't even imagine what it was like."

"No. I can't." I can see him tense up out of the corner of my eye. The hand that isn't on my knee is bunched into a fist, and his whole body looks like he's shaking. Not with fear, though, I realise after a moment. With anger. "If I ever get my hands on that bastard," he says slowly, "I'll kill him. I don't care what it takes. He deserves to die. For what he did to Silas, for that Brody kid..." Hunter's breath hitches a little. "For what he did to you."

"Hunter..." Tentatively I reach out to touch his cheek.

He tenses up under the brush of my hand. "The thought of you getting hurt, Millie, or worse..." He shakes his head. "It kills me. Every time I think about what happened to you back there, about the part I played in it-"

"Hey, wait." I pull him towards me so I can meet his gaze. "Hunter, that wasn't your fault. None of that was your fault."

"How can you say that?" he demands, his voice full of pain. "If I hadn't let Edith get in my head -- I mean, if I had just picked up on what she was planning..."

"None of us could have known," I insist. "We thought she was on our side. We couldn't have predicted she would turn on us."

"That's awfully understanding of you," Hunter replies dryly. "Considering... Well, you know." He swallows hard, taking my hand in his. "We never talked about what happened, really," he says quietly. "With Edith, I mean."

"You said it yourself," I say. "She got in your head. I think she got in *mine*, too."

"I shouldn't have let her," Hunter replies.

"Then why did you?" It's a question I've had for a long time, but I've only just worked up the courage to ask it.

Hunter waits for a long time before replying. "You have to understand, I've spent my whole life thinking I was a lost cause. Amelia was always the smart one, the powerful one -- between her and Dad, I was starting to think there was no hope for me. And then I met you, and..." He takes an unsteady breath. "And everything changed. To have these three other guys, and don't get me wrong, they're all brilliant, but they're all top-notch, and here I am..."

"You don't think you match up to them?"

Hunter shakes his head. "And being around you, Millie... You're this beautiful, smart, talented..." He throws his hands up hopelessly. "I didn't think I was worthy of you. Sometimes I still don't." Slowly he brushes a strand of hair out of my face. "All I can say is I'm sorry, Millie. For everything."

"No harm done," I tell him, and smile. "I shouldn't have reacted the way I did. *I* was jealous."

"Of Edith?" His eyes widen.

"I mean, yeah," I reply sheepishly. "I didn't think *I* could compete with *her.*"

"Then I guess we're in the same boat," Hunter observes. And then

449

he kisses me. It's light and tentative, almost scared, and before I even have time to reciprocate, he's pulling away. "I'm sorry," he says hastily. "I shouldn't have-"

But I interrupt him by pulling him back for another kiss. The relief of having put our feelings out in the open is overwhelming, and I find myself consumed by the desire for his touch, his comfort, especially in light of everything that's happened. Hunter's hands are light as they come up to rest around my waist, tightening as he pulls my body closer to his.

I can sense his barely contained excitement in spite of his efforts to be delicate. His lips move to the base of my neck (*a vampire thing?* I wonder), and I can feel his teeth working the skin there hard enough to leave a mark. I can feel his hands creeping under the hem of my shirt, but they stop before they can get where I really want them to go. "Don't stop," I murmur against his lips, sidling closer to him as I allow my fingers to tangle in his fiery hair.

Effectively given permission, Hunter hauls my shirt up and over my head, palming my breasts over my bra and soliciting a moan from me. My hands are on his belt buckle before I even have time to think. Before long we're discarding each other's clothes like our lives depend on it.

I move to roll over and pull him on top of me, but his hands on my hips keep me firmly in place.

"Here," he says, maneuvering me with his strong arms so I'm straddling him, "I want to see all of you."

I've never been on top before, and I move slowly as I guide him inside me so as not to hurt him. Hunter lets out a low groan, his lips meeting mine once more, and I begin to rock slowly into his lap as that familiar friction begins to heat up my whole body.

I don't know how long it lasts, that's how lost we are in each other, and I don't care. All that matters is the feeling of him inside me, soothing the anxiety and fear and pain, and by the time we come in unison it's all I can do to run my hands through his hair as he peppers my face and neck with soft kisses.

After a last moment of savouring the feeling, I pull away and crawl into bed, making room for Hunter beside me. There's the rustling of sheets, and moments later I feel a strong arm wrap around me as the vampire shifter pulls me flush against his chest.

"Thank you, Hunter," I murmur. "I needed that."

He presses a kiss to the back of my neck. "I should be the one thanking you. Are you feeling okay?"

"No worse, at least," I snark, before my tone dips back into one of disappointment. "This situation with my powers has me all messed up in the head. How am I supposed to help in this fight, how am I supposed to protect you guys when I can't even shapeshift anymore?"

"I wish I had an answer for you," Hunter replies.

"How did *you* do it?" I ask him, rolling over to look into his eyes. "Back before you learned how to shapeshift. How did you deal with those feelings?"

"Not well," Hunter confesses with a chuckle. "A lot of isolation, sulking—I mean, you saw me before. I resented the fact that I couldn't transform. But you taught me that maybe transforming isn't what's important at the end of the day."

"Yeah?" I smirk. "I changed your view, huh?"

"Don't get cocky," Hunter teases, but I can see the affection in his eyes. There's a pause, and he continues, "I do believe we're going to fix your magic, Millie. But until then, maybe..." He shrugs his broad shoulders. "Maybe there's some other way you can help in this fight."

"Like what?" I ask desperately.

"You're good at strategising, for one thing," Hunter reasons. "You're fast on your feet, too, and good at improvising. Landon told me about how you dealt with that other student earlier."

"Oh. Right." I blush. "But I don't think I'll be able to flirt my way out of a fight with an Academy agent, Hunter."

He hums, thinking for a moment. "There are humans who hunt shifters, right?" he says after a pause. "They don't have powers, but they've trained so much that they don't need them to go toe-to-toe with us. Think about those guys who attacked the convention centre."

"Mm." I'm starting to see where he's going with this. "You think I should try learning to fight?"

He shrugs. "It's worth a shot, right? I doubt most of the humans are expecting shifters with combat training. It could give you an edge —especially after you get your powers back."

"'After,'" I echo, chuckling a little. "You're such an idealist, Hunter Ash."

Hunter kisses me gently, running his thumbs over my cheek-bones. His movements are so sweet that it makes me feel like I've turned to jelly. When he pulls away, I see him drinking me in with his blue eyes. "I learned it from you," he says quietly, his voice barely above a whisper.

This brings unexpected tears to my eyes, and I can't help but wrap my arms around him and bury my face in his chest. If he feels the dampness on his skin, he doesn't say anything, just rolls onto his back so I can rest my head against him, his fingers stroking idly through my hair.

I still have no answers, and the future is still as nebulous as it was before. But falling asleep tucked against Hunter's chest, I find an escape.

CHAPTER 75

The train station is really only a train station in the most basic of terms, considering the size of the village, but I'm astonished when I see the sleek train that pulls up to the tracks as we bundle up onto the platform.

"Damn," Landon observes, crossing his arms. "You've got champagne tastes, Ash."

Hunter rolls his eyes. "Let's just say I've had about enough of sleeping on the floor in one-star motels for the time being."

"Lucky your dad is loaded," Silas agrees. "This isn't going to tip the Academy board off to where we are, is it?"

Hunter shakes his head. "Just because they pay well, that doesn't mean they have control of his finances." Seeing the doubtful look in the dragon shifter's eyes, he adds, a little defensively, "He isn't going to rat us out, Silas. He's been one of the dissenters on the board since day one."

"I hope you're right," says Silas, and with that, he leads our ragtag group across the station platform and up the train steps. The rest of us follow suit, Hunter and I supporting a still-woozy Shade while Landon watches me protectively from behind. The inside of the train car is plush, sleek and modern, and from the looks of it, the journey back to the city won't take long.

"Nice hickey," Landon murmurs in my ear as we move to get settled in our compartment. It makes me jump, and my hand flies to my neck and the mark that Hunter must have left last night. A burst of colour creeps into my face, and I open my mouth to respond, but the siren shifter just chuckles. "Hey, no judgement here. Not the jealous type, remember?"

Shooting him a relieved glance, I help Silas get Shade settled onto the seat while he moves to sit across from us. The others sit on the opposite side of the aisle, Landon already making some smart-ass comment about traveling in style while Hunter tries -- and fails -- to maintain his characteristic moody expression. After several minutes of silence, the engine roars as the conductor passes us by punching our tickets, and with that, we're off. The green fields and picturesque streams become a blur outside the window as the train picks up speed, and before long we're roaring through the countryside.

I'm sitting in the window seat with Shade leaning against me. He had a few lucid moments after a good night of sleep, but between the double-dose of vampire blood and witch magic, he's still more or less down for the count. I'm reminded of the day back when I was seventeen when I got my wisdom teeth pulled, but at least what few things the wolf shifter has said have made sense so far, abating my anxiety somewhat.

"Any progress on your powers?" Silas asks me. "I remember back when they drained me, waiting for them to come back was a gradual process. Do you think sleeping has helped at all?"

"Hmm..." I close my eyes for a moment, feeling for that familiar coolness in my stomach, but I might as well be a normal human again; all I feel is anxious and a little hungry. Shoulders slumping, I shake my head.

Silas hums in disappointment. "Well, it was worth a shot, at least. We're going to get them back and make that bitch Edith pay for what she did to you."

"Mollie, too," I say quietly. "It's her fault that she's dead." In all the chaos of the past days, I'm ashamed that I've almost forgotten the death of the one guardian I actually cared about. Guilt surges through me, as well as a rage I didn't even know I was capable of. Reaching into my boot, I withdraw the broken pendant she gave me when I was a kid, my fist clenching so hard that I can feel the metal digging into my skin. Another innocent life lost because of Hawthorne's treachery.

"What are you thinking?" Silas asks, peering curiously at me.

"That I'm going to get payback," I reply, and the sudden conviction in my voice surprises me. "Powers or no powers, I'm going to stop this."

"Hunter mentioned combat training," Silas says, shifting back in his seat. "I don't think it's a bad idea. Pretty badass, actually." And then he winks. Silas, the stoic dragon shifter, actually *winks* at me.

I can't help but smile a little. "The only question is where I'm supposed to learn how to fight."

"Well, that's an easy one," Silas replies, and nods in Shade's direction. "Shade can help you. He spent enough time in street brawls before coming into his powers that he could probably take anyone in a bar fight. Landon too, actually."

The information about Shade doesn't surprise me, but I raise my eyebrows. *"Landon?"*

"You guys gossiping about me over there?" the siren shifter teases from across the aisle. Laughing, he answers, "Don't let Aconyte pump me up too much, Boots. My parents *were* pretty keen hunters back in the day. I can handle a gun when I need to."

"Sounds like a plan," I say, grinning. The thought of me decked out in weapons and armour is borderline absurd, but the only thing more absurd would be going into this fight expecting diplomacy to work. "We'll just have to wait for Shade to come to, and then..."

"Shade has already come to, angel face," comes a mumble from my shoulder. I turn to see the wolf shifter looking up at me crookedly. His eyes, while still bleary, are as bright and silver as I remember, and my heart surges in my chest at the sight of him.

"Shade." Before I can stop myself, I'm pulling him into a tight embrace, kissing his cheek while desperately trying not to burst into tears again. "Holy shit, Shade, I was so worried about you."

"Easy, Boots, Easy," he says, his hand coming up to rest on my back. "You're gonna crush me."

Remembering his injury, I immediately pull back. "Fuck, I'm sorry."

"Don't worry about it," Shade replies. "I'm still kicking. A little worse for wear, though. Those bastards got me good."

"I thought you were going to die," I whisper, looking down.

Shade slides his knuckle under my chin and lifts my face up. He searches my eyes for a long moment and then kisses me gently, winding a hand through my hair as if hardly daring to believe I'm really here. "I thought the same," he admits when he pulls away. "Tell me you killed that fucker."

"Hawthorne?" Silas shakes his head. "If only. Glancing at me, he adds, "It sounds like we've got some catching up to do."

THE TRAIN CONTINUES its journey through the British countryside, the areas around us slowly becoming more urban the closer we get to London. The trip takes the better part of the morning, but after changing trains in Birmingham, time seems to speed up. There's no denying that I'm nervous —I suppose we all are, now that I think about it—but part of me still wonders what we're going to find waiting for us back in the city. Blockades? Armed patrols? How much control does the school board have over the rest of the humans, anyway? And if Hawthorne is smart—which he, unfortunately, is— then he'll be anticipating our return. The key will be outwitting him long enough for us to outnumber him.

If that's even possible.

After checking in to a five-star hotel in the centre of the city, courtesy of Hunter's expense account, we sit down in our suite living room to strategise.

"You don't think this is all a little conspicuous?" Silas asks, pulling back the curtains to glance out the window.

"You should have brought this up before I paid," grumbles Hunter.

"I for one think it's great," says Landon as he flops back on the couch.

"You would," I tease, elbowing him.

He catches my wrist and presses a kiss to my knuckles. "You wound me."

"It's not a bad idea, actually," Shade comments from where he's leaning by the bookshelf. "Hawthorne's probably combing all the abandoned buildings and cheap motels in the city for us. This should throw him off, at least for a bit."

"We can't keep doing this forever," Silas objects. "Going from hotel to hotel, lying low, *waiting*... We need to find someone who can point us to where Edith is."

"What about Mollie's place?" Landon suggests. "She lived there for god knows how long. Maybe there are some leads there."

"I hate to rain on that parade, but the last I heard, that whole apartment building was a smoking pile of ash," snarks Shade. "Anything she might have left there is probably burnt to a crisp by now, not to mention the fact that the Academy agents are probably still in the area. Besides," he goes on, "any magical signature she left behind is inaccessible to us without a witch. Sorry, Boots. No offense."

"None taken," I reply.

"So we're screwed, then," says Hunter, throwing up his hands. "We don't have anyone we can trust to tell us where she's gone."

There's a long pause, and then an idea comes to me. "What about someone we can't trust?" I ask suddenly.

The others all look at me like I've suddenly grown a second head. "You feeling all right, Boots?" asks Landon.

I roll my eyes. "Guys, I'm serious. I'm talking about her contacts— you know, that couple we asked for help who then turned on us."

Hunter's brow furrows. "You think?"

"Think about it," I insist. "Edith sent us to them in order to get me killed. She was probably planning on handing my body over to Hawthorne as soon as that siren made me jump out the window. Clearly, they're on the same side."

"So... what?" asks Silas. "You think we should just pay them a visit and ask nicely?"

I shake my head grimly. "Not so nicely."

Shade laughs. "Badass," he remarks, straightening up. "I'm in."

"Hold it," Landon protests. "Your injury-"

"Relax, Thyme, I'm fine," says Shade, waving him off. "Whatever Josie did has me back to almost a hundred percent. Besides..." His face hardens. "Nobody fucks with Boots and lives to talk about it. I think we're all in agreement there, right?"

The others murmur their assent almost immediately. But as much as their obvious care for me warms my heart, it also fills me with discomfort. I hate the way the dynamics have shifted like this. I haven't always had magical powers at my command, but the one thing I'd like to think I've never been is a damsel in distress. It no longer feels like we're all on equal footing; instead, I'm struck with a sense of inadequacy so strong it's almost crippling. "Okay," I say, getting to my feet. "But I'm coming with you guys. I want to be there to see this through."

The others look at each other with uncertainty, but to their credit and my extreme relief, nobody voices any objections. "Fair enough," says Silas. "We'll catch them early in the morning tomorrow, when they won't be expecting it."

With that settled, we depart for our rooms, each of us in our own mind. After getting ready for bed, I steal a paranoid look out my room window. Nobody outside that I can see, but...

The feeling of strong arms wrapping around me from behind draws my attention away. "Mind if I sleep in here with you?" Shade murmurs into my ear, making me shiver. "As I understand it, I owe you for saving my life, and there are quite a few ways I'd like to show my gratitude"

Grinning, I turn in his arms and wrap my hands around his neck. "I wouldn't have it any other way."

CHAPTER 76

"And you're sure this is the right area?" Silas sounds doubtful as he and Shade creep along behind Landon, Hunter, and me.

"Have I ever been wrong before?" asks Landon, grinning.

"Yes," Hunter replies. "Multiple times."

Landon laughs. "Boots, back me up, here."

I come to a stop at the next intersection and put my hands on my hips, squinting as I glance around. Yes, this definitely looks familiar, although I'd be damned if I had to remember the building number. I guess we'll just have to hope that between the three of us, we'll be able to find the right apartment. "Yeah, I think we're on the right track," I agree. "This is the neighbourhood, for sure. Second block on the left, if I'm not mistaken."

"Right. I remember." Hunter falls into step next to me as we resume our journey.

"This whole thing has me on edge," Silas confesses. He keeps glancing around to check for suspicious characters amongst what few pedestrians are out and about, and I don't blame him. It's a little before five in the morning, and the night is still dark, which only makes things worse. Every creeping shadow hides a potential enemy, every movement I glimpse out of the corner of my eye is enough to make my heart race. Could the Academy have put feelers out around here? Half of me is expecting someone to reach out and grab me from every dark corner and dead-end street. Having the guys around only makes me feel marginally better.

"Nervous, Aconyte?" Shade teases. Back to his smart-ass self in record time, but he's got a surprising spring in his step, considering what he's been through.

Silas snorts. "Hardly. I'm just saying, now would be the perfect time for an ambush."

You wouldn't even think they had been all over me less than a week ago, the more salacious part of my mind whispers, but I shut it down immediately. Now's not the time for fantasizing.

"I guess it's a good thing we're the ones doing the ambushing, then," Shade replies gamely. "These fuckers won't know what hit them."

"Keep your guard up," I warn as we turn down the side street, our shadows growing long under the light of the street lamps. "The guy, Caleb, is a siren shifter. That won't be a problem for most of you, but Jennifer is a dragon shifter. Powerful, too, from what I could tell."

"Sounds like fun," Shade mutters as we approach a block of posh apartment buildings at the end of the road. Hunter, Landon, and I come to a stop, craning our necks to stare up at them.

"I can't remember which one it is," I say, feeling my nerves start to go into overdrive. First my powers, and now my memory? Why did I even bother coming here?

"It's that one," says Hunter, nodding to the one on the right. "With the flower boxes outside the window. I remember."

Silas claps him wordlessly on the shoulder as we follow him one by one to the front door. "Allow me," says Landon, muscling to the front of the group, rolling his shoulders, and expelling another stream of soundwaves into the lock. Shade raises his eyebrows at me, but I hold up a hand to signal for him to be patient. A few tense moments later, I hear the sound of the tumblers clicking, followed by the hard *chunk* of the lock sliding back. Landon gives an exaggerated bow as he tugs the door open, the rest of us following him inside.

It's too early for a doorman to be here, so we march straight to the elevator without any trouble. As the lift slowly begins to rise, the other guys shift around me in a protective formation. "Think I should go last?" I ask doubtfully.

Silas winces. "I'm sorry, Boots, but..."

I hold up a hand to stop him. "It's okay. It's... probably a good idea." As much as I hate to admit it. Still, it's gutting to have gone from one of the most powerful members of our group to a glorified follower seemingly overnight. Once again I reach half-heartedly for my powers, and once again I sense nothing. Oh well. Worth a shot.

"How are we going to do this?" Hunter asks as we step into the hallway. "We don't want to attract attention."

"Something tells me we're going to attract attention either way," I observe. "People don't tend to take well to break-ins, even when they're not shifters."

"Nobody came to investigate last time, when they were attacking us," Landon points out. "Maybe these walls are soundproof."

"Or maybe everyone in this flat is in Hawthorne's pocket," Silas says. "We're going to have to be quick. Hunter, do you remember which unit it was?"

The vampire shifter furrows his brow, looking around for a moment. "This way," he says at last, pointing toward the hall on the left. "It was at the end of the hallway, if I'm not mistaken."

"You'd better not be," Shade snarks.

I allow the others to pass in front of me before addressing the locks on the door. The door looks strong and it's going to be hard to knock down. "Thoughts?" I ask. "Should Landon do his magical lock picking thing again?"

Silas shakes his head. "Both guns blazing, right?" And before any of us can respond, he's shifted into his dragon form, now large enough to take up much of the hallway. With one lunge of his muscular body, he throws his shoulder into the front door. It buckles on its hinges, and I see a light go on in the main room, but one more slam and it's crashing open, allowing us to pour into the apartment.

Caleb is standing in the kitchen entryway, looking bleary-eyed,

461

but his expression immediately twists the moment he sees us. "Jennifer!" he yells, shifting into a siren instantaneously.

Shade leaps into the air, and when he lands, he's in his wolf form, charging Caleb at top speed. The other siren doesn't even have time to react before Shade's pinning him to the ground, his teeth ripping into his shoulder. "Don't kill him!" I yell. "We need him alive!"

Shade glances up at me, doubt in his yellow eyes, but that's all the opening Caleb needs. Letting out a terrific siren scream, he pushes the wolf shifter off him and sends him sprawling across the floor. "Jennifer!" he bellows again.

"Honey?" A light goes on in the other room, and then his wife's face appears in the doorway. Her eyes land on me and her face twists into a snarl. "*You,*" she hisses, and then she too is shifting.

I realise too late that I'm right in the line of fire, but Hunter shoves me out of the way, already in his vampire form, to take the brunt of the fire she breathes in my direction. "Silas—" he says, already flagging.

Silas doesn't need telling twice, and with a roar he charges Jennifer, the two dragons locking together in a close-quarters fight. I'm left to watch helplessly, feeling more useless than I ever have.

Hunter moves to help Silas with Jennifer while Landon and Shade continue their attack on Caleb. The next time the siren produces a soundwave, Landon is ready to meet him, sending an equally powerful blast of force his way to neutralize the energy. With Caleb distracted, Shade has the perfect opportunity to pounce, and this time, he doesn't use his teeth. Instead, he lands on the siren's chest with such force that his head strikes the floor, making him lose consciousness. Almost immediately he shifts back into human form, allowing the others to assist with Jennifer. Between the four of them, they're able to wrestle her to the ground, and a quick command from Landon is enough to make her transform back.

I catch movement out of the corner of my eye and see Caleb struggling to sit up. "Oh no, you don't," I mutter, and sprint over to him without thinking. Dropping onto my hands and knees, I force him back onto the ground. "Just try it," I hiss, my mind already returning to what he tried to do to me the last time I was here. "You're outnumbered."

"What the fuck are you doing here?" he demands, his eyes flashing.

"We'll get to that in a minute," I reply, surprising myself with how collected I sound. "Just know that if you try anything, you're outnumbered."

Caleb steels a glance toward Jennifer, now subdued on the floor with the rest of the guys. He lets out a snarl of frustration, and then relaxes. "Crafty bitch," he pants. "Didn't think you had it in you."

"Nice catch, Boots," Shade says, striding over to me. He puts a foot on Caleb's chest, keeping him pinned to the ground, and stares down at him with a half smile. "Now," he says, still breathing heavily, "are you two going to play nice, or are things going to have to get *really* messy?"

IN THE END, things didn't have to get really messy. Whether because we have the upper hand or some other conniving, strategic move, they cooperate, and it's easy enough to wrangle them into the living room and onto the couch. I keep stealing looks at the door, wondering when the cavalry will arrive after having heard the commotion. But it's silent as the grave in the apartment building. Almost uncanny.

"Should've figured you'd come back to bite us in the ass," Jennifer spits from her place on the couch. "Fucking hybrids. Always more trouble than they're worth."

"About that," I say, crossing my arms, "we need to know about your friend Edith."

"*Friend?*" Jennifer laughs. "That's so cute."

"She's working with the Academy, right?" Silas persists. "She told you guys to jump Millie."

"We don't ask questions," spits Caleb. "We do as we're told, and the humans stay off our backs."

"Well," I say, "now you're going to do as you're told again. Tell us where Edith is. You must know, if you have connections to her and Hawthorne."

"Why the hell would we—"

But I don't let her finish, instead nodding to Landon, who hasn't yet transformed back. "Where is she?" he demands, the strength of his powers giving me goosebumps. "What was she planning? Who is she working with?"

I can see the woman struggling to resist, but Landon is working just as hard, and she realises she's outmatched before even a minute has passed. "There are communes," she grits out, her teeth clenched together. "Shifter communes, all around the U.K."

Silas' hackles go up at that. "You mean communities? Neighbourhoods?" he demands.

"A bunch of anti-establishment hippies," Jennifer says disdainfully, her whole body wound tight from the tension of trying to resist Landon's command. "They've been against your Academy since day one. Not too happy, either, after what happened in Boston. Sounds like the administration wants them dealt with."

"So they're sending Edith?" Landon squats so he's facing her.

"Their attack dog, you mean? Yeah." Jennifer sneers. "All I know is they've put her in charge of making sweeps for any shifter groups who don't support the humans. She's going to have her hands full, by the sounds of it."

"Which one?" I demand, taking a step closer. "Where is she going next?"

"Like I would know," Jennifer snaps. I glance at Landon, who just shakes his head, and my heart sinks. She's telling the truth.

"Where's the nearest one, then?" I ask. "If she started in London, she'll probably be working her way outwards."

Jennifer glances at Caleb, who looks like he would kill me if he got the chance. "Where did they say it was?" she asks. He hesitates. "Tell them!" Jennifer snaps. "Get them out of our hair."

"Oxford," Caleb replies at last. "In Jericho, right around the Osney Bridge. There's a whole district full of shifters there. Can't miss 'em."

"You're not lying, are you?" Shade asks, crossing his arms.

"Why don't you go there and find out?" Caleb fires back.

A tense moment passes. "I guess we will," I say at last, smirking a little. "But if you were, we'll be back. And I can't promise we'll be as nice the next time around." Nodding to the others, I back up. "Come on. We're leaving."

"We're just going to let them live?" Shade asks incredulously. "After what they did to you?"

"*Tried* to do to me," I correct him. "Besides, they're the only connection we have to Edith right now."

"She's right," says Hunter. "We can't risk losing them, not if they can point us to more of these communities."

Shade presses his lips into a thin line, and then nods, but not before stooping down to look Caleb and Jennifer in the eye. "Touch Millie again, and it won't matter what information you have," he tells them, his voice low and dangerous. "I'll kill you myself." With that, he stands up, nods to me, and the five of us retreat back towards the front door. I'm half-expecting the couple to stand and start fighting again, but they only watch us contemptuously from their place on the couch until we're out the front door and on our way back to the lift.

"It's as good a place to start as any," Landon says as the elevator begins its descent.

I nod in agreement. "Let's just hope these ones are friendlier."

CHAPTER 77

"I've never been to Oxford before," I say, tugging my jacket a little more firmly around my shoulders. We're making our way east along Botley Road, and in spite of the fact that the sun has finally come up, it's not getting any warmer. A chill humidity has settled in around the city, and I'm realising that I came woefully underdressed. "Not exactly how I pictured my first time here."

A cold breeze sweeps through the trees along the side of the highway, and I shiver despite myself. Silas, who is walking alongside me, puts an arm around my shoulders and pulls me flush against him. "You cold?"

"No." I can't help but press my face against his side. My nose has gone red and numb from the chill.

The dragon shifter chuckles, rubbing his hand against my shoulder to generate some friction. "You should've said something sooner, Boots. I run hot."

"Didn't want to worry you," I mumble, wishing I could disappear into his arms and fall asleep there.

"You're skin and bones, Boots. Of course we're going to worry," Landon says in his usual good-natured tone, but I can hear the concern in his voice as he sidles up to me on my other side, taking my free hand and rubbing it between his.

"Let's just hope we can find somewhere away from this fog," Hunter says. He's walking at the front of the group, hands in his pockets, and although vampire shifters tend to have lower body temperatures, he still seems put off by the weather.

"Speaking of which," says Shade, his eyes narrowing, "what are we planning to do if these guys tell us to fuck off? We're not exactly going to draw the right kind of attention, no matter where we go."

"Let's just hope they'll take us in," says Silas. Despite holding me close, there's a far away, melancholy look in his eyes.

"Hey," I murmur, squeezing him a little more tightly. "You okay?"

"I don't know," the dragon shifter replies. "It's just... Going to another one of these communities..." His voice trails off as he runs a hand down his face. "It's just been a long time, that's all."

"Shit," I mutter, once again kicking myself for my shortsightedness. "I didn't even think about that." Long before his arrival at the Academy, Silas and his parents lived in a neighbourhood similar to the one we're visiting now, populated predominantly by shapeshifters. From the sounds of it, he had a good childhood, up until the local shifters decided they didn't want to be jerked around by the humans anymore. This, I suppose, was back before the Academy had become so overt in their subjugation of shifters, but the goal of their actions was the same as it has always been: to find a way of keeping us on the fringes of society and at their disposal.

In the end, that's what happened—his parents, among others, were spirited away by Academy agents, never to be seen again, sowing the seeds of mistrust that would eventually lead Silas to finding out the truth about Hawthorne. In a sense, their actions were what led us to this point; if they hadn't suspected the humans from the start, would Silas even still be alive right now?

Would I?

"I'm sorry," I whisper. The words feel stupidly inadequate, but they're all I have to offer.

Silas doesn't say anything, but when I crane my neck to look at him, I can see that he's watching me with something in his black eyes

467

—sadness, yes, but also love. "They would have loved you, Boots," he says quietly, and presses a kiss to the crown of my head.

Nothing more needs to be said.

"So what does a shifter community even look like?" Shade asks, crossing his arms over his chest. "How will we even know it when we see it?"

"Caleb said we would recognise it," Hunter says, although he sounds doubtful.

"And we're supposed to trust him?" The wolf shifter snorts, shaking his head. "I still think we should've killed those bastards while we had the chance. Now they know where we're going. Who's going to stop them from siccing Hawthorne's guys on us the second we let our guard down?"

"Hawthorne's too smart for that," Silas replies. "He knows we'll have the advantage if we're with others of our kind. That's why he's leaving it up to Edith to take these groups down."

"Guess we'll just have to hope they've been practising," Landon says.

We've been walking for about twenty minutes and are now on the outskirts of Oxford; the river Thames stretches out alongside us as we make our way north, towards the Osney B ridge, and the water looks frigid and tempestuous. Rather appropriate, if you ask me. All along either side of the road are stately manor homes along with newer apartment buildings, creating a strange clash of old and modern that I can't quite wrap my head around.

Staying close to the pedestrian walkway, we follow the road up and over the blue and white bridge, a few cars puttering past us as we go. It's still too early for there to be a lot of traffic, but there's enough to put me on edge, and judging by the guys' expressions, I'm not the only one. I don't really let myself relax until after we're across, no longer exposed above the river, as the road slopes downward again along the opposite bank.

"Silas?" I ask gently, aware that this is a delicate subject for the dragon shifter. "Any idea what we should be looking for?"

Silas pauses, brow furrowing as he peers around at the banks of buildings. "We lived in the suburbs," he says at last. "Obviously we couldn't be too overt about it, considering most humans don't even know shifters exist. Then there was the Academy to worry about; we couldn't exactly flaunt our magic."

Landon frowns. "So you're saying... what, there's some kind of secret sign?"

"For us, it was an enchantment," Silas replies as we make our way down the street, the wind ruffling our hair. "Something one of the resident witches set up. To humans, it was invisible, but shifters could see the real name of the community on the gate."

"Keep your eyes peeled," I say. "It could be anywhere around here." What I don't say, but I'm sure the others have figured out, is that if *we* can track this place down, then it should be no problem for Edith. The possibility that she's already taken the whole district out crosses my mind, but I don't allow myself to consider it for more than a moment. I've had enough disappointments in the last few days to last a lifetime.

We lapse into silence as we pick our way through the area, peering down alleyways and side streets, on the lookout for anything that might jump out at us. For a while, we find nothing, and I'm just starting to lose hope when I hear a triumphant cry from behind us.

Glancing over my shoulder, I see Hunter standing back, looking up at the side of an enormous luxury apartment building. "I think I've got something," he says, beckoning the rest of us over.

We gather around him and follow his gaze to the brownstone wall around the corner from the entrance. At first, I don't see anything out of the ordinary other than a splash of faded graffiti that looks like it was scrubbed off a long time ago. It's only as I stare up at it that it morphs and shifts before my eyes, the colourful block letters transforming from an indecipherable mess into a series of five pictographs: a moon, a stylised pentagram, a minimalistic flame, a wave, and a droplet of blood.

"Subtle," Shade says approvingly. "Not bad."

"No sense waiting around," Landon says. "Come on, I'm freezing my ass off."

The rest of us don't need to be told twice and follow the siren shifter back around to the front entrance. An old-fashioned revolving door leads us into a posh lobby, complete with immaculate seating, tapestries on the walls, and a doorman who eyes us suspiciously as he watches us pass.

If we were lucky at Caleb and Jennifer's place, that luck has just run out; almost as soon as we're inside, an older gentleman sitting at the security desk gets to his feet. "Excuse me," he says, "may I ask what your business is here?"

I take the lead, just grateful to be out of the cold for a few minutes. "To be honest, we're not really sure," I reply as we approach the desk. "We're—" I pause, look around, and then lower my voice. If this is the wrong place... "We saw the mural outside," I say pointedly. "The... the special one."

The security guard gives me a thin smile. "I'm sorry, madam, but I don't know what you mean."

So much for subtlety. I decide to switch tactics. "Does the name Hawthorne mean anything to you?"

It's a gamble, and judging by the man's reaction, a mistake. "I think you had better leave," he says in a low voice, his eyes sweeping over our little group. And is it just me, or did they flash red for a moment there?

"It's not that," Hunter hastens to put in. "I mean, we're not with him. We're here with a warning. Hawthorne has his sights on us, and by the sounds of it, he has his sights on you guys, too."

"Get out." The security guard's tone has lost all civility. "We don't want or need whatever kind of attention you're trying to bring to us."

That's all the confirmation I need. "Please," I insist, leaning forward. "We have nowhere else to go. Hawthorne has people all over London, and by the sounds of it, his people are targeting groups just like yours. If we could just speak to someone your leader, maybe? Who's in charge around here?"

The older man's skin blanches at that, and when he opens his mouth to speak again, I catch a glimpse of fangs. Wasn't mistaken about the eyes, then. "Get. Out," he hisses, "before I have someone remove you."

I can feel myself growing more desperate. "Please," I implore him again. "We have nowhere else to go."

"That's hardly our concern," the security guard says. I'm aware of the sound of the elevator doors chiming, but don't look away.

"Come on," Shade says in a surly voice. "Leave them to Edith, if that's what they want."

"Edith?" The sound of a familiar voice finally pulls my attention away. The elevator doors stand open and holding them is someone I was beginning to think I would never see again.

Unwittingly, my eyes fill with tears. "Hazel?"

CHAPTER 78

The security guard stares at me like I've just sprouted a third arm. His eyes flick over to Hazel, the crimson already draining out of them. "You know these people, Hazel?"

"Know them?" Hazel exclaimed, making a beeline for the group. "*Know* them?" I'm glad I'm not the only one currently at a loss for words, and before I even have a chance to steel myself, Hazel is sweeping me into a bear hug strong enough to rival one of Silas's. "Holy shit," she exclaims breathlessly as she moves to embrace each of the others. "I swear, I was worried I'd never see any of you again!"

"Back at you," I reply. "How the hell did you survive that fire? And what about Xander and Ruby?"

"Fine, they're fine," Hazel assures me. "We wouldn't have survived if we'd tried to fight. We ended up jumping onto the roof of the apartment next door, if you can believe it. By then the crowd was big enough that the bastards probably realised it wasn't worth chasing after us."

"But how did you know about this place?" asks Shade incredulously. "*We* didn't even know about it, and we're from around here."

"Dumb luck," Hazel explains. "We ran into a wolf shifter on our way out of the city centre. Considering we had nowhere else to go, he really saved our asses. Leroy," she says, turning to the security guard, "these are my friends. Millie, Landon, Silas, Shade, and Hunter. They're all shifters, too."

"More strays?" the vampire shifter grumbles, looking none too happy. "Theo isn't going to like this."

Hazel goes a little pale at that. "You don't know that."

"Don't I?" The guard, Leroy, crosses his arms. "We're almost at capacity here, and you know it. A few more charity cases and they won't even be able to afford their mortgage."

"Well, that's not *your* problem, now is it?" Hazel asks, sounding a bit haughty. "Tell you what: I'll introduce them myself. Hell, I'll even bring Xander and Ruby as backup."

Leroy holds his hands up. "I'm just saying, it's your ass on the line, Van Buren."

"Noted." Hazel sniffs and then turns back to us. "Well, what are you waiting for? The landlord's going to want to meet you all."

"This Theo guy is the landlord?" asks Landon. "He's a shifter, too, I take it."

"Everyone living in this complex is a shifter," Hazel explains, beckoning us back in the direction of the elevator. "It's not like they advertise that, obviously, but I guess it's pretty easy to weed out applicants when ninety percent of the population can't shapeshift. Lucky for us, we don't have that problem."

Her optimism only makes my stomach sink, and I give her a guilty sideways glance as we step into the lift. "Actually, Hazel..."

The blonde frowns. "What?"

I feel a cool touch against my hand and look down to see that Hunter has moved to stand protectively at my side. "Boots had her powers stolen," he says. I appreciate him taking over for me; I'm not sure how many more times I can bring myself to rehash that trauma. "After we got separated, Edith and a bunch of lackeys showed up and brought her to some kind of... research bunker. They did what they tried to do to Silas."

Hazel's eyes go wide. "You mean they, like...?"

"It's temporary," I hasten to tell her. "At least, I think so."

473

"Something tells me that's going to make your job a little more complicated, Hazel," Shade remarks dryly.

To her credit, Hazel doesn't look flustered. "It'll be a hard sell, but nothing I can't handle. I can be charming when I want to."

In spite of her confidence, I can sense the others' unease as the lift continues up, all the way to the penthouse floor. Rather than opening onto a hallway, the elevator doors slide open to reveal one enormous apartment unit, bigger than some of the houses I've seen in my lifetime. Two burly men flank the doors on either side, and as soon as we move forward, their arms fly out to bar our way. "What are you doing up here?" one of them asks.

"New blood," Hazel replies. "I've got five new shifters here—on the run from the Academy, same as me." The guards look at one another, not seeming convinced. "He's going to want to meet this one," Hazel adds, nodding in my direction. "She's a hybrid."

That seems to be a magic word, as the guards pull away without further argument. "He's in his study," the second one says. "Try anything, and—"

"And I'm dead meat. Yeah, yeah, yeah," Hazel finishes for him, waving him off as she leads us into the penthouse. Considering how little time has passed, she seems to have made herself awfully comfortable around here.

On the other side of the dizzyingly large apartment is a door leading to an office. A panel of glass windows substitutes for the wall on the other side, providing a view of the sprawling city below us. Sitting at an enormous desk, his back turned to us, is an impeccably dressed man with silvery-white hair. He doesn't turn around until Hazel clears her throat, knocking gently on the doorframe. "Excuse me, Theo? Sorry to interrupt."

"No need to apologise, Hazel," the man, Theo, replies, and only then does he turn to face us. I'm astonished by what I see. Despite colourless hair, he's quite young—in his thirties, if I had to guess—and his eyes are the same gleaming shade of pale silver as his locks. They feel almost unnerving as they sweep from one of us to the next, pausing for a moment longer to linger on me. "I see you've brought guests." His voice is deep and rumbling, his presence commanding.

"With your permission," Hazel replies. "These are fellow runaways. Like myself and the Murakami twins."

"As I suspected," Theo says, nodding. "I trust you remember what I told you when the three of you arrived? That we've almost run out of space for new community members?"

"I understand that, Sir," Hazel replies. "I haven't forgotten. But—with all due respect—these are my friends."

Theo gives a thin smile that might be handsome if it looked genuine. "Hazel," he says, "I appreciate your tenacity, I really do. But as much as I would like to provide shelter for all refugee shifters, this community can't survive on good will alone."

"You're saying we need to pay to live here?" Shade sneers. "Fuck this. I thought we were all on the same side, here." He turns to go, but my hand flies out to seize his wrist, and he reluctantly stops.

"'Pay' is a subjective term," Theo says, unfazed. "I prefer the term 'contribute.' Survival against the humans requires unity, strength, and resources. If you don't have something to offer us..."

"But we do." Silas takes a step forward.

I blanch when I realise where he's going with this. "Silas—"

"Boots," he says, looking at me, "this is our only option." In spite of my hesitation, I know he's right, and bite my lip. I can't remember a time I've felt more put on the spot.

"I'd like to introduce you to Millie Brix," Silas says, his hand coming to rest at the small of my back. "She's a hybrid."

Something passes over Theo's face—a glimmer of recognition? — and his eyebrows raise almost imperceptibly. "Is that so?" His white eyes meet mine once again, nearly dazzling in their presence. "Is your friend telling the truth, Millie Brix?" he asks me. "Are you indeed a hybrid?"

"I... yes," I reply, swallowing hard. "I was."

"'Was?'"

I look to Hazel for backup, but she's fallen silent. Whoever this guy is, he's clearly the head honcho around here. "When I was a kid,

475

the Shifter Academy experimented on me, and the guys you see here," I explain slowly. "I was given the powers of all five species. Just a couple days ago, though, they kidnapped me. Experimented on me. I haven't been able to use my powers since then, but we're working on getting them back."

"Look," Hazel cuts in, "I know that a depowered shifter isn't exactly what you're looking for right now, but in terms of raw potential, Millie's off the charts. She could be a real asset to this fight once she gets her powers back."

I'm not keen on being used as a bargaining chip, but what other choice do we have?

"Hazel's right," adds Landon. "We've all seen Boots in action. We can vouch for her. If you're so hellbent on keeping the humans off your backs, surely a hybrid would be a valuable asset."

"Indeed," Theo says, steepling his fingers. His eyes haven't left me once since the hybrid talk began, and I can't shake the feeling that he's looking *through* me, and not at me. There's a long moment of silence as he mulls things over, and it goes on for so long that I have to break eye contact, if only to be out from under his impenetrable gaze for a few seconds.

And still he says nothing.

Silas' shoulders slump. "I guess we'll just go, then," he says, sounding defeated. "It's clear you're not—"

But Theo holds up a hand, and Silas quiets. You could hear a pin drop. "I believe something can be arranged," Theo says at last. "Not from a utilitarian standpoint, though."

I blink. "I... don't understand."

Turning to Hazel, Theo smiles. "I underestimated you, Ms. Van Buren. It seems my charity hasn't run dry after all." Then he turns back to me. "I find myself overtaken by a sense of camaraderie, Ms. Brix."

"Sir...?" I stare at him, hardly daring to hope.

Theo leans forward in his chair. "You see, Ms. Brix," he says deliberately, "our struggles aren't so different, yours and mine. It just so happens that I, too, am a hybrid." For a moment, I lose the ability to speak. I can only gape at him, this peculiar white-haired man who might be the only thing standing between us and me getting my powers back. Seeing my reaction, he chuckles. "Surprised?"

"I didn't..." I stammer. "I thought hybrids were rare."

"Oh, they are," Theo replies. "Exceedingly so. And I confess, you are the first one I've ever met in person. I had heard rumours of scientific experiments with the goal of replicating what was done to me by the witches when I was a boy, but I didn't believe them." Slowly he gets out of his seat, striding over to me and placing his cool hand under my chin. Gently, he raises my head to look up at him, the gesture exceedingly intimate coming from someone I've only just met.

Silas tenses visibly, and I can feel Shade start to lunge forward protectively. If Landon didn't reel him in, there would be no knowing what might have happened. It's only after a second passes that I realise he's using magic on me, probing at my powers the same way Mrs. Fairbanks did on that first day at the Academy. The fact that he doesn't even need to visibly transform in order to perform the spell is a testament to his power.

"Yes," he says at last, letting go of my chin and nodding his approval. "Yes, Ms. Brix. I believe you'll do quite nicely."

CHAPTER 79

"I don't like the way he was looking at you," announces Shade, cramming his hands into his pockets as he turns away from the windows to face me. We're standing in the living room of one of the lower apartments, one of the few open units left in the building, according to Theo. Rather than a suite, this time we've each been given our own studio, which I have to admit is surprising, considering the scarcity of space around here. Something about it tickles the back of my mind, but every time I follow that train of thought, I balk; it's clear that Theo thinks I'm worth the investment, and that kind of pressure doesn't sit well with me. I'm torn between disliking being thought of as a pawn and feeling even more desperate to get my powers back, if only to prove to him that he didn't make a mistake by letting us stay here. It's a complicated batch of emotions, and it's only made more so by the fact that this is the only other hybrid I've ever met.

He *was* right when he talked about camaraderie; much like my own parents, Theo's folks willingly gave him over to the coven who turned him. Humans, drug addicts, sold their only child to the cabal so he might have a chance at a better life, not knowing what his adoptive parents had planned for him. I can relate, even if the origins of our powers are different.

According to Theo, there have always been witches on the fringes of shifter society whose goals involve adjusting and perfecting shifter powers. He was as much a guinea pig to them as I was to the Academy—the only difference is that he's had years of training to hone his powers. It's obvious to anyone that he's the one in charge around here, and with good reason.

What that means for me, however, remains to be seen.

"He was just curious," I reply dismissively. "He said himself I was the first hybrid he'd ever met. I don't blame him for staring."

Shade snorts and shakes his head, turning away.

"What?" I ask incredulously, crossing my arms.

"Boots, it's almost adorable how naive you can be sometimes," the wolf shifter replies. "That's not the kind of look you give when you're *curious.* He looked like he was starving. His eyes were all over you."

That's enough to give me pause, and I can feel my cheeks heating up at the implication. "What?" I ask, taking a step towards him. "You think he was *interested* in me?"

"Don't act so surprised," Shade replies with a wan smile. "I don't blame him. Not saying I approve, but..."

I can feel my expression twisting into a grin. "Wait a minute, Ivis," I say teasingly, creeping up behind him and wrapping my arms around him. "Are you... jealous?"

Shade snorts. "Jealous? Please."

"You *sound* kind of jealous," I persist, pressing my lips to the base of his neck. He stiffens under my touch, his arms covering mine to pull my back more tightly against his chest.

"If I were jealous, I wouldn't have been down to mess around with you and Aconyte," Shade protests, although he isn't meeting my gaze.

"Yeah, about that," I say, pulling away and putting my hands on my hips. "You two have really come a long way since the Academy."

"Haven't we all?" Shade retorts, but I can see a glimmer of humour in his silver eyes. "I *trust* Aconyte. Just like I *trust* Ash and Thyme. This Theo guy, though..." He looks away, his expression grim. "You came so close to dying once already, Boots. I don't want to see you get hurt again."

479

"Well," I say, rolling up my sleeves, "I guess that's what you're here for, right? So are you going to teach me how to kick ass, or are you just going to keep brooding?"

"Brooding is what I do best, Brix," Shade snarks playfully, "but... point taken. All right, come here." He beckons me over to him, intertwining his fingers with mine as he pulls me towards the door.

"Wait," I protest, "we're not going to practise in here?"

"You think the shifters would pay for a place like this and *not* have some kind of training room?" Shade replies. "If they're that keen on keeping the Academy away, they'd be stupid not to."

"Fair point," I concede, and allow him to lead me out into the hallway. The rest of the guys have gone their separate ways for the time being. Hunter, still fatigued from the blood loss, went to rest for a while, while Landon and Silas mentioned something about taking a look around our new digs. It's nice to have some respite for once, although I know better than to let my guard down this time. Not after what happened with Edith.

Shade and I both look out of place in the luxury building. This is the type of place where rent would cost an arm and a leg, with tenants consisting of socialites and wealthy investors. At least *Shade* has a reason to be here. Right now, for all intents and purposes, I'm just like any other human.

Don't go there, I warn myself. *Don't go down that road.*

There's a laundry room in the basement and, just as Shade suspected, a large fitness centre. The floor is lined with foam mats, and I'm surprised to see practise dummies amidst the weights and workout equipment.

Ruby Murakami steps off one of the treadmills the moment she sees us and hurries to embrace first me and then Shade. "Hazel said you guys made it," she says, grinning from ear to ear.

"Barely," I joke. "Where is she, by the way?"

Ruby rolls her eyes. "On a date with Xander, I think. No idea what she sees in him, but if he's happy, I'm happy. You guys here to practise your powers?"

"Not exactly," Shade replies.

"Just some good old- fashioned martial arts," I add. "You want to join?"

"I'd actually better get back upstairs," Ruby says, dabbing at the back of her neck with a towel. "I'm sweaty enough as it is. I'll see you guys later though, yeah?"

"Definitely," I agree. It's only as she approaches the door that I think to call after her. "Hey Ruby?"

The dragon shifter turns around. "Yeah?"

I glance at Shade before asking, "Have you heard anything? About Theo, I mean? He's been awfully accommodating, considering the circumstances."

A strange look passes over Ruby's face, and she winks at Shade. "I'd say you boys had better watch your backs," she advises him. "Hazel said he looked damn near infatuated with you, Millie. Have fun with your training!" And with that, she breezes out of the room.

Shade is watching me expectantly, eyebrows raised.

"Okay, fine," I say, feeling a little self-conscious. "But I'm willing to bet it's just because we have something in common."

"Whatever you say, Boots," Shade says, pulling me close.

I kiss the tip of his nose, making him chuckle. "Enough talk. Let's get practising."

Shade obligingly leads me into the middle of the room, in front of the mirrors so that I can see my form. "I'm no athlete," he says, "but street fighting is sort of a specialty of mine. It's actually one of the better combat styles, since there are no rules. The goal is to do as much damage as you can, however you can. Go for whatever weaknesses you can find."

"What about shifters?" I ask doubtfully.

"Same concept," Shade responds. "Even when we've transformed, we all have soft spots. Dragons are big and powerful, but they're slow moving. Witches have magic, but they aren't durable for shit. Same thing with sirens. Wolves and vampires? Agile as hell, but they can't hurt you unless they get close to you. The trick is to strategise—use their own forms against them, if you can. As for humans..." He shrugs. "They're a piece of cake in comparison."

He moves to stand behind me, gently taking hold of one of my arms and extending it in front of me. "Punching," he begins. "You're going to want to hit with your first two knuckles. Keep your wrist straight and snap your arm out. The power comes from the speed." I follow his instructions and throw a punch. "Keep your thumb outside of your fist," Shade warns, "or you'll risk breaking it. Here…" He takes my hand and readjusts my fingers, his touch surprisingly gentle. The feeling of him so close to me is making my breath come in embarrassingly short bursts, and I would be lying if I said concentrating was easy.

"Same basic concept with kicking," Shade continues, his hands moving down my waist to come to rest on my thighs. His skin is warm, almost searing as he touches me, sending jolts of electricity throughout my body. "You're striking with the hard parts—the ball of your foot or your heel. For maximum power, you need to extend it completely. Try rotating your hip just a little when you kick…"

I lose track of time as Shade teaches me, minutes turning into hours in the training room. To be honest, I wasn't expecting to enjoy it—I've never been a super violence-oriented person, even after being imbued with dangerous powers—but the longer we practise, the more I find myself getting into it. I didn't realise there was so much strategy to it, from what spots to target on a person to how to best use their own weight against them in a takedown. I'm not under any illusions that I'll become a champion fighter overnight, but I surprise even myself with my own dedication. Shade, too, seems to approve of the job I'm doing, and I manage to get the upper hand once. Although it's up in the air whether he was just going easy on me .

"Keep your hands up," the wolf shifter warns, bouncing on his feet as he stares me down from the opposite side of the mat. "Protect your face."

"Right," I mutter, raising my fists.

"Remember what I told you," he says, lunging forward. "Look for an opening."

I try to remember the blocks he taught me, but they go out of my mind. Instead, I sidestep his incoming punch, grabbing hold of his wrist and pulling him off balance in a clumsy parody of a throw.

The wolf shifter seems surprised, stumbling, and I take full advantage, wedging my hip against his to help him fall onto the mat.

"Not bad, Boots," he says, grinning up at me from the floor. "Not bad at all."

"Yeah?" I lower myself onto him, pressing my chest against his with a coquettish smile. "You think I'm ready to take on Hawthorne?"

Shade grunts, his hands going to my hips, and I realise where my pelvis is. Flushing, I try to roll off of him, but he pulls me back down for a kiss. "You're not going anywhere," he murmurs against my mouth.

I break away to press my forehead against his. "We're in public, Shade."

"Good," Shade replies, grinning. "I like having an audience."

I snort, rolling my eyes and standing up before offering him a hand. He accepts and gets to his feet. "What time is it, anyway?"

Frowning, Shade checks his phone. "Almost six."

"Shit," I mutter, stretching my arms out behind me. I'm only just noticing how stiff my muscles have become. "We've been here a while."

"I think now's a good stopping point," my wolf shifter says. "We keep this up much longer and I'm going to get my ass handed to me."

The image is so absurd that I can't help but laugh. "I won't tell if you won't," I reply. "Come on, let's go find some food. I'm starving, and by the sounds of it, it's Landon's turn in the driver's seat tomorrow."

CHAPTER 80

For the first time in what feels like ages, I actually sleep well. And not because I'm half-dead or drugged out of my mind on vampire blood, but because I actually feel *safe* for once. What is this world coming to?

It's a wonder what being amongst friends will do to your morale. It hardly even matters that "friends" is a relative term here; the mere fact that we're no longer surrounded by people who are actively trying to kill us makes for a restful night. As much as Theo seems to promote the idea of a co-living situation, we're still left to fend for ourselves food-wise, so Hunter wanders out to pick up a pizza after my day of training with Shade.

We all gather in my designated apartment, and although it's a tight squeeze, it hardly matters; sitting and laughing over food makes me feel almost *all right* again, if only for the evening. The loss of my powers still hangs heavily over my head like a black thundercloud, but knowing I'm not alone makes a huge difference. The fact that I actually survived a day's worth of combat training with Shade has given me a much-needed boost as well. Although I doubt I could take on a shifter right now, the prospect of one day being able to hold my own without magic no longer seems so absurd.

Maybe things *are* going to be okay.

It's not until later that the others start turning in—Shade makes a quip about me having worn him out today and excuses himself, while Hunter leaves to continue practising his vampire form. Silas slinks quietly off to his room, and I make a mental note to check in with him at some point. Being surrounded by reminders of his childhood likely isn't doing his mental state any good, and I have to remember that I'm not the only one struggling right now.

I'm on the verge of following him out the door to ask what's wrong when someone slips his hand into mine, and I find myself being twirled in a dance maneuver that would look ridiculous if someone other than Landon had instigated it. Laughing, I spin into him, allowing him to pull me close to his chest and sway me back and forth to a tune that only he can hear.

"You're going to be sorry," I joke. "I've got the flattest feet this side of the equator."

"I'll challenge you on that," Landon replies. "Need I remind you that sirens literally have webbed feet? Great for swimming. Not so great for wooing."

I raise my eyebrows. "Is that what this is? You trying to *woo* me?"

The siren shifter grins before giving me a wink. "As great as hypnosis is, I tend to prefer the ladies in my life to like me for who I am. Not what I am."

It's an awfully strong sentiment coming from him, and I pause to peer up at his face, wondering what's gotten into him. "You okay?"

"Me? I'm fantastic." He grins. "I scored a moment alone with my girlfriend—what's not to like?"

"Girlfriend, eh?" I can't keep from smiling. "Is this official? Have you talked it over with the others?"

"Okay, okay, fine," Landon concedes. "*Our* girlfriend. But since they're not here right now..." Playfully, he buries his face in my neck, nipping gently at the spot Hunter bruised the other night.

A small sound escapes from me unbidden at the feeling of his mouth, and I don't resist when the siren shifter pulls me in the direction of the bedroom.

Landon isn't an intense person, more humorous than serious, and this translates into the way he touches me; his hands are gentle, and I'm sure he's aware of the way his breath tickles me when he murmurs something in my ear, something that would sound cheesy and over-the-top coming from literally anyone else. Gently he pushes me back onto the large bed, the feeling of his body over mine giving me a sense of safety and security.

It's only as I'm fumbling for his belt buckle when a muscle spasm strikes me hard in the back, all those hours of exercise finally catching up to me. I seize up, letting out a hiss of startled pain, and Landon immediately pulls back.

"What is it?" he asks, flirtatiousness replaced with concern. "Are you okay?"

"Mm, yeah, I'm fine," I grunt, pulling my shoulders back in an attempt to ease the sudden tension. "Just sore, I think. Shade's like a taskmaster."

Landon snorts. "Why am I not surprised?" Gently, he moves my hands away, instead lifting the covers so I can clamber gingerly into bed. "It's okay," he murmurs, kissing me gently. "We can wait until you're not... you know, dying."

I reach out to catch his wrist before he can move away. "Sleep in here?" I ask. The thought of spending my first night alone without my powers is almost unbearable, and I can see from his expression that Landon realises this.

Still, he can't help making a show of thinking it over. "Well," he says after a moment of hemming and hawing, "I guess it'll make waking you up easier. Scoot over."

I oblige, already groaning at the thought of another day of training. "You're really going to make me get up before sunrise?"

"Of course," the siren shifter replies, rolling onto his side and wrapping his arms around me. "If you can learn to shoot in the dark, you can learn to shoot anywhere."

Part of me wants to bicker, but my stiff body is protesting too much, and before I'm even aware of it, my eyelids are drifting closed. I don't even have time to be disappointed about not getting to have sex with him.

"RISE AND SHINE, PRINCESS." The feeling of lips against the back of my neck makes me shiver, and I come to gradually, rotating in Landon's arms so I can return the kiss.

"Five more minutes?" I plead.

"Nah, ah, ah," the siren shifter says, already throwing the covers off. "Up and at 'em, Boots. Let's go."

I laugh. "Never mind what I said last night," I say as I get out of bed and begin dressing. "*You're* the real taskmaster around here."

"Damn right," Landon says, preening a little. "Now get something comfortable on and meet me on the roof in five minutes. We've got a big day ahead of us."

It doesn't even occur to me to wonder how we'll manage this on the roof until after I'm out in the hallway, still rubbing sleep from my eyes and rolling my sore shoulders. I doubt most of Oxford will appreciate shots ringing out at four in the morning, but I'm too tired at this point to bother worrying about it. Instead, I drag myself to the lift and head up to the roof, already dreading what the day is going to bring.

I'm not sure what I was expecting up here, but it wasn't *this*. The whole thing is set up like a shooting range, equipment scattered all about and a row of fresh targets standing at the far end. As I'm gaping at this, Landon emerges onto the rooftop, a pistol in either hand.

"They can't seriously be okay with us firing guns up here," I exclaim as he hands one to me. I take it gingerly, half afraid to touch it, and hold it with two fingers as Landon watches.

"You're not giving these guys enough credit," he tells me. "This whole roof is enchanted —soundproofed, believe it or not. I've got the space reserved until noon, which should be plenty of time to get through the basics. Only downside is that the guns aren't ours, so you're going to want to make sure you don't break it."

"Easier said than done," I mutter.

The siren shifter laughs before launching into the basics of cleaning, loading, and unloading the pistol. It takes a while for me to get the hang of ejecting the clip, and even longer to remember to keep my finger off the trigger when I'm lining up the shot. But Landon, patient as ever, sticks with it, repositioning my hands as needed while he explains the basic principles of gun safety. "That one-handed shit you see in movies?" he says, shaking his head. "Bad idea. You want to hold it with two hands, no matter what. Your free hand is bracing your trigger hand. Get it?"

I nod. "Got it."

Landon fires off a shot to prove his point, and I'm stunned when it pierces the target directly in the middle. "You want to make sure the sight is lined up with your target," he explains. "Think of it as an extension of your arm."

I take a shaky breath and pull the trigger, wincing at the last second, and the bullet ricochets off the roof.

"Easy," Landon says, coming up behind me to adjust my stance. "Here, I'll show you. Keep your grip tight, okay? Exhale when you pull the trigger." Covering my hands with his, he helps me realign the sight with the target. "You ready?"

"I think so," I reply, swallowing hard.

With an ever-so-subtle touch, Landon slips his finger over mine and guides it down. The gun fires again, but to my amazement, this shot actually hit the target. More than that, even, it came damn near the centre.

"See?" Landon says, grinning triumphantly. "You're getting it."

I GUESS I'm fortunate that shooting is decidedly less physical than martial arts, and I find that I don't feel like I want to die by the time the sun comes up. It's going to take work— a lot of work. My accuracy still sucks without Landon's gentle hands on mine, but I'm surprised at how quickly I got over my fear of the actual shooting part.

Here's hoping I won't have to use it.

"That's it," Landon says, his hand slipping down to my waist to help straighten my posture. "Remember to breathe. I've got you." His free hand goes to my elbow, holding me steady as I count to three, let my breath out, and then fire. "Bullseye," the shifter commends.

I glance at the target and see the clean hole in the middle, and I barely remember to put the safety back on before I'm giving a little jump of excitement. "Holy shit! I did it!"

"Damn right, you did," Landon murmurs, and it's only now that I'm noticing he hasn't moved away from me, even though I'm no longer firing. His dark eyes drift to my lips, and in one fluid movement, he's kissing me again, one hand gently taking the pistol from me and setting it aside as his mouth moves against mine. The fact that we're in public registers, but I'm too caught up in the sensations he's resurrecting from last night to even care. "I think that's enough for one day," he says in a husky voice when we come up for air, and all I can do is nod furiously in agreement.

We practically stumble back into my apartment, already tugging at each other's clothes like our lives depend on it. Landon barely managed to return the guns before he was on me again, his ferocity astounding. My heart hammers in my chest as we return to the bed where we almost made love earlier, except this time there are no muscle cramps to get in the way. Soon Landon's hand is drifting between my legs, making me almost shamefully wet as he strokes at me gently, reducing me to a quivering mess.

Slowly we sink onto the bed, and I pepper my siren shifter's tan body with kisses as he fumbles the rest of his clothes off, his arousal obvious even beneath his jeans. His thumbs brush gently over my nipples as he pulls back to drink me in with his eyes, his gaze almost reverent as I lean back and bring him into the curve of my embrace. "Roll over," Landon tells me, his voice low with lust, and I do as he asks, adrenaline surging through me.

When he pushes into me, his movements are slow and deliberate —so much so that it's nearly enough to make me go crazy. It's almost like he's trying to tease the pleasure out of me, and when I glance over my shoulder at him, he gives me a knowing smile that just about reduces me to a puddle on the bed.

The pace he sets is agonising at first, speeding up ever so gradually as he reaches a hand around to stroke my clit while he moves. It's an exquisite feeling, and the sounds it elicits are borderline embarrassing, but I'm too caught up in it to feel self-conscious.

"Fuck, Boots," Landon groans from above me. "You're so tight." I feel his lips on my shoulder as he presses me into the mattress, his every thrust making me see stars as his fingers continue their deft ministrations.

"Landon..." I pant, lost in the feeling of him. The pleasure is all-encompassing, and my orgasm hits me all at once, like a tidal wave.

Landon follows not long after, his hips stuttering when he comes. As he lowers himself down on top of me, brushing back my hair to kiss me, all he can manage is a breathless, "Not bad for a first lesson."

I just laugh, still panting. Not bad at all.

CHAPTER 81

You would think, given everything I've been through, that I would know better than to get used to any situation that feels too comfortable. And you would be right. Nothing in my life has ever been permanent—none of the good things, anyway. Ever since I was a baby, it's just been one unfortunate incident after another. I'm accustomed to being left behind, so much so that it might as well be in my DNA. The worst part is that not even learning my true origins has been enough to prevent further tragedies. If anything, it's only brought more destruction to my life, and the one place I thought I would finally belong has turned against me, too.

The one thing that's gotten me through the past few months has been my connection to the guys. That I love them all is a foregone conclusion; my feelings for them run deeper than any I've ever felt before, and there's something so depressingly surprising in the fact that they've stood beside me through thick and thin. Especially now that the one thing we all had in common -—our powers—has disappeared, just like every other good thing in my life.

These are the nightmares that plague me as we settle into our lives at the commune: images of abandonment flash through my mind on repeat like a film reel, and some nasty voice in the back of my mind whispers that it's only a matter of time before the men that I love decide to cut their losses and get away from me before I end up getting *them* hurt, too.

If they notice how dogged I am by these ideas, they don't say anything, and I don't know if that makes it better or worse. At any rate, though, I can't help but feel a little melancholy about how nice it is here. After Mollie, I know better than to think this will last.

The days turn to weeks. I know I need to bring up the Edith situation with Theo sooner or later, but she has yet to make an appearance, and I worry that the moment I tell him she's planning an attack, he'll kick us back out onto the street. I'm not oblivious to the way he looks at me, either, but I seriously doubt it's for the reasons Shade suggested. I'm a novelty to him, nothing more, and without my powers, I'm like a broken weapon: nice to collect dust on a shelf, but otherwise useless.

My lessons with Landon and Shade are a much-needed stress relief. We practise several times a week, spending hours on end doing drills, sparring, learning about different weapons—and how to use them—and discussing how to apply human techniques to a shifter battle. Dare I say that I'm getting better? It's almost hard to believe, considering how long it usually takes me to get anything right, but my lack of powers spurs me on, and before long I'm feeling something I haven't felt in a long time: confidence.

I'm sitting on one of the benches in the lush courtyard now, flexing my sore muscles and trying, once again in vain, to get my magic working again. It's almost strangely quiet out here, and the sun on the backs of my eyelids is almost enough to make me nod off. It's not until a commanding voice sounds from the opposite end that I start awake.

"Enjoying the day, Ms. Brix?" I turn to see Theo approaching me, his hands tucked in his pockets and his head ducked a little. He exudes authority as he comes to a stop next to my bench.

"Yes," I reply, raising a hand to block the sun. "This training has been kicking my ass." Seeing his incredulous expression, I rush to add, "Not that I'm not still trying to get my powers back, obviously! I just figured, while I'm waiting..."

Theo chuckles and holds up a hand. "Relax, Ms. Brix. I didn't come here to scold you."

"I... oh." I blink, hesitating for a moment before saying, "You know, you don't have to call me Ms. Brix. You can call me Millie, if you want."

"Millie." He sounds like he's testing the way the word feels, a knowing smile appearing on his face. "Very well, Millie. Would you like to come for a walk with me? I feel it's been long enough for us to dispense with the formalities."

"You... want me to go for a walk? With you?" The invitation seems completely incongruous, coming from someone as regal as him.

Theo gives me a broad grin, his white eyes dazzling in the sunlight. "If it suits you."

I open my mouth to decline, citing some excuse about not feeling up to it, but it's been days since I've left the apartment complex and something in his handsome features is compelling—almost hypnotic. "Okay," I reply.

"You know, I didn't think people like you drank coffee," I observe, kicking myself immediately afterward for my brazenness. We're sitting in a hip coffee shop in the university part of town, two of the few patrons still here at this hour. I feel more comfortable in the shadows behind the string lights, and I find myself relaxing despite my best efforts.

Theo laughs. "'People like me?'"

I flush bright red. "I didn't mean... Shit. That came out wrong. You just seem so... Regal. I don't know. Your accent, the way you talk. You just didn't strike me as the type to hang out at a hipster coffee shop."

"Mm." Theo takes a sip of his drink, looking pensive. "I suppose I understand. I was born more than a hundred years ago, after all. My way of speaking has yet to catch up, it seems."

"More than a hundred years ago?" I stare at him, eyes wide. "You don't look a day over thirty!"

"The curse of my condition," Theo replies, a melancholy look on his face. "The witches wanted a weapon when they made me, and the best kind of weapon is one that can never break."

"I *do* age, but I... know the feeling," I reply glumly, staring into my cappuccino.

Theo's eyes are on me, I can feel them. It's not entirely unpleasant. "Do you know how many hybrids there are in the world?" he asks after a moment.

I shake my head.

"Me neither," he replies. "Truth be told, Millie, you're the only other one I've ever met. I find myself..." He presses his lips together, as if looking for the right words. "I understand you and the others you brought here are... close."

I swallow hard, avoiding his eyes. "Yes, I... suppose we are."

"I'm not one to step on toes," Theo goes on, leaning back in his seat, "but I don't think it's any secret that we share an origin, Millie. And that's... something to consider in our fight against the humans. I don't often feel drawn to those I bring into this community the way I feel drawn to you."

I gape at him, my heart fluttering in my chest. There's no denying that he's attractive, and there's something to be said "Theo, I..."

"I wasn't trying to make you uncomfortable," Theo replies, sounding off-balance for the first time since I've met him. "Forgive me. I... let's talk about something else."

Grateful for the reprieve, and struggling against a fresh flurry of emotions, I nod gratefully and turn back to my coffee. *Girlfriend.* Landon used the word girlfriend, and I agreed. Do the others think of me that way, I wonder? Would things be different if I weren't already spoken for? "How long have you been fighting the humans?" I ask, deciding to switch tacks.

"Long enough," Theo replied. "I was never forced to go to their Academy, but I've seen enough of what they do to our kind to last a lifetime. They want us silent and complicit. Our needs have never —*will* never—matter to them. Which is why I've built this community," he goes on, "I will do whatever it takes to see it remain safe."

I bite my lip. If there were ever a time to bring up Hawthorne and

Edith, this would be it. "About that," I say, straightening up in my chair. "This isn't easy for me to say, Theo, but there's a strong possibility that your community is already in danger."

Theo raises his eyebrows, looking ready to reply, when something over my shoulder catches his attention. His expression suddenly darkens as he runs a hand through his white hair. "I'm afraid we will have to postpone this discussion, Millie," he says in a stony voice. "We seem to be attracting undue attention."

Adrenaline floods through me as my eyes drift to the side, and immediately I see what he's talking about: a duo of uniformed officers is standing just outside the window of the coffee shop, the badges on their jackets are frustratingly familiar. "What do we do?" I ask.

Theo gets to his feet, holding out his hand to me. "We're not far from our building," he replies. "Stay behind me, and do as I say."

I nod and take his hand, allowing him to pull me to my feet. I'm not oblivious to the feeling of his thumb smoothing over my palm.

He positions his body in front of mine, which assuages my fear, but only a little; clearly they're closing in, if there are Academy agents this near to the apartment.

"Stay calm," Theo instructs. "Don't draw any attention to yourself."

"Okay." He leads me to the door, our drinks forgotten on the table, and in moments we're back out in the bright sunlight. My heart is racing in my ears. The two officers are within spitting distance, and I can feel their eyes on me despite my attempts to seem relaxed.

Theo's grip on my hand tightens a little as he makes a sharp right in the opposite direction of the apartment.

"Can we lose them?" I whisper.

"We can try," he replies as he leads me down the street in the direction of a busier street. If we can draw enough attention...

But almost as soon as we turn onto a connecting road, Theo stops dead in his tracks, his white eyes narrowing. At the other end of the alleyway are another two agents, and they're looking right at us.

"Look who just turned up," one of them remarks. "We've been looking for you for a while, Theo."

Without a word, Theo turns back around, but the other end of the alley is already blocked off by the other two officers, who must have been following us from the coffee shop. Shit. Shit, shit, shit.

"New plan," Theo announces, his eyes already beginning to glow with power. "Time to put that new training to use, Millie."

CHAPTER 82

The Academy soldiers don't seem to care that Theo is transforming, nor does it seem to matter to them in the slightest that we're in broad daylight in the middle of a busy district. I have time to wonder how many people they've paid off in order to stop any interference from the public, but that's the only rational thought that crosses my mind as they close in on us without any warning.

I know better than to try to use my powers, considering how close they are already, but in spite of the countless hours I've spent in the gym and on the roof, I suddenly feel like all of Shade's and Landon's lessons have gone out the window. Paralysed, I stand there, eyes wide, as the two agents at the end of the alleyway charge us, only thinking to get behind Theo at the last second.

My experience with hybrids has been, up until this point, restricted to my own abilities, so you can understand my surprise when Theo's entire body seems to light up with pure magic. It's nothing like I've ever seen before, and it's mesmerising in spite of our current situation. His eyes blaze with a blinding white light, his hair crackling with magical energy, and within seconds, his whole body is shifting. His mouth becomes a wolf's snout, while his back legs take on the form of a dragon. His hands become those of a witch, and it's

497

this that he puts to use, sending a wave of magical force shooting down the alleyway. It knocks the oncoming agents back. He seizes the opening to wing his tail in a wide arc, catching the man behind me in the side and knocking him into the wall.

I feel powerless as the first two attackers scramble to their feet, already digging for weapons—no guns, which I suppose I can be thankful for—but one of them is brandishing a knife while the other has produced a billy club.

Theo has already turned to push the others back, leaving me frozen in place as one of the agents runs me down. I crash to the ground; the wind going out of me in a rush, and he doesn't waste his opportunity, pinning me down as he swings his baton wildly. I barely have time to register what's happening before my arm is coming up in a clumsy imitation of one of the blocks Shade showed me, making me do it again and again until he was satisfied.

Here's something they don't tell you in combat training: a real fight is nothing like a practise fight. That's a lesson I learn the hard way as the baton connects with my forearm, sending a blast of pain all the way up into my shoulder. Still trying to get my breath back, I gasp again, gritting my teeth against the radiating sensation.

He still has the upper hand, and he knows it; eyes flashing, he grips the other end of his baton and bears down on me with all his strength, doing his best to crush my windpipe. My hands are in the way, giving me enough room to breathe, but he's stronger than I am, and panic tears through me as I realise he'll overpower me within seconds.

I'm vaguely aware of the sounds of fighting all around me, but there's no counting on Theo coming to my rescue; he has his hands full already. I push back against my attacker with all my strength, wishing desperately that I could turn into a dragon and throw him off, but that's not possible. For all intents and purposes, I'm just a normal human again.

A normal human with training, I remind myself.

Something Shade said about grappling echoes in the back of my mind: *Think about an animal in a trap. They don't worry about technique.*

They use their whole body. If someone is on you, you have to become an animal.

I become aware of the sound of yelling and I only realise after a moment that it's coming from my throat. A flicker of uncertainty crosses the agent's features as I begin to thrash underneath him, not caring where my elbows and knees fly. All that matters is getting him off of me.

Clearly, the guy wasn't expecting this much of a resistance, and I use that to my full advantage, swinging my arm in a wide arc so that my elbow connects with his nose. There's the sound of breaking bones, and blood immediately gushes down his face. Letting out a yell of pain, he pulls back, his hands flying to his nose, and that's the opening I need. I manage to untangle one of my legs, rotating my body to send him tumbling off me. What was it Shade had taught me for keeping an enemy down? Sidekick or front snap kick?

Doesn't matter, I think grimly, turning my hip over and strike him squarely in the chest. He falls backward, the tables temporarily turn. But I don't even have a chance to celebrate before another set of arms has wrapped around me from behind in a bear hug.

Swearing, I lurch forward, dropping my full body weight the way Shade showed me in order to upset his centre of gravity. The man goes tumbling over my head, giving me just enough room to scramble away and look frantically around for Theo. He's still in his hybrid form, a wall of fire and telekinetic force preventing the others from approaching. His eyes, still glowing with magic, meet mine, and he raises an eyebrow, probably not expecting me to have handled myself as well as I did. It's astonishing to me how, even though he's in multiple forms and fending off two armed assailants, he doesn't even seem to be breaking a sweat.

I catch a glimpse of movement out of the corner of my eye and turn just in time to see the baton guy coming at me, his face red with blood. I allow him just close enough to reach for me and then side-step him, shoving him clumsily from behind into the raging flames that Theo has conjured up. It's not the most elegant solution, but it's effective, and the other soldier is forced to go help his now on fire companion instead of continuing his attack on me.

Satisfied, Theo expands his force field to knock the other agents into the alleyway walls, temporarily stunning them, and then he's back in his human form. "Come on," he instructs, his voice surprisingly calm.

I don't need to be told twice. Clutching my throbbing arm, I race after the other shifter, around the limp forms of our assailants, and out of the alleyway. Now that the adrenaline is wearing off, I have to clench my teeth to fend off the pain, looking every which way as I follow Theo back in the direction of the apartment complex.

"Not bad, Millie," he observes.

I give him a weak smile. "Shade will be happy, at least." It's only as the shock and fear wear off that I'm struck with a strange sense of pride.

I stood my own back there. And I did it without shifting a single time.

I wince as a fresh bolt of pain goes up my arm, and Theo slows to a stop once we're outside the apartments. "Let me see that," he says, reaching out a hand.

"It's fine-" I protest, but before I can pull away, his cool fingers are already closing around my wrist, glowing with the telltale blue light of witch magic. Almost immediately, the soothing cold of a healing spell chases away the pain, and I breathe a sigh of relief.

"You fractured it," Theo says, letting go of my arm. "Don't worry—I fixed it."

"Just like that?"

"Just like that," he replies. "A century of practise, remember?"

"YOU SON OF A BITCH," says Silas, taking a step forward. "She could have been killed."

"She wasn't," Theo replies coolly. He's sitting on the other side of the desk in his office, the rest of us gathered in a cluster in front of him. My arm is still sore, but the worst is behind me, mostly replaced with exhaustion. "In fact, Millie did an excellent job defending herself. I'm impressed."

Hunter's eyes narrow. "You don't sound surprised."

"I admit, I was curious," says Theo. "There's no other way of gauging someone's skill besides seeing them in battle. You will be a force to be reckoned with once you get your powers back, I think, Millie."

"You two are on a first name basis now?" Landon asks, raising an eyebrow. He and Shade exchange a look.

"We just went for a walk," I assure them. "Considering Theo's putting us all up, it was the least I could do."

"Yeah. And you almost died because of it," Silas says.

"Wait a minute," Hunter speaks up, his face twisting with anger. "You planned this, didn't you?" He glares daggers at Theo. "This was some kind of a test."

"How very astute of you," replies Theo. "If you're asking whether I tipped the agents off, the answer is no. The humans have had us in their sights since long before the five of you arrived. I will admit, though, I was curious. If the occasion to see Millie in action presented itself..." He trails off, leaving us to fill in the details.

"Fuck," mutters Shade, running a hand through his shaggy hair. "You're lucky she did well. That's all I can say."

"It's fine," I say, although I'm not sure whether I'm reassuring them or myself. I guess I shouldn't be surprised; someone in Theo's position would want to ensure a return on his investment, especially if I'm taking up a bed that could go to a fully powered shifter. It sucks, but... we're not exactly in a position to complain. "I hope that was proof enough for you."

"It was," says Theo. "We'll need to make restoring your abilities our top priority, though."

Damn. I guess I should have known that was coming. I was on the verge of telling him back at the coffee shop, and this time there are no Academy hunters to interrupt me. No sense in waiting.

"Actually," I say, stealing a glance at the others, "that can't be our top priority, Theo." As much as I might want it to be.

"Oh?" Theo raises his eyebrows. "And why should my fellow hybrid not want her magic back?"

"I do want it back," I reply, "but it's more complicated than that. You need to know the real reason we came here, and it wasn't only because we were trying to escape from the humans." I take a shaky breath, steeling myself. If this pisses him off, makes him think twice about hosting us, then we'll be right back to where we started. "The girl who gave me my witch abilities," I say carefully, "she isn't on our side. She works for Hawthorne and the U.K. Academy. She's...actually the reason I lost my magic in the first place."

"Mm," says Theo, his pale eyes frustratingly unreadable. "Go on."

"She and some other agents have been sweeping the country, looking for shifter communities just like this one," I explain. "We have it on good authority that your commune is at the top of her list, Theo. And if we're right, then you guys are next. All of you."

CHAPTER 83

Theo's expression is frightfully stoic as he takes this in, his brow furrowed and his fingers steepled at his chin. "I see," he says at last. "And may I ask just who this 'good authority' is?"

I glance unsurely over my shoulder. "A siren shifter and a dragon shifter," I begin.

"We don't know much about them, other than that their names are Jennifer and Owen, and they live in Central London," Silas puts in.

"Why would two shifters want anything to do with the desolation of our community?" Theo asks, and although his expression is stony as ever, there's a nonchalance creeping into his posture that's worrying me.

"The same reason Edith would," Hunter speaks up. "They don't see a problem with what the humans are doing. If anything, they've probably been promised something in return for handing over shifters like us. It's—"

"It's unfortunate," Theo says slowly, "that there are such unscrupulous members of our kind still out in the world. It's also unfortunate that a group as savvy as yourselves would take such two-faced liars at their word."

"I had them under my siren song," protests Landon. "They couldn't have lied. It would have been next to impossible."

"Next to?" Theo asks, turning to him, and my heart sinks. No, no, no. This is going all wrong.

Landon retreats a little. "I mean... I guess there are some people who can resist..."

"Owen was the one who gave us this location," Shade mutters, sounding frustrated.

"So *he* wasn't coerced," says Theo, leaning back in his chair. "I appreciate what you are trying to do," he says, his white eyes lingering on me for a moment, "but I'm afraid that I can't act on information this tenuous."

"Look," I plead, beginning to feel desperate, "I know it's a lot to take in. But she's going to have people with her, *strong* people, and if this community isn't ready for them, it will be a bloodbath. We've seen it before, in Boston."

"I'm sorry," Theo says, "I truly am. But you have to understand the position I'm in. I am responsible for the lives of everyone in my care. I can't uproot them—some of these people have families, children. And if this attack is happening as soon as you claim, I doubt there would be sufficient time to relocate."

"Then fight," Shade protests, taking a step forward. "Spend whatever time you have organizing. Getting your people ready. They don't know that we know. Why not use it to our advantage?"

"There are more than a hundred shifters living in this building," Theo replies coolly. "Many are powerful, and all will do whatever it takes to protect this group. We are safe here, Mr. Ivis. As much as you refuse to believe it."

"This is a mistake," Silas says quietly. "There were plenty of shifters at the Boston convention, and they got taken out by a bunch of humans with weapons and armor. Shifters aren't invincible, Theo. We need to *strategise*."

"Thank you for that advice, Mr. Aconyte," Theo replies, "but I've made my decision. I understand your disappointment, but I have to think about what's best for this community. Should anything happen, I have the utmost faith in the abilities of my people."

"But-" I protest.

"That will be all," he says, cutting me off. "Thank you for coming out with me today, Millie. You've given me a lot to think about."

I know a dismissal when I hear one. Hunter and Shade look ready to keep arguing, but I give them a minute head shake and turn around, heading for the door. Silas jams his hands in his pockets and follows, with Landon bringing up the rear. Theo's stoic bodyguards remain stone-faced, although I catch them eyeing me curiously as I pass them by. How much has he discussed me with his inner circle, I wonder?

"This is such bullshit," Shade says as soon as we're in the hallway. "This could be our one chance to get a jump on them and he's throwing it away."

"Sounds like our luck has run out," Landon quips. "Again."

"We can't panic," says Silas. "We have to stick to the plan. This doesn't change anything. Edith will still be here, and she'll have friends. We need to focus on getting Millie in fighting shape, and when the attack happens, we have to be ready to take Edith alive."

"No promises," Shade says darkly, although I can tell he's mostly posturing.

"He's got some nerve, throwing you into a fight like that, Boots," says Hunter, shaking his head. "I'm glad you're okay. We all are."

"Well," Silas says, "I think I'm going to go think all this over. Maybe order some food. You guys want to join me?"

The others eagerly agree. "Anything to get away from this nonsense," says Landon, before turning to me. "What does our lovely paramour think?"

"I'm in," I agree. "I think I may check in on Hazel and the twins first, though. If it's going to be on us to fend off this attack, we need to make sure they're all on board."

"SO HE BASICALLY TOLD YOU TO fuck off?" Hazel asks over the rim of her wine glass. We're sitting on the roof terrace, taking in the afternoon sun a safe distance away from the shooting range. Xander set up a few deck chairs, and the alcohol was courtesy of Ruby -- considering the circumstances, it's exactly what I need right now.

"More or less," I admit, taking a sip of my own wine. A breeze ruffles my hair as I stare out over the rooftops.

"Jeez, this guy is worse than Russo," mutters Ruby. "Just another stiff in a suit who doesn't take anything seriously. It's like a single step below straight-up sabotage."

"I wouldn't go that far," I protest.

The twins raise inquisitive eyebrows at me.

Looking away, I go on, "I mean, he's a talented shifter. I've seen it firsthand. And he's... nice. Lonely, though." I shake my head. "I can't blame him. Being a hybrid is... It can be a bit isolating. I can't imagine the immortality part. It just seems so... depressing."

"Wait," Xander says, a smile creeping onto his face, "don't tell me you've got a soft spot for him, Boots!"

Hazel laughs. "Did your coffee date make you rethink things?"

"It wasn't a date," I insist, taking another swig of wine. "He just wanted company. And to see what I could do, I guess."

"'Not a date,' she says," Ruby remarks , grinning at Xander. "You sweet, innocent thing, Boots."

"What are you talking about?" I demand, going a little red in the face. "He just wanted to talk!"

"I guess you haven't been around here long enough to get much on Theo's background," Hazel admits. "Or maybe just not talking to the right people. The guy is... How should I put this? He's ambitious."

"That's putting it lightly," says Xander.

I cross my arms. "What does that mean?"

"There are only two things in the world that matter to Theo," Hazel explains, holding up a finger. "The people he protects and understanding the secrets of hybrids."

"Okay..." I say. "So what? I'm a hybrid. It makes sense that he would want to talk to me."

"He's more of a strategist than that," Ruby chimes in. "He hates the humans as much as the next shifter, but he's playing the long game. Trying to find new ways of turning this fight to the shifters' advantage. And one of those ways, according to him, is by using hybrids."

I snort. "Easier said than done, considering how rare we are."

"Exactly," says Hazel. "But with two of you here..."

My eyes narrow as she dances around the point. "Then...?"

"Shifting abilities are DNA-based," the siren shifter replies. "That's all I'm saying."

Her point finally hits me, and I feel my face go beet-red. "You're not saying... He wants to have a hybrid *child*?"

"There have been rumours." Xander leans forward. "He tends to send his own people off in search of other hybrids when he's not managing the community. He's a total gentleman, by all accounts, but you have to admit, it's... curious."

"Fuck." Sometimes, all you can do is laugh. I finish my wine in one gulp. "And here I was thinking he just wanted to spend time with me. That's probably why he's so invested in me getting my powers back. And that trip to get coffee today..."

"My guess is he wanted to test the waters," says Hazel. "If he's thinking of asking you to have a child with him, he probably wants to figure out where your head's at. Considering, you know, you have four boyfriends."

That only makes me blush harder, and the others laugh as I put my head in my hands. "God," I moan, shaking my head. "And he has to be damn attractive, too! What is my life coming to?"

"He's not going to pressure you," Ruby assures me. "Especially since he knows you're spoken for. But if he *does* bring the subject up, at least know it won't be totally out of the blue."

"I mean, it *would* be kind of an honour, wouldn't it?" Hazel says. "Hypothetically speaking, of course. Such a prominent figure in the shifter community, and a hybrid, too... The chance to create the first natural-born hybrid shifter. It has some appeal, doesn't it?"

"You've got to be kidding," I gripe. "This feels like a dream. You know what? It *is* a dream. You guys put something in this wine."

The others start to laugh, putting me at ease. Still, I don't like the nervous fluttering in my chest. Can my life get any more complicated?

THE LIGHTS ARE all on in Silas' flat, and I can hear muffled voices from out in the hallway. My mind is in turmoil over this latest revelation, and the alcohol is only confounding things more. The thought of having some kind of... arranged pregnancy with the man hosting us is absurd enough in the abstract, but whenever I think of the destruction the humans have caused, I can't help but wonder... *It's all a moot point, though,* I remind myself as I push open the front door. *He knows I have men in my life already. Men who probably wouldn't be too keen on seeing me hook up with this guy.*

Still a little wobbly from the wine, I try to be quiet as I peel off my sweatshirt and drop it on the couch, following the sound of the guys' voices toward Silas' room. It's only when I get to the door that I catch the first snippet of their conversation. "...are we supposed to do, exactly? Get in a circle with flowers? Get down on one knee? Just blurt it out?" That's Shade.

"You've clearly never romanced anyone in your life," replies Landon. "You need subtlety! We can't just dump it on her all at once. What the hell will she think?"

"It's just that we've never really talked about it," Silas says. "I think she knows—I mean, *I* certainly know, and I'm fine with it. I have a lot of respect for all three of you, and I think we can all make her happy."

"Still working on that part," Hunter mutters.

"Judging by the mark you left on her the other night, I'd say you're doing better than that," snarks Landon.

"Shut up," the vampire shifter shoots back, but there's humour in his voice.

"Look, the best thing to do is just let it come naturally, all right?"

says Landon. "We love her. Hopefully she loves us. That's what matters. As for the rest of the details, they'll work themselves out with time. It's not like anything about our relationship has been normal from square one."

"That's fair," laughs Silas. "She really is something else though, isn't she?"

"She really is," Shade agrees.

I linger by the door, my head pressed against the cool wood, and for the first time in a long time, I can't fight the urge to smile.

CHAPTER 84

Three more days pass, along with two more training sessions. Part of me wants to talk to Theo again, to try to get him to see reason and prepare for the upcoming onslaught, but the other, more vocal part, is afraid. Not just because I doubt he would listen to me anyway, but because, given the information Hazel and the twins gave me, my mind is in pieces when it comes to the enigmatic community leader. Do I think he would force the issue? No. He told me as much at the cafe. I'm more worried about my own reaction, and what loyalty to my heritage would mean for my relationship with the guys. My whole life has gotten quickly out of control, and the last thing I need is some kind of new wrench thrown into our already complicated dynamic.

That doesn't stop me from having some bizarre dreams, though. The salacious kind. I chalk it up to exhaustion and push the confusion from my mind, throwing myself into my training like my life depends on it. Fighting those hunters gave me a much-needed boost, and I'm eager to seize that momentum for as long as I have it.

Silas and I are sitting in his living room a few days later, tea mugs in hand, as we stare out the back window. It's early in the morning, not even light out yet, but I couldn't get back to sleep and found myself at his door instead. He's usually the early riser of the bunch, and can usually be trusted to be brooding in his room by the time the rest of us roll out of bed.

"It seems so quiet out there," I observe, taking a sip of my tea and nodding out at the street below. The city is still waking up, and the calmness is vaguely off putting. Wrong, somehow.

"I don't like it," the dragon shifter confesses. "It always puts me on edge. Especially now," he continues. "I've learned better than to let my guard down, after everything that's happened. First Boston, then Mollie's place..." He shakes his head. "Not even here."

"It must be strange for you," I venture, turning to look at him. "Being back in one of these places. I know it's not *exactly* the same, but... how are you doing?"

"Honestly?" He meets my eyes. "I'm not sure. This all hits so close to home, especially knowing what's coming. I... I miss my parents."

I reach into my boot and withdraw the broken pendant, the last remaining reminder of poor Mollie. "I can relate," I say quietly. "You think you've hardened up, that you can handle the loss, but then something happens and it all comes back to bite you again."

"I'm really sorry, Boots," Silas says, covering my hand with his. "You've been through hell these past few weeks."

"We all have," I reply solemnly. "All we can do now is use it as ammunition against Hawthorne."

"We will," Silas replies. "We—"

But we're interrupted by a knock at the door. Frowning, I look at him.

He shrugs and shakes his head before getting to his feet. Before he even gets to the door, the knocking comes again, this time sounding even more insistent. He pulls the door open, but the face on the other side isn't one I'm expecting. For a moment, I don't even recognise one of Theo's bodyguards. He looks disheveled, and in the low light I have to squint to see the marks on his face. Scratches?

"What's going on?" asks Silas.

"Don't know," the man replies, sounding out of breath. "Theo told me to find Millie Brix, make sure she gets out of the building safely. There are hunters here. A whole damn army of them."

My heart leaps into my throat as I jump to my feet. "Was there a witch with them?" I demand. "Petite, dark hair, about our age?"

"Look, I have no idea," grunts the bodyguard. "No one knows what's going on. They're on the penthouse floor. We're working on evacuating the building." It's only as he's saying this that I pick up on the muffled sounds of shouts and blasts from somewhere further down the hall. I don't even have time to feel vindicated; the situation is too urgent for that.

"Where are the others?" Silas demands, already stepping out the door. "Are they still here? Are they in their rooms?"

"Don't know," says the bodyguard. "I was told to protect Brix. Theo said that's all that matters."

"Like hell," I say, already sidestepping him to get a look around. All down the hallway, confused faces are peering out their doors, neighbours muttering uneasily to one another. "I'm not going anywhere without my friends."

"There's no time," the guard snaps. "We have to get you out of here." And before I can say anything else, he's grabbing my wrist and tugging me in the direction of the emergency exit. I let out a frustrated yell, Shade's drills already emerging in my mind, and wrench my hand free in a clumsy imitation of a wrist lock he showed me the other day. Clearly not expecting this, the guard grunts and takes a step back, giving me just enough room to shove him out of the way and rejoin Silas.

"We need to find the others," I say, panting.

"Come on," says Silas, already rounding the corner to where Landon's and Shade's rooms are.

The siren shifter is already stepping out into the hallway, rubbing his eyes. "What the fuck is going on?" he asks.

"Edith," says Silas. "She's here."

"Fuck," mutters Landon. "Are you sure?"

I nod, and that's all it takes to wake the siren shifter up. Hunter finds us just as we're pounding on Shade's door, looking relieved as he checks me over for injuries.

"Ivis, now's not a good day to sleep in," Landon calls. "Our witch problem is back."

For a terrifying moment, there's no response, and I wonder with panic if Shade is even here, but then his familiar voice rings around the corner. "Fuck, there you are!" Rushing up to me, he brushes some hair out of my face. "I was at your room," he pants. "For a second there I thought..."

"It's okay," I assure him. "I'm okay."

"Where is everyone?" asks Hunter.

"That guy said they were on the top floor," replies Silas. "Probably going after Theo first. They must have come from the roof."

"If Edith is here, that's where she'll be," says Landon. "No time to get breakfast, fellas. We've got a witch to catch."

Briefly I consider trying to track down Hazel and the twins, but I dash that idea; they're several floors below us, and if we go after her we'll be going the wrong direction while getting lost in the crush of evacuating shifters. No, we'll just have to reunite when this is all over.

Again.

Forgoing the elevators, we rush up the back stairwell, moving past a couple of others on our way up. It's only after one of the other doors flies open that I realise my mistake in taking the lead. Two armor clad agents immediately force their way into the stairwell, and they have me in their sights before I can do anything.

"Boots!" yells Hunter.

The first one is holding a rifle, so I do the only thing I can think of: I lunge to the right while sweeping my hands to the left, knocking him just off target enough for his shot to ricochet off the concrete wall.

Hunter, who's behind me, transforms and picks him up like a rag doll before tossing him over the edge of the stairway.

It was a mistake to watch, though, because in an instant, the second guard is on me. I barely have time to get my arm up in a block before he's shoving me backward, making me stumble and crash back into Silas.

A taloned hand steadies me—he must have already transformed

—and moves me behind him before unleashing a jet of flame at the second soldier. Whatever he's wearing, it must be fireproof, because the heat doesn't even slow him down.

Feeling movement behind me, I duck down instinctively, just in time for Shade to go leaping over my head in his wolf form. His strong jaws close around the man's shoulder, tearing at him savagely, and that's enough to make him go down.

We don't bother to wait around, picking up speed as we race up the stairs. Soon I'm feeling out of breath, cursing my lack of cardio, but the guys spur me on, some shifted and some not, as we make our way towards the penthouse.

I'm thoroughly winded by the time we shove open the door to the top floor, but adrenaline immediately takes over; it might as well be a battlefield. Almost everyone is transformed, with fireballs, spells, and claws flying in every direction. It's almost impossible to tell who's on which side, and for a moment we just stand there, trying to make sense of the situation.

It's only the sound of Theo's voice that snaps me out of it. "You're supposed to be safe, Millie!" He's in what looks like three different forms at once, grappling with a cluster of attacking shifters alongside a couple of his bodyguards.

"The witch," I shout, ignoring him, "where is she?"

"The young one? She was in my office."

I nod and move to go, then turn around and glance back at Theo. "Stay safe," I tell him.

Something crosses his face—a mixture of hope and regret—and he gives me a stoic nod. "Likewise."

That's all we have time for, as a roar alerts us to the presence of a dragon behind us. Whirling around, I just manage to get out of the way of the oncoming stream of fire, although the smell of burning hair tells me I got singed.

Landon helps me up, only for the beast's giant tail to catch him in the chest and send him sprawling backward. It's only as I look around that I realise with fear that I've lost sight of the guys.

Smoke and magic fill the entryway, making it impossible to see, and even yelling out their names, my voice is drowned out by the chaos.

Landon is struggling to his feet, unleashing a sonic blast to fend off the dragon's fire, and I catch a glimpse of what might be Shade duking it out with another witch, but there's no sign of Hunter and Silas. Eyes stinging, I squint and look around before settling on Theo's office. The others are nowhere to be seen, but if she's in there...

I'm frozen for a moment, torn, but the feeling of rough hands on my arms snaps me out of it. Craning my neck, I see a female siren shifter, and push back against the wall as hard as I can, weakening her grip. I pull free and charge for the office, operating on pure instinct. A long shot is better than no shot.

I struggle through the melee, narrowly avoiding a couple of latent spells, and shove open the door to Theo's office.

There, rummaging through his desk, is the girl who cost me my powers.

"Edith!" I yell, rage boiling through me.

Her eyes widen for a moment in shock before narrowing again. "Brix." With a flick of her wrist, she sends me flying back into the door, making my head spin.

By the time I get my eyes open, she's on the balcony, making for the stairs leading up to the roof.

Gritting my teeth, my head pounding, I struggle to my feet and follow her.

CHAPTER 85

The debris and overturned furniture impede my progress, but somehow I manage to get my feet under me and work my way across the office. I guess I'm in luck that she only cast the one spell; if she were so inclined, she probably could have paralysed me the way she did before. It seems she has greater aspirations, however.

As I stumble across the office, acrid smoke stinging my lungs, I can't help but wonder why she's heading for the roof instead of for Theo. Could there be reinforcements up there? But it's too late to back out now, and if I let her out of my sight, I could lose her forever. No, I'm going after her, come hell or high water.

Clenching my jaw, I yank open the sliding glass door leading onto the balcony, a burst of cool morning air hitting me in the face as soon as I make it outside. The sun is just beginning its ascent over the horizon, and far below us, the city is waking up; it won't be long before passersby start to notice the chaos unfolding in the apartment, if they haven't already. We don't have much time, and Edith knows it as well as I do.

Heart pounding, I steal a glance over my shoulder in the half-hearted hope that one of the guys might have followed me, but I can see nothing but explosions and indistinguishable figures.

You're on your own now, Brix, a voice in my mind whispers. *And no magic to back you up.* A surge of adrenaline rushes through me at the idea, along with a great deal of fear: I may have tangled with Academy agents before, but this will be my first time fighting a shifter without my powers. A very powerful shifter, at that.

I suck in a desperate breath—Edith's spell knocked the wind out of me, and the air is coming in wheezing gulps—and somehow manage to lunge out onto the balcony. By the time I actually turn in the direction of the fire escape, Edith is already disappearing over the top, and I hiss a curse as I lurch to follow her.

Taking a few deep breaths, I seize hold of the wrought iron ladder and begin to climb. My hands are trembling and my grip is unsteady. Due to fear or weakness, I can't say. At one point, my footing slips, leaving me dangling precariously over the edge with my heart in my throat, but somehow I manage to keep my clammy hands closed around the bars and struggle onward.

The effort feels like it takes everything I have, and I have to will myself not to look down; heights have never been my thing, and without my powers, I have no recourse if my body decides to take a sudden plunge. Wincing, I haul myself up and onto the roof, unsteady as I get my bearings and look around. The practise shooting range that by now looks so familiar is just as it usually is, with one key difference: two large, armor-clad agents who look none too friendly as Edith jogs up to them. I balk when I see that they're carrying rifles, and the smirk the witch shifter gives me when she looks over her shoulder is maddening.

She murmurs something to one of the men and then backs up; a moment later she's taking a flying leap from the top of the apartment building to the roof of the one next door, no doubt aided by magic.

I swear under my breath, but don't have time for frustration; a bullet glances off the concrete within a hair's distance of my foot, and it takes my all not to stumble back and fall over the edge. Some part of my mind is racing as I take note of the gouge mark the bullet left in the cement, and it fills me with hope even before I'm able to identify it.

Shotguns. They're using shotguns. What did Landon say...? *High power, short range,* or something like that. As I duck behind one of the chairs the twins, Hazel, and I were sitting in not so long ago, I'm already making quick calculations: the soldiers are on the other side of the roof, which means if I'm agile—or just extremely lucky—I might be able to stay out of their line of fire. Emphasis on *might*.

Not thinking, I upturn the little table and use it as a makeshift cover as I slip behind the projecting structure that houses the elevator. More shots ring out, nearly deafening in the early morning, and they come so close I can feel the air rushing past me. It's only once I'm on the other side of the cubicle that I allow myself to breathe, but my ideas seem to have run out. Fear floods my body, and I'm sickeningly reminded of the first time I ever shapeshifted, when those two guys tried to accost me in that abandoned building all those months ago. I had almost forgotten what it was like to be so utterly helpless.

Except I'm not helpless. Not even now. And when the barrel of the first shotgun sticks out from around the corner, I grab it without hesitating. The metal is blisteringly hot, but I ignore the pain in favour of upsetting the attacker's centre of balance, which somehow works.

He stumbles to the left, struggling to keep a hold on his gun, and by shifting to one side I'm able to kick him squarely in the chest, sending him toppling over the edge and onto one of the balconies below. His gun goes with him—damn—but that's one down.

Not bad for a human.

The second agent is savvier, and although I wait behind the wall for another few moments, hoping he'll make the same mistake, he doesn't. There may not be guns just lying around, but the shooting range has other things I can make use of, which I do after a moment's consideration. One of the empty weapons stands is light enough for me to move, and I fling it out in front of me in one direction while I skirt back around the elevator in the other. The movement draws the second agent's attention, and that's where he aims his shot. He'll only take seconds to reload, if that, but maybe...

He forgoes the half-loaded shotgun when he sees me charging him from the side, instead whipping out another one of those stupid baton things and angling it back. I'm not going to make the same mistake again, so I slide onto the ground long enough to aim a targeted kick at his groin. It's clumsy, and he's wearing body armour, but it has the effect I'm going for -- namely, making him step back, and allowing me to trip him.

With a curse, his legs get tangled beneath mine, and I'm able to get above him long enough to deliver a palm strike to the centre of his face, which happens to be left exposed by his helmet. The sound of his nose breaking gives me more satisfaction than I'd care to admit, but I don't take time to celebrate, instead picking up his discarded shotgun and racing across the roof in the direction Edith went.

The gap is disconcertingly wide, and I sling the strap over my shoulders so I can have both hands free when I jump. Steeling myself for a moment, I charge forward and leap, almost flaking out at the last moment. There's a split-second spent in mid-air, as if suspended, what looks like all of London spread out beneath me, and then my upper body is making contact—*hard*—with the side of the next building over. I scrabble for a grip, settling on a chimney pipe that's just barely within my reach, and struggle onto the roof before moving on.

For a moment I don't see Edith anywhere, and then I catch sight of her, two rooftops away. What follows is a game of cat and mouse, the closest thing to parkour I've ever done in my life, and it's only after it becomes clear that I'm not giving up that she finally turns around. Her expression twisted.

"It's never enough for you, is it, Millie?" she demands, her hands already glowing with power. "A hybrid, four guys chasing you, the whole world wanting something to do with you-"

"It's no cakewalk," I shout back. "The humans are the ones that did this to me! And if they get their way, they'll do it to you, too!"

"I'd like to see them try," Edith shouts. "It's about *survival,* Boots." She says the word as if it's a curse. "That's all there is to it."

Her hands are glowing more now, red from her transformation. *She's charging up,* I realise. *She stalling.* Two can play at that game.

"You're wrong," I reply, shuffling slowly to the left. Dare I reach for the shotgun? There's still a decent amount of space between us. It might be suicide. "The world is only like this because *they* made it that way. Don't you get it? We could be free, if the humans would stop treating us like second-class citizens!"

"Oh, grow up," Edith snaps, although I see something in her green eyes—doubt? "The humans will never respect us. Hell, we'll be lucky if they ever even *fear* us. So enough with this noble bullshit. So fucking idealistic—the perfect face for a rebellion that's going nowhere!"

The glow from her hands is nearly blinding now, but something gives me pause even as I grasp for the shotgun. "It's not too late," I tell her, and I mean it. At the end of the day, she's in the same situation as the rest of us. Just because she's on the wrong side now doesn't mean she can't be swayed. "You can still help us, Edith. I'll never be as strong as you. *You* could be the key to defeating Hawthorne."

"I..." She swallows hard, more conflict on her face than I've ever seen before. Her green eyes flicker back and forth, her mouth opening and closing as if she's having an episode. For a brief moment, her expression softens, the light from her hand dying down...

And then flaring back up again.

"I'll pass," Edith says coldly, and lets her magic out in full force. I roll to the side, but don't manage to get out of the way completely, and the burning feeling of the energy colliding with my side is excruciating. It doesn't go away, either, and I realise on some level that she must have cast some kind of torture spell. Low, even for her.

I drop to one knee, hissing with pain, but manage to pull the shotgun off my shoulder and set my sights. Through the agony, everything is a blur, the world moving in slow motion. The agent only got one shell into the gun which means I only have one shot.

But at this distance, one shot is all I need.

I exhale like Landon told me to and pull the trigger. The majority of the shot misses, of course, but one pellet connects with her thigh, a burst of red blossoming just above her knee. Stunned, she staggers back, her concentration faltering enough for her spell to subside, and

I have to sprint to make it to her before she falls off the edge of the roof. "Don't move," I tell her. "We can help you."

Edith looks at me with uncertainty, but then her eyes settle on something over my shoulder. I glance in that direction to see the lift doors opening on the roof of the shifter apartment. One by one the guys emerge, coming to an abrupt stop when they see what's happening a few buildings away.

I turn around just in time to see Edith summoning another spell, but don't realise what's happening until she's already placed the palm of her hand over her heart. "Nobody can help me," she says.

There's a flash of light, bright enough that I have to close my eyes, and then Edith Carlyle slumps over in my arms. Dead.

CHAPTER 86

And just like that, it's gone. Any hope of getting my powers back vanished right before my eyes as the witch shifter goes still and limp, her face still twisted in a confounding mixture of emotions. I would try to decipher them, but I find myself suddenly feeling disconnected from the experience, a bit like I would imagine a person might feel after a doctor tells you you're too sick to recover from something. Melodramatic? Maybe. But that's what I'm going through.

The world around me seems to go suddenly quiet, as if with Edith's death, the commotion in the apartment has abated all at once. And how appropriate, considering that all the colour in my world seems to have faded in the same moment, leaving my perception as grey and hopeless as a rainy day. Except this time, there's no sun to break through the clouds.

Edith. Gone. Forever out of my reach. Disappeared to the one place where I can't follow her. Anger and devastation battle for dominance in my harried mind, and it's all I can do to keep from throwing my head back and wailing. It feels like part of my soul has been taken away from me, no longer kidnapped but *murdered*, the ultimate insult for someone whose life revolved around magic she will never get back.

The fucking bitch. How could someone be that bitter, that resentful, to someone of her own kind? What would drive a person to betray everything the shifters stand for, all for a man who's proven about as trustworthy as a snake? Was screwing me over like this really worth it? Was she that jealous of my nature, that it led her to committing suicide?

Questions without answers, all of them. What are the stages of grief? Disbelief? Anger? Bargaining? Where am I now, I wonder? Somehow the "acceptance" feels like a foreign concept right now, as absurd as telling someone with an incurable disease to "just get over it". It feels like my breath is caught in my chest, adrenaline rushing through my midsection in spite of the fact that the immediate danger is out of the way.

A sick lump has risen in my throat, and it's only after a few moments that it dawns on me that I'm sitting here holding a dead body. A belated wave of disgust crashes down on me, and I let Edith's body drop to the ground, aware that I'm not exactly being respectful, but that's about the farthest thing from my mind right now.

Scrambling back on my hands and knees, I move away from the body as if it were a landmine, my breath coming in harsh gasps. It's not like I've never seen a dead body before; it's not even about the corpse. It's about what the corpse represents.

The battling emotions finally overwhelm me, and I turn away from the dead shifter, retching. *There goes my breakfast,* I think bitterly, my eyes watering as I clench them shut. *And there goes my only chance.*

The thought that I might still be in danger doesn't even occur to me until I look around, tears blurring my vision. It's eerily quiet on the roof, but now I'm becoming aware that the fighting is still going on, muffled by the building and beginning to spill onto the street, by the sound of it. Heart racing, I get to my feet, but whatever fight was left in me when I got up here seems to have died along with Edith; what's the point of even trying anymore?

The sound of the lift chiming makes my breath hitch. I whirl around, already fumbling for the empty shotgun—it might work as a club, if nothing else—but relief washes over me when the doors slide open and a familiar-looking timber wolf scampers out onto the terrace. If the situation were less bleak, I might have laughed at the absurdity of a wolf taking the elevator, but you can forgive me if I'm not exactly in a laughing mood right now.

Shade's eyes connect with mine from across the rooftops, and before I can stop him, he's bounding across the roof, not even slowing down as he approaches the ledge. His powerful hind legs propel him over the gap with ease, and he moves nimbly over to where I am in a form that will never be accessible to me again.

It's only after he approaches me that he slows down, shifting back into human form in one fluid movement, not stopping until he's within touching distance. "Boots," he says, sounding out of breath, and without his fur to obscure his skin I can see that he's taken a bit of a beating: the worst-looking cut over his eye will probably leave a scar, and his knuckles are covered in telltale bruises. "Shit, I couldn't find you anywhere." He looks from me over to Edith's body, his eyebrows furrowing. "What happened?"

"I chased her up here," I say, my voice trembling. "She was going to get away. I thought I could... I thought..." But my words are woefully incoherent, and as much as I hate looking weak in front of the guys, I can't help it. Whatever I was feeling when Hawthorne stole my powers, this is a hundred times worse.

Tears spill out of my eyes and down my cheeks, and I rub roughly at them with the back of my hand. I can't bring myself to look at Edith, afraid of what I might do if I dare. Shade seems visibly distressed to see me crying, no doubt out of his comfort zone with emotions so fully on display.

"Hey, hey," he says gently, sitting down next to me and taking my face in his hands. His large thumbs brush the tears away, but the unexpected tenderness only makes me cry harder, collapsing against him like my bones have suddenly turned to liquid. "Hey, it's okay. It's okay, Millie."

"Nothing about this is okay," I reply.

"You're alive," Shade insists. "That's all that matters."

"How can you say that?" I demand, pulling away from him. "Look at her! She's dead!"

"But—" he protests.

"But nothing," I snap. I guess this is the part where I enter the anger stage. "She was my only shot at getting my powers back, Shade. She was the whole *fucking* reason we came back to London in the first place! And look at her. She's gone."

Shade takes a hand through his sandy hair, looking uncertain as the meaning of words finally sinks in. "Fuck," is all he says.

"Yeah," I reply glumly. Sniffing pathetically, I draw my knees up to my chest and bury my head in my arms. "You might as well get going," I mutter without looking at him. "I've already ruined your lives. The least I can do is get out of your hair so you can go somewhere safe."

A hand comes to rest gently on my back. "Boots," Shade says, "with all due respect, what the fuck are you talking about?"

I stare at him incredulously, gesturing down at myself. "I'm useless," I reply in a stony voice. "My powers are gone forever now. I'm just a normal human again. There's no reason for you guys to keep me around. I'm just a liability."

"Millie," Shade says, touching my cheek. "Millie, please look at me." His use of my real name gives me pause, and I do as he says, as much as it hurts. "What on earth makes you think we're just keeping you around?'"

I shrug my shoulders. "You know what I mean. I was the thing that brought you all together in the first place. My magic—the magic you gave me—was our connection."

"*You,*" Shade insists as he pulls me closer. "*You* brought us all together in the first place, Millie. Not our magic."

"But the Academy-—" I protest.

"The Academy is a bunch of power-hungry assholes," Shade says firmly. "Don't give them credit for this—for any of it. We might have their experiments in common, but *they* aren't the reason we followed you. They're still not." He must see the doubt on my face, because he continues, "It wasn't your powers that made us all meet in detention that day, Boots. I don't know what it was—if it was fate, or the universe, or what—but that kind of thing doesn't happen because the Academy wants it to, okay? It happens because it was *meant* to."

I swallow hard, looking down at my feet. Part of me wants to believe him, and another part is insisting that he's just telling me what he thinks I want to hear. "I thought..." I clear my throat. "I thought that was why you wanted to help me get my powers back. To make us the same again."

"Fuck your powers," Shade says decisively, and it's unexpected enough to startle a laugh out of me. "Seriously, fuck them. You don't need them. I saw what you did to those two hunters back there. And that was unarmed, with no magic to back you up."

I glance across the rooftops, back to the evidence of the fight. Somewhere below us, the one guy must still be unconscious on the balcony. Without the adrenaline to speed up my thoughts, the reality of what I did is sinking in: somehow I managed to get the upper hand against a pair of trained agents. And then Edith, one of the most powerful witches I've ever met...

Somewhere deep down, I feel a warm flicker of an emotion I thought was lost to me forever. Pride.

"Maybe," I admit after a long moment of silence. "I just..." I just what? Thought that this play would somehow work out? Thought that I would stand a chance against an institution that's spent decades controlling shifters? Or maybe it's something else, something cocky and embarrassing that I buried so deeply. Managed to convince myself that what was important was doing the right thing. "I just thought I was special," I say quietly, the weight of the confession threatening to make me burst into tears again.

"You are special," Shade tells me, without an ounce of sarcasm in his voice.

I snort. "Right. I'm *normal* now, Shade. I'm just like every other human. Powerless."

"Your powers weren't what made you special," Shade says.

I blink at him, confused.

"You're special because you're *you*, Boots. You're Millie Brix. And that's why we fell in love with you."

His admission threatens to overpower me, and for a brief moment, I forget all about Edith, about Theo, even about Hawthorne. "You... love me?"

Shade rolls his eyes. "Jeez, Millie, what do you think? Of course I love you. We all do."

"I love you too," I reply, and those four words somehow make all the difference. Saying them is more liberating than I ever could have expected, and before I know it, I'm leaning in to kiss him, as if to make sure that he's here, that he's real. That he's telling the truth.

"Now that that's out of the way," Shade says when we finally break apart, "we need to figure out what to do about this." He nods in the direction of Edith's body.

"What do you mean?" I ask as he helps me to my feet.

"You can't think we're just going to give up that easily," he snarls. "We're going to go back to Josie, explain what happened, and figure out our next move. Together."

He squeezes my hand, and I return the gesture, nodding. "Together."

CHAPTER 87

Shade takes his time checking me over, and it's only now that I'm realising how much of a mess I must look. My chestnut hair is so tangled that the knots might never come undone, and I'm covered in enough scrapes and bruises to look like I've just come out of a war zone. And in a sense, I suppose I have.

"Let me see that," I say, stepping up to the wolf shifter and brushing some hair off the wound on his forehead. I frown. "Josie should take a look at this. It might scar."

Shade grins. "Badass."

I snort and roll my eyes. "You say that now. Even if scars *are* kind of sexy..."

Shade opens his mouth to reply when the sound of people on the ladder leading up from Theo's apartment catches my attention. Shade and I whirl around, already bracing for another confrontation, but I'm overwhelmed with relief when instead of an Academy agent, Hunter's face pokes up above the concrete. "Thank god," he mutters as he hauls himself onto the roof. "We thought you guys might have been taken."

Following behind him are Silas and Landon, looking no less battered than Shade. But they're alive, and that's what counts. One by one they hurry across the rooftops to where we are, embracing me wordlessly with barely disguised fear in their eyes. Silas, in particular, seems to have a hard time letting me go, his hands wandering over my body to check me for injuries. "It's okay," I tell him. "I'm okay." Well, kind of. "What happened down there?"

"We drove them back," Landon replies, hands on his hips as he catches his breath. "Bastards underestimated what a whole floor of pissed-off shifters was capable of."

"Not for long, though, if they have their way," Hunter says darkly. "Last we saw they were heading downstairs."

"Did the rest of the commune make it out?" I ask, for the first time remembering Hazel and the twins.

Silas shakes his head hopelessly. "I don't know."

My stomach sinks. "What about Theo?" I ask.

The others exchange an uncertain glance. "We lost track of him," Hunter admits. "We tried to get him to come up here with us, but he wouldn't leave his people behind. He might still be alive..." His voice trails off, and he sounds doubtful.

"Should've listened to us when he had the chance," mutters Shade.

"We can't worry about him right now," argues Landon. "We have to find Edith."

"Yeah, about that," says Shade, pointing in the direction of her body.

"She killed herself when I cornered her," I explain, barely fending off a fresh surge of melancholy.

"Fuck." Hunter runs a hand through his red hair. "*Fuck.* What does this mean?"

I throw my arms out hopelessly. "It means I'm screwed."

Silas, whose eyes are still fixed on the corpse, frowns. "How do you know?"

We turn to stare at him. "Her magic died with her, right?" Landon asks. "If there's anything left, it's probably lost its potency by now."

"So that's it, then," mutters Hunter. "Boots—I'm so sorry." He slides his hand into mine, and I lean into the comfort of his touch.

"Says who, though?" Silas insists. "Josie never said anything about bringing her in alive."

"You seriously think it will still work?" Landon asks incredulously. "You know shifter powers are linked to our life force. It's why the Academy couldn't keep running experiments on dead bodies."

"Yeah," replies Silas. "I also know that shifter magic is linked to our DNA. The witches understand this stuff better than anyone. I say we take her blood anyway and see what Josie can do."

"I..." I bite my lip, hardly daring to hope.

"It's worth a shot," Shade concedes. "It's not like we have anything to lose."

"Except Millie," Hunter points out, his grip on my hand tightening. "What if this fucks it up? What if it puts her in danger?"

"Boots is already in danger," says Silas grimly. "We all are."

"It's your call, Boots," Landon tells me. "You know we'll follow your lead." The fact that he can even say that when I'm now nothing more than a normal human warms me up inside, and Shade's earlier assurances echo in my mind. *You're Millie Brix. That's why we fell in love with you.*

Still... Do I dare to even hope?

The others are all watching me, waiting to see what I'll do. A moment passes, and then another, and I find myself reaching into my coat pocket for the vial I shoved in there a few days ago. I hold my hand out to Shade, not needing to say anything for him to understand; he pulls his switchblade from his pocket and places it in my palm. Unsteady on my feet, I return to Edith's body, and wordlessly kneel down to slice a broad cut along the inside of her arm. Her blood is already congealing, but I'm able to fill up the vial almost to the top, screwing the lid on tightly before returning it to my pocket.

Standing back up, I turn back to the others. "Let's go," I say. "There's nothing left for us here."

RIDING a dragon out of the city isn't exactly a reasonable option, considering the Academy presence, so we're left doing what we did to get here: taking the train. Landon, the gem that he is, actually managed to snag some of the supplies we pilfered from the nurse's office before leaving, and I take advantage as we stand waiting on the platform, dabbing some salve onto Shade's forehead before doing the same with the others' wounds.

"You're so gentle," Silas observes as I clean a scrape on his wrist.

"Glad my bedside manner is up to snuff," I reply, grinning.

"We should be the ones taking care of you," says Hunter. "If I were up there when that bitch attacked you..." His blue eyes go dark.

"There was something about the way she acted," I say slowly, not making eye contact with the others. "Right before she died, she..."

"What?" asks Shade, frowning.

I shrug my shoulders, not even sure where I'm going with this. In the aftermath of the fight, with my sensibility returning to me, I've had more time to dissect the way the witch shifter looked when I found her on the roof. Confused? Conflicted?

"I can't put my finger on it ," I admit as I toss the swab I was using and put my hands in my pockets. "It was almost like she..." *Like she had a moment of realization before she died,* whispers a voice in my head. *No, not realization. Clarity.* "I told her it wasn't too late," I explain. "I offered to help her."

"Then you're a better person than I am," mutters Landon. "The only help I'd give her is help dying more quickly."

"What did she say?" Silas asks, his eyes narrowing.

"She said, 'nobody can help me,'" I reply.

"So she was trying to rub it in," Shade reasons. "One last taunt before she fucked us all over."

"I'm not so sure," I admit, the wheels in my head spinning faster now. For all I disliked Edith, the one thing I couldn't see in her was a lack of self-preservation. She was out for herself, there was no doubt about that, but the strangeness of her actions is only growing clearer in my mind. "Why would she work with the Academy?" I ask. "Betray us to them? Maybe, if she were really that desperate to hurt us. But why would she *keep* working with them? That's what I don't understand."

"Easy," Landon quips. "Because she's crazy."

"*Is* she, though?" Silas asks, seemingly seeing what I'm driving at. "She was with Mollie long before she went after us. She said herself that she never believed in the Academy. Why would an independent shifter, one as powerful as she was, suddenly decide to work for them when she had nothing but contempt for what they were doing? When she *knew* that they would only try to hurt her?"

"For that matter, why would any shifter willingly work for the Academy?" I add. "Josie is the only faculty member who's shown any kind of doubt about what they're doing. We could take them if we were all on the same side. So why aren't we?"

"So... what?" Shade asks. "You think they're being forced?"

"Forced? Blackmailed? Threatened? I don't know," I reply. "I'm just saying, maybe we're not seeing the whole picture, here."

"I guess it's a possibility," Hunter admits doubtfully. "But that would mean my dad..." He trails off, leaving the implication hanging in the air.

There's a long pause as we mull this over, and as we're each lost in our own thoughts, the train comes chugging up to the platform.

"Come on," Landon says finally. "Our ride is here."

IF THERE WERE EVER a quintessential witch's cottage, it would be the one we find ourselves outside now. Ivy creeps up the walls, and the low fence and thatched roof practically scream "magic."

"At least we know we're in the right place," mutters Landon. "Remind me to get a vacation home like this."

I stride up to the door and tap the ornate knocker a couple times, glancing around for anyone who might have followed us from the station. So far, so good.

Josie appears almost immediately, her beautiful face lighting up when she sees me. "You made it," she says, beaming as she ushers us inside.

"Barely," Shade gripes. "We hit a bit of a snag."

"Here, in here," Josie says, leading us out of the quaint front room and into a bookshelf-lined reading room that's chock full of magical ingredients. "I've spent the last few days digging up everything we need. Now tell me about this snag."

We do so, and I pass her the vial of blood doubtfully. The witch shifter examines it, brow furrowing as she holds it up to the light. "This... isn't ideal," she confesses. "I have to admit, I was a little surprised that you didn't have her with you. Fresh blood is always best for these sorts of things."

"Will it still work?" questions Silas.

"I don't know," Josie admits, fumbling amongst her supplies before producing a bottle filled with shimmering liquid. "I've never done this ritual before. All I can assure you is that it won't *hurt* you, Millie... Although it will be painful."

I set my jaw. "No more painful than having to live the rest of my life without my powers. What do I need to do?"

Within a few minutes, Josie has drawn a pentagram on the floor. The smell of burning herbs and incense fills the room, and I can practically sense it vibrating with power. One by one, the guys cut their hands and allow their blood to drip into the bottle she produced, and I watch as the liquid slowly changes from silver to blood red. "You'll drink this when you're sitting in the pentagram," Josie explains, handing me the bottle. "You'll have to drink it all. Understood?"

I nod, pausing for a moment when I take the bottle. "Thank you, Josie," I tell her. "Seriously."

"Don't thank me yet," Josie says, and beckons to the rest of the guys. They move to stand in a circle around the pentagram as I kneel down in the centre, my hands shaking as I stare down at the potion. This one bottle could hold the key to my salvation.

"Are you ready?" Josie asks, her skin already turning witch-red.

I take a breath, steeling myself. "As ready as I'll ever be."

Josie nods, extends her arms, and within moments the whole pentagram begins to glow. Taking a deep breath, I tip the contents of the bottle into my mouth. The taste is awful, and even as it runs down my throat, I can feel a burning sensation.

"Not bad so far," I say, wincing as I try to lighten the mood. "It's almost like—"

But the rest of my thought is cut off by the sound of glass breaking.

CHAPTER 88

The world seems to slow down around me, but whether that's due to the magic or to the adrenaline, I have no idea. It all suddenly seems like it's happening far away, and although some part of me registers the fact that we're now in danger, there are other priorities at the forefront of my mind right now.

Namely, the pain. I've been hurt before, and back when I lost my powers, I thought having my life force sucked out of me was the worst possible sensation I could have ever experienced. Now, though... What started as a burning sensation in my throat has begun to radiate through my entire body, feeling like molten lava in my veins as the magic coursed through me like acid. Every cell in my body feels like it's vibrating, threatening to explode, and I'm not even sure being lit on fire would be worse than what I'm experiencing now. My eyes are clamped shut, and although my terror at the ensuing chaos is palpable, it is dwarfed by the excruciating burning that's now consuming me.

A few seconds—or has it been hours? — pass, and it's only now that I become aware of the scream rising in my chest. My watering eyes crack open, but the light in the room is suddenly too bright, almost blinding. My eyes are registering things but I'm barely even processing what I'm seeing. There are people in Josie's cottage that I don't recognise, save for their weapons and telltale uniforms, and...

And they're using powers. My pain-addled mind is able to pick up on that at least. Tears stream down my face, and I can hear one of the guys calling my name, sounding panicked, but it's all I can do to retain consciousness and keep air moving through my lungs. It's as if someone were pumping boiling water through my veins. The agony is in me and all around me, and before I know it I'm falling backwards, writhing on the floor as my hands bunch into trembling fists. *Breathe, Millie,* I tell myself. *Just breathe...*

And somehow I'm able to force myself to focus on what's happening around me. Landon is closest to me, and he's in his siren form, unleashing earth-shattering bursts of sound to keep the oncoming attackers from getting too close to me. It's cramped in here, and the sight of Silas fighting it out with another dragon is almost unbelievable in the confined space, but then a second dragon shifter lunges at him from behind. I try to make myself cry out, to get my stupid lungs to work long enough to warn him, but it's like I've been consumed by what Josie's potion is doing to me.

I'm helpless to stop it as the second dragon launches itself onto Silas's back, tearing at his scales viciously with its claws. It's only when Hunter grabs it by the shoulder and hauls it back that Silas is able to swing around and retaliate, but he knows better than to breathe fire in a confined space; the last thing we want is another Mollie situation.

"What's wrong with her?" comes the faint voice of Shade, and I realise that he's in his wolf form and talking to Josie.

He starts to move in my direction, but Josie grabs at him with a rose-tinted hand. "No!" she cries. "Don't touch her! If you cross the barrier..."

Letting out a snarl, Shade turns his attention on one of the other shifters, a witch who is halfway through summoning an enormous ball of energy. I don't miss the way his eyes dart back to me, panic written on his lupine face.

Afraid of what I'll see, I look down at myself, feeling disconnected from my body. Every vein and capillary is glowing through my skin, the same sickly red colour as the potion I drank, pulsating as if with its own life force. When will it stop? A horrible thought occurs to me: what if Josie was wrong? What if using Edith's blood messed up the ritual? Am I dying? Why did I think this was a good idea? Why—

But my admittedly limited train of thought is cut off as a fresh wave of energy courses through my body, making me cry out. Except it isn't heat this time, but an overwhelming cold, as if my blood has turned to ice.

And it's familiar. So familiar that I could cry. Because that ice that's now coursing through my veins is the same cool, calming energy that once powered my shapeshifting abilities—a magic I was thinking was lost to me forever. It's like being brought back to life, or meeting an old friend for the first time in years.

I sit up, leaning into the sensation as it chases away the pain, desperate to keep it from slipping away. Gritting my teeth, I stumble to my feet, adrenaline driving me as I shake the weakness off and seize on my shifter powers like they're my last lifeline. And what happens next is eerie in its repetition, like I've somehow cycled back to that fateful day in the abandoned warehouse when my entire life changed for good.

I don't even have to think about it. It comes as easily as breathing, a surge of magic so powerful that it sends me reeling. And then green scales are rippling up my arms while flame licks up my throat, my hair and eyes going black with witch power while my teeth sharpen to a set of strong fangs. I'm in every form at once, and for a moment I'm so stunned by the change that I can't even do anything.

That passes, however, when a wolf shifter lunges for Landon's throat. Not thinking, I'm suddenly moving, the vampiric speed powering me across the floor and out of the boundary of the pentagram in an instant. And then I'm tackling the wolf, tearing it off the siren shifter and throwing it across the room with a strength I would have once thought impossible.

"Boots?" Landon asks wonderingly as I help him to his feet. "Is that you?"

"Yeah, Landon," I reply. "It's me."

Extending both my arms, I do what I saw Theo do that time in the alley, shaping my magic into a force field around me while I wade into the fight.

One of the agents yells something, and the dragon Silas was fighting turns on me to exhale a jet of flame. Instead of letting it bounce off the force field, though, I draw the heat in, adding my own flame before releasing it back out in a blazing shock wave that knocks the dragon off balance.

Seeing my chance, I charge forward, shifting into my wolf form as I spring into the air while leaving the sturdy dragon scales. I land squarely on top of the other dragon and sink my teeth into its shoulder, eliciting a surprised cry of pain.

The feeling of someone grabbing at me from behind startles me, but there's a calm in the midst of the violence that keeps my brain working like a warrior's. With a burst of telekinetic energy, I shrug my attacker off like a bothersome fly, focusing on the dragon below me as I issue a demand in my siren voice, a voice that no longer even sounds like mine: "Why are you doing this?"

The dragon breathes fire again, but I push it back with a shockwave, forcing it back onto the floor. Vaguely I'm aware of the others turning the tide around me: Silas and Shade are tag-teaming two of the others, while Landon has used his own abilities to subdue the other dragon which has now shifted back into human form beneath his foot.

Josie and another witch have each other at an impasse, paralyzed by their own magic. Without thinking, I send a spell their way, breaking whatever enchantment Josie was under and allowing her to finish her attacker off.

It's only a momentary distraction, but it's enough for the dragon beneath me to extend a claw and grab hold of my throat, startling me as it cuts off my air. But even under duress, somehow I'm able to maintain my form, going as far as to shapeshift back into a vampire and use my superior strength to wrest its grip from my neck. Shade's instructions echo in my mind as I strike the giant lizard with my elbow before digging my knee into its side. Harder, harder, hard enough to crush a normal human...

And that's enough to do the trick. With a roar of pain, it writhes away, shrinking back as it shifts into the form of a human woman with dark eyes and equally dark hair. *So that's why the siren song didn't work.* There's something familiar about her, but I can't put my finger on it, instead, leaning forward to look her in the eyes and ask again: "*Why* are you doing this?"

The woman spits out a mouthful of blood. "Go to hell," she hisses.

I pull my arm back, caught up in the heat of the moment and ready to hit her again, when Silas's voice pierces through my fury. "Millie, stop!" He sounds both confused and in shock, and the sudden pain in his voice is enough to do what none of the other shifters could do: make me return to my human form.

Silas's hand touches my arm, and when I look at him I realise that he's shaking. All around us are the remains of the fight, which we appear to have won: a handful of unconscious enemy shifters, as well as the one Landon has bewitched. Miraculously, nothing caught fire, although the room is a disaster, and I feel a pang of regret for Josie's sake.

Shaking from the adrenaline and exertion, I look from Silas to the woman, who is still staring up at us with hatred in her eyes. "What?" I ask.

Silas's eyes are wide as he stares down at the woman disbelievingly. "It can't..." he murmurs. "It's not possible."

"What isn't, Silas?" I ask.

He points at the woman, not even sounding like he believes himself as he replies, "That's my mom."

89. EPILOGUE

Somewhere in the Scottish Isles, on an island away from the prying eyes of both humanity and the shifter community at large, there sits a small medical facility nestled in a tree-lined valley. There are many such labs scattered around the world, ostensibly for researching shapeshifting powers, but Hawthorne knows better.

He walks with purpose as he strides out of his office—more like a broom closet than something worthy of the Academy president, but such is the reality. The school board doesn't know that he and a contingent of his scientists are here, and that's fine by him; after so many years of doing what he does, the red tape has only continued to build up. The school board dragging its feet is a problem, yes, but it's no longer *his* problem. He has always put the greater good above bureaucracy, and he's certain that they will see things his way sooner or later. Sometimes it just takes a bit of a push.

The testing room is already prepared for him, cleaned up after the mess the shifters made last time, and the tables and machinery beckon him like an old friend. His scientist is setting something up when he enters, and as the door closes he turns around. In his hand is a beaker containing some kind of viscous liquid—shimmery, with a reddish tinge to it.

His future.

"Is that...?" Hawthorne asks, nodding at the beaker.

"Yes, sir," says his assistant. "Are you sure you're ready for this?"

Hawthorne smiles at the naivety of the question. He was born ready. "Yes," he replies coolly. "Let's not waste any more time. I have a score to settle."

DESCRIPTION

My powers are back, my men are safe, but the academy has a new enemy.
And we are all at risk if we can't stop him.

The days of being in foster care are long in the past and I have everything in the family I have found at the academy, but Hawthorne threatens everything. New powers, dangerous experiments and monsters rising from the shadows...we have never been in this much danger.

I fell in love with four men at the academy, I found myself, my powers and lost them once before. This time I won't stop fighting until I get my happy ending.

Hawthorne might have been ruling the academy once before but he never controlled the students.
And we are fighting back.

18+ Reverse Harem Romance which means the main character will have more than one love interest.

CHAPTER 90

It's funny how easily the tide of a fight can turn once personal feelings enter the equation. One moment, you're invincible, shocking even yourself with your ruthlessness and skill, and the next, you're being brought to a grinding halt, eyes welling up with tears as dueling emotions battle for your attention, whatever soft spot you've had hidden within you the whole time suddenly being torn open and left to fester. What used to matter doesn't matter anymore, and what you never thought would affect you has suddenly taken on more gravity even than the battle you've been fighting.

And *I'm* not even the one whose own parents are trying to kill me.

Silas, whose ability to take everything in stride, in spite of his own feelings and weaknesses, has always astounded me, is more than shocked as he stares down at the battered form of his mother, her eyes flashing with hatred and blood welling from her mouth. He looks *shattered*. The world around us has come to an abrupt stop, and not even the sight of the enemy shifters recuperating in my peripheral vision is enough to pull my attention away. It's like looking into the eyes of a ghost I've never even met before.

"*Mom*," Silas croaks, dropping to his knees in front of her. "You're alive? How...? What happened to you?"

"Oh, Silas." His mother turns to him with a loveless smile on her face, her eyes rolling in her skull like a rabid dog. "You were always so bright. Shame you've always had trouble seeing what's right in front of you."

"What did they do to you?" Silas persists. "Why are you helping them? I thought they *killed* you."

The other dragon shifter, a man now back in human form and pinned down by Landon, spits out, "We had our eyes opened. *That's* why." *He must be his father,* some part of me thinks.

"Silas," says Shade, moving to stand beside him, "we should really—"

"Shut up." The dragon shifter doesn't even look at him. "What are you doing here? What did Hawthorne do to you?"

"Are you deaf?" snaps his mother, struggling to sit up and clutching at a stitch in her side. "You might as well kill me now, Silas. It will save me from having to listen to anymore of your brain dead questions."

"Mom, please," Silas protests. "Let us help you. Tell us what you need—we can protect you from them. Whatever they have on you, it's not going to..."

But his voice trails off as his mother starts to laugh, a bitter, ugly sound. "Doesn't matter. Nothing you do matters."

I realise that I'm shaking, and it has nothing to do with the adrenaline of the fight; my mind is already racing backwards to Edith, the fallen witch shifter who seemed to express regret for betraying me even as she took her last breaths.

Nobody can help me.

"Don't say that," Silas tells her, sounding desperate, before turning to his father. "Dad, please—tell her we can help you both."

His father responds with a merciless, bloody grin. "Listen to your mother, Son," he says, the tone of his voice grating and sarcastic. "Be a good boy and let us out of here before we kill all of you. Family or not."

Silas looks as if he's just been slapped across the face. "You don't mean that." But whatever conviction was left in him before seems to be bleeding out before my eyes.

"Oh, but we do," says his mother, and before I have a chance to react, she's shifting her dragon tail into existence and using it to slam me hard across the chest, sending me flying across the room. In spite of having my powers back, it seems my reaction time is the same as it ever was. Which is to say, not very good.

It's still good enough for me to be in my vampire form before I even hit the ground, landing in a three-legged crouch just as the witch who had Josie paralyzed finally overpowers her, sending a bolt of energy straight into her body. She gets launched back, but my superior reflexes in this form are on my side, and in an instant I'm on the other side of the room, catching her before she hits the wall. She gives me a grateful look just as the chaos resumes, except it doesn't take long to notice that what's driving these hunters isn't strength or even magic; it's pure, unadulterated hatred, along with a sick conviction in what they're doing.

It's one thing to fight for a cause. It's another to actually *believe* in it.

That's the last coherent thought that crosses my mind before Silas' mother opens her mouth and exhales a blast of flame directly at him. He's not in his form yet, and the fire would be enough to immolate him... Except I manage to get my hands up just in time, conjuring a force field, much like how Theo did, in front of the man I love. It absorbs the full brunt of the heat and allows him time to shift, but I realise too late that it was all just a tactic to buy time. In the few seconds it took for us to regain our bearings, the others have already gotten up and changed forms, battered but otherwise full of fight. The next thing I know, his mother, now in full dragon form, dive bombs Landon and plucks her otherwise-helpless husband right out of his grip. "Hawthorne sends his regards," she tells us, before turning casually away.

"Stop!" the siren shifter yells, but it's no use; the command is impossible to hear amidst the commotion.

Then the enemy shifters, every single one, are leaving the way they came in, crashing out through the windows and disappearing into the still, blue sky.

"No!" Shade roars, bounding up to the window in pursuit, but it's too late. They're gone. "Fuck," the wolf shifter says, raking his hands through his sandy hair. "*Fuck!*" His eyes have already turned the golden colour of his wolf form. "We have to go after them," he says, rolling his shoulders back in preparation for another round. "If we leave now, we can take them out from the ground."

Silas, who has been looking borderline-catatonic, turns his scaly neck on the wolf shifter. "Like hell," he growls. "Those are my parents."

"Not anymore, they're not," Shade argues. "Whatever they are now, they're on the wrong side. If we let them get back to Hawthorne alive, we lose whatever advantage we had from them not knowing Boots got her powers back."

"Not. Happening," the dragon shifter hisses, staring down his snout at Shade.

"Silas," Hunter tries to reason with him, "if we can just capture them, figure out what they want—"

"*No!*" Silas bellows, flapping his wings in agitation. "They're my *family!*"

"Silas..." I shift back into human form and approach him like one might approach a wild animal, both hands in the air. For someone normally so stoic and unflappable, his agitation is heartbreaking. *What would I do if I were in his shoes?* I wonder.

Probably the same thing.

Slowly, I lift my hand to his snout and smooth my fingers along his bristling scales. The motion is gentle and slow, and I can feel him beginning to relax under my touch. "It's okay," I tell him, over and over. "No one's going to hurt them, Silas. Right?" I look around the room. Hunter and Landon give reluctant nods, while Shade kicks the wall in frustration, but throws his hands up. Gradually, the dragon shifter's tension eases, and he slowly transforms back into a human... only to collapse to his knees on the floor, silent and forlorn, his head bowed and his dark hair hanging in his face. I move to touch his shoulder, but he shrugs me off, looking utterly drained.

Landon approaches me and begins checking me methodically for injuries, his hands working from my scalp down to my shoulders. "I'm not a fragile flower anymore," I joke dryly.

"Believe me," the siren shifter says, planting a kiss on my forehead, "I never thought you were."

"You were unbelievable back there, Boots," Hunter says, his face lit up with admiration.

And at last, with the heat of battle finally dying down, I'm able to look around and see that he's right. The carnage before us catches me off guard; while the room was mostly clear before, now it's a veritable battlefield, with overturned potion bottles and destroyed books covering the floor, loose sheafs of paper fluttering down from where they were tossed up in the air. That's all secondary to what my eyes settle on next, though: a large smear of blood on the far wall, right where I flung the wolf shifter who was going after Landon. *Did I do that?* some part of me wonders, almost afraid to take in the sight. I was so caught up in the heat of the moment; I wasn't even paying attention to the damage I was doing.

That's never happened before. Not when I was fighting for my life against humans and shifters alike, not even when I lost my powers and had to learn to do things the old-fashioned way. Never, in all my time as a shifter, have I been capable of this much fierce destruction in so little time, and never have I been less aware of my own strength. As I look around, I'm only greeted with more traces of the violence I've inflicted in the aftermath of Josie's experiment, and for a few selfish moments, all thoughts of Silas' parents go out the window.

The only thing that pulls my attention away is a groan from Josie, who has slid to the floor with her hand clamped to her side. "Shit," I exclaim, and rush over to her, my angst momentarily forgotten. "Are you okay?"

"Yeah," the witch shifter spits out through gritted teeth. "Got nicked, though."

"Hang on," Hunter says, crossing the room to the backpack where we stored the medical supplies we pilfered from the Academy and tossing it to me.

Without needing further instruction, I rummage in it for a

moment before extracting a healing poultice and a compression bandage. "Will this do?" I ask, showing Josie the bottle.

"This looks like pure alchemy," the witch shifter says wonderingly. "Where did you get this?"

"Best not to ask," I reply as I dab a cloth with the solution and apply it to the wound in her side. To her credit, she doesn't even flinch, not even when I begin to dress the cut. "What do we do now?" I'm not sure whom the question is directed towards.

"It wasn't even like they didn't recognise me," Silas murmurs from his place on the floor. "They recognised me. They just didn't care."

"Just like Edith," Hunter mutters, crossing his arms as he turns to Josie. "Any idea what could make them turn like that?"

"I've never heard of that kind of magic," the witch shifter replies as I help her to her feet. "Brainwashing doesn't require the supernatural, though. Ask any cult member."

"Don't say that," Silas says, but without much aggression. "Please don't say that."

"I can do some research," Josie says after a moment's pause. "In the meantime, the five of you should plan on getting some rest. You'll need to be back on the move soon; if I know the Academy, they aren't going to stop at just one attack."

"I guess we have our marching orders," Landon says, without much humor.

I nod, but my mind is already elsewhere: namely, a certain witch shifter, dead by my hands, and the way I leapt back into violence just now without so much as a second thought. And something tells me, regardless of how much energy I just exerted, that I'm not going to sleep well tonight.

CHAPTER 91

A nd I don't.

I wish I could say that having my powers back and getting a reprieve from the violence have chased off my anxiety for good, but they haven't; if anything, the time spent alone with my thoughts only makes things worse these days. I can't even remember the last time I didn't have something to ruminate on, some immense worry that made me feel like the weight of the world was on my shoulders. Concern over the notion of what I'm now capable of battles in my mind with preoccupation with Edith, the role I played in her death, and whether or not the other shifters on Hawthorne's side are somehow being mind-controlled. Josie, after we help her restore some kind of order to her living space, retreats to her study to research the issue, leaving the rest of us to wander about the village while we collectively catch our breaths. A pall of unease has descended over our little group, one that has little to do with the fight. The implications of Silas' parents' brainwashing aren't lost on any of us.

If they, the key players in one of the shifter communities' earlier revolts, can be swayed so much as to turn on their own flesh and blood, what hope is there for the rest of us?

Rather than impose further on Josie, we rent rooms at the inn down on Gloucestershire's main drag (such as it is in a hamlet this small). As usual, we each get a space of our own; in addition to the beds being rather small, there's the added, unpleasant possibility of the Academy's hunters returning while we're still here. They tracked us down once - there's no reason they can't do it again. It's becoming clear to me as I stare out the window at the rapidly darkening sky that things are approaching a precipice: it's a race against time now, and we can't even be sure who our enemies are. Silas has kept to himself all day, and I can't say I blame him. I wish I knew what to say to make it better, but what? I can't even guarantee that it's going to be okay; none of us can.

At last I pull myself away from the window, draw the drapes, and slump onto my bed. Part of me wants to practice my powers, to see just what my new limit is now that my full potential has been unleashed, but the other is scared shitless. As early as yesterday, I was desperate for my shifting abilities back, but now that I have them back I can't even bring myself to use them, for fear of what I might bring out in myself. I don't like what I did today, and it's bothering me to no end that I could suddenly be capable of such carnage.

Eventually I heave a heavy sigh and crawl under the covers, willing myself to sleep, but it's no use; anxiety about my future—*our* future—is coursing through me, and I can't manage even the slightest bit of drowsiness. It's going up on midnight and I'm on the verge of giving in and trying a sleep spell in my witch form when the door to my room flies open, exposing a figure in the darkened hallway. I nearly fly out of bed, heart racing, and throw my hands up, ready to conjure something deadly to use against this unknown intruder, only to relax when I'm greeted by Silas' voice. "It's me."

My shoulders slump, and I immediately chastise myself for coming so close to hurting one of the men I love. *How appropriate,* a voice in my head chides. "I'm sorry," I say as he steps into the room, closing the door behind him. "You startled me."

"*I'm* sorry," Silas echoes, running a hand through his dark hair. The room is dimly lit, but I can make out the shine of his chocolate-brown eyes. "I couldn't sleep," he explains, adding after a pause, "I wanted to see you."

"I couldn't sleep either," I admit, sitting down on my bed and motioning for him to join me. He takes a seat next to me, hands folded in his lap as he stares at the floor. "My mind's racing, and I don't know how to turn it off. All this is..." At a loss for the right word, I throw up my hands in frustration.

"Complicated," Silas finishes for me. "It's complicated." He sighs, sounding more tired than he ever has before. "I'm sorry about earlier. After the fight. I... My parents—it caught me off guard, and I—"

"Hey, it's okay," I murmur, putting a hand on his arm. "That must have been a hell of a shock."

"That's putting it lightly," he says, and chuckles without much mirth. "It was like they were back from the dead. They were right there in front of me, and they looked at me like I was a complete stranger."

"This reeks of Hawthorne," I reply, chewing the inside of my lip. "Giving humans shifter powers isn't enough for him. He's trying to turn this into an autocracy."

"And my parents got caught up in the middle," Silas says, looking devastated. "I don't know which is worse: the thought of them being thrown in a cell all these years, just to be brought out and turned into minions, or the thought of them having been on his side all this time. Here I was, thinking they died for their beliefs, when really their beliefs died long before they did."

"Hey, that's not true," I tell him, turning to face him. Silas still isn't looking at me, his eyes downcast. Tentatively, I put a hand on his cheek and turn his face so his eyes meet mine. "Your parents did everything they could for shifters. Whatever this thing is, whatever the humans have done to them..." I run my thumb over his cheekbone. "Those people aren't your real parents. And we're going to do whatever we can to get them back."

Silas swallows hard. "What if we don't?" he asks, his voice barely above a whisper.

I don't even flinch. "We *will*. Come hell or high water, we will, Silas."

His expression softens, the slightest hint of a smile appearing on his face, and then suddenly he lunges forward and embraces me tightly, knocking me off balance. "I don't know what I'd do without you, Boots," he tells me earnestly. "You're a miracle. Sometimes I look at you and I still can't believe you even exist."

"I do," I assure him, stroking my hands through his unkempt hair. "And I'm not going anywhere. None of us are."

Silas presses his face into the junction of my neck and shoulder, and I can feel him smile as he replies, "I'll hold you to that." The kiss he places there is gentle, tentative, and I catch myself wondering if he, too, is put off by my sudden surge in power, but his grip on me only tightens as I reciprocate the affection and hum in pleasure. Eventually he pulls back long enough to give me a questioning look, to which I simply nod, pulling him in for another kiss. Permission granted, he kisses me with renewed voracity, his hands tangling in my hair as I paw at him in desire. Nothing else needs to be said; we both need this, need *each other,* and I've never been more aware of how delicate our situation is before just now.

I shrug out of my sleep shirt and Silas' hands immediately go to my breasts, his fingers gingerly sweeping over them as his tongue continues to explore my mouth. The deftness of his movements makes me let out a soft whine even as his lips mold against mine, and it feels like I can't get enough of him, even as I explore his strong features and toned body with my own desperate hands.

He moves closer, gently pushing me down onto the mattress, and then his body is over mine, the heat of it—warm, even for a dragon shifter—coming off him in waves as he traces the lines of my torso down to the hem of my sleep shorts. There's a question in his eyes, and I nod breathlessly. The next thing I know his hand is delving into my panties, nimble fingers stroking me open as I grow more wet by the second. An inquisitive finger brushes my clit and makes me squirm, and I can feel his gentle smile against my lips as he slides two inside me. The friction makes me moan, aided by the way his hips grind against mine, and the feeling of his thumb rubbing gentle circles on my clit is almost enough to have me coming undone.

Desperate to prolong the pleasure, I grab his wrist and pull his hand away from me before leaning into him and rolling both of us gently over. On top now, and better able to control the situation, I help him out of his shirt and toss it over my shoulder before getting to work on his belt buckle. Silas can't seem to keep his hands off me, alternating between stroking my by now utterly tangled hair and touching my breasts, my neck, my sides... And then I finally get his jeans off after a moment of fumbling with the zipper. My sleep shorts and panties follow, and for a moment after I bask in the sight of him: moonlight filtering in between the blinds casts an ethereal glow over his tall, muscular body, and I can't help running my hands down his sculpted chest, prompting a sharp inhale from the dragon shifter below me. "Sorry," he whispers, sounding a little sheepish. "I'm kind of ticklish."

You learn something new every day. I shoot him a goofy grin before slowly easing him inside me, going slow in order to accommodate his size. The pace I set is slow and gentle, all in the interest of keeping the painful reality of our situation at bay for just a little longer. I'm already wound up, and in spite of my care, it's not long before I can feel the first stirrings of my orgasm. "*Fuck*, Millie," Silas groans, dropping his head back down to the bed as his hands go to my hips, urging me to pick up the pace. I oblige, finding a steady rhythm that soon has my muscles tightening and my body spasming around him.

My orgasm strikes me almost out of nowhere, making me gasp as I brace myself with a hand against his chest. I clench around him almost instinctively, prompting another curse from Silas before he comes inside me, his fingers digging into my hips hard enough to leave bruises.

For a moment, we just stare at each other as we catch our breaths, each afraid of breaking the silence for fear of what will come next. At last, I open my mouth to speak, but Silas' hand flies up, cups the back of my neck, and drags me down for a passionate kiss. "Thank you," he murmurs against my lips. "I needed that."

"I needed it too," I reply. "I love you. You know that, right?"

"I love you too, Millie," Silas responds without a second's hesitation.

Smiling, I kiss him for another moment, savoring the contact, before climbing off of him and sliding under the covers and turning to look at him. "Do you want to sleep in here with me tonight?"

"I thought you'd never ask," he replies, and settles into bed alongside me. It's a tight fit, but we manage, the dragon shifter sliding a protective arm around my waist and resting his forehead between my shoulder blades. Our situation hasn't changed at all, but in the moment, maybe that doesn't matter so much.

And finally, as we lie there silent and tangled in each other's limbs, we sleep.

CHAPTER 92

"Rise and shine, lovebirds!" The sound of Landon's voice pierces through my haze of sleep, and for a moment I forget where I am... that is, until Silas groans and buries his face between my shoulder blades. Landon, who only seems to be further egged on by this, lets out his characteristic laugh, and in spite of being roused from a sound slumber, I can't help but grin as I rub at my eyes. Silas, for his part, pulls the blanket over his head, although not even the funk he was in yesterday is completely resistant to the siren shifter's charms. "We won't be having any of that," Landon goes on, marching over to the window and tugging the drapes back.

We're immediately greeted by a shaft of bright sunlight, making me blink my eyes furiously. "You know, in most other situations, this kind of behavior would be considered weird, Landon," I tease.

"Yeah, well, most 'other situations' don't involve one girl sharing four guys," Landon snarks back, his eyes twinkling. "Not that I'm complaining," he adds, and winks at Silas, who is only just now sitting up in bed.

"What's going on?" the dragon shifter asks, running a hand through his dark locks.

"Nothing," Landon replies, "except it's going up on eleven. If we're going to stay in town, we're going to have to at least move to another inn. We've already stayed in one place longer than we probably should have."

"Fuck, seriously?" I glance at the clock on the bedside table, and sure enough, it reads quarter to ten. I groan, leaning down to fumble for my discarded clothes. Modesty is something we seem to have collectively left behind, at least as far as I'm concerned. Once I'm fully dressed, I drag myself out of bed and stretch... only to be surprised at what I feel.

Normally, the day after a fight—especially a particularly violent one, like yesterday's—I'm stiff and sore, if not from outright injuries than from the exertion and adrenaline. Even *with* my shifter powers, that's how it's always been; the human body can only take so much punishment before it starts to complain and demand to recuperate. This much is made obvious just by glancing at Silas, who has donned his jeans but is still bare-chested: the dragon shifter's entire torso is littered with bruises, remnants of an untold number of cuts, scrapes, and blows from both magic and sheer, brute force.

But when I glance down at my own body, I see nothing of the kind. No cuts, no scratches, no scrapes—not even the telltale pattern of blue and yellow bruises I would have expected after my tangle with the agents on the rooftop yesterday morning (was it really only yesterday? It already feels like it happened ages ago...). Curious, and a little put off, I stretch my muscles again, longer this time, and once again, there's no pain, no stiffness, no exhaustion. In fact, I feel as if I've slept a whole day, already prepared to spring into action.

I feel like I could fight an army, and that scares me more than Hawthorne ever could.

"You okay, Boots?" I turn around to see Hunter poking his head in through the door. "You've gone pale."

"Shoo, vamp," Landon says teasingly. "You know what they say: three's company. Four's a crowd."

"Har har har," the vampire shifter mutters, rolling his eyes. "I'm serious—is she okay?"

"Yeah," I reply, and then shake my head quickly. "I mean, no. I mean... Physically, yes. I'm better than okay, actually. That's the problem."

"How is that a bad thing?" Landon asks, crossing his arms. "You're lucky. I feel like I've been run over by a train."

"Exactly," I point out, hauling my shirt back up to expose my torso (and not missing the longing looks each of the guys cast in my direction). "Look: no bruises, no cuts, nothing. I got tossed around pretty good yesterday. Between the fight at Theo's place and the attack during the ritual... I've *never* come out of a fight totally scot-free. Ever. And it's more than just that," I go on, dropping my shirt. "I feel *better* than okay. Like if you told me to run a marathon, I could do it, no questions asked. It's almost..." But I trail off. As absurd as it is, the word "superhuman" catches in my throat. Positive or not, it's abnormal.

And there's no guarantee that it *is* positive.

Hunter frowns, leaning against the doorframe. "That *is* weird."

Silas, holding his hand to his forehead like he has the world's worst hangover, makes a face. "Could it have been a side effect of the potion?"

"Josie never mentioned this," Hunter replies.

"None of us knew what to expect, though," Silas points out, tugging his shirt over his head. "Maybe this is some kind of added benefit. Your human form is less susceptible to damage."

"Could be a coincidence," Landon says, although there's doubt written on his face.

"Lucky coincidence," says Hunter.

"Yeah," I say. Damn lucky.

SHADE IS ALREADY OUTSIDE by the time we check out and leave the inn, perched on one of the low stone walls bordering the slow-moving river that crosses through town. "You guys have fun last night?" he asks me and Silas, with a pointed quirk of his eyebrow.

Silas rolls his eyes, which prompts a shit-eating grin from the wolf shifter. "Just saying, Aconyte, save some for the rest of us."

Silas waves him off, moving to stand in the shade of a nearby oak tree. "So," he says, jamming his hands in his pockets, "what are we doing?"

"I vote we check up on Josie," Hunter responds. "She might have some insight for us on this whole brainwashing thing."

"And if she doesn't?" Silas asks, in a tone of thinly veiled frustration.

Shade turns to him with an expression of surprising earnestness. "Then we'll keep looking until we find someone who does."

The dragon shifter scuffs his boot in the dirt, really *smiling* for the first time since yesterday. "Thanks, Shade."

The wolf shifter simply shrugs. "We're family."

The sound of a phone ringing nearly makes me jump, and I turn to see Hunter groping in his pocket. He frowns as he pulls his cell phone out and holds it up to his ear. "Hello?" There's a pause, and then his expression softens. "Hazel! Thank fuck!" I find myself letting out a breath I didn't even know I was holding. My best friend survived another day. "What happened?" Hunter asks. "Did you make it out? What about the twins?" There's a long pause, and then the vampire shifter nods and holds the phone out to me. "She wants to talk to you, Boots."

Not needing to be told twice, I seize the phone and press it to my ear. "Hazel!"

"Millie!" the relief in her voice is palpable, even from miles away. "Where are you? We thought you guys had been taken - we couldn't find you anywhere."

"We made it out," I reply. "We're all safe, don't worry. You?"

"Same here," she replies, "although Ruby broke her arm. She's recuperating now - it will take some time, but at least we're safe."

"Where are you guys?"

"Edinburgh," she replies.

"What-" I begin, but she cuts me off.

"That fight hit us hard," Hazel continues. "Theo nearly got killed.

A lot of the others weren't so lucky. There was no way of holding the base. There were just too many of them. He wanted to stay and look for you, Millie, but the rest of the group was in danger. We had to get out."

"So you went to Scotland?" I ask, confused.

"Yeah," the siren shifter replies. "There's a whole district full of shifters here, and they hate the Academy as much as anyone. They're putting us up, and Theo's working on assembling an army." There's a pause as she takes a breath. "He's taking the fight to the Academy, Millie. It's our only choice; we're out of time."

I suck in a breath. "What do you mean? Did something else happen?"

Hazel is silent for so long I'm starting to wonder if I lost the connection. "It's Hawthorne," she says finally. "We heard from some of the students back at the island. It sounds like..." Her voice catches, and she clears her throat. "It sounds like he gave himself shifter abilities, Millie."

She continues to speak, but I can't say I'm quite listening to what she's saying. My brain is still hung up on that last, dreadful bit of information, tunnel vision threatening to consume me as a faint ringing sound assaults my ears. It feels as if all the fight has been drained right out of me, and suddenly just staying on my feet seems like an impossible task. I slide down to the ground, putting my head in my hands. "...Millie? *Millie?* Are you there?" At last Hazel's voice comes back into the forefront as I beat off the panic attack threatening to overtake me. Sensing something amiss, Landon hurries over to me, sitting down next to me and rubbing soothing circles on my back. The motion helps bring me back down, and at last I'm able to respond.

"Yeah," I manage. "I'm here."

"Did you hear what I said?"

I clear my throat. "No, I'm sorry."

"He's gone insane," Hazel reiterates. "It's more than just the Academy now; he has groups of soldiers scouting the major cities, sowing chaos. More shifters are dead because of him. Whole communities are being threatened."

"But why..." I begin.

"If the rumors are true, and he does have shifting abilities, then he has no need for shifters anymore," Hazel says. "We're all expendable now, and he knows it. I think he's trying to install himself as some kind of... behind-the-scenes dictator. His goals go past the shifter communities, Millie. He wants to use his powers to rule the world."

The prospect is so cartoony and absurd that it's enough to make me laugh, but I can't manage even a chuckle. Hawthorne gave himself powers. Some way, somehow, he finally got what he wanted. And *that's* no laughing matter.

"What do we do?" I ask, although whom the question is directed towards, I can't say for sure.

"Did you get your powers back?" Hazel asks, point blank.

"Yes," I reply. "Yesterday. It's... a bit more than I bargained for. There are some odd side effects."

"Side effects?"

I shake my head uselessly, looking around at the guys, who are all listening intently. "I don't know," I admit. "It feels like I'm stronger than I was before. More durable." *More bloodthirsty,* adds a small voice in my head. *More prone to violence.* But I don't voice this last bit.

"Good. Brilliant." Hazel sounds relieved. "We need you, Millie. There's no way we can win this fight without you."

"But—" I protest.

"Hybrids might be our best weapon against Hawthorne," Hazel points out, "especially if he has more than one powerset. You're all Theo's been talking about—he thinks you're the one who will save us once and for all. They practically had to drag him out to keep him from looking for you some more."

My throat goes dry. Theo has made no secret of his... admiration for me, but this hits on a different level. If he truly wants to use me as some kind of trump card, what does that mean for me? For *us*?

"You have to come to Edinburgh," Hazel continues. "That's where the resistance is gathering. The Academy hasn't touched us yet, thank god, but if we want to keep it that way, we need someone with your powers here with us. This could be our last chance against Hawthorne, Millie."

"Okay, Hazel," I say, after a moment's pause. "We'll be there. We can leave today."

"Please hurry," the siren shifter says, and hangs up. Slowly, I look up and around at the guys.

This could be our last chance against Hawthorne, Millie.

No pressure, right?

CHAPTER 93

"I guess this means we have our marching orders, right?" asks Landon, slinging his backpack over his shoulder and jamming his hands in his pockets. "It feels like it's all about to come to a head."

"I've got some news for you, Landon," Shade replies easily, crossing his arms. "This all came to a head a long time ago. The rest of us are just stuck playing catchup."

I'm not sure whether that notion is comforting or panic-inducing, but either way, I manage a small smile as we follow the old cobblestone road that runs alongside the river. There aren't many people out and about, but now isn't the time for drawing unwanted attention - especially if it's coming from uninitiated humans.

Silas has fallen silently into step beside me, his tall form casting a protective shadow over my body, which somehow helps put me at ease. Hunter, on my other side, slips his hand into mine and squeezes it gently; I return the gesture without needing to say anything. That might be the best thing about this relationship, I'm realizing: we no longer need words to understand each other's emotions.

"Where in Edinburgh are they organizing?" asks Shade.

I frown and consult my phone for Hazel's text. "She said they've taken over a hotel... The Balmoral?" I shrug. "Never heard of it."

Landon's eyebrows shoot up, but before he can say anything, Hunter exclaims, "The *Balmoral?* How the hell did he manage that?"

"I take it it's a swanky place," Shade states.

"'Swanky' doesn't begin to cover it," Landon explains. "It's an honest to god castle. It also happens to be smack in the middle of the city center, so clearly Theo wasn't thinking about location."

"Any landmarks you can point me to?" I ask, just as we turn right and onto a small stone bridge leading to the other side of the river. From here, I have a good view of pedestrians coming from either direction, and it seems like the coast is clear.

The vampire and siren shifters exchange a look. "It's on Princes Street," Hunter replies after a moment. "My parents took me there on business once. Aim for the Scott Monument - I remember passing it on the way there."

I nod, a frown of concentration furrowing my brows. I'll be the first to admit I'm no geography expert, but I think I know the statue he's talking about. I hope. "Everyone hold on," I instruct, linking my free hand with Silas' and watching as the others do the same, forming a perfect circle. "I'm still adjusting to these new power levels, so I don't know if..." I don't even have time to finish the sentence before I feel another powerful surge of energy coursing through me the moment I invest the slightest bit of concentration. An image of the monument appears behind my closed eyelids, as clear as if I passed it every single day, and the next thing I know the world around us is shifting in the blink of an eye. A split second later, the stone bridge has become a concrete sidewalk, the sun now obscured by the shadow of the enormous gothic tower we now find ourselves standing under.

I barely even had to *think* about it, let alone exert myself, and I stumble back, nearly hitting one of the support columns before Shade catches and steadies me. "You're something else, Boots," he murmurs before letting me go.

I shoot him an uneasy grin. "Let's hope in a good way."

The park stretches long on either side of where we are, but it doesn't take Hunter long to get his bearings. "There," he says, craning his neck and nodding in the direction of the intersection to our east. "That's it—that big brown one with the clock tower."

We step out from under the shadows to get a better look, and lo and behold, there it is. It looks like it could have come out of a storybook, an enormous, imposing building that might once have housed royalty. Landon whistles through his teeth. "It's not exactly under the radar."

"There's something smart to that, though," Silas points out. "Theo's clearly strategizing. If there are as many shifters in the area as Hazel says, it might make them think twice if we're headquartered somewhere so obvious. It sends a message."

"We'll just have to wait and see if it sends the *right* one," Shade says, his expression darkening. I move to ask him what the problem is, but he's already moving past me, the look on his face uncharacteristically stormy.

"What's gotten into him?" Landon asks, falling into step beside me as we cross the grass, rejoin the sidewalk, and make a beeline for the hotel. Nothing suspicious is standing out, but the possibility that this could be a trap has crossed my mind. We're too far in it now to backtrack, though, that's for sure.

"I don't know," I reply honestly. "Silas just mentioned Theo, and he got all..." I shrug, searching for the right word.

"Possessive?" Landon quirks an eyebrow at me and then bursts out laughing when he sees my expression. "You know, maybe I ought to give that whole 'dark and brooding' thing a try. It's a nice aesthetic."

"You know I can hear you, Thyme," Shade calls over his shoulder to us.

"So am I right, then?" Landon demands. "Don't tell me Theo has you all in a twist. Jealousy is unbecoming."

"It's not *jealousy*," Shade replies, a little too quickly, and I can see the tension in his back and shoulders. "It's suspicion. Can you blame me for not tripping over myself to trust the guy?"

"He's taken good care of us so far," Silas points out, "and he clearly cares about shifter wellbeing. I mean, look at Millie: he practically took her under his wing."

"I know," Shade growls. "That's what I'm afraid of."

"We just have something in common," I insist, catching up to the wolf shifter. "You know how rare hybrids are, Shade." Still, there's a twinge of doubt, but I push it away. It's obviously just projection.

"Damn right, you are," Hunter says, grinning. "And with this new... boost, or whatever you want to call it, you'll wipe the floor with Hawthorne. He'll never even see it coming."

My shoulders slump and I look down at the ground, lost in thought. Shade, seeming to sense my unease, drops a bit of his glumness and glances at me. "Look, Boots, I didn't mean-"

"It's not that," I say with a sigh. "It's these new powers. It's like I'm back, and I'm *me*, but... Something's different. And I'm not sure if it's in a good way or not."

"Why? Because you're so much more powerful now?" asks Silas.

I nod. "I mean, you saw what happened to Edith. To your parents." It's a low blow to bring it up so soon, but if there were ever a time to make my feelings known, it's now, before we charge straight back into the fire. "What if they somehow get to me? You saw what I did back at Josie's, and that was after being rusty for who knows how long. If they turned me, who knows what I would be capable of?" I look to the others for an opinion, but their silence tells me everything I need to know: they've considered the same thing, and it worries them too, even if they don't say it. Sighing, I shake my head. "All this time trying to get my powers back, and now I'm starting to wonder if I should've just stayed human."

To my surprise, Hunter is the first one to speak up. "Don't talk like that." His ocean blue eyes meet mine, and I see nothing but empathy and affection reflected back at me. "This is who you are, Boots. It's who you're meant to be. And we'll do whatever it takes to keep you safe - to keep us all safe."

He looks around at the others, and they nod their agreement. "We're with you, Boots," Silas says finally, effectively ending the discussion and putting my mind at ease. "No matter what."

. . .

THE INTERIOR of the hotel is just as lavish as the exterior: everything seems to be gilded, with live palm trees, gold trim, and balconies visible all the way to the upper floors. Not for the first time, it crosses my mind just how lucky I am to have come from basically nothing to staying in places like this. It's a little melancholic to know that I'll never get to appreciate it for what it is; it's a means to an end for us, nothing more.

I'm expecting some kind of security, or at least some sort of grouchy bouncer like there was at Theo's last base, but to my surprise, the doorman ushers us in without a second thought. Another shifter, perhaps?'

Almost as soon as the concierge sees me, her face lights up. "You must be Millie Brix," she says, reaching across the desk to give me an enthusiastic handshake. "And your... friends?" she adds, nodding in the direction of the guys.

I nod. "We're—" Then, thinking better of it, I lean forward. "We're here for Theo."

"Indeed." The woman hurries out from behind the desk. "He gave us explicit instructions to look for someone of your description. Honestly, he's visited quite a few times, and I've never seen him all bent out of shape like this." Lowering her voice to a conspiratorial tone, she adds, "I take it you're... one of them, then? A shifter?"

"Er... yes," I reply after a moment's hesitation. "And yourself?" We might as well be talking about our favorite foods!

"Me? Oh, no, no," the concierge replies. "I'm just a normie, myself."

I can sense Silas' hackles go up. "Then how do you know-"

She holds a hand up. "It's all right. We at the Balmoral have been hosting your kind for more than a hundred years. It's a bit of a trade secret. We've never had one shifter rent out the entire place before, though. You guys having a party or something?"

"Something like that," I reply evasively. "Do you know where I can find Theo?"

The concierge blinks, her smile faltering just a little. "Why don't I show you to your rooms first, and then I would be happy to lead you to him."

"Oh." I shuffle my feet. "I was hoping I could talk to him now. It's... kind of time sensitive."

"In that case," she replies, after a moment's pause, "shall I take the gentlemen up?"

"Oh, no, no," Landon says, laughing. "We know better than that by now. We go where she goes."

The concierge looks suddenly uncomfortable, glancing over her shoulder for a moment before explaining, "The thing is, Ms. Brix, Theo is in recovery right now. He had a bit of a nasty accident before he came here and doesn't have the energy for too many visitors. He requested that when you arrived, I bring you to speak with him —alone."

Shade's eyes flash. "Are you fucking kidding me? The nerve of this guy—"

"Hey." I put a hand on his arm. "It's okay. I'll be fine. You guys go on up, and I'll meet you once I get the debrief from Theo."

"Good enough for me," Hunter says. "I could use a shower."

"Excellent." The concierge gestures to an underling, who hurries to her side. "Huel here will help you with your luggage. If you'll follow me this way, Ms. Brix..."

Casting one last glance back at the guys, I allow her to lead me through the lobby in the direction of what looks like a restaurant: spacious and bright, all bathed in the glow from a sun window. It's more or less entirely empty. "Theo is just at the table in the back corner, there," the concierge says, pointing. Indeed, I can see a figure with a familiar head of snow-white hair, his back to me.

Thanking the woman, I excuse myself, taking a deep breath as I make my way over to his table. He doesn't seem to hear me coming, and at last I come to a stop stiffly behind him. "Hi, Theo."

CHAPTER 94

For a moment, I wonder if he even heard me. I'm just opening my mouth to speak up again when slowly, he turns around in his seat. Those white eyes bore into mine, ethereal and unnerving in equal measure. His hair is slightly mussed, I see, but what's more shocking is the fact that his pale skin is mottled with fresh cuts, scrapes and bruises—much like Silas' was last night. Seemingly seeing my surprise, Theo smirks at me. "You should see the other guy."

Clearing my throat, the tension momentarily broken, I reply, "You look like shit."

"I *feel* like shit," Theo informed me, before lifting his left arm. To my surprise, it's in a sling.

"What happened?" I ask, my nerves giving way to my curiosity.

"Wolf shifter got to me," Theo replies. "Nearly ripped my arm right off. It was hanging by a thread by the time the others dragged me out of there. I... wasn't ready to leave," he adds, and his eyes flicker up to meet mine almost tentatively. A rush of... something hits me squarely in the chest, my cheeks flushing a little as I look down at the ground, suddenly desperate to not have him staring at me the way he is. Seemingly sensing my agitation, Theo pulls his gaze away from me, straightens in his chair, and gestures at the seat across from him.

"Please, sit." I do as I'm instructed, careful not to brush against his injured arm as I settle into the chair on the other side of the table. "Anything to drink or eat?" Theo asks, already rummaging for his wallet. "I'm buying."

"That's okay," I hasten to assure him. "Forgive me if my appetite isn't the best right now."

"Indeed," says Theo. "I've been told congratulations are in order. You're a shifter again."

"For better or worse," I mutter dryly, venturing a glance at him.

Theo smirks. "Thank god for that."

A moment passes, and then I clear my throat. "Out of curiosity, Theo, why did you want me to come here alone?"

Theo clears his throat. "Yes, about that. I hope this doesn't make you feel uncomfortable, Millie, but I..." He takes a breath. "You are special to me, and that's the long and short of it. Not in spite of your hybridism, but *because* of it." Leaning forward in his seat, Theo makes a move to reach for me with his free hand... but then seems to think the better of it and lets it drop to the table. The longing in his expression is palpable, so much that it's almost unbearable. "We're two of a kind, Millie," he says conclusively. "Whatever else we are, we share a story shared by almost no one else in the world."

"Except Hawthorne," I reply in a dismal tone. "And whoever else he's gotten his hooks into."

Theo's expression darkens, all the tenderness seeping out of his voice. "He isn't going to get away with this, Millie. One way or another, we're ending his despotism."

"How, though?" I ask, finally allowing the cracks in my disposition show. "He's brainwashing real shifters, Theo. I assume you've figured that out by now."

"I had heard reports," Theo admits. "Nothing concrete, though, nothing that standard manipulation wouldn't be able to do. I take it you've seen this firsthand?"

"Silas' parents," I reply quietly. "They used to be heads of their community. They were planning a coup. Until yesterday, we all thought they were dead."

"The dark dragon shifter's parents?" Theo's brow furrows. "I think I remember meeting them once or twice, back before the Academy's oppression became overt. They had some of the strongest convictions I'd ever seen."

"So what do we do, then?" I am. "Any ideas on what could be controlling them in the first place?"

"My first thought would be sirens," Theo says, "but not even the strongest of them is able to sustain their song for that long, and at that distance."

"Witches, then?" I prompt, wondering if it's possible Josie just isn't in the loop.

Theo shakes his head. "I grew up among witches," he reminds me, "and I never once heard of a spell that powerful. That said, though, a spell seems to be the only possibility. If the witch shifter were powerful enough..." His voice trails off and he looks thoughtful.

My thoughts once again return to Edith, the strongest witch shifter I've ever met. I'm having a hard time imagining someone stronger than she is. The prospect puts an unsettling feeling in my stomach. "Let's say it is a spell, then," I suggest. "What would we have to do to stop it?"

"The only surefire way would be to kill the witch who cast it," Theo replies. "There's no giving immunity to everyone in the world. We would have to take it out at the source."

"Cut off the snake's head," I say, nodding. "So how would we find this shifter, in theory?"

"Tracking isn't easy," Theo explains. "It's not something that can usually be done off the cuff. Some say it's impossible if you don't have the innate talent for it. I can't speak to that, but I do know that most tracking is done using an enchantment, not a spell."

"So, like, a magical item?"

The white-haired shifter nods. "But such items are exceedingly rare."

I groan, putting my face in my hands. "Nothing can just be easy, can it?"

Theo chuckles dryly. "If only. I *do* know someone who might be able to help us, though. He's here in the hotel."

I sigh with relief. "Can you get him down here to talk to us?"

"I can certainly try," Theo replies cryptically, before pulling out his cellphone and firing off a quick text. A moment later, his phone vibrates. "He's on his way down," Theo informs me. "Should be here any minute."

I nod, fold my hands in my lap, and wait. A heavy curtain of silence falls over the two of us, and I can feel the tension mounting before even a moment has passed. As nonchalantly as he does it, Theo is still watching me pointedly with his pale, otherworldly eyes. It's moments like these that make me wonder how I came out looking like a normal human.

My conversation with Theo back in Oxford is coming back to me in a surge, his unspoken but clear desire to be more than co-rebels, to further the hybrid cause as much as the cause of shifters in general. *He knows I'm taken*, I remind myself, but for some reason I still can't bring myself to look him in the eyes. Thankfully, we're given a reprieve when the sound of hurried footsteps comes from the side entrance to the restaurant. "Sir," says a voice, and as much as I wish it weren't familiar, it is.

Whirling around in my seat, I find myself face to face with someone I'd hoped I would never see again in my life, and I can't keep my mouth from dropping open. "*Lyle?*"

The American looks almost as shocked to see me as I am to see him. "Brix. No fucking way." Letting out a humorless laugh, he turns to Theo. "Joke's on me, right? You brought me down here just to see my reaction."

Theo's brows knit together in confusion, a look I never would have expected on him. "I'm sorry?"

Now it's Lyle's turn to look confused. "You mean...?"

"What is he doing here?" I demand, turning back to Theo. "He's on *their* side!" And I'm not wrong. The last time I saw the vampire shifter was back in Boston, when Hawthorne and Russo, an American Academy president, turned on the students who were there for our ill-fated visit to the peace convention. He was actively trying to prevent us from leaving, and if Hunter hadn't stepped in, he might well have succeeded.

"I could ask you the same thing," Lyle snaps at me.

"*I'm* here to stop the Academy," I snap. "And you? Taking a break from being Russo's lackey so you can live it up in Scotland?"

"Millie," Theo protests, "Lyle-"

Lyle ignores him. "It's been a long time since the convention, Brix. Long enough for me to realize Russo has completely lost her mind." A shadow crosses his face as he puts his hands on his hips, looking down at the floor. "I *fought* for her, damn it. I actually believed her bullshit." Raising his eyes, he says, "No one's more pissed off at me for not seeing what was going on than I am. So you can take your guilt trip and shove it right up your-"

"Lyle," snaps Theo, "you're not to speak to her that way. *Ever.*"

Chastened, Lyle raises his hands defensively. "It's all right," I say, my hackles lowering. "How did you manage to get over here anyway?"

"It's not that hard, when you're one of their prized RAs," the vampire shifter says, taking the spare seat at the table. "I told her I was going to track down a couple runaways, and just never went back."

"That was... bold of you," I admit begrudgingly. "I guess I can't fault you for tenacity."

"No one ever could," Lyle says, extending his hand to me. "Look, Brix, I know we got off on the wrong foot, and I know you don't like me. But we're on the same side here, whether we like each other or not. So what do you say?" He nods down at his hand. "Fresh start?"

I stared down at the proffered hand for a long moment before hesitantly taking it and giving it a brisk shake. "Fresh enough," I state.

"Well," Theo says, still looking somewhat taken aback, "I'm glad that's settled."

"So what did you bring me down here for?" Lyle asks, scooting in.

"We need your expertise," Theo explains. "It's my understanding that you know where a shifter might be able to... acquire certain enchanted items."

"I have been keeping up with the black market," Lyle admits, "but there are never any guarantees with these people."

"We don't need a guarantee," I tell him. "We just need possible."

Theo nods. "We're looking for a tracking device," he explains. "The key to stopping the humans might be in finding a single witch shifter."

"Those are rare," Lyle says, leaning back in his chair and pursing his lips.

"Can you think of anyone?" Theo prompts. "Location doesn't matter."

"Not off the top of my head," admits Lyle, "but I might know of an alternative."

"Which is?" I ask, drumming my fingers on the tabletop.

"I'm not the best person to explain it," Lyle replies, "but I know of a guy in Glasgow. He mentioned some kind of charm on the site I frequent - if we're lucky, he might still have it."

"Excellent," says Theo, and I feel a wave of renewed optimism. "Do you have his contact information? Do you know where we can find him?"

"Give me a few minutes," the vampire shifter replies, "and I can find out."

I DON'T REALIZE how mentally drained I am until after I leave the restaurant, feeling like I'm only just now letting out a breath that I've been holding for hours. The bubbly concierge greets me as soon as I leave the restaurant, and proceeds to escort me through the lobby into a lavish elevator leading to an equally lavish third floor. There are more guests mingling about up here, all of them shapeshifters of different ages and proficiencies. It's only as I'm approaching my room that I run into Landon, who is leaning against the balcony and watching the guests down below. "Hey," he says, turning to me. "How did it go?"

I can only look at him with a half-smile and reply, "If I told you, you wouldn't believe me."

CHAPTER 95

"I still can't believe we're actually listening to this guy," Shade snarks as we make our way down the Edinburgh street. It's been less than a day since our arrival, and by all accounts, dragging myself out of bed this morning should have taken a miracle (especially considering how far I jumped us yesterday), but once again, I barely feel the need to recuperate. Six hours of sleep and I'm already springing into action again in the morning. I barely even needed any tea to wake myself up. Needless to say, I can understand the guys' relative grouchiness, all things considered.

"*I* still can't believe you didn't rip his damn head off, Hunter," Landon jokes. "As far as assholes go, he's easily one of the highlights we've met so far."

"Are you sure we can even trust him, Boots?" Hunter asks, ignoring Landon's gibe. "Just because he *says* he's on our side now…"

"I wondered the same thing," I admit. "But it sounds like there are plenty of other rebels who can corroborate his story. And besides, Theo seems to trust him."

"Theo, Theo, Theo." Shade shakes his head sullenly. "The sooner we can get away from that self-righteous son of a bitch, the happier I'll be."

"Enemy of my enemy, remember?" Silas reminds him, casting an unreadable glance in my direction.

Silence overtakes our group, and I fall silent, unsure what to say. It's early yet, before the morning rush hour traffic really takes off, and the only sounds are the occasional chirping of a bird and the scuff of our soles on the pavement. In the heavy quiet, I tune in once more with my body—particularly, the almost overwhelming pool of power that's lighting up my stomach like the world's coldest thunderstorm. It feels as though my magic is trying to claw its way out, to wreak havoc and destruction on anyone unfortunate enough to get close to me.

Swallowing hard, I pick up the pace, speeding ahead of the rest of the guys. "Boots?" I hear Landon call after me. "You all right?"

"I'm fine," I reply quickly. "It's just chilly out here. That's all." Thankful none of them can see the blatant fear on my face, I pull my jacket more tightly around myself. It *is* chilly—more than chilly, in fact; it's fucking *cold*, especially for this time of year. A thick fog seems to have descended on downtown Edinburgh almost as quickly as we left the hotel, and it's making me shiver. The address Lyle gave me isn't really a proper address at all; according to him, the man we're supposed to meet, who only goes by the name Nathan, lives under the bridge that passes over the Water of Leith.

We make our way through the thick mist in silence, each of us mostly lost in our own thoughts, and although the sun is gradually rising in the sky, it doesn't burn off the fog like I would expect. In fact, the farther north we go, the thicker it seems to get. It gets to the point where I can barely see in front of my face, goosebumps sprouting on my arms. The feeling of a hand on my wrist makes me yelp, but my hand goes to my chest when I realize it's just Shade, who has caught up to me in the mist. "Sorry," he says, his hand slipping into mine, "didn't mean to scare you."

"It's okay," I reply. Shade's hand creeps up to gently chafe my upper arm. The motion helps warm me up; sensing this, he pulls his body flush against his side. "Is everyone staying close?"

"Barely," Landon gripes from somewhere behind me. "I lived in Scotland my whole life, and I've never seen weather quite like this."

"So am I going to be the one to say it, then?" Hunter's voice comes through the fog to my left.

"Magic, no doubt," says Silas. "I'll take that as a sign we're heading in the right direction."

"*Are* we, though?" asks Shade. "We could be going straight off a cliff and I wouldn't be able to tell."

"Boots," says Landon, "you wouldn't happen to have any light spells in that head of yours, would you?"

"Nothing I trust myself to cast," I admit. Knowing what's been happening lately, I might very well blind someone in the process. "Silas...?"

"On it," the dragon shifter affirms. Flickering embers rise in his throat, illuminating his tall figure with a flickering glow reminiscent of candlelight. It's not enough to burn the fog away, which is probably a good thing - starting a fire in public isn't exactly on my agenda for the day - but it's enough to at least get a better view of where we are. Turns out, we have indeed strayed from our path, at some point getting turned around completely. "Look," Landon says, pointing down in the glow of Silas' flames. "Let's follow the river."

Not needing to be told twice, the five of us work our way down the riverbank, becoming aware of the distant sounds of shouting and honking car horns. Clearly, this isn't a normal weather phenomenon —an omen if I've ever seen one—and it seems to have already caused a couple of traffic accidents. The strange thing is that the sounds around us seem muffled, like someone draped a blanket over the five of us. Whatever this is, it was clearly meant to keep intruders out, particularly intruders of the shifter disposition.

After what feels like an eternity, we're finally able to make out the form of the high metal bridge rising out of the mist. It's imposing in its own right, and the fact that I can't see what's beneath it only adds to its eeriness. "Nice digs," Landon quips. "It almost reminds me of —" But his voice is immediately cut off as something snatches him out of the mist, knocking the breath from his lungs.

"Landon!" I cry, pulling away from Shade and staring frantically into the mist.

The sound of a mighty roar pierces the silence, followed by a grunt in pain from the siren shifter. A dragon.

I roll my shoulders back. "Millie, wait—" begins Hunter, but I ignore him, whipping my dragon wings out and spouting a pillar of flame into the air. That lights up the world around me, giving me a view of the all-too-familiar dragon who is now shaking Landon in his jaw's.

I may not be great with faces, but I recognize Silas' father when I see him—and so, apparently, does Silas, who intensifies his own fire with a roar of dismay. I swoop in to rescue Landon, descending on the other dragon's back with enough force to make his mouth drop open. Landon tumbles downward, shifting into his siren form just in time to plunge gracefully into the water. The element of surprise is only going to get me so far, however, and Silas' father flings me off his back with one easy whip of his tail. Thinking fast, I use a blast of tele-kinetic magic to cushion my impact with the ground. "Boots," Silas yells. "You okay?"

"Don't worry about me," I call back.

"Millie." The pleading in his voice is enough to give me pause. "Don't hurt him."

A moment passes, and I nod. "I won't, Silas."

Shade has already leapt down the bank in his wolf form to help Landon out of the water, although to my relief, the siren shifter is more or less unscathed. Hunter, meanwhile, is standing in front of Silas to shield our light source from an unexpected blow. It's up to me.

Flinging my arms out in front of me, I shift immediately into my witch form. Force fields are still a relatively new concept to me, but I know enough to do what I need to do. Summoning a fresh wave of energy, I conjure a spherical force field around Silas' father and use it to carry him up and over our heads. I then launch it as far away from where we are as I can, not letting the barrier drop until I'm confident that the senior Aconyte has safely reached the ground. "That should keep him busy for a while," I say, just as Landon and Shade reunite with us. Hurrying up to the siren shifter, I throw my arms around him. "You okay, Landon?"

"As good as I'll ever be," he replies, before turning to Silas, who is still staring in the direction I sent this father. "I'm more worried about you."

"I don't know if I'll ever get used to it," Silas says flatly, before shaking himself. "Thank you, Boots. That was a close one."

"That son of a bitch Lyle set us up," Shade growls, his wolf eyes flashing. "This Nathan guy is working for Hawthorne, guaranteed."

"Working for *who?*" comes a voice from in front of us. Just like that, the mist begins to clear, revealing a stout, bearded man wearing, of all things, a *fanny pack.* "Bold of you to assume I'd do anything for that bastard. Whatever problems you've brought here, that's on you. You'd think the fog would be enough of a deterrent, but some people just don't know when enough is enough."

"You must be Nathan, I take it," says Hunter, crossing his arms.

The man, Nathan, sweeps into a bow. "In the flesh and at your service... depending on what the service is." His eyes land on me. "And who is this lovely specimen?"

I honestly can't tell if he's pulling my leg, so I ignore the question completely. "Lyle Morgan told us you'd be able to help us."

"Lyle Morgan?" Nathan scoffs. "Give me a break. Kid's slimier than algae."

"Maybe," acknowledges Silas, "but he said you might have a charm we need."

Nathan crosses his arms. "Depends on the charm."

"Shifters are being brainwashed," I say, not wanting to beat around the bush. "Our best guess is that a witch shifter is responsible. We need some way of tracking them down."

A slow smile creeps onto Nathan's face. "Interesting," he says, nodding. "I think I know what you need." Without any ceremony, he begins to rummage in his fanny pack before withdrawing what looks like an intricate wire medallion hanging from a cord. "I lifted this from a coven in France," he says, sounding proud. "This'll lead you to the caster of any enchantment you can think of. Trackers everywhere would kill for it. There is a catch, though," he adds somberly. "The person wearing it needs to be under the same enchantment."

"So..." I clear my throat. "We would have to put this on someone already being mind-controlled."

"Bingo." I reach for the amulet, but Nathan snatches it away. "I have a lot of buyers asking about this," he tells me. "You want it, we're going to have to talk numbers."

"Let's just take it from him," snaps Shade. "He's a human. It'll be easy."

He advances on Nathan, who takes a step back and holds out his arm. "I wouldn't do that if I were you, wolf boy," he advises. "You wouldn't believe some of the charms I have on me. You'll be dead before you hit the ground."

"It's fine," Hunter says, stepping forward. "Name your price." His wallet is already out, a wad of bills in his hand.

"*That's* more like it," Nathan crows. "Let's say an even thousand and we'll call it good."

Hunter rolls his eyes, but concedes. "Fine." He forks over the requisite amount of money, making Landon raise his eyebrows, before extending his hand. "The amulet."

But a wicked glimmer is already flickering in Nathan's eyes, making his heart sink. "You really are a bunch of pushovers, aren't you?" he says, grinning.

I see him reaching back into his pack and I cry out, but not even my new reflexes are enough to prevent the subsequent explosion.

CHAPTER 96

At first I'm not sure what's happened, which, added to the fact that the world seems to have fallen into slow motion, makes for a few panic-inducing seconds. The explosion is relatively small, like a burst of fire from an unattended tank of gasoline, but we're already confined by the bridge above us and the water below us. The heat wave strikes me painfully in the chest, scorching my face and bringing with it the smell of singed hair, but the force of it is what sends me stumbling back, careening into Shade in the process. The wolf shifter lets out a startled cry as he tumbles to the ground, shifting into his form as he goes, and that's all I get a glimpse of before the fog is back in full force, like a tarp hasn't just been thrown over my face.

"Shit!" I hear Landon say. And a steadying hand touches the small of my back. "Everyone okay?"

"The amulet," Silas yells, and a flash of fire and the flapping of wings next to me alerts me to his presence, speeding past with enough force to ruffle my tangled chestnut hair.

"Shade," I cry, throwing my hands out in front of me, "Hunter-"

"He's getting away!" Shade exclaims, charging past me in a blur of fur as his superior sense of smell guides him through Nathan's obfuscation.

Thinking fast, I shift into my vampire form, using my now superior speed to keep up with Shade's enhanced agility as he bolts through the mist. It's thicker than butter, but in this form I can sense every vibration of the air and water vapor around me, giving me a handy idea of which direction the wolf shifter is going.

I can smell human blood, too, and the source is moving rapidly away from us. *He* was *trying to screw us over,* I think as I continue my mad dash, *just not in the way we thought.* This prompts a fresh flood of anger and frustration, which propels me forward with a newfound enthusiasm. Hunter is somewhere to my right, keeping up with me, and a splash below tells me Landon has jumped into the river where he'll benefit most from his impressive swimming ability.

A column of flame briefly descends on us from above—Silas' doing, no doubt—and illuminates the space: we're headed for the green patch the river passes through, and I'm able to briefly make out the form of Nathan, running at a speed that should be impossible for a normal human. Although he's only barely outpacing us, it's clear that whatever charm or enchanted artifact he's using isn't something to be sneezed at. Even as the mist breaks for a moment, he turns around and throws something into the air—it looks like a stone, similar to the one used on us in the Boston Academy dorm. As soon as it makes impact with the ground, a pulsing wave of magical energy expands around him. I'm barely out of range, and can feel the force of the spell against my face, but Shade, just in front of me, isn't as lucky. He freezes in place, stalk-still, like a statue of a wolf in motion.

"Shade!" I yell, immediately dropping my pursuit of the items dealer to attend to my boyfriend. Thinking fast, I shift into my witch form, surprising myself again with just how *easily* I'm able to do so, and place my hands on his stiff fur. I remember learning about spells like this at the Academy, but I never learned how to undo them—one of the downsides to finding out your college is actually an authoritarian regime .

Hunter immediately comes to a stop next to me. "Boots—"

"Go!" I yell. "Stay after him! Silas will need your help!"

Hunter pauses, looking at me reluctantly for a moment before nodding once and taking off into the mist. Alone again, the sounds of the chase receding in front of me, I close my eyes, wrecking my brain for something to undo Shade's paralysis, but nothing comes to me. I'm barely able to stave off the panic long enough to allow my magic to the forefront, and do the only thing I can think of, something Shade himself taught me to do a long time ago. Taking a deep breath, I concentrate on my magic and visualize him moving again before sending a controlled wave of energy into his stiff body.

For a moment, it seems like nothing will happen, but then the wolf shifter springs back to life suddenly, his muscles vibrating with unreleased tension. He turns and stares at me with his golden eyes. "You didn't need to do that," he tells me.

I stare right back at him. "Yes, I did," I state. Shade looks at me with the closest thing to a smile that a wolf can manage before resuming his hunt, seemingly unfazed by his momentary crippling. Falling in beside him once more, I shift into my siren form, which slows me considerably, but I'm starting to think this will only end one way.

The fog thins as we give chase, and as we reach the edge of the enchantment's area of effect, I can make out the forms of Silas and Nathan in an empty clearing. They're staring each other down from opposite sides of the field, apparently at an impasse, with Hunter watching them. Silas' enormous dragon form dwarfs the squat man, but Nathan looks surprisingly confident as he glares defiantly up at him. I make a move to help, but the vampire shifter seizes my hand in an iron grip. "Wait!" he hisses.

"What-" I begin, but then Shade, seemingly noticing the problem, points at Nathan with his snout. He has the amulet in one hand, and in his other is what looks like a small wooden box.

"Easy, now," the human says, casting a nervous glance our way. "One more step and your charm is gone."

"He's bluffing," Silas growls, but I can see the uncertainty in his jewel-like eyes.

"Want to find out?" Nathan demands, his smirk only growing wider. "The second I put it in this box, it's over. Deactivated. Just a useless piece of wire on a string." Turning to me, he laughs a disgusting little laugh. "You know, for beings with powers we mortals could only dream of," he says, "you sure are willing to put your trust in us lowly humans."

"We paid for it," Hunter snarls. "You cheated us."

"I think we can consider this a learning experience, no?" Nathan taunts. "Always get your deals in writing. Now, if you'll excuse me, I'll be taking my leave. Give Lyle my regards. Or not." He winks at me.

"Don't move," I command, my siren song coming more clearly and musically than it ever has before. "Stay right there, Nathan."

I can see the dawning realization on the man's face, followed by a combination of abject terror and frustration. Slowly, I make my way towards him, my scales glistening in the now bright sunshine. I can see him struggling against my commands, but it's no use: I have him completely ensnared. "Hand it over, Nathan," I instruct him, my voice sounding musical to my own ears, "and we'll let you go."

To my astonishment, Nathan smiles in return. "Poor choice of words, Missy," he says. Before I can stop him, he turns around and hurls the amulet over his shoulder. I see it fly through the air and land directly in the river where it's immediately swept up by the current.

"No!" yells Silas, but I'm two steps ahead of him.

Not bothering to maintain my sway over Nathan, I swan dive straight into the river where a flash of familiar green scales alerts me to Landon's presence. I drop under the water, adjusting quickly to the feeling of using my gills, and yell to the other shifter underwater. "He chucked the amulet!"

"On it," Landon replies, and the two of us speed through the water with the speed and precision of a pair of mermaids or swordfish. My vision is completely clear, even in the muddy river; in fact, it's even sharper down here than it is normally. Together, we fly with the current in the direction the charm went, keeping our aquatic eyes peeled for any signs of gleaming metal.

I spot something shimmering against the riverbed and dive for it, but when I examine it, I see to my dismay that it's a rusted gold bracelet, probably lost in the river years ago. Letting out a cry of rage, I toss it to the side as I realize just how many discarded metal items litter the riverbed. We might as well be looking for a needle in a haystack. My shoulders slump, but the feeling of Landon's hand on my shoulder gives me pause. I turn to him and see the medallion dangling from his fingers. "Problem solved," he says.

Overjoyed, I throw my arms around him and pull him into a kiss under the water. Landon freezes in surprise, before embracing me back, his hands sliding into my hair as relief courses through both of us. When we finally break apart, the grinning shifter surfaces, and I follow suit. Together we make our way onto the riverbank: we've traveled a long way downstream, and I can just barely make out the figures of Hunter, Silas, and Shade rushing to meet us, all back in their human forms.

I stumble onto dry land, shifting back as I go, with Landon's arm wrapped tightly around my waist.

"Tell me you have it," Hunter says, panting from the exertion of the chase.

Grinning, Landon brandishes the amulet. "Never underestimate the power of underwater vision," he proclaims.

Silas laughs, relieved, and Shade runs his hand through his hair, his shoulders finally relaxing. Hunter claps Landon heartily on the back, and I'm barely back on the pathway when Shade presses his lips to my neck. "Thank you," he murmurs against my skin before pulling away.

No longer insulated by my aquatic form, I begin to shiver from the adrenaline and the frigid water. Hunter wraps his arms around my body, casting a wary glance down at me. "You all right, Millie?" he asks.

I nod. "Now let's get back inside somewhere. I'm covered in river water."

As MUCH AS Landon and I need a shower, our first order of business is to bring the amulet to Theo. He's not in the restaurant today; rather, he's seated regally on one of the plush couches facing the grand fireplace on the ground floor. He turns to us at the sound of our approach, and his eyes light up when they land on me... only to grow worried. "What happened to you, Millie?" he demands, his unwavering voice belying his concern.

"We went for a little swim," Landon replies. "About par for the course, I'd say. But we got the amulet." Reaching into my soaked pocket, I withdraw the shimmering charm, which seems to pulsate with power as I extend my hand to Theo.

A perplexed look crosses the hybrid leader's face, but then he shakes his head. Reaching out, he takes the charm from me, but his hand freezes for the barest of moments when his skin brushes against mine. For a split second, his composure seems shaken, but he recovers admirably and clears his throat. "Excellent," he says. "Tonight, we can discuss how to best implement the charm. For now, though..." The subtlest of smiles appears on his face. "I suggest the five of you go take a rest. It looks like you've had a long morning."

CHAPTER 97

To say that I'm tired wouldn't be a hundred percent accurate; by all accounts, I *should* be, and I think, on some level, I am, but it's not in a physical way. On the contrary, my body feels almost startlingly okay after this morning's events, a sensation that is as off-putting as it is comforting. I'm under no illusions about my own mortality. I can still get hurt, I'm sure, or even killed, but every physical symptom is more along the lines of "having taken a long walk" than "took part in a high-speed chase that also landed me in the freezing waters of a Scottish river." What, then, will it take to warn me when I'm overdoing it? It's as if that mental barrier has been brought down, and I'm now able to tap into reserves of strength the likes of which were never accessible to me before.

No, what I'm feeling now is more of a deep, profound mental exhaustion that has nothing to do with the fight or our pursuit of Nathan. Part of me can't help but wonder if this is how soldiers or international spies feel when they've put all of themselves into a fight to protect someone else, someone far away. I'm feeling burned out in the worst way, like I've been fighting this battle for decades, rather than months.

I feel *old*, and that scares me more than any surge in power levels possibly could.

It must show on my face, too, because as soon as we reach the floor for our landing, Hunter says, "You look run-down, Boots."

"I am," I admit after a moment of hemming and hawing. "I don't know if I over-exerted myself or..." But my voice trails off as I see I'm not the only one: Hunter's pale skin makes the dark circles under his eyes prominent, while Shade still seems to be shaking off the residual effects of the paralysis charm. Silas, in spite of our victory, is looking melancholy, and with good reason: we haven't even addressed the fact that his father made another attempt on our lives, seemingly without connection to Nathan. That means one of two things: either he's been following us on orders of one of the higher-up humans, or his consuming hatred of his own son has driven him here on its own. Frankly, I don't know which is worse.

Landon is the only one who doesn't seem at all fazed by what happened, but that doesn't stop him from turning a concerned gaze on me when he hears Hunter's remark. "It's not the new powers, is it?"

"I don't think so," I reply honestly. "I think, after everything we've been through, I'm just ready to breathe again. Like, without worrying Academy agents are going to storm the building or something."

"You and me both, Boots," Shade says, rubbing a hand on the back of his stiff neck. "I'm going to go lie down. That charm did a real number on me—I think it's given me a migraine."

"I'm sorry—" I begin, but Shade silences me with a kiss on the top of my head.

"Don't be," he says as he pulls away. "If it weren't for you, I would still be frozen in that damned field." Turning to go, he raises his hand to us. "See you guys at our next meeting with you-know-who." I don't fail to notice his eyes roll as he talks about Theo.

"Silas?" Landon asks, turning to the dragon shifter. "I don't know if I told you guys, but my suite has a hot tub."

My eyes go wide. "You're kidding." Landon gives me a bold smile, and I shake my head in disbelief. "No fair."

"Why do you think I brought it up?" Landon says, reaching out to run a hand through my wet hair. "You look like you could stand to warm up."

"I think I'll pass, actually," Silas says. "I've... got a lot on my mind."

"Understandable," says Hunter. "If you need anything, let us know."

"I will," the dragon shifter replies, before turning to me. "Thank you again, Boots," he says, the uncertainty in his eyes giving way to affection. "I mean it."

"I wasn't about to hurt your father," I reply quietly. Silas takes a step closer to me, touches my cheek for a moment, and then pulls away before wordlessly turning and heading around the corner to his room.

Landon, Hunter, and I are left to size one another up. "I hope that offer is good for all of us," the vampire shifter says, crossing his arms, "because I'm completely wrung out."

"Atta boy," jokes the siren shifter. "Boots?"

For a moment I'm on the verge of declining, but all propriety seems to have gone out the window. "Why not?" I ask, throwing my arms out to my sides.

"Yes!" Landon exclaims. "Now all we need is some champagne, and we can make this a party."

"I hear 'party' from you, Landon..." Hunter says.

The siren shifter elbows him. "Don't make me rescind the offer."

Hunter grins, and their lighthearted bickering lifts my spirits long enough for me to grab a change of clothes from my suite before following them to Landon's room. As soon as the lights are on I suck in a breath: the room was either meant for royalty or newlyweds—I'm not totally sure which—and it's dominated by a large, marble jacuzzi in the middle of the floor. I raise my eyebrows at Landon, who shoots me a grin—all the permission I need. For lack of a bathing suit, I strip down to my bra and underwear and clamber into the hot tub, not even bothering with a shower beforehand. Almost immediately I begin to relax as I slide into the steaming water, and a sound to my right tells me the others have followed my lead.

Hunter sighs in contentment as he gets in beside me, sliding his arm around my shoulders and leaning back against the wall. "You've been holding out on us, Landon," he mutters.

"Yeah, yeah, yeah." The siren shifter wraps his arm around my waist from the other side. "You can send me a gift basket or something."

AFTER NEARLY NODDING off in the warm water, I reluctantly drag myself out to take a real shower and rid myself of the remains of my dip in the river. Landon does the same, leaving Hunter to continue to bask in the hot tub. It's only after I'm clean, changed into dry clothes, and sitting on the couch, that I'm feeling better than I have all day.

"You had us worried back there, Boots," Landon informs me, coming to stand behind me. "This is really taking it out of you, isn't it?"

"I'm fine," I say. It's almost a reflex at this point.

"Boots." Landon tips my chin up so he can look at me, his hands dropping to my shoulders. "You don't have to pretend with me. With any of us."

"I..." My throat feels thick. "Thank you. I'm sorry. I forget sometimes."

"Shh, it's okay," the siren shifter says, his hand running through the hair at the base of my neck. "You can relax now." And slowly he begins to rub my shoulders, massaging away tension I didn't even know I was carrying.

"Mm..." I hum. "Shouldn't be letting my guard down."

"I'd say you've earned it," Hunter says from across the room, where he's pulling his shirt back over his head.

"Damn right, she has," Landon agrees, his hands caressing my neck and shoulders in slow, soothing movements that send butterflies flying through my stomach. I close my eyes, and when the siren shifter leans down to kiss me, I reciprocate with passion.

It's only when I open my eyes and see Hunter watching us pointedly from the other side of the room that I blush. This polyamory thing is new to all of us, something that's easy to forget when I'm being kissed by a gorgeous shifter. "Sorry," I hasten to say. "It's probably a little awkward for you to watch this."

Hunter shares a look with Landon, the corner of his mouth twitching into a smirk that, while out of place on the vampire shifter, he wears pretty damn well. "Who said anything about watching?" he asks, and crosses the room to where we are.

By now, the adrenaline in my stomach is giving way to excitement of the best kind, and I can feel my heart hammering in my chest as Hunter drops to his knees in front of me, pulling me in for a kiss of his own while Landon's hands continue to explore my upper body. My head is practically spinning by the time he breaks the kiss, leaving me searching for more, and the vampire shifter gives a low chuckle before sliding down my body, undoing the button of my jeans as he goes. A little maneuvering is all it takes before he has my bottoms off, drinking in the sight of my naked body like a starving man.

Landon's mouth claims mine again just as Hunter dips his head between my legs, his tongue sweeping over my pussy cautiously at first. The wave of pleasure the single, tentative action sends through my abdomen is too much to ignore, and I can feel myself getting almost shamefully wet as he focuses all his attention on my clit. Landon moves his lips to my neck, watching Hunter's actions intently as he sweeps my hair to the side, his hands dropping to my breasts, still covered by my shirt. I can feel his thumbs sweep over my hard nipples, toying with them almost lazily as the vampire shifter continues to wring pathetic noises out of me.

The feeling of Landon pinching my nipple gently makes me gasp, my legs snapping together almost involuntarily, and Hunter hums in contentment against my thigh as he gently pushes them back apart. My head falls back against the sofa as the two shifters continue their ministrations, neither focused on his own pleasure; I'm their complete center of attention.

Soon I'm writhing on the couch between the two of them, Landon's hands now expertly toying with my breasts as he covers my face, neck, and chest with kisses and soft bites. There will be marks there tomorrow, I'm sure, but right now, I couldn't care less. My clit is practically singing by now, and when I look down and see that Hunter's eyes have gone red with vampirism, I'm not surprised; no wonder he's so attuned to the subtle jerks and spasms of my lower body. His now crimson eyes bore into mine as he slides first one, and then two fingers inside me, stroking me in a maddeningly slow rhythm. They're taking their time with me, drawing my pleasure out as much as possible, but it's not long before I go careening over the edge, thanks to the smallest quirk of Hunter's fingers. I gasp as my orgasm overtakes me, but Landon covers my mouth with his, devouring the sound as I come undone under their combined touches.

That isn't the end of it, though. Hunter, smirking against my inner thigh, continues the movements of his tongue on my clit, albeit more slowly this time, and I've hardly recovered from my first when a second, equally intense orgasm comes creeping up on me.

"You're so beautiful," Landon says, pressing his mouth to my collarbone.

Hunter hums in agreement against my clit, and that's all it takes to make me come a second time. At last they have mercy on me, their hands caressing my bare flesh as I tremble from the aftershocks, the world around me a haze of relaxation and pleasure.

At last, the vampire shifter gets up and sits down next to me on the couch. "Not bad, Ash," Landon pronounces.

"Not *bad*? I made her come twice!"

"I guess we'll just have to find some time to break that record," Landon says, winking at me as he slides in on my other side.

"Don't tell me you guys planned this," I groan.

Landon snorts. "Hardly. You just looked like you needed it."

"I did," I admit after a moment. "I really did. Thank you guys. Seriously." Swallowing hard, I look at each of them in turn and say, "I love you."

"We love you too, Millie," Hunter says.

"Always," echoes Landon.

CHAPTER 98

I wake up the next morning nestled between Landon's body and Hunter's, their radiating warmth striking a sharp contrast to the cool hotel room. I'm tired in the best possible way, still basking in the relative calm of the moment before the reality of our situation sinks in.

"Morning, Boots," Hunter mumbles against my back when he feels me stir.

"Damn it, Ash, why'd you have to break the silence?" Landon griped. "If we had all just kept pretending to be asleep..."

"Sorry, Landon," I say, leaning forward to kiss him on the nose, "but no can do. God only knows how we're going to have to risk our lives today."

"Happens at least once a week," Landon agrees, grunting as he sits up. "I look forward to the day we can just go back to having a normal relationship. You know, without being in constant fear of getting brainwashed."

"One of those normal, every day, four-guys-one-girl polyamorous relationships, you mean?" I joke.

"Technicalities, technicalities," says Landon, waving me off. "Come on, let's beat feet downstairs. If we're lucky, they'll still be serving breakfast."

. . .

THEY WERE INDEED STILL SERVING breakfast, and the three of us now find ourselves sitting in the restaurant, a giant platter of gourmet pastries between us. We're at a huge table that stands in the middle of the room, no doubt at Theo's request. I'm still a little nervous about our next step, and a nagging thought has taken hold in the back of my mind, no matter how much I try to push it away: if the amulet requires a brainwashed shifter in order to work...

"There they are!" exclaims a familiar voice from behind us, which pulls me abruptly out of my thoughts. Turning around in my seat, my face lights up when I seek who spoke: Hazel, my first friend at the Academy. She's standing in the doorway of the restaurant, looking even more immaculate than usual, but she rushes over to us the moment she makes eye contact with me. "I heard you were here, but I figured you'd still be recuperating," she says as she sweeps me into a hug.

"Funny how we're always able to find each other when we get separated," I remark as I reciprocate her embrace. The bubbly siren shifter is among the most important people in my life, next to the guys, and I don't think it would be exaggerating to say I view her as a sister at this point. Knowing she's safe is a much-needed boost, and I can feel a fresh boost of optimism go through me.

"We're just telepathically connected," Hazel quips. "No big deal. Suck it, Landon."

"What'd I do?" Landon retorts, sounding mock-offended.

"Just don't go getting a big head now that you guys are official," she says, turning to Hunter. "That goes for you too, Hunter. Remember who introduced you." Scooting into the chair next to me, she adds, "Speaking of which, where are the others?"

"Right here," comes Shade's voice. I turn to see him and Silas making their way over. We make room at the table as Hazel embraces the newcomers.

"What about Ruby and Xander?" Silas asks.

"She's still recovering from the attack," Hazel replies. "As for

Xander, I have no clue, but I'm sure he's around here somewhere."

"Ms. Van Buren." Theo, flanked by two of his bodyguards, arrives and sits at the head of the enormous table. As soon as he arrives, it's like the energy in the room undergoes a dramatic shift: any pretenses of this being a fun, friendly hotel breakfast go out the window, replaced by the responsibility of a real, honest-to-God strategy meeting. And just like that, whatever fleeting positivity I felt when I woke up crumbles.

"Theo," Hazel says, nodding her head respectfully at the fair-skinned man.

"I take it the rest of you will be joining us?" Theo says, glancing around at the guys. His expression is stoic, but it carries the vaguest hint of annoyance... except when he turns his gaze on me.

"They will," I say, feeling as if I need to speak on behalf of the others. Out of the corner of my eye, I can see Shade's hands clenched into fists on the table.

Theo clears his throat, his eyes lingering on me for just a second. "I suppose that's fair, considering they will be involved," he says

"Damn right we will," says Shade.

"So this amulet," Silas says, changing the subject, "it needs to be given to an enchanted shifter in order to lead to the shifter who cast the enchantment. Right?"

"Right," says Hunter. "So we have to find someone we know is working for Hawthorne."

"Easier said than done," mutters Shade.

"Hardly," Theo responds breezily, his eyes flashing for just a moment as he looks at the wolf-shifter. "We happen to have recently acquired the location of one of Hawthorne's older research facilities. One with which Millie is well-acquainted."

I blanch. "You're not..."

Theo nods somberly. "If I'm not mistaken, you were taken there recently. When your powers were drained."

I squeeze my eyes shut for a moment, the painful memories flooding back to me. I had thought I was going to die. And in a way, I suppose, part of me *did*.

I'm back now, I remind myself, straightening up in my chair. *I'm stronger than ever. And I'm going to make him pay.*

"The base is still under Hawthorne's control," Theo goes on.

"Sounds like there will be plenty of opportunities to find an indoctrinated shifter," says Hunter.

"Indeed," says Theo.

"We can't just waltz in there and ask one of them to wear the damn amulet," Shade protests. "That place will be swarming with agents. We might not even make it in the door." He glances at me, and I can see the distress and protectiveness in his silver eyes.

"Not if you go in with both guns blazing, that's true," Theo replies, "which is why you'll be going in pretending to be indoctrinated yourselves."

Landon gapes at him. "You've got to be kidding me."

Theo levels his cool gaze on the siren shifter. "I assure you, I'm not."

"It's... not a bad idea," Silas admits. "We know we're high priority targets for Hawthorne. He'll want us alive, if only so he can have the satisfaction of knowing he brainwashed the people who have been causing him problems."

"You'll have to be convincing," Theo reminds us, glancing once more at Shade. "We still have no idea how this enchantment works. If they suspect anything, there's no knowing what they'll do to you."

Hunter snorts. "Sounds trivial."

"On that note," Theo says, getting to his feet, "I wonder if I might borrow Ms. Brix for a moment?"

Shade stiffens, and the others look at one another uneasily, but I nod and get to my feet. "Be right back," I say, feeling the wolf shifter's eyes on my back as I follow Theo into the next room. "Was there something you wanted to talk about?" I ask, swallowing hard.

"Yes." Putting his hands behind his back, Theo turns to me, his expression unreadable. "I think it would be best if you stayed here for this operation."

My eyes go wide. "What? Why?"

"This would be a dangerous task for anyone," Theo replies. "Considering all you've done already, all you've endured—"

"Theo, I can't send the guys in there alone," I protest. "You've seen me in action. You know I can take care of myself. And I have my powers back now."

Theo stares imposingly down at me. "I don't want you to get hurt, Millie."

I look back at him in disbelief. "But you would let *them* get hurt for me?" Theo's brow furrows, but he looks away, and it's all the confirmation I need. "I'm sorry, Theo," I tell him, taking a step back, "but I'm not letting them do this alone."

"Millie..." The rebel leader's voice is soft enough that it almost gives me pause, but I resist, turning on my heel and heading for my room. I'm afraid of what I might do if I look back.

I'M SITTING on the edge of my bed, picking at my fingernails and mulling over the morning's discussion, when the door to my room flies open. I immediately stand up, preparing for a fight, and barely have time to relax before Shade is striding across the room to me, slamming the door shut as he goes. "What are you—" I begin, but he interrupts me by pressing his mouth to mine.

"I couldn't just sit there," Shade murmurs when we finally break apart, his hands already on my shirt. "Not with the way that bastard was looking at you. Practically undressing you with his eyes, the fucking—" But he doesn't bother to finish, his lips connecting with mine once more as he pushes me back onto the bed, his hands fumbling deftly with my top.

"Shade," I manage, threading my hands through his sandy hair. "I want *you*."

The wolf shifter pulls back, drinking me in with his eyes as he tosses my shirt to the side and shoves his hand into my jeans. I can feel myself growing wet almost immediately and gasp with pleasure when he strokes me open with his finger.

I struggle out of my bra, all other plans and responsibilities rushing out of my mind in an instant. All that matters right now is *him,* his body over mine, the desire with which he's looking at me. Like I'm the only person in the entire universe. My bra drops to the floor, my fingers digging into his muscular back as he arches his finger inside me.

"Say that again," Shade mutters, lowering his mouth to my breast.

"Shade, I want you," I repeat, wriggling desperately beneath him to get him to touch me more. "I need you. Not Theo, *you.*" The wolf shifter sucks in a breath, his eyes flashing with a heady mixture of possessiveness, protectiveness, and passion that lights a fire in the pit of my stomach. Then his lips close around my nipple, and my thoughts become a jumbled mess. I can feel my orgasm building already, the feverishness and intensity of the situation only exciting me more.

WITH A GROWL OF PASSION, Shade rolls me onto my stomach, one hand dropping to my lower back while the other fumbles with his belt. My heart is fluttering in my chest, my whole body vibrating with pleasure, and when he withdraws his hand so he can push into me from behind, I can't help but moan. He sets a quick pace, finally able to release the stress of our predicament, of our feelings, and of the danger we're all putting ourselves in. He rubs my clit with surprising gentleness as he moves, peppering my back and shoulders with kisses even as the pleasure threatens to consume me. His hands are in my hair, caressing my skin, and between my legs, and before long I've been reduced to a melted puddle by his touch.

I come a moment later, gasping for breath as Shade follows suit. For a moment, neither of us move, the wolf shifter stroking my hair gently before helping me up, his arms encircling me as he kisses me tenderly. "Are you all right?" I ask as I finally catch my breath.

"Better now," Shade says, still breathing hard as he drops his face to my shoulder. "You?"

"Same," I say. "Do you want to stay in here with me for a bit?"

I can feel him smirk against my skin. "I thought you would never ask."

CHAPTER 99

T
he first thing I become aware of is the crashing of waves against far away ocean cliffs. Salt water sprays up from the sea below me, stinging my eyes and leaving a strong smell in the air. The sun is beaming down from a cloudless sky, reflecting off the steadily breaking waves with such intensity that I nearly have to squint as I look around. I crane my neck as I turn, not sure how I got here but hardly caring; it's such a beautiful day, and the world I find myself in is so relaxing, that it almost doesn't matter. There's something familiar about this place, like a long-forgotten memory from childhood that's been dragged back up to the surface after many years of being lost. I can't place it for the life of me, though.

I'm standing alone, high on the cliffs that jut out over the churning water below me. Blue waves stretch out as far as the eye can see, and I'm the only one here. There's something peaceful about it, almost comforting: the only sounds are the sounds of the ocean and the crunching of the dirt beneath my shoes.

Taking in a breath of the salty island air, I make my way down along the shoreline, the fresh breeze whipping my hair and carrying me easily along a well-worn dirt path. To my right is a mighty forest, so dense that I can barely see past the first row of trees, and again, there's something familiar about it, but I can't for the life of me place what it is. No matter; it's all in good fun, and besides, I could use a break from the constant toil of my real world... Whatever my real world is. I'm having a hard time remembering. The sunlit path leads gradually downhill, illuminated brilliantly by the glaring sunlight. It's peaceful here, although there isn't a person for miles around.

As a matter of fact, it's only now dawning on me how alone I am.

I feel the first stirrings of unease; that familiar feeling is only getting stronger as I go, but it's bringing with it a dull sense of fear that sits in the pit of my stomach like a demon. Swallowing hard, I try to push it away, but to no avail. The feeling of wrongness is unshakable, like a flash of intuition from my lizard brain that has my heart beating more and more rapidly in my chest. I need to stop, to take a breather, to try to get my head on straight again, but to my growing horror, I realize that I can't seem to stop moving. It's like my legs are working of their own accord, carrying me somewhere I don't want to go in spite of my best efforts. Panic rises in my throat, but I can't do anything to stop it; I'm unable to even cry out.

It's only as I'm making my way around a switchback leading down to the waterline that it dawns on me what feels so eerie about this place. There are no sounds at all, except for the crashing waves. No birds sing in the trees, no insects chirp, no distant animals chatter and roar. There isn't a single seagull in the sky, nor is there the sound of anything human for as far as my ears can hear. It's as silent and abandoned as the grave, and I can't break that silence for all that I try.

Adrenaline is coursing through me by now, fear threatening to take hold of me. I try to shift, to fight off this strange sense of possession, but it's no use; it's as if I never got my powers back at all, that comforting pool of magic in my stomach forever out of my reach. I want to call out - where are the guys? Where are Hazel and the twins? Where's Theo? The sense of growing dread only increases with every step down the path I take, my heart hammering in my chest and goosebumps creeping up my arms. I scan the area, desperate to see someone, *anyone*, who can tell me where I am and explain what's wrong, but the island is as deserted as a ghost town.

That is, until I arrive at the beach.

In the distance, I can make out a figure standing by the water, and I'm flooded with relief. Finally, I find my voice. "Hey!" I call. The figure doesn't turn around, so I try again. "Hey, hello! Can you hear me?"

But the person by the water doesn't even seem to notice me. I can't make out any distinguishing features, and the only thing that's clear from this distance is that they're standing stock-still, staring out across the water as if seeing something invisible to my eyes. The uneasiness has set in in full force by now, and I can feel my throat thickening as I follow the beach up to the figure of a petite woman, with short, dark hair and long, svelte limbs.

My eyes widen. "Edith?" Relaxing a little, I hurry up to her. Even if she *does* still hate me, at least she's another living being, and right now, that feels like a matter of increasing importance. "Edith, it's me, Millie Brix." When at last she's in reach, I touch her shoulder hesitantly, not wanting to startle her.

The moment my hand makes contact with her arm, Edith crumples to the ground on her back, as stiff as a board. *She's dead,* I realize, and my heart stops in my chest. Her green eyes are glassy and staring, and her flesh is rotting. I recoil in horror, stumbling backwards and falling into the sand in my haste to get away from the body. The moment I turn around, however, I'm greeted by the sight of dozens— no, hundreds—of other bodies lining the beach, all rotting, all dead, and all staring at me with those same blank, glassy eyes. It's only as I start to flee that I realize I recognize the faces: Samantha, Silas' parents, the old registrar worker, Mrs. Fairbanks. There are others, too, people whose names I don't know but whose faces I know: they're all shifters I've fought somewhere along the line, all under the sway of the humans, and all deceased.

Feeling like I'm running in slow motion, I race along the beach, but no matter how hard I run, more corpses appear around me. It's just as I'm rounding the corner that I notice four more corpses lining the shoreline, and I don't have to see them clearly to know who they are. Still, I can't stop myself from approaching them, my skin clammy and my breath coming in wheezing gasps.

The bodies of Silas, Landon, Hunter, and Shade are all lined up in a neat row, and all staring up at me. I open my mouth, but no words come out, so I do the only thing I can: I start to scream.

I sit bolt upright in bed, clutching the sheets to my chest and sucking in a choking breath. I'm shaking, gasping, my knuckles white from the strength of my grip on the sheets, terror still coursing through me, unstoppable. A strangled noise escapes me, which is followed by a wave of unbidden tears.

The feeling of strong arms encircling me almost startles me, but I'm only able to calm down when I hear Shade's familiar voice rumbling in my ear. "Boots, Boots, hey, take it easy. It was only a dream. It was only a dream..." He continues to murmur reassurances to me, stroking my hair as I lean into his embrace and desperately try to shake off the remaining images from the nightmare.

I'm not sure how long we stay like that, leaning on each other as the wolf shifter soothes me, but eventually, I'm somehow able to find my voice. "I'm sorry," I gasp, my trembling finally starting to ease up. "I don't know what... It felt so real... I thought you were—I th-thought you guys were—"

"Shh, it's okay," Shade says, pressing his lips to the top of my head. "I'm here. We're all here. We're okay."

His words are enough to calm me back down, but even as I settle back into bed, secure in the wolf shifter's arms, a horrible possibility occurs to me. What if that wasn't a dream? What if it was a premonition?

"Are you sure you're okay, Boots?" Hunter asks as we make our way down the street in search of an isolated spot to make the jump to the research facility. He and the others have been giving me concerned glances ever since I told them about the nightmare. "You look really worn out."

"I *am* really worn out," I admit, "but... thank you for your concern. I mean it." Forcing a smile, I glance around at the guys, who have been flanking me protectively since we left the hotel. "The stress is getting to me, I think."

Sure, that's one way to put it, but the truth is that there's more to it than stress. The nightmare has been eating at me all day, and I've only now identified what about it was bothering me so much: all the corpses littering the beach were people who could have—and probably were—brainwashed by Hawthorne. And all of them were people I had to fight through in order to get to where I am today. What that means for the guys is something I don't dare to even let myself consider. It's all too horrible to think about, but I'm not about to bring it up with the guys. Instead, I do what I do best: shove it to the back of my mind, compartmentalize, and ignore the possibility that, somewhere along the line, everyone I know and love has the potential to turn into my enemy.

Unless we put a stop to this.

"Are you sure you're good to teleport us?" Silas asks, brushing the back of his hand against my cheek. "Maybe it's better if we go alone."

"He's right," Landon says, his tone surprisingly somber for someone who's usually so lighthearted. It's clear that Shade didn't spare any details of my early morning breakdown, and while I appreciate their concern for me, their own assessment of the risk doesn't bode well for their chances without me going.

"You're starting to sound like Theo," I joke, hoping to lighten the mood a little. I see Shade's face darken when I mention the hybrid, but after what happened last night, he seems much more at ease with our relationship.

"We don't want to see you get hurt, Boots," Hunter tells me gently, taking my hand in both of his. "And it's obvious this is eating at you. You know we would do anything to keep you safe."

"I know," I reply, my eyes sweeping down to the ground. "That's the problem." Holding out my other hand, I nod to the others. The guys exchange an uncertain glance, but they follow my lead, forming a circle for the transport. Without another word, I close my eyes and let myself focus on that dreadful place where I almost lost everything that I am.

There's a telltale rush, a subtle shift, and then we're standing on the lush green grass of a field we narrowly escaped from not long ago. A chill runs down my spine as I look around; this is the same island from my dream, down to the very last detail. If that isn't a bad omen, I don't know what is, but it's too late to go back now.

"Remember the plan," says Shade. "We have to act enchanted, and mean it. No pulling punches, no matter what." His eyes meet mine.

"No matter what," I echo, nodding. It's showtime.

CHAPTER 100

Somehow, I make my legs move, choking back the cold, hard lump that is threatening to form in my throat. Everything about where I am feels surreal, and I have to remind myself not to present any nervousness as we make our way down the slightly sloping ground into the center of the field. The instinct to hide, to protect myself, is almost unbearable out in the open, and I can't help but wonder what kinds of enemies are watching us from the trees just beyond my line of sight. The crashing of the waves on the faraway rocks doesn't go unnoticed, and I strain to project an air of calm collectedness in spite of the terror that's threatening to overtake me.

"How are brainwashed people supposed to act, anyway?" Landon hisses out of the corner of his mouth as we make our way down the hill.

"No idea," I reply, doing my best not to let my nerves show. The last thing I need is for it to rub off on the guys and get one of them hurt. I'm not about to let that dream become reality. "Just act normal. Calm."

"Easier said than done," Shade mutters, but none of us say anything else. We're all too busy sweating bullets.

It's eerily quiet, the same way it was in my head last night, and part of me is desperate to have the suspense over with, for some hunter to jump out from the shadows and confront us, but it's dead silent. It doesn't occur to me until we're almost to the other side of the field that this facility might not even still be active, but I don't allow myself to pursue that line of thought. Theo's information is good. It has to be.

The low, concrete building looms at us from the other side of the valley, and I can feel my heart pounding harder with every step I take towards it. I'm expecting some kind of security, but there's nothing, and it's too late to turn around by the time the possibility of a trap dawns on me.

Silas quietly slips his hand into mine and gives it a squeeze. However hard this is for me, it must be ten times harder for him. Pretending to have met the same fate as his parents is a tall order, and the fact that he never even questioned doing it for me is heartrendingly romantic. I run my thumb over his palm in a silent display of reassurance just as we approach the front entrance.

And then, finally, a sound issues from the facility. The front gate slides open automatically, a low alarm announcing our presence, and it takes everything in my power not to shift and make a break for it. For a moment there's nothing but the sound of birdsong on the still air, but then I can make out the sound of footsteps echoing on the concrete walls. Pulling my hand free of Silas', I stand with my arms limp at my sides, looking as robotic as I possibly can as the newcomer emerges to greet us.

Except it's not a newcomer, I realize with a sudden intake of breath. It's so much worse. The petite woman who comes into view is none other than President Russo herself, head of the Boston Academy and confirmed crony of Hawthorne. All I can do is hope my theory about him is correct, that he didn't empower her as well. One hybrid is hard enough to deal with.

Russo stands still long enough to make me feel uneasy, her hand shielding her eyes as she stares at us in the glare of the sun. Realizing there's nothing to do now but go for it, I take a rattling breath and speak up. "We're here to submit to your disposal," I say, trying to keep all emotion out of my voice. *What was it that Silas' father said?* "We had our eyes opened."

For a dragging, horrifying second, I'm sure she's seen right through our lie, but then a smile begins to spread across Russo's face. "Is that so?" she purrs. "Is that really so?"

Hunter nods like an automaton. "We are at your service. Long live the Academy."

Not a bad touch, all things considered. It's so hammy that it would probably be absurd in any other situation, but none of us are laughing. Still looking like the cat that ate the canary, Russo leisurely closes the distance between us, crossing her arms over her chest as she sizes the five of us up. "When did it happen?" she asks, raising an eyebrow.

Damn it. Think, think, think. Casting my mind back to Edith, I swallow and reply, "Back in Oxford. After the attack on the rebel hideout." It's a shot in the dark considering we have no idea where the culprit is, and my heart damn near stops in my chest as I wait for her response.

Russo looks me up and down, taking my chin in her bony fingers and turning my head from side to side. Then she moves down the line, doing the same to each of the guys with what I can only hope is an approving look on her face. "Looks like we hit the jackpot," she says, her smile turning into a full-fledged grin. "Hawthorne will be pleased." She turns around, beckoning us to follow her with a lazy swipe of the arm. "Come along, then. We have a lot to catch you up on."

Exchanging a relieved look with the others, I follow her in; the guys forming a semicircle around me. Through the entrance we walk, the gate shutting behind us, and suddenly I'm once again trapped between the cold, concrete walls where I almost died once already. A chill runs down my spine, my arms covered in goosebumps, and I catch Landon giving me a longing look out of the corner of my eye, like it's all he can do not to fold me into his strong arms.

Steeling ourselves, we continue on.

Memories flash through my head, unbidden. Being strapped down to a table and pumped with chemicals, both magical and not. The fear of what will happen to me, the question of whether I'll ever see the guys again, the excruciating pain of being severed from my magic. It all comes flooding back, nearly strong enough to make me keel over from the trauma, and only the presence of the guys beside me can make me keep moving forward. Down the long corridor we go, the fluorescent lights casting an eerie glow over us as our footsteps echo on the stone walls. We round a corner, and suddenly there it is: the torture chamber where I was put last time, complete with the exam table and the rebuilt shelves full of alchemical ingredients. I stop dead in my tracks, unable to move forward as my eyes go wide and threaten to fill with tears. The others keep moving, and I see Hunter's blue eyes flicker nervously back in my direction as he passes me. They can't stop, and I shouldn't be stopped either, but I'm frozen in sheer terror.

Russo continues to disappear down the hallway, but I can't pry my eyes away from the laboratory. It's only when Shade, at the back of the line, passes and brushes his hand comfortingly over the small of my back that I'm able to move again, thankful that Russo didn't turn around. We follow her deeper into the bowels of the facility, and as we go, we pass room after barren room. Some of them are empty, but many aren't, and I see with dismay that the occupied ones are packed with shifters. They watch us go with dead eyes, and it's clear that they have no agency here. Whatever was done to Silas' parents was also done to them. And we're helpless to do anything but pretend not to notice.

It's only when we descend to a lower level that the space opens up, becoming a sort of bunker. The basement is well-furnished, complete with plush carpets and luxury furniture, and if it weren't for the lack of windows, I might mistake it for an actual apartment. Russo approaches a closed door and raps twice with the backs of her knuckles. There's a long moment of silence before it swings open, and I have to choke back my fear once more.

Hawthorne is standing in the doorway, close enough to touch, but this isn't the same human I remember from last time. There's something different about him, more ominous, and I see that his once-graying hair is now all black, a youthful luster to his skin that wasn't there before. His eyes seem to gleam—whether from deviousness or raw power, I can't be sure—and whatever humanity he once had is nowhere to be found. I feel Silas stiffen almost imperceptibly next to me, as do the others; the enemy is standing right in front of us. Even I have to beat back the instinct to shift and attack him. There's no guarantee that killing him will help us free the brainwashed shifters. He could easily have a contingency plan, and knowing him, he probably does.

No. Better to stay the course.

"What have we here?" he asks, looking us over with a maniacal grin.

"They say they've had their eyes opened," Russo replies simply, looking smug. "I thought it was fitting that they be brought to you. Considering the trouble they've caused, you should be the one to decide what happens to them."

"How interesting," Hawthorne croons, his expression unreadable. "Well, come in, why don't you? We won't get anywhere standing out here." He stands aside to allow us to file into what looks like his personal living space, and the ostentatiousness of it all is enough to make me sick.

When we're all inside, Hawthorne turns to me, puts his hands on my shoulders, and leans down to look me directly in the eyes. I feel like he can see straight into me with his piercing gaze, and I will myself not to blink or look away. "Millie Brix," he says. "On the right side of history, at long last."

"Yes, sir," I reply stiffly.

"Where did you say you came around?" he asks, tilting his head to one side.

"Oxford, sir," I answer. "After the attack."

"Indeed." He lets me go, turning away from me to face the roaring fire in the hearth. "I have to admit, I would have expected more from you, Ms. Brix. You've become something of a figurehead for these shifters lately, haven't you?"

I clear my throat. "A figurehead, sir?"

"Of course," he croons. "The hybrid prodigy. The rebel leader. The girl who will liberate the shifter community. Considering all you've done, I find it surprising that you were blindsided so easily."

"It happens, sir," Silas says in a robotic voice.

"And you, Mr. Aconyte," Hawthorne says, turning back around to stare down the dragon shifter. "All this time spent fighting, only to end up like your dear parents. A little disappointing, no doubt, but I suppose it's not unheard of. Coincidences, and all that." He takes a breath, squaring his shoulders. "All five of you, though? Interesting. *Very* interesting."

It's only as his eyes settle on me again that the first alarm bells begin ringing in my mind. He's looking at me like a predator, like I'm the food that he's playing with. *This was all too easy,* I realize, but it's too late.

"The only problem," Hawthorne says indulgently, pacing back over to us, "is that my asset was not in Oxford on the day of the attack. In fact, he never leaves his chambers. We bring our agents to him. Which you would know... if you had really seen the light." My heart slams in my chest, the dawning horror of our situation paralyzing me where I stand. "So, Ms. Brix," Hawthorne says, his expression conniving, "what are we going to do about this?"

CHAPTER 101

For a moment, all I can do is stand there, stunned, panicking, and wondering if I should stay the course or just throw in the towel. Deciding rapidly on the former, I manage to stammer out, "I don't know what you're talking about, Hawthorne. Sir." Even as the words come out, I can tell it's no use; Russo is closing the door to Hawthorne's quarters as we speak, just as I notice him rummaging in his pocket for a moment. Seconds later, he pulls out a small artifact, no bigger than a bottle cap. I can't tell what it is at first, but a closer look reveals it as a simple rune, much like the one used on us in Boston. Enchantment.

Closing his eyes, Hawthorne holds his hand out, and when he speaks, I realize it's not directed at me, or anyone in the room. "If you please," he says in a voice that is frighteningly calm. "I'm afraid I have to discipline some problem children." There's a pause, and he cocks his head to one side, as if listening to someone only he can hear. Just like that, the rune in his hand begins to glow with power, the light it's producing quickly becoming blinding.

Some kind of a remote enchantment? I have time to wonder. It dawns on me that he must be communicating with the spellcaster telepathically, if such a thing is even possible. *I* can't even do it after being given my powers back, and my blood runs cold at the thought of what that means for Hawthorne's own abilities. That's all I have time to consider, though, before Hawthorne is reaching out towards the first person he sees when he opens his eyes again: Hunter.

"No!" I yell. I don't think. My brain has already reverted back to fight or flight, my senses closing in on the sight of him brandishing his twisted mind control device at one of the men I love. On autopilot, I lunge to the left and knock the vampire shifter out of the way. He hasn't even had time to shift yet—none of us have. It's taken us that long just to process what's happening. Hunter goes stumbling to the side, out of the line of fire just as the rune releases a surge of energy.

I'm not that lucky. Right in the path of the power beam, I'm hopeless to do anything but take the brunt of the magic squarely in my chest. "Millie, no!" yells one of the guys, but I'm not even sure which one. My brain—no, my whole being—is already being consumed.

I've been mind controlled once before, back when we went to get help from some of Edith's contacts. That was a siren's song, and although it had felt all-encompassing in the moment, in reality, it was miniscule compared to what I'm now experiencing. A blip, really, nothing more. This is so much worse.

While the siren's enchantment made me into a marionette, a human puppet helpless to do anything but obey, the brainwashing spell is different. My body is still my own this time, but in an instant, my entire worldview has changed. The rune colors my thoughts, casting all my memories in the horrid glow of a brand new context. It's like suddenly seeing the world in monochrome, except instead of shades of black and white, it's now shades of chaos and control. My entire perception of my life and the people in it has been turned on its head. Some of the sweetest memories from my time at the Academy—making love to the guys, first learning to use my powers, finding a real home for the first time in my life—are no longer beautiful. I'm consumed by an overwhelming disgust and revulsion thinking about them, like they were just some embarrassing phase rather than my entire purpose.

I swear, I try to fight it. Even as these horrible new feelings wash over me, a small voice in my mind still yells that it's all a lie, that I need to resist, that the new worldview being forced on me isn't my own. But with every passing millisecond, that voice diminishes, like it's being pulled down a dark corridor until it's out of sight completely. Resisting it is like trying to catch air with my bare hands: impossible.

Hawthorne is looking at me with an expression of pleasant surprise on his face that quickly turns into a full grin. What once would have been frustration now becomes happiness within me. *Hawthorne is pleased,* I think, a smile spreading on my face to mirror his own. *That's good. I've screwed up so many times, I should be thankful he's given me this beautiful second chance.* "Isn't this an interesting turn of events?" he asks.

My smile broadens. "I can't believe it," I say wonderingly, all traces of my old attitude gone. "You saved me."

"No, Millie," Hawthorne says, putting his hand on my shoulder again in a way that's almost fatherly. This time, it doesn't make me cringe; it makes me *proud.* "You've saved yourself. I just helped show you the way."

"Millie, don't!" yells Hunter from behind me. That's enough to make me remember our audience, and I frown. A voice that once enchanted me is now as bothersome as a fly buzzing around my head. Why can't he just let me enjoy this new sense of clarity that I've been gifted?

Slowly I turn around, my expression hard and cold. The guys are all standing there, staring at me like they've never seen me before in their lives. Good. I feel the same way. The disgust that overtakes me as I look them over is surprising even in my altered state; how could I have once thought I loved these people? They're nothing but children, fighting stubbornly against the inevitable. No, worse than that; they're actively *hindering* Hawthorne's plans. Why can't they see that control is the only way to coexist? Shapeshifting was never meant to be democratized. It was meant as a means to an end, a source of power to shape the world, and they shouldn't have it. The thought that I once cared about these people makes me cringe. "Don't what?" I demand, moving to stand beside Hawthorne.

"Don't let him get to you," Landon begs, the fear in his voice palpable. "Please."

"*Please.*" I snort and shake my head. "As if begging will help. Get a grip, Thyme."

"What the hell have you done to her?" roars Shade, lunging towards Hawthorne. The Academy President raises his hand almost lazily, shifting rapidly into his witch form and sending out a pulse of telekinetic energy that sends the wolf shifter flying into the opposite wall.

None of the others have transformed yet—whether out of shock or sheer disbelief, I can't say—but now the spell seems to be broken. They shift all at once, but even in their forms, they're looking at me guardedly. *They're afraid to attack me,* I realize, and the thought makes me want to cackle. *They don't want to hurt me. This is rich.*

Hawthorne says exactly what I'm thinking. "This is a nice bit of irony, don't you think, Ms. Brix?"

"Absolutely," I reply without missing a beat. "Shall we convert them too? Whatever else they are, they could be useful to us."

"Oh, I hardly think that's necessary," Hawthorne says, pocketing the rune and taking a step forward. "Considering the trouble you've given me, I think it's only fair that the punishment fits the crimes, don't you?"

There's the most subtle feeling of doubt, but I squash it in an instant. I deserve whatever's coming to me and more. All the chaos I sowed for the Academy, all the blood on my hands, it was all leading up to this. The fact that I've been given this new lease on life is more than I deserve. I'm lucky Hawthorne believes in second chances. "Yes, sir," I reply.

"You son of a bitch," Hunter yells, leaping towards Hawthorne.

I calmly step between him and the man I'm now loyal to, blocking his path. "No can do," I croon, grinning at the way the vampire shifter's face twists in horror. "If you want to get to him, you'll have to go through me. And something tells me you won't want to do that."

"No," Hawthorne responds, "but they'll have to. They'll have to because you're not going to give them a choice. The only question is, who to start with?" Furrowing his brow, he gives the guys a once over before settling on Silas. "Appropriate, I think," he says. "Almost poetic, considering how he turned you against me in the first place. Dispose of him if you please, Ms. Brix."

"Gladly," I say, rolling my shoulders back and turning on Silas.

The dragon shifter, who up until now has been completely silent, looks utterly devastated. His heartbreak is written on his face, the flashes of his parents' fate practically playing right before his eyes. "Millie, please," he whispers, holding up his hands. "Don't do this. Fight him!"

"That's your first mistake, Silas," I croon mockingly. "I'm not going to fight him. I'm going to fight *you*." And with that, I shift into my vampire form and lunge at him.

Silas barely has time to transform into a dragon before I'm on him, pummeling with supercharged blows that glance off his scales. He whips his tail out, catching me in the side and sending me stumbling, but doesn't breathe fire. Even though I'm actively trying to kill him, he still doesn't want to seriously hurt me.

Pathetic.

With a hiss, I storm forward again, using my witch magic to form a force field around myself and physically knock him over as I charge him. Silas yells out in pain as he goes flying into a wall.

"Millie," commands Landon desperately in his siren voice, "get Hawthorne out of your head!"

Except he isn't in my head. There's nothing in my head except for me, the new and improved Millie Brix, and no siren song can change my convictions. Vampire again, I grab Landon by the throat and toss him effortlessly across the room. Hunter grabs me from behind, and his superior strength is enough to give me pause... Until I call on my dragon magic and blast a stream of fire over my shoulder. He has no choice but to pull away as he fights the scorching heat, and a solid kick to Shade's side as he charges me is enough to get him out of my hair for now. *I'll deal with him next,* I decide.

By now, Silas has regained his footing, and a flap of his massive wings makes me back up just as he pulls out all the stops and shoots a fireball on me. Crying out, I shift into my own dragon form, effectively nullifying the heat, and lock my jaws around Silas's as I rake at his scales with my claws. He thrashes with his tail once more, nearly knocking the wind out of me, but I hold my ground, biting down with all the strength I can muster.

"*Please,* Millie!" Shade yells from the corner of the room. "We love you!"

Again, I feel the slightest flicker of doubt, and again I push it away. It's too late for these kinds of platitudes now, and besides, Silas is running out of air. I can feel him weakening under me, unable to breathe with my teeth clamped around his snout, and ever so slowly, his muscles begin to fail...

Only for the door to blast open with the force of a magic I've only seen before in one other person. "Millie, stop."

Standing in the doorway is Theo himself.

CHAPTER 102

For a moment, it's like all other sensory input goes out the window. It has nothing to do with his feelings for me, which are not only irrelevant now, but disgusting; my only loyalty is to the Academy and to Hawthorne. That's where it always should have been, and where it always will be. How pathetic of him to think there could have ever been something between u! Given my relationship with the guys, which is also disgusting and irrelevant, he's left with the air of a schoolboy with a silly crush. It's almost laughable.

That's not what gives me pause now. Rather, his very nature is what makes me freeze in my tracks. Theo is a hybrid, and a natural-born one at that. He wasn't created in a lab the way me and Hawthorne were. His abilities are innate, and his skills are the stuff of legends, making him arguably the most important potential asset we have. And yet, in spite of the obvious futility of resisting the Academy, still he fritters his power away on a fight he can't hope to win. It's as frustrating as it is contemptible, and it sows a disdain in the pit of my stomach that nothing else can compare to. My head snaps to look at Hawthorne. His hand is back in his pocket, no doubt touching the stone, but for some reason he still hasn't used it. Does it need to be recharged? Or is it dependent on the spellcaster's own energy reserves?

It doesn't matter, I think, folding my hands daintily behind my back. *I've seen the light. That's what's important at the end of the day.* With this in mind, I eye the rebel leader with a cold composure. "Fancy seeing you here, Theo." I practically spit his name out. "Decided I couldn't be trusted on my own? Probably a smart idea, in retrospect."

Theo's eyes drift from me to Hawthorne and the guys and then back to me. "I was afraid of this," he says, a twinge of regret in his voice. "This was why I didn't want you to go. You're too valuable to be taken advantage of by the Academy."

"Taken advantage of?" I ask, taking a step towards him. "Taken *advantage* of? That's rich." I snort and shake my head. "You're the one who's been taking advantage of me. From square one, all you've cared about is your own damned legacy. Why waste so much time on a cause that's so clearly worthless? It's ridiculous."

"You're wrong," Theo tells me in a stoic tone of voice. There's frustration hidden just below the surface, along with a haunting sense of melancholy that makes me pause for a fraction of a second. Is he... *disappointed* in me? I shake the idea off. It doesn't matter what he thinks. It doesn't matter what any of them think. "You've spent all your time as a shifter standing up for what's right, Millie," he goes on, his pale eyes boring into mine with a surprising intensity. "Hell, you're the direct result of the Academy's abuses! How can you not see that?"

"Don't you get it?" I hiss back at him. "That's the whole point, Theo. The Academy *made me.* I wouldn't be standing here if it weren't for the humans. I owe them everything; I don't owe the shifters jack shit." Cocking my head to the side like a predator observing my prey, I change the subject. "How did you figure out this was going to happen, anyway? Did you follow us here?" I chuckle. "Stupid of you not to bring backup. You know you're outnumbered."

"I've told you since the beginning," Theo replies slowly, "I've always felt a connection to you, Millie. Call it love, call it camaraderie, call it a sixth sense. Call it whatever you want. I knew something was wrong from the minute you left. And it looks like I was right."

"Isn't that sweet," I purr. "The legendary Theo's in love. Unfortunately for you, my allegiances have changed."

Crossing my arms, I move to stand beside Hawthorne, who looks as pleased as punch. "You heard her, Theo," he says, putting his hand on the top of my head like a proud parent. "It would be easier if you just joined us, you know. We could use someone with your abilities on our side."

"I'll die first," Theo replies without missing a beat.

"Boots, please," Landon calls to me, his voice seeming far away. The hope has mostly gone from his tone, replaced with resignation.

I ignore him. "Use the rune," I tell Hawthorne. "Fix him. Hell, fix all of them, while you're at it."

"Not so fast," Hawthorne says. "I still deserve satisfaction for all the problems the rebels have caused me. Even better if your boy toys can watch while you tear this bastard's throat out."

A wicked grin slowly spreads across my face, and I loosen my neck, already itching for another fight. It's funny; before, after getting my powers back, I was afraid of myself. The bloodlust scared me, as did the ease with which I doled out violence. Now, though, it's like I've been reborn. The idea of a violent fight sends a surge of excitement through me. "Gladly, sir," I say.

Theo holds up his hands. "I don't want to fight you, Millie."

"That's too bad," I tell him, "because I'm just about ready to rip you limb from limb."

"This isn't you," the rebel leader protests. "Remember everything you've done!"

"Useless," I snap, and shift into my witch form before turning on the guys. "You might want to close your eyes for this. Your precious figurehead isn't going to leave this room alive."

"No!" Shade yells, lurching forward, but Russo grabs him by the arm and pulls him back just as half a dozen other shifters make their way into the room. Things have just gotten a lot more interesting.

"This should be good," Hawthorne says, and crosses his arms.

That's all it takes for the apartment to descend into chaos. Russo may be human, but the guards she summoned are not, and before the guys can meddle in my business anymore, the newcomers are shifting into their forms. Rules of engagement don't exist here. Without any fanfare, the Academy shifters descend upon the guys, who are left to shift back and defend themselves, essentially distracted from my dealings with Theo and Hawthorne. A shame, since I was hoping to watch them die or be converted personally, but we can't always get what we want. With a snarl of aggression, I round on Theo and extend my arms.

My telekinetic blast hits him squarely in the chest, but he's already shifted his lower half into his vampire form, anchoring himself to the ground with his supernatural strength. "Millie, I know you're still in there," he says. His voice is eerily, frustratingly calm, and even though rage is pouring off me, his pale eyes seem to be looking right into me. "You can pull yourself out of this. I know you can."

"Like hell," I hiss, transforming into a wolf and charging him. I fly into him, my teeth tearing into the untransformed flesh of his upper torso as I use my own momentum to hurl him onto the ground. Shade's training, it seems, is still coming in handy. I'm on top of the hybrid shifter in seconds, snapping my fangs furiously at him.

Theo gets his arms up and summons a force field of his own. It expands in a rapidly growing bubble, forcing me away from him. I dig my heels in, but it's no use; he's been around longer than me, and his magic is stronger. But I'm more tenacious. Shifting into my siren form, I let out a scream of pure sonic vibration that connects with his bubble. I can see the energy field vibrating from the pressure of the waves, and Theo lets out a grunt as he concentrates on keeping the barrier up.

Hawthorne and Russo, meanwhile, are watching both fiascos like fans at a sports match, and the pride on Hawthorne's face makes my heart surge in my chest.

"Why don't you fucking fight back?" I yell at Theo at an even louder volume.

That finally does the trick. His force field fragments momentarily —only for a split second, but it's enough of an opening for me to expel a jet of fire in his direction. The hybrid leader is forced to leap out of the way, losing his concentration and allowing the barrier to drop. Sprouting my dragon tail, I swipe it in his direction, sending him flying off his feet. He collapses in a heap, and when he drags himself back up, there's a trickle of blood running from his nose, which is clearly broken. It's hardly a surface wound, nothing compared to some of the violence I've seen, but seeing the blood on Theo's pale face makes me freeze in my tracks.

I hurt him, I think. *I actually hurt the rebel leader.*

The feeling it elicits in me is strange, and I don't like it. It's like the slightest hint of uncertainty wells up in my stomach, a flicker of doubt as he stares defiantly back at me, still not doing anything to hurt me. Frustrated, I yell again, "*Fight me,* damn it!"

"No, Millie," Theo says, his voice startlingly calm. "I'm not going to fight you."

There it is again, that pang of unease that I felt when I was fighting the guys. Gritting my teeth, I shift back into my vampire form and lunge at him once more. When Theo speaks again, it's in his siren voice. "Don't."

The command isn't enough to fully incapacitate me, but it *is* enough to slow me down. Theo himself shifts into his vampire form, putting up his hands to block the pummeling that I rain down on him the moment I get my senses back. I put my whole weight behind the blows, angry at the sudden cracks that are appearing in my convictions. "You were always meant to lead the shifters," Theo pants as he stumbles backward under the force of my punches and kicks. "You've been at the heart of the rebellion this whole time. You're so much stronger than you know."

"Shut up!" I yell, sprouting dragon claws and raking them across his arm. Blood wells up from the cuts, and once again I have to fight to resist the sudden disgust I feel at myself for the injury I've caused. *This is right,* I tell myself. *I'm doing the right thing.*

"We need you," Theo continues, still in that terrifyingly calm tone of voice, and still without making any offensive moves against me. He's only doing the bare minimum to protect himself, I realize. "The rebellion needs you. *They* need you." Our arms still locked together, he nods in the direction of the guys, who are fighting tooth and nail with the other shifters. I make the mistake of following his gaze and seeing them being beaten back. The cracks in my armor grow a little more.

"Enough of this," I hear Hawthorne command. "Finish him off."

With a burst of renewed energy, I summon the biggest blast of fire that I can from deep in my chest and exhale it directly onto Theo. His vampire body goes up in flames, and even the stoic rebel leader is unable to keep from screaming in pain as his legs give out. The smell of burning flesh fills the room, the sounds of suffering and violence all around me. But it's the look in Theo's eyes that makes me freeze: that same half-plaintive expression of disappointment and lost hope.

I tell myself not to give in, to stay focused on what truly matters, but then I hear one of the guys—I'm not sure which one—let out his own cry of pain, as frightened and anguished as Theo's.

And just like that, I snap out of it.

CHAPTER 103

For a moment, it's like having a bucket of cold water dumped over my head. No, more accurately, it's like finally being allowed up for air after being held underwater almost to the point of death. Suddenly the world is too bright, the colors too vibrant, all of my senses thrown out of whack by the abruptness of the shift. Whereas the first shift came almost as a relief, bringing with it the freedom of having my ideas shaped around apathy, this one comes as a shock. No more than a couple of seconds have passed, and Theo is still lying on the ground in front of me. All around me are the sounds of battle, but whatever bloodthirst Hawthorne induced in me is gone, shaken off like some kind of meddlesome pest.

The carnage...

I realize I'm shaking as I stare down at Theo, his body still smoldering from the heat of the flames. My eyes drop to my hands, which are shaking, covered in scrapes, bruises and blood. Blood that isn't my own. My ears pick up on a cry of anguish, and it's a moment before I notice it's coming from me. *What have I done? What the hell have I done?*

"What are you doing?" Hawthorne's voice, sounding like it's coming from far away, makes its way to me from across the room. "Kill him, Millie!"

But the command doesn't hold up anymore. The guilt, disgust, and shock of what I just did is too much for even the most potent of brainwashing spells. Finally, I get my body to work, and this time there's no malice behind my actions—nothing but cold despair and desperation to make things right. Thinking fast, I shift into my dragon form, the bulk of my reptilian body immediately dwarfing those around me. There's no water around here, but if I can just use my mass to help Theo...

I drop to the floor, pressing my armored torso over Theo's body. The effect is immediate, considering the heat-resistant properties of my scales: the flames are smothered in an instant, giving way to smoke and ash as I roll off of the other hybrid shifter. For a terrifying moment, I wonder if he's dead already, but I notice that his chest is still moving, albeit shallowly, and that's all I can do for now.

"Millie, stop it! Kill him!" Hawthorne yells, and out of the corner of my eye, I see him shift into vampire form. It's the first time I've witnessed him change forms completely, and it only fuels the anger bubbling up in my chest.

"Boots!" I hear Silas say in a tone of triumph. I turn to the other dragon shifter, our eyes meeting briefly, and nothing needs to be said. On the same wavelength, he disengages from the shifter he's currently fighting and flanks me, and together we expel an enormous blast of flame directly onto Hawthorne. He should really know better than to pit his vampire form against two dragons, but it's clear that he hasn't quite learned the strategies of transformation yet, which is our saving grace. The flames lick at his skin, blistering it the same way they did Theo's. Unfortunately, he gets his hands up in time to surround himself in his own force field, rendering our attacks useless.

Grabbing the rune again, Hawthorne shouts out to his mysterious collaborator. "Again! Bewitch her again!" The blast of light hits me dead-on, but this time, it has no effect. My convictions are rock-solid. It's as if the trauma of what I did to Theo has granted me immunity against the spell's effects, and with a broad sweep of my tail, I knock Hawthorne off his feet. With an outraged roar, he turns to his other minions. "Kill them, all of you! No one leaves this building alive!"

That's all the warning I get before one of the enemy witch shifters summons a glyph under our feet. Immediately I feel the strength going out of my limbs, but I manage to shift into my witch form and summon a counter-spell of my own, the two sigils lining up underfoot and effectively neutralizing one another. It takes energy to maintain, but I have enough cycles left to conjure a force field around myself, each of the guys, and Theo. The enemies' barrage continues, but we're at a stalemate. The tide, for now, seems to have turned.

"She won't hold out forever," Russo yells to Hawthorne from across the room.

"Maybe not," Landon grunts from within his force field, "but we will." Extending his arms, he lets out a fresh wave of sound vibrations that encases us in another layer. It's not as strong as the barrier I created, but the combined strength pushes the rest of our attackers back. From his place on the floor, Theo also summons another layer, and between the three of us, we're completely ensconced.

Hawthorne meets my eyes, his expression one of pure hatred. "This isn't over," he says after a tense moment, before turning to his cronies. "Evacuate. We return to the Academy. We'll have the numbers there." Shooting me a vicious smile, he adds, "Enjoy this while it lasts, Millie Brix. Next time, there won't be a second chance. I'm going to kill you, and I'll make sure it hurts."

"I fucking dare you," Shade yells from his own spot. His wolf's eyes meet mine, and I can see the relief on his face at the confirmation that I'm back to my old self.

That's all that happens before the others make their retreat, stalking out of the apartments and up the stairs. I maintain the barrier long enough to wait for their footsteps to retreat completely before letting it down, pausing to telekinetically move a chair in front of the door to barricade it. Then I shift back into my human form, breathing hard. "I'm sorry," I pant, rushing to the guys. "I'm sorry, I'm sorry, I'm so sorry."

They all but flock to me, enfolding me in their arms in a group embrace. "Shh, it's okay," Hunter murmurs against my scalp. "It's okay, you're okay."

A ragged sob escapes me. "I can't believe I... I-I almost..."

"You broke free," Silas says, brushing my hair out of my face. "That's all that matters."

"I knew you were still in there somewhere," Landon says, grinning. "Hawthorne will never tie you down, Boots."

It's only after a moment that I remember Theo and pull myself away from the guys to rush over to him. Almost as soon as I reach his curled up form, my heart leaps into my throat. The situation isn't good. His entire body is covered in what look like third-degree burns, charred and scorched beyond recognition. The fact that he's even still breathing is a miracle in itself. Kneeling beside him, I shift into my witch form again, already scrambling for some kind of spell, but then his hand bats mine away. "Don't," he rasps. "Save your energy. It's too late."

"No, it's not," I insist, my eyes welling up with tears. "It can't be. We have supplies. We can get you to Josie. You're not going to die, Theo!" But I'm not sure who I'm even trying to convince. One look at him is enough to tell me that he's beyond any help I'm able to give. Moving him would probably kill him.

"It's okay." Theo reaches up and strokes my cheek with the backs of his knuckles. "I told you you were special, Millie Brix."

"I'm not," I say, my voice shaking. "Look what I did to you."

"If this is what got Hawthorne's hooks out of you," Theo says, taking a labored breath, "then it's a sacrifice I'm happy to make. I'm sorry that I didn't... That we didn't..." There's an adoration in his eyes that makes my heart break. "You need to lead them," he tells me. "Take the fight to Hawthorne."

"What? No!" I protest. "I'm no leader, Theo. I can't—"

"Yes, you can," he says. "You will. The others will follow you. You can't let him get away with this. Please," he adds, taking my hand. "Consider it a last request." There's a dry smile on his face.

I realize I've started to cry. "I don't know how," I whisper. "I'm not you."

"No," Theo replies simply. "You're better."

"Theo..."

"Don't let them win," the hybrid leader says, and then he dies.

I stare at him for a long time, crying silently. The feeling of Hunter's hand on my shoulder almost makes me jump. "This isn't your fault, Boots," he says.

"How can you say that?" I demand. "I killed him!"

"No, Hawthorne killed him," Silas says, his voice filled with disgust. "Everything that's happened, all this tragedy, it's all because of him. And we owe it to Theo to take him out, once and for all."

"I don't trust myself to," I reply, voice trembling.

"You don't have to," says Landon, kneeling down beside me. "We do."

Trembling, I look up from one of my boyfriends to the next. In spite of everything I've done, the faith and love in their eyes is profound and unshakeable. They believe in me, even when I don't.

And maybe that's enough.

Slowly, I get to my feet. "I can try," I say at last, "but we're still screwed. We couldn't even get someone to wear the amulet."

"I'm not so sure," Landon muses. "Do you think that amulet works on former mind control victims?"

The corner of Shade's mouth twitches. "There's only one way to find out."

THE AMULET VIBRATES as it pulls me along, tugging me instantly in one direction as we make our way up through the foothills. We're on another island in the region, just a short flight away from the now-abandoned facility. It makes sense that the spellcaster would be quartered here. My only hope is that he hasn't left by the time we get to him. We don't speak much as we follow the medallion's trail, each lost in our own thoughts. We sent Theo's body out to sea; it's not much, but I couldn't bear to leave him on the basement floor. It was the least he deserved.

"What if it's not working right?" Hunter pants as we ascend the top of the cliff. "Could it be misleading us since you're not technically enchanted anymore?"

"Even if it's right, the spellcaster is going to have guards," I reply. "We'll just have to hope Hawthorne isn't there too."

"I wouldn't mind the chance to rip him limb from limb," Shade growls. "After what he did to you, Boots…"

"I don't think he will be," says Landon. "They don't know we have a way of tracking the guy down. There's no reason they wouldn't go straight to the Academy."

"It's possible," Hunter agrees. "Maybe we'll get lucky."

Silas, who is at the head of the group, stops in his tracks as he crests the hill. "Lucky isn't the word I would use," he says, and points. Where the ground levels off, we find ourselves face-to-face with a cottage, although "cottage" might be too generous of a term. It's more like a shack, run-down and battered by the wind and the water. The amulet around my neck pulls even harder at me, nearly dragging me forward as it points directly at the source of the enchantment. Whoever it is, they're in that house.

The only problem? There are two very familiar-looking figures flanking the entrance, and now I understand Silas's hesitation; it couldn't have been more cruel if Hawthorne had set it up on purpose, and for all I know, maybe he did.

Standing on either side of the cottage door, their hands behind their backs and utterly dead behind the eyes, are Silas's parents.

CHAPTER 104

"Mom," Silas rasps. "Dad."

"Son," sneers his father. "Have you finally changed your mind? I didn't think you had it in you."

Silas shakes his head. "We're here for the spellcaster."

His mother cackles. "Isn't that sweet? What was your plan, exactly? To ask us nicely? To bargain? Maybe you thought you could somehow talk us down?"

"It's happened before," I snap, stepping forward. If I could break free of the enchantment, maybe they can, too. "We're not here to hurt you," I insist. "Please. Remember what you used to stand for."

"Idealism," Silas's father spits. "Pathetic, sugar-coated idealism. And we're never going back."

"That's the spell talking, not you," I insist, reeling back Theo's fight with me as I search for a way to get through to them. "I know you're in there somewhere. I was, too."

"Shame, that," muses Silas's mother. "You would have been such a valuable asset, too."

"It's no use, Boots," Landon murmurs to me. "They're not going to listen."

At that moment, the door to the shack rattles open, and a scrawny figure appears in the entrance. It's a guy, I realize, and he can't be more than a few years older than me. Hell, he might even be mistaken for an Academy student. The only difference, however, is his eyes, and when he turns them on me, I nearly freeze to the spot. They're filled with a terrifying, unadulterated hatred, one that can't even be chalked up to mind control. No remorse, no mercy, not even a flicker of doubt.

Who the hell is this guy?

"You're the one who broke free," he says flatly, stepping forward. Silas's parents move to flank him, but he shakes them off and extends a bony finger in my direction. "I guess congratulations are in order." A sickening smile spreads across his face.

I don't take the bait. "Undo the enchantments," I tell him. "All of them."

It's futile, and I know it. The spellcaster barks out a laugh. "And why would I do that?"

"Because they're my parents," Silas says, hands clenching into fists. "Last chance, you son of a bitch."

"Who, these fine folks?" The spellcaster glances between Silas's mother and father. The corner of his mouth twitches up, and without any warning, he shifts into his witch form. Moments later, he's lifting the other shifters up telekinetically before sending them flying over the stony cliff.

"No!" Silas yells in anguish, and that's when all hell breaks loose. He's the first one to transform, his mighty wings launching him off the ground as he bolts towards the spellcaster. I can see the retaliation coming from a mile away—the dragon shifter is blinded by emotion—and shift into my wolf form in a mad dash to prevent catastrophe.

The spellcaster pulls a similar move, lifting Silas up in the air with obvious intent, but I barrel into him at the last moment, breaking his focus just as Hunter sprints forward. Arms outstretched, he crashes into the witch shifter like a missile, but rather than cast another spell, the scrawny man shifts again.

For a moment, I don't even believe my eyes as I find myself staring down a new vampire. *A hybrid,* I think with a sense of dawning dread. *Another hybrid. And he's on their side.*

That's all I have time to process before the spellcaster is turning on me, locking an arm around my throat. His vampiric strength practically crushes my neck, but I manage to shift into my siren form and yell, "Get off!" The command works, and I feel his grip loosen for a split second as he visibly battles with my siren song. Within moments, however, he's shifting again, changing into a wolf and tackling me.

Shade appears out of nowhere, knocking him off my body, only to yelp as the hybrid locks his jaws around his throat. The aggression is terrifying, and I'm still so flabbergasted that a fellow hybrid would be behind this that I can't seem to think straight. Thankfully, I don't have to; Landon lets loose a supersonic blast that, while deafening, makes the hybrid cringe back. I follow Hunter's lead and shift into my vampire form so we can flank him, but in the blink of an eye he's shifted into his dragon form, spraying a jet of fire out and around us in a circle. I'm forced back, the heat on my vampire skin unbearable, and a cry of pain escapes me.

"Millie," Hunter yells, even as he bites back his own pain.

"Get behind me," I tell him, just as I shift into my dragon form. Falling in line with Silas, we circle the spellcaster high above the others. At the very least, this should keep him distracted from the rest of the guys. His dragon form is bigger than either of ours, though, and one swipe of his tail is enough to send me spinning out of control. I steady myself with my wings long enough to breathe fire in his direction, but it's no use; even if he were susceptible to the heat, he's too agile even for Silas to keep up.

Thinking fast, I extend an arm and conjure a force field—not around myself, but around him. "What the fuck are you doing?" he yells from within the bubble, but I ignore him as I try to decide what to do.

Not about to be on the receiving end of my magic, the enemy hybrid shifts into his witch form once more, holding up his own hands as he fights to undo the barrier I've created around him. Immediately, maintaining it becomes harder; I can feel his energy pushing against mine with enough force to make me pant from exertion. I can hear the guys calling to me from below, but I can't even focus on what they're saying. It's suddenly become an impossible task, and I can feel myself faltering.

I have to let go of the dragon form, I realize. I won't be able to contain him while I'm multitasking. Dropping to the ground, I shift completely into my witch form and channel a fresh burst of stamina into the force field. The hybrid does the same, and before I know what's happening, both of our barriers are bursting in a massive explosion of energy that sends me stumbling back. It's like a bomb going off, and it's only after the blinding light and debris clear that I see the result: the spellcaster has been completely vaporized. Just like that. The result of two powerful hybrids going head-to-head until nothing is left but ashes.

I stand there, staring and catching my breath, as the guys convene around me.

"Boots," Landon says, putting a hand on my arm, "you okay?"

For a moment, I feel like I've lost the ability to speak. "He was like me," I say at last, my tone wondering. "He was a hybrid." Who was he, I wonder? How did he end up willingly subjugating his fellow shifters?

Is that what I could have been, if I had taken a different path?

It's not a question I have an answer for, and I find myself turning away as I struggle not to be sick. The only thing that distracts me is a nudge from Shade, who silently points down the cliff towards the beach below. Silas's parents are below us, sprawled out on the sand in positions hauntingly similar to the corpses in my nightmare. Their bodies look utterly destroyed, but to my surprise, they're still alive by the time we approach them. With the spellcaster dead, they should have their minds back, but not much more; it's clear that, as with Theo, it's too late to get them medical attention.

"Silas..." I say, but my voice trails off. The dragon shifter turns to me, and I see the question in his eyes. I give his hand a squeeze before letting it go. "Take as long as you need," I murmur.

He nods, pulls away from me, and his form grows distant as he kneels in the sand between his parents. I don't feel right coming any closer. I can hear their voices, but the sea breeze makes it impossible to hear what they're saying. Maybe that's for the best—this isn't the kind of moment that's meant for outsiders.

Landon, Hunter, Shade, and I turn away, standing in silence as the last member of our group says goodbye to the parents and to the childhood that was taken from him. I'm not sure how much time passes, but eventually, the tall dragon shifter comes back to us. "I floated the bodies out to sea," he says. "It was the least I could do."

"What did you—" Shade clears his throat. "Did they...?"

"They died as themselves," Silas says quietly, shrugging his shoulders. "That's the best we can hope for."

I can only nod, slipping my hand silently back into his. I desperately want to embrace him, to soothe his pain and whisper that it's going to be okay, but it isn't my place. Grieving and processing will have to wait, as horrible as that is. We're not done yet.

"What do we do now?" asks Hunter.

"The only thing we can do," replies Shade.

I nod slowly. "We get the rest of rebels and we move on the Academy. One way or another, we're ending this."

OUR PARTY IS silent as we step out of the hotel and onto the Edinburgh street. Filing out of the building behind us are all the remaining rebel shifters Theo gathered, leaving his intent when he went after us. I don't know if it's going to be enough, but there's no time left. Without a word, the guys and I lead our army in the direction of downtown.

A short teleportation later, we're standing on the shores of the island that's come to dominate my life this past year. I can see the campus rising up in the distance, past the lush green hill we're now standing on. It's strange to think that the first time I saw this view, I had no idea what kind of war was coming next. The whole place is surprisingly unchanged; there's hardly a cloud in the sky, and the weather is idyllic. Birdsong fills the air, and if I didn't know better, I wouldn't think anything was amiss.

Slowly we move forward, and as we descend the hill, dozens of figures become visible below us in the quad. The whole place is packed; students, faculty, and teachers are all standing there stiffly, and it doesn't take a genius to see that none of them is on our side. *Have they been waiting for us?* I wonder. *Did they know we were coming for them?* Maybe killing the spellcaster tipped them off. It doesn't matter, really—by now they've seen us. We're committed.

Landon takes my wrist gently before I can continue forward, and I realize that he and the rest of the guys are hanging back. Eyes wide, I turn back to them. "We can't stop now," I tell them.

"We know," replies Hunter.

"But if anything happens," adds Shade, "to you, to any of us..." His voice breaks, and an uncharacteristic fear flashes in his gray eyes.

"We love you, Millie Brix," Silas says simply. The others nod somberly, their eyes never leaving mine.

"I love you too," I tell them. "All of you."

None of us needs to say anything else; one by one, they each approach me and press a kiss to my lips. I savor the feeling desperately, wondering if this will be the last time. There are, after all, no guarantees. Silas's parents were proof enough of that. But the moment ends all too quickly, and soon enough we're huddled together once more, staring down at the army that awaits us. I glance at each of the guys in turn and then take a step forward. "No going back," I say, rolling my shoulders. "Now come on. Let's finish this."

Ó

CHAPTER 105

It all started here, on a remote island in the Scottish Isles, so I guess it's appropriate that it should all end in the same place. Poetic, in a way, like the path I've been following for so long—often unwittingly—has at last come full circle. It feels both like it's been more than a single year since I first discovered my powers, but at the same time, it's as if hardly any time has passed at all. Between coming to the school, meeting the guys, and first pulling on the thread that unraveled the corruption in the human ranks, I've become a new person, literally and figuratively.

The question at the forefront of my mind now, as I lead our group out of the main building and into the quad, is whether that will even be enough. Hawthorne having powers is bad, and from what I've seen, his newfound magic puts him on par with me. The only thing I have on my side is experience, and even that doesn't hold up very well against his army of brainwashed minions.

Silas and Shade are to my left, and Landon and Hunter are to my right, flanking me. Behind us are the Murakami twins, Hazel, and Josie, who is breathing hard from her prior exertion; she's done an admirable job so far, and it's astonishing that she's even still on her feet after expending as much magic as she already has. We won't be able to count on her for this last push, I'm afraid, and it doesn't take a genius to see that Hawthorne has us outnumbered. We may have the students on our side, but he has the faculty, and one look across the courtyard at the enemy posse is enough to tell me that they're practically foaming at the mouth.

There's a moment of eerie silence as the two opposing groups face each other down from opposite sides of the quad, like two armies about to do battle. In a way, I suppose we are, although most armies aren't being mind-controlled by a cabal of witches, so...

"And here we are," says Hawthorne, spreading his arms out as his voice rings out over the courtyard. "A fitting end to our saga, isn't it, Ms. Brix?" His eyes flash with thinly veiled madness, and I can see how bloodshot they are; when was the last time he slept, let alone ate? His veins are prominent and dark, the corruption of his newly acquired magic permeating his entire body. The other school board members look similarly affected, although the corruption isn't as far along for them—is there a chance of undoing it, when this is all over?

"Well, Millie?" Hawthorne prompts me again in the silence outside. "I have to admit, I was expecting something with a bit more flair, coming from the girl who's at the heart of this little game of ours. Freedom fighting doesn't leave much free time, I suppose."

Shade makes an angry noise and lunges forward, but I catch him by the wrist. "Don't," I murmur in a low voice. "Wait for him to make the first move."

"Is that really it?" Hawthorne sounds almost maniacal at this point. Months of waiting for this standoff, and now I'm not playing ball; I have to admit to a little satisfaction at that. "No smart remark? No rallying cry for your ragtag army? Nothing at all to say for yourself?"

"Just one thing," I reply. My voice rings out clear and steady, in stark contrast to the fear bubbling up inside me. Mollie's words echo in my mind then, and I close my eyes for a brief moment: *Fear happens to everyone, Millie. What matters is what you do in spite of it.* Whether from the nugget of wisdom or the fact that, one way or another, this all ends here, a wave of calm washes over me, and when I open my eyes, the whole world has melted away, save for

Hawthorne. "I hope you've been practicing," I say, and then I leap into the air. I'm shifting into my dragon form before I hit the ground again, launching myself across the open space at top speed.

It's as good a cue as any, and just like that, the nervous tension evaporates. The opposing groups charge each other like enemy troops, and within seconds the whole quad has erupted into a horde of battling shapeshifters. By the time I clash with Hawthorne, I've shifted my upper half into my witch form so I can use the technique Josie taught me to keep track of the guys; it takes a bit of concentration to keep psychic tabs on them as they join the fray, but I need to know that they're safe. If anything else happened to them because of me...

That train of thought is cut short when Hawthorne, now also in his dragon form, comes crashing down on top of me, knocking the wind out of my lungs. I get my hands up in front of me and release a pulse of telekinetic magic; it isn't hard enough to send him flying, but it's enough to push him off for a moment, and a moment is all I need.

I shift fully into my vampire form just in time for his slashing claws to lash out at me. There's a small surge of pain, but he doesn't break my sturdy skin, and I have speed on my side. My hand flies out to catch his wrist, pulling his giant form forward just enough to knock him off balance. It's becoming clear that he's not used to being in his other forms yet, which I'm aware could be my saving grace.

Reaching out with my mind, I check on the others: Hunter and Silas are somewhere behind me, teaming up against a duo of wolf shifters, while Landon and Shade are making short work of one of the former board members. The teachers are the real issue, and without being familiar with their magic signatures, it's hard to tell who's on our side.

Doesn't matter, I remind myself, gritting my teeth and whirling around to leap onto Hawthorne's back. He lets out a roar of frustration and pain as I pry at his golden scales with my hands, actually managing to pull one loose. Before I can target the wound, however, Hawthorne is shifting out from underneath me, soon standing in front of me in his vampire form. We circle each other for a moment, fangs bared, and I catch the movement out of the corner of my eye a split second before he's on me. Now it's my turn to be put on the defense, grabbing onto his upper half as he tries to grapple me onto the ground. Locked together, we each lean into our supernatural strength, but we're evenly matched. Almost.

Opening my mouth, I exhale a fireball straight into Hawthorne's midsection. Still a vampire, his reaction is painful and immediate as he lets out a yell of pain and releases his grip on me. Seizing the opportunity, I lunge forward in my wolf form and tackle him to the ground, powerful jaws clamping down on his wound.

That probably wasn't such a good idea, I realize, when he lifts up his arms, now shifted into witch form, and launches me back with the same kind of telekinetic push that I so often favor. I struggle to get to my feet, but the waves of energy just keep coming, keeping me doubled over like the world's strongest gust of wind.

Thinking quickly, I allow my upper half to shift into siren form before unleashing a sonic screech on par with the force he's directing at me. The pulsating sound waves neutralize his magic, allowing me to struggle back to my feet.

All around us, the battle rages; out of the corner of my eye, I see Hunter being knocked over by a dragon's tail, and that brief moment of distraction is all Hawthorne needs. The next thing I know, my arm is exploding with pain as a pair of wolf's jaws clamp down on my shoulder. My knees buckle, the distraction of the pain overwhelming for a moment, and then my legs go out from under me.

Hawthorne might be an asshole, but he's no idiot. Seeing his opening, he goes in for the kill, unlocking his jaws long enough to make a lunge for my throat. Winded, thrashing, and thrown off my game, I squeeze my eyes shut in preparation for the killing blow, only for the weight to suddenly disappear from my chest. Struggling to sit up, I widen my eyes in amazement when I see Amelia Ash shoving Hawthorne off of me, her red eyes gleaming in the sunlight. Panting and a little dazed, I accept the hand she extends to me. "Thank you," I tell her sincerely.

"Don't thank me yet," she replies, before taking off to assist her brother.

I'm barely able to get my bearings before Hawthorne goes in for another attack, this time from his siren form. I roll out of the way of the incoming soundwaves before seizing on one of the benches and hurling it at him with my mind. The bastard manages to deflect my witch magic with his own, and a horrible realization comes to me as I watch him shrug off blow after blow: we're going to kill each other. We're evenly matched, and for all his bluster, Hawthorne isn't giving in. The insanity on his face tells me everything I need to know: he would rather go down with this ship than see all his work be undone.

Am I willing to do the same?

Frantic, I scramble for some idea, anything that might give me an edge over the man who has dogged my footsteps for as long as I can remember, but it's hopeless. Anything magical I can do, he can counter just as easily.

And then, as clear as if someone else were speaking to me, a thought rings loud and clear through my mind. The answer comes to me so easily that I can scarcely believe I didn't think of it before.

I shift back into human form.

"Give up?" Hawthorne demands, breathing heavily as he shifts back into his dragon form and advances on me. "I can respect that," he says, his fanged jaws snapping with rage. "I'll make it quick, Ms. Brix."

I brace myself for the impact, and when it comes, it takes everything I have not to scream. Hawthorne's massive jaws latch around my arm, his teeth shredding my shoulder and dampening my shirt with blood. The pain is unbearable, but secondary to my task; all I have to do is not pass out, give it one last push...

Faintly, I'm aware of someone yelling my name. Out of the corner of my eye, I see Landon watching me with wide eyes, already moving to come help me. The battle around me seems to slow down, the magic flying through the air, looking for a moment as if it were traveling underwater. My arm is being crushed in Hawthorne's jaws, the pain all-consuming...

I close my eyes and think of my parents, think of Mollie, of Josie, of Hazel and the twins, of the *guys*...

And then I unleash my witch magic, the hand still in Hawthorne's mouth lighting up from the sheer power of it. His dragon's eyes widen when he realizes what's happening, but it's too late; a split second later, an explosion of energy is bursting out of him, tearing his body apart from the inside out. I'm soaked in blood, but the grip on my shoulder loosens as he dies, collapsing in a heap in front of me before slowly turning back into his human form. His body is mangled, his head an unrecognizable pulp, but I could swear I can still feel the hatred rolling off of him in waves.

Cradling my battered arm in front of my chest, I stare down at the corpse in disbelief. The sight is gruesome, and I'm still in a great deal of pain, but it's all dimmed against the reality of what's just happened.

Hawthorne is dead.

We won.

It would be nice to be able to say after that everything came to a neat close, tied up with a bow, the conflict reduced to a distant memory. But real life doesn't work like that, as much as we want to. As tired as we may be, there's always another battle to be fought.

The only difference is that this isn't a physical battle.

"How are things going?" I ask, leaning across Hawthorne's desk to meet Josie's eyes. It's strange being on this side of the president's desk, especially after having been on the receiving end of more than one of his stern lectures over the months. It feels almost surreal somehow, like I've walked into a dream.

The aftermath of the fight is as bloody and unromantic as one might expect. For all that I wanted to avoid violence, there was never going to be a way around it entirely. Corpses littered the quad when I finally stepped away from Hawthorne's body, those of both students and faculty, on both sides. It's enough to make my stomach turn. Not for the first time, I wish the guys were here by my side, but they're busy helping with the cleanup process, leaving me as the impromptu leader in the aftermath of Hawthorne's destruction.

"Slow," Josie replies, reaching up to massage the back of her neck. She's never looked older than she does in this moment, and I can't blame her; this has aged all of us, probably irrevocably. "The hex ran deep. Even now that I've removed the glyphs from under the registrar's office, there's residual power that still needs to be siphoned off before classes can resume." She hesitates for a moment, taking a breath. "*If* classes resume."

"Not having the entire campus susceptible to mind control is a good place to start," I acknowledge. "After that, though..."

"We're going to have to find a way to keep the Academy open," Hunter's father speaks up. He and the surviving board members—all shifters—are standing in the back of Hawthorne's office, watching my discussion with a mixture of hope and trepidation. Hazel and the Murakami twins are standing behind me by the windows, and their presence puts me at ease. It's nice to know that I'm still among friends, especially with our world reeling the way it is.

"Agreed," says one of the other board members. "We've been fielding calls from the other Academies left and right all morning. People want answers, and without Hawthorne..."

"You cut off the head of the snake, Millie," Josie puts in. "The question is what we're going to do with what's left."

"Why are you all looking to me for answers, anyway?" I ask, turning from one faculty fellow to the next. In spite of everything I've accomplished, I can't help but feel a little small in the presence of all these people who were once my superiors. "I just killed him. I didn't mean to take his job."

"You were the face of this revolution, Millie," Hazel reminds me.

"Indeed," agrees Hunter's father. "You may not have been the only one, but you've been at the heart of it this entire time. It seems to me that your voice should carry weight as we decide how to move forward."

I swallow hard, glancing over my shoulder out the window. The carnage is still widespread outside, and I catch a glimpse of Silas and Landon speaking to a couple of the other students. Silas's eyes meet mine for a moment, and he winks at me, the corner of his mouth quirking up in that crooked smile I've come to love so much. *They're all looking to me, aren't they?* I realize.

"Whatever happens next," I say, choosing my words carefully, "we need to make sure the humans aren't in a position to take over the Academy again. The shifters have to be allowed to govern ourselves and decide how to educate ourselves moving forward." I pause for a moment, hardly believing what I'm about to say, and then continue. "The Academy has to stay open, though."

Ruby's eyebrows knit together. "I beg your pardon?" she asks, blinking. "After everything that's happened?"

"Look," I reply, turning to her, "I get it. But we have to remember why the Academy was started in the first place—to *help* shifters, not to oppress them. There are still thousands of kids getting powers every day, with no way of knowing how to control them." I take a shaky breath, glancing at Josie. "I was one of them. If you and Samantha hadn't found me that day, I probably wouldn't be here right now."

"No one's arguing that the Academy should stay open," Hunter's father agrees. "The question is how we want to rebuild. We need shifters we can trust running the Academy—no more of these human sycophants. From the President down to the instructors."

"How about Josie, then?" I ask, nodding at the witch shifter. "She's the reason I'm still alive. She helped me get my powers back."

Josie gives me a melancholy smile. "That's a kind offer, Millie," she tells me, "but I'm afraid this fight has taken a lot out of me. I would be happy to stay on as a faculty fellow, or even a teacher, if that's what you think is best, but I've never been leader material. You, on the other hand..."

My eyes go wide, my face blanching. "Me? President of the Academy?"

"She has a point," Xander pipes up. "You have access to every shifter form, Millie. On top of that, you were the one who uncovered what the Academy was doing in the first place. I can't think of anyone more qualified to be in charge."

The idea is so absurd that I almost burst out laughing. Me? In charge of the school? Have they all lost their minds?! I was a student here less than a year ago... "I think you're giving me too much credit, you guys."

"Hardly," comes a new voice. I lift my gaze to the door to see Hunter striding into the office, followed by Shade, Silas, and Landon. The gang's all here, and I'm immediately put at ease. The vampire shifter, looking nothing like the meek, brooding guy he once was, moves to stand beside his father. "I don't know about the rest of you, but there's no one I would trust more than Millie to run this place."

A surge of pride wells up inside me, and when my gaze drifts over to the other guys, the expressions on their faces—love, pride, and unwavering faith—nearly bring tears to my eyes. My mouth suddenly feels dry.

"Agreed," Shade says, nodding.

"My parents would have thought the same," Silas adds, a flicker of melancholy passing across his eyes. "It's a shame they were never able to know you, Boots. Really know you, I mean."

My eyes move to Landon, questioning. The siren shifter shrugs, grinning. "Ditto."

Hunter's father steps forward, extending a hand to me. "What do you say, Ms. Brix?"

I hesitate for a long moment, biting my lip. The idea of being in charge is intimidating, equal parts scary and enthralling. How long have I wanted to make a difference? How much thought have I given to what I would do *after*, when all was finally said and done? What would *my* parents think if they were around to see me now?

"I won't be able to do it alone," I say finally, gingerly accepting Hunter's dad's hand and shaking it. "And I'll want to make sure we have people we can trust running this place. Clean out the corruption from top to bottom."

"It goes without saying that you would have a say on the new order," Josie says. "Considering how many instructors have died, we're going to need to start by finding replacement professors. The sooner we can have things running the way they were meant to be run, the better."

"Any suggestions as far as instructors?" Hunter's father asks me. "I understand options are limited now, but..."

But a grin is already spreading on my face as I look around the room, from the guys to the twins and Hazel. "I wouldn't worry about finding new teachers," I reply. "I have a couple of ideas."

"Nepotism strikes again," Landon jokes, elbowing Shade and eliciting a glare from the wolf shifter. "Talk about putting the lunatics in charge of the asylum, am I right?"

Hazel groans, Hunter rolls his eyes, and I'm left to laugh, although whether from relief or at the bad joke, I can't tell. It feels like a world I've been carrying on my shoulders for the past months has finally been lifted, leaving behind an immense lightness that not even the siren shifter's bad humor can damage.

"The biggest trick the humans pulled was convincing us that *we* were the lunatics," I remind the others. "This is the way it should be."

Silas nods slowly. "The way it should be."

EPILOGUE

G o *figure,* I think as I step out of Hawthorne's office—*my* office, I remind myself—and into the administration hallway. *And here I was thinking I would never be comfortable in this place again.*

All around me, the school is decked out for the holidays: garlands, enchanted evergreen trees, and intricate wall sconces line the hallways. The smells of oranges and cinnamon fill the air, and outside, the campus grounds are covered in a fresh blanket of snow. Winter is upon us, and I couldn't be more content.

It's strange to think that months have already passed since Hawthorne's defeat. Soon I'll be turning twenty, and if there's anything more surreal than *that,* I can't think of it. To say that the transition has been an easy one would be dangerously sugar-coating it, and, not for the first time, I find myself basking in gratitude yet again. It's been a rocky road. With new students trickling in everyday, courtesy of Josie and Amelia Ash, Samantha's apt replacement, I've barely had a chance to breathe through it all. The guys have taken to teaching classes like ducks to water, and although some of their teaching styles—Shade's and Landon's, namely—are... unorthodox, to say the least, there's no denying that they're getting results.

Outside the window, a gaggle of new students sweeps across the quad, in a hurry to get inside and out of the cold. After some debate, we decided to forgo the uniforms moving forward. They did nothing except encourage stratification, which is the exact thing I want to avoid now. We need to start seeing all shifters as equals, and neither look down on the new students, nor give them inflated egos. Egos are where all these problems started in the first place.

I stretch my arms over my head, stifling a yawn. It feels like I've been in my office for two days straight, going over propositions from the board and requests from the faculty, who are all still getting their sea legs. I haven't seen the guys in a while; between their work and mine, free time has been limited, and I find myself wondering if any of them is on an off period right now.

That was the biggest downside of taking over the Academy, one I didn't foresee—although I probably should have. Love has had to take a backseat, and part of me still feels melancholy about that. This isn't to say our passion for one another has dwindled in the slightest over the past few months—if anything, the distance has only made it stronger, and the guys are getting along better now than they ever have. But that doesn't make the distance any easier.

"The illusive headmistress makes an appearance," comes a voice from behind me. I turn around to find myself face to face with Hazel, her arm linked with Xander's. Walking alongside them is Landon, the expression on his face only slightly less humorous than usual.

"What are you doing outside your office?" he asks in a tone of false surprise. "I thought you pretty much lived in there now."

I roll my eyes, slugging him playfully on the arm before turning to hug Hazel. "Nobody told me there would be this much *paperwork*," I complain. "No wonder Hawthorne went crazy."

"You're no Hawthorne, Millie," Xander informs me. "And it sounds like you're already doing a better job."

"Don't give her a big head," Hazel tells him jokingly. "We'll have to deal with her if her ego gets as big as Landon's, here."

"I beg your pardon," Landon snarks back. "*I* wasn't the one who took a window out while showing off in front of my students."

Hazel flushes, but laughs it off. "Fair point, Thyme."

"So you and Ruby are sticking around, then?" I ask, turning to Xander. "We'd be lucky to have you aboard."

"There was talk of going back to Boston," the dragon shifter replies, "but I think the U.K. is more our speed. Besides," he adds, shooting a glance at Hazel, "I've got more than one reason to stay here."

"All right, you two," Landon jokes. "We all know you're adorable. You're making me self-conscious." Extending a hand to me, he asks, his voice suddenly surprisingly serious, "Do you want to go somewhere, Boots? I'm getting tired of looking at the inside of this building and I haven't been here nearly as long as you."

I meet his soft brown eyes and nod, slipping my hand into his. His thumb brushes other the pad of my palm, seeming to sweep away my stress and exhaustion all at once.

A moment passes, and then another, and finally Hazel coughs. "Let's give the lovebirds some space," she says to Xander, tugging at his hand. "Where did you say Ruby had gotten off to?"

"Giving the groundskeeper an earful, if I remember right," Xander responds, and they turn to go. "We'd better go track her down before she rips the poor man's head off."

"See you guys," Hazel calls to me and Landon over her shoulder as they retreat down the hall. "And happy holidays!"

Landon and I reciprocate the farewell, turning to face one another in the silence of the admin building. For a moment neither of us says anything. "So..." the siren shifter says finally.

"So..." I echo. It's a little awkward at first, considering that the last time we were together, there was a gaggle of first-year students waiting for him to start his lesson.

Landon takes a step forward, casting a surreptitious glance around.

"What is it?" I ask incredulously.

"Just making sure we're alone," he answers. "You know the rules about PDA."

I open my mouth to ask what he means, but before I can he's closing the distance between us, his lips brushing tenderly against mine. My body melts into his, and for a moment I forget where I am. It's funny how you can know someone for a year and still feel like you've been with them all your life. His hands go to the base of my skull, fingers twining in my hair, and I'm on the verge of wrapping my arms around him when my stomach suddenly lets out a loud growl.

I jump away from him, blushing furiously, and grin sheepishly up at my fellow shifter. "Sorry," I mutter. "I just realized I never ate lunch."

Landon frowns, glancing at the clock on the wall. "Better late than never," he says, grinning, "and lucky for you, I know a place in my hometown that has a great winter menu."

I raise my eyebrows. "Your hometown? You mean all the way in Scotland?"

Landon crosses his arms, eyeing me sternly. "Are you saying our master teleporter can't jump us a few hundred miles?"

"You're giving me too much credit," I inform him, but the admiration on his face is heartwarming nonetheless. "I mean, if you're comfortable with the possibility of being stranded in the middle of the ocean somewhere..."

Landon just chuckles. "Lucky for you, Boots, the ocean is kind of my place."

MAYBE I'M NOT GIVING myself *enough credit,* I think as I sit at the booth at the end of the restaurant, watching as Landon makes his way back over from the counter, two steaming mugs of mulled apple cider in his hands. Even after having my powers amplified by Josie's potion, acknowledging my own ability feels craven somehow, like even after everything that's happened, I'm still not worthy of my success.

"You're thinking too hard, Boots," Landon informs me as he passes me one of the mugs. It's the perfect follow-up to the roast dinner that preceded it, as cozy as a home cooked meal, and damn near as comforting. "I can practically hear it, and I'm no witch."

"Sorry," I reply, cradling the cider in my hands. "It's just a little surreal, still. That's all."

"You're telling me," the siren shifter jokes. "*I'm* in charge of teaching these kids about the ethics of mind control. *Me*. Whose bright idea was that, anyway?"

"Mine, you ass," I exclaim, letting out a burst of laughter. "You're selling yourself short, Landon. Between you and Hazel, the students are in good hands."

"It's just strange to think that *we* were students here, not that long ago," Landon says, sounding thoughtful. "If you'd asked me a year ago where I thought I would end up, this is about the furthest thing from what I would've said." He reaches out with his free hand to take mine. "That said, though," he adds, his voice gone surprisingly soft, "I can't picture myself anywhere else."

"Would you still say that even if I weren't in charge?" I ask, only half joking.

There's no levity in Landon's expression when he nods. "I go where you go, Boots," he tells me. "You know that."

"Yeah." I take another sip of my drink, hesitating for a second. "Sometimes I don't believe it, though."

"Yeah?" He raises his dark eyebrows. "How come?"

I shrug my shoulders evasively. "It's not that I have a problem with how things turned out, per se," I explain, the sudden need to get my thoughts out almost unbearable. "It's just that, with everything wrapped up the way it is, sometimes I just feel like..."

"Like it's all too easy," the siren shifter finishes for me. "Like it's somehow not over."

"Right," I say, relieved that he understands where I'm coming from. "And even though Hawthorne is gone, who's to say someone like him won't show up again? The humans did it once already, and that was without having access to the ability to give themselves shifter powers."

Landon's expression turns somber. "Hawthorne was a symptom," he says pointedly, "not the cause. And if we're not careful, the humans

649

will try something again. I wouldn't be surprised if they blew the lid off our existence completely, just to sow chaos."

"I'm not sure if I have another fight like that in me," I tell him, as honest as I can bring myself to be. The truth is that this past year has taken it out of me, and I'm sure I'm not the only one. None of us signed up for this, at the end of the day; we were as much victims of circumstance as the shifters who preceded us—the only difference is that we were in the position to do something about it. "If one of the other Academies lets their guard down, if they somehow manage to continue Hawthorne's experiments..."

"Then we'll stop them," Landon says, his grip on my hand tightening. "We'll end it the same way we ended this, and we won't stop until the world is safe for us. For all of us."

I swallow hard, suddenly overcome with emotion. This all feels like more than I deserve, especially after the carnage that has followed me ever since my arrival at the Academy. "I guess," I say slowly, "if I have you guys with me, then maybe it will be all right. No matter what else happens."

"And we'll always be with you, Boots," Landon tells me without missing a beat. "We're never leaving you. Ever." His hand moves up to caress my cheek, his touch surprisingly ginger.

I close my eyes, leaning into his touch as my hand covers his. "How did I get so lucky?" I ask softly, marveling at the fact that we're *here,* we're *alive,* and that most of all, we're *safe.*

Landon just grins at me, the smile working its way through my chest to settle into my heart. "I could say the same thing to you, Boots," he says, and when he leans across the table to press his lips to mine, I reciprocate without a second thought.

THE REGISTRAR'S office is eerily peaceful when I knock on the door, still a little unused to being able to just waltz into whatever room on campus that I please. "You know you don't have to knock, Millie," comes Josie's muffled voice, sounding a little amused.

"Sorry," I reply as I step through the door. "Force of habit."

"Well, your timing is good," Josie replies, getting up from the desk and passing me a file of papers. "I have the latest dossiers on possible first year recruits. All I need is your sign-off, and then Amelia and I can head out again."

"At this rate we'll be overflowing," I say as I examine the documents.

"That's a good problem," Josie says with a smile, and then excuses herself.

Moments later, Amelia and Hunter emerge from the records room. "I'm just saying, I think you could stand to be a little harsher with your grading," she's saying to him. "People aren't going to learn if you don't incentivize them, Hunter."

"*Positive* incentive, Amelia," Hunter replies, stopping dead in his tracks when he sees me. A smile spreads across his face. "Someone really intelligent taught me that once."

I grin, ducking my head as Amelia turns to me. "Hey, Millie," she says. It's amazing how all her former hostility has melted away; fighting on the same side tends to do that to people. "How's it going?"

"Not bad," I reply. "I figured I would stop by and see if Hunter was around."

"I'll take that as my cue to leave," Amelia says with a sly smile as she heads for the door. "Don't get up to *too* much trouble, you two." And with a wink in her brother's direction, she's disappearing out the door.

Hunter steps around the desk and pulls me into a tight embrace. His chest is warm, and I bury my face in it for a moment, basking in the feeling of closeness. "Missed you," he mumbles into my hair, and I can feel him smile against my scalp.

"It's been a while," I agree, pulling back to look him in the eyes. I have to crane my neck; sometimes I'm still surprised by how tall he is. His ocean blue eyes are bright, full of energy in spite of the long week he's put in preparing for the holiday break. "How are your students?" I ask when I finally pull away from him.

"They're doing well, I think," the vampire shifter replies. "I'm still not sure I'm totally qualified to be *teaching* them, but..."

"Hey." I take his face in my hands. "They admire you, Hunter. That's the most important thing. They look up to you. They know what kind of difference you've made in this place."

"And I'm sure the fact that my father's a board member isn't influencing their opinions in the slightest," he remarks dryly.

I interrupt him with a kiss, pulling him close in the warmth of the office. "You're cute when you get self-conscious," I mumble against his mouth.

I feel his smile broaden. "I know." Pulling away, he interlocks his fingers with mine. "Come on," he says, tugging me in the direction of the door. "Are you up for a drink?"

"Depends on what kind of drink," I reply. "As awesome as your blood is, Hunter, I think I'm more in the mood for something alcoholic."

"Good," he says as we leave the office. The air outside is bitterly cold, hitting my face full-force, and I shrink against it, unable to keep from shivering. This doesn't go unnoticed by Hunter, who pulls me against his body, his arm draping around my shoulders. "I've got something better in mind." Tucked into his side, I allow him to lead me down the path and off to the right, away from the faculty building.

"Where are we going?" I ask.

"The board members' cottages are this way," Hunter explains. "I think it's high time I introduce my girlfriend to my parents. Officially, I mean."

My blood immediately runs cold. "Excuse me? Parents?"

Hunter laughs. "Relax. They already know we're dating, Boots."

"Yeah," I protest, feeling color creeping into my cheeks that's decidedly not due to the cold, "but I'm willing to bet they don't know you're not the only one who's dating me."

We continue to follow the cobblestone path, skirting around the outside of the quad in the direction of the faculty quarters. A few clusters of students are still milling about, done with classes for the day and eager to get back to the warmth of the dorms. As we pass by the academic building, a couple of freshman girls ogle Hunter, starstruck looks in their eyes as they whisper to one another about the President and her significant other. If Hunter notices the attention, he pays it no mind, looking at me like I'm the center of his universe. It's enough to chase my self-consciousness away entirely, and by the time we arrive outside the cottage marked "Mr. and Mrs. Ash," the worst of my nerves have abated.

Hunter knocks on the door, his grip on my hand tightening almost imperceptibly. There's a pause, and then the face of a red-haired woman appears in the doorway. She's the spitting image of Amelia, and her expression brightens the moment she sees Hunter.

"Sweetheart," she exclaims, pulling him into an embrace. "What a nice surprise!" I've seen her around, between the previous administrative visits to the campus and the ill-fated Boston conference, but I never put her association to Hunter together until now. Her blue eyes sweep over me, and I can't get over the feeling that she's assessing me, deciding whether I'm worthy of her son.

Her gaze lingers on Hunter's and my joined hands for a moment, but her warm smile doesn't waver for an instant.

"Mum," Hunter says, "I'd like to officially introduce you to Millie Brix. She's my, uh... girlfriend." He sounds like he's almost marveling at the word.

There's a beat, and then another, and I'm on the verge of panicking and making a break for it when Hunter's mother extends a hand to me, her smile growing. "It's a pleasure to finally meet you, Ms. Brix," she says warmly. "I've heard a lot about you. Come in, please—it's freezing out here."

A FEW MINUTES later I'm shrugging off my scarf and curling up next to Hunter on his parents' loveseat. The space is pretty small in here, not surprising, considering the board members' cottages are mostly reserved for the rare occasions when they visit the campus. They've been spending a fair amount of time here recently, though, helping with the transition process and voting on measures I've proposed as President. It's still bizarre that people decades older and more experienced than me are suddenly deferring to me about the management of the Academy, but if there's one thing I've learned from all of this, it's that humans and shifters have greatly differing definitions of the word "normal".

"Blood?" asks Hunter's mom, turning around to reveal her shifted form, fangs prominent. In her hand is a wine bottle, but something tells me its contents didn't come from grapes.

I turn to Hunter, raising my eyebrows. He's already in his vampire form. "I know you said alcohol," he murmurs to me, "but blood is just as good to us vamps."

"There's a first time for everything," I reply gamely before shifting into a vampire.

Looking pleased, Mrs. Ash pours some of the thick red liquid into a glass and hands it to me. I take an experimental sniff, marveling at how something that would normally smell disgusting now makes my mouth water. I can't resist drinking deeply, relishing in the taste, and Hunter eyes me with an affectionate grin. "Well?" he asks.

"I'll take this over pinot grigio any day," I joke, making both him and his mother laugh.

"I apologize that my husband isn't here right now," Mrs. Ash says, taking a seat across from us in a plush leather armchair. At the far end of the room, a roaring fire in the fireplace is helping to heat the building up, but I find myself clinging more steadfastly to Hunter for warmth. "He's been called back to Europe to discuss reopening the French Academy. This new push of yours to get the other teaching sites reopened all over the world is... surprising, I have to say."

It's the type of question that could make a person balk, but there's no hostility in her tone—merely curiosity. "It is," I acknowledge, "but considering the number of new shifters we're finding every day, we have to make sure they can all be taught safely. Even better to start up a school that we can rebuild from the ground up."

"Better for preventing corruption," Hunter adds. "Millie is trying to prevent more young shifters from being handed over to the humans for experimentation." He casts me an admiring look. "There's more to helping shifters thrive than just teaching them how to use their powers."

"Speaking of which," says Mrs. Ash, "I understand I have you to thank for teaching Hunter how to finally shift, Millie."

I blush a little. "Hunter was the one to make the change, Mrs. Ash. I just helped him along."

"You're being too modest," Hunter teases me. "Mum can vouch for me. I was a lost cause."

"Hardly," I protest, unsure how to react to the compliment.

"You made my son into a real shifter," insists Mrs. Ash. "More than that, though, I don't think it would be exaggerating to say you brought him back to life, Millie."

I blink, looking from mother to son. "It's true," Hunter says quietly, his voice suddenly tender. "I didn't see a place in this world for me, Boots. Now that I think about it, you were as lost as I was. Maybe more. No parents, no community..."

"I had you," I reply quietly, my heart leaping in my chest under his smoldering gaze.

"And he had you," Mrs. Ash adds.

"Damn right I did, and I didn't even realize it at first." Hunter pulls me closer, and even though his vampire body is cold, I still feel warmer than ever. "I don't care where my place is in the world anymore," he tells me seriously. "As long as it's with you."

I'm stunned into silence, unsure how to react to such a raw display of affection. For a moment, a sense of discomfort at the public nature of his confession settles over me but then Hunter's mother speaks up and breaks it with a single question. "So why does he call you 'Boots', anyway?"

The time clicks by easily after that, and with the metaphorical ice broken and the blood flowing, the conversation grows ever more entertaining. Mrs. Ash plies us with the classic "meeting the parents" stories—mostly referring to Hunter's childhood and his early difficulties mastering his shifting abilities—which Hunter takes in stride.

By the time we stumble back out of the cottage, swaying on our feet and laughing like there's no tomorrow, we're past the point of being tipsy, and without having touched a smidge of actual alcohol. "Okay, okay, you're right," I manage to tell Hunter through the giggles, still in my vampire form and with no plans to shift back for the foreseeable future, "you were right—blood is better than booze."

"You're only realizing this *now?*"

I collapse into his side, more laughter taking hold of me. "Don't rub it in," I tell him teasingly.

"I'm just saying," he replies, ruffling my hair with a hand, "you owe me for introducing it to you."

"I guess I'll just have to come up with some way of repaying you," I reply, linking my arms around his neck.

Hunter raises his eyebrow. "Is that a promise?"

"Let's find out," I tell him, and pull him in for a kiss.

The cold doesn't even make a difference.

FOR SOMEONE who's been on the wrong side of a detention room more often than the right one, Shade has by far been the biggest surprise in the aftermath of our fight with Hawthorne. To be honest, I had the most doubts about putting him in charge of his own class, considering his temper and general disdain for academics on the whole. But his understanding of the mechanics of shapeshifting is more progressive than that of anyone else, even many of the former Academy professors, and there was no question that he should have a shot.

What's surprised me is how quickly he's taken to the whole thing, almost as if to spite anyone who had misgivings. His methods are decidedly Shade-like, which might spell trouble for anyone else, but they have, in fact, made him one of the most popular instructors at the new Academy. The only downside? When you have a whole school clamoring to be taught by you, you're not left with a great deal of free time. It's always the same issue.

An issue that's presently on my mind as I make my way through one of the upper floors of the academics building, on my way to the Intermediate Wolf Shifting classroom. It's been a while since I've seen my temperamental boyfriend, and although there's been talk behind the scenes of constructing a wing in the faculty housing for me and the guys to all live in the same space, nothing concrete has happened yet. There are more important things to concentrate on.

Nonetheless, I can't stop from smiling when I approach the class-room and hear Shade's commanding voice exclaiming, "Seriously, Ryerson?! Is that the best bite you can manage? My grandmother could do better..." His voice trails off when he catches a glimpse of me leaning in the doorway, and he grins. "All right, guys, that's enough for today," he says. "Take the extra five minutes to... do whatever it is you guys do."

The students get up in a flurry, already chattering with one another. A couple of them cast longing gazes in Shade's direction, but he's already making his way over to me. "Hey," he says once everyone has left, closing the door behind him and kissing me quickly. "Been a while, Boots."

"Unfortunately," I agree, basking in the feeling of his body pressed against mine. "It feels like I haven't seen any of you guys in weeks."

"Yeah, way to neglect your significant others," the wolf shifter jokes. "God forbid you have a school to run."

"And I'm not the only one," I reply, laughing. "You've really taken to this teaching thing, haven't you?"

"For God's sake, don't tell anyone," Shade says. "I've worked hard for this reputation, Boots."

I cross my heart. "Your secret's safe with me, Shade."

"I know." He pulls me close again, and this time when he kisses me, he takes his time with it, humming with contentment when he feels me smiling against him. "So what do I owe the pleasure, Boots?" Crossing his arms over his chest, he gives me a disarming look with those silver eyes.

"Is just wanting to see you enough?"

The wolf shifter chuckles. "I don't believe you."

"What—seriously?" I snort, shaking my head. "I swear, you're as bad as Hunter sometimes."

Laughing, Shade runs a hand through his sandy locks. "You know, I'll take that as a compliment."

I put my hands on my hips. "Wonders never cease." Moving back to perch on the edge of one of the desks, I eye him for a moment. "You know, considering how things worked out between the five of us..."

Shade raises his eyebrows. "This should be good."

I swat him lightly on the arm and continue, undeterred. "I'm just saying, it's a little surprising how, well... *well* everything has worked out. Us. This." I make a sweeping gesture with my arms. "I just... realize that it's not exactly normal, that's all."

"Boots," Shade says, his eyes glinting with mischief, "what about any of us is 'normal'?"

I laugh, rubbing the back of my neck. "Fair point. We all started out in the same place, as babies. It just..."

"Makes sense," Shade finishes for me. There's a moment of silence, and he bumps the inside of my foot gently with his own. "Four shifters and a hybrid."

"Yeah," I say, my smile diminishing just a little.

The change doesn't go unnoticed. "What is it, Boots?" asks Shade.

"Nothing," I reply, pinching the bridge of my nose. "I wasn't always a hybrid. That's all."

"True," Shade agrees. "You used to be a human. We were shifters since birth."

I nod slowly, unable to meet his eyes. "I've been... struggling with that a bit," I confess. "The idea that there won't be any more hybrids." Seeing Shade's brows furrow, I rush on. "I'm not saying I'm not happy we stopped him," I explain, already regretting bringing this up. "It's just—knowing that those experiments were what created *me...*"

"Who says you're the only hybrid out there?" Shade points out. "I mean, Theo was a hybrid. Why shouldn't there be others?"

I can't help but feel a pang in my chest at the mention of the name. The white-haired, white-eyed community leader still crops up in my thoughts from time to time. There was never anything between us, not really, but he represented possibilities. Sometimes I still wonder what things would be like now if I had taken him up on his offer to continue my bloodline, to bring more hybrids into the world.

If I had taken that path, would he still be alive right now, I wonder? Would *I*?

They're all questions without answers, and I have to shake myself to come back to the present. "I suppose there could be," I acknowledge. "Theo was made by witches, not humans, so maybe..." But the possibility is both exhausting and maddening. To have history in both the human world and the shifter one, to feel like a freak even amongst freaks, isn't something that can be properly explained. "I just wish there were more of us," I admit. "A community. And with Theo gone, there's nothing I can do to continue that legacy."

"Hey, now," Shade says, that annoyingly charming smirk in full bloom on his face. "Who said Theo was the only person you could have a legacy with?"

Part of me wants to roll my eyes at the posturing, but the other is more focused on the butterflies that have erupted in my stomach. I settle for shuffling up to him with what I hope is a coy smile on my face and saying, "I wasn't aware you guys were offering."

"Can't speak for them," the wolf shifter says, reaching down jokingly to press his hand to my stomach, "but I don't mind the idea of a few little Shades running around."

"Sounds like a discussion we'll have to have as a group," I tell him sternly, grabbing his hand and bringing it up to my lips. "A long, *long* way into the future." Gently, I kiss his knuckles, smiling as I peer up into his gray eyes.

"I can live with that," Shade replies, moving next to me and slinging an arm around my shoulders. "Now come on. Let's get out of here before those guys from admin figure out where you went."

SHADE ISN'T the only one who subverted my expectations.

This is a fact I'm pondering as I wander down the hallway of teachers' offices, searching for Silas's. The dragon shifter was the guy I fully expected to take to being an instructor, more so than any of the others. His temperament is perfect for it, and his head is in the right place—or at least, that was how it seemed to me. *And I wasn't wrong,* I think as I stop outside his office and peer in through the window. *He's doing incredibly. His students love him. But...*

Silas's office is empty, and the lights are off. Frowning, I continue down the hallway until I reach one of the side exits and make my way out onto the grounds. *But he's sad,* another part of my mind speaks up.

And who can blame him? Of all the people affected by Hawthorne's evil, Silas has to have been struck the worst: losing his parents to the Academy as a kid, thinking they were dead for years, only to meet them again and find out that they were brainwashed by the enemy. Their deaths—their *real* deaths—must have felt like the ultimate slap in the face to the dragon shifter. The icing on the cake after being tortured and nearly killed himself after I showed up.

Do I blame myself? No, but the guilt is there all the same, my mind still spinning with *what ifs* whenever I catch Silas's dark eyes from across a room.

Maybe that's why I start to walk when I catch a glimpse of a strapping figure sitting by himself on one of the benches by the far side of the quad. There's snow on the ground, and thick flakes of it have begun to drift down from the thick clouds in the sky, gathering in his dark hair and leaving a dusting on the bench. Pulling my coat more tightly around myself, I wade through the deep snow drifts in the direction of the first guy I shared secrets with.

His back is to me, and the snow muffles my footsteps, so he doesn't appear to notice me until I've taken a seat next to him on the bench, wrapping my arms around myself. "Hey," I say, feeling like I'm too loud in the quiet of the afternoon.

Silas turns to me, smiling. "Hey," he echoes, leaning over to press a kiss gently to my cheek. "I'm sorry I haven't seen you the past few days," he says, looking down. "I was... I guess I'm just a little out of it."

"You seem down," I venture, leaning forward to look at him. "Do you want to talk about it?"

"You're a sweetheart, Boots," Silas tells me. "I'm fine."

"It's your parents, isn't it?" Almost as soon as the words are out, I wince inwardly, wondering if I've overstepped. Silas is the strong, silent type, and even after all this time, I can still never be sure what he's thinking.

The dragon shifter heaves a heavy sigh, shifting his body to look me in his eyes. I'm expecting him to say something—to rebuff me, or to assure me that I have nothing to worry about, but instead, he remains silent. He watches me long enough that I start to grow restless, pulling my eyes away from his just in time for him to reach up and brush some snowflakes out of my chestnut hair.

"They would have loved you," he says, his voice sounding rusty in the cold. His hand lingers on my face, as if he hardly dares to believe that I'm here, that I'm *real.*

I cover his hand with mine, shifting closer to him on the bench. For a minute he's terrifyingly unresponsive, but then he leans gently against me, tall enough that his cheek rests on the top of my head. "I would have loved them, too," I tell Silas quietly. "They were good people, Silas. I've never doubted that."

"I miss them," the dragon shifter admits, sounding almost sheepish. "It's stupid, I know, considering I spent twenty years thinking they were dead, but... I can't help but feel frustrated. Like they abandoned me."

"You lost them again," I finish for him. "Silas, I'm so sorry."

"At least I had time with my parents, though," Silas says, straightening up. "You never even got to meet yours."

"I was angry at them for a long time," I admit. It's the first time I've confided in anyone about this. "After I found out they left me on purpose, that they never wanted me in the first place... I spent so long missing them, building up this image in my mind of the family I wanted but never had."

"Sounds like we're in the same boat," the dragon shifter observes. "Just a couple of battered shifters with no family to speak of."

"That's not true," I tell him, pulling his face down so I can look him in the eyes. "We have each other. *You're* my family, Silas. You, Landon, Shade, Hunter... I love you."

"I love you too, Boots," Silas tells me. "I've loved you ever since I met you, I think. And..." He takes a shaky breath, the heat of it coming out in plumes and calling to mind his dragon form. "And I think that's enough."

He leans down and kisses me; the feeling sending sparks of electricity down my tense shoulders. I'm reminded of the first time he kissed me, after revealing the nature of my hybridism to me in the face of overwhelming scrutiny from Hawthorne and the humans.

Silas's arms encircle me, his mouth breaking from mine only so he can bury his face in my neck. His nose is cold, making me shiver, and I can't help flinching, letting out a short giggle.

"Save some for the rest of us, Aconyte," comes a familiar voice. I pull away from Silas and turn to see Landon making his way through the snow, seemingly unbothered by the cold in spite of how lightly he's dressed. The siren shifter grins as he comes to plop down on my other side. "If I'd known this was where the action was, I would've come outside sooner."

"You know people are going to give us strange looks if they catch us all out here together," Hunter points out, moving to stand across from me. "You should hear the things my students are saying. "I can't tell if they resent you or want to *be* you."

"It's not our fault we're so fucking handsome that she can't keep her hands off us," comes Shade's voice. The wolf shifter, bringing up the rear, stands behind me. And just like that, the four loves of my life are flanking me on all sides. I can't tell if it's real or imagined, but I could swear the temperature feels suddenly warmer.

"So did we miss any good gossip?" jokes Landon.

"We were just taking a minute to take it all in," Silas responds.

"It's been a hell of a ride, hasn't it?" Hunter asks.

"Damn right," Shade says. "But for some reason, I think we're going to be okay."

I smile, in spite of the snow that continues to drift down on us. Surrounded by the guys I love, safe in the knowledge that I'm exactly where I need to be, I can't help but agree.

106.BONUS EPILOGUE

MILLY

10 YEARS LATER

The Snow is cold as it brushes against my cheeks, dotting my nose with it's flakes. The wind howls through our house in the forest, close to the school we all run together. Years have passed since we fought for the academy, for each other and the life we have now but sometimes, on nights like this, it is so close. My nightmares never have faded, but I'm not alone to face them and that is all that matters in the end.

Landon comes out onto our balcony, the sweet scent of hot chocolate drifting in with his scent. I grin as he hands me a hot mug of the nice hot chocolate we have before leaning on the railing next to me.

"One of those nights, huh?" He questions. I trace my eyes over him, noting how the years have only made him more handsome. The same can be said of all my men sleeping in our home. We all worked for seven months to build this house and enchant the forest and land around us so no students can come here.

About a year later, Hazel demanded her own house nearby and now there is a sweet cottage just down the path to our left.

"I believe certain hormones are making me sleepless," I whisper. Landons' eyes drift down to my baby bump, the wonder we all assumed would never happen. About four years ago we decided to try for a baby, not caring who the father would be but we were not blessed. At some point, we stopped trying and accepted the students at the school might be all the family we could have.

Which we accepted.

Then our miracle made his or hers arrival into our life. I'm only four months along but my bump is big. I'm yet to feel her or him kick.

He moves over and places his hand on my bump over my white cotton shirt. "Be nice to your mother, little one."

I chuckle, even as I feel something like a flutter. I place my hot chocolate down and place my hand next to Landons'. There, the flutter becomes stronger and I blink.

"I think the baby is saying hello," I chuckle in wonder. He falls to his knees, his eyes bright and wide, and presses a kiss to my bump.

"Hello, baby."

ABOUT G. BAILEY

G. Bailey is a USA Today and International Bestselling Author of
fantasy and paranormal romance.
She lives in England with her cheeky children, her gorgeous (and
slightly mad) golden retrievers and her teenage sweetheart turned
husband.
She loves cups of tea.
Chocolate and Harry Potter marathons are her jam and she owns way
too many notebooks and random pens.

f

ABOUT REGAN ROSEWOOD

Regan Rosewood is a new author from England, where she lives just down the road from G. Bailey.

She has a cute cat and an addiction to reading.

f

I knew nothing about mates until the alpha rejected me...
Growing up in one of the biggest packs in the world, I have my life planned out for me from the second I turn eighteen and find my true mate in the moon ceremony.
Finding your true mate gives you the power to share the shifter energy they have, given to the males of the pack by the moon goddess herself. The power to shift into a wolf.
But for the first time in the history of our pack, the new alpha is mated with a nobody. A foster kid living in the pack's orphanage with no ancestors or power to claim.
Me.
After being brutally rejected by my alpha mate, publicly humiliated and thrown away into the sea, the dark wolves of the Fall Mountain Pack find me.
They save me. The four alphas. The ones the world fears because of the darkness they live in.
In their world? Being rejected is the only way to join their pack. The only way their lost and forbidden god gives them the power to shift without a mate.

I spent my life worshipping the moon goddess, when it turns out my life always belonged to another...

This is a full-length reverse harem romance novel full of sexy alpha males, steamy scenes, a strong heroine and a lot of sarcasm. Intended for 17+ readers. This is a trilogy.

CHAPTER
ONE

"Don't hide from us, little pup. Don't you want to play with the wolves?"

Beta Valeriu's voice rings out around me as I duck under the staircase of the empty house, dodging a few cobwebs that get trapped in my long blonde hair. Breathlessly, I sink to the floor and wrap my arms around my legs, trying not to breathe in the thick scent of damp and dust. Closing my eyes, I pray to the moon goddess that they will get bored with chasing me, but I know better. No goddess is going to save my ass tonight. Not when I'm being hunted by literal wolves.

I made a mistake. A big mistake. I went to a party in the pack, like all my other classmates at the beta's house, to celebrate the end of our schooling and, personally for me, turning eighteen. For some tiny reason, I thought I could be normal for one night. Be like them.

And not just one of the foster kids the pack keeps alive because of the laws put in place by a goddess no one has seen in hundreds of years. I should have known the betas in training would get drunk and decide chasing me for another one of their "fun" beatings would be a good way to prove themselves.

Wiping the blood from my bottom lip where one of them caught me in the forest with his fist, I stare at my blood-tipped fingers in a beam of moonlight shining through the broken panelled wall behind me.

I don't know why I think anyone is going to save me. I'm nothing to them, the pack, or to the moon goddess I pray to every night like everyone in this pack does.

The moon goddess hasn't saved me from shit.

Heavy footsteps echo closer, changing from crunching leaves to hitting concrete floor, and I know they are in the house now. A rat runs past my leg, and I nearly scream as I jolt backwards into a loose metal panel that vibrates, the metal smacking against another piece and revealing my location to the wolves hunting me.

Crap.

My hands shake as I climb to my feet and slowly step out into the middle of the room as Beta Valeriu comes in with his two sidekicks, who stumble to his side. I glance around the room, seeing the staircase is broken and there is an enormous gap on the second floor. It looks burnt out from a fire, but there is no other exit. I'm well and truly in trouble now. They stop in an intimidating line, all three of them muscular and jacked up enough to knock a car over. Their black hair is all the same shade, likely because they are all cousins, I'm sure, and they have deeply tanned skin that doesn't match how pale my skin is. Considering I'm a foster kid, I could have at least gotten the same looks as them, but oh no, the moon goddess gave me bright blonde hair that never stops growing fast and freckly pale skin to stand out. I look like the moon comparing itself to the beauty of the sun with everyone in my pack.

Beta Valeriu takes a long sip of his drink, his eyes flashing green, his wolf making it clear he likes the hunt. Valeriu is the newest beta, taking over from his father, who recently retired at two hundred years of age and gave the role to his son willingly. But Valeriu is a dick. Simple as. He might be good-looking, like most of the five betas are, but each one of them lacks a certain amount of brain cells. The thing is, wolves don't need to be smart to be betas, they just need the right bloodline and to kill when the alpha clicks his fingers.

All wolves like to hunt and kill. And damn, I'm always the hunted in this pack.

"You know better than to run from us, little Mairin. Little Mary the lamb who runs from the wolf," he sing songs the last part, taking a slow step forward, his shoe grating across the dirt under his feet. Always the height jokes with this tool. He might be over six foot, and sure, my five foot three height isn't intimidating, but has no one heard the phrase *small but deadly*?

Even if I'm not even a little deadly. "Who invited you to my party?"

"The entire class in our pack was invited," I bite out.

He laughs, the crisp sound echoing around me like a wave of frost. "We both know you might be in this pack, but that's only because of the law about killing female children. Otherwise, our alpha would have ripped you apart a long time ago."

Yeah, I know the law. The law that states female children cannot be killed because of the lack of female wolves born into the pack. There is roughly one female to five wolves in the pack, and it's been that way for a long time for who knows what reason. So, when they found me in the forest at twelve, with no memories and nearly dead, they had to take me in and save my life.

A life, they have reminded me daily, has only been given to me because of that law. The law doesn't stop the alpha from treating me like crap under his shoe or beating me close to death for shits and giggles. Only me, though. The other foster kid I live with is male, so he doesn't get the "special" attention I do. Thankfully.

"We both know you can't kill me or beat me bad enough to attract attention without the alpha here. So why don't you just walk away and find some poor dumbass girl to keep you busy at the party?" I blurt out, tired of all this. Tired of never saying what I want to these idiots and fearing the alpha all the time. A bitter laugh escapes Valeriu's mouth as his eyes fully glow this time. So do his friends', as I realise I just crossed a line with my smart-ass mouth.

My foster carer always said my mouth would get me into trouble.

Seems he is right once again.

A threatening growl explodes from Beta Valeriu's chest, making all the hairs on my arms stand up as I take a step back just as he shifts. I've seen it a million times, but it's always amazing and terrifying at the same time. Shifter energy, pure dark forest green magic, explodes around his body as he changes shape. The only sound in the room is his clicking bones and my heavy, panicked breathing as I search for a way out of here once again, even though I know it's pointless.

I've just wound up a wolf. A beta wolf, one of the most powerful in our pack.

Great job, Irin. Way to stay alive.

The shifter magic disappears, leaving a big white wolf in the space where Valeriu was. The wolf towers over me, like most of them do, and its head is huge enough to eat me with one bite. Just as he steps forward to jump, and I brace myself for something painful, a shadow of a man jumps down from the broken slats above me, landing with a thump. Dressed in a white cloak over jeans and a shirt, my foster carer completely blocks me from Valeriu's view, and I sigh in relief.

"I suggest you leave before I teach you what an experienced, albeit retired, beta wolf can do to a young pup like yourself. Trust me, it will hurt, and our alpha will look the other way."

The threat hangs in the air, spoken with an authority that Valeriu could never dream of having in his voice at eighteen years old. The room goes silent, filled with thick tension for a long time before I hear the wolf running off, followed by two pairs of footsteps moving quickly. My badass foster carer slowly turns around, lowering his hood and brushing his long grey hair back from his face. Smothered in wrinkles, Mike is ancient, and to this day, I have no clue why he offered to work with the foster kids of the pack. His blue eyes remind me of the pale sea I saw once when I was twelve. He always dresses like a Jedi from the human movies, in long cloaks and swords clipped to his hips that look like lightsabres as they glow with magic, and he tells me this is his personal style.

His name is even more human than most of the pack names that get regularly overused. My name, which is the only thing I know about my past thanks to a note in my hand, is as uncommon as it gets. According to an old book on names, it means Their Rebellion, which makes no sense. Mike is apparently a normal human name, and from the little interaction I've had with humans through their technology, his name couldn't be more common.

"You are extremely lucky my back was playing up and I went for a walk, Irin," he sternly comments, and I sigh.

"I'm sorry," I reply, knowing there isn't much else I can say at this point. "The mating ceremony is tomorrow, and I wanted one night of being normal. I shouldn't have snuck out of the foster house."

"No, you should not have when your freedom is so close," he counters and reaches up, gently pinching my chin with his fingers and turning my head to the side. "Your lip is cut, and there is considerable bruising to your cheek. Do you like being beaten by those pups?"

"No, of course not," I say, tugging my face away, still tasting my blood in my mouth. "I wanted to be normal! Why is that so much to ask?"

"Normal is for humans and not shifters. It is why they gave us the United Kingdom and Ireland and then made walls around the islands to stop us from getting out. They want normal, and we need nothing more than what is here: our pack," he begins, telling me what I already know. They agreed three hundred years ago we would take this part of earth as our own, and the humans had the rest. No one wanted interbreeding, and this was the best way to keep peace. So the United Kingdom's lands were separated into four packs. One in England, one in Wales, one in Scotland and one in Ireland. Now there are just two packs, thanks to the shifter wars: the Ravensword Pack that is my home, who worship the moon goddess, and then the Fall Mountain Pack, who owns Ireland, a pack we are always at war with. Whoever they worship, it isn't our goddess, and everything I know about them suggests they are brutal. Unfeeling. Cruel.

Which is exactly why I've never tried to leave my pack to go there. It might be shit here, but at least it's kind of safe and I have a future. Of sorts.

"Do you think it will be better for me when I find my mate tomorrow?" I question...not that I want a mate who will control me with his shifter energy. But it means I will shift into a wolf, like every female can when they are mated, and I've always wanted that.

Plus, a tiny part of me wants to know who the moon goddess herself has chosen for me. The other half of my soul. My true mate. Someone who won't see me as the foster kid who has no family, and will just want me.

Mike looks down at me, and something unreadable crosses his eyes. He turns away and starts walking out of the abandoned house, and I jog to catch up with him. Snowflakes drop into my blonde hair as we head through the forest, back to the foster home, the place I will finally leave one way or another tomorrow. I pull my leather jacket around my chest, over my brown T-shirt for warmth. My torn and worn out jeans are soaked with snow after a few minutes of walking, the snow becoming thicker with every minute. Mike is silent as we walk past the rocks that mark the small pathway until we get to the top of the hill that overlooks the main pack city of Ravensword.

Towering buildings line the River Thames that flows through the middle of the city. The bright lights make it look like a reflection of the stars in the sky, and the sight is beautiful. It might be a messed up place, but I can't help but admire it. I remember the first time I saw the city from here, a few days after I was found and healed. I remember thinking I had woken up from hell to see heaven, but soon I learnt heaven was too nice of a word for this place. The night is silent up here, missing the usual noise of the people in the city, and I silently stare down wondering why we have stopped.

"What do you see when you look at the city, Irin?"

I blow out a long breath. "Somewhere I need to escape."

I don't see his disappointment, but I easily feel it.

"I see my home, a place with darkness in its corners but so much light. I see a place even a foster wolf with no family or ancestors to call on can find happiness tomorrow," he responds. "Stop looking at the stars for your escape, Irin, because tomorrow you will find your home in the city you are trying so hard to see nothing but darkness in."

He carries on walking, and I follow behind him, trying to do what he has asked, but within seconds my eyes drift up to the stars once again.

Because Mike is right, I am always looking for my way to escape, and I always will. I wasn't born in this pack, and I came from outside the walls that have been up for hundreds of years. That's the only explanation for how they found me in a forest with nothing more than a small glass bottle in my hand and a note with my name on it. No one knows how that is possible, least of all me, but somehow I'm going to figure it out. I have to.

FIND HER WOLVES HERE...

Printed in Great Britain
by Amazon